CATWALK

— INCLUDES THREE NOVELS —

catwalk

strike a pose

rip the runway

ALSO BY DEBORAH GREGORY

CATWALK

– INCLUDES THREE NOVELS –

catwalk

strike a pose

rip the runway

DEBORAH GREGORY

LAUREL-LEAF BOOKS

Catwalk copyright © 2008 by Deborah Gregory
Catwalk: Strike a Pose copyright © 2009 by Deborah Gregory
Catwalk: Rip the Runway copyright © 2011 by Deborah Gregory
Cover art copyright © 2011 by Claudette Barjoud

All rights reserved. Published in the United States by Laurel-Leaf, an imprint of Random House Children's Books, a division of Random House, Inc., New York. This work contains two previously published works, *Catwalk* and *Catwalk: Strike a Pose*, published in the United States by Delacorte Press, an imprint of Random House Children's Books, a division of Random House, Inc., New York, in 2008 and 2009, respectively.

Laurel-Leaf Books with the colophon is a registered trademark of Random House, Inc.

Grateful acknowledgment is made to Nine Lives Entertainment, LLC, for permission to reprint lyrics from "These Lies" by Alyjah Jade, copyright © 2010 by Alyjah Jade. All rights reserved. Reprinted by permission of Nine Lives Entertainment, LLC.

Visit us on the Web! www.randomhouse.com/teens
Educators and librarians, for a variety of teaching tools, visit us at
www.randomhouse.com/teachers

Library of Congress Cataloging-in-Publication Data is available upon request.

ISBN 978-0-385-73930-6

RL: 5.0

Printed in the United States of America
10 9 8 7 6 5 4 3 2 1

First Edition

Catwalk

Catwalk

DEBORAH GREGORY

dedication

For my purrlicious friends "Pashmina," "Angora,"
and "Nole." Thank you for stroking my fur
and helping me unleash my feline fatale.

Meowch forever!

acknowledgments

Molto grazie to Stephanie Lane, a fabbie editor who truly earns purr points to the max. Most importantly, I must pay homage to the feline fatales who've made their mark in my life—and on the world—from Lynn Whitfield and Tonya Pinkins to Tina Andrews and Anath Garber. And to my best friend, a fashionista to the finish line—Beverly Johnson, the first black supermodel in America. Nothing will ever change that. Scratch, scratch!

Catwalk Credo

As an officially fierce team member of the House of Pashmina, I fully accept the challenge of competing in the Catwalk competition. That includes granting unlimited access to photographers and television crews at all times during the yearlong process. I will also be expected to represent my crew to the max, abide by directions from my team leader, and to honor, respect, and uphold the Catwalk Credo:

*Strap yourself in and fasten your Gucci seat belt. By entering this world-famous fashion competition, I acknowledge that I'm in for the roller-coaster ride of my young, style-driven life. Therefore, whenever I feel like screaming my head off or jumping out of my chic caboose, I will resist the urge; instead, I will tighten a notch on my fears like a true fashionista.

*Illustrate your visions, but don't be sketchy with crew members. My commitment to my House must always come first. Nothing must stand in the way of my Catwalk obligations—*nada, nyet, niente, Nietzsche!* And when someone or something presents itself as an obstacle, I promise to call upon my crew to summon the strength necessary to cut off the interference like a loose, dangling thread.

*Rulers are for those who rule with purrcision. The true measure of my success will be not how I slope the terrain to fame but my ability to align my tasks and tantrums with those of my crew. I must always remember that grandiosity could land me in the half-price sale bin like Goliath—who was toppled by a tiny but well-targeted rock.

*Be prepared to endure more pricks than a pincushion. Now that I've made the commitment to a goal sought after by many other aspiring fashionistas, I must be prepared for *cat*iac attacks. Therefore, I will honestly share my fears and concerns with my crew, so that I can be pricked back to the reality that I am *not* alone in this not-so-chic and competitive world, nor will I achieve fabulosity solely on my own merits.

*Become a master tailor of your schedule. I must face the fact that my time has now become a commodity more valuable than Gianni Versace's gunmetal mesh fabric from the seventies. Despite my daunting tasks, I must always find the time to show up for my crew and attend my bimonthly Catwalk meetings throughout the year. Together we can make our dreams come true, one blind stitch at a time.

*Floss your teeth, not your ego. Now that I'm part of a crew, carrying on about my accomplishments like I'm the Lone Ranger of Liberty prints is not cute; neither is grungy grooming or having food crouched between my teeth. I will carry tools of my trade with me at all times, including a container of dental floss and a hairbrush, so that I can be prepared for prime-time purring and on-camera cues that may come at me off the cuff.

*Ruffles don't always have ridges. While everyone is entitled to an opinion, I will not allow myself to become hemmed in by well-meaning wannabes outside my crew. My individual style is only worthy when it becomes incorporated into the collective vision of my Catwalk crew. I will also resist the temptation to bite anyone else's flavor to the degree that it constitutes copying, or I will be asked to pack my tape measure and head back to the style sandbox on my own.

*Pay homage and nibble on fromage. As a true fashionista, I must study the creative contributions of those who came before me so that I can become the maker of my own mélange. I will also publicly give the fashionistas who came before me the props they're due whenever name-dropping is appropriate. Despite my quest for individual development, I must acknowledge that I will always channel influences from the past, present, and future.

*Click out your cat claws to defend your cattitudinal stance.** When others turn bitter, I must bring on the glitter. Competition always brings out the worst in foes—and even friends—because everyone will try to gobble the biggest slice of the fashion pie and no one settles for crumbs without putting up a fight.

*Always be ready to strike a pose.** Even if I am not a model in the House of Pashmina, I cannot expect to strut the catwalk without getting a leg up on the competition first and saving my best riff for last. When it's showtime, I will be prepared to do my assigned task to help bring the House of Pashmina to the finish line.

*Act fierce even when you're not feeling it.** Never let the competition see you sweat. While going through this creative process, I may feel doubts about my direction. I will feel free to bounce my ideas off other crew members, but never reveal sensitive information to outsiders! Not all fashion spies have been sent to Siberia—they hide among us, always ready to undo a dart or a hemline.

*Keep your eyes on the international prize.** As a fierce fashionista, I intend to get my global groove on by sampling style and culture around the world. In order to show my appreciation for the global access that style grants me, I commit to practice a foreign language for five minutes a day and double up on Saturdays because we're going to win the Catwalk competition and stage our style at a destination to be determined—over the rainbow! *Ciao, au revoir, sayonara!*

My younger sister, Chenille, says that I prance instead of walk. I should, since my motto is *Sashay, parlay!* Even Fabbie Tabby knows how to work it like a cat on a hot tin ramp. You can tell by the way she prances on the heels of my bare feet as I patter down the creaky hallway to the bathroom. My mom hates when I walk around without shoes on the craggy wooden floors, but I'm feeling too wiggly this morning to be on splinter patrol. Once I hit the cold faux-marble bathroom floor, I fling open the purple paisley plastic shower curtain, swiping Fabbie Tabby in the process.

"So *sari*," I apologize to my kitty sister, to whom I bear a striking resemblance. See, we both have the same ultraslanty hazel eyes, pushed-in nose with wide-splayed nostrils, and bushy sprout of golden auburn hair (mine on my head; hers from head to tail). The only way we differ: Fabbie has a plumpalicious hinie, which I push out of the way so I can squeeze sideways into the too-tiny shower stall, but then I stub my big toe *hard* on a chipped tile. Serves me right for *dis*missing my beloved boo.

I'm feeling like a bona fried frittata today for good reason. It's my first day back to school, and now that I'm a junior I'm *finally* eligible to run in the most important elections in the fashion galaxy: house leaders in the annual Catwalk fashion show competition. If I don't snag one of the five highly coveted nominations, however, then I will *not* have a reason to survive like Gloria Gaynor.

"Oh, no, not I! I will survive!" I screech along to the hyped hook of my mom's favorite disco song like it's a motivational mantra. Chenille swears that I sound like a cackling jackal. So *what* if I can't sing? I'm just trying to put myself on blast, okay? What I desperately need right now is a blast of hot water, because everything is about to be on like popcorn.

Everything except the hot water, I realize after I turn the screeching knob and watch the pathetic dribbles sputter from the shower nozzle.

"Chenille!" I scream at the top of my lungs, because now I'm feeling *extra* crispy. Serves me right. I can't believe I let that early-bird specialist take a shower first when I know how rickety the hot-water situation is. All you have to say are the words "broken" or "repair" and our landlord Mr. Darius's English takes a magic carpet ride to Babbleland. It doesn't matter how many times my mother complains and the repair guy futilely descends into the building's danky Tomb Raider basement.

The water situation remains chilly to tepid. The truth is, that relic of a boiler needs to be replaced with a new one from this century. And despite the fancy-schmancy name of our housing complex—Amsterdam Gardens—there are merely a few wilting shrubs on the premises. Any green thumb Mr. Darius has is from counting the thick stack of Benjamins he collects monthly in rent.

"Get out of here—*caboose babaluse!*" blasts Mr. Darius, his loud combustible rant rising from the courtyard into my second-floor bathroom window. That's precisely why we call him Big Daddy Boom behind his back.

Standing over the bathroom sink, I brace myself to swipe at my underarms with a washcloth soaked in freezing cold water and dabs of Tahitian vanilla soap. If you ask me, loitering knuckleheads like the ones Mr. Darius just shooed out of the courtyard have it easy breezy: they don't have to sweat the big stuff, like entering the Wetness Protection Program or getting nominated in the most important election any budding fashionista worth her Dolce dreams could run for.

Shivering, I hightail it back to my bedroom, catching a glimpse of plodding Chenille in her bedroom, already dressed in a gray polo shirt under her signature blue denim overalls and wearing black Puma sneakers. She's huddled over her bureau, carefully placing her precious hairstyling tools in the compartments of her gray melton cloth organizer. I scan the handygirl getup she's chosen to wear on her first day as a freshman at Fashion International, the fiercest high school in the Big Apple. I still can't believe Chenille was accepted into Fashion International's auxiliary program, designated for aspiring hairstylists and makeup artists. She should be toting a toolbox instead.

Personally, I think she should have followed in her friend Loquasia's Madden clunky-booted footsteps and applied to Dalmation Tech High School, which is directly across the street from our school. Fashion International is located on Thirty-eighth Street between Seventh and Eighth Avenues, in the heart of the most famous fashion district in the world. "You dropped a clamp," I mumble at her. Chenille studies the gray fuzzy area rug by her feet like a forensic examiner but comes up empty. "Psych," I say, deadpan.

Chenille squints at me with her beady eyes, then announces: "I'm taking the train with Loquasia."

"Whatever makes you clever," I shoot back. I walk into my bedroom, pulling out my pink sponge rollers and throwing them in my Hello Kitty basket caddy. *Puhleez*, I'd rather go bald like Shrek before I'd let Chenille touch my fuzzy goldilocks. Springing my spiral Shirley Temples into place one by one, I glance absentmindedly at the poster on the wall above my bed: Miss

Eartha Kitt poised in a black pleather Catwoman jumpsuit. One of my best friends, Aphro—which is pronounced like *Afro* and short for her fabbie name Aphrodite—gave me the poster for Christmas last year. She snagged it through a *major* hookup: Aphro's foster mother, Mrs. Maydell, worked for years as a maid on Eartha Kitt's Connecticut estate.

As you can sorta see, our household principles are divided into two distinct halves: Chenille is the yin and I'm the bling. What else could explain how she and my mother are both morning people while Fabbie and I are confirmed night creatures? I bet you Chenille shot straight up in her coffin at the crack of dusk, pecking along with the pigeons outside her bedroom windowsill until it was time to hoist her beauty-salon-cum-backpack onto her petite back and head off for her first day as a freshman.

"Pashmina!" my mom yells out. I'm naked, so I don't respond until I put on my favorite pair of pink cotton bloomers with the big cat's eye on the rear, which always make me feel like someone's got my back, or at least is watching my butt.

"Wazzup?" I yell back.

"I'm leaving twenty dollars on the dresser for you," Mom yells, her sharp voice rising above the din of the spritzing. My mom is addicted to hair spray because it provides her wigs with hurricane hold. "You never know what or who you're gonna tangle with," she warns us.

The phone in the living room rings loudly, making me jangly. Mom is not into any technological advances that soften sound. I stand quietly by my bedroom door and listen closely as my mom answers the cordless phone stationed on the Plexiglas end table. Suddenly, she gets an extra crispy tone in her voice: "I can't believe you're calling here before nine!"

I cringe, praying that it's not one of my crew.

"I don't know. . . . I *said*, I don't know, okay? I'll send it when I can," my mom says in a tart voice to the intrusive person on the other end.

My stomach wigglies rotate like they're on a spitfire grill. I realize that Mom has hung up on yet another creditor. She thinks we don't know, but they've been hounding her lately like a basset on a bone mission. Suddenly, I feel guilty: if Chenille and I weren't too old to be sharing a bedroom, we wouldn't have had to move to a bigger apartment. Like a *chatte noire*, I retreat stealthily to my bedroom, which Mom and I have spent the whole year pinkifying from floor to ceiling, including the wooden dresser we found on the sidewalk. Every weekend last year, Mom, Chenille, and I took the subway downtown to the Upper East Side to hunt for furniture discarded like empty cans of tuna by the resident snooty-patooties.

I snap the back closure on my petal pink bra, then carefully ease my skinny legs into my pink fishnet pantyhose, but I can't seem to dissolve my guilt. We're always stressing about money. That's why I'm motivated to get a part-time job pronto—hopefully from the job board postings at school. Of course, I know my mom wanted to move out of the Boogie Down Bronx for her own reasons: to be closer to her job and maybe even to get away from Grandma Pritch. My throat still automatically constricts every time I think of her forcing gooey oatmeal down my throat when we had to live with her. Mom left us with Grandma Pritch when I was three years old and didn't come back to get us until I was five.

Now Grandma Pritch is living all by her lonesome in the Edenwald Projects on Baychester Avenue, across the street from where we used to live. She's so old her eyes are going; last week she tried to take a shower in the hallway closet, then caused a ruckus in her building, claiming someone had swiped her shower stall! Shoot, she may be old, but Grandma Pritch *still* gives me the fritters.

My mother, who most people call Miss Viv, is an assistant manager at the Forgotten Diva Boutique, a plus-size clothing store (with *snorious* clothes for old-school customers) on Madison Avenue and Seventy-second Street. She was a sales assistant for a long time, but two years ago she got a promotion, which is how we were able to move into this three-bedroom apartment on the verge of a nervous breakdown. But I'm not ungrateful: as long as I have my own bedroom, I don't care if the ceiling collapses, because I'll just carry on like Chicken Little—dust myself off, then sashay through the soot, okay?

Chenille's modus operandi, however, is more like the Road Runner's, because it's only seven o'clock in the morning and she's already stationed by the front door for a hasty exit.

"Bye, Ma," she shouts before she slams shut the heavy metal front door.

I wince at the fact that Miss Wannabe "Snippy" Sassoon left without saying goodbye to me. I'm so over her, or maybe it's the other way around, because it seems that the taller I've become, the less Chenille is feeling me. Maybe it's the fact that we're now two grades apart even though I'm only one year older. (I was in the IGC program in junior high for intellectually gifted children [I hate the way that sounds] and skipped eighth grade.)

Suddenly, I realize that Chenille has the right idea about time management: it wouldn't be a bad idea to get to school early today. I hold up the new outfit that Felinez and I worked on for two weeks.

"Wow, this is the whammy-jammy!" I exclaim.

It's my ode to cheerleader chic: the pink pullover knit sweater has the letter *P* glued on the front and pink pom-poms hanging off the bottom edge and will be worn over a pink checked pleated wrap skirt fastened on the side with a giganto pink safety pin. Felinez also put a fuzz ball on the toes of my pink pleather boots: if you look closely you can see roll-around eyeballs pressed into the center of the fuzz ball. The pièce de résistance, however, is the matching shoulder bag. Using pink mop fibers, Felinez made me a bag that shakes ferociously like a big, bouncy cheerleader pom-pom. Staring in the beveled antique mirror, I put on my CZ (cubic zirconia) bling: first, my favorite eBay snag, a black Naughty Girl Lolita watch with floating pink crystals inside; then my French Kitty rhinestone cat pendant primed inside with Frisky perfume and dangling on a Mexican silver chain. My mom gave me my latest kitty *cadeau* for my fifteenth birthday last May. One day, I'll be able to wear bona fide *blang*, like a Hello Kitty diamond pendant by Kimora Lee. I stuff my pink satin meowch pouch into my purse—it's a little drawstring pouch that Felinez and I came up with for carrying essentials. You can wear it on your wrist or on your neck, or put it in your purse. Even Fabbie

Tabby has one—she wears it on her collar. Inside is one quarter, her phone number, and some biscuits, in case she ever prances too far over the rainbow.

Now I grab my hot-pink Kitty decal–littered note-books and head to my mom's room to retrieve my designated ducats. My allowance is skimpier than I hoped for, but I'm determined to stretch it longer than my Chinatown-find fishnets, which are cramping my crotch area, okay.

I walk into the kitchen, where Mom is already stationed in her favorite little niche, drinking a cup of Belgian Blends mocha and reading yesterday's *WWW*, *Women's Wear Daily*, which she brings home from the boutique every night. She never eats breakfast and I don't either—even though she yells at me for doing the same thing she does.

"Please change the litter already," my mom instructs me without looking up from her newspaper. She is now dressed in the tailored attire associated with her "Miss Viv" professional personality—a hot-pink wool blazer, black wool trousers, and a black turtleneck sweater, most likely cashmere, which she craves. (There was a reason why my mom named both her daughters after luxury fabrics, pashmina and chenille, okay.) It's my job to take care of Fabbie, and one that I do gladly. Chenille obviously is not a cat person, and my mom has enough to deal with.

"Is that jacket new?" I ask Mom, checking out her outfit while I open the refrigerator and take out the carton of pink grapefruit juice and my *Vogue* magazine (I like to keep my fashion as fresh as my juice).

"I told you not to leave your magazines in the refrigerator," Mom snaps without looking up. Now it's my turn to ignore her while I indulge in my favorite morning ritual—sipping and flipping. I don't know why she acts so janky about my storage habits—it's not like we're running a gourmet garage in the refrigerator. See, my mom is a medi-okra cook, which is why we mostly eat take-out chow. Besides, she's so tired from working that she doesn't have time to cook.

Humming, I continue gulping juice and scanning the pages of my cool magazine until I get my fill of Juicy Couture, Gianni Versace, and Kate Spade.

"You excited about today?" asks my mom.

"I'm hyped," I respond. "I've got to get nominated."

Mom looks puzzled, which makes me realize that she doesn't remember about the Catwalk competition. She was just asking a general question, like it's my first day in kindergarten and I'm gleeful about showing off my new Princess Potty Mouth lunch box. (Awright, I did love that thing—stuffed it with PB&J sandwiches till the hinges rusted off.)

I realize that now is not the time to stand mute like a dummy (Catwalk code for mannequin). "Don't you

23

remember, all I talked about last year was I couldn't wait until I was eligible to run for house leader nominations in the Catwalk competition? Hello—well, that time is now!" I shriek, trying to stimulate Mom's brain cells, which must be suffocating underneath her Beverly Johnson frosted shag wig.

"Okay, don't get huffy with me. What happens if you get nominated?" Mom asks warily.

"The five candidates with the most student votes get appointed house leaders," I explain carefully, hoping my mom will grasp how important this is to me. "*Then* I get to pick the students that I want to be members of *my* house—the House of Pashmina."

"So what else do you get besides that? I don't like the idea of you spending all that time involved in nonsense. You could get a part-time job and bring some money into this house," my mom says, tipping her hand. Now I see why she feigned an amnesia attack—she was hoping I'd forgotten all about my little dollhouse dreams. Well, I'll show her—time to bring out the hot-glue guns!

"I know it may not seem like much to you, but I could snag a one-year modeling contract with one of the five big model agencies. All of them have representatives attending the Catwalk competition fashion shows in *full force*," I say, zapping her hard.

Mom knows Fashion International's policy on modeling as well as I do. They have a not-so-tacit agreement with the model agencies not to sign students under sixteen, and even then, only students who have competed in the Catwalk competition are eligible. But the real prize is that every year at least three student models from the winning house are given one-year, $25,000 modeling contracts. So why shouldn't I keep my eye on the grand prize?

"And how much is this gonna cost me?" Mom asks, turning defensive.

"The Catwalk Committee provides each house with monthly expense funds. And I'm in charge of the budget—and submitting the monthly expense reports to the Catwalk director," I counter, my face flushed.

"Yeah, well, I know how these things work. Just remember that my money is funny right now," Mom says sternly.

"I know," I say, exasperated.

Ↄ ↄ

"Geez, *I know*," I repeat to myself, barreling down the stairway. When I get to the first-floor landing, I'm blindsided by the latest graffiti scrawled on the wall in screaming red letters: TREVA AND TINA 4REAL. *Get a life*, I moan inwardly. I gallop like a moody mare across the courtyard, then catch myself and switch into my sashay for the rest of the long stretch to the sidewalk. That's what's digable about being your own fashion representative: whether you live in a brokendown palace like I do or on a fabbie estate in Connecticut like Eartha Kitt, when you step out into the urban jungle, the only thing people see is your style.

"Pashmina!" Stellina screams, jarring me out of my schemes and dreams; I didn't see her crouched on the bench across from the monkey bars.

"How ya doing, Pink Head?" she giggles, calling me by my nickname. "That outfit gets *major* purr points!" Ten-year-old Stellina cups her tiny hand into a cat's paw.

I howl involuntarily because it's funny to see myself mimicked by someone with such purrlicious potential. Stellina is one of the poised posse of kids who live here and look up to me because I want to be a model. They really gobble up every Kibble 'n Bit of instruction like I'm serving it à la mode.

"How come you sitting out here?" I ask. Stellina and her best friend, Tiara, went away to a Fresh Air Fund camp for most of August. But now it's back to school, so everybody is springing into action.

"I'm waiting for Tiara—her mother left for work already, so she snuck back upstairs to change her clothes into something more bling-worthy," Stellina explains, rolling her eyes. I feel bad for Tiara because her mother must be color-blind: what else could explain her forcing her daughter to mate checked skirts with polka-dot turtlenecks?

At least that's one drama I don't have to deal with: my mom doesn't stress about my dress—even if the creditors are about to knock on our door.

"Whatchu up to?" Stellina asks, panting like a puppy for the 411.

"I got ants in my pants about getting nominated for house leader," I reveal.

"Oh, that's jumping off today?" she asks earnestly, then squinches her nose. "You mean the fashion show thing, right?"

"*Oui, oui.*"

"What do you mean by house—you go to some-body's house?" she asks.

"No. It's like—um, we call it a house—a fashion house." I'm struggling to figure out how to explain it in terms she would understand. "You know, like the House of Baby Phat or the House of Prada."

"I got you," she says wisely. "So it's Prada or *nada*!"

"I hope so. The winning house gets to say *sayonara*. If I don't win, I'll be watching eggs fry on the sidewalk for another summer," I lament. Judging by the puzzled expression on her face, I realize that I have to explain further. "The winning house gets a trip somewhere over the rainbow."

27

"I got you." Stellina nods knowingly. "I wanna go back to camp next summer. It was real fun. But all that swimming was hard on my press-and-curls!"

"Awright, I'm out."

"See ya, supermodel!" Stellina says with a final sigh. "Can I be a model, too?"

"No doubt," I assure her.

As I descend into the subway, I indulge in my favorite fantasies: in the first, I'll spot a model clutching her portfolio, on her way to a go-see; in the second, I'm spotted by a famous photographer or agent or some other Big Willie fashionista who thinks I'm already ripping the runway, but they just can't help asking, "Are you a model?" I haven't seen one model yet, but I bet they ride the iron horse because it's the best way to get around, given the gridlock. I stop to dig absentmindedly into my pom-pom purse for my Fashion International MetroCard, and some harried passenger torpedoes my leg with an oversize shopping bag that must be loaded with bricks, because my knees buckle involuntarily.

I turn to look at the offending "bag lady," but she doesn't even say sorry. Luckily, my fishnets are intact and I make it to school in one piece, clutching my Hello Kitty necklace like it's a good-luck charm, confirming my one true belief: in the fashion jungle, only the accessorized will survive.

FASHION INTERNATIONAL 35TH ANNUAL
CATWALK COMPETITION BLOG

New school rule: You don't have to be ultranice, but don't get tooooo catty, or your posting will be zapped by the Fashion Avengers!!

YOU'RE NOT KATE SPADE, SO DON'T THROW SHADE. . . .

While some of us are planning on participating in the Catwalk nominations today, others have let it be known to the powers that "busy bee" that they won't be participating in the nomination process today. For the broken record, there is a reason why only junior and senior students who major in Fashion Buying and Merchandising, or Fashion Marketing, and have maintained a 3.5 grade point average or higher are eligible for the prestigious position of house leader. As Catwalk Director Fabianna Lynx (Ms. Fab) has explained, house leaders must possess strong management, planning, budgeting, and executive skills. Therefore, it doesn't make dollars and sense for someone who likes to doodle all day (yes, I'm talking about Illustration majors!) or get their click on (wannabe Francesco Scavullo photography majors) to be in charge of a Catwalk house. On the other hand, someone who prefers snapping their fingers like a general and keeping their team members' egos in check would soar in such a position. So why don't we all manage our own inflatable

egos and show up to today's first Catwalk general assembly meeting to
participate in the task of nominating
qualified candidates? Still don't want
any part of this democratic process? Sorry to hear that, but may
I suggest dropping out of school
altogether? Then perhaps, one day in
your player-hating future, you can ob-
tain a GED by visiting the Web site
www.thatsyourproblemnotmine.com.

9/8/2008 07:30:22 AM
Posted by: Spadey Sense

2

I can't believe that the school year has just begun and Shalimar Jackson is already back in business with her horse and phony show, jamming up the security checkpoint line in the process. This time Shalimar is pretending that her four-legged constant companion J.B. *still* has a Limited Access Fashion Pass when everybody knows the Fendi fiend was banned last semester. But leave it to Miss Jackson to crank out a Coty Fashion Critics' Awards performance before she even snags a house leader nomination.

"He *does* have a pass—I swear! I left it at home cuz it got sucked into my Dirt Devil by accident and I haven't had time to get it out of the lint bag!" whines my biggest Catwalk rival. Petulantly, Shalimar stomps her foot in protest, but instead the clunky heel of her brown lizard "Shimmy Choo" lands on the precious toes of Willi Ninja, Jr., as he tries to cut the line.

"*Ouch!*" snaps Willi, whose feet will no doubt be insured by Lloyd's of London one day, given his star status in voguing—our fave phys ed class.

"My bad," quips Shalimar. "I thought I was light on my feet."

"Yeah, well, you're *heavy* on my corns!" retorts Willi, another Catwalk rival.

The crowd in line snickers like bloodthirsty spectators at the Colosseum in ancient Rome, except in this case, it's the House of Ninja against the House of Shalimar—*coming soon to a runway near you!*

Our favorite security guard, Flex, is more interested in a certain someone's departure. "Shalimar, let's go," he commands. "If Ms. London sees J.B. in the mix, I'm gonna lose my job." He motions like a drill sergeant for the too-short model wannabe to step out of the conga line. We all dig Flex because he's like his namesake and doesn't get supa bent about drippy incoming Mambolattes or the sharp paraphernalia that other schools consider dangerous objects but ours considers merely tools of the trade.

After all, this is Fashion International High School, and we're desperately determined fashionistas who are more interested in taking a bite out of the big time than taking a bite out of crime. Don't get me wrong: fashion school is not a fairy tale. There are many times when clashes, crises, and competition make us wanna click out our cat claws and slice each other into grosgrain ribbon. However, the only physical violence I've ever witnessed within these lime green, cobalt blue, and hot-pink walls was during my freshman year when Chintzy Colon, who happens to be standing in back of me in the line, sliced her index finger with an X-Acto knife in fashion marketing class. At the time, we were all busily crafting promotional materials that were abracadabra fierce for our dream business plans when a certain senorita lived up to *her* name by "cutting the corners" too closely on her fold-out brochure. Led by her bloody finger, Chintzy fled to the Fashion Lounge, crying hysterically, like a five-year-old being chased by a Weeble balloonicle in the Macy's Thanksgiving Day Parade.

I turn around deliberately to check out this *lesser* Catwalk contender. Chintzy averts her eyes from mine as if she is still wincing from last semester's macabre memory, but I'm not swayed by her deception. It's no Victoria's Secret to me why she spent last year networking, noshing, nose-grubbing, and numbing her tootsies: the Chintzy cherub is angling for a dangle despite her phony protestations—*"Oh, you think I could get nominated, mija?"*—echoing down the halls.

"*Hola*, Pashmina. *Que bonita.* Those are bootylicious," Chintzy coos, staring down at my feet. Her gushing proves my *punto*: she's definitely on hype patrol.

"*Muchas gracias*," I reply, since I can't return the saccharine-spiked compliment. Chintzy is wearing a white vinyl miniskirt, which to me is like kryptonite—white induces inertia followed by fashion death if worn after Labor Day. I twirl one of my bouncy ringlets, frazzling the curl like I always do when I'm nervous. I'm not stressing about Shalimar, because I know she's a *shoe*-in. Both of Shalimar's parents work on Wall Street, and let's just say the business of Benjamins must be booming right now, judging by Shalimar's extensive Choo collection.

Chintzy, on the other hand, doesn't have a dad—I don't mean like my situation, because she has met her dad—but I know he doesn't visit—and her mother is a secretary at Avon and raising four kids solo. (On Career Day, we all had to go around and share, but afterward Chintzy kept the 411 flowing like true confessions.) Nonetheless, Chintzy has me worried. Obviously, she's not as crafty as Zorro with an X-Acto knife, but she knows how to sprinkle on that Splenda smile to land enough votes to edge me out of the top five. Suddenly, I fast-forward: I can already see Chintzy during our election campaign, her table crowded with jumbo pans of juicy chorizos—Latin sausages—and glass pitchers of Puerto Rican virgin sangria in an attempt to get everybody punchy enough to put her name into the ballot box. Maybe I should be taking notes, because Chintzy's affable nature worked like a *brujería* spell on our fashion marketing teacher. Even after Chintzy bungled her brochure for her business plan for ChicA Public Relations, she still snagged the same grade I got for mine—a disappointing B-plus. My ego was squashed like mushed plaintains.

"Wazzup, Miss P.P.! Work your initials, Churl. That sweater is off the hinge-y!" Willi squeals, posing like a prom queen, since he cut the line courtesy of his girl, Dulce, who is five Prada pumps ahead of me. Dulce turns to glare at me with her Spadey sense; if you see Dulce, you see her red patent-leather Kate Spade tote bag clutched to her side like a life preserver.

"Thank you, Mr. N. You are what's up, okay?" I hurl at the sneaky Ninja.

"*Soooo*, inquiring minds need to know. Are you *in*?" Willi taunts me.

"In there like swimwear," I shoot back with my best poker face, even though I don't know whether Mr. Twirl Happy is referring to the Catwalk competition or voguing classes—both of which he thinks he has locked up. And he freakin' does. Willi Ninja, Jr., is, after all, the adopted son of voguing legend Willi Ninja, who brought the fun underground modern dance form to our school curriculum. Suffice it to say, I'm green with Gucci Envy that his heir apparent was born with a pose at his elbows instead of a pacifier in his mouth. Mr. Willi is luckier than Miss Piggy: I mean, they both get to be the ham and eat it, too! I, on the other hand, don't even know my father's name. Sometimes I think: How am I ever gonna compete with that kind of legacy?

"*Pobrecito*," Chintzy announces sadly. She's eyeing J.B., who is wearing a white satin cape draped around his tiny shoulders as he exits with Shalimar, who has finally given in to Flex's command to step off. Another round of snickers emanates from the crowd in approval of Shalimar's grand finale. J.B.—James Brown—is Shalimar's hyperactive Maltese. He's aptly named for his fast-moving, feverish footwork, reminiscent of the late Godfather of Soul himself. Unfortunately for Shalimar, J.B.'s jaws are just as quick as his feet: last June, he chomped on Ms. London's Fendi briefcase, prompting his ban from school. What a psycho Twinkie he is.

"Take a bow," I mutter under my breath, secretly eyeing the dynamic duo's exit while I pretend to be staring at the prominent square lime green sign perched on the wall directly to my right: NO VOGUING IN HALLWAYS, PLEASE.

Obviously, Fashion International isn't like any other school. That's why exchange students from all over the world vie for admittance to this fashion mecca, where there are more perks than the Mega Millions lottery: the coolest guest lecturers, a Fashion Café with an international menu that prohibits split pea soup because of its dreadful color, and a hands-on

36

curriculum that includes model appreciation and voguing classes. Properly behaved purse-size pets are even permitted to attend with their student owners as long as they pass the only tests they're required to take: a charm barometer and weigh-in by Principal Confardi, who then grants a Limited Access Fashion Pass, which means the pets are allowed everywhere in school except in physical education classes or the Fashion Café. During those periods, pets must be checked into the Petsey Betsey Annex downstairs—an animal lounge with trained attendants funded by designer Betsey Johnson.

But not all pets are deemed acceptable, as witnessed by another prominently placed sign in the hallways: NO PET SNAKES PLEASE. *The only reptiles we want to see are on your purse!*

At long last, I feel the tickly paw scratch on my neck (my crew's secret Catwalk salutation) that I'm craving. I turn around to see Angora, who has slithered into the line behind me. Chintzy doesn't seem to mind, because she just shoots me an apologetic look, like she's used to making way for budding supermodels.

Like me, Angora has got her own agenda. That's why she majors in fashion journalism: so she can become a model *and* fashion personality; in other words, a bona fide "model-blogger." I can already picture her frame by frame on a *Rip the Runway*–style show like the one supermodel Tidy Plume hosts on the Teen Style Network. If you don't know who Tidy Plume is, then just hand in your All Access Fashion Pass *pronto soon*, okay. Tidy is a *major* Victoria's Secret model, so major that it's written into her contract that she must *always* close their annual fashion show wearing the blinged-out Fantasy Bra—diamond-encrusted, sometimes to the tune of eight hundred karats and $6.5 million.

"What's the matter, *ma chérie*?" Angora asks, seeing the pained look on my face. Angora may be near-sighted, which is why she always has her glasses—baby blue cat's-eyes trimmed with a delicate scattering of crystals—perched on her upturned nose, but she registers everything like a human scanner. Like right now. I gently tug at my fishnets, but she intuitively deciphers that I'm feeling kaflustered about the tall task ahead of me today—that is, getting nominated as a house leader.

"You need a tutu to do ballet, but anyone at any time can *wiggle*," Angora snickers, yanking my fishnets up after we walk past the security checkpoint. Angora loves to talk in sound bites—obviously honing her fashion-hosting skills.

"*Meowch, mijas!* Sorry I'm late," screeches Felinez, bouncing toward us, her wild dark hair flapping as much as her red cheerleader-style pom-pom purse. Although she is clutching the new looseleaf notebook she crafted over the weekend, husky Felinez still manages to ensnare me in an octopussy grip. "I missed you, Pink Head," she coos.

I giggle because we just saw each other, but that's just the way Felinez is. "Lemme see," I say, peering at the cover of the red vinyl–bound looseleaf on which she decoupaged a Barbie postcard framed in red crystals. " 'Every morning, I wake up and thank God for my unique ability to accessorize,' " Angora coos, reading the inscription. "That is *très* adorable."

Obviously, the postcard speaks volumes about Felinez's career goals. She couldn't breathe unless she was making something—and for me, Felinez is the ultimate accessory. We met in kindergarten at P.S. 122 on Tremont Avenue in the South Bronx. Even back then we were a couple of funky fashionistas—making fun of all the wee wee wannabes, snapping on their corny outfits like I was baby Dolce and she was Goo-Goo Gabbana, when we were just budding style gurus still nibbling on Gerber's. I had trouble pronouncing Felinez's name back then, so I started calling her Fifi, and the nickname has stuck ever since. By the time we were nine, Felinez could already turn a sow's ear into a silk purse with all the stuff she found in the garbage. To this day, Felinez would prefer to take a Dumpster dive in a back alley than a trip to a shiny shopping mall. I hate that we're not in the same grade anymore because I got skipped, but I stop myself from saying it. Instead, I hold her tight and mumble, "Nothing is gonna tear *us* apart, Miss Fifi!"

"This is what you two spent all weekend doing?" interrupts Angora, eyeing our matching shoulder bags and pleated skirts. Her blue eyes are opened so wide, they look opalescent.

"*Oui, oui,* croissant!" I say, imitating Angora. She's from Baton Rouge, and I just love the way she lays on her Southern drawl like greasy sweet peppers in a French flambé. Angora herself is a tasty mélange of French Canadian and Choctaw Indian, with a dash of Cajun thrown in for spicy seasoning.

"Well, I figured we're gonna need more than a few cheers to get those votes today," Felinez says, wincing while she tries to pull her skirt down because she's self-conscious about her adorable chubby legs. Felinez is my inspiration—*por vida,* for life. But I know why she stresses so much. It was just a few years ago that we were shopping on Thirty-fourth Street at one of those tiny boutiques—as in the sizes were too small for Felinez and she couldn't fit into this pink thermal top with cute red cherries on it that I had also tried on. I will never forget the hurt expression on her face: it was the first time Felinez felt more like a float in the Puerto Rican Day Parade on Fifth Avenue than a yummy sundae with cherries on her top.

"Tell me you didn't weigh yourself again this morning," chides Angora.

Felinez pauses for a second—like she's Chintzy and going to give us the PR version (as in publicity, not Puerto Rican, which is half of what Felinez is)—then realizes that she's talking to her crew and lets out a fart as well as the truth.

"*Sí, sí,* I did," she says, embarrassed.

I know my best friend's ritual by heart: every morning after she pees, she takes the scale out of the oven in the kitchen and puts it on the floor and weighs herself naked—but not before she moves the scale around on the floor like an Ouija board until she finds that magical spot that tips the indicator to a lower number. Then she puts the scale back on the warm grate in the oven, slamming the oven door in disgust, vowing never to weigh herself again.

"Did your parents leave yet?" Angora asks. Felinez's parents are in a band called Las Madres y los Padres, a Latin hippie group that pays homage to the love-and-peace music from the sixties. They're always on the road, doing gigs on cruise ships and wherever else they can pocket a groovy paycheck.

"That's why I'm late!" Felinez says, exasperated. "My mother kept me up all night, changing her mind a million times about her costume! First it was a pink ruffled top with purple paisley bell bottoms, then she was like, 'No, *nena*, make me a yellow top to wear with a miniskirt!' I was like, 'Yellow is not *lo mejor color* this year unless you're Big Bird on tour, *esta bien?*' Oh, she drives me *tan loca!*"

Of course, Felinez is the one appointed to make the "freebie" costumes for Las Madres y los Padres. Luckily, her father and the other male band member aren't as outfit-obsessed as Felinez's flamboyant mother, who calls herself Madre Cash and is *muy* demanding. Madre Cash wears the kookiest hippie-style costumes you've ever witnessed, and when they return from their world tours, she works Felinez like Spinderella on her over-worked sewing machine.

"I can't believe she kept you up like that, when she knew you had to go to school," I say, flopping my purse on the floor so I can dig for one of my gooey gloss wands.

Felinez gasps. "*Mija*, you know it's bad luck to do that! If you wake up broke tomorrow, you'll be sorry!" she scolds me.

"Yeah, well, I have a news flash for you, Senorita Fifi. Your *brujería* prediction must be retro, cuz I woke up broke *this* morning!"

Felinez laughs nervously. She takes *brujería* very seriously. I also know that she's so happy to see her parents

42

when they come back between their gigs that she'll do anything to keep her mother in stitches—literally.

"I know, *mija*, but that's not what made it worse. You'd think Michelette would help. No, she's sitting there watching the same episode of *Betty la Fea* a million times!" Michelette is Felinez's older sister, the one who actually takes care of Felinez and her seven-year-old brother, Juanito. Michelette works in a video store and can rent all the movies she wants, but instead she's obsessed with the Colombian soap opera. Their cousin in Bogotá tapes the new episodes of *Betty la Fea* and sends them to Michelette at least once a month. In return, Michelette tapes the episodes of the American version—*Ugly Betty*—and sends them to her.

"Should we wait for Aphro?" asks Felinez.

"Nah—I've got to get inside a bathroom stall *pronto soon* to fix my twisted fishnets so they can stop cutting off my circulation because they're not long enough, which is the short story of my five-foot-ten life!" I say, unleashing a mouthful. We're all nervous about today.

"Okay, let's get ready to Tanqueray," Angora says, pushing open the hot-pink door to the Fashion Lounge, then sniffing the air. "New Stick Ups."

I smell the fresh aroma, too, even though I can't place the scent.

"Orange blossom with a tinge of *santal*. Perfect for *moi*. God, I've missed this place!" Angora says, staring at our favorite sign on the freshly painted hot-pink wall, adjacent to the row of pale pink porcelain sinks with shiny gold faucets. Unlike most of the signs around our school, this warning is delivered in three languages so there can be no misunderstanding:

WEAR A SCARF, BUT DON'T BARF, PLEASE!

POR FAVOR, USA LA BUFANDA, PERO NO GRUNYAS!

S'IL VOUS PLAÎT, PORTEZ DES ECHARPES, MAIS NE VOMISSEZ PAS!

"This weekend, Daddy and I went to the *supermarché*—and finally got an odorizer for my room. Now I can smell magnolias every morning," Angora informs us.

I love how she makes a trip to the supermarket sound like a Parisian experience. Unlike me, Angora has a dad she loves. It took a lot of wrestling, but her mother unwillingly let her only daughter come live with her dad, Beau Le Bon, in the Big Apple. He is a supa-cool cartoonist and creator of Funny Bunny—you know, the goofy rabbit that tells jokes when you press his stomach.

"Is the odorizer shaped like a bunny?" I ask. I'd be surprised if her dad let her buy anything normal. Their whole house looks like an Easter treasure hunt—from rabbit salt and pepper shakers to porcelain eggs from Bergdorf Goodman.

"No, but he made me hop to the counter carrying it," Angora chuckles, shaking her head.

"You look so pretty in that top," Felinez says to Angora, who's wearing a fuzzy scoopneck sweater with short sleeves. She always manages to look so cuddly.

"Yeah, it's just the right salmon color—like expensive smoked lox, instead of Bumble Bee!" I heckle.

"Five purr points," coos Felinez. Purr points are our ratings system, used for everything from boys to bustiers.

Angora plops her book on its edge till it teeters over. "What's that?" Felinez asks.

"*The House of Gucci,*" Angora, who reads voraciously, states. "What a *frothy* bunch. Far more eccentric than the Addams family. I mean, when they got into a fight, they threw five-hundred-dollar handbags out the window!"

"Yeah, well, the only house I'm interested in right now is my own," I mutter nervously.

"The House of Pashmina. Well, I'll be *dirndl!* I love the sound of that," Angora says, blinking rapidly, then posing, reminding me of the test shots she did when we first met freshman year in modeling 101. Angora posed with her white Ragdoll cat named Rouge, and they almost looked like sister and brother with their matching blue eyes and pristine auras.

"There's no way a certain person is getting

nominated," Felinez starts babbling, under her breath but loud enough for inquiring minds to latch on to.

I look toward the stalls just to make sure no one is eavesdropping. I mean, the walls in our school really do have pierced ears.

"Just transpose the letters in her name and you'll come up with the two words that best describe her!" Angora says smartly.

I pause for a moment trying to catch on, but I come up blank. "Chin and Neitzche?" I ask, chuckling.

"No, I wasn't talking about her," Angora corrects me.

"Well, I was," Felinez says. She *despises* Chintzy.

Suddenly, I catch Angora's spelling drift: "OH!" I snicker, cupping my paw to touch hers in recognition of pure genius at work. Felinez realizes at the same moment that Angora is referring to Shalimar.

"*Sham. Liar!*" we screech in unison.

"Awright, it's showtime," I say, signaling for us to go our separate ways. I'm off to textile science, while Angora is headed off to voguing 101. It has taken me two years to convince her to strut her gait. "Promise me you'll pose instead of pout," I say, trying to encourage her. I know Angora could vogue if she would stop feeling so insecure about freestyling. "Just dig into your spicy heritage!" I assure her.

"Thank you for that genealogic encouragement,

chérie, but I can't move like you!" Angora says, already starting to pout.

"Ah—you promised," I warn her.

"Okay voilà!" she retorts. "Just keep expecting miracles to be whipped up like soufflés!"

I run off to my class, with Angora's taunt teasing my eardrum. I guess I do expect miracles. Shouldn't everybody?

FASHION INTERNATIONAL 35TH ANNUAL
CATWALK COMPETITION BLOG

New school rule: You don't have to be ultranice, but don't get tooooo catty, or your posting will be zapped by the Fashion Avengers!!

ENUF WITH THE SUPA-DUPA SUR-PRISE . . . ??

Anyone who claims they wannna be in the Catwalk competition for reasons other than the prestigious perks should cross the street to Dalmation Tech—and let us normal fashionistas speculate about the goodies that will be bestowed on winners this year. So far, we've heard that Louis Vuitton, Ooophelia's, the Limited, and Radio Shack are providing gift certifi-cates. As for the designer mentorship, it will most likely be with a certain flower empowered mogul. That's right, someone who knows a showroom intern at Betsey Johnson says calls with Catwalk Director Fabianna Lynx were exchanged and the Flowered One will also be one of this year's judges. (This scoop is bona fide despite the fact that the intern in question was fired for swip-ing samples.) As for the hush-hush destination for this year's trip, *you can* stop ruminating about Gay Paree before you crash your "model" airplane into the Eiffel Tower. The Catwalk committee would *never* pick the *same* destination two years in a row. *Bon-jour!* We've also heard about the top-secret communiqués written in invisible ink passed around among

Catwalk officials all summer that revealed such sensitive information. So
now that we're back to school, let's
get back to Fashion Journalism basics,
shall we? If you know the **who, what,**
or **where** about the above, then decipher the code for us before we read
you!

9/15/2008 8:00:02 AM
Posted by: Fashionista1005

49

3

By second period, I'm ready for my close-up at the Catwalk general assembly meeting. Angora, on the other hand, is ready for a meltdown. I wait outside Studio C to retrieve her from voguing 101, but she bolts out, staring blankly ahead like a zombie. She doesn't even register my gagulation over the tastiest Toll House morsel in fashion town exiting before her. This fashionista is taller than most of the guys, which means he's model material, as opposed to the rest of the shorties at our school. I discreetly check out his chiseled cheekbones and the zebra-striped mink hat plunked on his head, both of which hype his purrlicious appeal. So does the portable supersonic sound system he's carrying under his arm. Much to my chagrin, however, Shalimar suddenly appears next to the beauty with a boom box, ready to suck him up like sushi.

"It was a thousand-dollar ice cream sundae!" Shalimar brags, peering into his piercingly blue slanty eyes, which are framed by thick blond eyebrows. It's obvious that Shalimar is still searching for a new taste sensation despite the fact that for her sixteenth birthday, her parents took her to Serendipity 3 restaurant on the Upper East Side, where she got to indulge in the world's most expensive sundae. All morning, I've been hearing dribbles (but seen no nibbles, mind you) about this Golden Opulence Sundae: five scoops of Tahitian vanilla ice cream covered in 23-karat edible gold leaf, then topped with chunks of rare Chuao chocolate.

"Is there *anything* she won't devour?" I whisper to Angora. "I can't believe you didn't tell me you were taking a voguing class with the Mad Hatter!"

Angora is too vogued out to care about the latest object of my ogle. "If one more person asks me why I'm not in intermediate voguing with *Pashmina*, I'm going to hold a press conference!" Angora marches away quickly, sending Morse code distress signals with each clomp of her powder blue suede UGG boots. By the time we hit the second floor, she's out of breath and has to rest by the Hall of Fashion Fame passageway.

"Are you okay?" I ask. Angora's asthma goes into full throttle when she's kaflustered.

"I'm just fine and dandy. I hid in the back of the class so Mr. Blinghe wouldn't call on me. I think I need a chin splint from hiding my face in my palm—that's all," Angora says, struggling to regain her normal breathing.

"It was just the first day—and I'm sure Shalimar's shade didn't help," I offer.

"Oh, *plissé*! I can forget about modeling in a Victoria's Secret fashion show, okay? I don't need Je-T'aime's crystal ball to read the *Women's Wear Daily* headline of the future: Angora prance? Not a chance!"

Je-T'aime is Angora's dad's Creole psychic from Louisiana. He doesn't make a move without her. In Angora's case, I decide to coax the wilting magnolia into putting one UGGed foot in front of the other. If I get elected, I'll need my star model to be prance-ready by spring, and that's why I'm hoping that voguing classes will help Angora unleash her inner feline fatale. According to Willi Ninja, the unspoken fashion rule is: if you can vogue, then you can work the runway for points on the Dow Jones, okay.

"If I didn't think you could be as fierce as Tidy or Tyra, I would tell you to move back home with your mother and master the art of hyping hush puppies!"

"*Perch. Prance. Payday!*" Angora giggles, repeating another of my mantras. Then she pulls out her inhaler to rebalance her oxygen intake. "His name is Zeus," Angora adds nonchalantly.

"What was he doing with the beatbox?" I ask.

"He's a deejay—'hip-hop addict,' that's what he called himself. Mr. Blinghe made us introduce ourselves because 'voguing is about connecting with others,'" Angora repeats wearily.

"Does he want to model, too?"

Angora nods.

"Now, there's a new hyphenate," I offer.

"What do you mean, *chérie*?"

"A model *and* a deejay. What should we call him?"

"Speaking of hyphenates, take a look at this one," Angora says, perking up. She whips out the *Little Brown Book*, the magazine for Bloomingdale's insiders. (Her father's Funny Bunny antics have their perks now that parents are dropping carrots on his likeness, sold at Toys 'R' Us.) Angora opens to the page featuring Nacho Figueras, an Argentine polo player and the face of Ralph Lauren's new men's fragrance. "*Purrr*," I hum approvingly. "A professional polo player *and* a model. I think Zeus is tastier, though. Oh, I got it—what about 'model-spinner'?"

"I like that," Angora says, smiling sweetly at the photo collage of Tidy Plume.

"Your eyes are prettier because they peer deeper into the soul," I coo to Angora.

"Her breasts are bigger though. I want those breasts, *chérie*," Angora counters.

"It's an indisputable facto that A-cup means A-list."

"Then add an addendum to our Catwalk Code: B-cup means more Benjamins!" Angora quips.

"Sounds like a *booby* trap to me."

Senior-year design major Nole Canoli and his five-member entourage turn the corner and walk ahead of us into the Fashion Auditorium. Elgamela Sphinx, the model in the bunch, towers over the rest of them and breaks out her supermodel-in-training smile. "Hi Pashmina and Angora," she coos.

As for Nole Canoli, the word on the street is he could be the next Gianni Versace. That means, a designer who is bling-worthy. Nole has a pudgy round face set off by his thick black Gucci glasses. He also has an egg-shaped head that probably glows in the dark because it's so giganto and closely shaven. Oblivious to our presence, the bling-worthy one walks into the auditorium. "It's turning into a real Macy's Thanksgiving Day Parade," I observe.

Angora nods knowingly as I reminisce about my fave cartoon balloons. When I was five years old, my mom finally rescued us from the gingerbread house before Grandma Pritch cooked Chenille and me in her oven. I started kindergarten a few weeks later, and on Thanksgiving the three of us went to the Macy's Thanksgiving Day Parade. I held my mother's hand tight because I thought if I let go maybe she would float away. My little hands were freezing, but I was in heaven watching all the gigantic balloons travel by. Sonic the

Hedgehog. The Weebles. Snoopy. The only one missing was my favorite, Miss Piggy.

Angora nudges me from my childhood memories to clock Nole Canoli in action. "Anyone with that much hot air *has* to be deflatable." Nole air-kisses Liza Flake, who attends the Fashion Auxiliary program for hairstyling. Every chance she gets, you can spot her whipping out her turquoise faux crocodile portfolio, which is filled with test shots taken by photographers who use hairstylists, makeup artists, and fashion stylists to transform the models being tested into primp-ready posers. Rounding out the Canoli entourage are makeup artist Kimono Harris and hairstylist Dame Leeds, both in the auxiliary program. "Mini Mo," as the supa-petite blusher is called by her friends, always wears China red lipstick and her dark, straight hair is cut in a geometric precision bob, sorta like Aphro's (except Mo's hair requires no "assisterance" from Revlon Realistic Relaxer). Probably the most pampered member of Nole Canoli's entourage, however, is Countess Coco, whose tiny head topped with a foxy mane sticks proudly out of the black Prada bag thrown over Nole's right shoulder. She's a purebred Pomeranian with bulging eyes and equal attitude.

Speaking of entourage members, as we descend into the doorway of the auditorium, Aphro, who is seated midway, finally waves us down like a desperate housewife in Times Square trying to hail a cab. Even from rows away, we can hear Aphro's armful of silver and gold bangles jangling to their own fashion jingle.

"*Scratch, scratch!*" coos Aphro, sitting next to Felinez. They both extend their cupped hands and we all cross paws. Then Aphro unleashes one of her signature snorts—a laugh so hearty it sounds like a happy hog lapping up slop at its trough. It's part of what makes the mighty Aphrodite such a purrlicious Babe. Aphro majors in Jewelry Design and invented her own hip-hop moniker by adopting "Biggie" as her middle name. She wants to start a jewelry company called Aphro Puffs. Let's just say that the self-proclaimed "model-blinger" takes the advice of our marketing teacher, Ms. Harness, very seriously: "You're never too young to start branding yourself."

Angora and I plop down in the cushy hot-pink theater-style seats next to our crew.

"Okay—time to thread the needle," Aphro pipes up, which is Catwalk code for taking care of business. "Let's take bets. What's the supa-dupa surprise gonna be—a person, a place, or a *thang*?"

"Winner gets a Mambolatte," Felinez chimes in.

"Oh—all right. I think it's gonna be a person. A special mentorship with someone like—ooh, I got it—a French designer in Paris, like Yves Saint Bernard!" Angora says satisfied.

"Um, I think it's gonna be a place," Felinez says

confidently. "Like the Catwalk winners get to stay at the Four Seasons Hotel in Paris, where they'll plan a party?"

"Right! Y'all are all wrong! It's definitely a *thang*—like the Queen of England donating her royal jewels to the winning team, *ayiight*," quips Aphro.

"So *sari*," I counter, ready to throw mystery into the mix, "but it's none of the above."

My crew gives me the look that I know all too well: *Whatever makes her clever!*

Despite my excitement about what's about to jump off, I lean on Angora's shoulder and sneak a yawn.

"Pash—if I tell you something, you won't get upset?" Angora says, leaning closer.

I respond warily, "Wazzup, buttercup?"

"You need a spritz," Angora says, palming her vial of Bitty Kitty fragrance into my hand.

"I should have known that Tahitian vanilla soap wasn't going to hold up," I whisper. "I had to take a bird bath this morning because the hot water went to a hootenanny, leaving me high and dry."

Angora smiles at me, but I'm so embarrassed that I can feel the eye on the backside of my bloomers blinking in discomfort.

"God, I'd like to undo Mr. Darius with a seam ripper!" I mumble.

"Not to worry, *chérie*—only I can tell you smell," Angora whispers into my ear.

"Thank you for the blast," I say, spritzing on more of the Bitty Kitty fragrance before handing it back to Angora.

Yet another Catwalk opponent, Chandelier Spinelli, and her best friend, Tina Cadavere, scurry to grab seats in our row. Two steps in, Chandelier slides back out apologetically, like she's forgotten something terribly important—"Forgot her false teeth maybe," I whisper to Angora. Flinging her suede cutout scarf once around her neck, Chandelier unwittingly whacks Tina on the nose. "I'm sorry, Miss *Fluff*!" she squeals. Tina lets out a round of heckles as the dizzy duo scurry to another aisle.

"Tina the Hyena is on the loose," Angora observes. When we were freshman, Chandelier was real cool with me until she started throwing shade—as in Gucci twisted horsebit–hinge eyeglasses. By sophomore year, she went from tore up from the floor up to chic chitty-bang-bang with Nole Canoli and his crew.

"All I wanna know is how Miss *Chan-de-lee-ay* started hanging with Guccis?" shouts Aphro drawing out the pronunciation, which garners snickers from the nearby seats.

We shush Aphro in unison, but to no avail.

"Someone tell me please, then I'll shut up!"

"Maybe her father got promoted to head nurse,"

Felinez offers with a giggle. In sociology, Chandelier mentioned that she lives with her father and that he's a male nurse at a hospital in Brooklyn.

Aphro twirls the ends of the purple chain wrap draped around her neck like a detective meditating on clues. She designed the scarf from knitted links intermingled with chain mail; unwrapped, it would trail for miles. Aphro was in the same modeling 101 class as Angora and I. Hands down, Miss Aphro is the best catwalker among us, which is why the anointed strutter will be choreographing our fashion show. See, scoring points in the Catwalk competition depends as much on the choreographed posing and prancing as it does on a house's fashion theme and scheme.

At last, the auditorium has filled up with students who want to put their dibs in. Our principal, Mr. Mario Confardi, skips onto the stage with his signature sprightly gait. He smoothes down his fuschia silk tie, which contrasts sharply against a pale pink shirt and superbly tailored dark gray gabardine suit. Everything about our steely principal spells professional, which is why I suddenly sit up straight in my chair and poke Felinez to do the same. Mr. Confardi steps to the mike in clipped choreographed motion, his every move revealing the hidden Confardi code clearly deciphered by the most perceptive fashionistas among us. Loosely translated, it means: *I'm serving it up like pancakes, so you'd better grab my guidance while it's hot!*

Standing like a model on the catwalk patiently posing for the photographers stationed below the ramp to capture fashion shots, Mr. Confardi waits for our catty chatter to cease without having to signal us. That's also Confardi code. Our top fashion dog may be short with a slight build, but he is *très* commanding—and chic. Take his wardrobe: he's aways Dolce down in the suit department but pinches his pennies for Prada when it comes to his footwear—usually baroque brown lace-ups with perforated and stitched toes.

"Good morning," Mr. Confardi announces in his piercing voice. "Glad to see you could make time in your busy schedule to place your nominations—including you, Countess." Mr. Confardi motions to Nole Canoli and Countess Coco, who is clearly on the fast track to divadom, judging by her well-placed paw on the armrest.

Mr. Confardi continues with the words we are all waiting to hear: "Welcome to the nomination process for house leaders for the Thirty-fifth Annual Catwalk Competition."

We all clap. "Bring it on!" someone shouts. I turn and catch Anna Rex's stone-faced profile: that long aquiline nose and dark straight hair pulled back severely into a ponytail. Not one facial muscle registers excitement, not even a twitch. On last year's Catwalk blog, one of the house leaders claimed they vetoed picking the stoic one as a model because she is obviously a Botox-injection regular. While that rumor has still not been verified, one thing is true: Anna Rex maintains a 4.0 grade point average without breaking a sweat. There are five Anna Rex disciples—all superskinny, with an obvious clique code that requires them to always wear black and never smile in public. It's also no secret that Anna Rex and her calorie-conscious cronies are the reason why the school implemented its no barfing policy in three languages. They never eat in the Fashion Café, but they can be seen outside the school smoking tiny clove cigarettes, supposedly hand-rolled in Dutch Teepees by a Surinamese Indian Chief, or so claims the snobby one.

A hush washes over the auditorium as Mr. Confardi continues his shrill spiel: "Our founding principal, William Dresser, had a unique vision when he created the charter for Fashion International forty years ago. He wanted an educational environment where a passion for fashion could truly flourish."

Speaking of unique visions, I can't help my wandering eyes, which search the crowd for just one more peek at Zeus. Not a zebra stripe in sight. My fashion lights are dimmed.

"Our founding father also created the format for the

Catwalk competition so that the most talented of our students could walk right into a fashion career—almost literally—after they graduated," Mr. Confardi continues. "To facilitate this process, the five competing Catwalk houses must be helmed by a committed leader."

Angora, Fifi, and Aphro turn and beam at me like I possess the key to fashion *paradiso*. I blush instinctively.

After Mr. Confardi winds down, he announces: "Now for the driving force behind the Catwalk competition, Ms. Fabianna Lynx!"

As we all clap, Ms. Fab grandly walks up the steps onto the stage with her pampered, pudgy white bichon frise, Puccini, hot on her heels.

"Sashay, parlay!" Aphro shouts out. It's giggles all around. As if on cue, Puccini plops his fat white extra-furry body down on the stage like a pancake next to Ms. Fab as she proceeds to adjust the microphone stand to accommodate her six-foot-tall stature. More giggles.

"Check the outfit," I whisper. Ms. Fab's style can be spotted from the last aisle in the auditorium: today she is wearing a leopard-print ankle-length denim dress with leopard-fur trim around the scoop neckline, and calf's-hair leopard-print mules with red piping. Puccini is wearing a matching outfit—a leopard-print denim coat—minus the mules. We all know that Ms. Fab makes both their outfits because, as she says, she wouldn't be caught dead shopping at the Forgotten Diva, no offense against my mom.

"I heard she used to carry secrets for the Soviet Union in her lynx muffler," Angora offers about the so-called Lynx legacy, which fascinates us all.

"I bet she was the most furbulous double agent to grace the Kremlin," I concur.

Ms. Lynx looks ready to speak, so we wait with bated breath. "Good morning, my fellow fashionistas!"

"Good morning!" we shout back.

"Candidates nominated today will be eligible to run in the Catwalk elections. And next week, you will cast your ballots at the Catwalk election. The final five will be responsible for selecting their team members, delegating duties, and presenting a style vision that will culminate in one of the five full-concept fashion shows, which are held at Bryant Park."

Angora and I take a deep breath. We are definitely at the starting gate. Let the fashion games begin.

"Okay, shall we begin placing nominations?" Ms. Lynx says, looking down at Puccini as if he will be contributing. "Oooh, Puccini, don't you just get goose bumps at this petticoat junction?"

Puccini lifts his head and peers at Ms. Lynx, then drops his chin back on the floor with a defined *plop*.

"I had the honor of becoming the Catwalk director

twenty years ago, when our founding father was still here," Ms. Fab says, then takes a pause, which Aphro feels compelled to fill.

"*And* we heard you were sleeping with him!" she blurts out.

Sometimes I think Aphro has Tourette's syndrome. What else could explain why things just slip out of her mouth like hazardous emissions?

"He may be gone, but I believe he's watching with pride," Ms. Lynx goes on spookily, luckily not having heard Aphro. "*Okay*. I now move for nominations to begin. Raise your hand if you second."

Hands fly up, and I feel the excitement buyers must feel sitting at a Sotheby's auction, waiting to get their bid on with their numbered paddles.

"Farfalla and Sil Lai will assist with nominations," Ms. Fab explains as her two assistants ascend to the stage.

Nole's hand flies up first. "I nominate Chandelier Spinelli."

"I second that," someone else says.

Chandelier blushes and accepts the nomination.

Everybody claps, including Angora, who can't help herself; after all, her mother runs Ms. Ava's Etiquette and Charm School in Baton Rouge. Meanwhile, I keep my hands to myself and instead try to gauge my odds of beating Chandelier to be one of the top five contenders.

I also hide my disappointment that Nole nominated *her*. Aphro, Angora, and Fifi are oblivious. They hold their hands high like they're totem poles.

Farfalla calls on another student.

"I nominate Chintzy Colon," someone says.

"I second," says another.

Both Chintzy and her Splenda smile accept to a strong round of applause. Now I'm starting to sweat. Chintzy got nominated before I did?

Both Willi Ninja, Jr., and Shalimar Jackson also get nominated. Finally, Angora gets her nomination in. "I nominate Pashmina Purrstein," she announces loudly.

"I second that!" Aphro yells out.

After all the usual suspects and a few long shots such as supa-shrilly Chantez Winan get nominated, Ms. Fab asks the question we've been waiting for. "I move that we close the nominations. Does anybody second?"

A sea of voices second Ms. Fab's motion.

Sil Lai reads the list of Catwalk house leader candidates. "If you are one of the thirteen candidates that I just called, you have one week to launch your campaign. The election will be held next Monday," she explains. "At that time, all students will be eligible to cast a ballot. The day after Election Day, the poll results will be posted outside the Fashion Café. Please read the Catwalk competition rules and regulations *carefully*."

Ms. Lynx sashays back onstage, grinning like a spotted Cheshire cat. Sil Lai runs center stage to hand Ms. Lynx the Big Willie bronze statue. Ms. Lynx holds the Big Willie statue like it's an Academy Award—and to us, it is.

"This is what you will work so hard for—our school's ultimate symbol of promise, potential, and dedication. Each year, a Big Willie is bestowed upon the winning house. Good luck to you all!"

Ms. Lynx waits for the thunderous rounds of applause to die down. "I'm sure each and every one of you is also familiar with the $100,000 prize and college scholarships that will accompany this prestigious award—thanks to our generous corporate sponsors. What everyone has been dying to know, of course, is this year's destination for the all-expenses paid two-week trip."

I sit up in my chair, my appetite whetted for more than a Mambolatte all of a sudden.

"The winning team will be whisked off to . . . Firenze, where they will stage their fashion show as the opening collection in *Pitti Bimbo*!"

"Italy! Knew it!" I scream, cupping my hands to Angora. Firenze is Italian for Florence, where the junior fashion collections—Pitti Bimbo—are held every summer.

"But hold on. We do have one extra perk this year

that has managed to stay hush-hush on the plush," Ms. Lynx goes on. "Someone please hand me the note written in invisible ink!" she giggles, motioning to Farfalla, who eagerly marches toward her with a satin leopard tote. She plops it into Ms. Lynx's outstretched left hand.

"Break it down!" Aphro shouts, because she can't stand the anticipation anymore. None of us can.

We watch as Ms. Lynx opens her spotted tote like it's Pandora's box, but all she pulls out of it are a pack of leopard tissues. Coughing, Ms. Lynx puts her hand to her ample chest and waits for her throat to clear before she resumes speaking: "For the first time, we have an unprecedented surprise."

"What is it!" someone screams.

We all burst out laughing. "Let me catch my breath, will you?" Ms. Fab insists. "Okay, okay. I am incredibly pleased to announce that for the first time in the thirty-five-year history of the Catwalk competition, you will have more than just memories to savor, because this year the entire process will be taped, then televised by the Teen Style Network!"

"Omigod!" Aphro shouts, like a supa-giddy contestant on *The Price Is Right*.

I drop my jaw like a sun-kissed guppy, then announce, "I *think* I won the bet!"

Amid a cacophony of screams and shout-outs, Ms.

Fab smiles before she explains that film crews will have unlimited access to Fashion International.

"I expect everyone to come to my office and sign a waiver. If you don't sign a waiver, you cannot be captured on tape—and I know everyone is dying for their close-up, right?" coaxes Ms. Fab. "Oh—the episodes will begin airing next spring. But please be advised, our faculty has absolutely no control over the footage the network uses, so please do *not* prance to my office putting in requests!"

Suddenly, I freeze. "What does that mean?" I say to Angora. She squinches her nose and smiles.

"We are counting on *every* student—whether you are a Catwalk House member or not—to remember that you are indeed a representative of Fashion International and are expected to carry yourself like a true fashionista," Ms. Fab warns.

Now I tug Angora's fluffy sweater sleeve. Her blue eyes are beaming so brightly they look like metallic Christmas balls dangling from a well-lit, overdecorated tree.

"I can't do this," I moan.

"What do you mean, *chérie?*" Angora asks.

It's easy for Angora to get excited by the possibility of roaming cameras. I shudder thinking about a camera crew following me home to my dilapidated neighborhood. "Great. Maybe they can tape the drug dealers on

114th Street while they're engaged in a transaction!" I gripe.

"So what?" Aphro says with a shrug. So what? At least Mrs. Maydell keeps their home spotless. "Don't let 'em come to your house."

"That's right, *mija*," seconds Felinez.

"Well, we have to get into a house first before we can worry about them following us home," Angora advises. "Let's just take one Baby Phat step at a time."

"Right now, we're taking one Baby Phat step into the Mambo Hut and buying you a Mambolatte!" Felinez says.

"Afterward, let's hit the job board—and pray," groans Aphro. "I've got to make some money."

"I hear that," I moan.

"Me *tambien*!" Felinez joins in.

Chandelier throws a glare in our direction. "Fasten your Gucci seat belt, girls, because we're in for the roller-coaster ride of our style-driven lives," I predict.

"That's good for our Catwalk Credo," Angora advises. I whip out my pad and scribble. Then I poke Aphro to watch Chandelier as she air-kisses Nole into oblivion.

"Oh, Gucci hoochie, *puhleez*!" Aphro chortles.

For once, we don't poke Aphro into silence.

New school rule: You don't have to be ultranice, but don't get tooooo catty, or your posting will be zapped by the Fashion Avengers!!

BLING BLING IS THEIR THING. . . .
Some misguided soles circle around their hoop dreams instead of facing them head-on. No, we're not talking about the electronically tainted types at Dalmation Tech populating those skanky basketball courts in hopes of channeling video-gaming addictions. We're talking about certain fashionistas right here at Fashion International who have banded together into posses based on the bling quotient of their baubles and bangles. One so-called *purrlicious* posse comes to mind: we see them every day, prancing around our bubble-gum pink hallways with primp-ready purpose, intent on reinventing the fashion wheel with their kitten-size talent. So far, these feline flashers number four, which is why we have aptly dubbed them the "Bling Quartet." Perhaps it's time to define the real meaning of the term "fashionista"—an emblem most of us wear like a badge of honor because we value its connotation of a person with fashion humility who relies on the *established* and *enduring* design icons from Pucci to Gucci for inspiration. My advice to real fashionistas who are *serious* about earning their street cred on Seventh Avenue: stay away from

the Bling Quartet's glare, or you'll get a sunburn. And don't be fooled by their bling ambition, which they believe will outshine the rest of us at the Catwalk competition. We know who is the 23-karat topping on *this* opulent fashion sundae—and who is *definitely* not the cat's *MEOWCH*!

9/17/2008 4:00:03 PM
Posted by: Shimmy Choo to YOU

4

One week after the Catwalk nominations, it's time to hit the campaign trail. The thirteen house leader candidates, as well as our "committee members" (aka our closest crew), have been allowed to exit last period earlier than the "civilian" students so we can set up our Catwalk election tables in the corridor on the main floor. Despite the twenty-minute grace period, time is not on our side. When the bell chimes at three p.m., it will be helter-skelter as the fashion locusts descend on our tables to get up close and personal with the candidates—and the freebies. Then at five o'clock sharp, the schmoozefest will be officially over so everyone can cast their ballots at the voting booth set up in the Fashion Annex.

Despite my sweaty underarms and pounding heartbeat, running my Catwalk election campaign is more fun and ghoulish than celebrating Halloween. Not only do we get to wear costumes for the occasion, but we've also had our share of tricks *and* treats.

Speaking of tricks, Shalimar Jackson and her jaded

cronies sneak up the back stairwell, flinging open the fire exit door so quickly that they alarm us with their cacophony of terror. I don't mean to stare, but Shalimar's stretchy Lycra dress is so short she looks like a peacock plucked of its plumes. Her equally hard stare makes me feel embarrassed about the back alley location of my election station. Okay, so it's not really in a back alley, but my table is pushed so far into the corner of the dimly lit hallway that if I turned my back and accidentally lost my balance, I'd probably knock open the fire exit and go tumbling like Alice in Wonderland down the stairwell into a rabbit hole.

"Bling, bling, bling!!" heckle Shalimar and her best friend, Zirconia, running past us.

"*What* was that?" I ask, stunned by Shalimar's latest shenanigans as her bubble butt bounces off to her election table, which is in a prime retail location at the end of the wide and brightly lit intersection.

"I didn't want to mention it, *chérie*, but someone posted an entry on the new Catwalk competition blog, referring to us as the Bling Quartet. I guess we're supposed to be, um, supa-show-offs," Angora reports hesitantly.

"Did Rouge rip out your tongue? I mean, *now* you're telling us this?" I ask nastily.

"What happened? I didn't know the Catwalk blog was already up," Felinez demands.

Neither did I. I'm so mad at Angora for not keeping our ear to the street. "You're supposed to be the reporter, so start reporting!" I advise her sharply. I may have a few blind spots—like my hissy catlike temperament—but that doesn't mean I like being blindsided by a Shimmy Choo–wearing chortler. "Who was it, do you know?" I ask, even though I don't want to know.

"Take a Gucci guess," Angora says.

I snatch the paper place marker with my name off the bare table in disgust so we can begin setting up.

"We might as well be positioned behind a scaffold. Then at least we could put up a sign, 'Open During Construction,' " I gripe.

"I'm telling you I think somebody bribed *somebody*—that's what's up," huffs Aphro.

Angora breaks into a skeptical smile.

"We're not pulling your weave. It's true!" Aphro continues. Angora is naive about the wicked ways of the Big Apple. "Trust, Kentucky Fried Chicken is not the only source of greasy fingers in this gritty city."

"Oh, come on, *mijas*, it's the last day," Felinez says, rubbing my shoulders.

I throw the kitty tablecloth on our table with extra vigor. Angora runs her hand gingerly across the tablecloth, an adorable hot-pink faux fur fabric trimmed with winking cat's-eye sparkling decals. Sometimes, Angora seems so fragile—her delicate touch, her soft

74

nature. Maybe that's why I can't help pushing her around. I don't mean to, but I guess that's *my* nature.

"*Chérie*, I'm merely a kitty in the city just like you—clawing my way to the top. Why don't we work together?" Angora says, her eyes blinking rapidly because she's upset.

My nerves are on edge because Chintzy Colon has just plopped some homestyle Boricua hors d'oeuvres on her table, which is adjacent to ours, and the aroma is overwhelming.

"We *would* have to be set up next to her chorizo factory!" moans Felinez.

Anna Rex's black lace–swathed table is to the left of Chintzy's, and she doesn't seem too happy with the pungent odors, either. The sight of Chintzy's edible wares must be causing her sensory overload. I can tell by the deliberate way Anna keeps folding her promo pamphlets, as if she has obsessive-compulsive disorder. Anna turns up her nose, whispering furtively to her disciples, who are as skinny as she is and also dressed in black. She's probably nervous about her whole campaign going up in smoke, even though in Anna's case that wouldn't be such a bad idea.

Meanwhile, Moet Major, whose table is to the left of Anna Rex's, prances up and down the hall, showing off her new black satin baseball jacket with HOUSE OF MOET embroidered on the back in golden letters.

"A little presumptuous, no?" I hiss.

Felinez shakes her head in agreement. She's freaking out, too: she worked so hard over the past week supplying us with our treats—namely, matching babydoll T-shirts with our slogan emblazoned on the front in fuchsia letters: STYLE SHOULD MAKE YOU PURR. Felinez also made Angora a blue catsuit so stretchy it yawns and a purple one for Aphro, as well as matching catty masks with tinted plucky whiskers. Now Angora is opening up her powder blue travel bag on wheels, chirping away anxiously—another one of her nervous habits.

"You dragged that on the bus?" Aphro asks, impressed.

Angora hates the subway and the scurrilous furry friends who hang out on the train tracks like crew. As a matter of facto, she won't set foot down under unless she's with us; otherwise, she travels everywhere on the bus. Considering the route Angora takes to school—straight down Broadway—it's not a bad idea. She lives with her father on Eighty-ninth Street off Riverside Drive, an area that has the added green benefit of Riverside Park right by her tootsies. Even after two years, Angora is still getting used to the city and all its noise.

The mention of a bus has obviously jarred her memory about her morning jaunt. "Have you ever been on one of these new, super-long buses? I mean, I don't know about all that snaking around," Angora starts in. "Those buses are sooo long, they scare me. I actually don't think the front of the bus knows what the back is doing all the time." Angora sways from side to side to make her point as she pulls a huge bag of furry items out of her bag. We watch in amazement. She really should be a reporter. I could even see her doing the weather: *It's raining Dolce and Gabbana booties today*, mes chéries!

"What have you whipped up like a soufflé today?" Felinez asks, imitating Angora.

"Okay, I thought this would be *très* adorable— they're fur balls for the wrist or the hair. They go with our feline fatale message," Angora says, her eyes widening, which means she wants our approval. I pick up one of the fluffy pink pom-poms on an elastic band with a paper tag attached to it that says in tiny letters: EARN YOUR PURR POINTS TODAY.

"Fur balls, get it? Rouge tried to eat one this morning. Like the ones she spits up aren't big enough!" Angora's cat, Rouge, has a finicky system: she is constantly coughing up something or sniffling from allergies, and only bottled water touches that finicky tongue.

Felinez spurts out what I'm thinking: "*Mija*, this must have cost a lot, no?"

Suddenly I feel guilty. Angora is down for our cause, so how could I snap at her even if her father does have funny money to funnel for furry excesses. I guess I would be jealous if Angora didn't despise her psychotically perfect control freak of a mother so much.

"They kept me up all night," Angora says proudly.

"*Tan* coolio," coos Felinez, arranging the fur balls on the table so we can get on with our flow.

Suddenly, the cackling from the corner table reaches a high pitch. I glance down the hallway and stare involuntarily at Shalimar as she shimmers away in her metallic gray turtleneck minidress. Her friend Zirconia is wearing a matching sweater dress in vanilla, all the better for showing off her matching bubble butt.

"Leave it to the knit wits to put the emphasis on 'sachet' instead of 'sashay,' which carries more clout in my prop portfolio, okay," I observe, watching carefully as the bubblemint twins pile ivory sachets on their table.

"Hold this end," Aphro says, nudging me back to our duties. I grab the end of the hot-pink banner with our election campaign slogan in spotted pink letters—STYLE SHOULD MAKE YOU PURR—and step onto the chair so we can tape it above our table.

"*Purr*fecto!" Felinez says, nodding approvingly.

Stepping down from the chair, I put the basket of pink satin meowch pouches on the table just in time to catch another back stairwell entry.

"How you doin'?" asks this guy, his face settling into what looks like a permanent smirk.

"Feline groovy," I respond, handing him a meowch pouch, which causes him to snicker sweetly.

I have never seen this goofy cute guy before, but apparently Felinez has, because she greets him by his name. "Hi, Ice Tray!"

Before he can even respond, she shoves a pamphlet into his hand and starts our spiel: "You can earn your purr points today by voting for Pashmina Purrstein!"

"I can do that," he says, breaking into a grin that reveals his giganto rabbit front teeth. Running my eyes up and down his downtrodden decor like a human scanner, I take in his graffiti-tainted hoodie and Hefty Bag–gy jeans that are falling so far down his butt you could make a deposit in his coin slot.

Angora greets him with her usual charming curiosity. She is so nice to everybody. I have to thank her later for keeping her eye on the prize: voters.

"Where did you get your name?" Angora asks, using a technique we learned in Salesmanship: always focus on something about the customer to stimulate interest.

"It's my tag," he says proudly.

"You mean, like your design label?" Angora quizzes.

"Nah—more like for my art."

Suddenly, I realize that Ice Tray is referring to the

intricate doodlings left behind by grafitti artists on practically any surface in the Big Apple that will take to spray paint. All the buildings in Amsterdam Gardens are "decorated" by taggers. For all his blustering, Mr. Darius has never caught anybody defacing the property, and of course, he's too cheap to get the walls repainted.

"It's *très*—you know, like French?" he explains proudly.

"Oh," Angora says, beaming.

"Wazzup with your name?" Ice Très asks Angora.

"She looked like a goat when she was born—without the horns, of course," I quip.

"Oh, you mean cuddly—like *you*," he teases.

"Actually, my mother thought it was a pretty name for a girl with good breeding—she is very proud of her French heritage, by way of Canada," Angora interupts.

"What about *your* name?" Ice Très asks me.

"My mother wanted her daughters to live in the lap of luxury, I guess," I say, shrugging because I realize it sounds pretentious. It sounds more endearing when Mom says it.

"*Ayiight*. Well, I'm trying to get to Paris in a few to study art," Ice Très informs us.

Now I wonder what he's doing at our school, but he clears that mystery right up—at least geographically.

"I just moved here from Hamilton, Washington.

We had to outrun the Pineapple Express," he says. I have no idea what he's talking about, but Felinez perks up at the sound of an exotic dish. "See, we was always getting flooded out. Tropical water coming up from Hawaii made the river situation a little too hectic round our way, so my family got tired of that and we moved here."

Felinez listens with sympathy as he continues, "Thought about going to High School of Visual Arts, but everybody knows the honeys are over here!" Ice Très chuckles, winking and blinking again—at me.

"Wow, that's deep," I retort, impressed—not—at how he turned a natural pineapple disaster into a shallow move for honey dipping.

"I know, right," he says mischievously. "Nah, on the real, I wanna open my own company, Fashion Thug, you know, with hand-painted denim joints and whatnot—and jeans that fit big booties *specifically*."

Felinez winces and makes a face behind his back like, *Don't do me any design favors, graci-ass!*

I take a closer look at the graffiti on his jeans, checking out the details, which causes Ice Très to jump on an explanation like a firefighter with a water hose. "These are from PRPS—you know, it's pronounced 'purpose.' I got a lot of their joints from Pieces on 135th. Their wash is *sick*!"

"Pamphlets, please," orders Aphro, signaling that

our chat with Ice Très is over. Time is tick-tocking away.

"Awright, check y'all later." Ice Très breaks out.

After he walks away, Angora says approvingly, "I think Mr. Ice Très is *très* smitten with you."

"*Claro que sí.* Nobody is ever smitten with me!" Felinez says, pouting. "Not when you two are around."

"I'm sorry, but I am not interested in members of the thugeration," I say offhandedly, even though I think with the right makeover Ice Très could be even tastier than a croissant. But Felinez is right: whenever guys come flocking like geese, they treat her like she's a hologram. What's up with that?

Aphro, however, is oblivious to Felinez's feelings: "So is that a no on a hug from a thug?"

"Yes," I say firmly.

"Yes to a hug, or no to the thug?" Aphro continues.

"Yes—I mean, no!"

Luckily, the bell rings. "Showtime!"

Watching the students pour into the hallway, I tap my feet impatiently. It will take them forever to snake down the corridor to us—especially now that Chintzy will be plying potentials with chunky chorizos! I also can't help but notice how many guys stop to congregate by Shalimar's scentsation. Even Ice Très stops to do a buffalo stance. Shalimar pushes one of her sachets up to his nose, causing him to break out in his rabbit grin. Now

I know he's not a true artist; if he were he wouldn't have fallen for Shalimar's sham (and I'm not referring to her pillows, either).

"Maybe we should have padded our booties for the occasion," I say, wincing.

"Someone is green with Gucci Envy," chides Angora.

As usual, Angora is on *punto*.

"Maybe I'd better rethink my position on, um, aspiring visual artists," I say pensively. "After all, I am originally from the Boogie Down, where graffiti art was born on the cars of the IRT subway line." Staring at him with my mouth open, I wonder if Ice Très sensed that I wasn't digging his doodlings. "Close ¡·'" Aphro shouts.

"You talking to me?" queries Zeus, who I didn't see hovering in back of me.

"No—not you!" shrieks Aphro, letting out a snort.

Now I want to gaspitate over zebra stripes, but instead, I quickly snap into election mode. "Hi, I'm Pashmina Purrstein and I'm running for Catwalk house leader."

"I'm Zeus," he says, grinning. I try not to stare at his chiseled cheekbones. Zeus, on the other hand, is trying to show me his artistic side. "I dig your slogan— 'Style Should Make You Purr.' I can do a lot with that visually—I'm a graphic artist. We have three cats, too."

"Who's 'we'?" I ask, wondering if he means his

family. I'm always curious about other people: if they have more than I do—like a real father, or even a mother who *maybe* talks about their father sometimes, hello.

"Oh—my mom and dad. And I got two sisters. You'd dig my mom; she's crazy about cats. My dad was upset when she brought the third cat home. But she was like 'What do you want me to do? Cats are like potato chips, you can't have just one!'"

Angora laughs loudly. She just loves sound bites. Zeus stands like a statue and rests his left hand on the back of his hat, which I gather now is like his security blankie. "I'm serious. I could do a lot with your catty theme—um, visually. I major in display and whatnot."

"Yeah, you said that before," I say, nodding. But before I can continue, Zeus fills me in on the rest of his credentials like he's auditioning, when I'm the one trying to snag a vote—and maybe even more than that.

"I'm also a deejay, so I could hone in on your whole vibe—you know, laying down rap over tracks."

I'm not surprised by Zeus's allegiance to hip-hop—anybody could spot the flavor he savors. "Yeah, Angora told me you're a deejay. But you're a model, too, right?"

Zeus blushes *big*-time, staring down at his sneakers. Definitely Adidas. "Yeah, I'm trying to get a hookup with Vanna Snoot. She's a customer of my father's," he admits like he's embarrassed.

"Straight up?" interrupts Aphro like he said the

magic password. Vanna Snoot owns Snoot, Inc., the fiercest model agency in New York. As if reading our minds, Zeus elaborates. "My dad owns a custom tailor shop on Fifty-ninth Street under the bridge."

"I think I've seen that shop," I say. His dad's shop is next to the Snoot agency. We've all canvassed the block hoping to get a glimpse of the goings-on inside Snooty Central, which is housed in a three-story pink building with gilded window shutters that beckon like an attraction at Madison Square Garden on Halloween: scary but inviting.

"My dad makes a lot of clothes for her—and the models, too," Zeus continues. "Anyway, he's trying to get me an appointment. He showed her a Polaroid—I couldn't believe he did that, man."

"Can he get you an appointment?" I ask.

"She wants to know—can you get us an appointment, okay?" Aphro asks him point-blank.

"I hear you. Word is, Vanna doesn't see anybody," Zeus says, undefeated. "And you know the policy about students from Fashion International."

I sigh knowingly. The only model wannabes from our school who get snagged by agencies are winners from the Catwalk competition.

"See, that's why I want to lead a house," I confide. The reason we're all hyped about Snoot, Inc., is that they break new faces.

I wonder if Zeus is a "friend of Dorothy's." Not all the guys in our school are gay, contrary to the snickerings from the bozos across the street. Like Ice Très so aptly put it: everybody knows the fiercest honeys go to Fashion International.

"Um, you know about our theme?" Angora asks Zeus.

"Yeah, I can see it," Zeus says astutely.

"And we're definitely catering to the Kats and Kitties!" I say, interrupting her.

"Well, you've got my vote," Zeus says, beaming.

After he leaves, Angora announces: "Wouldn't it be great to have him in our house?"

"Well, I've got to get elected first," I say, staring longingly after Zeus's shadow.

Now Nole Canoli and his best friend, super-exotic Elgamela Sphinx, stand swooning at Chandelier Spinelli's table. Nole holds a pair of her giveaways—chandelier earrings, of course—to Countess Coco's furry, pointy ears.

After a few more snickers, Nole's entourage marches down the hall.

"Oops, here come the cattle," Angora says, beaming. My eyes lock with Nole's, and he looks like a deer caught in the headlights. I know he's voting for Chandelier Spinelli, but I break into a grin and hand him a fur ball anyway.

"Ooh, that would look so cute on Countess's

collar!" coos Elgamela, who wasted no time dangling Chandelier's sparkly giveaways from her own perfect earlobes, further accenting her Arabian princess aura. Today, she even has an amber crystal stuck in the middle of her forehead.

"Oh, that's my version of a Bindi!" she explains giggling, catching me staring and tossing her long, dark wavy hair. Suddenly she's fascinated by something we have, too. "What's that?" Elgamela asks, pointing to the pink satin meowch pouches.

"Felinez makes them," I announce proudly. "They're called meowch pouches and you can wear them on your wrist or around your neck. And you *are* such a feline fatale."

"Here, *mija*, take one!" Felinez says, shoving one in Elgamela's hand. She hesitates for a second, which prompts Aphro to chortle. "Girl, we know you're voting for *Chandelier*, but don't be bashful when it comes to booty!"

"Spoken like a true pirate," Nole says, giggling.

After they leave, I feel a twinge of sadness. "I wish we could snag Nole for our house, no?"

"Pash, I thought you said you despised his gawdy Gucci tendencies?" Angora asks, quoting me verbatim.

"Yeah, well, I'm prepared to believe his hype. Everybody says he's gonna be the next Versace," I offer, pouting.

A student interrupts our little huddle and I automatically snap into vote-for-me mode. "Hi, I'm Pashmina Purrstein. I'm running for house leader."

"I know who you are. My textile science class is next to your runway class. I saw you in action, too," the girl says, giggling. I scan her quickly and notice that she's hiding behind her big black sweater—kinda like Felinez used to before she began expressing herself bigtime.

"Um, you know anything about our style philosophy?" I ask her gently.

She shakes her head in the negative.

"What's your name?"

"Janilda."

"Look, Felinez and I have had it up to here with the plus-size clothing market. We're even sick of that distinction. New millennium girls kick it in every size—and that's what the House of Pashmina will be featuring in our fashion show," I say proudly.

Janilda's pretty eyes brighten.

"And that's not just for the Catwalk competition. My career goal is to open a chain of stores—Purr Unlimited—that will break boundaries by offering our fly private label collection in every size."

"We're gonna be like that Florida orange juice company—own the land, the growers, the oranges!" Felinez shouts.

"You got your strategy *down*." Janilda chuckles.

"You never met Felinez before?" I ask, surprised.

"Um, no, I've seen her around," Janilda explains.

"Oh—when you said textile science—"

"Yeah, but I *major* in textile science."

"Oh. Felinez majors in accessory design, but she will be my right hand, my partner in our enterprise. And, um—"

"But aren't you, like, going to be a model? I mean, a major model?" Janilda asks.

"For true." Because I understand that not everyone is up on our whole modelpreneur philosophy, I break it down further for Janilda.

"You are *major*!" she coos when I finish. "I like that—'modelpreneur.' Well, you've got my vote!"

Janilda bounces away.

"We're gonna be the Ben and Jerry of the fashion *mundo*—scooping up profits, *big-time*!" I coo after her.

Angora and Felinez cross paws with me on that one.

But just when I think I can celebrate my victory, along comes Chenille.

"Hi, Chenille!" coos Angora, shaking a fur ball against the front of Chenille's overalls.

Chenille looks down at the fur ball positioned at her ample chest, then grabs it and even reads the slogan before announcing to me: "Oops, you missed a spongie." My mouth drops open as I clasp at my curls, searching for a runaway sponge roller. *"Psych,"* Chenille hisses.

Where's Grandma Pritch when I need her? I think, glaring at my sourpuss sister.

"Um, gotta go. See you later," Chenille says dourly.

I watch Chenille waddle down the hall in her baggy denim overalls and suddenly I get a flashback to the sixth grade. One day after class, I saw Chenille standing in the hallway, gabbing away with her friends, with my favorite black crochet shoulder bag flung over her shoulder like it was hers. I was so pissed that I walked up to Chenille and took my bag off her shoulder, turning it upside down, dumping all her stuff on the floor. Chenille's arms started flailing all around, but that's where the advantage of being a foot taller came in very handy. I just pulled her hair and kept her at arm's length. Too bad a school monitor appeared out of nowhere and escorted us both to the principal's office. Obviously, the principal was none too happy when she figured out that we were sisters. "You two should be ashamed of yourselves!" she hurled at us. I wasn't, but Mom was. She said that I was selfish and didn't even reprimand Chenille for borrowing my bag without asking me. Ever since then, I guess you could say my sister and I have been on a Rocky Road binge.

"Well, so much for Ben and Jerry," I muse out loud.

"Chérie, she's gonna vote for you," Angora says.

"She'd better do my hair—for free!" Aphro chortles.

"If I were you, I'd spend my ducats on a *real* hair-stylist," I hiss back. The magic hour is upon us and I start packing up our toys so we can go home.

Aphro senses my discomfort and throws a fur ball at my head. "I'm just gonna *weave* that one alone!"

New school rule: You don't have to
be ultranice, but don't get tooooo
catty, or your posting will be zapped
by the Fashion Avengers!!

TRUE PIRATES <u>LOVE</u> THE "BOOTY." . . .

Last night, thirteen Catwalk candidates plied us potential voters with
stylin' spiels and swag before we
headed to the Fashion Annex to cast
our ballots. The campaign antics may
be over, but the drama quotient is
about to quadruple seven times a Pucci
scarf square once the election results
are posted on Thursday! In the meantime, I feel compelled to break down
last night's booty (and I'm not referring to Shalimar in that skintight
Silverado Express dress either, which
made her look like she was having
chipmunks in reverse!). After I
chomped on Chintzy Colon's **chorizos,**
which were exactly how I like my
fashion—*hot, hot, hot!*—I proceeded to
angle for a pair of danglers from the
candidate with the highest fabulosity
factor, Chandelier Spinelli. Now,
that's when I couldn't help but overhear *another* candidate complaining
about the expenses incurred for her
"She Shells." If Chantez Whining,
oops, Winan, wanted to make a *splash,*
she should have been asking herself:
"Is this bootylicious enough for ya,
babe?" I was not born yesterday, so I
can tell when someone's freebies have
been lifted from the dirty shores of

Jones Beach—for free—thereby counter-
acting the whole inherent pleasure
of receiving goodies and giveaways!
Obviously certain candidates should
keep a dictionary right by their Lee
press-on nails so they can look up the
definition for the word "swag" and
start appreciating its acronym: *stuff
we all get* (and deserve)!!

9/23/2008 10:45:34 AM
Posted by: Miss FLUFF

5

The next day I sniff my underarms and detect the distinct smell of Swiss poodle. In one hour, the names of the five elected house leaders will be posted outside the Fashion Café. I'm bouncing off the walls worrying about the results, which is why I shimmied out early from physics so Felinez and I could rendezvous in the Fashion Lounge.

"How come walking up and down the bathroom doesn't make time go faster? Newton was a *fig*," I complain nervously.

Felinez is more concerned with fashion reality than the laws of motion. "What is that stain, *mija*?"

She is pointing to the ashy white ring on my brown suede fringed moccasins. "I can't believe it!" I shriek.

"You stepped into water with alkaline properties," Felinez says in her distressed Boricua accent.

"Alka-*what*? The toilet in my house overflowed this morning!" I cry in disgust. "I *had* to sop up the water so I could take a shower. If I waited for Mr. Darius to come, we would have floated away in a tsunami!"

Felinez knows firsthand the fringe benefits of living in a brokedown palace. "Really, *mija*, he is the worst landlord. You should report him," she advises.

"To whom?" I counter. "Note to fashion self: shower with sheep in my sleep instead. It'll be safer!"

Right now, I hope Felinez also knows how to remedy my ruination. I was psyched about debuting my Power-to-the-Prairie outfit today, from the brown faux suede fringed miniskirt to the beaded ceremony necklace. "All this in the hopes of snagging a pow wow in Zeus's tepee," I moan, stroking the embroidered succotash headband I tied around my forehead after I tamed my frizzy hair with Elasta QP Glaze, which is Miracle Whip for girls like me who are knotty by nature. Trust, it's the only way I'm able to work my native plaits.

"I knew you liked him!" Felinez squeals.

"Oy, wait till he sees me. He's gonna call me Dances in Toilet Water!" I predict.

"Don't worry, I got the Nu-Hide cleaner from leather class in my locker. I can fix it," Felinez assures me.

"Thank *gooseness* my best friend is such a GENIUS!" I quip in my goofy voice. "Let's go by your locker, then hit the job board before the zoo lets out."

Speaking of animals, Chandelier barges into the bathroom with Tina the Hyena. Chandelier, however, is acting more like an anxious antelope. She gallops to the sink and stands so closely to me that the blast from her breath opens my pores. "Who needs Bioré strips when you're around," I mumble under my breath. Instead of apologizing, she stares at me wide-eyed like her pupils are adjusting to the reality of competing in the food chain.

"I thought of you," she says, rubbing lipstick from her teeth, "when I was getting a root canal yesterday."

"Silly me. I thought having capped teeth made excavation a moot point," I counter.

Chandelier stares down at the ring around my footsies, then cuts to her Gucci loafers, then to Tina, like she's doing a Woodbury Common outlet commercial. "Exclusive edition," she declares to Tina.

"*Puhleez.* They grind those out like Parks sausages!" I retort angrily. Felinez snickers loudly as we flee the Fashion Lounge. "God, she's such a primping *predator.*"

After we zap the water stains, we dash for a ducat alert at the job board. I send a text message to Aphro and Angora to meet us outside the Fashion Café later for the "showdown at the okie-dokie."

Meanwhile, Felinez is fretting about her Italian homework. "*Io sono malata,*" Felinez says, reading from her notebook. " '*Malata*' means 'sick' and not 'mulatto'?"

"Mos def."

"How do you say 'mulatto,' then?"

"I don't know, but I bet you in Italian they say something less slavery-oriented," I shoot back. Every

Black History Month, my mom makes us watch *Roots* together, and inevitably she blurts out, "I hate that word, 'mulatto.'" Probably because that's what I am, even though she never told me.

"God, I can't wait till we go to Italy," Felinez says, psyched, then cringes. "If we win, I mean."

"We'd better," I retort, echoing our Catwalk Code: *Act fierce even when you're not feeling it*.

Felinez smiles assuredly.

"Let's sashay by Ms. Fab's office," I whisper to Felinez, in an effort to quelch my own anxiety.

"*Por que?* What for?"

"Maybe we'll get first whiff of the It List," I say sneakily. Creeping closer, we get a whiff, all right—of a conversation not meant for our ears. "That's a good idea for reaction shots," advises Ms. Lynx, her voice of authority trailing into the hallway. "But you should stick around the Fashion Café afterward—and do try today's special, jambalaya gumbo. I hear it's divine."

"Any reason why?" asks an unfamiliar voice.

"There's nothing like Cajun peppers to put blush back in your cheeks. Oh—you mean—well, you'll see," Ms. Fab adds emphatically.

We stand still like undercover fashion spies trying to decipher Ms. Lynx's cryptic instructions.

Seconds later, four scruffy-looking men and one petite woman pop out of Ms. Fab's office. I freeze when I see the familiar logo on their equipment bags: TEEN STYLE NETWORK. I quickly examine my ceremony necklace like I'm searching for hidden hieroglyphics. Luckily, the crew seems too distracted to notice us. The lady has a pixie haircut and is dressed in grungy sneakers, jeans, and a green camouflage jacket. She points at one of the neon signs in the hallway: LEAVE YOUR CORNS ON THE COB. NO BARE FEET, PLEASE.

"Jay, get a shot of that," she orders, motioning to one of the guys hoisting a camera bag.

Jay hops to the task.

"Omigod! Ay, *dios mio!*" Felinez shrieks, once we're out of earshot. "Do you think Ms. Lynx is on the jinx?"

Instinctively, I know what Felinez is referring to. For the past twenty years it's been a secret tradition at FI to kick off the Catwalk competitions with a quickie voguing battle known as a pose-off once the leaders have been chosen.

"Don't be *radickio. If* she knew about our pose-off, we'd all be banned to Style Siberia," I shoot back, but my shuddering shoulders aren't so convinced. See, end-of-season markdowns aren't the only thing fashionistas can count on: disobey any of Fashion International's cardinal rules—like "no voguing in hallways"—and suspension is imminent. The loophole that fashionistas have hidden behind for twenty years, however, is this:

nobody said *anything* about voguing in the Fashion Café. People who already have props wouldn't understand why we would risk suspension for something that seems so silly, but they don't understand. See, we can't control the outcome of the Catwalk competition, but at least *we* decide how we're gonna set it off.

As we approach the job board, another thing becomes Swarovski crystal clear: we also can't control the competition for all the job postings. "This is a mob scene. We might as well be standing in a line for a fashion show at Bryant Park!" I huff.

"I know, *mija*. You'd think they were giving away swag!" Felinez groans, trying to jockey for space in the huddling masses. I reach into my purse to retrieve my pink pen and jab Diamond Tyler in the chest. Turning swiftly to meet her gaze, I'm relieved that her Victoria's Secret push-up padded bra with revolutionary patent-pending technology obviously softened the impact of my intruding elbow. (During gym period, I saw her in the cute scallop-edged "Secret" in the locker room.)

"I voted for you!" Diamond blurts out.

"Now, that's what's up," I respond gratefully, but I can't help but notice that Diamond has a serious case of ring around the eyes.

"Is everything cool?" I ask her.

"I was up all night with Crutches," she says, and

seems relieved someone noticed. Crutches is Diamond's cat, who was born with weak legs and has trouble walking.

"I've been taking her to swimming lessons, and the muscles in her back legs are getting stronger, but she was moaning all night cuz I pushed too hard," confides Diamond.

"Yeah—but it'll be worth it. Crutches'll be sashaying in no time!" I chuckle.

"That sounds more like Fabbie," Diamond offers shyly, a troubled look clouding her misty green eyes. "God, I never have any luck with these jobs. I think I'm gonna try the animal shelters."

"Really? You mean volunteering?" I ask. What I really want to ask her is, doesn't she need the seven dollars an hour like we do?

"*Mija*, this one looks good," Felinez says, interrupting the currency exchange. She points to a posting for the Betsey Johnson boutique.

"Omigod, I would do a kitty mambo in my bloomers just to work there," I concur. Diamond grins at me like she wishes she had my gusto. Little does she know that it comes from having nothing to lose but my hopefulness. Felinez continues to scan the postings for an assistant schlep job in any designer showroom, which would be primo for her.

"Oooh, this one," I say, pointing to a posting for

Ruff Loner showroom assistant. "No ducats, but internship credit."

"No way, José. I don't care if I have to fold the same pashmina scarf fifty times as long as we work together!" Felinez testifies like a preacher.

"Stick to a showroom," I protest, pulling out my cell phone. "It's time you put your pattern-making skills to a test."

"If I can't work with you, then I'd rather spend all my time making the accessories for our fashion show," Felinez declares defiantly. "At least *that* freebie means a chance at flying the Friendly Skies—for free!"

"Hold up, Tonto. Let's wait and see if there will be a House of Pashmina, then I'll demand you devote your every waking *minuto*," I advise her, positioning myself in a corner for privacy so I can get a leg up on the competition. Just to make sure, I suck in my stomach.

"You think they're gonna see your flat stomach on the phone?" Felinez asks, whacking me in the midsection.

Shooing her away, I speak in my professional voice. "Um, hello, I'm calling from Fashion International." Meanwhile, the girl on the other end informs me in her brittle British accent, "We're not taking any more applicants at the moment. *Not* from Fashion International."

Humiliated, I hang up. "Do you think she could tell

on the phone I'm black?" I ponder out loud because I can hear my mother's voice ringing in my ears. She got played back in the day trying to snag A-list jobs. And even when she did get hired at two-star boutiques, she was constantly reminded that the cocoa color of her skin stood in the way of a payday or promotions.

Felinez, however, snaps me back to reality—literally. "No, Pocahontas, I don't think so!" she says, yanking one of my braids to make her *punto*.

"Well, Miss Prickly Pennyweather didn't know how fabulous we are!" I gripe, writing down more job postings in my notebook, but I decide to wait until later to resume cold calling so I can put on my cheerful voice.

Despite our layover at the job board, we arrive outside the Fashion Café before the Catwalk announcement is posted. Some of the usual suspects are posed in place.

"Wazzup, pussycat!" yelps Ice Três. He has a chartreuse messenger bag slung over his shoulder. It's tagged with his wannabe brand, FASHION THUG in silver metallic letters. I gaze at his sly smile and realize that he may not be as tasty as a Toll House, but he is definitely crunchy. Maybe it's time to yank Shalimar's silver spoon. That's what up, until Zeus rolls up on us. Today, he's carrying his sweet sound system with a purpose known only to us. "I'm ready to crank it up," he confesses, crossing paws with Ice Très.

I stand with a hand on my hip, checking them out while they start riffing about an assignment in Illustration, then switch to the subject of sneakers. Suddenly, Zeus realizes that I'm being left out of the mix. "We're serious sneakerheads, ya dig?" he explains.

Meanwhile, Shalimar must also be digging Ice Très, because she rolls right up. "I thought you were waiting outside biology for me?" she asks him boldly. I marvel at her sudden switch in taste sensations: obviously Zeus is no longer the cherry on top of her "opulent" fashion sundae.

"Oh, I thought you said chemistry," shrieks Ice Très, guffawing like Roger Rabbit on helium.

Speaking of infectious laughs, Angora and Aphro finally arrive on the fashion scene, too. Aphro lets out a signature snort to release her anticipation. "It's time to flip it like burgers, baby, *ayiight!*" she yelps.

"No doubt," adds Ice Très, getting his flirt on, until Shalimar puts his moves into deep freeze.

"Can I talk to you for a second?" she asks him in her best Mrs. Softee voice, pulling him aside.

Ice Très shrinks inside his hoodie, smiling coyly as he's dragged to the sidelines.

"What's up with that?" Aphro asks me.

"Shalimar is obviously *hood*winked," I say offhand-edly, trying to keep the situation Lite FM.

"I wonder what she put in those sachets? Maybe we should have taken a whiff," adds Felinez.

"Probably some of that Frankenstein stuff," Aphro says with conviction.

"Frankincense," Angora says.

"Whatever." Aphro snorts again, becoming fasci-nated with the burnished metal symbol on my ceremony necklace. "Oooh, what's up with this?" asks Aphro. She loves symbolic trinkets from around the world.

"I think it stands for 'unity' in the Iroquois tribe," I say, trying to remember. I got it last year at Ooophelia's, but I haven't worn it yet because I wanted to work it with the right cultural theme, like I always do.

At last, Ms. Fab's assistants, Farfalla and Sil Lai, ap-proach with the important papers in their hands.

"And the winner is!" Aphro says, jumping up and down. Everybody giggles. Except for Shalimar. She stands with Ice Très at her side like she's a presidential *shoe*-in. Now Aphro squirms her way up front while I stand pondering whether Ice Très is feeling Shalimar over me.

"No way, José," Felinez says out loud, resting her paw on my forearm to balance herself as she stands on her tippy-toes to no avail. "Can you see?"

"Not a whiff," I reply as Sil Lai posts the It List on the pink velvet board.

"*Chérie*, I can't see either," Angora adds, squinting.

Chandelier Spinelli squeals. "Guess Miss Piggy can see," I observe, clutching Felinez's sweaty paw. By now, Aphro has managed to elbow her way to the front of the fashionmongers and yells out loudly to us, "*Pashmina Purrstein, that's what I'm talking about! We're in the house. We're in the house.* Omigod. Omigod!!"

"*Yes!*" I scream, raising my cupped hand in the air.

"*No!*" someone screams through their cupped hands like they're maneuvering a bullhorn.

"Oh, snap!" yells someone else amid a round of hyena heckles. I don't turn to glare at the source of the dis. Instead, I let Felinez envelop me in a bear hug. Then I close my eyes and press my head down against her fuzzy hair.

"We did it, *mija*!" Felinez says, gurgling against my chest, clutching me tighter. I inhale the sweet scent of Fanta orange soda that always clings to Felinez's clothes. Sometimes I fiend for Fanta because of Felinez, but I've only seen those delicious orange cans in one place: "Uptown, baby, where they sip it down, baby!" I sing in my goofy voice.

Felinez giggles, then says, "Stop, *mija*. You're giving me cramps!"

I let go quickly. "Oy, I can't take two floods in one day!"

Felinez doubles over in laughter or pain; I'm not sure which, so I shut up for a *segundo*. Now Felinez's face turns red.

"I'm just playing!" I say, hugging her again. "Seriously, I can't do anything without you—not since I'm six." This time when I open my eyes, Chintzy Colon is standing nearby, staring at me, her eyes wet from fresh tears like she's a newly crowned beauty pageant contestant.

"Congratulations," I coo, over Felinez's shoulder.

"I didn't get it," Chintzy says, wincing. Then she hides quickly behind her Snap-On Smile. "I'm happy you won, though. You deserve it, Pashmina."

Now I feel janky about snapping on her. Chintzy can be cool, even if she's fortified by artificial sweeteners.

"I hope you'll choose me to be in your house," Chintzy says.

Felinez grabs my hand, so I slither away without responding, and we make our way to Aphro. I make sure, however, that we end up right near Zeus just in case he wants to beam me up.

"See, told you I voted for you!" Zeus says enthusiastically, then motions with his index finger to the lunchroom. "I'ma check you inside."

I grin like I'm flattered even though I was hoping he

would drop a few more corn niblets in my direction. Felinez senses my longing and pulls my sleeve like a ventriloquist so I'll gush on cue instead and not miss my five minutes of fashion fame. "God, I feel like Miss America!" I say.

"Don't say that, *mija*. You'll jinx yourself—cuz they always get caught in scandals!" Felinez warns me.

"Well, maybe I'm taking notes for my own scandal!" I declare joyously, staring at my name, the third on the list, before I make an observation that causes my smile to crumble like blue cheese. "Why is Shalimar's name first?"

Shalimar Jackson

Willi Ninja, Jr.

Pashmina Purrstein

Anna Rex

Chandelier Spinelli

"Because it's in alphabetical order, Miss Paranoid!" Angora says, wrapping her arms around me.

"Oh, right!" I respond, just in time to spot another sore loser: Moet Major who has cleverly folded her black satin baseball jacket emblazoned with HOUSE OF MOET over her arm.

"That's what they have sample sales for," Aphro says, referring to the sales where designers discard their surplus stock to make way for the next season.

"Yeah, I guess she let the cork out of the bottle

big-time," I reply. Nonetheless, I feel bad for her, because that could have been me, so we hustle inside the Fashion Café and step to the counter.

"How's the shrimp?" Felinez asks chirpily.

"So fresh, it'll crawl on your plate by itself," Velma, the crabby food attendant, shoots back.

Felinez takes a plate, then advises me to try the crab salad—so she can taste it, of course.

"No thanks, it sounds too itchy." Instead, I turn around to scratch my deep desire: to see Zeus, who is perched at a table with his sound system on top of it. He beams at me from across the room. "He's braving the fashion frontier!" I say excitedly.

While I'm busy ogling Zeus, all eyes are on Willi Ninja, Jr., who has just pranced into the Fashion Café, grinning from ear to ear, with his crew in tow. Doting Dulce stands to his side, meting out her Spadey sense. She clutches her red patent tote like she's a fashion victor.

Suddenly, I overhear Shalimar explaining our private pose-off to Ice Très in a voice louder than a boom box: "We never know when the pose-off is happening until a few hours before. I'm telling you, it's kept more top-secret than the designs for Barbie dolls, which are kept locked in the Mattel corporate vault!" she shrieks.

"I wish someone would lock her up in a vault—on time delay—and eat the key!" I grumble at my gumbo.

"Would you listen to Miss I Wanna Be Down? She'd better get that *bourgie* tone back in her voice before her parents cash in her stock options," Aphro observes accurately.

"I can't believe she's digging him," I say, puzzled.

"*Puhleez.*" Aphro hmmphs. "She's just sprinkling him to show us she can can."

Secretly, I wish Ice Très would spread some of his sprinkles around again, like he did during elections. "I wonder what she really put in those sachets," I repeat, shaking my head as Shalimar continues to babble:

"The trick is to hang loose and be ready for the signal. Like with musical chairs. Cuz once the hankie is dropped, you're supposed to stop whatever you're doing and start posing for points."

"She did *not* say for points," Aphro blurts out in disbelief. "She is such a shamorama. And always gotta explain everything in such big 'O' detail."

Leana, the other Fashion Café attendant, starts in: "You lucky I don't know how to vogue—cuz I'd show y'all how the real heffas shake it!" Cackling loudly, Leana drops a dollop of gooey gumbo on Shalimar's plate.

I turn just in time to catch the Last of the Mohicans: Nole Canoli and his crew making their timely entrance. His late arrival signals that the pose-off is about to be on. Dame Leeds looks around the café like an undercover spy, then snags a broom and runs to the door. He slides the broom sideways into the door handles, securing them. Now that the door is barred, absolutely no one will be allowed to enter the Fashion Café until the pose-off is *finito*.

"So much for the Teen Style Network," I say with relief.

The crowd breaks out into a loud round of claps and piercing yelps. Nole and his crew join Chandelier and Tina at their table, letting it be publicly known where his allegiance stands. After exchanging air kisses, Chandelier cuts her slice of pizza with a plastic fork and knife, like she's Princess Kryon at a socialite luncheon.

I'm too excited to sit down, and I can't afford to take my eyes off Willi Ninja, Jr. None of us can. We're waiting for our five minutes of fame.

In true dramatic form, Willi Ninja, Jr., signals the chef to hook him up with the special. "But don't worry about a napkin, cuz I'm gonna use my hankie! *OOPS!*" he yells loudly, dropping his white cotton hankie with a flourish on the floor, and falling into a vogue step before his body hits the shiny pink-and-gray linoleum.

Zeus cranks up the music: bold lyrics delivered in the falsetto voice of a male singer over the spaced beats of hip-hop music.

"*This is house, my house! In my house we work our*

theme like the Dream Team. *The theme of my house is more than a feeling. It's homage to house maximus à la mode. It's an attitude I'm taking straight to the bank. Homage to house maximus. Bank on my house. Next to Gucci, they get loosey. Next to Prada, there's nada. Next to my house there is victory maximus. Homage to house. For real fashionistas. Because that's what's up. You must obey the rules in my house, so repeat after me. This is house, my house! And this is my homage maximus. Pose struck!"*

The music vibrates with thunderous bass as all the students in the lunchroom break out in elaborate poses to profess our undying love for fashion. My lungs are filled with pride as I quickly observe that every single student has stepped to the Catwalk challenge. As usual, some of the more dedicated voguers have elevated their posing to a higher level by jumping on top of a lunchroom table. I stay on the floor so that I can meet Willi's gaze as he challenges each of the other four house leaders—including me. Ninja, Jr., approaches me, utilizing the clean, sharp movements inspired by martial arts that earned his legendary father the moniker he passed on to his adopted son.

Screams of "Work, supermodel or be worked!" are heard over the hypnotic hip-hop beats.

I beam at Angora, Aphro, and even Felinez, who is no slouch in the voguing department. She has her own salsafied ways of moving, which I love. Angora moves carefully, but I can tell she is serving her soufflé, as she would say. One day, I know that Angora is gonna break out and vogue like a real supermodel. I know she can.

I try to quickly take it all in: Willi Ninja, Jr., approaches Chandelier's camp. Nole is holding Countess Coco and voguing, beaming like a proud fashion papa. Elgamela Sphinx gyrates her hips like a dreamy genie rising from a bottle. I know Elgamela is going to make the fiercest catwalker, and I feel a twinge of sadness that she won't be in my house. Now I cut my eyes over to Shalimar, who is voguing with Ice Très. Once his eyes meet mine, he slithers toward me and vogues in my face, trying to press his body against mine. I block him with my outstretched arms, pushing him away. Shalimar's shady eyes rest on me, so I decide to go with Ice Très's flow just to set her off.

"Twirl!" Aphro shouts, watching Willi Ninja, Jr., who has just picked up Elgamela. In return, she stretches out her arms with complete abandon. After he puts her down to a round of applause, Willi Ninja, Jr., picks up the hankie and stretches his arms in a final pose, signaling the end of our pose-off.

Zeus turns off his tasty track, "Homage to House." Then Dame Leeds removes the broom from the doors to the Fashion Café, but not before we get off another round of victory claps. For one more year, fashionistas have pulled off our private pose-off without prying eyes upon us.

"Major purr points for Miss Angora," I say proudly.

Once the doors are swung open, the Teen Style Network crew waltzes in. Their timing is perfect—for us. Zeus zooms past me with his sound system tucked under his arm, obviously on his way to his locker to hide the evidence. "Did you lace those lyrics yourself?" I shout after him.

He nods in the affirmative and hustles over quickly. "I'm honored to have been a part of this. I've never seen anything so tight before!"

"Well, you get major purr points for mixing," I profess. Now that it's official, I *have* to lure Zeus into my house. The top cat in the hat could seriously hook up the music for my fashion show.

As if reading my mind about plucking potential candidates for my house, Zeus offers, "Have you seen Dame Leeds's portfolio?"

"No," I say, wincing. Zeus seems tight with Dame Leeds, but Dame Leeds leads to Nole Canoli, and that fashion trail can only lead to Chandelier Spinelli.

"You know Dame?" Aphro asks, impressed. She rests her head on my shoulder, still out of breath from posing.

"For a minute," Zeus says, fiddling with his hat.

"He never talks to us," Aphro says matter-of-factly.

Dame Leeds's ears must be buzzing like a yellow-jacket, because he motions for Zeus to come over. Zeus shrugs and humbly says, "I'm glad you dug the track."

As Zeus trails off, Aphro yells after him: "I think she digs more than that!"

I shove Aphro like a harried passenger on the IRT: hard and with no regard.

FASHION INTERNATIONAL 35TH ANNUAL
CATWALK COMPETITION BLOG

New school rule: You don't have to be ultranice, but don't get tooooo catty, or your posting will be zapped by the Fashion Avengers!!

PUERTO RICAN PRIDE IS MORE THAN A PARADE

After the nominations for the house leaders were posted yesterday, there were five winners and eight losers. Like in all elections, there were **mucho** factors at play—such as fashion, foes, and just plain forgery. Sorry, but call me a stickler for creative arithmetic, *esta bien*? For example, everybody knew Willi Ninja, Jr., was going to be nominated—he was even given the honor of dropping the hankie for our pose-off. If you ask me, that's not what a real election is supposed to be. I mean, I'm not into hating or anything, but just because someone has inherited his pedigree from a parent who was a voguing legend—even if said legend did model in fashion shows for Claude Montana in Paris—that doesn't make him qualified to be the best house leader, *esta bien*? What about candidates like Chintzy Colon or Sarabelia Rodriguez, who couldn't possibly win because they don't have the same kind of street cred or, for that matter, enough Latin constituents to shoulder the vote? Does that mean they aren't qualified to lead a house? *Yo pienso que no.* I don't think so. Latin influence on fashion extends way beyond Carmen Miranda wearing fruit baskets on her head, even if that was a popular theme with drag queens like Tropicana and Flotilla de Barge in last year's Puerto Rican Day Parade. Doesn't anybody care that in the thirty-five years since the Catwalk competition began, there hasn't been one Latin house leader elected? Not one? *Por que?* Doesn't that go against the multicultural mission that our school's founding father, William Dresser, had for Fashion *International*? This is why I'm strongly advising fashionistas with a conscience to use the Teen Style Network coverage this year to voice our pride in all things multicultural. Then maybe next year a Latin candidate will stand a chance of getting elected and being noticed for more than just her tasty chorizos! Must Latin talent always wear bananas on their heads to get noticed? *Parate,* okay? Stop signs are red for a reason!

9/25/2008 10:35:44 PM
Posted by: Cha Cha Heels

6

The hallways are buzzing like beehives from the success of our pose-off. Even Ice Très is trying to store honey for the coming winter. "You posed for purr points. I'm digging it, pussycat," he coos, winking coyly at me as Aphro and I sashay down the hall.

"Then why don't you come to my house?" I offer boldly. If Shalimar wants a pillow fight, let the goose feathers fly.

"You haven't seen my portfolio, but you want me in your house?" he counters coyly.

"Rewind. This is prequel to a sequel, hopefully. I said *come* to my house, not *be in* my house. And bring your portfolio if you want. We're having a preinterview strategy meeting," I explain, then hit him with the time and locale like a professional house leader.

"Okay, your crib, I got you," Ice Très says, accenting his nod with another wink.

I try to pretend that I'm just scouting talent, which I am—*sort of*.

Meanwhile, Aphro's trying to suppress a smile, but

Ice Très's goofiness is even melting her sugar cane shell, not that she'll admit it. "That's a *lot* of winking and blinking, if you ask me," she says, and hmmphs as we exit the apiary.

"Who's asking?" I gently nudge Aphro down the stairs and squeal, *"Showgirls!"* Last Saturday night we all watched this *scandalabrious* movie on TV at her place about two competing Las Vegas show-girls prancing around with the most awesome plumage on their heads. Anyhoo, one of them pushes the other down a flight of stairs to secure star status in the show. Sure their ways are wicked. Just like the fash-ion biz.

"Well, it could lead to a hoodwink, that's all I'm saying." Aphro continues. I ignore Aphro because I'm feeling hyped by the fact that Ice Très accepted my pre-screening invite. "Purr points. He's good." I giggle, mar-veling at Ice Très's dead-on imitation of *moi*. "M.O. to the I."

Aphro and I head to the job board for more cold calls, but after fifteen calls, "chilly" would be a more ap-propriate word.

"What a buzz-kill. Don't they know I'm the leader of the House of Pashmina?" I gripe to Aphro while I force myself to keep dialing for dollars.

Finally, we get an appointment at Loungewear Lulu, a flagship boutique on West Broadway off Grand, which manufactures its own line of leisure and loungewear—or so explains the nasal person on the other end of the phone.

"I've never heard of this designer before. Have you?" Aphro asks me, twirling one of the feathered ends of the sequined purple lariat artfully wrapped three times around her long graceful neck, setting off the short, chic, sharp lines of her Cleopatra bob.

"No, I can't say I've seen Lulu riffing about ruffles on the Teen Style Network," I declare, "but that's what I dig about the fashion biz—another day, another designer."

Chenille walks past us, barreling toward the exit. "Hey, Chenille. Was you at the pose-off?" Aphro asks.

"No, but I gotta *pose my way* to a client," my show-off sister announces proudly.

"Well, sashay to a payday," I suggest sharply. Chenille takes my hint and saunters on her merry way. Secretly, I feel a twinge of Gucci Envy that my younger sister is snagging ducats before I do, but I say, "I don't understand how she plans to get into one of the houses if she can't even represent at the pose-off."

"I know. It's *unbeweavable*," retorts Aphro.

"Bet this. I won't be calling on Shrek's secret assistant to be in my house—and she can take that to Banco Popular," I sassyfrass.

My cell phone does a ringy-ding. "It's my mother

calling again." I assure her that I'll be home by six o'clock to let Mr. Darius in to fix the toilet. But I protest, "You think he coulda came this morning?"

"Never mind that. It's not like there was anybody home who needed to *use* the toilet," my mom gripes in the agitated tone she gets when she deals with Mr. Darius.

"Well, it's a good thing Fabbie didn't have company," I joke, but Mom is not in the mood, so I quickly change my iTune. "Don't you want to know where I'm going now?" I ask teasingly, then blurt it out before she responds. "I have a job interview in SoHo!"

I should have known, however, that my mom would take this info to negative town: "Can't you find something further uptown? I don't like the idea of you traveling so far, especially at night."

I stand still, tapping my foot, listening to my mom as she drones on about the sharp increase in predators on the prowl for pubescent flesh.

"Well, I guess I'm lucky I'm not wearing my red hoodie today to tempt the hungry wolves," I retort, anxious to eighty-six this conversation. Instead, I succeed in further pissing off my mother, who drops the latest crime statistics before she releases me from her rant.

"*Bad* kitty! I *should* be declawed," I grumble after snapping my cell phone shut like a Venus flytrap.

"What you *shouldn't* have to do is deal with Mr. Darius," counters Aphro.

I shrug, unfazed. "Frankly, I think Big Daddy Boom should watch a few reruns of *Flip This House* and pick up pointers. Consider yourself lucky Mrs. Maydell is a home*owner*."

"Actually, she ain't, and Mr. Maydell lets us know every time *they* get into a fight," Aphro says, and provides a gruff demonstration: "*This is my house—I'm the one making the mortgage payments around here so y'all better straighten up and fly right!*"

Mr. Maydell is kinda scary; according to Aphro, he's always ready to rumble with her younger foster brother, Lennix, for the slightest infractions.

I feel a breeze by my ear as Chandelier and Dame Leeds whiz by us, chomping on strategy cuds like hype-hungry cows. "I've got all the members I need to win. Getting the rest of my team together is going to be easy breezy," Chandelier brags.

"I heard that, Miss Thing," agrees the dramatic hairstylist. "And you know I'm going to work it for points on the Dow Jones. I'm thinking we should feature short hair so we can angle the dangles—chandelier karats!"

I try not to cringe as I concede that Dame won't be working his dangle-proof drama for our house.

"What about you, Miss Pashmina?" Chandelier

turns and asks me in her taunting voice. "Who's down with feline fatale? *Meowch!*"

Aphro and I pretend we don't hear her, so she continues dropping lines from her brag book. "Don't know why I'm bothering going on this job interview, because I know it's already mine!" she says with assurance, then pecks Dame on both cheeks like they do in Europe.

"Snag it, Gucci girl!" shrieks Dame, pecking back before he hurries down the hallowed hallway.

"Oh, bye, Miss Aphro . . . scratch, scratch!" Chandelier singsongs before grandly descending down the stairs to the doorway of the main entrance, where the attention deficient can get stroked by the ogle-ready Dalmation techies who linger outside after school.

"Why she always putting me on blast?" Aphro asks, her eyes blazing.

"Because she knows you call her Gucci hoochie behind her back." I giggle as Aphro and I walk toward the less frequented Eighth Avenue exit, for those of us whose own initials are enough, like Bottega Veneta.

"*Chan-dee-le-ay* better not be going on the same job interview we are." Aphro groans in protest as I fling open the door.

"Don't even trip—" I start in, ready to squash her doubts, but squash my riff instead when I spot the Teen Style Network crew crouched right outside the pink wrought-iron gates. By reflex, I adjust the headband plastered to the center of my forehead. The lady hones right in on us like a heat-seeking fashion missile. "Hi, I'm Caterina Tiburon. I'm the field producer for Teen Style Network—assigned to cover the Catwalk competition," she announces, confidently extending her right hand. Her handshake is firm and forceful in contrast to the soft, rumpled condition of her drab, baggy khakis and pocket-plenty camouflage jacket. Secretly, I wonder if Caterina Tiburon has gone AWOL from the U.S. Army. She isn't exactly what I expected a producer from the Teen Style Network to look like.

Before I respond to her courteous introduction, I tug down my mini from the micro end. "Hi, I'm Pashmina Purrstein."

"You're one of the house leaders, right?" she asks rhetorically, her eyes darting around at the other students coming out of the building.

"Yes," I say proudly.

"We knew she would get elected," Aphro chimes in. "True talent always rises above the din of the sales bin!"

I keep the Silly Putty smile plastered on my face despite the fact that Aphro sounds like one of the shady fabric merchants on Orchard Street—desperate to move bolts of raw silk that will unravel as soon as you get them home.

Caterina smiles faintly, then cuts right to *her* yardage requirements. "I'd like to get you on camera."

I freeze, but luckily my lips move. "Abso—um, yeah . . . of course," I say, fussing with my headband again.

"Not now," Caterina clarifies, excusing herself; then she whispers to Jay and a tall guy crouched next to metal cases of camera equipment. After she finishes, the tall one comes over. "By the way, I'm Boom," he says, extending his hand. I wonder what they're up to, but the way Boom cracks a smile puts me at ease.

"I'd like to schedule some time with you—I'm interviewing all the house leaders," Caterina says firmly.

"Um, okay. We can do it tomorrow, whenever you want. We can meet in Studio One downstairs—right next to the Hall of Fame?" I offer.

"If you don't mind, I'd like to see you in your natural habitat first. This is the more candid up-close-and-personal take before we get into the nuts and bolts—of fabric—of the competition," Caterina continues. I can tell she's trying to make a joke because she senses my hesitation.

"Nuts is right," I joke back, then get embarrassed that Caterina might get the wrong impression of me.

"Look, it's just establishing shots," Caterina continues, using production lingo. "I already have an appointment with Shalimar Jackson. We're going over to her apartment to tape her at seven o'clock while she holds a meeting for her social club."

Now my apprehension is bona fried. Shalimar is going to be shot in her Limoges-laden penthouse with the members of a *bourgie*-woogie organization, all of whom go to private schools like Huxley, Baumgiddy and Tense. That makes the fur on the back of my neck stand at attention.

"Um, okay. Lemme check with my mother first," I say, stalling. "I know she usually has her bridge club on Wednesday nights. I'll call you on the cell as soon as I clear the schedule?"

Caterina hands me her card, and I scribble my cell number on a page and tear it out of my Kitty notebook. "I look forward to it," she says.

After they leave, Aphro says, "You are so shady."

"What was I supposed to say—Spades?" I quip. Spades is a card game that my mother plays with gusto, but Hector, her quasi boyfriend, hasn't been around lately for her to even do that. Aphro and I played with them once, since it requires four players.

"What's the name of Shalimar's social club again— Hansel and Gretel?" I ask sarcastically.

"Jack and Jill," answers Aphro. "You got elected house leader for a reason. You don't have to front for anybody."

"Yeah, but you gotta come over."

"Let her come over Thursday. I mean, you did invite Ice Très," Aphro points out.

"Now, that's a plan." Why not have the Teen Style Network shoot us while we're having our first prestrategy meeting? "I mean, we gotta get the Catwalk flyer together to post on Friday."

Now that the Catwalk house leaders have been chosen, I have to begin interviewing and snagging some more fierce members for our house.

"You're definitely gonna help me with some catworthy choreography?" I ask Aphro, getting ten poses ahead of myself.

"I got you," Aphro says as she reflects on the bold moves from the pose-off. "Did you see Elgamela? I didn't know anybody could do that with their belly button."

"Too bad she won't be doing that for us," I lament, reflecting on the sad fact that Chandelier has snagged our favorite model. "Well, we'd better scurry on down to SoHo."

"I don't 'scurry.' I take the subway like the rest of the animals in Manny Hanny," Aphro quips as we descend into the gloomy underworld. Dramatically, Aphro sidesteps the puddles of dirty water scattered on the grimy, slippery floor of the train station. "Well, I guess you ain't the only one who sprung a leak today."

"This is true, but I pity the peeps who don't have access to the iron horse like we do," I say, like it's a consolation prize. "Gets you wherever you're going—pronto."

Aligning with my predictions: fifteen minutes later we arrive in the puddle-free, pricey shopping strip on West Broadway.

"SoHo is *sweet*," proclaims Aphro like a fashion mantra. "Definitely the spot for Purr Unlimited."

I gaze longingly at the endless stretch of stores ahead. The first three blocks on West Broadway are the most important retailwise, and for this privilege, boutique owners pay a premium rent. "Sixty dollars per square foot!" I exclaim.

"Sixty times at least five hundred square feet for even the smallest store. Do the math—that's serious sweating each month," adds Aphro. I know she secretly hopes to have a store, too, for her Aphro Puffs jewelry line. Something small and tasty like the Tarina Tarantino jewelry boutique on Greene Street—my fave, of course, since she's a devotee of Russian Hello Kitty.

"All Big Apple landlords are *greedy*," I announce like it's a revelation, at least to me, which makes me feel the pressure about picking slots for Catwalk house members. "Since we can't have Nole Canoli, we gotta think of another designer who can fulfill our vision," I fret.

Aphro stares blankly at the gray blazer and slacks in

the window of the Banana Republic store. "Meanwhile, *they've* obviously got enough bananas to open yet *another* one."

"What about Diamond Tyler?" I ask.

"I know you dig her animal sensibilities," Aphro says, like she's hesitating.

"Yeah, but she is a *good* designer."

"We've just got to look at portfolios, that's all there is to it," Aphro says, shrugging. "I dig Nole's stuff, but I can't say I've really checked anybody else, that's all I'm saying."

I hate when Aphro does that. For somebody who riffs raw, she can flip the script and act so cagey. I know she digs Nole. Who doesn't? Hello! I'm so busy fuming at her that we walk silently for the next three blocks. When we get to the fourth block on West Broadway going west, we stop in front of a store obstructed by a scaffold. I can't see the building number we're looking for. "This has got to be it," insists Aphro.

"Nah, it *can't* be," I snap, staring at the pay-less-and-look-it outfits propped in the window. "Are you sure this is the right address?"

"There's a sign, right there," Aphro huffs, pointing at the small block-letter sign displayed in the corner of the window: LOUNGEWEAR LULU.

My attitude sinks to the level of my moccasins.

"Should we even bother going in?" I ask, turning meek at the sight of unchic.

"We made an appointment. What if they call the school and tell them we didn't show up?" Aphro points out, attempting to push the door open to no avail. I press the buzzer instead, which chimes with a spooky echo.

"Almost all the boutiques in the Big Apple have buzzers because boosters are always mopping instead of shopping," I remind her. Boosters then sell the stolen merchandise through an underground network, which costs the retail industry billions in lost revenue. "But I bet this is not a mopping stop on their itinerary."

Once we're buzzed inside the fun house with the distorted designer duds, I examine the rows of packed racks of clothes directly in front of me. Front and center of one rack is a white jumpsuit covered with hordes of invading sequins. "I think Chintzy would like this. It could go with her white go-go boots," I observe glumly.

On the top of each rack are hand-blocked signs with the word SALE! in glaring red letters. *Subtle*. This is the kind of store, my retail instructor would say, that conducts sales all year round. Seemingly out of nowhere, a tiny, frail woman with ashy white skin and even ashier long hair appears from behind a mirrored door. She's wearing a long black empire-waist dress.

"What can I do for you two ladies?" she asks in a squeaky voice, approaching us slowly like a zombie from *Dawn of the Dead*.

Escape! I want to squeal, but instead I announce that we're from Fashion International. The scary lady's eyes widen, or so I think, until I look closer and realize that this is their perpetual state. Some of my mom's best customers at the Forgotten Diva boutique are also afflicted with the same Popeye pupils—no doubt the handiwork of an overzealous plastic surgeon.

"I'm Lulu Fantom," the lady says, breaking out into a fit of giggles and revealing teeth that look like they've trotted on the yellow brick road.

After we tell Lulu our names, she breaks into another round of giggles, which makes me wonder if she's making fun of us? I hate when people trip about my name. So does Aphro. But when Lulu asks us about our majors at school and we tell her, she giggles again. That's when I realize we're probably witnessing her signature snorkle.

"I design my collection myself," Lulu starts in as she proceeds to show us around the store, confirming our worst fear: she is, indeed, the designer behind the duds in this haunted house, established in 2004—the same year designer Faux Sho' introduced his fake Mongolian lamb maxicoats that had women looking like Swamp Things.

"I can't keep these in the stock," Lulu continues, proudly showing off a pair of ivory gaucho pants with white sequins up the side. "I just love this fabric."

"Is it muslin?" I ask in disbelief.

"Yes, I just love it; it gives the illusion of linen at half the cost," she boasts.

In my opinion, muslin is the hillbilly of fabrics, but I decide it's best to keep my thoughts to myself. Cuckoo Lulu continues to gush over a few more of her "signature pieces," before she makes it crystal clear that the tour of her haunted house is over. Even though neither of us is interested in blemishing our supa-scanty résumés with a stint at Loungewear Lulu, I feel insulted when we're ushered out of the store without so much as a half-meant *I'm looking at lots of applicants, but I'll be in touch. Toodles!*

Once outside, we adjust to the letdown. "I think she's running a *boo*tique, not a boutique!" I exclaim, getting depressed.

"She was definitely peekaboo scary!" Aphro adds.

"How about we try a few more real boutiques while we're down here?" I suggest.

"No doubt," Aphro responds cheerfully.

By the fifth real boutique and apologetic round of "Sorry, but we're not hiring," the two of us are ready to click our kitten heels and head home. "I hope Felinez didn't get kicked to the curb like we did," I say as we walk quickly to the subway station on Spring Street. "We gotta at least look in the window," I say, and Aphro knows exactly what window I'm referring to. We turn onto Greene Street so I can swoon at my favorite store. "Ooh, look at the new bag candy!" I say, staring hungrily at the lipless Pink Head of the rare Russian Hello Kitty cameo pendant dangling from a lucite beaded choker. "Oy, I can't believe I don't have one of these yet."

Aphro shakes her head at me. "My jewelry is gonna be more fierce."

Now it's Aphro's turn to swoon, so we stop for a *segundo* in front of the Jimmy Choo boutique. "Shimmy Choo," I groan, using the Catwalk code name for the former Malaysian cobbler whose sought-after heels help everyone from Beyoncé to Lindsay Lohan sashay to stardom. "I sure could use a little shoe therapy right about now," Aphro says, prompting me to whip out my cell phone and call Angora for feline support.

"Stop sole searching, *chérie*," Angora hisses through the receiver. "We live in a cold, cruel world. That's what my mother says anyway, and she's always right."

By six-thirty, I wish I could say the same thing about my mother, because it's obvious I rushed home for no reason. Mr. Darius has stood me up. *Again.* I'm so annoyed I could scream from the rooftop. And I would if the door up there wasn't locked with prison-issue chains. My cell phone rings and I run to my bedroom to grab it out of the brown suede fringed messenger bag I was carrying today. Fabbie is plopped on top of my bag and she won't budge. "Move the caboose!" I yell, then toss her like a salad, but I've already missed the call. I'm worried that maybe Mr. Darius called my mother or something. I don't want her to think that I wasn't here holding down the fort like a true Apache. But I see from the missed call prompt that it was Felinez, so I hit her back.

"What's up, pussycat?"

Felinez alternates between barks and screams into the receiver before she blurts out to a salsa beat, "Ruff! Ruff! I got a job. I got a job!"

"You'd better work, supermodel!" I scream into the receiver, before I register an alternate reaction: *God, how come Felinez got a job and I didn't?*

Felinez is so busy babbling about her new position as an assistant to the assistant at the Ruff Loner showroom that she doesn't notice that I've missed a salsa beat.

"And I get to recatalog the patterns from all the past seasons," she babbles on, before she finally pauses for a breath and says, "*Mija*, how did it go in SoHo?"

"Well, let's just say SoHo was so low I had to hurry home and lick my wounded paws," I joke.

Suddenly, there is a loud rapping on the door. "Hold on!" I yell, scrambling to get by Fabbie, who now is sashaying ahead of me to the door like she's a fluffy Goodfrill Ambassador.

When I open the door, Mr. Darius stands like a stone statue, not moving even a facial muscle.

"Um, hi Mr. Darius. Are you going to fix the toilet?" I ask, holding the cell phone to my chest.

"No. I come tomorrow. There is flood in the basement. We gotta fix," he says unapologetically.

"You gotta be kidding!" I shout, losing it. "You gotta fix the toilet. My mother is coming home soon."

"You try the thing," he says, motioning with his hands like we're playing a game of charades.

"The plunger?" I guess.

Mr. Darius ignores me. "Try fix it, maybe."

"No, it doesn't work!" I blubber. "When are you going to fix it?"

"I come tomorrow," Mr. Darius says, clearly annoyed, being led by his protruding stomach as he walks away.

"Hello! What time?" I balk, stepping into the hallway in an attempt to stonewall him.

"I don't know," Mr. Darius says, shooing me away.

"I gotta know what time," I insist.

Mr. Darius's eyes catch a tiny twinkle as the corners of his mouth turn up involuntarily. "Okay. Okay?"

"Six o'clock," I command, pointing to the face of my French Kitty watch.

Mr. Darius nods his head slightly, then waves his hand like he's shooing me away again.

"Oy," I groan, closing the front door. Then I resume my Catwalk leader mode, getting back on the phone and filling Felinez in on the Teen Style crew sighting after school.

"Omigod. I wish I was there!" Felinez says. She ran off to her appointment at Ruff Loner before Aphro and I left to go down to SoHo. "So, are you calling her back?"

"Calling who back?"

"The producer. Caterina. You said she wanted to see you in your natural kitty habitat?" Felinez reminds me.

"She did not say that!" I giggle. "Oh, right. Lemme—Omigod, I just thought of something so shady, I may go into total eclipse!"

"What happened? *Que paso?*" Felinez screams in anticipation.

"Operation: Kitty Litter," I respond, deadpan.

"Ay, *dios mio*, what are you up to, *mija?*" Felinez says, with a giggle.

"Operation: Kitty Litter" is the code name we invented and have used for all our covert secret operations since grade school.

"Aphro is right: we get the Teen Style crew to come

over and shoot us having our first preinterview strategy meeting. *And* I tell Mr. Darius to come over at the same time to do the repairs," I explain.

Felinez gets quiet.

"Blue Boca? Come on, don't you get it? They could get him! On camera, I mean. Maybe he'll think it's the fashion police or something! At least he'll be embarrassed when I hit him over the head with the plunger!" I crow, trying to jump-start Felinez's enthusiasm. Blue Boca is a nickname I gave Felinez one summer when a heat wave so blazing struck the city that all she did was suck on blue ices that turned her tongue spooky blue. "I just want to see the look on Mr. Darius's face when Caterina instructs Boom to stick a camera on him. *Comprendo?*"

"*Mija*, maybe he'll get really mad," Felinez warns.

True to my stubborn nature, I ignore her apprehension. "Operation: Kitty Litter is a go. Signing off!"

New school rule: You don't have to
be ultranice, but don't get tooooo
catty, or your posting will be zapped
by the Fashion Avengers!!

WHO'S AFRAID TO PRANCE TO A
PAYDAY? . . .

Not all students at Fashion International fantasize about becoming a
supermodel or a "modelpreneur," as the
most ambitchous among us like to call
ourselves. Some of us are intent on
fashion domination by using our man-
agerial skills and creative vision.
Take me, for example. Nothing matters
more to me than providing a platform
for my unique take on style from a gay
perspective. That's why I feel qualified to lead a house in the Catwalk
competition—NOT because I happen to be
the best voguer in school! Yes, my
adopted father, vogue legend Willi
Ninja, was responsible for providing
the student body at Fashion International with a more appropriate
physical education elective than basketball, fencing, and calisthenics
classes. Although he is no longer with
us, we should all continue to express
our gratitude for his making such a
valuable addition to our curriculum as
voguing classes, and sparing us from
being subjected to the bouncing ball
and other boring antics associated
with butch sports. However, I feel compelled to clarify what voguing actually

is, given what I witnessed during yesterday's pose-off. Voguing is a dance form that originated in Harlem ballrooms back in the day, and it combines various techniques from the martial arts, jazz and modern dance, gymnastics, and yoga, among other disciplines. And thanks to the dazzling voguing displays presented by Elgamela Sphinx and Miss Aphro Biggie Bright, I'm going to add belly dancing and hip-hop to the eclectic beat-driven blend. Beyond this, there is also an exquisite execution that distinguishes it from other dance disciplines. Voguing is structured around distinct hand and arm movements, so the trained voguer must keep time with the beat of the music as well as accentuate various changes in rhythms. Therefore, simply primping and POSING to the beat is only ONE aspect of voguing. Also, for the record, Jody Watley and Malcolm McLaren, NOT Madonna, were the first two recording artists to feature true voguers in their music videos. Nonetheless, the Material Girl received maximum exposure because of her blonde ambition, if you catch my drift. Given my posing pedigree, all I would have to do to gain the same exposure would be to pull down my pants and stick my butt out of the school window!! Contrary to shady belief, I have no intention of following in my adopted father's footsteps like his godson Benny Ninja, whom I revere completely, and who thankfully may be joining our school's faculty (no disrespect to Mr. Blinghe). But, see, I intend to dance to my own fashion beat because I don't have to pose for a payday. Now if you don't mind, I must get ready for my Teen Style Network close-up, then win the Catwalk competition. Click. Dial tone. Good-bye!!

9/30/2008 12:45:45 PM
Posted by: Twirl Happy1992

7

Staring at the sign-in sheet in the reception area of Ms. Lynx's office, I shriek when I see that Chandelier Spinelli has already booked her time slot for Studio C to conduct interviews for team members. Sure, she may already have Nole and Elgamela in the Gucci bag, but she still has to enlist talent for her house like the rest of us: by *any means necessary*. Channeling Zorro, I boldly scrawl my name on the sign-in sheet in the slot for Tuesday from four to six p.m. Then I plop down on one of the gilded chairs with the leopard seat cushions to wait for the blank team member forms that I'll need to submit after I have selected all my house members. But first, Farfalla has to win *her* battle with the temperamental Xerox machine.

"*Madonna, ancora! Ma, venga!*" Farfalla yelps, shoving the paper tray into its compartment. Pressing the Start button to no avail, Ms. Lynx's dramatic assistant turns to coaxing: "Oh, *please, per favore, va bene?*"

I smile at her, embarrassed, then avert my eyes to

the spotted plaque hanging on the closed door of Lynx Lair: WEAR FASHION, OR BE WORN.

Still no Xeroxes, so I scan the wild inhabitants of Catwalk Central: the bobcat heads mounted on the walls, the carved cheetah bookends standing menacingly on their hind legs, and, crouched in the corner, the leopard ceramic statue with the gaping jaw.

Suddenly, the door to Ms. Fab's inner sanctum swings open, and out pops another predator. I stare down at the leopard-skin area rug sprawled by my feet as Chandelier's babble spills into the reception area. "I can't believe I got the job!" Chandelier squeals, tossing her stiff, spritzed hair that's like an overtamed lion's mane. Then, turning toward Farfalla, Chandelier grandly announces: "I got a job at Betsey Johnson!"

Like a well-trained fashionista, Farfalla feigns bright-eyed interest even though she's preoccupied with her Xerox crisis. *"Bravo!"* she chortles.

At last, Chandelier floats into the hallway on her fashion-job cloud while my mind starts spinning like a dreidel. How did Chandelier snag a position at Betsey Johnson? What was she doing in Ms. Lynx's office?

Ms. Lynx steps out of her lair and looks at me quizzically. "Just waiting for forms," I inform her.

"Dov'e Sil Lai?" Ms. Lynx shoots to Farfalla.

"Lei andata in giro per il tuo cappuccino, ma espero che ritorna subito!" frets Farfalla.

The commanding Catwalk Director continues speaking to Farfalla in Italian. By now, I'm lost in translation, so I sit mesmerized fantasizing about living *la dolce vita* in Italy for two weeks in July.

"Ecco, finalmente!" Farfalla says, refueled by the humming sound of Xerox copies ejecting into the tray.

Finally is right. Now I'm armed with the necessary forms. *"Grazie!"* I say, then hightail it into the hallway, but not fast enough to avoid Chintzy.

"Oh, hey, wazzup," I say, bracing myself.

"When are you interviewing?" Chintzy asks eagerly.

"I thought you wanted to be in Shalimar's House?" Yesterday I watched while Chintzy stood Splendafied by Shalimar as she dangled a hookup with Grubster PR, one of her father's investment clients. Of course, the conversation went hush until I faded to fuchsia down the hallway.

"No way, José," Chintzy responds.

"My flyer will be up tomorrow, okay?" I say, stalling. "Right now, I gotta hustle and flow to the Fashion Annex to do research for a quiz!"

As I clomp in my pink classic Swedish wooden clogs down the stairs, I'm so preoccupied with Chintzy's sudden desire to walk feline that Zeus spots me first.

"I knew it was you!" Zeus says, his pale blue eyes squinting at me like I'm a magical looking glass.

"Oh, I guess you heard my herd," I say, embarrassed.

"Where you roaming?" Zeus asks, chuckling.

"To the library to check on zebra migration patterns," I jest.

"That's always interesting."

"Nah—actually, another kind of pattern. Tartans for textile science. I still can't tell the difference between the Barbecue Plaid and the Braveheart!" I reveal.

"Oh, the last one's easy—check out Mel's kilt," he advises, but realizes by my blankety that I don't get it. He quickly adds, "In the movie?"

"Right." I nod, trying to picture the Scottish plaid in question, but all I can envision are Mel's bushy calves. "Are you into kilts?"

"Could be," he answers.

I decide it's time to bite the catnip. "You'd be an asset to my house—whether you bared your legs or not."

Zeus breaks into his squinty-eyed grin again.

"We're starting our preinterview strategies tonight at my house at six *sharpo*," I babble, holding my breath. "Consider yourself in if you can make it."

My cheeks start burning. Why did I put him on blast like that? Shrieking inside, I decide to take it back. "You probably have something more important to do, like scrubbing your sneaker collection."

"Nope. Consider me in there like swimwear," he says calmly.

"Oh, I get it—it's Posture Like Pashmina Day," I quip, scribbling my address on a sheet of paper in my Hello Kitty notebook. Then I get embarrassed because I don't want to spill the refried beans about Ice Très.

Zeus squints at me like he wants to ask what I meant, but instead he just riffs, "No doubt."

I hand him the scribbled-on paper and he breaks out, explaining that he has to head uptown.

Right after school, Felinez, Aphro, Angora, and I have to head downtown to the Alley Kat Korner on Avenue A to buy some kitschy items for our first close encounter with a camera: pink-frosted cupcakes, paper plates and cups, and pink popcorn. "These kernels will pop for the camera." I giggle while Angora picks out posies.

Operation: Kitty Litter is about to jump off at six o'clock tonight at my apartment. That is, if Mr. Darius and the Teen Style Network crew show up. In the meantime, we get busy pinkifying my crib.

"Does Zeus know about Operation: Kitty Litter?" Angora asks as she places the flowers in the metallic blue floral vases she's supplied for the occasion. I'm secretly grateful she left her dad's rabbit vases at home where they belong.

"Um, no. And hopefully Mr. Hairiest Darius is on his way," I say.

"I'm glad you didn't tell him. As Ms. Ava says, sometimes the truth is just plain inappropriate."

"No wonder enrollment in your mother's etiquette school is so high. Fiberoni coaching along with napkin placement. *Quel resistable*," I add, imitating Angora and throwing our prized pink faux fur tablecloth over the scratched wooden dining room table. "Zeus was psyched about coming over."

"Angora, the flowers are beautiful. *Que bonita!*" Felinez says, sniffing the bouquets of pink roses and delicately spotted yellow Peruvian lilies. Angora has arranged bouquets around the living room and left one as a centerpiece on the dining room table.

"These are my mother's favorite—the Dreamland Bouquet. I should send her a bunch to christen her new home on Hysteria Lane," Angora declares, going on to explain the indignities her mother has to endure "living in a smaller house, like less fabbie neighbors. Speaking of Fabbie, where is my little darling?" Angora keeps cooing until Fabbie Tabby hops onto the couch and waits for Angora to come and pet her to death. It's a ritual they have.

"Anybody up for a sip and a flip?" I ask, grabbing the jumbo bottle of ginger ale out of the fridge and the *Vogue* magazine nestled next to it.

"Hit me, Pink Head," Aphro says, lunging at the *Vogue* like it's the Holy Grail. "Yo, would you buy a magazine if I were on the cover?"

"Yeah—*National Geographic*!" I reply, wondering about another model with cover potential. "I can't figure out if Zeus is on the loose?"

"Well, he's gotta be gay, straight, or *très* taken." Angora smiles, then shrugs. "My mom was also giving me dating advice last night on the phone."

"From the woman who still thinks spam is canned lunch meat? *S'il vous plaît!*" I heckle, taking a swig from the bottle of ginger ale, then belching with gusto.

Felinez grabs the bottle from me and takes a swig. "That is so ghetto!" Aphro squeals.

"No, it's not! Ghetto is when three people take swigs from the same bottle—not two!" Felinez counters.

"Well, then ghetto couture is inviting Ice Très over," I slide in nonchalantly.

"I thought you invited Zeus over?" Angora asks, blinking at my boldness.

"Yeah, well, I like them both—and according to the game of Spades, whoever has the two of clubs wins the kitty!" I giggle, meowching Felinez.

"Explain?" Angora asks.

"We gotta teach you Spades," I reply, making a note to my fashion self. "Once the cards are dealt, whoever has the two of clubs gets to pick up the six cards left on the table, which are called the kitty. Then they can discard any six cards they want," I explain. "So maybe I'll be doing the discarding!"

"*Mijas*, the real question is, why would a tasty *sabor* like Zeus wanna join our house?" Felinez interrupts.

"He digs our theme and our dream—and hopefully me too," I say wistfully. "That reminds me. Chintzy Colon also wants to join our house."

"No way, José!" Felinez objects.

"She could be an asset," I counter, because I'm not at all surprised by her reaction.

"I'm telling you, *mija*, she's a sneaky señorita!" Felinez says, taking a bottle of pills out of her purse.

"Okay," I snap. "Note to fashion self: shelve this discussion until later. And what is that you're trying to shove in your blue *boca*?"

I grab the bottle out of Felinez's hand despite her protestation: "Michelette took them—they really work!"

"'Burn, Baby, Burn'?" I say, scanning the label. "Do you see what that says? 'These statements have not been evaluated by the Food and Drug Administration.'"

"Maybe they don't have time to evaluate everything!" Felinez argues.

Aphro lets out a snort. "You need to stop."

"That's easy for you to say. You're skinny. What about me?" Felinez blurts out.

She is freaking. "I hope you can keep it locked down in front of the camera crew," I warn her.

"*Por que no?* Why not? You're gonna show them the leaks in the ceiling! All you wanna do is embarrass Mr. Darius! Why shouldn't I show them my cracks? Pudgy, *pobrecita gordita* Felinez! Your best friend—*por vida!*"

"Fifi Cartera, I cannot cope right now. Can you please put a baste stitch in your ego until we can mend it properly later?" I beg my best friend.

Suddenly, there's a knock at the door and I'm so relieved to be off kitty pity duty that I lunge for it. I fling it open only to see my favorite zebra-striped mink hat. Zeus catches the kaflustered expression on my face. "I'm still invited to be a member, right?" he asks, smiling.

"Abso-*freakin'*-lutely!" I say, flopping my arms around his carved muscular torso, which is hard as stone, probably from his skateboarding antics out on Monyville, Long Island. I get my blush on—again. The rest of my crew senses my seismic reaction like they're earthquake experts, so I try to render their reading inaccurate by turning the dial to Lite FM: "How did you get up here without ringing the intercom?"

"Oh, right," he says, wondering if he did something

wrong. "These two little girls let me in. They ran up to me in the courtyard, and asked if they could feel my hat!"

It figures. Everybody wants a piece of Zeus for conservation. "Don't tell me: Stellina and Tiara, right?"

"Yeah. They're really hyped," Zeus says, nodding.

"They are our resident models-in-training," I explain, then babble on about my plans to open the House of Pashmina fashion show with trot-ready guest tween models.

Zeus keeps nodding, then looks at me like he didn't see me earlier. "I dig this look. It's different from the other day?"

"Yeah, this is my Diehard-Dutch-Girl look," I say, blushing, then patting the front of the cotton flowered kerchief tied on my head.

"By the way, how'd your interview go at Betsey Johnson?"

I freeze. So does Aphro. We look at each other like, *Where'd he get this tiddy from?*

"Ice Très told me," Zeus pipes up, sensing static. "I guess Shalimar told him?"

"What *what* in the butt?" Aphro blurts.

Zeus doubles over laughing from Aphro's outburst.

"Um, I think what Aphro is trying to say is, we did not have an interview at Betsey Johnson. Chandelier got that job, anyway," I say, trying to keep the situation

149

static free. Zeus nods, puzzled. Now the intercom rings. I answer it and hear Caterina's voice. "I'll be right down," I inform her chirpily.

As I walk out the door, Angora comes to close it behind me. "I can't believe Ice Très isn't here yet."

Angora purses her lips. "He'll be here."

"Handle her," I whisper, this time nodding toward Felinez. Angora winks and nods. Fifi is definitely stressing. But she's right about one thing: maybe I *am* more interested in pulling a prank than taking care of business. Suddenly, I start having second thoughts. Well, they're here and I have to explain somehow why my building looks like the "before" shot on *Extreme Home Makeover* while Shalimar's looks like the "after."

My neighbor, Mrs. Paul, walks out of her apartment and joins me at the elevator bank, clutching the faux tortoiseshell handle on her vintage purse like she's carrying a pitchfork inside. Mrs. Paul never smiles, at least not at me.

When the elevator comes, Mrs. Paul gets in first. "It's hot in here. Or is it me?" I ask, flapping my crocheted babydoll tee against my chest for ventilation.

"Don't get lippy with me," Mrs. Paul mumbles.

"Right," I say politely, fleeing from the elevator as soon as the door opens to the lobby. I can't help it; my clunky wooden clogs clop heavily onto the faux marble floor. Stellina and Tiara bolt to the front door and announce to the camera crew, "Pink Head taught us how to vogue! You wanna see?"

"Who's Pink Head?" Caterina asks, amused.

"Me. It's my nickname," I explain. "It means a friend of felines who worships at the altar of pinkdom." *Pink Head, Blue Boca.* Now the nicknames that Felinez and I annointed ourselves when we were hot totties seem radickio. But Caterina beams, so I stop blushing. She then instructs the camera crew to start filming the tiny fashionistas in action. "How old are you?" she asks Stellina.

Striking a pose, Stellina bats her lashes and replies, "I don't give out *that* information."

I shrug, and grin in approval. Some of my neighbors gather around to see what's going on. "Lord, what they giving away?" Mrs. Watkins asks, rushing over. She works at the supermarket across the street and becomes so excited at the prospect of a freebie that she almost drops one of the three grocery bags she's juggling.

"We're primping for prime time," Tiara explains matter-of-factly.

Mrs. Watkins beams with pride. "Shoot, I ain't too old to be a model. Y'all should have me in the competition. I would tell them people at Piggly to get Wiggly cuz I'm gone!"

After a few minutes of clicks and more cackling, Caterina motions for the crew to head to the elevator.

Mrs. Watkins follows us. "Heard someone in Queens won sixty-three million yesterday," she announces to anyone who'll listen. Mrs. Watkins is referring to the New York Mega Millions lottery. She buys tickets every week. "How come nobody in Harlem ever win?" No one answers her. Meanwhile, Boom the cameraman pans the lens across the graffiti-lined walls. "Oh," I say nonchalantly, "we've been trying to get that cleaned up forever, but our landlord, Mr. Darius, won't do anything."

Caterina quickly changes the subject. "Of all the supermodels, who do you like?" she asks, shoving the microphone in my face.

"The ones who personify feline fatale," I quip.

"What about Tidy Plume?" Caterina asks, which makes me realize she doesn't know what I'm talking about.

"Um, no, she's more like couture confection."

Caterina goes blankety.

"A Barbie doll. Too perfect," I explain, sounding calm, but I'm sweating profusely and worried my underarms may start venting despite the extra applications of Arrid Extra Dry that I glommed on for this uncertain occasion.

"Um, I think that Tyra Banks or Moona—" I start in, but I can tell Caterina's gone blankety again.

"She's the model from Somalia, the SNAPS cosmetics spokesperson? I think she has feline fatale appeal," I continue, realizing that my teacher Ms. London is right. Black models don't get the hype that white models do, or Caterina would be up on Moona, too.

The silence is thick in the elevator, but I'm grateful for the small things at the moment. "Thank gooseness it's working, because yesterday it wasn't," I say, smiling apologetically. When the elevator door opens onto my floor, I shut my mouth like a Venus flytrap at the sight of Chenille. True to her stoic nature, she ignores the camera crew and glumly announces, "I'm going down to Reesy's."

I nod approvingly like a good older sister and quickly usher the film crew inside: Chenille can make her coins, but she is *not* stealing my camera cues.

Once inside, I secretly hope that Ice Très has beamed himself up to my apartment like Scotty in *Star Trek* while I was gone. One look at Angora, however, tells me that's not the case, so I go into my Catwalk house leader mode, initiating introductions all around. Then I hesitantly inform everyone. "We're having a few, um, technical difficulties but hopefully Mr. Darius, the landlord, will keep his appointment to remedy the bathroom situation soon," I say emphatically into the camera.

Suddenly, I feel embarrassed, but Zeus switches on his brilliant smile. "The fashion show must go on," he declares, snapping his fingers.

"I heard that," Aphro seconds as we all head over to the dining room table to get down to Catwalk business.

Zeus takes a black portfolio emblazoned with a zebra lightning bolt decal from his backpack.

"Fabbie Tabby, time to start the meeting!" I yell.

On cue, Fabbie hops onto the table and plops down. Boom and Caterina let out approving yelps, and two cameras zoom in for a close up on Fabbie's whiskers.

"I love the color contrast—turquoise and lime green," I comment on Zeus's skateboard graphics. "No animals in the mix?"

"We'll be getting to that," Zeus says confidently.

After we finish goospitating over Zeus's portfolio, I pass around Xeroxes. "I need your input to create the Catwalk Credo, which will serve as guidelines. Here's what I've scribbled so far."

I watch Zeus's face as he reads my outline: "I dig that: 'As an officially fierce member of the House of Pashmina, I solemnly swear to abide by the directions of my team leader, to represent my crew to the max, and to honor, respect, and uphold the Catwalk Credo.' "

"We also have to make up a list of all the positions we need to fill for our house," I continue.

"Photographer," Zeus says. "I mean, we should be documenting our whole Catwalk process along the way."

"*Brillante*," coos Felinez.

"I know somebody lethal—he's in my visual display class," Zeus lets on.

"Explain?" Angora asks.

"Lupo," says Zeus, shoving a handful of pink popcorn into his mouth. "Lupo Saltimbocca. He's hyped about becoming the next Francesco Scavullo. He's outta sight."

"Got it," I say, recognizing the name of the famous fashion photographer from the seventies. Scavullo was a star in the *Vogue* magazine stable back in the day. "Okay, so we're gonna set up in Studio C for Tuesday from four to six for interviews. Please let Mr. 'Salt in the boca' know so he can be there or be square."

"*Saltimbocca*—it means 'jump in the mouth,' an expression to use when something is supa-tasty." Zeus chuckles.

"I heard that. Just what we need," adds Aphro.

"That reminds me," I say. "Not everyone is down with our cause. So I think the flyer should put it right out there: 'Only cat lovers need apply.' "

"Let's take a vote," Angora seconds.

"I've also written down the definition of feline fatale style—'adorable and playful but fiercely clever, and

pays homage to our catty companions regardless of sex.'
I mean gender," I say, blushing.

"*Brillante!*" Zeus says, imitating Felinez. "I'll put a
pink cat illustration on the left of the flyer."

"That's outta sight!" I say, imitating Zeus.

"Awright—let's talk about models!" Aphro yells out.

"We're gonna need to sign up seventeen more models," I say. "So far we've got three. And figure ten kids
as guest models to open the show."

"One lead designer, one assistant designer," adds Felinez, then explains to Zeus, "I'm the accessories designer, and Aphro's the jewelry designer."

"What about Nole Canoli?" Zeus suggests.

"Nole is down with Chandelier Spinelli," I say
pleasantly, since Ms. Lynx has warned us to "behave instead of beehive"—even though I'd like to sting Chandelier.

"Maybe Ice Très—for the second designer?" adds
Zeus, swinging his second fashion strike.

Angora's blue peepers rise above the rim of her
cat's-eye glasses, and I feel the gnawing disappointment
from Ice Très's dis full force. Not that I'm about to drop
that tiddy right about now.

In the meantime, Caterina has her own recipe for
"reality" television. "How did Chandelier enlist the
most talented designer at FI for *her* house?"

Note to fashion self: Caterina's khakis may not be

"crisp," but her behind-the-scenes snooping is bona fried.

"Chandelier is a Gucci hoochie. Some people are impressed by that," Aphro says, venting.

"I, um, don't think Nole Canoli is the only digable designer in school," I offer feebly.

Everyone looks at me like they're waiting for me to drop the winning Lotto numbers.

"Um, I think Diamond Tyler is purrworthy, too," I add.

"Oh, she's the one stressed about her cat, right?" Zeus asks with concern.

"Who don't you like?" Caterina interjects.

"*Miss* Jackson. She's such a Fendi fiend," Aphro blurts out.

"What Aphrodite is trying to say is . . . ," I begin, pausing to formulate my thoughts.

"She can runway, but she can't hide!" Aphro says with a sneer.

Boom chuckles, lightening the situation.

"We have our own definition of what 'fashion-forward' is." Now I decide to look directly into the camera. "Not everyone is down with that. There are competitors who would rather stick with the tried, even if it's *not* true. We believe when it comes to fashion trends, sometimes you just have to drop it like it's hot. Now drop that—*boom!*"

Suddenly, there's a loud rapping sound on the door. Everybody shrieks with laughter at the timing of the interruption. I shoot Angora a look, however, like *It better be Ice Très*. Much to my chagrin, however, the first face I see when I open the door is the sullen one of Mr. Darius. Amazingly, he is with a repairman, who is carrying a toolbox and a plunger.

I usher them in like they're dethroned royalty. "Kats and Kitties, *this* is Mr. Darius, my landlord."

Mr. Darius steps inside, and once he sees the cameras, his eyes start rolling like pool balls.

"Don't mind the film crew," I say sweetly, regaining my nerve for Operation: Kitty Litter. "They've been filming the building, too! Isn't that exciting?"

Mr. Darius starts mumbling to the repairman, and they hurry to the bathroom. I follow them so that Boom, Jay, and Caterina will follow me.

"The toilet's broke and the hot water hasn't been working," I lament.

Mr. Darius mumbles to me, "Please go."

I trot back to the living room and wait for Mr. Darius to come back with a prognosis, but he proceeds to leave in a hurry, without saying a word.

"Mr. Darius, is the toilet fixed? Oh, did you see the crack in the ceiling?" I ask pleadingly.

"No, no. My wife wait in car. She get angry, I keep her waiting," he says, eager to get away from me.

"Well, maybe she could come up," I suggest. "Have some pink poporn?"

Mr. Darius's kernel of patience with my on-camera charade finally pops, causing him to let out a minor explosion in the hallway.

"We have fizzies, too—ginger ale?" I squeak as he exits hastily down the hall. "*See ya, Mr. Darius!*" I say, shutting the door.

"Bravo!" yelps Angora, clapping loudly. "That's what I call effective Catwalk leadership skills!"

Caterina grins at me, while Angora decides to turn the table, asking, "Who decides what footage you're going to use?"

"The network has final cut," Caterina reveals.

"Are you going to let the competing houses see each other's footage to create more drama?" I ask.

"They'll see it when it airs," Caterina says firmly.

"Do you leak stuff to the media?" counters Angora.

"We do send them footage, or 'items,' in the hope that they'll give us some coverage," Caterina admits.

"What's an item?" Felinez asks.

"Newsworthy tidbits, like the stuff we read in the gossip column in *Women's Wear Daily* or 'Page Six' in the *New York Post*," Angora explains proudly. She *is* the fashion journalism major among us.

"So, you mean there may be something printed about us in the newspaper?" I ask, getting excited.

"Could be. The news editors decide what they'll print or air," Caterina continues. "We're gonna shoot a lot of footage—there'll be plenty of opportunities for media coverage." Then, in her clipped tone, Caterina commands: "Okay, how about some questions now?"

"Abso-fre—" I say, then stop myself mid-word.

"Pashmina, I sense there is tension between you and your sister, Chenille. Does she want to be in the House of Pashmina, too?"

I gagulate at Caterina's candor and start mumbling. "No, maybe she doesn't, but she understands that I'm an, um, aspiring modelpreneur," I say, diverting the drama from my cranky sister. My mother will skin me like a rabbit in a Maxmilian fur trap if I dis Chenille on camera.

Luckily, Angora steps up to the fashion plate. "Not everybody is on board with our agenda. They just think we have it easy. But they don't realize, if a model doesn't plan her career carefully, she'll have nothing more than some pretty pictures and a pocketful of poses when it's all over, and there's no greater fashion tragedy than a marked-down model."

Caterina instructs the camera to go to Zeus for input. "Um, my family isn't totally cool with what I'm down with. I mean, if that's what you want to know," he reveals. The camera keeps rolling, so does Zeus. "I think they'd rather I do something else. But I see modeling as a way to help my family. I mean, my dad works hard. He's a custom tailor and has his own shop, but he could have been a designer, I mean he's got the skills."

"Were you deejaying in the Fashion Café yesterday when everyone was voguing?" Caterina continues.

Now my clunky clogs come in handy—because I kick Zeus on his left Adidas under the dining room table. After a few seconds of silence, Caterina realizes that we aren't going to break from twenty years of covert tradition, not even for our five minutes of fashion footage, so she continues probing with supa-catty questions.

"Who's the bigger threat—Shalimar or Ninja, Jr.?"

"They are not our enemies—merely the competition," I respond calmly. The four of us do the Catwalk handshake on that one.

"What is that you're doing?" Caterina asks.

"That's our Kats and Kitties handshake," I explain proudly. "You know, crossing paws."

After fifteen more minutes of sound bites, we take a snack break, then get back to our meeting. By the end, we've compiled a list of all the candidates we need to assemble for team members and we complete the copy for the flyer I'm putting up on the Fashion Board.

"Ayigght, I'm gonna hook up the cat graphics and the type tonight on my computer, and I'll have the poster ready in the morning. Cool?" Zeus asks, beaming at us.

"Abso-*freakin'*-lutely!" I say emphatically.

After the Teen Style Network crew leaves, we start squealing. "You were fierce!" declares Aphro.

"Really? I felt like a Bazozo," I say jokingly, referring to our Catwalk code for dunce.

"Miss Biggie Grande, you're gonna have to stop with the hoochie shout-outs, or we're gonna end up in the haters' corner," warns Felinez.

"For true," I second, issuing a gentle warning before dolloping praise on Fifi: "You were on *punto*, too," I say, giving her a much-needed hug. I think all that model talk sometimes does bother her now that Aphro and Angora are in the mix.

"Caterina is *très* inquisitive," notes Angora, who is helping me clean before my mom gets home from work, which will be *pronto*.

"Mos def," I concur. "I bet she even knows where all the squirrels in Central Park bury their acorns."

"Well, you definitely put your landlord on blast, that's for sure," Aphro teases.

Zeus looks at us, puzzled. After we brief him on Operation: Kitty Litter, he gets his heckle on heartily. "Well, I definitely think you got his attention. I don't know if that ceiling is gonna get fixed, though," he says, trying to suppress his laughter.

We all laugh so hard that my disappointment about Ice Très's disappearing act melts away. Who cares, cuz I definitely earned my zebra stripes today by snagging Zeus for the House of Pashmina—even if I don't get to keep him all to myself.

New school rule: You don't have to be ultranice, but don't get tooooo catty, or your posting will be zapped by the Fashion Avengers!!

BOYZ IN THE HOODIES

Ever since I was a young fashion thug tying up the laces on my first pair of Adidas Superstars and leaving my mark on my first legit slab of vertical concrete (the 20-foot overpass on Highway 20), I knew I wanted to represent street style for brothers everywhere. See, back in the day, fashion was all about name-dropping, from your hoodie to the bangle on your hot toddy's arm, but today you can jet to Shanghai or South Central and see our raw flavor served full strength. I'm not gonna front—I did snag those style sentiments from a certain delovely. Anyway, as for the new-school definition of a brother: it's anybody who isn't trying to jack up my street cred just because they're making paper on Wall Street or shouting from their seat in the House of Representatives. See, we're all representatives in this thing called life. As for a "house," the time has finally come that I'm going to be part of one that'll make fashion *he*story. Straight up this Catwalk competition at Fashion I is dominated by the delovelies, but I will still represent. If the music business can clean up its act and end the pirating of video vixens to sell records, then the fashion business should stop the propaganda that style is for sissies. But I won't lie: a de-lovely with a style vision of her own (like the aforementioned) is like a virgin slab of concrete. I'll never be able to resist the temptation to leave my mark. So, there's nothing else I can say to the ones tempting me right now except "Tag, you're it."

10/01/2008 10:45:44 AM
Posted by: Fashion Thug

8

"I still can't believe Ice Très stood me up," I bemoan to Felinez, slamming my locker shut. "Wait till I see him, I'm gonna be so shady—"

"I know: it's total eclipse time," Felinez interjects, because she understands my dark side too well.

What I don't understand is why I can't stop *obsessing* about the Fashion Thug—that is, I can't stop until Zeus strolls up with the fabbie flyer we'll post on the fashion board. He opens his black vinyl messenger bag and holds up his handiwork like it's a delicate soufflé. "Think potential Kats and Kitties will dig that?"

"You put the 'fly' in flyer!" I squeal, marveling at our tagline: ONLY CAT LOVERS NEED APPLY.

"Check the groovy graphics on the borders. *Hello!*" adds Aphro.

Angora takes notes on the curlicues. "*J'adore* this typeface. Is it from Font Book?"

"Nah, I designed this jammy myself. We can use it for all our graphics needs—the programs for the fashion show, our little hype handouts, everything," explains Zeus.

"*Major* purr points," Angora concurs.

"Okay, let's tack and roll," I order, grabbing the flyer and Felinez's arm. Aphro is chaperoning Angora to the ladies' room.

"Non-Catwalk business," I inform Zeus with a wink while we stand there whispering among our fabbie three selves.

Zeus smiles knowingly: "I got two sisters. I got you," then jets to his locker in the next row.

"Oy, now I'm getting like Ice Très," I comment to Felinez as we walk to the fashion board. "Winking and blinking."

"What happened?" Felinez asks in an agitated tone.

"What's bothering you, Blue Boca?" I ask, taking the spotlight off myself.

Felinez's apple-size cheeks turn bright red as she explains what happened on the way to school this morning. "Outside the bodega, this fat guy with his stomach hanging out of his T-shirt yells at me, '*Hola*, fat ass!' So I turn and blast, 'Who you calling fat?' He laughs like a stuffed *puerco*. 'I said, *flat*. FAT asses I like, *mami*!'"

"What a jerkaroni," I snarl, comforting Felinez, at least until I see Ice Très helping Shalimar put up *her* flyer. Now I'm the one who needs to be comforted. My mouth open like a guppy's, I read the overly hyped header on Shalimar's poster in disbelief: CALLING ALL FASHION THUGS. HOLLA. Suddenly, that's exactly what

I'd like to do: scream and make some noise. "So now she's into ghetto couture?" I hiss under my breath, grimacing at the musical-chair turn of events. Ice Très has obviously become her graffiti guru. Fifi pries the pink tacks out of my hand to prevent me from sticking them into Ice Très's pointy head instead of on the corners of our prized poster. The guilty one grins in my direction, instinctively realizing that he's just escaped the wrath of a killer kitty. Meanwhile, I pretend I can't see the brightness of his rabbit teeth bouncing off the fluorescent lights.

Felinez nudges me back to business. She points to Chandelier's poster—the most blinged-out on the board. "She must have gotten here at six a.m. with the other fashion vampires," I comment as we walk away. "Well, at least we beat Anna Rex and Willi Ninja, Jr."

Against my will, I turn to stare at Ice Très. Shalimar winces at me and points to the meowch pouch strung around my neck on a piece of pink rawhide. "What you got in there—voodoo mojo? Don't think it's working!" she giggles. I ignore her and try to meet Ice Très's gaze so I can level my signature shady glare, but now *he's* pretending he doesn't notice, his head shrinking into his Rocawear hoodie.

"I can't believe I've been *hoodwinked*." I wince, walking away to lick my wounds in private.

Now Anna Rex and Elisa Pound whiz by us, their

poster in hand. "Sorry I'm late," Anna moans to her black-clad disciple. "I had to beg my mother to give me money for Alli."

"I wish I could go get Alli, too," Felinez laments.

"Who's Alli?" I ask her, secretly wondering if she's losing it. That's when I discover the only thing she's trying to lose is weight, as usual. "Alli" is the half-dose of the prescription drug Xenical—a fat-blocker pill—with disgusting side effects I can't repeat.

"This one *is* approved by the FDA, though!" Felinez blurts out. "But I wish it didn't cost fifty dollars a bottle."

"Yeah, well, that's not the only price you pay. Do you really want to become known as Senorita Poops-a-Lot?" I ask. "I hope when we win the competition, you have better things to do with your prize money."

"Well, I hope people show up for our interviews later!" Felinez counters sarcastically.

About that, Fifi is right. "And I hope we don't get any *LOSERS*," I add nervously, twirling a loose strand of hair at my temple at full throttle. "Even if they have been approved by the FDA!"

r ٦

At four o'clock sharp, Aphro, Felinez, Angora, and I are the only ones sitting at our appointed table in Studio C. Tapping my meowch pouch against my chest, I order everyone to fill out their membership forms. Then I cup my head in my frozen hands. "If nobody shows up, I'm gonna have a meltdown like five-day-old mac and cheese."

"Well, at least Zeus is down for the twirl. He'll be here," Aphro says, jabbing my elbow. "My lips are chapped. Gimme your lipstick."

Aphro swipes the Baked Brownie Swirl Stick from my hand and pops open the tube. "This ain't frosted, is it?"

"Of course not," I reply.

"Good, cuz I was about to get frosty with you," she hmmphs.

I know that Aphro hates bling-bling on her *boca* because she thinks it makes her lips look too plumpalicious, even though I wish I had a smoocher like hers.

"Speaking of frosty, *chérie*, I'm going to risk my life telling you about a certain blog entry," Angora starts in, intently filling out her form. "Ice Très is waxing his Magic Markers about joining a certain house—"

"Shalimar's. We know," says Felinez.

"He's also hoping that all admiring 'delovelies' consider becoming his design muses. I guess that's what he meant by 'Tag, you're it'?" Angora reflects.

"Delovelies? He's not a designer—he's a dunce," comments Aphro.

"Also on dunce detail—Delilah Diddy waylaid me

after textile science today to show me pictures of her cat and her sketchbook," I report to my crew about one candidate too anxious to wait for the scheduled interview rendezvous. "Her style is so predictable, the only things she should consider designing are crystal balls."

"*Je comprends*," Angora says, concurring.

"Oy, maybe we should forget about cat lovers. At this rate, I'm gonna need a CAT scan!" I moan in jest.

Suddenly, there's a loud cackling outside the studio and I look up, hoping the graffiti artist will grace us with his wearable denim art and goofy grin. Instead, I realize it was merely a caco*phony* orchestrated by Chandelier and Tina, who hurriedly walk by, peering into the studio on the fly.

"I don't think he's coming," Aphro snarls, reading my troubled mind.

Now I feel like a dunce—and compelled to share my secret obsession with my crew. "Remember those Pepe LePone peep-toe slingbacks? I saw them on sale at the Shoe Shack, but I didn't buy them? Then I went back the next week hoping they had slashed the price some more, but somebody else had already snatched 'em. Remember how I couldn't stop obsessing about them? Well, that's how I feel about Ice Très, okay."

"So you're saying, you're not really interested in a guy until he's been marked down?" Angora interprets.

"No, that's not it. Pink Head's saying she wasn't

feeling Ice Très till somebody else was!" blurts out Felinez.

I shrug. I don't know what I'm feeling anymore.

"Well, I know Shalimar ain't feeling Ice Très's fashion thuggery. She *must* be peepin' something else—" Aphro starts in, but smacks her lips instead, blotting her freshly applied lipstick.

We all giggle uncontrollably while Zeus appears in the doorway with a supa-shortie in tow.

"This is my man Lupo Saltimbocca," announces Zeus, his flash-ready smile lighting up the studio. Maybe Aphro is right. Maybe I don't think I'm good enough for Zeus. I know that's not what she said, but maybe that's what she was thinking. He's got it made in the shade, while I have to deal with family drama.

Lupo blushes and looks up at Zeus, who is a head taller than him. He has a really big nose and a grin that's goofier than Ice Très's.

"Come on, now. I had to put you on blast. Show them your work," Zeus instructs Lupo, obviously eager for us to give his recruit our feline seal of approval.

Lupo clumsily opens his portfolio, and a pile of photos plops on the floor. I watch him pick them up, hoping he has more luck loading his camera. "These are some of the models I shoot already," Lupo explains excitedly, his big brown eyes getting pop-eyed. I zoom right in on the head shots of Elgamela that landed on the top of the heap, while Aphro homes in on the silver lily pendant dangling on a platinum chain around Lupo's short, thick neck.

"Did you make that?" she asks.

"No, I'm not a designer," Lupo clarifies.

"I know, but it's handmade," Aphro continues.

"Yes, by Agnello. He makes jewelry back in Firenze," Lupo explains in his thick Italian accent. "This is the, how do you say, the symbol, yes, for my region. *Gigli*."

"The lily pad is the symbol for Firenze?" asks Felinez, trying to help Lupo. "We're all taking Italian."

"Oh, bravo," says Lupo, impressed.

"See, we're trying to do more than order ice cream in Italian—that is, if we win," I giggle.

"Gelato, *per favore*!" Lupo giggles, too. "I can help you with that, you know?"

"Ordering gelato?" Felinez asks, her mouth salivating. "Where—here?"

"No, I can help you study Italian," he clarifies.

"Well, that settles it—" I start, realizing what an asset Lupo really is to the House of Pashmina.

"You're in there like swimwear!" Zeus says, finishing my sentence.

"Seriously, though—these photos are hot!" I exclaim, flipping through his portfolio and noticing eight more photos of Elgamela posed in slinky black Lycra outfits against a stark white backdrop. I wonder if Lupo is obsessed with her. Maybe he has already interviewed to be in Chandelier's house just to be close to his model muse.

Right on cue, Zeus adds, "You know that Chandelier wants him in her house, but I told him this is the move."

"Do you know Elgamela?" Lupo asks, turning to me. "For me, she is incredible." Sensing my hesitation, he quickly adds, "You are very beautiful, too. And you." Now Lupo is pointing to Aphro. "I want to take pictures of both of you."

"Oh, you're definitely in with us now," Aphro says, smoothing down her straight bangs.

"We love Elgamela. I mean, she hit the fashion trifecta—tall, exotic—and she can dance," I say.

"Not as good as you," Lupo squeals at Aphro. "I saw you in the café. *Madonna*, you were *marveloso!*"

Now I'm getting the impression that Lupo pulled Zeus's strings for an intro, and not the other way around.

Aphro tilts her head like a peacock. "Well, I try."

"See, Elgamela is friends with Nole and Dame—and *Chandelier*," I continue, getting back on the Catwalk track.

"Yes, but Elgamela loves me. If we want her, I tell her that, no?" Lupo says earnestly.

Zeus nods behind Lupo's back. "He's the man, I'm telling you—things can be done, tassels can be pulled."

Suddenly, I get hopeful. "Really? Then make it happen. I've got to hand in these sheets," I say, pointing to the formidable stack of empty member forms that will need to be filled out and delivered to the Catwalk director's office by Friday morning.

"Can I come in?" asks Diamond Tyler, knocking on the door.

"I didn't think you would show," I say like a bad hostess, I guess because I'm relieved that she *did* come.

Diamond stands in the doorway, her hands shoved in the pockets of her Free People Reindeer Love parka.

"Girl, don't just stand there. Come on in and take your jacket off. The pawnshop's closed!" Aphro yells out.

"Such great energy. I love her!" gushes Lupo. He's definitely feeling Aphro. Diamond chuckles and plops her cute aqua-and-pink-striped Yak Pak on the floor, the two pandas perched on the front pockets positioned by my pink Mary Janes like they're gonna smooch my toes.

"How's Crutches?" I ask, watching as Diamond squirms on the edge of the chair.

"Oh, great! Now they've got her swimming with this new pussy paddle."

Lupo and Zeus snicker, then burst out laughing. "Sorry," Zeus says, trying to stifle his guffaws.

Diamond earnestly explains about the physical therapy contraption before she veers into her latest source of discomfort. "Did you hear about the sheep on the Grand Concourse?" she asks, turning to Felinez since they both live in the South Bronx.

"No," Felinez responds guiltily. "I didn't, um, count any sheep?"

Lupo giggles. I think that's his calling card, along with the Nikon camera he has taken out of the case and strapped around his neck.

"There are five slaughterhouses right on Tremont," Diamond explains seriously. "Well, one of the sheep escaped with the USDA clip hanging off her ear. She ran right into the street. She could have been killed. I mean, she's escaped death twice. Really."

I try to understand what she's saying, then I get it.

"We're petitioning to get her sent to a farm in Westchester," Diamond goes on, "instead of being returned to the meatpacking district to be killed. The meeting is tonight, so I gotta get uptown."

"I got you," I say, eager to accommodate her busy animal-activism schedule. "Show us what you got, cuz I don't think Aphro has seen your designs."

Diamond gingerly lays her sketchbook on the table

and I turn the pages with tender care. "Sweet," I comment with each passing page. I really do dig Diamond's vibe, even though I can sense that the rest of my crew has doubts about her skills.

"What kind of stuff do you want to do?" Diamond asks hesitantly.

"We're gonna feature regular and plus sizes for the Kats and Kitties," I say proudly. "And we'll open the show with a few fashions for kids, too."

"That's what feline fatale style is all about: *all sizes*," Felinez says.

"I like that," Diamond says, nodding approvingly.

"Yeah, we do too," Zeus pipes up.

"I love all sizes too," seconds Lupo, and the two of them start guffawing again.

"I think I'm gonna have to separate you two till recess," I warn them.

Then I turn my head and mouth to Angora: *I don't think he's gay.* She nods back at me in agreement.

In the meantime, Lupo focuses his camera and starts clicking away. The flash from the Nikon startles Diamond, who puts her head down and tries to cover her face.

"We must document the whole process, I think?" explains Lupo. "For the fashion show, we can have a photo collage on the walls behind where the audience is sitting, no?"

"That's *meowverlous*!" I coo in my British alter ego voice. Zeus and Lupo are making me giddy.

Diamond gets excited too, and pulls out another notebook of design sketches.

"Wow. Now, these I dig. The babydoll dresses—this one with the eyelet bib and the ruffles," I say, tapping the page.

"And you can wear it on or off the shoulders. We could put some cat's-eye shapes beveled with rhinestones around the neckline," Diamond suggests. "And put some cat's-eye tattoos on the model's shoulders?"

"Nice," says Zeus. Judging from the phoenix on his right arm, it's not surprising tattoo sightings would get a rise out of the graphic artiste.

"We could do a whole babydoll segment. That would look great with headbands," adds Felinez.

"For jewelry, I wanna make some necklaces with cat charms dangling from them," adds Aphro.

"Oh, that totally works with this kind of neckline," Diamond says, then turns to Felinez. "I really like the meowch pouches you're wearing."

"Oh, yeah. We want the models to carry those instead of the wristlet clutches everybody else is doing," explains Felinez.

"What's your thought on pom-poms?" I ask.

"If you've got them, you'd better shake 'em?"

Diamond says, shrugging as if she suddenly realizes that she is indeed auditioning.

Zeus, Lupo, and Felinez giggle.

"Well, I think we should give it a twirl, no?" I say to Diamond, hoping she'll say yes. "I mean, I know you can't stay, but we'll see what the cat drags in." What I really want to say is: *I pray that Nole Canoli smells the catnip and careens around the corner any* segundo.

"Is there any designer at FI you dig?" Zeus asks her outright.

"Yeah, your friend Nole Canoli. I mean, he was in my draping class and, well, he's a genius," Diamond says, like she's telling us something we don't know. "Have you asked him?"

"Yeah, I asked him," Zeus admits. "He joined Chandelier's house. She, um, did her interviews yesterday. I saw him there."

I wince, of course, because Zeus has reminded me that we're scrambling for talent.

"I'm happy you came to see us. I knew we had the same style sensibilities," I say sincerely.

"You know what, I can stay," Diamond decides on the spot.

"*Meowverlous!*" I squeal again.

Diamond relaxes into the chair, like she has let go of caring for all the animals in the world except for the desperate felines in front of her. "So, did you get a job?" she asks me, seeming genuinely interested.

"Um, no, but Felinez did," I say, turning to Fifi.

"It's just an internship, so don't be jealous!"

"What about you?" I ask, wondering if Diamond will be able to contribute to our burgeoning demand for design supplies.

"Yes!" Diamond says excitedly; then she drops the doggie bag. "It's at the Animal Care Center on 110th Street. Volunteering, you know."

"Oh, right," I say, then change the subject. "We'll discuss the Catwalk budget later, but I'm getting about three hundred dollars for the first installment."

"Hola!" shouts Chintzy Colon, who walks into the studio with a tall blond girl in tow. I've seen the girl in the library, but I don't know who she is, even though it's obvious she hit the genetic lottery and we're talking the Mega Millions jackpot.

"Your flyer was so cute!" the girl coos, interrupting Chintzy. She's even taller than I am, and blonder than Angora. "You won't believe, but my name is Kissa Sami!"

Now Lupo's eyes really get pop-eyed. "You're a model, right?" he asks.

"I will be soon!" Kissa coos. Lupo aims his camera at Kissa and clicks away. She poses without any prompting. "Do you want me to walk now?" Kissa asks, looking around to see who's in charge.

"Yes, please," I command, watching her sashay—sort of stiffly, but with definite potential.

Aphro jumps up and gives Kissa some instruction. "Push your hips forward, then let it flow. Don't move your arms so much." Kissa walks again, this time more assuredly.

"You have beautiful eyes," I say, noticing how her eyes are slanty but blue and icy clear, not hazy like Zeus's. "Where are you from?"

"Finland," Kissa coos, then tells us how psyched she was to be chosen for FI's student exchange program. She goes on to explain how long the waiting list is—longer than the one for a highly coveted Birkin Bag at Hermès (and that one is six years!). "My best friend was crushed—she couldn't come. We dream together to be in the Catwalk competition!"

"Did you make up your name?" Aphro asks, half-joking.

"Oh no. It means 'cat' in Finnish. We have seven at home. I swear!"

"Seven Kissas, or seven cats?" Lupo asks for clarification.

"Seven furry, not seven tall like me!" Kissa giggles, then pulls out pictures from her shoulder bag. "You don't believe."

"Oh, we believe," I giggle, looking at the photos of her most beloved feline—a black cat she tells me is named Kuma. "My mother went to a sushi restaurant and she misunderstood the waiter. She thought he told her that 'kuma' means 'black' in Japanese, but it turns out it means 'bear'!" While the kitty coo-fest continues between Kissa and Angora, a few more students enter the studio.

"I got this," Aphro says, and handles them while I conduct an interview with Chintzy Colon.

Chintzy sits down and smiles on cue. "You must have been upset that you didn't win, um, one of the house leader positions," I begin, broaching the touchy-feely.

"My mother was more upset than I was," Chintzy says, but I wonder if she's merely on spin patrol as usual. "I mean, I'm not sure I could handle the stress anyway, um, now that I'm going to be working—" Chintzy stops like she's spilling the refried beans.

"Where are you working at?" I ask, trying to fend off an attack of Gucci Envy.

Chintzy hesitates, then blushes. "At Grubster PR."

"Oh, so Shalimar hooked you up?" I ask, blushing brighter than Chintzy. Sometimes being right feels worse than being wrong.

"Um, she got me an interview, that's all," Chintzy says apologetically.

"So why don't you join her house, *mija?*" Felinez asks, butting in.

"My sense of style is closer to your vision?" Chintzy says like it's a question, swinging her leg nervously. Now the question on my lips is why she's wearing Cayman Crocs, those ubiquitous holey plastic clogs that should be relegated only to tiptoeing around the tulips.

"I also think your house is the most fun. Everybody else takes themselves so seriously," Chintzy adds for good measure.

"That's true, *chérie*," Angora says, looking up from her interview with Liza Flake, a hairstyling major in the Fashion Annex. "We are just one big furry ball of fun and michief."

Liza smiles at me and says, "I see your sister is in the program now!"

"Yes," I say, then divert the drama by pointing to her photos. "What's that—you did a shoot?"

"Yeah, my first one!" Liza says, excited. "For Elgamela—she's really working hard on getting her portfolio together. I think she's definitely gonna win one of the modeling contracts in the competition."

"We agree," Angora says diplomatically.

"Did you interview her yet?" Liza asks, like she hopes we did. "I told her I was coming here."

"Um, no, but who knows? The night is still young," I say, then divert the drama again. "I love her hair swept up like that."

"We could do upsweeps like this for the show—with chopsticks?" Liza offers.

"Love, *love*," Angora coos. "Did you interview with anyone else?"

"Well, yeah, but I don't want to start any bidding wars," Liza says, running her fingers through her bright red hair.

"Name your price," I say sarcastically.

"I get to pick the lead stylist," Liza quips.

Now I wonder if she's serious, so I put her to the test. "Who do you have in mind?"

"Dame Leeds?"

I can't help but think, we are definitely not picking the lucky numbers tonight.

"We'll take your offer into consideration," I say politely.

"Is that hennafied, Miss Redhead?" Aphro blurts out, breaking the heated negotiations.

"Freakin' yes," coos Liza, lightening up. "Seriously, though, I like what you guys are doing. The every-size concept. My mother is plus size, and she is always on the major frus about the frumpy clothes. Unify—that's what I think."

"My mother is assistant manager of Forgotten Diva on Madison," I add in agreement.

"Oh, I didn't mean anything bad," Liza says, embarrassed.

"Oh, puhleez. My mother knows. Her customers are old school, or else they'd be petitioning for fiercer threads. Trust," I assure her.

"So, are you gonna get back to me for real?" Liza asks nervously.

"We'd love to have you for the hairstyling assistant."

Liza shifts in her chair for a second, then asks the obvious. "What about your sister?"

Angora shoots me a look, and I know exactly what she's thinking: she wants me to heed her mother's advice, which is exactly what I do. "She's so busy with clients from our, um, neighborhood, she's not stressing the extra responsibility."

"Not even for a piece of a hundred thousand dollars and Louis Vuitton luggage—*and* a trip to Italy?" Liza asks in disbelief, spieling off the goodies like a game-show host. "Well, I'm in it for the loot. And that's the truth."

"Well, sometimes the truth is just plain *appropriate*," Angora says, and we all giggle at the inside joke.

Meanwhile, a few more students come in and sit at the studio table, so I turn my attention back to Chintzy, who has been waiting patiently for a grand finale. "But what would you do—in the house, I mean?" I ask her.

"Be your assistant, and I can help with the PR when the time comes. I can also be one of the dressers for the models backstage at the show," Chintzy says, like she's adding on extra helpings of duties for good measure.

Felinez is talking to Mink Yong from her geometry class but still finding time to glare down my throat. Nonetheless, I make a decision. "Okay, Chintzy, let's do it."

"Great!" Chintzy says, sprinkling me with her smile, then reaching over to hug me. Felinez glares at me like she did in kindergarten after I snatched all the pink crayons, which I deemed only for *my* domain, hence my nickname.

"Bye!" Chintzy says, bouncing off the chair and almost right into the bosom of Jackie Moore and a few more designer candidates, all of whom Diamond recognizes instantly.

"Hi, Jackie," Diamond says sweetly. Roger Rivet nods at her and makes it clear that he is strictly business. Frail and tiny, he unzips his portfolio and places a well-manicured (and frosted?) hand on top of it like he's posing for a hand cream ad. The three design candidates take seats as Shantung Jones takes a twirl for Aphro. Roger stares at his hand like he's about to dig for gold under his nails instead of focusing on the fierce fashion model.

"Now, you know you're gonna have to change your hairstyle?" Aphro tells Shantung teasingly, because they're both wearing the same exact dippin' do—an asymmetrical blunt-cut bob with razor-sharp bangs.

"When Naomi wears her hair like that—for me, she looks *bellissima*," declares Lupo. Aphro hates any comparisions to the British supermodel who whacked her maid with a cell phone and landed herself in an orange sanitation vest—and I don't mean on the runway, okay.

Shantung giggles, her cinnamon-specked eyes sparkling.

"We'll discuss her hairstyle later," pipes up Liza Flake, like she's the head britch in charge. Only problem is, she isn't.

Aphro throws me a glance like, *Is she the assistant hairstylist, or the lead?*

I make a note to my fashion self to handle that skirmish—as soon as we find someone above Liza's level, thank you. Truth is, any distraction is welcome, because I can tell that Diamond is definitely not feeling Roger's designs, and let's just say I'm definitely not ready-to-wear them either.

Lita Rogers's sketches are a little more appetizing. "I like the lace tops and gypsy skirts," Diamond says.

"My family is going to invest in my clothing line as soon as I graduate," Lita tells Diamond.

"Oh, so you got it like that," Aphro says, demi-joking, demi-serious.

Lita shifts her gears into gratitude mode. "I know I'm lucky."

"What's your line going to be called?" Diamond asks sweetly.

"Lollipops," Lita says, grinning proudly. "I've had the name picked out for a while. My father is going to get it trademarked."

"That's tasty," I say politely. Angora's silence, however, is palpable.

"*Chérie*—what say you?" I ask, grinning. My mouth is starting to hurt from all this interviewing.

"There is a famous strip club in Baton Rouge called Lollipops," Angora informs us hesitantly.

Lita's face turns beet red. She flaps her sketchbook shut tighter than a Venus flytrap. "Really?" she asks in disbelief.

Angora nods. "Ms. Harness, our fashion merchandising teacher, is right. Research is everything."

"I gotta go," Lita informs us, still red-faced.

"I'll let you know," I tell Lita, trying to smooth her ruffled fashion feathers. After all, it's still a tasty name, and it's hard coming up with an original name someone hasn't already used for their schemes and dreams.

"Um, I have to go too," Roger Rivet informs us, and I give him the same we'll-be-in-touch spiel.

Jackie Moore looks at us like a deer caught in headlights. She pulls out a skimpy sketchpad filled with swimwear designs. "Yellow bikini," I say, observing the bling-bling string set.

"Are we going to do swimwear?" Aphro asks.

"Um, it's possible," I say, but I can't help but wonder where Jackie is picking up her color cues.

"I'm from Florida," explains Jackie. "It's always sunny—that's why I'm into yellow."

I thank Jackie for coming and scribble a few notes on my pad. Heather Bond is next in the hot seat. After Jackie jets, she sits on the edge of her chair like she's ready to eject herself on my cue. Then she nervously opens her sketchbook for our perusal. "I'm into vinyl. I think that goes with feline fatale—big-time."

"I agree," pipes up Diamond, obviously looking out for the hides of all her four-legged friends.

Aphro, however, has an opinion about that one. "I prefer leather—soft as butter and not Parkay, thank you."

"A black pleather catsuit would be cute for the show," I interject. Although Heather's designs are strictly fade to black, I'm trying to see whether she has any diversity.

"Is black your favorite color?" Diamond asks.

"Um, yeah, I guess it is," Lita says, shrugging and sealing her coffin. She definitely seems more like a design disciple for Anna Rex, even if she doesn't know it.

After two *more* hours of noshing and networking, we decide to wrap up our session like a fashion falafel.

"Thanks for stopping by!" Felinez says giddily. She hugs Shantung Jones so hard, the frail model winces as if her tiny bones are being crushed. "Next time we'll have party hats and piñatas!"

Lupo grins and walks out the door after Shantung. I tap him gently on the back and mouth, *Stay*.

He breaks into a big grin and resumes his posturing.

"Okay, so now that it's just inner crew, I want to get some feedback." I instruct everybody to sit down.

"I can't believe you invited Chintzy into our house without asking the rest of us!" Felinez blurts out.

"Okay, you're right. My bad. But I knew what you were going to say, and I don't agree with you," I say firmly.

"I'm telling you. She's a sneaky senorita!" Felinez says, her face flushed.

"She's going to be our assistant, and she's gonna help with our publicity campaign. I think she's an asset—on some level," I say, kaflustered.

"That's a croc—like those *fea* clogs she was wearing!" Felinez cries. "You never liked her before!"

"Okay, you're pissed. Now you can pick whichever model you wanted out of the—" I count the number of model sheets we've collected and render the final tally. "Okay, we saw twenty-five models so far. I know you want Mink. Kissa. Who else?"

"Jaynelle—and the guy with the corkscrews," Felinez says, still pouting.

"Dreads—that's Benny Madina," I remind her. "Okay, he's in. Who else do you want?"

"Shantung." Felinez folds her arms across her chest and continues to pout. "Never mind, *mija*, you don't listen to me!"

I figure Felinez is cranky because we haven't eaten dinner, so I let it go. "Shantung, of course."

"We still don't have a lead designer," Aphro reminds me.

"Jackie is tacky," I moan.

"I agree," adds Angora. "Yellow is only a fashion color if you're Big Bird. What about Roger?"

"All those hanky hemlines. No, thank you. I wanted to pull out a tissue and blow my nose," I respond.

"Heather 'Pleather'?" asks Aphro.

"Well, at least she's into catsuits. Lita with the dirndl skirts and crop tops was too sickeningly sweet. Yuck," adds Angora.

"So we *still* don't have a lead designer," Aphro repeats.

"I know," I shout, finally losing it. "What do you want me to do!"

"Need a moment?" Aphro snarls.

I take a second to chill before I blurt out, "Look, Di-amond can do it. I'm leaning toward her. I'm telling you, she's a gem in the rough."

"Rough is right. You sure she won't crumble under the pressure? I mean, she seems more interested in us not eating lamb chops than in winning a competition, okay?" shouts Aphro. "I mean, no disrespect for her vegetarian plan and whatnot."

"We've got her back," I insist.

"Ayiight," Aphro says, sounding unsure. "You're the boss, Miss Ross."

"That's right, you are," says a familiar voice. I look up and there is Ice Très, darkening the doorway.

I smile at him automatically, probably from smiling all afternoon at interviewees. Suddenly, I feel my throat tighten and announce, "I gotta get some water."

I ignore Ice Très, but he trails behind me. "Can I holla at you for a sec?"

"You've got my undivided attention from here to the water fountain. Let's see if you can hold it," I bark at him.

"I just wanna explain what happened," he says with a grin.

"I know what happened," I counter. "So it's a wrap, falafel, and a shish kebab. Get it?"

"Got it," Ice Très concedes. "Look, I didn't want to mix business with pleasure. I thought if I joined

Shalimar's house, then we could just be friends. Know what I'm saying?"

"Um, no, but I'll be right up," I say, bobbing my head down to sip some water from the faucet. When I finish, I stand back up and announce, "Time's up."

"Okay, how 'bout Friday we hook up? Around six? I'm going to see Zeus spin."

"I was going anyway," I say, not giving in.

"You can stretch me to the limit with your catty stance. I deserve that. But we're cool?" Ice Très asks pitifully.

"Chilly," I say, then run back to the studio to retrieve my crew.

My crew is all ears when I return, except for Aphro, who is all mouth, as usual.

"I cannot believe you agreed to hook up with him!" she snarls. "A five-year-old could have cooked up a better story in his Creepy Crawlers Oven than that one."

"Back to business, big mouth, if you don't mind," I warn Aphro.

"Whatever makes you clever," Aphro hisses, and storms off.

Lupo runs after her, which annoys me. "You'd think she was a runaway sheep with a USDA clip on her ear in need of sanctuary," I say, agitated. "Are you two gonna stand there like dummies?" I shoot at Angora and Zeus, who are posed so still they look like mannequins in a Macy's window.

Angora purses her lips and says, "This dummy is going home. And remember, we've only got till Friday to hand in the membership forms."

New school rule: You don't have to be ultranice, but don't get tooooo catty, or your posting will be zapped by the Fashion Avengers!!

FASHION 101: DON'T FALL FOR FAKE FENDIS

Ever since I can remember, I have wanted to be head of the class. Perhaps my leadership skills come naturally to me since I'm the oldest of four kids and my mother died when I was six years old. During the difficult years that ensued, fashion became my refuge in what I considered to be a cruel and not-so-chic world that could snatch my mother in such an untimely death. While my father worked long, endless shifts as a male nurse at Brooklyn Hospital, I'd keep the four of us entertained by staging elaborate fashion shows in our tiny living room. (To this day, I think my little brother Socket is the best male model on the catwalk.) Becoming one of the lucky ones granted entry into Fashion International has given me an all-access fashion pass.

First of all, I'm armed with valuable insider 411: for example, did you know it was *not* French designer Paul Poiret who created the narrow, elevated ramp used in fashion shows known as *le podium* in gay Paree, but rather British designer Lady Duff-Gordon who staged the first catwalk-style fashion show in 1904? Secondly, FI has afforded me the incredible opportunity to stage my own fashion show this year in the prestigious annual Catwalk competition. (Nole Canoli, I want the world to know that you are the star jewel in my fashion crown!) Perhaps the most important lesson that I've learned at Fashion International, however, wasn't taught in any of the classrooms. Let's just say it's the uncredited addendum to the course Fashion 101. So listen up, aspiring house leaders: the secrets to any leader's success are assembling the most formidable team and always keeping an eye out for true talent. On the flip side of the fashion token, never ever fall for the fake Fendis hiding among us, or you'll develop a serious case of toxic schlock syndrome that will prevent you from competing at the top of your fashion game. . . . That's all for now. See you at the shows, *darlings*!

10/05/2008 12:35:00 PM
Posted by: Gucci Girl

9

Aphro is still all up in here about our designer duel at the interview finale. At least Felinez and Angora are trying to squash it like two-day-old beef jerky, which is exactly what it is. Literally. Call me paranoid, but I even think Aphrodite has been blasting her mighty "Biggie" mouth to Lupo Saltimbocca. After all, he didn't stay and watch my back; instead, he ran toward Miss Blunt (Bob) like he was going to live up to his last name and jump in her mouth. Or so I grumble to Felinez, who squeamishly mumbles back at me, "*Mija*, I'm just trying to A-B-C my way out of it, *esta bien?*"

"Pash, I think he tried," Angora says gently, adjusting her powder blue beret one micromillimeter away from her forehead. I'm not surprised that Angora instinctively knows why I'm *really* upset with Lupo. She's got it like that.

"Well, Loopy made it sound like all he had to do was click his camera and Elgamela would wiggle her belly button for him," I whine, nervously shoving my hands into the pockets of the shrunken denim blazer I decorated last night with paw prints from a metallic marker, secretly inspired by Ice Très. On the back, I sewed a CAT JUNKIE appliqué. I know that I'm exaggerating Lupo's claim, but I'm upset that he didn't come through on the promise of procuring the next Cleopatra for our house.

In the meantime, Aphro has agreed to meet us by Stingy Sami's newsstand this morning before we go to school. When she finally arrives, she squints at me like she's looking through the scope of a shooting gallery rifle to knock down a plastic duck. At least it's an improvement from yesterday. After I grunt "Hello," we proceed to forage the newsstand like press-poaching possums in search of any tasty tiddies that miraculously have been fed to the gossip columns by Caterina and her crew about the Catwalk competition.

Sami nods knowingly at us before staring off into space, the bit on his high-tail pipe clenched between his teeth. The newsstand owner has given up trying to stop fashion freeloaders—meaning students from FI—from thumbing mags and rags without forking over a finder's fee. But everybody else has to pay the piper. Once we saw him chase a lady in a wheelchair away after she threw a quarter at him for the pawed-over copy of the *New York Post* she was reading.

"I swear if I see Shalimar's name, I'm calling the

sham police," I hiss, carefully turning every page of the *New York Post*.

After scouring every single newspaper in the newsstand, including the *Daily Tattle*, we finally decide to let it go like disco.

"I can't believe we haven't even gotten an honorary mention yet," Angora says, breathing heavily.

"God, are we not worthy? Are we not worthy?" I moan.

We're not the only early-morning fashion desperadoes. A tall blond fashionista with a short, stubby ponytail, whom I've seen in the hallway at FI, crowds the newsstand and pleads with Sami. "Tell me you have the new *Vogue*. Puhleez?"

We giggle at his apparent fresh-fashion jones because we know it all too well. All of a sudden, the ponytailed pleader looks at me like I just jumped out of the pages of *Vogue*. "Omigod, hello! I'm so preoccupied, I didn't see you standing there in all your kitty fabulousness," he coos adoringly to me.

I'm puzzled pink because I don't think we've ever spoken.

"Sorry, let me rewind. Hello! I'm Bobby Beat. Okay, it's my professional name, because I serve the makeup instead of applying it, or so I've been told," he giggles, putting his hand to his chest.

"Where are you from?" Angora asks, honing in on his accent.

"Brooklyn," Bobby says, giggling again.

"Word?" inquires Aphro. "I'm from the BK, and that ain't no accent I ever heard."

"Oh!" Bobby squeals, hitting Aphro on the shoulder with a flicked wrist movement. "Brooklyn, Michigan!"

Angora sighs sweetly.

"Anyhoo, I've been hoping I'd run into your fabbie felineness, because I couldn't make the interview."

I smile back at him, flattered, as he babbles on.

"I had to do makeup for my sister's friend's test shots. Um, she's sending in photos for the next round of auditions for *You'd Better Work, Supermodel!*" Bobby explains earnestly, which piques our budding supermodel interest.

"She's eighteen?" Angora asks rhetorically, because we know the television show's eligibility rules by heart. We also know that *Supermodel* provides one winner a season with a $100,000 one-year modeling contract with the Snoot model agency.

"Yup, she's a freshman at FIT like my sister." Bobby nods knowingly. "But honey, don't stress it. With those cheekbones, there is only one way you won't get a modeling contract from the Catwalk competition." Bobby pauses, and we wait with bated breath until he continues, "If you don't have me as the makeup artist in your house!"

"I hear that," Aphro says, finally lightening up.

"*Chéri*, what about your cheekbones?" Angora asks approvingly. "You look like you could model too."

"Oh, I know, but I can't stand the thought of trudging around all day on go-sees. I'm trying to get paid, *chérie*," admits Bobby Beat. "I know what I want: to be the next Kevyn Aucoin," he continues, referring to the late makeup artist, a graduate of Fashion International back in the day.

"Well, show us your legendary beat," I challenge him.

He whips out his book, which is half the size of most portfolios I've seen so far. Bobby senses my apprehension and quips, "It's the new millennium, *chérie*. Time to downsize."

We all huddle together and look at Bobby's test shots. "I'm very into Booty Dust, applied with a sponge, not a brush," he confides, pointing to the sparkly accents on the eyes, shoulders, and cleavage in the photos.

"I definitely dig that," I comment. "It makes everything pop in the photo."

"Who needs kitty litter when you have glitter!" Bobby says excitedly.

We guffaw grandly while a paying customer with an obvious Chinatown version of a Marc Jacobs quilted satchel steps up to the newsstand to buy a newspaper.

"Knock-knock," Aphro whispers to me.

Sami shoots us a look like it's time for us to take our fashion show on the road.

"Aw, Sami, don't be so stingy!" Bobby giggles, forking over five dollars for the September issue of *Vogue*.

"I thought you wanted October?" I ask.

"I do," Bobby Beat explains, "but I spilled orange juice on my September issue this morning at breakfast, and I hate stains—even on the ads, so I might as well get a replacement while I'm here."

"I read my *Vogue* while I'm sipping orange juice too," I giggle.

"Sipping and flipping!" Bobby coos. "Gucci, Pucci, and Juicy, oh my! By the way, what was that 'knock-knock' at the counter? You weren't referring to knocking me off, I hope!"

Aphro lets out a snort and we explain. "Nah. That's our code word for clocking a designer knockoff!"

"I *love* you tabby cats!" howls Bobby, who goes on to tell us his own code name: *SpongeBob*.

"I *love* you, SpongeBob!" I shout back.

"Now, tell me before I sign on," Bobby says with confidence, "who is the lead designer gonna be?"

The smiles vanish from our faces like we're

busted piñatas at a pity party. "Um, Diamond Tyler," I squeak.

Bobby looks disappointed too. "*Chéries, mon amis,* my new dear friends, she has sparkle potential for sure, but how do you say 'V for Versace'?" he moans, referring to Nole Canoli's online identity.

"That's what I said," hmmphs Aphro.

"Don't you just love the Catwalk blog?" Angora asks, veering away from the ensuing drama.

"Honey, first thing I do when I get up and take the chamomile eye pad off is turn on my Apple and read the blog!" claims Bobby Beat. "I *loved* Nole's."

"Is there any reason you want to be in our house?" I ask to keep the flow going.

"I mean, why not Willi Ninja, Jr.'s?" Angora adds.

"Oh, because I'm a queen, we should stick to-gether?" Bobby Beat retorts. "Is that what you're ask-ing, Miss Blue Beret?"

Angora pales two shades. Before she recovers, Bobby keeps pulling out stitches with his seam ripper. "I have been wielding brushes like Picasso and doing my mother's and my two sisters' makeup since I was potty trained. I *love* being around girls and glam and glitter. Does that answer your question?"

"You checked all the right boxes on the catty ques-tionnaire," I assure him. "Just one more question: what's your real last name?"

"Harmon. My grandparents changed their last name when they got to Ellis Island. It was German, like Harmensnauzer or something. But they didn't want to get dissed. It was right after World War Two and all."

"That's totally cool," I say, reassuring him, though I'm the one who really needs it. Forget about having *second* thoughts about Diamond. I'm having triplets!

Luckily, Bobby Beat babbles all the way to school, and we all stay lost in our own thoughts. I start perking up when he shares the source of his inspiration during his tender toddler years. "I loved all the original divas. Diana Ross, Eartha Kitt—can you believe that purr?" he coos.

Even Aphro warms up to Bobby, telling him about her foster mother's former job at Eartha's estate. As soon as we approach the front of Fashion International, Angora whispers in my ear, "Well, somebody is worthy." At first, I think she's referring to the Dalmation dogs from the technical school across the street, because I see them standing in a pack in front of our school as usual, ogling our roster of groovy girls. Then I realize that she is referring to Caterina and her crew, who are standing around like they're waiting for something to jump off. I notice Shalimar and her chic chortlers huddled together, engaging in a chorus of "Omigod! Omigod!"

"What's with the caco*phony*?" I ask, trying to keep

the situation Lite FM since Bobby Beat is in our midst. "That should be the new tagline of her house—printed right on T-shirts: 'Omigod'!" Nonetheless, I watch, transfixed, as Shalimar bats her Lee press-on lashes while she carries on in her shady corner. Meanwhile, Ice Très is trying hard to make eye contact with me. When that doesn't work, he tries the flip side and bum-rushes me.

"This place is wild," he says, grinning from ear to ear as he gets in my face.

"Yeah, a real urban safari," I quip, wondering what his *punto* is.

"The bet is she ain't gonna show," Ice Très continues, which makes me realize we're not on the same fashion page.

"What happened?" Felinez asks him.

"We're waiting for Chandelier," Ice Très responds.

"Why?" I ask, disappointed he wasn't referring to a famous fashionista sighting.

"Where y'all been?" Ice Très asks, like we're clueless kitties. "You ain't heard?"

"Awright already with the Sesame Street cue cards," I grumble. "Spill the refried beans."

"Snaps, I can't believe you're not on this. Awright, it's like this. Well, let me put it this way: Chandelier's father was indicted for chopping up body parts and selling them!" Ice Très says, delivering the news-breaking blow like the first reporter on the scene. "And at six thirty-five p.m., Chandelier's father was taking the perp walk outside arraignment court for participating in a *lucrative* cadaver operation."

"What, *what?*" I ask in disbelief, forgetting my deep freeze on Ice Très.

Angora shrugs and gives me a look like *Don't blame me*.

"Geez. It's not enough to have your ear to the street anymore. You've got to get down there with your nose," I moan, embarrassed that we've been trumped by the tagger. "I'm *gagulating*."

Chintzy Colon catches my glance and runs over, eager to serve up every gory detail of the latest drama like they're chorizos hot off her homemade grill.

Between her excited spurts, I gather that Lee Spinelli, a nurse at Mount Morris Hospital and formerly of Brooklyn Hospital, was involved in a black market body parts ring headed by a dentist. "It would take forty-five minutes to take out the bones, then another fifteen minutes for the skin, the upper arm, lower arm, thigh, abdominal area, and more," Chintzy babbles, like she's spouting a recipe.

"Can you believe it?" interjects Angora, who got briefed quickly by peeps on the side.

"No, actually, I can't," I admit. "Is this an early Halloween gag—like somebody's pulling my leg?"

"Nah!" counters Ice Très. "It's on the real. Body snatchers be making *bank*. They be parceling out a whole body and delivering to the highest bidder."

"Like who?" I ask, still not believing the hype.

"Tissue banks—and we're not talking Kleenex, okay. Research facilities—fresh or frozen, you can get a fresh elbow à la mode—or some freeze-dried brains, okay."

Angora picks up the news feed where Chintzy left off. "It's true, *chérie*. Chandelier's father and the rest of the cadaver crew were so busy that they often ate lunch or dinner in the dissecting rooms. He went from earning fifty thousand dollars a year as a nurse to making a hundred eighty-five thousand. . . ."

Suddenly, Aphro gets a shopportunity alert: "That's how come Chandelier started featuring Gucci all of a sudden!"

"Speaking of label dropping—she was so worried about us so-called fake Fendis that she didn't even realize there was one right under her nose," Angora says sadly.

We watch as the crowd outside multiplies intensely. Everyone is completely aghast about the Chandelier blast.

"The pelvis went for five thousand dollars?" Felinez squeals, getting creeped by all the statistics. "Ay, *dios*, I hope mine goes for more than that!"

"I'm sure they'd get at least twenty thousand for your butt!" I blurt out before I realize how insensitive it is. It's bad enough Felinez has to contend with all the stuffed *puercos* in the world who target juicy girls' body parts. "Sorry, Blue Boca. I was on a Tootsie Roll." I wince.

All of a sudden, Mr. Bias, the assistant principal, steps outside and announces loudly, "Okay, everyone, proceed to your homeroom classes. Right *now*, please."

Reluctantly, we all shuffle toward the front door, wondering if we're going to be graced with a Chandelier Spinelli sighting. Even her best friend, Tina Cadavere, is nowhere to be seen. Ice Très taps me on the shoulder and leans close, which gives me the creeps. "Hold on," he whispers. "I'm just trying to tell you something." I figure whispering is in order with this turn of eerie events. "I left you a little something in the stairwell by the Fashion Annex," he coos.

I nod like I know what he's talking about, but I don't. "Look forward to Friday," he says, and jets in front of us.

"What was that?" Angora asks, concerned.

"I don't know but apparently there's a prize for me behind door number three, if you catch my drift," I report, revealing all the details of the secret location. "Now I'm wondering if this is Ice Très's definition of a treasure hunt."

"Speaking of hunted," whispers Angora, pointing to Nole Canoli, who is huddled in the hallway by the security checkpoint. He's clearly trying to hide in plain sight. I can tell by the way he has his back turned to everyone but Kimono Harris, Dame Leeds, and Elgamela Sphinx.

"Doesn't he look a little pale?" I whisper.

"Yeah, even Countess Coco looks a little peaked," adds Angora. "I mean for a Pomeranian, her pallor is off!"

"So is yours," I warn her, then hope she isn't offended.

"I'm still tired from our interview session," confesses Angora. "That was *exhausting*."

Suddenly, I feel deflated too. "The only item we're getting on 'Page Six' is gonna be about Chandelier, the heiress to a chop shop dynasty!"

"I know," admits Felinez. "But I wonder if she is going to show her face—or fibia—in school again?"

Suddenly, a lightbulb appears over my head. "You think she's gonna drop out?" I quiz, secretly plotting a coup like Haiti's dethroned leader Papa Doc, who we're studying in history class.

Felinez and Angora get the picture. "Or maybe she'll be cut from the Catwalk competition like a dangling thread," says Angora.

Nole Canoli whizzes by us with Countess Coco perched in his Prada bag. He is trying desperately to keep his head down, as if he is shielding his face from probing cameras on a perp walk. We all watch warily as Caterina and her crew march down the hall toward an unknown destination.

"I bet you she's going to Ms. Fab's office," Angora predicts.

Meanwhile, I ponder our possibilities. "Even if Chandelier doesn't drop out, there's definitely too much squeal appeal. I mean, what's she got to offer now: 'Gee, my Dad can get us a fabbie deal on tendons and ligaments'?"

Aphro has had enough. "I'm out," she informs us. Angora attempts to say something, but I put my hand on her shoulder to tell her not to bother. "She can keep stressing me if it makes her happy," I say.

"Let's take the back stairwell, then," Angora says.

"Might as well," I concur. My curiosity has been piqued by Ice Très's mysterious message outside the bottle. When I swing open the door and spot the huge heart shape with Cupid's arrow sprawled wall to wall in the stairwell, my heart sinks like a sunken treasure. It's a message all right: SOS!

"Maybe this is just a clue?" Angora says weakly, her blue eyes popping in utter disbelief.

"He must be sniffing spray paint," I reply, shocked by this blatant disrespect for Fashion International's cardinal rule: don't scribble or dribble on the walls.

We stare at the huge metallic black-and-silver letters left courtesy of the misguided graffiti artist: WAZ-ZUP, PUSSYCAT? THIS IS 4REAL. ICE TWICE.

"Omigod," Felinez moans.

"Maybe no one will know he's talking about you?" Angora says hopefully.

"He might as well have hired the Goodyear Blimp and scrawled my name across the sky. *That* would have been more subtle!" I wince.

I check my Kitty watch and realize it's time to get to home period. "Geez," I say, looking back at Ice Très's handiwork. "A good marker is a terrible thing to waste."

By lunchtime, the speculation about the subject of the tagger's ardor has reached a peak second only to a Chandelier sighting and the unveiling of the spring fashions today in the Mercêdes-Benz Fashion Week shows at Bryant Park. "Wazzup, pussycat!" a chorus of shriekers yells in my direction. I ignore them and run into the Fashion Café like it's safe passage to the Underground Railroad. "The situation is outta control," I gripe to Felinez because my nerves are on edge.

"It's not your fault," Felinez says, trying to reassure me. Somehow she has regained her appetite and is hovering at the lunch counter, with her arms bent like chicken wings, unable to make a decision about her order.

"Velma, what should I get?" Felinez asks our favorite food attendant.

"Angel hair capellini," Velma shoots back.

"I'll have the same," I say. "This suits our continuing exploration of Italian culture."

"*If* we make it to Italy." Felinez grunts. "I don't know if I can go through a year of this roller coaster."

"Puhleez. A roller-coaster ride is more predictable," I grumble in return. Suddenly, a lightbulb goes on. I take out my Catwalk notepad and begin to scribble some thoughts for our Catwalk Credo. "Strap yourself in and fasten your Gucci seat belt," I read out loud.

"*Très bon,*" says Angora, looking over my shoulder, then adding her tasty thoughts to the Catwalk Credo until we come up with the remainder of the tenet right there on the spot. *Whenever I feel like screaming my head off or jumping out of my chic caboose, I will resist the urge; instead, I will tighten a notch on my fears like a true fashionista.*

"Yoohoo!" shouts Bobby Beat, zooming by us with his food tray poised gracefully at his waist. "Can you believe the drama today? Talk about Zorro—somebody left their mark in the stairwell! I'm so outta here after lunch!" he coos.

I'm relieved that Bobby Beat doesn't know that I'm the secret source of inspiration for our urban Zorro, and I have no intention of telling him. I also instinctively know what Bobby's early departure means. He is one of the lucky seniors who have been granted access passes to the one event we juniors have yet to witness: the fashion shows taking place at Mercedes-Benz Fashion Week.

"Oh, I am so green with Gucci Envy," I admit. Bobby laughs it off. "Oh, look at the credo we're creating. You'll get a copy, of course, at our first official team meeting." My stomach ties in knots as I say that. *Please, God, let me get my team assembled before I'm disgraced,* I silently plead.

Bobby Beat takes the glasses off the top of his head and puts them on to read the credo. "Truly fabulous!" he agrees. I exhale, satisfied that I have at least channeled some of my agitation into something constructive for our cause. And I also managed to snag a bona fide makeup artist for our house. "Okay, I've got to twirl," Bobby says excitedly. "After the shows, I have to get to work."

"When do you work?" I ask, my ears perking up at the mention of a job.

"Honey, I work twenty-four-seven," Bobby says evasively.

"Yes, I should have known, Superman—the glasses were a clue," I coo.

Bobby air-kisses each of us on each cheek, including Angora, who blushes. "Mademoiselle Blue Beret, that's how they do it in Europe—so get used to it!" he advises.

I'm relieved that the static between them was squashed. I would have felt fried if we didn't snag Bobby Beat for our house. When he sails away, Felinez says, "See, not everything is bad. I really like him."

"Yeah, I do too. Let's perch in our catty corner," I say, feeling inspired by Bobby Beat's effusive energy. "If he beats like he talks, then he's the second Rembrandt."

"*C'est vrai!* That's the truth," Angora agrees.

We always sit four tables back from the entrance of the café, which affords us a panoramic view of the floor show, as we call lunchtime antics.

Zeus and Lupo burst through the door, looking wild-eyed—like everyone is today—obviously searching for clues of intelligent life in fashion land. They spot us and sit down to cross paws. "I just wanna give you a heads-up. Ice Très is in Mr. Confardi's office."

"Why do I get the feeling the other platform shoe is about to drop," I moan, mortified that Zeus knows about my situation. I've even given up hope that he's ready to tango with me. Why would he want to? I'm the object of affection of a magic marker gone haywire.

"Pashmina?" Zeus repeats, and I realize he has been trying to bend my ear some more. "I just saw the camera crew coming out of Ms. Fab's office, too."

"You don't think—?" I freeze, wondering if I'm gonna be the source of more shame for my house.

"Nah, nah," Zeus says, waving his hand like a freestyle paw.

I start coughing wildly.

"You all right? *Va bene?*" asks Lupo.

I cough and nod at the same time, then sip some water till I regain use of my larynx. I try to resume eating. That's when I notice a long dark hair resting on my pasta.

"Not mine," Zeus says, running his fingers through his wild wavy hair. "Want me to take it back?"

"Yeah, get Velma to handle this, cuz I don't think that's a hair from an angel," I explain, handing him my plate of capellini.

My cell phone rings and I shriek because I forgot to turn it off. Even a fashion toad would know that today is definitely not the day to break any more Fashion International rules like the one clearly posted on the wall of the Fashion Café: EAT YOUR JELLY, BUT NIX THE CELLY.

Angora covers me while I discreetly grab the phone out of my purse and see that the number belongs to exactly the person I'd like to avoid right now, the prying Teen Style producer, Caterina Tiburon.

"*Tales from the Crypt,* part two?" I moan, getting paranoid.

"Answer it!" Angora orders me.

"Hello, Kaflamma Central," I answer in the voice of my chirpy alter ego.

Caterina doesn't miss a beat. Obviously in her line of work she's seen more than her share of fashion alter egos—or just plain egos.

"I wanted to give you a heads-up," she begins.

"Wazzup?" I query hesitantly, wondering why I am suddenly the recipient of so many heads-up today.

"Tune in to Channel Two news tonight, five o'clock—there might be a segment of interest to you."

"Omigod!" I shriek before I realize what I've said. Felinez and Angora snicker. "Is this about Chandelier?"

Felinez and Angora close in on me like an invasion of body snatchers is about to take place. In her typical cagey fashion, Caterina doesn't give me a straight answer. "It just may be something of interest to you."

"Awright. I'm on it," I say, sick to my stomach as I sign off. Then I tell my crew what Caterina said.

Zeus comes back with a fresh plate of capellini. I push it away. "I'm sick," I confess, reporting the phone call to Zeus. "I think we might be getting the ax."

"You mean, like, cut from the competition, or losing a limb?" Zeus asks.

"Could be either," I say, kaflustered. "Forget about catfights. With these latest developments, I honestly think fashion is going to the dogs—*for real*."

FASHION INTERNATIONAL 35TH ANNUAL
CATWALK COMPETITION BLOG

New school rule: You don't have to be ultranice, but don't get tooooo catty, or your posting will be zapped by the Fashion Avengers!!

YOU'D BETTER WORK, SUPERMODELS. . . .

Today was the official start of Mercedes-Benz Fashion Week in New York City—the only place in the world I would rather be than Paris, Milan, or Firenze next June (opening the Pitti Bimbo show, if I'm lucky—and I think I will be now that I have hooked up with the most purrlicious house in the Catwalk competition this year!). Anyhoo, back to foundation basics: I waited three years for the moment I could walk into the glamour-fortified tents at Bryant Park with an access pass—instead of hiding in the folds of the tent for a behind-the-scenes peek! More than 100 spring collections will sashay the runways under the over-guarded tents during the course of five days at Bryant Park, and other nearby venues (because not every design house can afford to sell their embryos in exchange for a spot in the park!). The spring shows are held every year in the fall and the fall shows are held in the spring. (Got it?) The fall fashions you are seeing in the stores now were shown earlier this year—that means last spring, when I was merely a junior, so those collections were not christened by my eyes! The lag between showtime and

218

shipping gives the press and retail buyers ample time to manipulate the fashion crystal ball so you will think you've made your own selections to hang in your closet. (You don't honestly believe you have been put on this planet to make your own choices, do you?) Anyhoo, I adore the anticipation, the music, the models, the fashion makers pacing to and fro with scissors, sandwiches, and sponges—and, of course, the goodie bags placed so delicately on each guest's chair! Street-smart fashionistas remove the appointed goodie bag from their seat and plop it immediately into their kiss-lock purses to be on safe side. (Swag looting is on the rise, so guard your goodies with a vengeance, my dears!) More than the goodie bags, I honestly just love seeing inspired fashion brought to life. By the way, I spent more than three hours in line with my fellow senior fashion classmates to get our student access badges with nothing more than my sponges and Booty Dust, which I applied generously to everyone in line. I say, who needs kitty litter, when you have glitter? It's simply all-purpose! Anyhoo, I'm not bwitchin' about the long lines that come with being a die-hard fashionista. I don't even mind that I cannot take off my Dolce loafers right now because my feet are so swollen. I've decided that I'll just sleep with them on.

The other reason why I was so electrified today is because I also met some feline fashionistas with whom I plan to align myself so we can "scratch, scratch" out the Catwalk competition at our school next June! With no disrespect to the creativity I witnessed today at Mercedes-Benz Fashion Week, the Catwalk competition means more to me because I will finally be an important ingredient in a fierce fashion enchilada. Sorry, I must be getting famished again—gotta go get my sponges and Booty Dust out, so I can beat some more faces. . . !

10/10/2008 11:45:22 PM
Posted by: SpongeBob

10

Next period, I have model appreciation. I'm so scared that I'm going to be dragged like an alley cat into another scrappy situation that I don't even look up from my notebook in class. "The Trinity of Terror was not a left-wing Palestinian organization but the reign of which three supermodels?" asks the teacher, Ms. Boucle. Her ample chest heaves with anticipation while she waits for a response. "Anybody?" No one volunteers. "Pashmina?"

I feel a poke in my back that startles me back to reality. I look up and see everyone staring at me.

"What, what?" I ask, embarrassed by my trip to the Bozo sphere. Ms. Boucle pushes her thick red glasses up on the bridge of her nose disapprovingly. Ruthie Dragon, who is seated in front of me, raises her hand energetically.

"Yes, Ruthie," Ms. Boucle says, putting her hands on her hips and throwing me a glance like *I'm watching you Pinkie*.

"Um, it was Linda Evangelista, Christy Turlington,

and Naomi Campbell!" Ruthie says enthusiastically. I am so over her. I thought we were on the same fashion page, but she didn't even show up for my team interviews. Then I find out that she's joined Chandelier's house, or perhaps I should say chop shop.

Suddenly, there's a loud outburst right below our second-floor classroom, which faces Thirty-eighth Street. A few students jump up and peer out the half-opened windows to check out the action. Even Ms. Boucle adjusts the extra-wide red lizard belt trapping her waist and waddles over to the scene of an unfolding drama. I sit frozen in my chair, paralyzed by my own fears. Ruthie Dragon turns from the window and shoots me a look like *You'd better get over here and check this out.* I make a fire-breathing face at her like *Don't make me slay you, okay.* I figure the commotion outside probably has something to do with Chandelier. No doubt she's finally gracing us with her notorious presence. And with the chop shop heiress's dumbfounding luck, her father has probably already bribed his way out of prison by donating a few hardened arteries to the Police Athletic League.

"PASHMINA!!"

The guttural scream from outside is so visceral, my veins turn to warm milk. Now everyone in class turns to look at me. I jump up and run to the window. Ice

Très stands tall, looking up at the window, waving like he's looking for someone—me. Mr. Confardi hovers by the entrance and barks at him, "A suspension isn't enough? We can head right to expulsion if you'd like. As a matter of fact, why don't you apply to the School of Visual Arts, where your *talents* would be more appreciated!"

"I'm sorry, Mr. Confardi. I just wanted to say good bye to someone real quick before I jet," Ice Très offers in a feeble voice.

"Friday, awright?" yells Ice Très, still waving to get my attention. I stand still like a dummy—a real one—because I can't help wondering, *How did I ever get myself involved in this corny kaflamma?*

"Everybody go back to your seats, please," orders Ms. Boucle. "The show is over!"

⌐ ⌐

Felinez is waiting for me outside class, and I'm so embarrassed that I'm the one who's now walking like a fashion felon on a perp walk. Shalimar is standing squarely outside like she's waiting for me and ready to rumble. In her case, however, that merely means extra-heavy doses of lash batting. She's wearing a brown flowered wrap dress. "I see we've been reduced to wearing consignment shop finds," I say, observing the vintage of Shalimar's nineties-looking Diane von Furstenberg dress.

"She's already handed in her forms to Ms. Lynx's office," Felinez informs me like it's good news.

"So?" I hiss back. Just what I needed—an annoying reminder that I haven't handed in my team membership forms yet.

"So that means she just got a strike since Ice Très got suspended," Felinez says defensively.

"Oh, right," I say apologetically, scanning the Catwalk rules and regulations in my mind: *Any infraction by team members results in an automatic strike, which will be calculated into the judges' tally for your house's final overall score.*

"We should consider ourselves lucky he didn't show up to the meeting, *mija*. That's all I'm saying," Felinez adds.

"Luck is a funny thing, isn't it?" I muse, staring at Shalimar head-on. Shalimar turns away sheepishly. "That also means Ice Très got disqualified as a team member in her house as a result of his suspension. Now I can see it. She's become unglued at her Shimmy Choos."

Angora joins us and, true to her journalistic nature, delivers an update. "Calls from Chandelier were fielded by Mr. Confardi's office. I got that from a reliable source. Even better," she says, trying to look over at Shalimar, "you missed a certain person's Coty Fashion Critics' Awards performance in Ms. Lynx's office fourth period. And I got that from an even more reliable source."

"Crocodile tears?" I ask in disbelief.

"*Au contraire,*" Angora tells me.

I gloat for a *segundo,* then turn glum. Shalimar may be shedding real tears, but I am far from shedding my real fears. "We don't have a leg up on the competition yet," I say apprehensively. "What we do have is a head's-up from Caterina that we have to deal with."

"Let's wait for Zeus," advises Angora. "We need all the back-watching we can get in this lipstick jungle." I smile, realizing that she is already quoting quips from Bobby Beat, our latest addition to the House of Pashmina.

ᖓ ᖆ

As soon as Aphro comes out, then Zeus, we all head uptown to my house. Zeus stays zip-lipped on the subject of Ice Très. But Aphro is anxious to gloat and just can't miss the shopportunity to seal it with a dis. "I told you to watch out for Mr. Blinking and Winking," she snarls at me.

I nod like I'm listening.

"Hi, Pashmina," screams Stellina, running out of the courtyard as if she's been waiting for me. "The cameras were here!" she says, like she's giving me gossip so hot her little fingers are scorching.

"I know," I say with a giggle. At least I can feel proud about one thing: how hyped Stellina and Tiara are about being included in the Teen Style camera crew's visit to my humble abode.

"They were talking to Big Daddy Boom," she continues.

"I know," I say, secretly hoping my on-camera prank doesn't backfire on me one day.

"Can I touch your hat again?" Stellina squeals to Zeus.

"Sure—cuz you have that Midas touch," Zeus answers. He can tell by the look on Stellina's face that she isn't following his drift, so he just smiles and bends down so she can get her paws on his plushness.

As usual, Mr. Darius is in fine form. He and José, his assistant, are assembling the massive mountain of recyling bags that must be left curbside for pickup by the sanitation trucks tomorrow morning.

"Don't you ever wonder where all this garbage ends up?" Angora asks.

"I'm sure Mr. Darius wishes it would just disappear daily," I observe. Suddenly, Angora starts breathing heavily and stops for a second to catch her breath. She takes out her inhaler and we all wait in silence for it to kick in.

In the meantime, I watch Mr. Darius in action. Now he's yelling at one of the homeless guys, who we call Mr. Sunkist because he pushes around a shopping cart that's always filled to the brim with empty soda cans. He spends most of his day taking the bottles and cans to the Piggly Wiggly supermarket across the street to collect the deposit money. "Every week, ticket I get!" Mr. Darius yells at Mr. Sunkist, who has already ripped open one of the recyling bags to plunder discarded bottles and cans.

"He's definitely scary when detonated," Zeus observes, nodding knowingly at the explanation of Mr. Darius's nickname. We head upstairs to my apartment, and I'm surprised that my mother is already there, sipping a cup of her favorite Belgian Blend at the dining room table. I called earlier and told her about Chandelier, and that I was bringing my friends over to watch the news. Maybe this is her way of showing support. "This beter be good," she says, looking at us curiously as we all pile into the living room. Leave it to my mother to know how to make me more nervous than I already am.

Anxiously, we sit down. It's only five minutes till

the five o'clock news. "An invite for ringside seats at Mercedes-Benz Fashion Week couldn't be more coveted than a seat on the gently worn black leather couch in my living room right now," I blurt out, trying to keep the situation Lite FM. "Well, maybe I'm exaggerating just a notch on my Gucci belt. *Not.*"

"Chenille, come in here," my mother says, much to my chagrin.

Angora catches my horrified look. "Why don't we just invite the Terminator," I mumble.

Chenille saunters in and flops into the butterscotch leather reclining armchair—the withered cousin of the black leather couch, both pieces snagged on Sixty-seventh Street last summer during our furniture-foraging escapades. Judging by the smirk on my younger sister's face, she would rather be somewhere getting paid to scorch someone's scalp with a hot comb than sitting with us.

"So, I hear you're working the press and curls," Aphro inquires like she's with the Labor Department and verifying hourly wages.

Chenille nods her head as if she's bored with bringing in the Benjies. I wish I knew where she hid her money, because I'm tempted to engage in a sticky-finger stint of my own.

"I made twenty dollars this week," Chenille boasts.

"Do you put in tracks?" Aphro asks. Luckily, Aphro is sitting next to Angora, or she'd get a swift kick from my smug pink suede UGGed foot.

"Yeah," Chenille says matter-of-factly, like she's the extension expert behind Beyoncé's bouncy weave. "If you buy the hair, I'll do it for twenty dollars a track."

"Twenty dollars!" shrieks Aphro. "For that much, I'll put my own tracks in with a hot-glue gun!"

"That sounds like a good investment to me," Angora says sweetly. "After all, hair extensions are career extensions!" Angora is always so nice to Chenille and tries to get me to see her hidden potential, which must be buried deeper than Jacques Cousteau's treasures in the Bermuda Triangle, cuz I sure can't find it.

"Okay, shut up, everybody. *Cayete la boca!*" shouts Felinez as the *Five at Five* newsroom anchors start spouting away.

After fifteen minutes of sitting stiff as a board lest I miss one word, I relax into the couch. Nothing so far about us, or even anything interesting, until one of the anchors announces, "More indictments are expected against the body-cutter ring as new charges are filed by the Brooklyn district attorney's office."

"Omigod, listen up!" shrieks Aphro as we all sit on the edge of our seats.

The anchor turns the story over to a reporter

outside the downtown arraignment court. We watch as a group of men in suits walk in wearing handcuffs.

My mother senses the commotion and hovers over the couch. "Which one is her father?" she asks impatiently.

"Probably the one in the Gucci suit," I say. "How do you say, 'Can I get a refund?'"

My mom doesn't smile at the joke that I cracked for her benefit. She's always complaining about the snobby, cheap customers who return clothing they've purchased but obviously already worn and the way they feign innocence when they're declined because of sweat stains or driblets of red wine.

We're all glued to the television as the reporter does her stiff riff: "Five medical professionals—including nurse Lee Spinelli, embalmer Joseph Ricola, and ex-dentist Michael Minelli, the alleged leader of the notorious body-cutting ring, were indicted earlier today on one hundred and twenty-two counts of body stealing, grand larceny, forgery, racketeering, and other charges. According to that indictment, more than a thousand corpses were harvested from area funeral homes without permission from next of kin. . . ."

"No way Chandelier is coming back to school after this," Angora predicts. "I mean, who would sit next to her at lunchtime watching her cut a slice of pizza with a plastic fork?"

Zeus starts fiddling with his zebra-striped mink hat, which means he feels a brainstorm coming on.

"I see steam rising," I say, egging him on.

"I'm gonna hit Dame right now on the cell. I bet you Chandelier has called Nole Canoli and hit him with the hardness!" Zeus says, lit up like the Christmas tree in Rockefeller Center.

"Wow, that's not a brainstorm—that's a hurricane," I mumble.

"Might as well, cuz ain't nothing on the news but the news," Aphro seconds.

It's true. "We've been watching for thirty minutes and there is not a fashion sighting in sight," Angora reports. "Not even an early Christmas push for *très* tawdry tartans!"

Zeus is talking on his cell phone to Dame Leeds. "Word. That's what's up?" He gives us a thumbs-up sign, which we're hoping means he's managed to snag *scandalabrious* tidbits on the Chandelier crisis.

As a matter of fact, we're so anxious to get our gossip grub on that we almost miss the anchor announcing: "Now we go to our latest inductee in the Smiley Wiley 'Shame on You!' Hall of Fame."

"Hey! Isn't that your building?" yells Aphro, pointing to the television screen. Sure enough, newscaster Smiley Wiley is standing in front of Amsterdam

Gardens. I see Stellina jumping up and down in the background.

"Oh, *that's* what she was trying to tell us downstairs," I say, realizing that I misinterpreted her excitement. It wasn't a blast from the past. She was talking about *today*.

A voice-over continues: "Acting on an anonymous tip, Channel Two learned that landlord Nakheir Darius, who owns the high-rise building complex Amsterdam Gardens, located on Amsterdam Avenue and 114th Street, has been terrorizing his tenants for years with illegal threats of rent hikes and evictions, and postponing basic building repairs, even withholding heat by denying access to the boiler room facilities to repair technicians."

The camera cuts to footage of the lobby, elevator shafts, and then Smiley Wiley, who was obviously camped outside our building today, chasing after Mr. Darius himself. "Mr. Darius, is it true that tenants have gone without hot water for two weeks?" Smiley Wiley shoves the microphone toward Mr. Darius, who shields his face from the camera and motions for the camera crew to leave.

"Get out of here now!" Mr. Darius shouts.

"What about the unauthorized rent increases? Is it true tenants are subjected to ten percent rent increases despite the rent stabilization guidelines enforced by the city council?"

"Get out, you idiot!" Mr. Darius repeats.

Facing the camera, Smiley Wiley says in a deadpan voice, "Mr. Darius's favorite phrase seems to be, 'Get out, you idiot.' As a result, today we induct into the Smiley Wiley 'Shame on You!' Hall of Fame landlord Nakheir Darius. Welcome, Mr. Darius!"

"Omigod, we're going to get evicted," I shriek in disbelief.

Chenille throws me a dirty look like *You've really done it now. We're going to be homeless!*

Surprisingly, my mom's reaction is exactly the opposite. "Well, I hope that gets him off his lazy behind once and for all. Cuz I'm sure not paying this rent increase," she announces.

I realize that Mom has kept more to herself than I thought. "You mean he asked to raise the rent?"

"Yes indeed, he did—and we haven't even lived here a year yet!" she reveals, flashing a rent bill in her hand. "Free market rates, my butt!"

"Oooh, he is low-down," Aphro says, shaking her head.

"That was great," Zeus says, beaming at me proudly.

"Thank God they didn't mention me or the

Catwalk competition," I say, finally realizing that Caterina probably orchestrated the leak to help me. "I wonder how Caterina pulled this off?"

"She probably knows one of the producers," Angora offers. "But who knew that television shame could lead to fame! I love it." Her eyes beam with pride at the producer's handiwork.

Zeus, on the other hand, is anxious to share *his* handiwork. "Well, you wanna hear what Dame Leeds said?"

We're so wrapped up in the drama, we forgot about the cadaver crisis. "Tell, but don't kiss!" Aphro says, slapping him on his arm.

"Nole Canoli did speak to Chandelier," he says, pursing his mouth like he's savoring the tasty tidbit he's about to put on the grill for us. "She's not coming back to school for a while," he says, nodding.

"Ay, *dios mio!*" Felinez cries.

"If she doesn't come back to school soon, she's gonna get disqualified from the Catwalk competition," I say, scanning the competition rules in my head. " 'No house leader is allowed any more than five missed school days in the designated year,' " I read aloud.

"If that's the case, then bring it on," Zeus says. Slick minds think alike.

"Holy Canoli!" I say, licking my lips. Suddenly, I

feel a breath of fresh air hitting my lungs. Even Angora seems like she's breathing easier.

"Wow, doesn't it look like my living room got bigger?" I say in amazement, looking around.

"No!" shrieks Felinez, "but our opportunities have!"

"So, do you Kats and Kitties want to stay for dinner?" my mom asks with a smile. I can't believe Mom is so calm about my Operation: Kitty Litter caper. I thought she would throw me in the frying pan and turn me into a burnt frittata—her specialty.

"I want to stay!" Felinez squeals.

While my mother fiddles around in the kitchen, Chenille goes to help.

"I hope she ain't planning on frying any extensions!" Aphro says, then does her snorting laugh. Obviously the mere thought of being able to snag Nole Canoli for our house has gotten her off my grill.

While we're waiting for my mom to whip up a frozen dinner, we start talking about everything that has been going on with the Catwalk competition. "Wait till you meet Bobby Beat," Felinez says enthusiastically to Zeus, her big brown eyes widening. Then she starts playing with a pink toothpick between her teeth that she pulled out of her meowch pouch.

"Oh, that is tick-tacky," I tell her, slapping her hand. "Next you'll be carrying sausages in there!"

Suddenly, there's a loud rapping on the door. "See, *la policía* are coming to arrest you for that!" Felinez bursts, embarrassed. I freeze like a statue in a wax museum.

"Who is it?" I yell, but no one answers, so I look through the peephole and see Mr. Darius. I press my hand to my chest and mouth my horror to my crew: *It's him!*

Everyone stands alert, like a dressing team behind the scenes at a fashion show.

I take a deep breath and open the door. "Hi, Mr. Darius!" I squeak, like Miss Piggy on helium, much to my chagrin.

Mr. Darius breaks into a forced smile. "I just to tell that we sorry for problems and make sure to fix soon," he says. I'm so shocked that I could almost faint. My mother comes to the door and he gives her a forced smile too. "I come to fix soon—everything."

"Oh, good," Mom says, looking at him matter-of-factly. "I got something for you, too. Hang on, I'll be right back."

My mom motions for Chenille to hand her the rent bill. She then hands the bill to Mr. Darius. "I won't be paying the rent this month. That should make up for all the time we didn't have hot water or heat. And please fix that amount. I won't be paying any increase, either."

Mr. Darius humbly nods to my mother. "No problem."

"Good night," my mom says. Translation of her body language: *We're done here, you fool!*

She closes the door.

"You read him with relish—and a hot dog!" I say proudly.

There's another rap on the door. This time Mom opens it. It's Mr. Darius again. Sheepishly, he hands her the casserole dish he has in his hand. "This my wife make—please enjoy."

"Oh," my mother says, suddenly pleased by all the attention. "What is it?"

"Kobideh kebab," says Mr. Darius. "My wife make."

"Well, thank you," Mom says, softening.

This time, after she closes the door, I squeal: "Thank God! Now we don't have to eat Lean Cuisine!"

I am so hyped by what happened that I can't resist the urge to hug Mom, even though I know she doesn't go in for that sort of cuddly behavior, especially in front of my crew.

We all go the table and eat the food Mr. Darius brought, which is actually pretty tasty. "This is the jointski," Zeus comments. "It kinda reminds me of my mom's cooking. It's similar to Mediterranean food."

I nod like I agree. I'm fascinated by what it must be

like to have parents who were born in another country. "I have to check your mom's cooking real soon," I say, then get embarrassed. I don't want Zeus to think I'm inviting myself over.

"Actually, my girlfriend is a better cook than my mother. On the real," Zeus says, smiling proudly.

Suddenly, I feel like someone just did a touchdown on my chest. I pause for a moment to catch my breath. Angora does too and gives me a look that could easily be translated as, *Well, now you know he's not gay!*

"What kind of food is this?" Felinez asks, chowing down the kebabs and oblivious to my deep-dish disappointment.

"The kind you eat," quips Mom.

After we suck up two bottles of ginger ale, Zeus heads out because he has to go home to Long Island. He lives in Monyville, which is near the "five towns," as he explained it.

"Heading off to Moneyland," Aphro teases him.

"Mos def," Zeus says, yawning with his arms stretched over his head and his hands clasped on top of his mink hat.

I hug Zeus, too, amid oohs and ahhs from Felinez and Aphro. I ignore them.

"From now on, I think we should heed our own advice," Angora starts in. "The time has come to strap ourselves in and fasten our Gucci seat belts."

My mom chuckles and hands Zeus his Starter jacket. "That's original."

We explain to her about the Catwalk Credo. She seems like she's proud of me. What I neglect to tell her is that we haven't assembled our whole team, and that the other four houses are all in place—even if one is about to fall like a house of cards.

New school rule: You don't have to
be ultranice, but don't get tooooo
catty, or your posting will be zapped
by the Fashion Avengers!!

DON'T HATE THE PLAYERS, OR THE
FASHION GAME. . . .

Everybody talks about relying on
your instincts to survive in the fashion game, but sometimes you should
just rely on the facts, okay? You can
call me superficial, you can call me
shady, but the bottom line is that you
call me, period. So when I received
a phone call this morning from Chandelier Spinelli, whom I've adored
and supported throughout her fashion
metamorphosis (stop, rewind; actually, I'm the catalyst behind it),
telling me that she was going to take
a hiatus from school due to a personal
crisis, I felt it was necessary for me
to publicly state my game plan. Let it
be known right here that I did NOT
abandon Chandelier Spinelli in her
darkest hour of need. I live with a
single parent myself—one who is inca-
pacitated and requires a Hoveround
Power Chair just to get around because
of her weight problem and because she
needs hip replacement surgery, which
she cannot afford, okay? So I know
firsthand the drama that a parent can
put you through. (Everyone feels sorry
for single parents, but you should
feel sorry for their kids, okay?) I
might act fabulous, but that does not

240

mean that I'm not honest about who I am. So let me get out my seam ripper and pluck out some useless stitches: no one cares that when I was six years old I started dressing my Barbie dolls in hand-stitched clothes, each sequin and bugle bead given more attention than the parts for my Tonka trucks. Sure, that will make a good sound bite for the Teen Style Network, but the truth is, the only thing anybody cares about is if you're a winner or a loser. I may not be the most fabulous designer of all time, because we all know who that designer was (Gianni, may you rest in haute couture heaven), but I don't believe that there is another designer currently in the fashion galaxy who is more FABULOUS than I am. Now, that's as honest as I'm ever gonna be. My freshman design teacher, Mr. Rocailles, gave me a piece of advice, which has stuck to me like Velcro. He said, "The fashion business is like musical chairs. When the music stops, you'd better quickly plop your ass on another chair, or you're out of the game." And that's exactly what I intend to do. I'm going to bestow another house with my talent, because I sincerely believe it is my destiny to be a winner in the Catwalk competition. So, please, don't hate the player OR the fashion game!

10/15/2008 9:30:35 AM
Posted by: V for Versace

11

When I get to school, there's a message in my Catwalk in-box to report to Ms. Lynx's office. My pulse quickens because Ms. Lynx has never summoned me before. I'm supposed to submit my team membership forms to her office today, "But why is she on my case so pronto?" I speculate nervously to Felinez. The indelible image of Zorro's banned cousin waving wildly as I watch from my fashion tower frightens the froth off my steaming hot cappuccino. "Oh, I get it. I might be joining Ice Très in Style Siberia after all."

"You'd better go now, *mija*," Felinez warns me.

"No way, José," I say. "I have to get cap-happy first."

"*Cuidate*—be careful," Felinez sighs, waving her hand in defeat as she heads off to textile science.

I trot in the opposite direction to sociology but get ambushed around the bend by Willi Ninja, Jr., who's intent on providing a private lesson in the collective behavior of nosy human beings. "Did you stand up for your man?" he asks, posing in a defensive pirouette stance.

"What?" I ask, blushing shades of paranoid pink. I should have known peeps would be offering their own versions of the brou-haha.

"Well, he got suspended because of you—the least you can do is defend his honor," Willi Ninja, Jr., says, provoking my posture.

"Th-that is radickio," I stammer. But the truth is, I do feel guilty as charged.

"Is it, Miss P.P.?" Ninja, Jr., says, eyeing me carefully to see if I'll bend like saltwater taffy. "Better check your in-box. I'm sure he sent you a broken arrow to mend."

"I checked my in-box," I say, now getting paranoid times squared. I wonder if Willi Ninja, Jr., saw the note from Ms. Lynx. That's it—he's probably already peeped the situation!

Willi Ninja, Jr., pivots and turns to get the last word. "Well, all I can say is: one down, three to go. . . ."

It figures the pedigreed poser already assumes he has the Catwalk competition on lockdown, but the battle hasn't even begun. "Don't make me snap my clutch purse!" I call back, marching away defiantly. That's it! I've had it with peeps pushing me around. Time to stop tap-dancing gingerly and bring in the noise!

I send a text message to Zeus: "Make it happen." He'll know exactly what I mean. Then I march right into the Lynx lair.

Sil Lai looks up from her desk and purses her

lips. "You haven't submitted your team membership forms yet?"

"No. Not yet," I say, my voice zooming from squeaky to leaky in seconds. "I had a message that Ms. Lynx wants to see me?"

Sil Lai looks at her computer screen, opens a document, then looks at me with that Botox face, which makes it hard for me to read between her lines. "She's busy. I put you in for fourth period," Sil Lai informs me.

Fourth period? I'll have a catiac arrest before then. I look around the office and see Farfalla, stationed in her cubicle. I wish she manned the reception desk, because I could read her like the *New York Times* style section—backward and forward. But Farfalla doesn't look up, and as usual, she seems buried in work, like an archaeologist at an excavation site.

"I spoke to Mink," Sil Lai says, still stone-faced.

I wait for Sil Lai to drop an Altoid (a minty hint), but *nada*, so I decide to take her probe further.

"I can't believe she joined my house!" I gush, but realize immediately that I sound like I have no self-esteem—and I'm not talking about the clothing label, either.

Now the phone rings and Sil Lai gives me a look like I'm dismissed. Scurrying out of the office, I pop the collar on my Flower Power burnout sweater to ward off the chilly thought of fashion exile.

After sociology, Zeus is hovering on the horizon to give me the heads-up. "Definitely getting used to buzzwords involving body parts," I say, smiling. I stare longingly at his beautiful long dark eyelashes and wonder what his girlfriend is like. Probably a model too.

"It's on—lunchtime at Petsey Betsey," he informs me proudly.

"I knew you'd come through," I say softly. What I really want to say is, *Flotsam and jetsam the girlfriend, because I know you're tickled pink over moi. M. O. to the I.*

"You heard? Moet Major has been nominated by proxy vote as the replacement house leader. She's forming her own team, though. Chandelier is definitely out on a limb," adds Zeus, snapping me back to my challenging reality.

"Let's pray I'm not next," I say, shuddering, then spill the refried beans about my current concerns.

He gets a troubled look in his eyes.

"What?" I ask.

"Nah. Nothing." Zeus shakes it off.

I send a text message to Diamond, Aphro, Felinez, and Angora: "Operation: Kitty Litter is in full effect."

Although Diamond Tyler doesn't bring Crutches to school, it should have come as no surprise to me that she is a frequent visitor at the Petsey Betsey annex. "How's Crutches coming along?" the attendant, Bubba Barbieri, asks her. Diamond gives him a detailed update, then segues into her current cause: rescuing Sheepish Sally who was desperately trying to save herself from the chopping block by saying baaah-bye to the wicked city.

When the rest of my crew arrives, Bubba grants us access to the waiting area after administering a warning: "You're not allowed in the pet playground."

Zeus gingerly folds his six-foot frame into one of the bright orange wooden chairs with the giraffe-shaped backs.

"These were hand painted by Garo Sparo and donated to the school," Diamond informs us. "He's one of my favorite designers."

"That's a cool name—is he into birds or something?" Zeus asks.

"No, it's spelled S-P-A-R-O. But he does volunteer at the animal shelter. That's how I got my job. He's an amazing designer. He does a lot of corsetry work—evoking style from the Victorian era," Diamond explains, babbling. It's clear she's nervous—and truth is, so am I.

"He's gonna let me intern at his studio," she continues. "I mean, so he says. Maybe later in the year."

"We're not interested in interning," Aphro blurts out, like she's not impressed. "We need jobs paying some real paper, okay."

I smile warmly at Diamond to make up for Aphro's aversion to "freebies," which is what she calls internships.

"Have you found anything yet?" Diamond asks, concerned. But she only manages to irritate Aphro—again.

"You make it sound like we're lost," she says, then gives one of her signature snorts.

Zeus spurts out a laugh. He can't help himself because he's still not used to the Babe squeals that emanate from Aphro's smoocher.

Right now, I'd like to stick Aphro Biggie's head in a trough to cool her off.

At last, Nole and most of his entourage—Dame Leeds, Elgamela Sphinx, and Kimono Harris—enter the Annex. Nole kisses Countess Coco on her nose, then hands her over to Bubba, cozily tucked in her black Prada carrier.

"Okay, Countess, no funny business today with the biscuits. Even Your Highness has to share," Bubba warns the fiery-haired Pomeranian.

Meanwhile, Diamond is fixated on Elgamela's bandage dress in juicy orange, which looks very similar to the French designer Hervé Léger's hand-sewn numbers, favored by Beyoncé. It's probably just a knock-knock, even though Elgamela is so fierce she could wear a dress made out of real Band-Aids and still earn purr points.

"Omigod, Nole, did you make that?" Diamond coos, pointing to Elgamela's mummy-tight curve hugger.

Diamond is obviously wearing on Nole's nerves, because he winces and shoots back, "Don't disrespect Hervé like that. And why would I steal his trademark?"

The delicate designer's face cracks like a cubic zirconia. So much for Operation: Kitty Litter. Maybe sticking my head in the odor-absorbing clay would have been a better idea.

"Today's my birthday. My dad got it from the designer consignment shop near where we live," Elgamela coos humbly. "He just got so tired of hearing me whine about it that he bought it for me!"

Nervously, I clear my throat before I speak to ensure that no squeaky sounds emanate against my will. "Wow, that's nothing like the reject consignment shop near my house," I babble, then repeat the motto plastered in the dingy window of Second Time Around: "Why go to JCPenney when you can save at Secondhand Benny's!"

"That's hysterical," Elgamela squeals back, her exotic accent lilting on the words. Elgamela quickly tells us all about Cherry Hill, New Jersey, where she grew up; it is apparently chock-full of designer-obsessed housewives. "My father owns Chirpin' Chicken on Second Avenue. I work there after school," she goes on. "That's why I smell like chicken half the time. Can't get it out of my pores."

"Really? I didn't know that," Felinez says, surprised.

"What—that you can't get the smell of chicken grease off your skin?" Elgamela asks, amused.

"No!" Felinez tries quickly to divert any more drama. "That you worked, um, as a chicken. I mean, that your father was rich. You know what I mean!"

We all laugh hysterically.

"It's right off Sixty-second Street," Elgamela explains. "Come by any time after school—wings are on me. I'll even throw in a breast and a leg!"

"Awright—as long as you chop it up Benihana-style," laughs Zeus, crossing paws with Nole. Suddenly, I realize that maybe Elgamela is Zeus's girlfriend. *Duh!*

Just then, Elgamela breaks into her dimpled smile, beaming at him. There was definitely no riddle to her rave reviews: she is charmed and dangerous. All of a sudden, Ruthie Dragon, who is out of breath, comes running into the reception area. I refrain from blurting out, *Look what the cat dragged in—a dragon*. Good thing too, because as soon as the traitor catches her breath, she blurts out to Nole, "Sorry I'm late!"

Nole introduces us, but I gently inform him that we already know each other—unfortunately. What I want to ask is why she's here: the haters' corner is in the other annex.

"Okay, so you know why we're here. Dr. Zeus said you wanted to see me," Nole says, wrapping his arm around Elgamela's slender waist.

"We want you in our house," I say, opting for the direct approach, because sometimes the truth *is* plain appropriate.

"Yeah, well, I want Ed McMahon to knock on my door and tell me that I've won a million dollars. I might actually have a shot at that," Nole retorts, staring intently at me.

Despite the barking in the background, the room gets so quiet you could hear a dog biscuit drop.

"Well, have you interviewed with any of the other houses yet?" I ask, stalling for time so I can put on my fashion game face.

"Like whose—Anna Rex's?" Nole asks, challenging me. "Why do you think she wears black all the time? Olives in a jar have more color coordination sense than she does. At least they made sure to get stuck with red pimentos!"

"Puhleez. After she loses, she can always get a job working at Vera Wang," Dame Leeds snarls, leaning his shoulder against the safari mural on the wall, right on the large rhinoceros's behind.

"Why there?" Diamond asks innocently.

"Black is de rigueur for all Wang employees," Angora says. God, Diamond is definitely not earning any karats today.

Dame looks at Angora, impressed, then adds, "Churl, I knew one of the showroom sales assistants. Miss Thing showed up to work one day in pink—and Vera gave her a pink slip to go with her outfit!"

"Speaking of pink . . ." Nole pauses, then pulls a tube of hand cream out of his black leather briefcase. "Do you always wear it?"

He carefully opens the tube of Kiehl's hand cream and moisturizes while waiting for my response. Now I'm afraid to answer because I don't want to blow my shot at snagging the infamous Holy Canoli, as he's been aptly nicknamed by Dame Leeds. I try to conjure up an image of the designing drama queen helping his semi-invalid mother out of her Hoveround. It works.

"When I'm not, I'm thinking pink," I answer, then take my honesty to another level. "I dug what you had to say," I stammer, referring to Nole's much-buzzed-about blog entry. "My mother raises us by herself. Me and my sister. I've got to win that prize money and snag

251

a modeling contract because I can't take the Payless situation much longer."

Now Nole shifts gears. He sits down carefully, like he's afraid the chair is going to break. This is the first time I've ever noticed that he's insecure about his pudgy figure. "Please. Every time we have to buy five cans of cat food, my mother starts her Poorvarotti aria!" he admits. I'd heard that Nole's mother is Italian and his father is black, although I don't get the impression his dad is in the family photo album, if you catch my drift.

"You have cats?" I ask, surprised.

"Why do you think I'm here? You think my Gucci loafers are my most prized possessions? No, it's my Persian cats, Penelope and Napoleon. And of course, Countess," explains Nole, dropping more catty details. "They're both snooty by nature, and Penelope has already had two nose jobs. I mean, she did have collapsed nostrils."

Of course, Diamond backpedals again to talk about Crutches.

Nole nods but interrupts to praise me. "I like your all-size philosophy. I want to design a line like that too."

"What's your line called?" Aphro asks.

"Nole Canoli," he responds, like *What else?* "I'm over people associating me with a deep-fried tube of

252

pastry filled with ricotta cheese. It's time 'Canoli' is associated with *chic*ness."

"I heard that," Aphro seconds, who jumps at the chance to explain the philosophy behind her funky jewelry collection, Aphro Puffs.

"And all this time, I thought your name was spelled like the Afro pick!" Nole snickers. "I was gonna call my company Chic Canoli—and make my logo two Cs like Chanel's—but I didn't want the fashion police coming for me with trademark trauma, okay?"

"Speaking of trauma—have you heard from Chandelier?" I boldly ask.

"You know I have," Nole retorts. "She's down for the body count. What can I say? And all she was trying to do was win the competition so she could get that corporate mentorship at Betsey Johnson, then take over the fashion business to help her brothers and sisters."

Now I feel guilty for bad-mouthing Chandelier. We had more in common than I ever realized.

"It's hard when you're fierce," Nole says knowingly, stroking together his freshly moisturized hands. "Night after night I fantasized about becoming famous, lying there in my bed on sheets with a thread count so low I'm embarrassed to tell you."

"Puhleez—how do you spell Maxicale without

counting to a hundred, hello? I'd sure like to forget," blurts out Dame Leeds.

"So, pink purrlicious one. Does everything match?" Nole asks teasingly.

At first, I don't comprehend, but the image of Hello Kitty watching my butt promptly brings Nole's probe into sharp focus.

"Well, take a guess," I say playfully.

"My guess is you always wear pink ones," Nole says, smirking, then turns to Dame. "What do you think?"

"Sometimes they're purple," quips Dame. "Let's make a bet. Loser buys all of us the first round of gelato in Firenze."

Suddenly, I realize that Nole is baiting me. "So do we have a deal?"

"About the gelato?" teases Nole.

"No, about you joining my house as lead designer," I say firmly. "Do we have a deal?"

"In principle," Nole stalls. "I have certain conditions."

"Shoot."

Nole turns to Diamond. "I'm the lead designer and I get star billing?"

A look of relief washes over Diamond's face. "Please. I was the one who suggested you in the first place. I'd be honored to work with you."

"Male fashions make up at least thirty percent of our Catwalk collection," Nole tells me, continuing the negotiations.

"Done," I say.

"My crew is in: Dame is lead hairstylist, Liza Flake is second. Kimono assists Bobby Beat. Elgamela, of course, is star model. And Ruthie Dragon will be me and Diamond's assistant," Nole says. "*And* my cat closes the show in the bridal gown."

I hesitate for a second, because I would like to slay Ruthie Dragon instead of having her join my house now, but I guess fashion beggars can't be choosers. I have also dreamed about Fabbie Tabby walking down the runway in the Catwalk competition for as long as I've wanted to win it. The truth, though: as long as my show closes with a feline, my vision remains intact, so I find myself saying with a sigh, "Done and done." Immediately I can't help but wonder if I have indeed sold my soul for a shot at stardom. I take some blank team membership forms out of my Hello Kitty tote bag and hand one each to Nole, Kimono, Elgamela, Dame Leeds, and Ruthie.

I think Nole secretly wonders the same thing: I can tell by the way he fingers the blank form, then puts it down on the empty chair next to him and rubs his hands in despair. "Again." He sighs as if he is exhaling the disappointment of the Chandelier drama. But somehow I don't think he wants to admit that to us, not yet. Instead, he switches to his signature smirkiness: "I hate those little cuts I get on my hands from cutting fabric. Sooo not chic."

We all laugh. Even Aphro. I take off my game face and watch with glee as the pets romp around in the playground where Countess Coco is holding court. Five minutes later, I'm clutching the last signed membership forms that I need to fulfill my first official task as a house leader. Now I feel fortified to face whatever drama awaits me in the Lynx lair. One down, one to go. I sigh. Then I make the one announcement I've been dying to make: "The House of Pashmina will have its first official team meeting tommorrow at three-thirty sharp. All team members are required to attend."

Sil Lai still doesn't crack a smile when I hand her my membership forms, but now I don't care. The door to the inner sanctum of the Lynx lair is opened, and Sil Lai motions for me to enter. Puccini, who is resting in his leopard bed, looks up at me loopy-eyed, like he's been daydreaming but I've brought him back to some reality. Ms. Lynx is scribbling furiously with a leopard-patterned pen, so I let my eyes roam over her office walls. It's true what I've heard: all the walls are plastered with photos and magazine tear sheets of her back in her modeling days. I'm not at all shocked at how thin she is in the photos because I'd already heard that she was obviously a much smaller size than her present "diva size" 22.

Now Ms. Lynx looks squarely at me, and her intense dark eyes activate another round of stomach fritters. "Do you always wear pink?" she asks, finally smiling.

I break into a grin but refrain from revealing why I'm so amused: two people have asked me the same question in one day. I hear my mother's voice ringing in my ear, *When something's not broke, don't fix it.* "Well, when I'm not, I'm *thinking* pink," I say, smiling warmly.

"Well, that's why I wanted to see you," Ms. Lynx starts in, causing my stomach to flip-flop. "What I mean is, because you are a house leader, I'm going to need you to be discreet about certain events that have occurred recently. That means *on* camera and *off*, if you follow the bouncing ball?"

"I follow it," I say, my voice squeaking. I'm frozen inside. I wonder who told her that I was bad-mouthing Chandelier. Or is she referring to Ice Très and his misfired Cupid's arrow? Neither of which is going to earn me any purr points—forget about my final tally!

"In any case, gossiping is not encouraged, but now,

with the Teen Style Network being granted full access to the faculty and student body, I find it imperative to encourage everyone to take a proactive approach," continues Ms. Lynx in her commanding voice.

Now I feel dizzy because I'm not sure if Ms. Lynx is reprimanding me or is merely on spin patrol.

"Yes, I feel—I mean, I hear you, Ms. Lynx," I say, nodding cooperatively.

I'm so relieved that I'm obviously still in the fashion game that I take a *segundo* to decompress on the spot. "Um, I just handed in my team membership forms," I announce, like a proud mother who just delivered a big litter of kittens.

"Good. I knew you would," Ms. Lynx says sharply. "Now, I've referred you for a sales position. It's for a new boutique that will be opening in Harlem. The owner is an old friend, and the two of you certainly share a shade in common."

"Wow," I say, gingerly taking the piece of paper from her hand. "Thank you so much."

"Don't thank me yet. She's quite a handful, but as I always say, if you can't handle a designer's roar, you'll never survive in the fashion jungle."

I nod furiously like an obedient lion tamer while the words from Gloria Gaynor's disco hit rush to my brain: *Oh, no, not I! I will survive!*

"Make sure you get your budget forms in to me on time," Ms. Lynx says politely.

I assure her I will, then run to the bathroom to deal with the flood under my arms. Now I know what the expression "dodging a bullet" means, because I feel like I just dodged a fashion missile big enough to topple the Eiffel Tower in gay Paree!

New school rule: You don't have to
be ultranice, but don't get tooooo
catty, or your posting will be zapped
by the Fashion Avengers!!

THEY SHOOT BLACK MODELS, DON'T THEY?

Like most girls blessed with five
feet ten inches of fierceness, I have
fantasized about becoming a supermodel since I can remember. And I do
remember exactly when my fantasy
began: I was in kindergarten and stole
one of Taynasia's blond Barbie dolls.
She was this bourgie girl who lived
down the block and I knew she wouldn't
miss it, so I took it, and I was
right—she didn't miss it. So there I
was, sitting cross-legged in front of
the television set in the living room,
stroking the hair on this stolen blond
Barbie doll. All of a sudden, this
beautiful brown girl who looked like
the Queen of Sheba—or what I thought
the Queen of Sheba should look like—
came walking out on TV in front of all
these people, wearing a skimpy outfit
that reminded me of Jane from *Tarzan.*
Behind the Queen of Sheba were all
these other pretty girls wearing similar skimpy feathered outfits. Then a
guy came out and they all started
kissing him and everybody in the audience was clapping. My foster mother
happened to come out of the kitchen at
the time and asked me, "What on earth
are you looking at?" I pointed at the

screen to the black girl standing there, smiling like I had discovered the Holy Grail. "Lord!" my foster mother said. "Those girls look like they escaped from a bikini chain gang!" I laughed so hard that my foster mother started laughing too. So you see, that day really stood out in my mind for two important reasons: First, I saw a girl who looked like me and everybody loved her. Second, I found out that I had a very unusual laugh that some compare to Babe the Pig, and it made people laugh. It was years later that I realized the model was the infamous Naomi Campbell and that she was strutting in a Todd Oldham fashion show for his summer collection. I happened to see the same exact footage in the video archives last year in FI's fashion library while I was researching a term paper on the history of black models for Model Appreciation. And thanks to the black supermodels—who, I discovered during my research, reigned on the runway back in the day—from Pat Cleveland, Billie Blair, Beverly Johnson, and Iman to Veronica Webb, Tyra Banks, and Naomi Campbell, I have grown up with the opportunity to do more than sit on the sidelines watching fashion shows on a television screen. And little brown-skinned girls growing up now don't have to steal blond Barbie dolls anymore. We can steal brown ones. (I'm just messing with you. Hopefully, you'll be able to at least ask your mother to buy you one.) Next June, my

dream is finally going to come true
when I model in my first televised
fashion show. It will be shown on
the Teen Style Network as part of the
Catwalk competition. I also happen to
believe that I am the proud member
of the house that is destined to win
in more ways than one. Well, what I'm
trying to say is, brown-skinned girls
like me can become a part of fashion
history. So next June: LET THE STRUT-
TING BEGIN!!

   10/24/2008 11:30:45 AM
   Posted by: Aphro Puffs

12

Caterina and her crew have piled into Studio C for the first official House of Pashmina Catwalk team meeting. Aphro, Angora, Zeus, Lupo, and Felinez are already in the house, so we're waiting for the rest of our team to arrive. Lupo is clicking away, taking candid shots of the Teen Style camera crew as they set up. Caterina turns away. She definitely doesn't dig being photographed herself, so I try to put her at ease.

"Wow—how did you know about the meeting?" I greet her with glee. Naturally, *I* didn't call to tell her about it because that's against the reality show rules and regulations.

"That's my job," Caterina says matter-of-factly.

"Did you happen to catch the five o'clock news?" I ask carefully, because I know she knows *exactly* which daily edition I'm referring to.

"Oh, no," she says, sounding genuinely sorry. "We were running around like crazy because of the shows."

"Oh, right," I say, embarrassed. How could I think my landlord's induction into Smiley Wiley's Hall of

Shame could trump coverage of Mercedes-Benz Fashion Week? "Well, I wanted to thank you for that, um, heads-up you gave me."

Caterina stares at me blankly, pretending she didn't hear me. Instinctively I sense that I've stepped on the toes of some unspoken producer protocol. That's when it dawns on me that what she did fell outside her line of duty, so I realize I should just drop it like it's hot.

Caterina brusquely changes the subject to fit her agenda. "Is it okay if I ask you some questions on camera before everyone comes in and the meeting starts?"

"Absolutely," I say. Boom and the rest of the crew get the camera equipment and lighting set up pronto. Of course, I should have known Caterina was cornering me for some salacious sound bites. Sure enough, she drops the boom.

"How do you feel about Chandelier Spinelli dropping out of the Catwalk competition because of her father's indictment?" she asks, straight-faced.

Now I feel like a kitten cornered in a bulldog pen. Ms. Lynx's admonition rings in my ears. I decide I'd better choose my words carefully.

"I'm sorry that I won't be getting the opportunity to compete against Chandelier Spinelli. I thought she was a worthy opponent. We, um, I hope that she will come back to school again soon." I stop abruptly. As my fashion merchandising teacher says, sometimes less is more.

"What about Ice Très's expulsion from the competition—do you think that was a fair result of his suspension?"

"All's fair in fashion and war," I blurt out, then shriek inside. *Just keep it Lite FM,* a voice inside warns me.

"Knock-knock!" screams Bobby Beat from the doorway. I squeal at his acknowledgment of our Catwalk code, then introduce him to Caterina and her crew.

"Can we interview you for a second?" Caterina asks him.

"Yes, ma'am!" Bobby Beat says, beaming at the prospect of being on camera, and asks if he can primp first.

"Actually, let me get a quote from you while he gets ready," Caterina says to Lupo, and it's obvious she has forgotten his name. This time Zeus, well, jumps in on that tip, and even explains what Lupo's last name means.

"Why did you join the House of Pashmina?" Caterina asks Lupo candidly.

"Oh, because we have the most beautiful girls?" Lupo says, laughing goofily. He looks over at Aphro, and Caterina asks the cameraman to get a shot of Aphro arranging her folder of tear sheets and sketches for one of her jewelry classes.

Meanwhile, Bobby Beat is brimming with ideas that he can't wait to share with me. "Omigod, SNAPS cosmetics has this new bronzing powder with a hot-pink base for highlighting the cheekbones! I think that would be so fabulously feline for the show. What do you think?"

"Bronze it is," I agree.

"Actually, I'd like to start by bronzing *you*. We can't have you on camera like this—not even for reality television. Honey, as far as I'm concerned, reality is something you create."

Caterina overhears Bobby Beat's bite and zooms right in on us. "Don't look at us, just keep going," she instructs us. Bobby doesn't, well, miss a beat. He whips out his makeup kit and commands me to hold still while he touches me up. Then he starts babbling about the latest booty in the beauty biz. "Can you believe someone just bought a tube of lipstick and mascara for fourteen million dollars from H. Couture Beauty cosmetics?"

"What, what?" I ask in disbelief, but Bobby commands me to keep my mouth shut while he outlines it with Very Berry lip liner.

"The mascara casing has twenty-five hundred blue diamonds and the lipstick casing has twelve hundred pink diamonds," Bobby claims, then puts a tissue between my lips for me to blot. "And it comes with concierge service and complimentary lash and lip refills for one year."

"Well, tell them my lips are available anytime," Aphro offers.

"That's good to know," quips Lupo, breaking out in his goofy grin.

Bobby motions for Angora to come over for a quick fluff with his mighty brush. As soon as I notice that Felinez isn't looking, I mouth to Bobby to offer "Miss Fifi" a lip plumping as well.

"Miss Fifi," Bobby Beat says loudly, "could you bring your booty into my beauty booth, please?"

I shake my head at Bobby, but he doesn't get it. He just makes a face at me like, *What?* I make a note to my fashion self to tell him later to refrain from referring to Blue Boca's body parts.

Now some of the other team members pour into the studio. Between Lupo's flashbulbs and Caterina's camera crew, as Angora so rightly observes, "It feels just like Mardi Gras!"

When Nole Canoli enters with his crew, who are now my crew, Caterina and, well, her crew, really go into full-tilt boogie.

I make another note to my fashion self that I must warn all the members of my team not to gossip about other Catwalk contenders in front of Caterina and her crew. As a matter of fact, I make still another note to add that to the Catwalk Credo, which I will circulate at our next team meeting.

When Boom sticks the microphone close to Nole's face, he brushes imaginary lint off his black Gucci shirt, then adjusts the Prada carrier so Countess Coco's tiny visage is visible for the camera. I wouldn't be surprised if Nole actually knew Countess Coco's better side for photography.

"You were close to Chandelier Spinelli, weren't you?" Caterina asks Nole, blindsiding his, well, good and bad sides.

Nole's cheeks turn so red, it looks like he's having an allergic reaction to kaflamma. "Professionally we were close," he says carefully. It's obvious he is really struggling to distance himself from the aftershock of Chandelier's scandal.

"Have you spoken to Chandelier since her father's indictment?" Caterina asks him.

"Yes, I have, but that conversation is private, and I want to respect her while she is going through a difficult time," Nole says calmly. He then smiles warmly, as if to prove to Caterina and her probing camera that he is not some pushover she can control like a Ouija board. His tactic seems to work, because Caterina backs off and asks him a more relevant question: "Who will be your designing partner for the competition?"

Nole perks up and motions for Diamond Tyler to

join him. Then he introduces her. "Diamond's talent is truly uncut. I mean, she is brilliant but serves up humble pie. She's sweet but salty, tender but tough when she has to be, and she can whip out outfits as sublime as a chocolate-marshmallow soufflé," Nole says, beaming.

Angora gazes at Nole and I can tell she is also impressed with his sound bite savvy. "What's your design philosophy?" Caterina asks Nole.

"Whatever it is I'm feeling that day," Nole admits. "All a designer has is a personal vision, and you have to sell it to yourself first, like a sales associate at Barney's working on straight commission, or else nobody is gonna buy it!"

All of a sudden, Kissa and Mink barge into the studio in a fit of giggles, until they spot the camera crew. I introduce them to help them adjust to the "Smile, so you won't get Punk'd" feeling. It's four o'clock, and at last all members of the House of Pashmina are present and accounted for. We sit down at the long conference table, and I instruct everyone that first we're going to go around the table counterclockwise and introduce ourselves. "Tell us a little bit about your overall career goals and what your position is in the House of Pashmina."

After the introductions, I begin the meeting. I look down at the table at all the faces staring at me and the Teen Style Network hovering in the background and the truth of Bobby Beat's words hits me: *Reality is something you create*. And I created this.

I snap out of my *Surreal Life* moment to begin the meeting. "Okay, everyone, to begin with, I want to welcome you to our first official Catwalk competition meeting for the House of Pashmina."

"And we have you to thank for that," Chintzy Colon says, breaking into her Splenda smile. Then Zeus puts his hands together to clap, and everyone else follows suit.

"Bring it, don't fling it!" Aphro shouts out.

I grin. I love Aphro and wouldn't want to be doing this without her, Angora, and Felinez front and center. Angora winks at me and I wink back. Even Dr. Zeus has come to mean something to me, even if it isn't what I want it to be. I glance at Elgamela, Nole, Dame, Lupo, Liza, Diamond, Kissa, and Mink and realize how lucky I am to have snagged such five-star talent. The clapping dies down and everyone gets real quiet. I instinctively sense that everyone is waiting for me to christen our meeting, so I do just that: "By entering the prestigious Catwalk competition and committing to abide by directions from the team leader," I announce proudly, "each of us is publicly acknowledging that we're in for the roller-coaster ride of our young, style-driven lives. It is my duty to inform you that for the next seven

270

months, you will find it best to strap yourself in and fasten your Gucci seat belt."

Nole snickers, then puts his hand over his mouth and blushes. "Sorry!" he squeals softly.

"By the same token, I humbly ask you to please call upon me or one of your Catwalk crew members to share your fears and concerns so that one of us can prick you back to reality that you are not alone. You can also feel free to reach out to me whenever an obstacle presents itself that prevents you from fulfilling any of your Catwalk duties—or whenever you simply feel like screaming your head off. If you cannot reach me at the exact moment you feel the urge to pull out your seam ripper for reasons other than deconstructing a seam, please get in touch with my assistant, Chintzy Colon. Her number, like everyone else's, is right there on the team membership form, which I'm about to pass out. I am here to inform you that there is no one in this room who can hide in plain sight—not for the next seven months, anyway."

Bobby Beat lets out a scream as if to demonstrate a crew member in crisis. Lupo clicks away like he's coming to Bobby's rescue, which causes me to grin uncontrollably.

"Now I'm going to pass around Xeroxes of the team membership forms. Each of you gets a complete set," I say, passing out the packets I stayed up all night copying at the Kinko's by my house. I glance absentmindedly at Dame Leeds's beaming face. "This way, you have contact information for each team member right at your fingertips, and you can also refer to it in case you forget a crew member's duties—or yours, for that matter. I know the introductions were a lot to take in today."

"Well, I can help each of you remember everything you need to know about me right now," blurts out Dame Leeds. "I do press and curls—not pressing! So see Miss Ruthie when your wrinkles are wearing you down—the ones on the samples, that is, not on your face!"

I can see why Nole and Dame are thick as thieves—they both have endless quips on their lips. Ruthie Dragon, on the other hand? I'm still trying to decipher the connection between her and Nole. She raises her hand and waves at Dame's joke. She is, after all, the appointed pressing person, since she is Nole and Diamond's assistant. I still feel uneasy about having her in the mix, but I realize that every leader must make small sacrifices to accomplish the greater good.

"Now I'm going to hand out another form. It's called the 'I've Got the Hookup' sheet," I explain. "Each of us is bringing more to the table than meets the eye. In order to have a bird's-eye view, I need for you to tell me about your connections. Try to think of anything or anyone in your life that you have access to that could be useful to us as a team. As you'll see on the form, I've made some categories to help you begin this process. One category is 'People I Know Who I Don't Realize I Know.' Under that box, you should write everyone from your babysitter to the boot maker round your way who could possibly could be called upon for a favor that would benefit our fashion show."

Bobby Beat raises his hand. "Now, does the person have to be a style diva?"

"What do you mean?" I ask.

"Well, my mother's best friend, Mrs. Hawkins, works at the Spanx factory right on Steinway, and I know she could probably hook us up with some tights for the show, but she herself wears these dresses that come in prints with the biggest flowers—native to the borough of Queens before the settlers took over Astoria, if you catch my drift and smell the pollen."

One of the Teen Style Network camera crew lets out a chuckle. Obviously, Bobby was describing one of his relatives too.

"That's a very good point you've brought up, Bobby. Maybe we should all acknowledge the fact that a fashionista is someone who is smart enough to judge others by something more than their outfits. And I certainly think that someone who has access to fine hosiery such as Spanx is a person worthy of such consideration," I say, phrasing my point carefully.

Now everyone in the room bursts out laughing.

"No, I'm serious!" I protest. "I'd certainly like to think that attending FI has already provided each of us with an insight into human behavior, even though I know most of us also show appreciation for our unique ability to accessorize by getting on our knees and thanking God every morning."

Felinez smiles at my recognition of her true talent. "Does anyone have any more questions about the hookup list?" I ask. "Okay, so for our next meeting, I'd like each of you to have your hookup sheet ready to be handed in. After I've reviewed them, each team member will be given a complete master hookup list."

Liza Flake raises her hand. "What about if we can't come to the next meeting?" she asks. "I start my internship next week at Vidal Sassoon, and I don't think I'll be able to come."

"That brings me to meetings," I say, nodding. "As a team member, you'll be expected to attend every meeting—that's two a month. No exceptions. If you absolutely cannot make a meeting, your absence must be cleared with your team leader first—that would be me—and we're talking documentation will be asked for. So don't even attempt to offer up an excuse that doesn't come accompanied by serious paper-work—doctor's note, court affidavits—you name it, no document is too official to bring with you if it's going to support your excuse, okay?"

I notice that Liza has turned as cool as an air conditioner flipped to the MoneySaver switch.

I stop to take a sip of water. "Before we continue, I must humbly ask each of you a very important question. Please feel free to collectively answer honestly: how many of you sitting in this room right now really want to divvy up the hundred-thousand-dollar cash prize, gift certificates from Louis Vuitton, the Limited, Radio Shack—need I go on?—*and* go on an al[1] expenses paid, two-week trip to Firenze, Italy, next June and open the fashion show at Pitti Bimbo?"

I watch Liza Flake's face closely to gauge her response. Like everyone else in the room, she shoots her hand straight up.

"Okay, good, because for a second, I didn't think we were on the same fashion page," I say firmly. "Now let's talk schedule."

I pass out another round of forms. "This is your Cat-walk schedule sheet. Every meeting, you will be given an updated one. But right now you must face the fact that your time has become a more valuable commodity than Gianni Versace's gunmetal mesh fabric from the seventies. I've already told you your task for our next meeting. I think that's a good start. Any questions?"

Diamond raises her hand. "When do we talk about designing the collection?"

"Next meeting," I assure her. "I will be given my fashion budget as well as the design challenges we'll be expected to complete. Last year, for example, the five competing houses had to create an ensemble constructed out of biodegradable materials. Also, the collection must contain five categories. That's the same every year."

"I hope this year's design challenge is edible," Nole quips.

"Oh, that reminds me," I say. "On the hookup form, you'll see a category for child models. We are definitely doing a children's fashion segment to open our show—because that's an integral part of feline fatale fashion. So if you know any child models—we're going to have to have them come in and try out—make sure to write down the contact. We really need about ten guest child models—I didn't write on the form, sorry," I say absentmindedly, perusing the form. "They should be under the age of twelve. That's what's still considered a child these days, anyway."

"What if we don't know any children?" asks Mink shyly.

"That's totally cool—I mean, fine. As a matter of fact, anything on the hookup form is merely a way for us to pool resources. No one is expected to *fab*ricate connections of any kind. And please—while I want you to eat, breathe, and live the Catwalk competition until that Big Willie statue is in our possession next June, no one should start hanging around schoolyards under the pretense of luring kiddies for our fashion show! Understood? *Vous comprenez? Capisce?*"

"Scratch, scratch, we feel you!" shouts Benny Madina, the tasty morsel with dreads who was Felinez's male model pick.

"Awrighty, that concludes our business for today. And I just want to say, regardless of what happens over the course of the next seven months, it has been an honor to spend this time with you. I'll never forget it." I really mean it. "So, if we could all join hands before we run and state our Catwalk mission together. This is how I would like us to end every meeting."

I stand up at the head of the conference table and join hands with Felinez on my left and Angora on my right. "If you could repeat after me, please," I say, bowing my head and taking a deep breath before I continue: "As an officially fierce team member of the House of Pashmina, I fully accept the challenge and obligations of competing in the Catwalk competition.

My commitment to my house must always come first so that I can become the fashionista only I can be. Meowch, forever!"

Afterward, Caterina tries to get my attention as she hovers in the doorway before departing with her crew. I excuse myself from Chintzy, who has run over to give me a folder of tear sheets of ideas. "I can't give this my attention right now," I tell Chintzy gently. Now I see what it means to be a house leader: you're really the gatekeeper of everyone's dreams locked up inside in a safe place, waiting to be unleashed.

I go over to the door. "Um, thank you, again," I say to Caterina, even though I know she won't acknowledge what I really mean. "That worked out okay."

But Caterina surprises me. "I'm glad," she says honestly, then switches back her producer gear to drive. "I guess I'll see you around campus."

"I hope so," I say, shifting my gear, too.

Nole walks over with Dame and taps me on the shoulder, then reaches over to give me a series of air kisses on both cheeks. "I made the right decision," he whispers in my ear.

I nod in agreement.

"So did I win the bet?" Nole asks me, amused.

"I'll let you unpack my suitcase in Firenze and examine my panty selection so you can see for yourself," I say, giggling.

Dame Leeds's eyes open wide. "Oh, no you didn't, Miss Thing, cut a side deal! That's a no-no. Put it in the Catwalk Credo—I insist!"

I assure Dame I will.

Now Aphro grabs me to get away from the meeting. "You were fierce," she says, hugging me.

Suddenly, I look at one of my best friends and understand what Ms. Fab was trying to tell me earlier about surviving in the fashion jungle. I look Aphro squarely in her face and tell her, "No, no, *you* are fierce." This time I mean it.

FASHION INTERNATIONAL 35TH ANNUAL
CATWALK COMPETITION BLOG

New school rule: You don't have to be ultranice, but don't get tooooo catty, or your posting will be zapped by the Fashion Avengers!!

GLITTER TO YOUR OWN GROOVE. . . .

As long as I've been a student at Fashion International, I've prided myself on living on the cutting edge and getting to know who I really am underneath the faux fur. The truth is, most of the time I feel like I'm walking on imaginary eggshells. That's probably why every day I try to dress fiercely so I can meet and greet the world in a manner that is much groovier than the way I actually feel inside. What I didn't know is that there are lots of people in the world who are just like me. I discovered this recently because I made an assumption about one such person, only to discover that underneath our different layers of flavor, we are remarkably similar. We each use our passion for fashion to rise above our background, to overcome our shortcomings, to camouflage our disappointments in a world that she so aptly described, if I may paraphrase her, as not so chic and even downright cruel.

I want to publicly apologize to this person for never giving her the benefit of the doubt or for taking the time to get to know who she was underneath her faux fur. As I move forward in my ambitious attempt to manifest my dreams—right now through the Cat-walk competition—I plan on changing my current modus operandi. For starters, every time I come in contact with someone—whether they be a frenemy, a ferocious friend, or an outright foe—I'm going to ask myself, *What are their dreams?* If I take the time to answer that question, then I have a better shot at dealing with the person as a human being. In other words, just like me.

So here's to scratching beneath the surface. May you sparkle madly and glitter to your own groove. Meowch forever! . . .

10/25/2008 12:00:55 PM
Posted by: Feline Groovy

Glossary

Abracadabra fierce: Snap-your-fingers fabulous. As in, "Did you see the paisley jumpsuit that opened the Betsey Johnson spring show? It was abracadabra fierce!"

Angle for a dangle: To maneuver a situation or jockey for position. As in, "Don't be fooled by Nole's protestations. He's just trying to angle for a dangle. I know for a facto he's dying to go to dinner with you."

Back in the day: Referring to an earlier era. It is a sign of pure respect in the fashion game to pay homage to the players who came before you and paved the way for your future reign.

Battle: When one voguer challenges another, in or out of a fashion show or ball.

Beam me up: Star Trekkies started this riff. Now fashionistas use it to put someone on blast or to vibe with someone. As in, "Zeus can beam me up anytime, cuz I've fallen for him!"

Big Willie: A major player in the fashion game.

Someone who has earned street cred. Can also be a reference to the "Big Willie" statue—the prestigious bronze dress-form trophy bestowed upon the winner of the annual Catwalk competition at Fashion International High School. The award's name was chosen in honor of the school's founding father, William Dresser.

Blang: Bling squared. Blinding dazzle.

Blankety: Blank. As in, "I tried to tell her he's not feeling her, but she went blankety."

Bling-worthy: The opposite of CZ (cubic zirconia) in value and merit. Something or someone who is considered a bona fide "gem." As in, "You're always falling for the CZ. Tadashi is the most bling-worthy banana in the bunch."

Bona fried: Bona fide to a crisp. Legit. As in, "Trust me, Ms. Boucle, I have a bona fried reason why I didn't do the homework assignment."

Bootylicious: Fierce footwear. As in, "Those Shimmy Choos are bootylicious."

Braggedy: Someone who flosses like a broken-down braggart. As in, "Did you hear Chandelier carrying on about her job interview? She is so *braggedy*."

Bumpin': Purely fabbie.

Bwitch: Phat.

Cacophony: Discord. Phony flow. Talking loud and saying nothing.

Cadeau: French word for *gift* or *present*. Pronounced "ca-doe." A useful expression for kitties who want to milk it: *"Je voudrais un cadeau s'il vous plaît!"* Translation: "I would like a present, please!"

Catiac arrest: When you just can't take it anymore. Much more painful than a cardiac arrest. As in, "If I don't get nominated, I'm going to have a catiac arrest!"

Catitude: That special feline quality that leaves the peeps gaspitating and proclaiming, "She's fierce!"

Catwalk: A narrow, usually elevated platform used by models to "sashay, shimmy, and sell" designers' clothing and accessories during a fashion show. The British term was originally coined after designer Lucy Christiana, aka Lady Duff-Gordon, staged the first fashion show in London in the early 1900s.

Chat noir: French for "black cat."

Chica-boom!: Extra special. Extra fabulous. As in, "That dress is definitely chica-*boom!*"

Churl: *Girl* and *honeychild* rolled into one. As in, "Churl, please, you'd better be on time or I will drop you like a bad habit."

Click, dial tone, good-bye!: Dropping the communication line on someone who is getting on your nerves.

Coinky dinky: Coincidence. Can also have a sarcastic connotation. As in, "I got the pink lizard

Shimmy Choo slides for Christmas. And so did you? What a coinky dinky!"

Coin slot: The crack between the butt cheeks. As in, "Excuse me, Fifty Cent, can you pull up your pants, please, cuz I'm not trying to insert two quarters in your coin slot!"

Crossing paws: Playing your cards right. Making things happen. Hanging out with a purpose. As in, "While you were out lollygagging, I was crossing paws with Caterina coming up with ideas for our Catwalk collection!"

Crunchy: Someone who is cute, but not as tasty as a Toll House morsel. As in, "Check out the crunchies. Twelve o'clock dead ahead."

Crutch: A best friend or true crew member. As in, "You'd better come with me to the dentist, because I need my crutch."

Dolce dreams: When you're pining for more than polyester and only Dolce & Gabbana will do.

Down for the twirl: Down for a specific cause. Or, a fashionista ready to rip the runway.

Drop an Altoid: A minty hint. A tasty hint. As in, "Who's opening Mercedes-Benz Fashion Week? Come on, drop an Altoid!"

Ducats: Loot. Cash. Benjamins. As in, "Just put some ducats in my bucket and we'll be *skraiight*, awright?"

Extra crispy: Angry or annoyed. As in, "Don't take that extra-crispy tone with me, young lady."

Fabbity: On the fab tip.

"Faboo is not you": Despite your daydreams, you are not fabulous.

Fabulation: A compliment for fierceness. As in, "Mamacita, that outfit deserves a fabulation."

Fashion forward: Taking inspiration from all around you instead of following trends.

Fashionation: An obsession with fashion in a good way.

Fashionista: A male or female who is true to the fashion game.

Feeling wiggly: Feeling jittery, nervous, hyper-anxious.

Feline fatale: A girl with catlike qualities—feminine, graceful, mysterious—who also possesses strong instincts. As in, "Ciara is such a feline fatale."

Flossy: Someone who is conceited or down for showing off at the drop of a tin bangle. As in, "She's so flossy!"

Flurry: Thoughts that circle wildly like a 1950s skirt. As in, "I just got a flurry. Why don't we let the junior models work the meowch pouches in the show?"

Friend of Dorothy's: Cute gay boy. The Dorothy in question is the main character in *The Wizard of Oz*.

Furbulous: Fabulous on the warm, fuzzy edge. Associated with feline fatale sensibilities.

Glitch: Someone who tends to clog the flow. As in, "Please don't bring Taynasia to the party. She is such a glitch."

Green with Gucci Envy: Jealous to the max.

Growing whiskers: Getting too upset. As in, "Stop growing whiskers and calm down please."

Gucci hoochie: Someone who is obsessed with established designer labels and afraid to define their own sense of style.

Hervé Léger: French haute couture designer known for his trademark mummy-tight, body-sculpting bandage dresses which are sewn entirely by hand and have been worn by fashionistas from Alicia Keys to Naomi Campbell.

Horse and phony show: The act of performing elaborate antics that are merely designed to cover the fact that a scam or sham is being perpetrated right before your eyes.

Hot off the griddle: News or gossip so scandalabrious that your fingers are still scorching. "Honey, I got news for you hot off the griddle: Shalimar got nominated as one of the house leaders!"

Hush-hush on the plush: On the Q.T. On the DDL (down down low). In other words, the person is telling you: "Just don't say you heard it from me!!"

Hype patrol: Publicity push for anything from a media event to a sweet sixteen party to a new designer or a hot new product. As in, "I'm gonna be on hype patrol all week so I can get nominated as a Catwalk house leader."

Jitters and fritters: Not your garden variety type of fears; this type of high anxiety occurs when the stakes are high or you're reaching for the sky.

Joints: Favorite songs or clothing items. As in, "You got the new PRPS jeans? I already got one of them joints—that wash is *sick!*"

Kaflamma: Drama times two. As in, "If we don't get to our Catwalk meeting on time, there is going to be some serious *kaflamma!*"

Kaflempt: Upset. As in, "I'm feeling kaflempt today."

Kaflustered: Discombobulated. Kaflempt. When you're feeling wrecked about a situation.

Kanoodling: Acting smoochy with someone.

Kibbles 'n Bits: Loose change.

Kitten smitten: Someone who gets the feline's charm. A friend of cats and cat girlies alike.

Knock-knock: Catwalk code word for spotting a designer knockoff.

La dolce vita: Italian for "the sweet life."

Lap it up: To indulge in a good thing like getting compliments, or taking an extra sniff from a cashmere sweater.

Le podium: French for runway—the narrow, usually elevated platform on which models sashay during a fashion show.

Lite FM: Opposite of heavy or stressed. As in, "Don't let Shalimar see that you're sweating her bankroll. When she does her presentation, just keep it Lite FM."

Loony spurts: Fits of temporary insanity. As in, "I can't believe Ms. Lynx left me that nasty voice mail. She must be suffering from loony spurts."

Major: Fierce times seven. As in, "That hat is major."

Manny Hanny: Manhattan. The Big Apple. Aka: "Make Money Manny Hanny."

Medi-okra: Average. Mediocre.

Meowch pouch: A feline fabbie drawstring pouch for carrying important essentials such as MetroCards, lipstick, keys. Can be worn on a string around the neck, or around the wrist. Designed and created by Felinez Cartera.

Meowching: Gossiping, sharing notes, or cupping your hands together in the Catwalk handshake with a member of your crew.

"Meowch forever!": "May the power of feline fatales reign for infinity!"

Milk Dud: A party pooper. As in, "She is such a Milk Dud."

Modus operandi: Mode of operation. Rolling like that. As in, "Would you check out Tiara's modus operandi? Now, that's what I'm talking about."

Ma chérie: French for "my dear."

Moi: French for "me." Pronounced "mwah." As in "Are you talking to *moi?*"

Mos def: Most definitely. As in, "I'm mos def heading over to Mood Fabrics to check out the latest Gaultier gauze prints."

"Mother Goose is on the loose!": Catwalk code warning to watch your back when something is about to go down. The Catwalk crew also use it when they're referring to hiding from the Catwalk director, Ms. Lynx.

"My pockets are nervous": When you're fresh out of ducats in the bucket. As in, "My pockets are nervous. Can you spring any Kibbles 'n Bits till Saturday?"

Numbing the tootsies: Pounding the pavement. Walking the extra mile to success. As in, "I've been numbing my tootsies for weeks. I know I'm getting nominated for class president."

Off the hinge-y: Even more fabbie poo than "off the hook." As in, "That Tracy Reese satin trench coat is off the hinge-y!"

"Oh, plissé": "Please, don't try it!" Pronounced "plee-say."

One Big Face: A hundred-dollar bill.

291

Persnickety: Uppity. Highfalutin.

Pink Head: A friend of felines who worships at the altar of pinkdom. Also Pashmina's nickname and the name of the jewelry collection by Tarina Tarantino.

Pose-off: A fashion posing contest. The movements are derived from the posing aspect of voguing. True voguers, however, will incorporate intricate dance movements into the competition or contest.

Prada or nada: When knockoffs will not do the trick. The real thing or bust.

Presto: Something or someone that is abracadabra fierce. As in, "We need some serious prestos to put on the seats at the fashion show."

Prêt-à-porter: French word for ready-to-wear. In fashion parlance, it means clothes that are manufactured as opposed to *haute couture*, which is custom made.

Pronto soon: Right now. Same as *tout de suite*.

Pure fabbieness: When something is just utter perfection. As in, "Have you see the new Dolce and Gabbana hobo bag? It's pure fabbieness."

Psycho Twinkie: An annoying person. As in, "Sharpen your claws, girls, here comes that psycho Twinkie Shalimar again!"

Purrfecto: Better than perfect.

Purring: Throwing around compliments or bragging. As in, "She's always purring about Dr. Zeus like he invented rhymes. Puhleez!"

Purrlicious: Tasty. Exceptionally fabbie. As in, "I think Zeus is purrlicious."

Purr points: Rating system on a scale of 1–10 for an object, fashion item, or person with feline fatale qualities. As in, "Did you see the new Fendi clutch? I give it five purr points."

Purr-worthy: An object, fashion item, or person with feline fatale qualities.

Put on blast: To hype. Also, to call someone out. As in, "Why did you have to put me on blast like that?"

Radickio: Utterly and completely ridiculous. "Did you tell Chandelier she looks radickio in those polka-dot gaucho pants?"

Read with relish (and mustard): When you really tell someone off. As in, "I'm gonna read you with relish (and mustard) if you don't stop lapping up my props!"

Runway: A narrow, usually elevated platform used by models to "sashay, parlay" during a fashion show.

Sassyfrass: To say something smart-mouthed.

Scandalabrious: Describes a scandal so thick, it's dipped in Crisco, then refried. As in, "Chandelier's father got arrested for chopping up body parts. How scandalabrious is that!"

S'il vous plaît: French for "please." Pronounced, "see voo play." As in, "Why should I do your homework? *S'il vous plaît.*"

Sham-o-rama: It's the one place that's always open

for business in the urban jungle: everywhere you turn, there is someone trying to pull the wool over somebody's eyes in the name of getting ahead. Word of advice: don't fall for it!

Shopportunity: A combination of favorable circumstances for the purpose of shopping till you drop.

Snap your clutch purse: Go off on somebody. Tell someone off.

Snooty-patooties: Snobby rich people.

Spin patrol: A press release version instead of the real deal. As in, "Chandelier is just serving spin patrol. I know she gagged when her father got arrested for selling body parts!"

Sprinkle: To shower someone with tasty sweet nothings. As in, "Stop trying to sprinkle me. Aren't you dating Zeus?"

Stroking her fur: Boosting someone's confidence. As in, "I know why you're stroking my fur, but it's not gonna work."

Super winks: Deep, sound sleep. As in, "I'm in serious need of some super winks."

Swag: The freebies and promotional incentives that are given away in goodie bags at fashion shows and other fashion clothing and product launch parties and events. Acronym could stand for Stuff We All Get.

"Thank gooseness": "Thank goodness."

Thread the needle: Do whatever it takes to get the job done. As in, "I can't believe you still haven't turned in your illustrations. Just thread the needle already!"

Tiddy: Tidbit. As in, "Now, that's a tiddy for your ears only."

Times squared: Magnified twice. As in, "There are times squared when I just want to click out my claws and scratch Shalimar's face into grosgrain ribbons!"

Tout de suite: French for "right now." Pronounced "toot sweet." As in, "You'd better whip it together, because we have to be in Ms. Lynx's office *tout de suite*."

Très: French for "very." Pronounced "tray." As in "Zeus is *très* tasty!"

Twirl: To battle. Also a command used in voguing battle. As in, "You think *you* got the yardage? Then let's twirl!"

"Wake up and smell the catnip!": "Stop daydreaming!" "Stop pretending!" or "Stop sleeping on your game!"

Whatever makes her clever: Not stressing over someone else's actions. As in, "I told Taynasia I'd take her to school, but she blew me off. Whatever makes her clever."

"What's the fuss, glamourpuss?": "Chill out and stop making a scene."

Wickster: Someone who is a tad bit wicked. As in, "Shalimar is a real wickster, so don't lean too close, because she'll singe your eyebrows off!"

Work it for points on the Dow Jones: To capitalize on a situation. Or, to prance on the catwalk like your paycheck depends on it!

Yanking my weave: New-school equivalent of the old-school expression "yanking my chain." As in, "Knock, knock—stop trying to yank my weave—that's not a real Louis Vuitton bag!"

Catwalk

strike a pose

Catwalk

strike a
pose

DEBORAH GREGORY

dedication

For Anath Garber, a purrlicious person to the maximus, and her lucky daughter, Karina. I'm forever grateful for all your shape-shifting to help me reach my feline fatale potential.

And to all the kats and kitties around the globe who are priming to pose for points on the Dow Jones. *Sashay, parlay!*

acknowledgments

Muchas muchas to Random House Delacorte Press dedicated editor Stephanie Elliott and ferocious designer Kenny Holcomb. And to Benny Ninja, the father of the House of Ninja, for keeping Willi Ninja's legend alive and the time-honored tradition of voguing. The days of voguing at the Club Shelter and the new Loft will always be a part of my youth. It was at these underground house music clubs that I learned that to strike a pose is akin to meditation—and to finding inner balance and grace in this crazy world.

And to the most legendary catwalker of all time, Pat Cleveland, who ruled the runways back in the day from New York to Milan to Rome to Paris to Tokyo. . . . For the fashion record, La Cleveland, who sublimely channeled Josephine Baker into her unique runway presence, will eternally stand as the ultimate example of the saying *You'd better work, supermodel!*

Catwalk Credo

As an officially fierce team member of the House of Pashmina, I fully accept the challenge of competing in the Catwalk competition. I will grant unlimited access to photographers and television crews at any time during the yearlong process. I will also be expected to represent my crew to the max, to obey directions from my team leader, and to honor, respect, and uphold the Catwalk Credo.

*Strap yourself in and fasten your Gucci seat belt. By entering this world-famous fashion competition, I acknowledge that I'm in for the roller-coaster ride of my young, style-driven life. Therefore, whenever I feel like screaming my head off or jumping out of my chic caboose, I will resist the urge; instead, I will tighten the belt a notch on my fears like a true fashionista.

*Illustrate your visions, but don't be sketchy with crew members. My commitment to my house must always come first. Nothing must stand in the way of my Catwalk obligations—*nada, nyet, niente,* Nietzsche! And when someone or something presents itself as an obstacle, I promise to call upon my crew to summon the strength necessary to cut off the interference like a loose, dangling thread.

*Rulers are for those who rule with purrcision. The true measure of my success will not be how I scale the terrain to fame, but my ability to align my tasks and tantrums with those of my crew. I must always remember that grandiosity could land me in the half-price bin like Goliath—who was toppled by a tiny but well-targeted rock!

*Be prepared to endure more pricks than a pincushion. Now that I've made the commitment to strive toward a goal shared by many other aspiring fashionistas, I must be prepared for catiac attacks. Therefore, I will honestly share my fears and concerns with my crew so that I can be pricked back to the reality that I am *not* alone in this not-so-chic and competitive world and will not achieve fabulosity solely on my own merits.

*Become a master tailor of your schedule. I must face the fact that my time has now become a more valuable commodity than Gianni Versace's gunmetal mesh fabric from the seventies. Despite the complexity of my tasks, I must always find the time to show up for my crew and attend my weekly Catwalk meetings throughout the year. Together we can make our dreams come true, one blind stitch at a time.

*Floss your teeth, not your ego. Now that I'm part of a crew, carrying on about my accomplishments like I'm the Lone Ranger of Liberty prints is not cute; neither is grungy grooming or having food between my teeth. I will carry the tools of my trade with me at all times, including a container of dental floss and a hairbrush so that I can be prepared for prime-time purring and on-camera cues that may come at me off the cuff.

*Ruffles don't always have ridges. While everyone is entitled to an opinion, I will not allow myself to become hemmed in by well-meaning wannabes outside my crew. My individual style is only worthy when it becomes incorporated into the collective vision of my Catwalk crew. I will also resist the temptation to bite anyone else's flavor to the degree that it constitutes copying, or I will be asked to pack my tape measure and head back to the style sandbox on my own.

*Pay homage and nibble on *fromage*. As a true fashionista, I must study the creative contributions of those who came before me so that I can become the maker of my own mélange. I will also publicly give the fashionistas who came before me the props they're due whenever name-dropping is appropriate. Despite my quest for individual development, I must acknowledge that I will always channel influences from the past, present, and future.

Click out your cat claws to defend your cattitudinal stance. When others turn bitter, bring on the glitter. Competition always brings out the worst in foes—and even friends—because everyone will try to gobble the biggest slice of the fashion pie and no one readily settles for crumbs without putting up a fight.

Always be ready to strike a pose. Even though I may not be a model, I cannot expect to strut the catwalk without getting a leg up on the competition first and saving my best riff for last. When it's showtime, I will be prepared to do my assigned task to help bring the House of Pashmina to the finish line.

Act fierce even when you're not feeling it. I will never let the competition see me sweat. While going through this creative process, I may feel doubts about my direction. Therefore, I will bounce ideas off other crew members, but never reveal sensitive information to anyone else! Not all fashion spies have been sent to Siberia—they hide among us, always ready to undo a dart or a hemline.

Keep your eyes on the international prize. As a fierce fashionista, I intend to get my global groove on by sampling style and culture around the world. To show my appreciation for the global access that style grants me, I pledge to practice a foreign language for five minutes a day and double up on Saturdays, because we're going to win the Catwalk competition and stage our fashion at a destination—to be determined—far, far away! *Ciao, au revoir, sayonara!*

Don't get it French twisted: the number one reason I *desperately* wanted to become a house leader in the Catwalk competition this year is the chance to cinch and sparkle on the fiercest catwalk in Manny Hanny (that's New York to nonfashionistas)—the elevated platform in Bryant Park assembled twice a year to officially unveil the Mercedes-Benz Fashion Week designer collections. But I must also confess a scintillating second reason: to get my grubby paws on the Catwalk budget!

See, the elected house leaders, aka "the fabbie five"—Willi Ninja, Jr., Anna Rex, Moet Major (who became a house leader by default after Chandelier Spinelli was disqualified; more notes on that scandal later!), Shalimar Jackson, and *ahem, ahah*, the feline fatale of the fashionable litter, Pashmina Purrstein (that would be *moi*)—are in charge of our own fashion show expenses. Of course, it's not a straight-up shopportunity, but delegating ducats to create the purrlicious vision for the House of Pashmina is definitely a clothes encounter of the third kind. The furbulous Catwalk competition will be staged next June in front of a panel of celebrity judges and oodles of *très important* invited guests. Today, however, we're getting the first installment of the Catwalk budget as well as the assignment for the Design Challenge, which must be turned in to the Catwalk office in a few weeks.

This explains why, at four o'clock, I'm still perched with my kitten heels in the Catwalk competition office, waiting like an anxious game show contestant for Ms. Fabianna Lynx's trusted assistants, Farfalla and Sil Lai, to hand each of us the "envelope, please." Okay, the truth is I'm crouched in a far-flung corner of this wild habitat—my elbow dangerously close to the gaping jaw of the four-foot-tall stuffed leopard statue whose urban territory I'm invading because my new Catwalk rival, Moet Major, is trying to upstage me, literally.

"We'll see who prances to a payday, that's all I'm saying!" she boasts. Hovering too close for fashion comfort, Miss Moet flings the long asymmetrical bang on her burgundy spiked boy cut while pivoting on her left and then her right Adidas. She flexes her outstretched arms until they stress the seams on her tiny black satin baseball jacket—HOUSE OF MOET embroidered on the back in mustard yellow letters.

We're all on pins and needles, because we don't know how much we're getting for our first installment of the Catwalk budget. We also don't know the secret assignment for the Design Challenge, which can garner the winning team a surprise bonus as well as make or break our chance of ultimately snagging the Big Willie trophy next June. Willi Ninja, Jr., is so anxious that he pops the cork on Moet. "The Muhammad Ali of muslin? Churl, please, may I suggest you step out of the ring before you snap, crackle, *fizzle!*" snarls Willi, who is stationed diagonally across from me, next to the closed door on Ms. Lynx's inner sanctum.

To punctuate his *punto*, Willi renders one of his signature Ninja moves: one sharp snap with his fingers, followed by a full-circle hand movement, then a finger pointed at the object of his disdain.

"*Ding, ding, ding!* Round's over," Shalimar announces like a gruff sportscaster. "Yes, I said it—so put that in your blog entry for all I care!"

Everybody gets hush-hush. We're all guilty of putting Shalimar's pretentious platitudes on blast in our Catwalk competition blog entries. "Miss Shallow—I mean Shalimar—what else should you expect for dribbling on about a thousand-dollar Golden Opulence Sundae exploding with chocolate peaks from the undiscovered mountains of Peru?" chortles Willi Ninja, Jr. "May I suggest that on your next birthday, you do us all a favor and just blow out the trick candles on the cake—and keep your wish of global domination to yourself? Ah, Choo!" Willi pretends to sneeze at Shalimar's Shimmy Choo burgundy calf-hair pumps.

"I wish they would burn sage in this office to clean out the negative energy," huffs Shalimar, prissily. Meanwhile, Farfalla is having a fit of her own. "*Non ancora!* Not again!" she whispers, harshly, flailing her arms in protest at the photocopier.

"It's time to hit the Easy Button," suggests Anna Rex, deadpan.

I shudder, because the Staples shout-out reminds me of the technical difficulties awaiting me at home. Last night, while I was updating the master hookup list for my next Catwalk meeting, my computer froze like a Popsicle.

"That's it, *finito!*" Farfalla moans, clearly giving up on her limited mechanical skills. I pull at my corkscrew curls, secretly praying that Ms. Lynx's dramatic assistant doesn't make me late for my job interview at Jones Uptown boutique, which is right about now! I can't afford *not* to get this job. First of all, I desperately need the ducats (money at home is tighter than Betsey Johnson's waist cincher); second, Ms. Lynx herself provided the intro, so I have to represent. That's right—out of all the students at F. I., she referred *moi* for a job at Laretha Jones's new flagship boutique in Harlem, because, she says, "We both share a passion for the same shade—pink."

At the moment, Willi is feeling his own shade, or I should say *shadiness:* "Come on people, bring on the *challenge*, so I can say boo to Mr. *Benjamin and his friends!*" he groans, confident that the TBD (to be determined) bonus is merely a twirl away. In case you didn't know, Willi is the adopted son of the late Willi Ninja, whose voguing legacy extends from the West Side Highway piers to *le podium* in Paris.

We're all ready for the challenge. Shalimar Jackson and Anna Rex are even analyzing plays from last year's biggest losers. "No, see, you're wrong. Dropping the ball on the Design Challenge is definitely the reason why the House of Barbie didn't win last year," explains Shalimar, coolly. She is seated by Sil Lai's desk, her legs crossed, swinging her left foot with the calculated precision of a hockey player guiding a puck with his hockey stick into a goal.

"So Miss P. P. What say you?" Willi asks, prompting me to deliver my own analysis of the House of Barbie's demise.

"Barbara Beaucoup made a mistake with her take on last year's Design Challenge—turning night into day. She thought it meant to go non-coloric with her collection. In my opinion, that's what caused the judges to go total eclipse on her house's score," I say, authoritatively.

"Black is back," insists Anna Rex, like she's channeling enough dark energy to levitate whatever the challenge might be this year.

"I heard that, cuz I'm gonna be coming with it like the other side of midnight!" seconds Miss Major, feebly.

Then she reluctantly smacks her raisin-branded lips like she's finally grasping her place on the fashion food chain: house leader by default.

Here's the scandal: Chandelier Spinelli's house came tumbling down after her father was indicted for participating in an illegal "chop shop"—and we're not talking Caddies and Benzies, okay? Apparently, Mr. Spinelli, who was a nurse at a Brooklyn hospital, and four colleagues were caught red-handed divvying up human limbs and organs to sell to the highest international bidders! Once the *très* tawdry scandal hit the front page of the *Daily News*, Chandelier developed a bad case of post-traumatic press disorder, and she's currently in hiding while her father awaits trial for his alleged participation in the hamstring ring. (According to a bona fried reliable source, the MIA house leader is holed up at her aunt Voltage's Séance Parlor in Carroll Gardens. The source is one of my best friends, Aphro Biggie Bright, who also lives in the B.K.L.Y.N. and has eyes in the back of her bob.)

Suddenly, the door to the Catwalk office flings open and we're faced with a physical challenge. Caterina Tiburon and her four-member Teen Style Network camera crew pile into the tiny room. In case you haven't heard, for the first time in the Catwalk competition's thirty-five-year history, all the gores galore will be televised as part of a reality show on the Teen Style

Network! (I know, I can't believe it—cinch and pinch me, *purr favor!*) *Catwalk: Strike a Pose* will begin airing after the winning house is announced and more prizes than the Mega Millions lottery are bestowed on it. Trust, I'm not exaggerating about the fashion looty toot: the winning house gets to open the Pitti Bimbo collections in Firenze (*ciao*, Manny Hanny!); at least three of their models will receive modeling contracts with Snooty Model Agency Inc.; and members of the winning house will snag gift certificates galore from fiendish faves like Macy's, the Limited, and Louis Vuitton. And the cash prize? One hundred thousand dollars divvied up among the lucky house's members.

"Hi, fashionistas! So how was your Thanksgiving?" Caterina asks, her hazel eyes flashing as she scans the cramped office for sources of salacious sound bites. After missing us in action at our secret Pose Off ceremony for the appointed house leaders in the Fashion Café last month, Caterina is determined to catch any future ops of Fashion International High School's fashionistas in flagrante, if you catch my drift.

"You're getting too predictable, like Tory Burch accessories," quips Willi Ninja, Jr.

"And I might be getting as overexposed," shoots back the pushy producer. "So what's on today's menu?"

"Citrus poached octopus?" I offer, knowing full well that the Catty one, as we've aptly dubbed Caterina, isn't interested in the specials being served in the Fashion Café. "Seriously, we're waiting to get the scoop on the Design Challenge."

"Churl, please, we're waiting for our first installment of the Catwalk budget. Stop pretending you don't need the *loot to toot* your fashion horn!" heckles Willi, calling me out.

"Now *that* sounds appetizing," Caterina concurs, then pauses, waiting for more bites. Boom hoists the camera onto his shoulder and points it in my direction, or perhaps at the gaping jaw of the stuffy leopard statue. Smiling nervously, I back up so Boom can get a close-up of Stuffy's porcelain white incisors.

Shalimar jumps on the chance to shift the focus to her "catty corner." "Well, it's *not* as appetizing as the Prêt-à-Portea served at the Berkeley hotel in London, where *we* spent Thanksgiving."

"Oh, did you all go?" queries Caterina.

"A field trip to London? Keep hope alive, *okay?*" snipes Moet, sucking her teeth.

"No, Sh-Shalimar is referring to the Browns, or is it the Joneses? Oh, pardon *moi*, of course, it's the J-J-Jacksons!" snarls Willi Ninja, Jr., referring to Shalimar's well-heeled parents, who work on Wall Street. Like we did about her sixteenth-birthday outing, we've heard ad infinitum about her family's Thanksgiving foray to the land of the Earl Grey empire.

"I went with my family," concedes Shalimar, batting her DiorShow(off) Mascara–fortified lashes. "Every day from two to six p.m. in the Caramel Room, the hotel serves fashionista's afternoon tea—inspired by the collections."

"Oh," says Caterina slyly. Obviously, Shalimar's shade boots—right down to her Shimmy Choos—make for entertaining *foo*tage. I conjure up images of Caterina filming Shalimar in her Park Avenue penthouse apartment, sipping tea with her Jack and Jill social-club cronies. Last month, after the nominations for house leaders were posted, Caterina requested face time with each of the fabbie five in our "natural habitats."

But leave it to the serenely eerie Anna Rex to conjure another image that chips at Shalimar's fine bone china service. "Um, I'd think twice about recommendations for certain establishments," she starts in, her frail arms crossed defensively across the bodice of her long black turtleneck dress. Regal Rex was standing so still by the coat closet that I thought she was pretending to be a mannequin—for real. "I think the notice from the health department plastered on the gated front door of the maddeningly popular parlor explained the origin of its mysterious shutdown at the height of the holiday season."

I marvel at Anna Rex's delivery: she didn't even break a sweat while breaking it down. Willi Ninja, Jr., marvels, too, because he squeals: "Ooh, drop the boom on those mouse droppings, churl! They closed that place like it was Pandora's litter box!"

Caterina beams at the possibility of a "catfight." She shoots a surreptitious glance at her camera crew, no doubt to make sure they're capturing the electrifying exchange.

Boom captures another round of quibbles 'n bits among Shalimar, Willi, and Anna before I decide to seize five minutes of frame for my other BFF, Angora Le Bon.

"Oh, I forgot. You know Angora's father, Beau Le Bon, created Funny Bunny, right? Well, a twenty-foot Funny Bunny balloon got added to the Thanksgiving parade lineup this year," I interject, bouncing to my own beat. Angora's father is an illustrator who has risen to fame on his furry cartoon creation.

"Did you go?" Caterina asks.

"Yup. We were numbing our tootsies together outside Macy's!" I giggle.

Caterina smiles weakly at me before switching back to the prying game. "So, who has ended up with the most members in their house?"

The five of us all look at each other like Pricewater-houseCoopers representatives before the ballots for the Academy Awards are tallied: our lips are *sealed*.

"Who has the least? That's what I want to know,"

counters Shalimar Jackson, glaring directly at Moet Major. I raise my penciled auburn eyebrow in disbelief. Why would Shalimar even go there after the whole Ice Très scandal? Ice Très is the graffiti artist who got suspended after tagging one of the walls in the stairwell professing his true love for *moi*. (It was way more horror-frying than it sounds.) Not only was he suspended, he was also disqualified from Shalimar's house. Since his return, I've been avoiding the Urban Thug designer like gaucho pants.

Apparently, I'm not the only one stunned by Shalimar's shady lapse. "Keep sipping those loose tea leaves, churl. I hear you're *scrrrreeching* by with thirty. *Trrrrenta*. Three *zero*. Okay! And I'm talking about your whole house—so how many of those are models? Good luck getting a fierce *chevron* on the catwalk with those skimpy *skrimps*!" snaps Willi Ninja, Jr., referring to a catwalk formation of three models in an inverted V-shaped angle, known as a chic chevron.

When the snickers subside, I strike a blow: "Last year, the House of Moore had forty-six members—more than any other winning house in the Catwalk competition's thirty-five-year history." What I don't add is that the House of Pashmina is six members deficient of that winning combo platter.

Then Caterina goes in for the fashion thrill. "Pashmina, do you honestly think if Chandelier Spinelli wasn't disqualified, you would have managed to snare star designer Nole Canoli for *your* house?"

"The question really is, would the house of Chandelier have won? We'll never know, will we?" I say, hoping I don't come off trifling. Nole Canoli was tight with Chandelier, but now he and Elgamela Sphinx, hairstylist Dame Leeds, and makeup maven Kimono "Mini Mo" Harris are members of my house. I know what peeps think, but why did Caterina have to put me on blast—on camera? I turn like a cornered kitty just in time to see the *Fabulous* one herself swing open the door to her inner sanctum and step out grandly. Puccini, her pudgy white and woolly bichon frise, is hot on her d'Orsay leopard pumps.

"Presto, darlings, *presto!*" Ms. Lynx announces, handing a stack of envelopes to a fretting Farfalla, who drops them on the leopard carpet. Puccini sniffs at the salmon-colored envelopes like he's desperate for a whiff of Snausages. Meanwhile, Ms. Lynx places her heavily bejeweled hand onto her forehead like she's about to collapse from parting with a few Catwalk coins. (I'm not joking; there was a reason for Farfalla's frenzy earlier. Word is she practically has to write a writ of habeas corpus to get an extra pack of copier paper approved by her tightfisted and, as you can see, ferocious boss.)

The long-awaited Lynx and doggie show is not lost on Boom. He quickly swings the camera down at her pumps and Puccini, then back up, right into her MAC-attacked face for a compelling close-up. We all wait with bated breath for Ms. Lynx to drop parting instructions.

After a few calculated heaves, Ms. Lynx releases a complimentary crumb: "Congratulations are in order. I must say I'm *quite* pleased." While she pauses, we all register the Catwalk-encoded message: *Kudos for keeping your fashion traps shut on camera about the Chandelier Spinelli scandalabra!*

"Now, back to business. Right before the Christmas break, all five houses must submit their Design Challenge assignments to this office. Your designs will be kept top secret and will be privately judged by the Catwalk Committee. The winning team will be posted on the Fashion Board when classes resume in January. Please remember that losing the Design Challenge does not mean your team will lose the Catwalk competition—it merely means you should sharpen the scope of your collection. Conversely, winning the Design Challenge does not grant you immunity or guarantee that you'll win the Catwalk competition—a panel of very accomplished fashion judges will decide that. But it will bequeath you with a three-hundred-dollar bonus that must be used toward your Catwalk budget."

"That's all?" groans Moet Major. Ms. Fab ignores her not-so-bubbly outburst to continue her spiel: "And let me remind each of you that Catwalk expense reports must be filed with this office the first of each month. Not the second, or the third, or your legs won't be the only things in need of shaving. We're talking points, people," stresses Ms. Lynx. "And *detail* on your expense reports will be more impressive than creativity. In other words, submitting in*accurate* expense forms will send you packing to Style Siberia—instead of Firenze. You heard it here first—from my mouth to your fears," Ms. Lynx warns us.

"How do we know if we do the Design Challenge, um, the right way?" asks Moet. Like she didn't fizzle out the first time.

This time Ms. Lynx doesn't ignore her outburst. "The answer to that question is obvious. A misinterpretation is better than no interpretation. *Tutti capito? Understood?"* Ms. Lynx motions for Farfalla to turn up the AC and fans herself profusely.

"Capito!" we echo in unison.

"What exactly is the Design Challenge?" inquires Caterina.

"Don't ask me. Ask them," commands Ms. Lynx, now extending her jeweled hand toward Sil Lai to get this rodeo on the road. Sil Lai takes the cue and crisply requests, "Could everyone get in line, please?"

"Head of the class," quips Moet Major, swooping into the line first, causing a chain reaction. She bumps into Shalimar and her hefty sidekick—an ample Fendi black Spy bag, which still protrudes massively despite the fact that her banned-from-school Maltese, J.B., is no longer perched inside. Shalimar's Fendi luggage knocks into Willi while she steps on poor Puccini's paws.

"Oh, my goodness," yelps Ms. Lynx. "If you can't maneuver your way around a poised pooch, how are you going to navigate Seventh Avenue!"

Willi Ninja, Jr., snickers. "Not so *Major*."

Sil Lai ignores the commotion and motions for me to come up front.

"Pashmina, sign here, please."

I obey, scribbling my signature in the Catwalk registry, and then grab the envelope from Sil Lai. I open it with a flourish and chuckle at its leopard interior. "Totally Fab," I mumble out loud.

Caterina makes another attempt at finagling a footnote: "Now that you've gotten your first *expense check*, does the Catwalk competition seem more real?"

As I formulate a frothy flow for the camera, I notice the sharp contrast between Caterina's authoritative voice and her hide-in-plain-sight camouflage gear. "Abso-positively," I concur, "but I'm keeping my eye on the prize like Ms. Lynx suggests."

"Look who's trying to w-w-work it for points on the Dow Jones," huffs Willi Ninja, Jr., but I ignore him and peek inside the envelope—carefully thumbing my three-hundred-dollar Catwalk check.

"So what's the Design Challenge?" Caterina asks again. I unfold the Catwalk competition letterhead with the bold leopard border.

"It's something I won't be stressing about," I lie for the sake of the sound bite. "Because I think, um, I've gathered the most formidable design team possible—including Felinez Cartera, who is a brilliant accessories designer. Together, we're ready to render an interpretation of feline fatale fashion that will scratch out the competition."

I stare right into the camera without blinking and force a smile. "I have to go now, to a job interview," I inform her.

"For what?" asks Caterina.

I tell her about Laretha Jones's new boutique opening and how it melds with my desire to be a "model-preneur." "If I'm going to run Purr Unlimited, I'm going to need lots of retail experience," I explain carefully.

Caterina gets a twinkle in her eye, like she's proud of me, but in the next second she's back to trying to sucker someone else into spilling the trade secrets. Better them than *moi*.

2

I flee from the Catwalk office, my blurry eyes stuck with Krazy Glue to the Design Challenge, when I hear a familiar voice ignite the deserted hallway like a brush fire:

"That sure wasn't snappy, *nappy*!" hisses Aphro, one of my three official BFFs with whom I currently have a bona fried beef jerky. "What's up with your weave?"

It's futile dodging Aphro's bogus missile; instead, I reach for my outta-control curls and freak at the frizz formation.

"Hmm. Hmm. Told you," smirks Aphro. Like she should talk: it's true that I yank my *real* hair compulsively when I'm nervous, but she's addicted to Dax hair dress (aka ghetto grease) and the scorching hot comb to keep her short, Naomi Campbell–wannabe bob flatter than her training bra.

"What are you doing here? I thought you had to jet," I say, puzzled by Aphro's stakeout. This morning, she told us that she had to scurry after school, but didn't reveal the reason.

"I don't feel like dealing with *that* drama right now," she tells me.

"Does it have to do with your family?" I ask, trying to act concerned. Aphro lives in Bed-Stuy, Brooklyn, with her foster parents—the Maydells—and three other foster children, including nine-year-old Lennix, whom she's really close to.

"No, it doesn't," she snaps, snappily.

"Oh, I see," I mutter nervously, but what I really want to say is *Wish I didn't have to see you right now!* I just found out from Chintzy Colon, my assistant in the House of Pashmina, that Aphro cackled to Lupo Saltimbocca, our house photographer, about my D.D.L. crush on Dr. Zeus. Dr. Zeus is the nickname for Zeus Artemides, the tasty mink-zebra-hatted deejay, graphic designer, and model, who's also in our house.

Right now, I'd like to hit smug Aphro over the head with a leftover turkey drumstick from Thanksgiving. Biggie Mouth, on the other hand, is intent on playing tug-of-war with me. "Let me get with it!" she insists, petulantly. Her bangles jangling, she lunges full force for the envelope in my hand, which contains the privy communiqué.

"Don't come for me, Miss Aphro Puffs," I retort while holding the envelope out of her long-armed reach. Aphro Puffs is the name of the blang jewelry empire the budding model-blinger hopes to helm. Another hyphenate waiting to happen in our house,

Aphro is the jewelry designer as well as the choreographer and, last but not least, one of our star catwalkers for the fashion show.

I run down the hallway to get away from her claws but Aphro snags my hoodie in a heartbeat.

"Hold up," she snorts.

I hate that I can't run nearly as fast as Aphro because of her Wonder Woman legs, despite our being practically the same height—five feet, nine inches—give or take a centimeter. I lean against the wall to catch my breath, coincidentally right under the neon-lime-green-bordered metal plaque by the stairwell, which clearly states in bold black letters:

YOU MAY BE DESTINED FOR A FASHION
STABLE IN YOUR NEAR FUTURE, BUT YOU
ARE CURRENTLY AT SCHOOL, SO NO
GALLOPING IN THE HALLWAYS, PLEASE.

"Awright," I sigh, giving in. Together, we examine the contents of the Catwalk envelope like fashion forensic scientists. " 'Take things you see every day in your environment and turn them into fashion'?" I read out loud, puzzled pink. "It kinda sounds like the Riddle of the Sphinx, don't ya think?" I moan, removing the check from the envelope. But before I can shove the designated ducats into my Hello Kitty wallet, Aphro manages to snatch it for a preview.

While she revels in the zeros on paper, I marinate for a minute.

"Do you think it means take the stuff we see every day and make it represent on the runway?" I mutter absentmindedly.

Aphro reluctantly hands me back the check, her big brown eyes widening, which means she is thinking outside the sandbox. "Stuff we see every day could be regular stuff we wear every day—like that raggedy pink bathrobe of yours covered with balls of acrylic pile, or those silly-cat-head fuzzy slippers. Ya dig?"

"Could be. Or, your noisy bangles. Ya dig?" I retort.

Aphro lets out one of her signature snarkles—a cross between a pig's happy snort and the scary squeals that emanate from a roller coaster at the moment when it sharply plummets at a ninety-degree angle.

"Obviously, this will be the first order of business at our Catwalk meeting," I sigh.

I zip up my Free People pink kitten hoodie carefully, wondering how much time Aphro's been spending with Lupo. "How come you never pick up your celly lately?" I ask, but I already know the answer to that one. Judging from the latest cackle I've peeped, I suspect that my best friend has been jumping into Lupo's mouth *mucho* lately. (His last name, *Saltimbocca*, literally means "jump in the mouth" in Italian. I swear!)

"Why—you my long-lost mother now?" she says, defensively.

I'm not going to let Aphro bait me. I know she doesn't know where her real mother is. The last time she saw her, they were snuggled together on the couch, watching *The Wizard of Oz* and eating graham crackers, before a caseworker came and took Aphro away with her little blue vinyl suitcase in tow. She never saw her mother again.

Aphro continues to stare at me with her sizeable pout puffed out. I decide it's time to attack: "You obviously have been in the loop with Loopy—a *lot*. And, I can't believe you flapped your lips to him!" I hiss at her, making a slur of Lupo's name.

"What, you jealous? You should just get with Zeus already and stop pretending you're the Princess of Pink all alone in your Chicken Little castle waiting for the ceiling to collapse," Aphro snarls, leveling her "Bed-Stuy glare" at me.

"Zeus has a girlfriend, so how desperado should I behave? Duh?" I say.

"That's never stopped you from following the yellow-brick road before," Aphro says, challenging me.

"If it's all right with you, I'm going to my job interview—*late*," I announce, coldly, before marching off.

"Let me go with you," Aphro says, her voice softening as she trots behind me.

"No!" I whisper sharply, turning around to put her on blast. "You're so secretive—and shady, too! You say you don't like Lupo. 'He's too short. He talks funny. His nose is too big.' But now you're kanoodling with him?"

"We had lunch—fusilli. It's pasta shaped like corkscrews—like your hair when you're not pulling it out!" snaps Aphro. "And who says I like him? I'm just trying to get some photos for my portfolio, okay?"

I glare at Aphro. Lupo promised he'd take feline fashion shots of us for our modeling portfolios—but "us" seems to be transforming into "her."

"I should have known there was an angle to your dangle," I say, nodding.

"As if you would ever go out with a short guy either," counters Aphro. "You're only feeling Zeus cuz he's model material."

"At least I'm honest about it!" I blurt out, walking away.

Aphro pleads with me. "Lemme go with you. I just can't deal with a situation right now."

I'm tempted to force Aphro to show her hand like in a poker game, but I give in. "*Awright*," I say, mocking her, "you'd better click your heels and follow me down the yellow-brick road."

Once we get outside, I'm startled by the two lingering Dalmation dogs huddled by the pink gates. Directly across the street from Fashion International is Dalmation Tech High School, stomping grounds of computer and mechanically inclined students. They inhabit grungy gray hallways that no self-respecting fashionista would dare darken. Every day after school, members of their pimply student body camp outside the fabbie pink gates of Fashion International, licking their chops at the sight of budding fashionistas in the hopes that we'll throw them a bone—*not*. By four o'clock, however, they've usually scrammed—with their tails tucked between their baggy-panted legs.

"Can't believe they're still here," snarls Aphro, rolling her eyes at the partners in cyber crime clinging to each other in the hopes of bolstering their computer-chip-operated egos.

The shorter one raises his eyebrow at me.

"Puhleez, who are you trying to hoodwink?" I snap without flinching.

Shortie's confidence crumbles like Piggly Wiggly blue cheese. His smirk vanishes and he stares down at his dingy "No Edition" sneakers.

Aphro sticks her arm through mine as we skip away.

"You ain't all that," snipes the taller one, receding like the Grim Reaper into his gray hoodie.

Looking back, Aphro shouts, "Yes, we are!"

When we reach the Fortieth Street entrance to the subway, Aphro reminds me to call our crew to give them a "catty" update: "Felinez has probably given birth to five purses by now."

"Yeah, well, I'd better call my mom first—cuz she'll *charge* five more purses she can't afford if she doesn't hear from me!" I counter.

Once I get my mom on the phone, I remind her that I'm headed to a job interview and will be home late. She reminds *me* not to talk to any strangers, despite the fact that I'm almost sixteen and quite familiar with her shrill drill. Then she proceeds to ply me with the latest statistics: "Seventy-six new sexual predators in our neighborhood," she says, curtly. I focus on the background noises instead of my mother's voice: the shrill beeps from an electronic cash register and women's voices—probably customers. My mom works as an assistant manager at Forgotten Diva Boutique, a plus-size clothing store, on Madison Avenue. My mom now senses I'm lost in la-la, because she raises her voice. "I want you to go online tonight and print out the updated list and give it to Chenille, too."

"What are the chances of me printing out the faces of sexual predators if I can't get my computer to work, huh? Do you have any stats for *that*?" I snap at her, impatiently.

"Just turn the computer off for a while; sometimes that works," offers my mom, feebly, "and watch that tone, you hear me?"

"Okeydokey," I say, squashing what I really want to say: *How about a dial tone!* Things between my mom and me are supa-tense right now, because she's not sure about this whole Catwalk competition thing. She also seems tired all the time—which is probably why she snaps at me instead of talking.

"She thinks that I'm gonna be pressuring her for funds to front our fashion, that's what it is," I say out loud, flipping my cell phone shut. "I wish I could shut her off for a while."

"I hear that," Aphro says, giggling, twirling her lariat necklace, "but I sure hope *she* didn't!"

I wait until we get off the subway at the 135th Street station to call Felinez. She is so desperate for info she sounds like she's been chomping on piñatas.

"Three hundred dollars, *mija!*" Felinez screams into the phone after I break down the booty like a proud pirate. She's screaming so loud, I have to take the phone away from my ear. Aphro and I are standing in front of the window of a supa-fly boutique called Montgomery, on Adam Clayton Powell Boulevard and 136th Street.

"Aphro puffs," I coo, pointing to a black satin appliqué of a black girl with big round eyes and Afro puffs sewn on the front of a white T-shirt.

"Omigod, I have to have that T-shirt!" Aphro declares. "I'd better get a j-o-b to snag that—okay."

Meanwhile, I continue to fill in Felinez: "I know—you're in charge of buying accessories supplies, but don't get too hide-happy," I warn her.

As for the Design Challenge, Felinez already has a plan for bagging the Benjamins: "*Mija*, it's the garbage can! Something you pass every day, right? That three-hundred-dollar bonus is ours!"

"You must be sipping salsa sauce. So we're supposed to design trash can lids that can be worn as headgear?" I ask, baffled.

"No! The stuff inside!" Felinez screams excitedly.

"Of course, I should have known," I moan. I met Felinez "Fifi" Cartera in the first grade in the Boogie Down, where I lived until last year. Ever since, the two of us have made quite a pair of hyperactive kittens: when I get nervous, I yank my hair, while Fifi Dumpster-dives to find materials she can recycle into pouches, purses, belts.

Now I can hear her older sister Michelette screaming in Spanish. "*Dejame!* I'm not getting off the phone!" Felinez retorts.

Michelette works at the Champagne video store, where she has her pick of films, but all she does is obsessively watch episodes of the Colombian soap opera *Betty, la fea.* Exasperated, Felinez drags me into their latest Bronx tale. Apparently, Michelette is threatening to move to Bogotá with their aunt Flamingo, which would leave Felinez and their younger brother, Juanito, in the lurch, since their parents travel most of the time in a cover band called Las Madres y los Padres.

"Why would she want to live with someone who doesn't even have a DVD player?" I ask, puzzled.

Suddenly, a truck backfires and sends me practically diving right into the metal trash can on the corner. The burly men in the truck even have the nerve to start whistling at us.

"Maybe it's time to call Geico!" I snarl at them, then end the call to Felinez.

"Did you call Angora yet?" Aphro asks, getting me back on track.

"For the second time," I insist, "I'd have better luck paging the Easter Bunny."

As we turn the corner, Aphro starts to say something, then backs out: "Never mind."

"What are you hiding?" I ask her, getting spooked out by her secret. "Does it have to do with something at home?"

"Why you keep asking me that?" she retorts, defensively.

"Because I know the dealio," I say, not backing down. Her foster mother, Mrs. Maydell, is really nice, but Mr. Maydell is gruff around the edges. Aphro senses what I'm thinking: "Yes, he's always on Lennix, but he leaves me alone."

Nonetheless, I can see the tears welling in Aphro's eyes behind the usual bluster. She shakes her head, then pats the bangs down on her bob as if she's trying to straighten out something. We walk silently to the front of the Jones Uptown boutique, which is obviously under construction, judging by the brown paper–lined windows. "Ms. Lynx says Laretha can be a handful," I warn Aphro, then repeat Ms. Lynx's advice in my head like a mantra: *If you can't handle a designer's roar, then you'll never survive in the fashion jungle.*

"Well, I hope she's got some talent—to go with that noise," Aphro says, ringing the loud buzzer of the mystery boutique. We stare at the windows, trying to get a peek inside, to no avail. "I wonder when this place is gonna open."

"Not soon enough," I say, sighing. "The only thing I need more than a job is a job right now."

"I hear that," Aphro seconds, then rings the buzzer again. We both get quiet at the sound of jingling keys being inserted into the lock on the other side of the door. Seconds later, open sesame, the glass door swings and a brown-skinned lady with a purple head wrap sticks her head out.

"Can I help you?" she asks. I shriek inside, wondering if I screwed up my appointment. When I called earlier, I told the lady on the phone that I was referred by Ms. Lynx. She rushed me off before I could elaborate but I heard commotion in the background, so I didn't push it. Now I can see that all the commotion is probably construction-related.

"Yes, I'm Pashmina—"

"Lord, I forgot," she says, eyeing me up and down. "I thought you weren't coming."

"Oh, you said before closing, so I came as soon as I could," I start in, noticing she looks supa-stressed—probably about opening her store on time. I know the drill: store announcements are mailed at a bulk postage rate; trunk shows are planned; opening discount incentives are given. We covered it all in my Retail 101 class.

"That's fine—I got so much going on in here, I don't know what day it is," she says, shaking her head, then opening the heavy door wider to let us in.

"I'm Laretha Jones."

I smile back at her warmly. Aphro is too busy gaping at the iridescent violet moiré wall treatment. "Oh, this is *major*," she squeals.

Aphro releases a few more oohs and aahs at the purple tiered shelves and racks, next to a lilac wood display case. A man on a ladder is painting an into-the-woods-type mural on the wall near the dressing rooms, but apparently it's not to Laretha's liking. "Those are not trees, those are twigs!" she complains. While the two

337

have a heated discussion about forest foliage, I examine the layout carefully, but I can't help feeling puzzled pink. Ms. Lynx said that Laretha and I shared a shade in common. I shake my curls, trying to recount the encounter in Ms. Lynx's office.

"Would you like to see the rest of the store?" Laretha asks me.

"Yes!" I say, enthusiastically. "This really *is* major."

Laretha shows us the back area, which is packed with inventory covered in plastic. "This is where the sewing machines are going to be," she explains, "and the cutting table."

"Is this your first boutique?" I ask.

"Yes, indeed, but I worked for years on Seventh Avenue, which is how I know Ms. Fab," Laretha explains. "She modeled for Adolpho. Back then, I was his design assistant."

"Oh, I remember seeing one of the Adolpho ads in her office," I say, recalling the photo of Ms. Fab in a pink and gray tweed suit holding a large Saint Bernard on a gold chain leash by her side.

"Ooh, yes, Ms. Fab was something fierce—she still is, just bigger and I'm sure feisty as ever," Laretha chuckles.

"That's for sure," Aphro blurts out, but I pinch her in the side.

Laretha beams at Aphro. "So who are you?"

"Oh, my bad," Aphro says, putting her hand over her mouth like she's embarrassed. "I'm Pashmina's best friend."

"Well, that's nice. But what is your name?"

"Oh, Aphro. Aphrodite Bright."

"That's a very interesting name," Laretha says like she's intrigued.

I'm wondering why Aphro left out the Biggie— maybe she didn't want to appear too gangsta, even though I think her adopted moniker suits her perfectly.

"Well, take a peek at my collection. It's sort of early spring," Laretha says, motioning to the racks.

"Ooh, look at this!" Aphro says, lifting the plastic on one of the suits on the rack, a purple mohair duster with fringes. "You know, purple is my favorite color."

"Mine too," Laretha says, ending the color-wheel mystery.

"Oh, um, it is?" I ask, weakly.

"After my sojourn to Africa, I had a spiritual awakening and wanted to embrace the royal colors of the motherland," Laretha informs us.

Laretha gazes at my pink outfit and smiles. "I used to love pink before my spiritual awakening but sometimes you have to let go of childish things. Now the only pastel I can be around is lavender. It's so serene and peaceful."

"Pashmina is a hard-core pinkaholic!" snorts Aphro.

Suddenly, I feel immature, wondering why Laretha

and my best friend are being so shady with me, but soon Laretha offers an explanation.

"It's funny how something starts out as a color, but ends up an attitude," she says.

"That's what I always say. Pink is not just a color, it's a cattitude!" I blurt out, without thinking.

Laretha smiles at me absentmindedly, because she is gazing at the lavender seed-bead lariat around Aphro's neck like she's just found herself another piece of serenity. "Now *that's* interesting."

"Oh, I make them," Aphro says, humbly.

"Is that right?" Laretha asks, rhetorically. "Well, then we have to get some of your stuff up in here."

"Really?" Aphro asks, bringing the rhetoric full circle.

"Aphro's company is going to be called Aphro Puffs," I offer, proudly.

"I like that. I almost started making jewelry when I was back in high school. My parents wouldn't hear of me going to a school like y'all do, so I had to go to Bed-Stuy High School right around the corner from us—"

"Bed-Stuy High! I live four blocks from there!" exclaims Aphro.

"Get out of here. I grew up there. Been in Harlem since I got married, though. Who's your family?" Laretha asks, staring at the dusty haze on a counter's surface.

Aphro hesitates before she calmly announces, "Mr. and Mrs. Maydell—they're my foster parents."

Laretha stops swiping dust from the counter in midair. "My mother raised lots of foster kids. Ain't that something. I wonder if they know each other," she muses, then looks closely at Aphro. "Are they treating you right?"

"Oh, Mrs. Maydell is real cool," Aphro says, refraining from revealing the tenseness between her and Mr. Maydell. "She works for Mos Def sometimes."

"Really?" Laretha says, clearly impressed by Mrs. Maydell's association with Brooklyn rap royalty. "What does she do?"

"She's a domestic," Aphro says, nodding. "She used to work in Eartha Kitt's estate in Connecticut. May she rest in peace—Eartha, I mean, not my foster mother."

Now Laretha is further impressed. I can tell by the way she nods. "Now you're bringing me way back." She breaks out into a grin that makes the gap between her front teeth appear wider. "When I first started designing for Adolpho, we'd take buyers out during market week to the piano bar at the Carlisle Hotel when Eartha Kitt was performing there, cuz we always knew the buyers would come back to the showroom the next day, and place bigger orders!"

"That's the power of the purr," I say, chuckling.

"Oh, y'all too young to know about Miss Eartha," Laretha says, shaking her head.

"I have a poster of her as Catwoman in my bedroom. Mrs. Maydell got it for me!" I share excitedly.

"Ain't that something. Lord, there will never be another Eartha," Laretha says, staring at me, like she is noticing me for the first time. "Is that all your hair?"

I'm not sure which answer will grant me access to Laretha's royal treatment, so I opt for the truth. "Today it is," I giggle.

"Well, that is some head of hair," Laretha says, beaming at me.

"I know. It's unbeweavable," I giggle.

Laretha beams at me again, then quickly announces, "I could stand here all day with you two, but I have a store to open—and I'm still sitting here under construction."

"I hear you," I say, nodding and looking around in amazement. I can't wait till I have my own store one day. "You know, I major in fashion merchandising and buying."

"Oh, so now you tell me," Laretha says, nodding.

For good measure, I throw in another career cachet: "And my mother is assistant manager at Forgotten Diva."

Laretha, who must be about one Reese's Piece away from a size 18, stares at me blankly.

"The plus-size boutique—on Madison?" I say, hesitating. My mom already hipped me to the reality about women and sizes: sometimes they act like they don't know anything about plus-sizes so it doesn't look like they shop there.

Sure enough, Laretha says, "Oh, I don't know that store."

I decide to tell Laretha about my plans to open a retail chain called Purr Unlimited.

"You know, unlimited—as opposed to all the limits everybody places on women's sizes?" I add for good measure.

Now Laretha looks at me with newfound respect. I take a deep breath, waiting and hoping she'll offer me a job. Despite our shady difference, I would still like to work for her. Aphro takes the words right out of my mouth.

"You know you should give Miss Pashmina a job," blurts out Aphro, swinging the ends of her lariat as if to punctuate her point.

"I know that's right," Laretha chuckles.

Suddenly, the crashing sound of a paint can falling off the ladder in the back interrupts our exchange.

"Now you did it!" yelps one of the construction workers.

Laretha hurries to the back of the store to survey the situation. While we wait, Aphro stares inside the empty display case. "I wonder what kind of jewelry she's gonna have."

"Obviously yours," I say with pride.

"I hope so," Aphro says.

Seconds later, Laretha rushes to the front of the store, sweating. "We have a real crisis. The construction worker knocked over the varnish and that is definitely going to set us back a few hours."

"Well, thank you for taking the time to see me," I say, nervously.

"Pashmina, it was truly a pleasure. And Miss Aphro, we are definitely going to have your jewelry up in here," she says, politely.

"Oh, trust, I will definitely be making my way uptown more often now that you're here!" Aphro says, excitedly.

Once we're outside, Aphro declares, "You definitely got the job. Don't sweat it."

"I hope you're right, Miss Aphro *Biggie* Bright," I say, walking her to the subway.

Aphro seems less stressed, but still preoccupied about something. Still, I decide to flip the switch to my own drama.

"I don't know what I'm gonna do if my computer isn't working. I have to print out the hookup list," I say, thinking out loud. For the past month, all my team members have handed in every connection they have that could be useful for our Catwalk fashion show committee purposes. Now I have to compile them into a master list and make photocopies to hand out at our Catwalk meeting tomorrow after school. Aphro flinches but then reassures me: "Why you sweating? There's probably nothing wrong with your computer." Before she descends the downtown stairwell of the subway, she turns around and declares, "I know you like to put me on blast, but you know we're tight, right?"

"I know," I say, truthfully.

"We'll be ruling the runways—for real," she says, regaining her usual cocky composure.

"I know," I say, matching her energy level. "But right now I'd be happy if I could control my computer!"

New school rule: You don't have to be ultranice, but don't get tooooo catty, or your posting will be zapped by the Fashion Avengers!

DING, DING, ROUND'S NOT OVER . . .

Just because I'm down with hip-hop style doesn't mean I don't understand things on the traditional tip—like politics. For example, right now in American history class, we've been breaking down a leader who I can relate to: former president Richard Nixon. Here he was, vice president under Dwight D. Eisenhower, then ran for president and lost by a very close margin to John F. Kennedy in 1960. Then he came back swinging and ran for governor of California in 1962. Sure, this second loss made our future leader bitterly announce that he was leaving politics and "you won't have Nixon to kick around anymore." But the visionaries knew Tricky Dick was just getting started when he reemerged as a presidential candidate in 1968 against Hubert Humphrey, screeching by on a victory in one of the closest elections in our country's history. Then he ran for reelection in 1972 against George McGovern. This one was a landslide victory, with 60 percent of the popular vote. That's because people realized Nixon was a true contender. Now, I don't want to get into that other stuff about the break-ins and Watergate, cuz if you wasn't sleeping in history class, you should be up on that well-documented shady situation. But the man at least had the dignity to step down after he realized they had him on audiotape and stuff (which today would be like getting peeped on YouTube).

Another historical point I can relate to: after Nixon resigned as president, Vice President Gerald R. Ford succeeded him. Now, just because G wasn't nominated in the first place doesn't mean he wasn't legit enough to be head of state. Which brings me to a present situation that will soon be recognized as official fashion history: I may have become house leader by default—a first in the Catwalk competition's 35-year history—but I'm an authentic leader, nonetheless, and I'm definitely "too legit to quit." So I want to commence the record with the following guarantee: there ain't gonna be any smoking guns while I'm in office. No audiotapes, downloads, or newspaper articles about someone in my family up to some shadiness—cuz there are no bones in the closets (no disrespect to my predecessor, whose father got caught up in an alleged but true skeleton scandal). My aunt, whom I live with, is visually impaired but she keeps everything in check in our "White House." Trust, come next June, there is just gonna be a lot of smoke when I come out blazing at the Catwalk competition. Believe that.

Posted by Black Satin at 11:17:20

3

Aphro isn't the only one who doesn't want to go home. What else could explain why I'm slouching my shoulders and dragging my feet instead of "representing" in the courtyard of my building complex? We live in the Amsterdam Gardens, on West 114th Street, which I've nicknamed Chicken Little Central because it seems like the ceiling is always on the verge of collapsing. All it takes, however, to snap me back into Catwalk sashay mode is a shrill salutation from the rear. "Hey there, supermodel!" shouts Mrs. Watkins, one of my neighbors. Everybody in Building C knows that I'm going to be a model, so they're always calling me out.

Turning around, I straighten my shoulders and flash the on-camera smile that I learned in Modeling 101. Ms. London's instruction still echoes in my ear: *Widen your eyes and stretch the corners of your mouth, but not too far like the Joker!*

"Hi, Mrs. Watkins," I say, cheerfully.

"The jackpot is up to seventy-three million today. Yes *indeed!*" she exclaims. Mrs. Watkins buys a Lotto ticket every week—and by the way she talks about it, she makes you feel this could be her lucky day, or yours.

"Well, I hope you hit the big time," I say, secretly wishing the same for myself. Then I share an international tidbit that Felinez told me: "The El Gordo lottery in Madrid is three billion dollars!"

"I wish I lived in Spain, but I'd better be winning something here. Shoot—been buying these tickets for twenty years. My number's gotta come up sometime," she professes, tightening her grip on the shopping bags she's hoisting in both hands. Mrs. Watkins works across the street at Piggly Wiggly supermarket and is always loaded with bags brimming with bulky items. I open the door for Mrs. Watkins, and she walks into the lobby.

"I sure hope we have heat up in here," she says, wishfully.

"I know," I second, looking around for our landlord, Mr. Darius.

"He better had done something, cuz that trifling boiler has been fixed more times than the New York State lotto!"

Nodding in agreement, I follow Mrs. Watkins inside, but turn to see if anybody else is coming so I can hold the door. Alas, I spot Mrs. Paul, another neighbor, who lives across the hall from me. I wish Mrs. Paul would play the Lotto, because maybe she'd feel lucky enough to smile sometime. I wait patiently while she barrels toward me like a bulldog, with a cute, curly-haired boy wearing a dingy green plaid shirt and high-water brown tweed pants.

As if reading my mind, Mrs. Watkins says in a hushed voice, "Heard her daughter went back to Georgia. Left her son up here. What on earth she got him wearing? Poor child."

I nod but keep my eye on Mrs. Paul, who finally barges through the door. I smile, but experience has taught me not to be too chirpy or she'll give me the evil eyeball.

Sure enough, Mrs. Paul glares at me, swinging her vintage black vinyl purse like she's about to whack me.

"Hi," I say quietly to the boy as he whisks by.

The dimples set in his face as he beams at me.

"Come on, Eramus," commands Mrs. Paul.

"Eramus. What a cool name," I say, involuntarily. He beams at me again as we walk toward the elevator bank.

"So who is that you got there?" asks Mrs. Watkins, even though she obviously knows that Eramus is Mrs. Paul's grandson.

"Never mind all that," Mrs. Paul shoots back at Mrs. Watkins.

"Well, hold on to your hot sauce. *She* actually spoke to those less worthy," Mrs. Watkins mumbles under her breath. "Today must be my lucky day, indeed."

I feel a giggle come on, but I instinctively squelch it, since Mrs. Paul is not above tattling to my mother. Last summer, she scolded my mother for letting me wear Juicy sweatpants. She thought the Juicy logo plastered on my butt was "false advertising." (We're still not sure if she meant that the word was too suggestive or that my butt is too skinny to be considered "juicy.") The four of us crowd into the empty elevator and Eramus stares up at me again, his big brown eyes twinkling.

"How old are you?" I ask him.

"Eight," he answers.

The elevator opens onto Mrs. Watkins's floor. "Good night, all," she says, making a point of brushing her big shopping bags against Mrs. Paul's nubby wool vintage black coat.

Mrs. Paul bristles at the contact, but Eramus and I say, "Good night!" in unison. Then we giggle.

When we get to my floor, Mrs. Paul marches down the hall to her apartment with Eramus. He turns and stares at me, and I'd swear his eyes are pleading, "Help me!"

Shaking my head, I go inside my apartment. Ramon is sitting at the dining room table, reading a Home Depot catalog, which is like his Bible. I wish Ramon was equally obsessed with computers, but no such luck. "She's in the bedroom," he says, his eyes darting in that direction. The dim spotlight above the dining alcove reflects off Ramon's skin, which resembles undercooked bacon. My mother does not refer to Ramon as her boyfriend but I guess you could say he is. They broke up over the summer, but two weeks ago he resurfaced and hopefully so will the dilapidated bathroom, if you catch my drift.

"Okeydokey," I say, then duck into my room quickly, because I've got to get the hookup list ready pronto. Unfortunately, I'm not quick enough to avoid my sister, Chenille. She waddles down the hallway with a frosted blond wig on a white Styrofoam head in her hand. "Is that Mom's?" I ask in disbelief. I know that the Beverly Johnson shag wig is the jewel of her wig collection.

"Yup. Gotta get it ready for wig class tomorrow. No point in using one of their ratty ones when I can do Mom's," Chenille says, showing off. It's bad enough my younger sister is already clocking ducats aplenty from her burgeoning press-and-curl clientele in our building complex, but now even my own mother has succumbed to her styling shadiness.

"Geez, now I've seen it all," I mutter out loud.

"No, you haven't seen it all," counters Chenille with that stupid smirk on her face.

"What's that supposed to mean?" I ask.

"Well, let's just say I saw more in the hair annex today than wig heads. These heads were attached to bodies—and they were whispering about *the House of Pashmina*!"

"Why would I listen to someone—over the age of five—who hoards Halloween candy under their mattress?" I say, realizing that Chenille is probably pulling a *"Psych!"* We do it to each other all the time, but she's just not as good at it as I am.

"You'd better stay out of my room," warns Chenille, trying to mask her blushing cheeks.

"Puhleez. I was looking for my flat iron—cuz I know you stole it!"

"You're lucky I'm not holding it in my hand right now," Chenille says, glaring at me.

"It figures that would be your weapon of choice!" I say, sneering all the way to my room.

Slamming my bedroom door shut, I turn on my computer and stare at the screen, waiting patiently for it to turn that beautiful shade of sky blue that Angora adores. *Please, Cyber God, crank it up!*

As I wait, I decide to try Angora again. Luckily, she picks up the phone.

"Bonsoir!" she coos.

"Where've you been?" I ask.

"Oh, Je'Taime's here," she says, apologetically. Angora lives on the Upper West Side with her father. Je'Taime is her dad's psychic from Baton Rouge. I can just see the head-wrapped high priestess with the long false eyelashes and acrylic tips on her fingernails coddling Angora and her dad with her crystal ball predictions and motherly gumbo. Angora adores Je'Taime as much as she despises her mom, the manners maven behind Ms. Ava's Etiquette and Charm School in Baton Rouge.

"*She* called today to tell me that she is now to be referred to as an international protocol consultant," Angora says, exasperated. Angora never refers to Ms. Ava as her mom.

"That sounds very Inspector *Chérie*," I giggle in my French accent.

"I know *she* was really checking up on *us*. She should just stick her fingers in her garden in Hysteria Lane instead of my business. I mean, it's not like she really cares about me."

"You sure she doesn't care about you?" I ask in disbelief.

"The only thing Ava Le Bon cares about is money—and manners, in that order," claims Angora. "And I sure don't want her money, or manners like hers, *merci*."

While Angora is talking, my manners abruptly go AWOL. I can't hear a word of her angst, because I'm too busy pondering the tiddy Chenille just dropped on me like a think bomb. "Have you heard anything—about me?" I ask, interrupting her family flow with my paranoia, and repeating Chenille's foreboding verbatim. "Aphro is spooking me and suddenly Chenille is peeping intel about, um, my organization?"

"I'm not sure what is going on with Aphro, I noticed it, too, but I think Chenille just wants your attention. That's why she provokes you," Angora advises me. "If you would just see her potential. I mean she really is talented, Pash."

"Okay, that's a wrap and a falafel on that style-free subject," I say, curtly.

But now Angora is like a dog with a bone: she just won't leave it alone. "You should be an only child and see what it feels like."

"Sign me up—*pronto!*" I insist.

"*C'est la vie.* Can I hear about your visit to the Lynx Lair, *s'il vous plaît?*" pleads Angora.

"Oh, right," I say, remembering she is hyped to hear about the Design Challenge. I break it down. "Benjamin beckons."

"*Absolument.* Things you see every day?" repeats Angora, mulling over the challenge. "That would be all the rabbits overrunning my apartment!"

"Oh, no!" I counter. "We're not featuring the animal kingdom on the runway, okay? Please think *feline, chérie.* Feline! Not lions and tigers and rabbits, oh, my!"

"Okay, you don't have to get testy," Angora says. She gets so easily offended by my Boogie Down bluster.

I try to tone it down for her, but I guess I'm always bringing my Bronx ways. "Sorry," I whisper.

"Okay, *chérie*," Angora says, back to her peaceful blue aura. Then she hops on another Funny Bunny alert. "Dad is waiting for his first net profit statement, which means the royalties are gonna make us like royalty!" she squeals in her bouncy Baton Rouge accent. "That means he's gonna give me money for our fashion show supplies!"

I feel a twinge of jealousy, but I let it go like disco and focus on the finance. "So what is a net profit statement?" I ask. I learned about licensing agreements in my fashion merchandising class. Basically, a Big Willie fashion designer or a celebrity slaps their name and design philosophy on a product that they don't really make. In exchange, the designer gets a percentage of the action from the company that is manufacturing and distributing the product to consumers.

"Well, in Hollywood they do things differently than the fashion biz. The person who created the idea gets a percentage of what's left over *after* the film studio's expenses, so that's what 'net' means, as opposed to 'gross'—which is *before* expenses."

"Well, that sounds 'gross' to me. I mean, who's to say what the studio's expenses are? The sky could be the limit, no?" I counter.

"We'll see when it comes," Angora says, sighing.

"So speaking about expenses—how much did we get for the Catwalk budget?"

"Enough to buy fabrics as soon as we get the sketches in," I reply, excitedly.

"Oh, I'm definitely in the Mood to go shopping," squeals Angora. Mood Fabrics is the place to be. After every season, all the major design houses, from Versace to Betsey Johnson, sell their fabric remnants to Mood, the premier designer outlet, located on Fortieth Street. Mind you, these remnants are not run-of-the-mill. They're sublime fabrics that were designed exclusively for the designer by a prestigious textile mill in Europe or the Far East. "And how was the job interview, *chérie?*"

I sense a tinge of embarrassment in Angora's voice. I know she feels guilty because she doesn't have to look for a part-time job, thanks to the Funny Bunny gravy train that is about to spill over.

"Well, it wasn't exactly what I expected, but I think I got it," I say, trying to convince myself.

"I bet you did," Angora says, reassuringly.

While talking to Angora, I press the Documents icon on my desktop, but it doesn't budge. Angora senses that something is wrong. "I can't believe it," I say, freezing, just like my computer screen. "I *hate* this. The last thing I need right now is to have to buy a new computer!"

I start banging the computer tower to see if I can get it to work.

"What are you doing?" asks Angora.

"Sometimes banging the thing gets it to work!"

"Well, now that you have a check for three hundred dollars, you can buy a new one," Angora says, giggling.

"That's not funny-*bunny*!" I hiss at her. Even the thought of misappropriating Catwalk funds and facing Ms. Lynx's wrath makes me shudder.

"Okay, listen. I'm going to send an e-mail to all our members about the Design Challenge so everyone will come prepared to the meeting. And hop over here in the morning and we'll type the hookup list here, okay?" suggests Angora.

"Great. Now I have to get up an hour earlier. I'm totally psyched!" I gripe, jokingly. Really I'm grateful to Angora for being one of my best friends. When I hang up the phone, I grab Fabbie Tabby's furry cinnamon body and hold her close to me, collapsing like a soufflé onto the pinkified bed. Whenever I feel frightened, her warm body and heavy breathing remind me that somebody does care about me. She surrenders to my grip and flops down on her pudgy side, defeated. She knows she can't get away from my needy paws when I'm in a state like this. I don't even bother to get up and take my clothes off. Lying there, I fall into a deep dream and see myself, Angora, Felinez, and Aphro as our alley cat alter egos, homeless and looking for something—anything—to eat. Aphro warns me not to stick my nose into a discarded can of tuna. "There's something foul in there," she warns me. Somehow I know she's talking about something else. I spend the rest of my dream attempting to figure out what she's really trying to tell me. But she just stares at me, her piercing brown eyes squinting and the fur of her black coat rising. I try to swipe her with my paw, but even as a cat she runs faster than me. "You'll never catch me," she taunts me, climbing magically to the top of a tenement building. "And you should stop spending so much time chasing after your own tail."

When I wake up, the only thing I realize is, even as a cat Aphro gets under my fur—and now I'm convinced, she is definitely hiding *something*.

4

It's been forever since my dilapidated desktop has taken an unplanned trip to Style Siberia and gone into deep freeze.

"Pash, the Red Cross is not coming to your rescue, so you're going to have to rely on the kindness of strangers," coaxes Angora. Her shady plan for thawing my computer crisis: instead of noshing on today's exotic lunch special in the Fashion Café, we're descending upon the Dalmation Tech "dog pound" across the street.

"You mean the kindness of strange students," I protest.

"*C'est vrai, chérie.* Zeus says their bulletin board is littered with listings 'from computer show-offs pimping their services for next to *nada*' or so he put it," relays Angora.

"Well, let's hope Mr. Tasti D-Lite is right," I giggle to mask my irritation with Angora for ad-lipping with the mink zebra hatter about my technical difficulties. But that's Angora—always aiding and abetting. She probably thought Zeus could lend a helping paw because he's a visual merchandising major, but little did she know he's a dunce on the download just like the rest of us.

Aphro thinks our plan is pointless. "You shouldn't be going across the street," she warns us.

"Do you have a better idea?" I ask her.

"No, but maybe you should just wait until someone else can fix your computer," she offers.

"No thanks. I'm already falling behind on my Catwalk duties," I gripe.

Aphro bails from our bid and we can't figure out why, but I'm through with trying to figure out Aphro anyway. Anna Rex cuts in front of us without a poised "pardon me" to make a hasty retreat to the Fashion Lounge. "No doubt for a barf attack," notes Angora. Victoria's Secret is out—about Anna Rex and her crew, anyway: black is de rigueur for them, probably to cover the stains and dribbles from their rampant bulimia bouts. I make a sour face, but Angora misinterprets it.

"Aw, come on, Pash, you look like a kitten without a mitten," coos Angora. "Aphro is right. You should tell Zeus how much you *j'adore* him."

"Puhleez. Now you sound like Ms. Ava."

"*Arrête. Stop.* I cannot discuss my mother before lunch," pleads Angora.

"Oh, no, I can't deal with this before lunch, either," I moan. Ice Très is sauntering in our direction with that smirk on his face that makes me melt.

"Yes, you can!" Angora says. She tugs at my arm like I'm a child, because she thinks I'm getting chilly feet about our latest Operation: Kitty Litter.

"I'm not talking about that. I mean *that*!" I say under my breath, trying to subtly turn my eyeballs in Ice Très's direction without moving a facial muscle so Angora can catch my drift.

But the Urban Thug designer is upon us before we can flee the fashion scene. "Wazzup, pussycat?" Ice Très says, sweetly, like he just hollered at me yesterday.

Ice Très does his trifecta tease: grins widely, showing off his big goofy white teeth, sets off his dimples and makes his chocolate brown eyes twinkle, then winks. It works every time. I can feel myself melting against my iron will. I continue to stare up at Ice Très, remembering how much I like that he's so tall. "Oh, hi. I haven't seen you in a minute," I say, telling a fiberoni. Truth is, my Fashion Lounge appearances have multiplied like white rabbit boleros in my attempt to avoid this lethal eye contact with the infamous tagger.

"Yeah, well, I've been out of pocket for a minute. My mom was hospitalized—cuz of her diabetes," he explains, sadly.

"Oh, is she okay?" Angora asks, sounding concerned.

"Yeah, I get her moving every morning now to

362

golden oldies. She had to step up the exercise and cut out the red velvet cake—know what I'm saying?" he chuckles. "But we're dealing with it."

I know that's not the only reason Ice Très has been absentee, but there is no need to point out his much-publicized suspension. He probably feels foul for being disqualified from the Catwalk competition. Sure enough, Ice Très gives me props for my enviable position. "That's crazy cool, you hanging in there, Miss Boo-Kitty Leader."

"Catwalk leader," I say, correcting him.

"But check this, I wanna show you my new sketches for my line—since you're gonna snag the Big Willie come June," he jokes, buttering me up like a Parisian croissant. His ploy is working, too, because I can feel my crust flaking off. Of course, Ice Très is referring to the sought-after bronze dress-form trophy bestowed upon the winner of the annual Catwalk competition. The award's name was chosen in honor of F.I.'s founding father, William Dresser.

"What about Shalimar?" I ask, looking for further strokes. All of a sudden, I wonder if Miss Earl Grey still plans to be serving him tea in her family's penthouse digs now that he's out of her fashion house.

"She's got skills, no doubt, but you're the prize," he says, winking and blinking. "Come hang out with me next Friday at Native—this fly spot uptown—so I can show you what I'm up to. You know I've got to maintain my reputation."

"Um, what reputation?" I ask, pretending I'm not fully familiar with his self-proclaimed fame.

"You know—I'm the notorious tagger from Highway 20. I told you that, right?" he says, having the decency to blush from his own bold hype.

"Yes, I think I read that in the Catwalk blog," I say absentmindedly, as if I don't recall every line of his blog entries verbatim. Nonetheless, it's definitely time for Shalimar to share, whether she likes it or not. "Awright—pick me up."

"Awright—seven o'clock?"

"That's groovy," I second.

"Awright—I gotta jet—take care of this prescription thing for my mom," he explains.

I refrain from telling him what we're up to, and luckily so does Angora. She just smiles sweetly at him as we bid him *adieu*.

"He is *très* charmed and dangerous," Angora says, like she's a dating expert.

"Do you think he's going out with Shalimar?" I ask, gloating.

"I don't know, Pash," admits Angora.

"Well, you must have heard the word on the street, no?" I say, trying to stimulate the brain cells underneath her Helene Berman powder blue beret with the satin bow on the side.

"Um, no, I haven't—but I suggest we start *crossing the street*," Angora says, taking my arm. "I wonder what is up with Aphro."

"Who knows? But I'm not down with it," I groan.

We exit school to meet Felinez, who has agreed to tag along. "I can't believe you'd pass up today's special—yuca corn bread and jalapeño sausage dumplings—for this humiliation," I say, beaming at Felinez, who is propped against the pink wrought iron gates. I know that the only thing Felinez loves more than sniffing foil leather hides is aromatic dishes served steaming hot. Instead, she decided to settle for a quick snack run to Stingy Lulu's newsstand to snag some crunchies.

"I'm such a glutton, um, for punishment?" admits Felinez, abruptly shoving a bag of Mariquitas plantain chips into her bounty-full hobo bag.

"Well, I must be, too, because I'm never going to stop hounding you for that hobo—no matter how many times you adamantly say no!" coos Angora. She is always pumping up Fifi's product. Today's handcrafted offering: a black leather fringed hobo bag lined with opulent white rabbit fur. She made it for her final project last semester.

"Well, you're gonna have to get in line, cuz I swore

to Chenille I'd leave it to her in my last will and testament!" Felinez says modestly, wiping the crumbs from her mouth.

"Puhleez, she's lucky you even speak to her," I gripe. I know that Chenille digs Felinez's fashionable handiwork, which says a lot, since I wouldn't put *fashion* and *my sister* in the same sentence. That reminds me to ask Fifi about intel. "Have you heard anyone say anything about me, or the House of Pashmina?"

"You mean aside from the usual—that we're stuck-up?" Felinez asks, sounding confused.

"Chenille knows something—I think," I explain to her.

"Well, you should ask her," suggests Felinez.

"Trust me, that was a waste of time," I reply.

"Well, wait till you see what I sketched for the meeting later!" Felinez says, moving on.

We turn our eyes to Caterina and her Teen Style Network crew, who are camped by the pink pansy trees. "Not one sound bite about my computer crisis," I warn Felinez and Angora under my breath.

They nod in silent agreement as we put our fashion game faces on and wave wildly at the Teen Style crew. Flanked by my best friends, I slowly drag my kitten heels across the wide traverse to the treacherous terrain known as Dalmation land.

"Now I know what it must have felt like for the

brave Indians crossing the fifty-three-mile Bering Strait sixty thousand years ago!" announces Angora when we reach the other side. Then she pats her pale blue beret in place like it's a security blanket.

Felinez giggles nervously.

"Knuckleheads dead ahead," I whisper with dread, trying not to look into the two sets of hungry eyeballs shielded by dark gray hoodies stationed in our path.

Felinez glares directly at them while tugging at the hem of her red corduroy skirt.

"What a pudgy predicament!" the shorter one snickers like a goofy chipmunk.

My cheeks flush instantly. "Well, if it isn't the dingy duo!" I hiss back, remembering their stint last week on *our* fashionable turf. Angora tries to smooth their rough edges by beaming at them like they're official members of the Dalmation Tech welcoming committee.

But Felinez has had it up to her hobo. "No more, *graci-ass!*" she gripes. Obviously, the thought of encountering more Dalmations who stare at her like she's spicy lunch meat is more than she can stomach. Felinez rifles through her beloved bag and whips out a brochure—stuffing it defiantly into Angora's hand. "Here, *está bien.* I'm gonna do something more productive—like finish the sketches for later!"

"Come on, Fifi. Stop. *Parate!*" I coo in Spanish, trying to coax her.

Angora sighs sweetly. "Okay, *chérie*," she concedes, quickly stuffing the glossy brochure into her Princess Lion white and gold shopper.

By now the Dalmation dog packs have multiplied to watch Felinez's bouncy exit.

"Don't go! They don't love you at Faggots International like we do!" barks one of the Dalmation dogs.

"They're just plain *rude*!" Angora frets loudly to me, causing the scrutiny to shift back to us.

"Let's get inside. We've got more eyes on us than the shoplifters at Macy's!" I warn.

"They're just plain rude!" chortles one of the boys in a fluttery voice, imitating Angora's Southern accent.

Angora purses her lips, twitching her mouth sideways, which she does when she's trying to digest sour thoughts. I put my arm gently on her shoulder, then strike a brave pose, flinging open the dilapidated, dingy gray metal doors to enter the school's elaborate security checkpoint.

"Computer theft must be on the rise," comments Angora, coolly, trying to regain her sweet composure.

What I'm more interested in, however, is the glossy brochure sticking out of her bag. "What did Felinez give you?"

"Oh. That. Um, Beau wants to take me and Je' Taime to Colombia for Christmas, which we have to book soon," Angora explains, hesitantly. "So Fifi got me, um, some travel packages." She gingerly hands me the trifold brochure to look at.

"Oh, right," I say, recalling how psyched Felinez is that her parents' band will be performing in the Cali Fair, which is held from Christmas to New Year's Eve. According to Fifi, the Cali Fair rivals Carnival in Rio with its salsa marathon concerts, *calbagatas* (horse riding parades), and masqueraded movers and shakers. "Well, I'm glad somebody is going."

"I wish Felinez was going with us," Angora says, wistfully. After all, the Carteras have lots of relatives in Bogotá. John Cartera, Felinez's father, makes up the Colombian half of Felinez's Latin equation. It would mean so much to Fifi to see her eighty-five-year-old *nena* (great grandmother), who takes her false teeth out at the dinner table to eat a plate of *platanos* "gummy-style."

"Well, let's hope Dad's check arrives in time, or we won't be going, either," says Angora, blushing like she's embarrassed that Funny Bunny is funding her holiday hoopla.

Angora's angst is cut short by the menacing security guard's barking order: "Open your bags, please."

We hop to it and hold our breath while he checks our bags. He's so thorough I'm surprised he doesn't call in some real Dalmatian dogs to conduct a sniff test.

Afterward, Angora conducts her own sniff test:

"The hallways are in desperate need of Stick Ups," she concludes, twitching her sensitive nose as we head to the security desk for our visitor's passes.

"I wonder how Lurch knew we aren't students here," I muse, jokingly.

"Because we're not gray?" concludes Angora, looking around at the scant few female students on the move in their non-coloric baggy pants and sweatshirts.

"Ghetto wear," I observe, disapprovingly. I hate anything that smacks of uniform, and lots of urban gear fits that category too neatly, if you ask me. At that moment, my point is proven. Loquasia Madden, Chenille's crony who lives in Building B across our courtyard, whizzes by, giving me the strangest look followed by a smirk.

"She knows something, too," I say, getting paranoid.

"She's your sister's friend—what do you expect?" Angora says while she's trying to navigate us safely through the inquisitive masses. "Okay, this way."

"Well, I guess we're right on time—to be the lunch special today," I say as we ease up to the Computer Annex bulletin board. We're immediately flanked by grungy boys wearing clunky glasses.

Like a fashion journalist on assignment, Angora ignores the eyes on us and whips out a pad, pointing with her blue feather-topped pen: "Let's see—this one looks, um—"

"Catchy?" I say, wincing at the GET THE FACTS notice in bright red letters warning about the rise of meningococcal meningitis in teens.

"Not that one—this one," Angora says, placing the plumage on her pen at the ad in question.

"Oh. Less infectious," I say. I read the listing in question.

YOUR PC AND ME: COMPLETELY COMPATIBLE. FAMILIAR WITH MICROSOFT WINDOWS, MEMORY INSTALLATION, INTEL PENTIUM DUAL-CORE PROCESSOR REQUIREMENTS, AND LCD MONITORS. MAJOR: COMPUTER TECHNOLOGY. WILL WORK FOR A LETTER OF REFERENCE FOR AFTER-SCHOOL CREDITS. CALL ME: CHRIS MIDGETT, 212-555-HELP.

"That can't possibly be his name, can it?" I ask in disbelief. The eavesdropping ears behind me answer instead of Angora.

"Yep, that's his real name, but maybe I can help you?"

I turn abruptly to face the nosy intruder. "My computer is frozen," I reveal.

"Is it a Mac?" he asks.

I stammer for a second, because I'm busy peering into his glasses, which are so thick I wonder if they're bulletproof.

"No, it's a PC," interjects Angora.

"Oh," he says, snobbily. "Well, I could look at it. . . . But mostly everyone has a Mac now."

"Right. I'll run right over to Apple and charge one—in pink," I say, sarcastically.

Mr. Mac Attack turns sheepish. "Well, I'm just telling you—nobody is into the disk operating system anymore. It's virus city."

"Um, you know what? We're good," I reply.

Mr. Mac Attack treats our lack of interest like it's a phase in his computer programming. "So, you go across the street?" he asks rhetorically.

"Yes, siree," Angora says, sweetly.

"You're models, right?" he asks, his lip twitching.

"Almost, but we're not *flattery* operated," I say, determined to move to final phase.

Mr. Mac Attack does his version of freezing, because he stands as still as a statue while we ignore him and scribble down a few more freebie listings. Then I drag Angora by the arm away from his gooey gaze.

Once we're outside, Angora lays on a dose of Ms. Ava's instruction. "Pash, you don't have to be so mean."

"Yes, I do," I retort.

When we're safely back on our side of the "strait," Angora takes a deep breath.

"Are you okay?" I ask, concerned. Angora was born with an asthma condition that she almost never complains about.

She nods. "It's not my breathing—it was the dreary decor I did not adore."

"I have two words for that dog pound—*Extreme Makeover: Home Edition*," I add.

"Pash, that was four words."

"I'm being generous today," I quip. "Ramon could do wonders with that place." After a moment's pause, I add, "Well, let's hope he keeps doing wonders at my house."

Heading to the side entrance of school, I whip out my cell phone to dial Chris Midgett. "I hope this is worth it," I moan after I leave a number on the answering machine.

"How does he sound?" Angora asks me.

"Like someone who can fix my computer," I retort.

Deep house music pipes up over the loudspeaker—our cue for changing periods—which means we have to hustle to get to the next class. (At Fashion International, loud bells are prohibited.) I have fashion merchandising and Angora has fashion journalism class.

"You know, I wish you could go with us to Colombia for Christmas," Angora says, looking back at me longingly.

"Trust me, I know," I coo. And I really do. "But I'm going to Native next Friday—and that sounds exotic enough for *moi*!"

FASHION INTERNATIONAL 35th ANNUAL CATWALK COMPETITION BLOG

New school rule: You don't have to be ultranice, but don't get tooooo catty, or your posting will be zapped by the Fashion Avengers!

REAL MODELS DON'T EAT TRUFFLES. . . .

I'm tired of apologizing for the genetic fact that I was born tall and skinny with innate sophistication, which is why I look totally chic in Chanel, even at the age of 16. The truth is, if the fashion biz did not demand models to be precisely what I am naturally, then I wouldn't have a career to look fashion-forward to, or a place in the world that's tailor-made for my 23-inch waistline. I know there have been rampant rumors about my so-called sordid methods for being so naturally thin. What's sordid is this kind of speculation without proof. We all judge each other rather harshly at F.I., because that comes with the fashion territory, and I wouldn't even pay it any attention if any of my personality assessments were true, including the one that I'm also snobby and superficial. Since we're being televised and will have to watch this footage for a long time, perhaps we should all point out our positive traits as well. So that's why I'm pointing out one of the reasons I wanted to become a house leader in the Catwalk competition: to be an advocate for tall girls' right to stand out and not have to slouch in order to make those less endowed feel more secure. I, for one, want the Teen Style Network footage to reflect how well-rounded we are as students. And compassionate. Did you know that my TALL counterparts around the globe who aren't in the fashion industry aren't as lucky as I am? Take Leonid Stadnik from Podolyantsi, Ukraine, for example, who is recognized by the Guinness World Records as the tallest human in the world at 8 feet, 5 inches tall. Likeable and qualified, Stadnik had to quit a job he loved as a veterinarian because of his height. Why is it the ailing animals he treated seemed at ease with his towering presence, but Stadnik's boss got tired of craning his neck upward to shout orders, and therefore fired him? Or why wasn't the doorway of the Antsi Animal Clinic made higher to accommodate Stadnik?

Speaking of discrimination, there are people of average height and looks roaming the hallways of F.I. who are more interested in gossiping about what's going on in the House of Anna Rex than the gossamer chiffon gowns in Giorgio Armani's spring collection. I've been hearing grunts that the models in my house are all skinny, tall, and blond. First of all, fashionistas at F.I. are trained to be as discerning about dart and dovetail details as we are about "information disbursement." So that is not totally accurate: all the models in my house are NOT blond! But why should I have to apologize for my artistic choice in models, anyway? The Houses of Ricci and Chloé don't. Nor does the House of Gucci, who clearly acknowledge by their choice in mannequins that the longer the neck and legs, the longer the return on their orders. That's why I will be using mannequins that will make the most of my design strategy.

There is one other thing that becomes tiring when you're tall and skinny: people asking how you remain so thin. Do you know what I crave for dessert? Attention, that's what. Not $1,000 Golden Opulence Sundaes. I'd rather obsess about the Sonia Rykiel cashmere tube skirt I could buy for the same amount—and how totally chic it will look on me and the models in the House of Anna Rex.

Posted by Who's Blonder at 13:22:05

5

At five o'clock on the polka dot, most of my crew is inside Studio C for our bimonthly Catwalk meeting. That includes Aphro, Felinez, Angora, Dame Leeds, Lupo, Nole, and Diamond Tyler. Dr. Zeus strolls in at one minute past, wearing his mink zebra-striped hat, a black turtleneck, baggy black cargo pants, and Adidas sneakers. He walks up to me and gives me a tight hug with his taut, muscled arms, then kisses me on my cheek. "I got a great idea for the scrims on the runway," he says.

I beam at Zeus approvingly, despite wishing his ideas involved *moi* personally.

By five-fifteen, it seems that all my team members have arrived. I stand at the head of the conference table to address the furbulous forty. After carefully scanning the room, however, I notice that one adorable kitty is missing. Instantly, I switch gears from heady head of state to fretting Fabbie Tabby who has just given birth to the largest litter in feline history. "Anybody seen Liza *FLAKE*?" I ask, directing my probe at Dame Leeds, who is the lead hairstylist and Liza's immediate boss in the hierarchy of our house. "An answer in this lifetime would be groovy."

Sucking his teeth, Dame crosses his arms against his tangerine cashmere sweater. "She was *supposed* to be here with my sketches!"

Lupo Saltimbocca, who is sitting with his arm resting on his prized Nikon camera, decides to lighten the tension: "Pashmina. What did you do to your hair today? I *love* it. *E molto bellissimo*. It reminds me of fusilli!" he says. Involuntarily, I twirl one of my curls. "*Fusilli*—funny how that word keeps coming up," I mumble under my breath.

Aphro throws me a weird look, which reminds me that I still have to get to the bottom of *that* barrel of crabs. At last, my assistant, Chintzy Colon, tries to put Liza in the loop. "I saw her running out of algebra class early today, and I tried to say hi and that I would see her later, but she didn't answer me," she offers, her head swaying, which causes her thick, dark ponytail to swish to the side like a horse's mane.

Felinez rolls her eyes at Chintzy, to whom she has an aversion, like artificial sweetener. A stern glance at Fifi, however, swiftly communicates *Keep your eyelids to yourself!* I'm not going to lie: I was also skittish about the PR Chica myself, because she ran against me in the Catwalk elections and plied half the student body with homemade chorizos during her campaign. (The *PR* stands for *public relations*—Chintzy's major—not *Puerto Rican*, although that applies to her as well.) Now I'm glad that Chintzy was so persistent about joining my house. She's turning out to be the one fashionista I can rely on.

"All the members of my house know they're supposed to clear absences with me prior," I state, annoyed. "If anyone else has a valid reason for not attending a meeting, now is the time to let me know—not *after* you pull a Houdini." I glance over disapprovingly at divo Dame, who should keep his assistant hairstylist in check. "Absolute-*tamont*," he says in accordance.

"Well, I got a job at Tracy Reese!" belts out Ruthie Dragon. Ruthie is Nole Canoli's and Diamond Tyler's appointed design assistant. Adding my model appreciation classmate to the roster was the one concession I had to make to get Nole Canoli to join the House of Pashmina. "It's not gonna interfere with me coming to meetings, though. *And* I can borrow shoes and accessories from the wardrobe closet for our show! Well, some, anyway."

"Wow, pieces from Reese's. That's quite a coup," I say, squelching my Gucci Envy. As I circulate our latest hookup list, I secretly wonder how Ruthie, out of tens of dozens of students, snagged the position with the only black designer garnering respect right now on Seventh Avenue. I hand the thick stack to Kissa, one of the models, to pass around the table. Swiping her honey blond–streaked eye-covering bangs to the side, Kissa hands the stack down to Bobby Beat, our lead makeup artist, whose bangs are even blonder and longer than hers. The rest of his hair is tucked neatly into a stubby, short ponytail. "Ooh, you are so Too Faced today," he quips to me. My cheeks burn from embarrassment as I wonder what he's getting at, until I realize that he is referring to my golden beige sparkly eye shadow—from Too Faced Cosmetics. "Oh, thank you," I say, graciously.

While the sheets are still making their way around, Chintzy chirpily asks, "Didn't you just get a job, too, Miss Aphro?"

Aphro squirms in her chair before she responds. "Oh, right—um, I just found out."

I shriek inside. By the look on Angora's face, I realize she's as puzzled pink as I am.

"I'm going to be working at this new designer's boutique—um, Jones Uptown—in Harlem as soon as it opens," Aphro spurts out.

"That's faboo!" exclaims Bobby Beat, clapping his hands together. "Who is the designer?"

"Laretha Jones—it's her first time out the gate," explains Aphro, like she's describing a Thoroughbred at Belmont.

"Is she a black designer?" asks Ruthie Dragon, curiously.

Aphro nods. "She worked for years for Adolpho on Seventh Avenue. Ms. Fab—um, I mean, Ms. Lynx—was even the showroom model there back then."

I crumble again inside while Miss Aphro sits there repeating spoon-fed fashion herstory! I earnestly try to make eye contact with Miss Bright, but she won't look at me; instead, she gazes blankly at the conference table, twirling the ends of the lariat wrapped around her neck like a lasso.

"Oh, I never heard of her," admits Bobby Beat, apologetically.

"See, everybody is always sleeping on *black* designers," quips Ruthie Dragon. "But let Jessica Simpson or some other tawdry no-talent-of-the-moment come out with a clothing line—that they ain't even designed—and everybody from *Women's Wear Daily* to the London *Tatler* puts them on blast like they're *haute!*"

"Preach!" quips Nole. "That's gonna change, though, when my Canoli label drops and kicks off a Black renaissance like *haute* buttered soul!"

"I can dig that," Zeus says with a nod.

Twirling my curls furiously, I ignore the fashion forecasting, obsessing about Aphrodite getting mighty employed.

"Well, black designers aren't the only ones who have it bad," interjects Diamond Tyler. "I mean, I can't believe what they're doing to police dogs in Düsseldorf."

"Break it down, Diamond," chides Nole Canoli. Even Countess Coco's ears perk up at the prattle. As usual, Nole's prized Pomeranian is perched in a black Prada bag.

Flustered, Diamond explains: "The German and Belgian shepherds have been fitted with blue plastic-fiber shoes, supposedly to protect their paws, but it's really so they can work longer hours in the harshest weather conditions. In an interview, the police spokesman had the nerve to say, 'The dogs don't like it, but they'll get used to it.'"

Suddenly, there is a loud knock on the door.

"That better be Miss Liza before I reprise her!" Dame exclaims, dramatically popping up from his chair to open the door. Turns out, of course, it's the usual suspects—Caterina and her four-man crew.

"Can we come in?" asks Caterina, rhetorically. While her crew plunk down their equipment and hurry to get into focus, Caterina apologizes profusely for interrupting. "I would have been here on time but the meeting for the House of Moet ran over," she reveals.

"Speaking of Moet's house, lemme tell you what I heard be going on when the lights are out in her real habitat," blurts out Benny Madina. Benny is one of our models, with chiseled chocolate features and long copper dreadlocks.

"Ooh—what?" asks Nole.

"Well, you know Moet lives with her aunt, right? Well, honey, before she goes to bed every night, Ms. Mabel takes out her one false eyeball and sticks it in a tub of Vaseline!" Benny dishes like a gawdy gossip columnist. "Even the bedbugs don't bite at night, cuz they too scared that eyeball is watching them!"

"You need to stop, cuz you are wearing me out with the T and crumpets," snickers Nole.

Zeus and Lupo burst out laughing, causing a ricochet of cackles.

"Awright, lights out on the fun house—let's turn to Catwalk topics," I say, sharply. "I'd like to begin with ideas for the Design Challenge, shall we?"

Surprisingly, Aphro's hand shoots up first. I take a deep breath and look Aphro straight in the face, hiding my angst. "So what do you have?"

Aphro plops her purple macramé tote on the table, then pulls out her purple folder. Lupo Saltimbocca breaks out in a grin, clicking away with his camera. His job is to document our whole Catwalk competition process until June, but I'm now convinced he must have enough photos to open an Aphro photo gallery exhibit *pronto*.

"What do we pass every day, right? Graffiti. It's everywhere—on walls, buses, the subways. So," Aphro says, pulling a stack of faux ivory, Lucite, and black resin bangles out of her bag with a flourish, "we could engrave bangles with words and phrases from the graffiti we see every day."

"Oh, I love that, *chérie!*" coos Angora.

"Does it have to be slip-on bangles, though?" asks Felinez. "I hate those—they never slip on my hand!"

"Mine either," moans Phallon, the plus-size model in my house.

"We should get hinged bangles, no?" I ask Aphro directly.

"We could," Aphro says, hesitantly.

"Does it have to be bangles, though? I mean, can't we put the graffiti on something else? Everybody is wearing bangles now," counters Chintzy, flashing the Splenda-fortified smile that drives Felinez cuckoo.

"No, no, I dig it," I say, dismissing Chintzy's objection. "Um, the first one has to be 'Tink Pink.' Everybody says 'Think Pink,' but the House of Pashmina is all about creating our own messages."

"'*Perfecto*,'" seconds Lupo.

"No, '*Purr*fecto,'" I say, then spell it out. "That will be the second engraving, and the third will be our battle cry: 'Sashay, Parlay'!"

"How about 'Powder to the People'—my personal fave?" suggests Bobby Beat.

"It's a keeper," I say, beaming at Bobby.

"Don't the sayings have to be things we pass every

day? I mean, that's what the Design Challenge says, right?" interjects Ruthie Dragon.

"Yeah, but the things we pass every day aren't just outdoors. They're things from our own indoor environments. I have those sayings scribbled on my walls, so who's to say it's not from our everyday life?" I say.

Ruthie Dragon stares at me, clearly tense, but I ignore her.

"I think we should put the sayings on the garments, too. Like you said, graffiti is everywhere," suggests Nole, stroking Countess Coco's head.

"Well, why can't we do both?" offers Diamond Tyler.

"Done—and done," I order.

"Why does it just have to be graffiti?" asks Kimono "Mini Mo" Harris, who is Bobby Beat's makeup assistant.

"Actually, I was just going to amend our direction," I say, nodding. "The sayings can come from advertisements, posters, billboards—anywhere, really."

"There's an old poster for the play *The Color Purple* by my house. I mean, it's practically peeling off, but every morning when I look out the window, I see it on the back of the building facing me," claims model Mink Yong, who lives in Hell's Kitchen off Eighth Avenue and Forty-ninth Street.

"We don't want to take any trademarked messages—otherwise we could get into a copyright infringement thing," I say, pondering Mink's suggestion.

"Yeah, but something like 'The Color Purple' could play off the fact that it's Aphro's favorite color," Angora says, sweetly.

"Yeah, that it is . . . ," I say, my voice trailing off. Ruthie Dragon breathes fire in my direction again, so I say for her sake: "You can't copyright a title, anyway—unless it's a trademarked advertisement slogan or something—so we could definitely go with that one."

"Are you sure?" Ruthie asks, challenging me.

"We covered it in fashion business class," Chintzy offers.

I smile at Nole as if to say, *Well, at least one of our assistants isn't sleeping in class.*

Now Felinez shoots up her hand. "My idea is kinda similar," she says sheepishly, whipping out her sketches. "I mean, all the advertisements we see on the bus shelters and the phone booths—and everywhere. We can make our own ads," she explains, holding up her sketch pad. "So these are plastic tote bags representing the glass bus shelters, and the ads will be printed on the front and back of the totes. And on the big belts and hats, too." She shows us a few sketches. "One could be like a fake movie poster: 'Strut, Pussycat, Strut!' "

"That is sooo cute!" exclaims Elgamela Sphinx.

She blushes at the prancing cat in a micro mini in the middle of a street in Times Square, the title in neon lights blazing on a movie marquee above her. I watch as Zeus beams at Elgamela. I wish he would look at me like that.

The next sketch is a tote bag featuring the fake poster for a spooky TV series: *Bad Blood*.

"Ooh, that is wicked," squeals Elgamela.

"Um, maybe a little too wicked for me. Can we please stay away from ads with vampires dripping blood? Leave that sort of nourishment for the House of Anna," I suggest, then get embarrassed, because I don't want to be caught saying anything controversial on camera. But it's too late; Boom's lens is coming right at me amid a round of "Ooh, shade boots!" from Dame Leeds and associates.

Felinez blushes and moves to the next set of sketches. One is for Feisty Feline Cat Food, featuring an adorable plump Persian, and another is a fake "Cat-woman" movie poster.

"Now we're back on track," I say, smiling.

"I dig the belts," coos Diamond. The wide see-through belts have a montage of the advertisements and big pink sequined buckles.

"For the guys, we can use see-through duffel bags with the advertisements—sorta slung over their shoulders?" suggests Felinez.

"This is gonna work. I want bags, belts, and a few vinyl hats, too, okay?" I advise Felinez.

She nods approvingly.

"Okay, so I think we'll do the kiddie wear, then the urban wear segment," I inform my crew, looking around for approval. "And the bangles will be worn with coordinating active and street wear with slogans on them—and we've got the bags with the advertisements and various posters. We'll call the two-part segment of the fashion show "Word on the Street." I pull out my pad and start scribbling.

Now Zeus raises his hand. "What I wanted to do is light the scrims onstage with colors from the traffic lights—green lights, red lights, yellow lights. I can do sequences with blinking lights on the traffic signs, so it will be like subliminal messages."

"Traffic signs of our own making," I suggest. " 'Feline Crossing One Mile Ahead.' 'Kitty Trail Next Right.' "

"Exactly," says Zeus, nodding enthusiastically.

"Okay, I think we've nailed the Design Challenge," I say, then pause. "Um, Aphro had a good idea. We should do a segment with sleepwear—raggedy bathrobes, pajamas, cat-head bedroom slippers—like the ones we wear every day?" I suggest.

"Does it have to be raggedy?" Nole says, snobbily.

"Yes, raggedy—and we'll throw newspapers on the

floor that we pick up and read while standing at the end of the runway," I say, thinking out loud.

"I'm not designing anything with threads hanging off of it—or that looks like it's been eaten by bats. Otherwise I could just pull stuff out of my mother's closet!" gripes Nole. His mother, Claudia Canoli, maneuvers through most of her life from her Hoveround chair. She is obese and needs to have hip-replacement surgery that she can't afford. Nole told us she works for an Internet real estate company out of their apartment and sits around in her bathrobe all day, almost never leaving the house, except to run errands.

I decide it best not to challenge Nole in front of the camera. "They don't have to be raggedy," I concede, "but we will do bathrobes and pajamas—and the kids will be included in that segment, too."

"Well, put me in pajamas with Felix the Cat—that's what I wore when I was little," Zeus says, heckling.

This time, the snickers are needed, so I allow them before I move on. "Now for the moment we've all been waiting for—sketches for the collection. Diamond, Nole, what do you have for us?" I say, waiting with bated breath.

Without a flourish, Diamond shows us the sketches so far. "Even before the graffiti idea, I got the idea to embroider sayings across the rear of the sweatpants," Diamond says, proudly.

I feel my cheeks burning, but I bite my tongue to refrain from telling Diamond that her idea is dated. I conjure up the image of me in my Juicy pants that Mrs. Paul disapproved of. Dame, on the other hand, decides to make a dig. "Why on earth would we want to do something that everybody from Juicy, Lucy, and Victoria has done in shrill overkill? Honey, the secret is out. Where have you been?"

Diamond blanches like an almond. "Victoria's Secret uses stamped letters!" she says, her voice cracking. Blinking hard, Diamond is struggling to fight back tears.

"Um, Diamond, I love script embroidery, but on the back of terry cloth jogging pants, it does bite into Juicy's joint," I say, sweetly.

"I—I don't think so," she stammers. "There were designers doing it before Juicy."

"Exactly," Nole says, with a defeated sigh.

"Awright," I say, deciding to make a declaration. "Let's stick with our original idea and stay away from script scribblings—period."

"What about doing cat heads on the rear in rhinestones?" counters Diamond, like she's not down for the count—yet.

"Baby Phat does that," Chintzy says.

"Theirs are stenciled, but Hello Kitty does it—on scarves and hats—so good-bye to that idea," I sigh. "But I have one."

Everyone stops fidgeting in the seats and sits as still as a statue to hear what I have to say, like E. F. Hutton has spoken. "We put cat tattoos on the models' bare shoulders for the baby-doll dresses and tops segment."

"That's very feline fatale," says Angora in agreement.

"Where are the sketches for baby-doll off-the-shoulder dresses and tops?" I ask.

Diamond looks at me blankly, which means she hasn't done them yet, so I egg her along. "Okay, what else?"

"These are poodle-neck pullover terry tops that I wanted to pair with the pants," Diamond continues.

"Feline fatale and poodles?" I ask, surprised at Diamond's obvious U-turn into a stranded fashion desert.

"No embroidered logos, no rhinestone cat heads, no poodle necks. Done—and done squared," seconds Nole, motioning for Diamond to continue. She is totally frozen like an out-of-season mannequin in a Macy's window waiting to be re-dressed.

"Keep going, Diamond," orders Nole, a little too brusquely.

Now Diamond looks like she's melting and closes her sketchbook in resignation.

"Don't pack up your crayons and head to the sandbox by yourself, girl," blurts out Dame.

"Please . . . show us the rest of what you got," I say, softly.

Diamond ponders her position, smooths back her brown curly hair, then pouts. "For the third segment, I thought we should do some catsuits for the girls and scuba suits for the guys."

"Now that's what I'm talking about," coos Aphro, enthusiastically. We all study the sketches, laying on the oohs and aahs like junk-box jewels.

" 'Slink, Don't Slouch,' " I say, brainstorming more slogans. "That's another slogan. Chintzy, write that down, please," I instruct my assistant. "I think we should pair the walking-advertisement belts with hot pants and vests and catsuits. Zip-up patent leather boots will set these off lovelily, too."

"I think we should stay away from black, though," suggests Dame.

"But I like it for hot pants and catsuits," I say, looking around for approval.

"I agree, *mija*," says Felinez. "Think slink." Felinez is in charge of organizing all the footwear and accessories except for jewelry, which is Aphro's department.

"What about leather pants?" asks Dame Leeds.

"Do you have leather pants money?" I ask him. Realizing that the camera is on, I quickly shoot him one of Chintzy's snap-on smiles.

"We're doing lots of, um, *leatherette*, anyway, with the catsuits and hot pants and vests. I think that's enough," offers Diamond.

"Pleather is not leather, honey," quips Dame. "And this is the sort of sketch I was going to suggest." Obviously Dame had been sitting at the conference table concocting a replacement sketch, since Liza didn't show up with his original ones. And here I thought he was talking about hairstyle sketches. I look at the amateur rendering of a leather jacket with zippers, gadget pockets, and a spaceship collar that looks like it's about to take off—*not* set it off.

"That's very interesting," I say, lying for his sake.

"So can we use it?" Dame asks directly.

I glance over at Nole, who isn't letting me off the hook. I know because he has taken out a tube of Kiehl's hand moisturizer and he squirts some into the palm of his left hand before carefully massaging it on both of his paws. This is Nole's nervous habit, how he takes himself out of the moment, like my hair-pulling.

"No, I don't think so," I say, hesitantly.

"Well, excuse me, Miss Donatella!" Dame says with a huff.

I decide it best to cut off Dame's designing moment like a loose thread. "Okay, so what do we have for evening?" I query Diamond and Nole.

"For evening—corset tops paired with long tattersall skirts, tapered pants, and tapered long skirts with bustles," advises Nole.

"I know what would look *très* romantic to wear with that," interjects Angora, smoothing down her beret in the front. "Berets with big satin bows in front," she says, proudly.

"Wow, I dig that!" I say.

"That sounds cutesy," Aphro replies. "And feline fatale style should be bursting at the seams with scratch appeal."

"And that's exactly what we'll be doing to fit into those things!" shoots Phallon, letting out the tension with her own seam ripper. "Busting out!" Clearly she's a little insecure about fitting her 38DDD *bust*line into the Carmen-style corset tops with velvet ruffle trim and hook-and-eye closures up the front.

"Don't worry—at the show the dressers will have you trussed up like a turkey!" says Nole.

"That's exactly what I'm worried about!" counters Phallon, thoroughly annoyed. She squirms in her chair, obviously uncomfortable. I can tell she's wearing one of those high-waisted girdles, which my mother never leaves home without, by the way she pushes up her rib cage to catch her breath.

"Oh, come on, Phallon. It will be fun," coos Elgamela, batting her fluttery eyelashes.

"Fun for you. Not for me! And fun for the audience if one of Phallon's ta-tas topples on them!" warns Phallon.

"My vision for feline fatale fashion has always been for both regular and plus-size models to wear the same silhouettes—and not be confined by their size," I explain, gently. "I can assure you that the corset top will be constructed to accommodate your—um—you."

"It better be," groans Phallon. Now everyone in the room is focusing on her size-16 form spilling over the tiny conference room chair.

It's Lupo, not me, however, who tames her size tantrum. "*Bella*, I will shoot photos for you in the corset and you will see how beautiful you will look—and you can use for your portfolio, no?"

Phallon melts like butter on a hot griddle under Lupo's simmering gaze. "You would do that for me? Good. Cuz I sure could use some photos. And I'ma hold you to it!"

I want to blurt out, *Well, you'd better stand in line, cuz I'm first!* But I stick to the agenda, winding up the meeting. "So, we'll have some more sketches next week, no?" I ask, directing my question at Diamond.

"Yes, we will. Beachwear, the off-the-shoulder tops and dresses, and the wedding gown," says Diamond, siphoning off the tension.

Now Nole shoots me a knowing look. He thinks his cat Penelope is going to close the show. I've got to figure out a way for Fabbie Tabby to sashay to the finish line. Penelope is one of Nole's prize Persian cats, with a pancake-flat nose that I'm convinced is the product of a botched alley-cat rhinoplasty procedure.

"Okay, so I'm thinking the call of show is gonna be about thirty-two looks," I say, calculating how many outfits will be in our fashion show.

"That's it?" challenges Ruthie Dragon. "The winning house last year had forty-two looks."

"I know that," I say, self-consciously, ever mindful of the probing lens in the corner. "And when you're the house leader and fashion show producer, you can orchestrate fifty looks if you want!"

"That's right—Wall Street is crashing, so why shouldn't we?" pouts Nole Canoli, sucking in his pudgy cheeks.

Camera or no camera, I realize it's time to let Nole know who's in charge: "I'm sorry that we don't have the unlimited budget to stage a scene from *The Fifth Element* for you, but even designers showing in tents at Bryant Park are showing sparer collections. Zang Toi's spring collection only had twenty-six looks."

"Pash is right," pipes up Bobby Beat. He whips out a sheet of paper like it's an analytical flowchart to support his argument at a board meeting. "Here's the program for the Mara Hoffman spring collection show I went to." He pauses for dramatic punctuation. So does everyone else who isn't a senior—the only students allowed to darken the doorstep, or rather the tents, at Bryant Park with their F.I. student access passes. "Thirty-five looks to be exact. And the show was flawless—well-received by the buyers *and* the press." As we all know, in the fickle world of fashion, where one week you're in and the next you're out, the approval of the latter is far more important than that of the former. Fab press always means fab orders. Not the other way around.

"Well, can we at least match that number?" insists Nole Canoli.

"That we can do. You and Diamond bring me sketches for five evening looks next meeting."

"Done," concedes Nole.

"Okay, fashionistas, so we're off shopping for fabrics and supplies soon—and ready for a sampling at our next meeting. Can I get a meowch on that?" I ask, signaling it's a wrap and a falafel.

"Meowch indeed," says Chintzy Colon, enthusiastically.

Felinez shoots her a look like she wants to scratch her eyes out.

"Oh, and please don't forget—I need your submissions for child models, because we'll be doing that audition soon!" I remind everyone.

As my team members start trickling out, Caterina approaches, finally coming out of her observational cocoon. "Pashmina, a few questions, please."

"Shoot."

"Do you think the Catwalk budget is enough to create your, um, elaborate vision for the show? Or is it unfair to expect so much for so little?" queries Caterina, sticking the mic near my face.

I wince at Caterina's catchall phrase for my vision and wonder what the other houses are doing. Only Caterina would know. Catching myself, I cut to the bottom line, though: "I'm glad they give us something! Whatever sacrifice we have to make by pooling all our resources together—working part-time, getting donations from family members—we do what we gotta do. The competition may be wicked, but the prizes are *worth* it."

"Yes, but I heard Diamond mention something about a wedding gown? Come on—that's a tall order even for a bride-to-be, let alone *students* participating in a fashion show competition," Caterina says, baiting me.

I wince again—this time at Caterina's calling us out like we're Crayola cronies instead of fashionistas in training—but I shut her down: "Well, first of all, that was going to be our little secret. But nobody gets to see this footage before the competition is over, right?"

"That's right. You know that," Caterina assures me.

"Okay, well . . . we were going to have—I mean, one of our cats is going to close the show . . . in the wedding gown," I whisper, furtively, like I'm Karl Lagerfeld revealing secrets for the House of Chloe couture collection.

"What do you mean, 'we'? Penelope is closing the show!" screams Nole.

"Says who?" I counter.

"Says me, or I'm walking right over to Ms. Lynx's office and having you disqualified for lying!" snarls Nole, turning nasty.

The crew gets quiet at the prospect of a real catfight.

I switch my gears, pronto. "Nole, listen, all the models have to begin their runway training in a few weeks, right?"

"So?" retorts Nole.

"So what if Fabbie Tabby and Penelope walk the catwalk in a Pose Off so we see who will get trained to close the show?"

"Oh, please, Penelope will leave Fabbie Tabby curled up in a fur ball!" boasts Nole.

"So we have a deal?" I ask.

"In principle," concedes Nole, hesitantly.

Caterina goes over to huddle with her crew. Now Zeus, who has been hovering over the Catwalk hurricane, moves in and envelops me in his arms. "It's all good," he whispers, hugging me tighter.

I feel myself melting in his arms. Instantly, I'm fantasizing that he's finally broken up with his girlfriend, the one-star cook, and is ready for my style soufflé instead. I can dream, can't I?

6

Felinez is not impressed with my recipe for invoking Cupid's spell, because she cuts in and bluntly asks, "Are we going to Subway?"

Zeus shoots me a look like *Don't let me stop you.* "Sorry, but I gotta go meet my dad," he confesses, a troubled cloud passing over his sparkling dark eyes.

"Okay," I sigh, acknowledging the collapse of my fashion fantasy starring Zeus and me. "Wazzup? You seem preoccupied."

"It's deep. The landlord raised the rent again on my dad's shop, and he seriously can't afford it—so he's tripping about that. I'ma run by there now," Zeus says.

"These landlords are biting the flavor out of the Big Apple," I say, sympathetically. "The rents are so radickio the only retailers who can afford them are Victoria's Secret, Banana Republic, and the Gap. New York is gonna turn into one gap-ing secret republic stuffed with so many bananas at its core it'll topple the Statue of Liberty!"

"That's what I'm talking about. My dad says soon, finding an old-school tailor—well, he didn't use that term, but you know what I mean—is gonna be a black-market situation. I'm not joking, you're gonna have to slither in an alleyway and go up five flights, then tap three times on a trick door to get your pants altered without a *crooked* hem!"

"I heard that," I say, giving Zeus an extra hug. "My mom is seriously worried about the rent drama in New York, too. Even Madison Avenue boutiques, like the Forgotten Diva, are affected. They have to clock $110,000 a month in sales just to cover operating expenses, inventory, and salaries."

"Wow, that's deep pockets," Zeus says, tipping his hat, then lingering for a minute.

I turn my attention to Fifi and her needs. "Speaking of down under, do you mean the subway below, or the Subway between slices?" I ask for clarification.

"What do you think, Miss House Leader?" she riffs. Of course, I know that Felinez always likes to hit Subway before we take the subway. She is one senorita who does not miss a Happy Meal—or a sad one. "We gotta make it quick, though, because Chris Midgett is coming over."

"Interviewing circus performers for the fashion show? That's a slick move," says Zeus, nodding.

Embarrassed, I explain about my computer crisis. After all, Angora already filled him in. Now Felinez and Angora throw in a few giggles for good measure.

When Caterina comes back, I motion with my eyes for them to can the desktop drama. "Um, Pashmina, one last question?" she says.

"Shoot," I say, all smiles. But suddenly, I get paranoid; maybe Caterina already knows. It would be in keeping with her scorpion nature to sting me without warning.

"How was your job interview the other day?" she spurts, nonchalantly.

I'm stunned by her arachnid effect. Even Angora and Felinez both stop in midgiggle.

Does everybody know I didn't get the freakin' job! I want to hurl back. Instead, I decide that in this instance, the truth is appropriate. "Actually, Aphro got that job. It's a hot new boutique. Jones Uptown," I say, smiling on cue.

Caterina grimaces slightly. I guess she *didn't* know. She scuttles over to Aphro with the mic.

As far as I'm concerned, it's a wrap—and a falafel—so I motion to Felinez for us to jet. I'm not supposed to leave until everyone has cleared out, because I'm responsible for closing up Studio C after the meeting, but I'm not in the mood to deal with Aphro right now. Even Dame Leeds is giving me the hairy eyeball. "Um, can I get with you for a second, Miss Purrstein," he says, authoritatively.

I want to stomp my foot and pout like Felinez used

to do when we were little and I swiped the pink crayons out of her box: "*No más*. No more!"

Instead, I hear myself saying, sweetly, "Wazzup?"

"Listen, I know I'm responsible for Liza showing up—or not showing up—whatever. Trust, I will deal with that situation. But I don't see why you had to penalize me for her disappearing act," blurts out Dame, defensively.

Now I'm following the drift of his drama. "That's not why I vetoed the sketch, um, the design," I say, puzzled. "I just didn't feel it represented the House of Pashmina, that's all."

Out of the corner of my eye, I realize that Craig, the other camera guy, is catching our exchange on his handheld video camera. My cheeks flush as Dame continues to singe my leadership with his hot comb: "Well, you could be more open to suggestions, that's all I'm saying!"

Now I'm stinging like Dijon mustard, but I nod attentively at Dame, hoping he'll just press on. Frantically searching for the right thing to say, I blurt out, "Dame, you and Liza are valuable team members. Can't we table this until our next meeting?"

Finally, Dame stops in his drama tracks. "Well, good, cuz don't get it French twisted, okay?"

"Oh, I won't. I don't, I mean," I say, smiling sweetly as he sashays down the hallway.

Satisfied, Craig shifts his camera in another direction. I'm embarrassed but I exhale deeply, then turn to address my team members with a warm good night. "Awright, everybody. You don't have to go home, but you gotta get up outta here!" I shout. As everybody exits, I stand by the door, waiting patiently. Mink and Kissa strike a pose as they come through the door, giggling. "Sashay, parlay!" I giggle back. Taking inventory, I realize what I need most in my fashion-biz survival kit: always be equipped with equal parts purrlicious sound bites, ego salve, and outfits!

Aphro walks out the door without looking at me, tagging behind Angora. Angora at least turns and mouths at me, *I gotta go*, before they head down the hallway.

Felinez and I watch them in silence while I make sure the door to Studio C is locked. "She knew you were going to be upset about the job thing," blurts out Felinez.

"You knew?" I ask, testily.

"She really needs the job, too, *mija*," Felinez says, rubbing my arm.

"Since when are you fending for Biggie Mouth?" I ask, pouting.

"Since I understand trying to fill an empty purse," declares Felinez.

"Yeah, it's definitely not raining Benjies right about now. Speaking of . . . spot me five so we can hit Subway?" I ask, licking my lips for an Italian sub. Tonight is my mom's bid whist card game night and I know that Ramon, her boyfriend, or whatever she calls him, is there. I'd rather eat before I go home.

We wolf down the Italian sub sandwich layered with hot sliced peppers and dripping with oil and vinegar—just the way Fifi likes it. Felinez also gets a bag of potato chips and a bag of nacho chips. "You're such a side hog," I blurt out before I catch myself.

But Felinez just giggles. Then I start giggling. Now people are staring at us. I suck on the straw in my 7UP—and try to slurp away the whole Aphro thing.

"God, I'm really pissed," I moan.

"With who and who and who?" asks Felinez, knowing my dark side all too well.

"Dame for putting me on blast—on camera. And Liza—I mean, what's with not showing up? And Aphro, cuz she definitely does not have my back. And, most of all . . . at Ms. Lynx," I admit. "I mean, she steered me down that thorny path. Clearly, Laretha Jones was not '*tinking* pink,' okay?"

"I think she was really trying to help you get a job. I mean, she said they hadn't actually seen each other. How was Ms. Lynx supposed to know about her African odyssey?" Felinez assures me, giggling.

As soon as I hit my courtyard, I hear someone whistling the *Catwoman* theme song. I look up at the second floor window, and of course, it's Stellina, my *numero uno* groupie. "I gotta go home," I yell up to her. But she's not trying to hear that. "No! I'll come right down!" she coos.

"No! I'll be right there—but just for a *segundo!*" I warn her. As it is, Mr. Sunkist is tearing past the jungle gym, forcefully steering his "borrowed" Piggly Wiggly supermarket shopping cart, which is piled high with the empty cans he collects. He drops a few on the way, then dramatically bends over, swaying to pick them up, and puts them teetering on top of the pile again. "Got any for me, you tall drink of water!" he asks me giddily.

"Not today," I say, calmly. Mr. Sunkist earned his nickname for the obvious reason. And I know that his cuckoo behavior must mean he's "off his meds," as my mom explains it. When he's taking them, he walks around quietly like a zombie, going about his business. I worry about Stellina running around outside at night in case any of the assorted boogeyman types are also on the prowl. My mother's "AMBER Alerts" are obviously wearing off on me. Instead of waiting for the elevator, I head to the stairwell to walk one flight up to Stellina's apartment. But not before I examine the handiwork of the latest tagger to deface the graffiti-splattered walls.

AMERICA IS NOT A COUNTRY. IT'S A
CORPORATION. BUT THE REVOLUTION WILL
BE TELEVISED. MAD MIXXER [COPYRIGHT
THAT!]

Climbing the stairs, I ponder the tagger's MADness as it relates to my own terms: see, the Catwalk competition will be televised, which will make me part of the fashion revolution, so one day I won't have to be part of any corporation except my own, like Kimora Lee or Tyra Banks, with their high-yielding legs and enterprises.

"What took you so long?" quips Stellina as I burst into the hallway. She is hanging outside her door, canned laughter from the television set spilling into the hallway.

"I was pondering the revolution," I announce.

Stellina squinches up her nose, looking puzzled, but gets right to her agenda: "Did you meet Eramus Tyler?"

"Oh, is that his last name? Same as one of the designers in my house," I say, nodding sweetly at my future runway model.

"Yup. His parents got a divorce and his mother got a job in Atlanta, so she left him with—well, you know who, so don't sue!" Stellina says, flashing her naughty nine smile.

"My, you're a busy little bee," I say. "Maybe you want someone to come buzz in your bonnet."

She looks at me, seeming puzzled again, but this time she catches on. "I'm not feeling him. Yesterday, he was in the elevator with a sketch pad and showed me what he was drawing. No fierce outfits or anything."

"Well, what was he drawing?" I ask, curiously.

"I don't know. It was green—I think it was supposed to be the Incredible Hulk but it turned out like a Ninja Turtle. You see all that grease he got in his hair? And those corny outfits? That plaid is so sad."

I already know that Stellina must be feeling him or she wouldn't be taking his fashion inventory.

"Take it easy on greasy," I advise. "It's bad enough he's stuck with a grandmother who carries a pitchfork in her purse instead of a tube of MAC lipstick so she'd look more glamourette than Grim Reaper, okay?"

"Why waste the good stuff on that trout pout!" shoots Stellina, poking out her mouth and pursing her lips together sternly like Mrs. Paul's.

I double over in laughter until my giggles are drop-kicked by Stellina's sudden U-turn to my least favorite subject—my sister. "Speaking of greasy, Chenille pressed Taynasia's mother's hair today—and she got ten dollars!" shoots Stellina, her eyes sparkling like Lotto balls.

I nod knowingly, even though I'm pressed at the thought of some Hamiltons or even Washingtons not wandering my way. "So, you think I can talk to your mother?" I ask, deflecting from my sister's booming enterprise.

"I already asked her if I can audition to be in your fashion show and she said yes!" Stellina announces loudly. Then she turns and yells into the apartment. "Pashmina is here. I told her I'm gonna be in her fashion show!"

"You are so sneaky—I caught you in the act," I say, shaking my head. "Look, um, you have to audition, because the other members of my house have to approve the junior models. Okay?"

"I got the job. But I understand—auditioning is just a formality," Stellina says, bugging her big eyes.

"Exactamundo," I say, making a note to my fashion self to talk to Mrs. Warren and double-check if this is cool. "Auditions will be in January; then we'll start runway rehearsals after that if you're selected."

"Who else do you want to be a junior model?" she asks, like she's vying for selection approval.

"Well, let's see. We have Felinez's brother, Juanito, and Aphro's foster sister, Angel—"

"Can Tiara be one of the other models?" asks Stellina.

I should have known that Stellina would try to hook up her best friend, who is also nine, but I don't want to tell her that Tiara is not runway material, because she, well, marches like a penguin on thin ice at the North Pole.

"Um, lemme get back to you on that. See, I have to give the other team members in my house a chance to bring their junior talent to the table. Ya dig?"

"I dig. You don't like Tiara," Stellina says, astutely.

"That's not true," I say, trying to deflect from a dis.

"Okay, well, who's gonna be doing the training, cuz I can teach you a few moves, okay?" she informs me, gleefully. Then she pops out the door and struts, twirls, and perches herself in the doorway.

"Aphro," I start, realizing that I'm avoiding referring to Aphro as my best friend, "is the designated runway modeling trainer."

Suddenly, Mrs. Warren yells out to Stellina from the living room. "You'd better get in here and do your homework!"

"I already know how to work the runway. Okay?" she giggles.

"Right—well, soon you'll be showing all my team members that sashay. I'm counting on you," I say, coaxing her. "And I'll talk to your mother about everything."

"Awright, gotta go, supermodel," Stellina whispers, "and tell Eramus a little dab'll do ya!"

I shake my head, laughing. "Will do ya."

I take the elevator to my floor and stand in front of my apartment, fishing for my keys. I know that my mom is busy with her cronies at the card table and they are wickedly serious about bid whist.

I hear Mrs. Paul's door creak open, so I turn, and I see Eramus peek his head out. He waves at me like a shipwrecked survivor on a deserted island.

"Hey, wazzup?" I say, tilting my head to the side. I refrain from telling him that I was just talking about him.

"Hi," he says, sweetly. His dimples deepen and his eyes twinkle. What a cutie patootie.

"So, what are you up to?" I ask, smiling back at him. I can't help noticing that he is wearing the same dull green plaid shirt with brown high-water pants from yesterday. I wonder why he's rockin' the same dingy outfit two days in a row. I gotta figure out how to prime his purrlicious potential.

"Nothing," he says, shyly.

Within the next few minutes of awkward silence, it slowly dawns on me it was no accident that Eramus stuck his head out of the door at that precise moment. He was probably waiting for me to come home. The elevator door opens and a short, brown-skinned boy with wire-rimmed glasses and a heavy backpack steps out. He smiles at me warmly as he walks down the hall.

"Are you Chris—um," I start, but I decide not to say

his last name, just in case it isn't pronounced like the word *midget*. Maybe it has a French twang to it—like *Brigitte* with an M. One thing is for sure: there is truth in advertising, because Chris is definitely short.

"Yup, that's me," he says. "Are you Pashmina?"

"Yup, that's me," I respond. I try not to stand too close to him so I don't tower over him and make him feel uncomfortable. I realize that with my heels, I'm almost a head taller than him.

Awkwardly, I introduce Chris to Eramus. Now they both stand there, grinning without saying a word. Luckily, the raucous cackling from my mom's card game crowd inside my apartment breaks the silence. "Take me to Boston, baby!" someone screams out, which is the code for getting a winning bid whist hand.

"Well, I'll see you later. Maybe tomorrow, okay?" I say to Eramus.

"Okay," Eramus says, shyly, then recedes back into the apartment like an apparition.

Chris smiles at me, his chubby brown cheeks glistening. I look at his tan zippered Windbreaker and the sage green cotton button-down shirt he's wearing underneath—both so neat and clean without a stain or a crease. Suddenly, I get the image of a raccoon eating an acorn without dropping a crumb. "So where do you live?" I ask, apprehensive as I open the door to Chicken Little Central, aka my apartment.

"Queens," he says proudly. "Astoria."

"Oh, that's nice," I say, nodding approvingly. Inside, however, I feel slightly embarrassed. I can just picture the house he lives in—nice and neat, with clean hand towels and a white wrought-iron fence outside and big fat juicy cucumbers and tomatoes growing in the backyard garden.

When I open the door, the bellowing from my mother's best friend, Lonni, greets us like a blast of hot air: "Mind your ugly business!" she shouts out as she slams down a card on the table with a flourish. Then she winks at Ramon, who is seated to her left, and rubs her hands on her close-cropped platinum blond Afro like it's Aladdin's lamp.

"You need to be shaving somewhere else!" counters Mr. Chisolm, stroking his gruff beard, "cuz I can tell by the hair on your forearm that it's gonna be a full moon tonight—and I'm about to get paid!" Mr. Chisolm slams his hand down on the table. "*Bam!*" he shouts. Amid the oohs and aahs, I take it he is going to Boston, too. Mr. Chisolm looks up at me, which shifts the attention of everyone in my direction—including Chenille, whom I cannot believe my mother has allowed to watch her card-playing cronies. Chenille gives me a smirk like she's having a four-star day: clocking Benjamins earlier, now learning bid whist.

Everyone else seated at the card table gives Chris

the once-over, like he's lunch meat I'm about to layer in a Subway sandwich. I clear up that gourmet mystery—pronto—especially for salacious Lonni. "This is Chris—um . . ." I stall, still refraining from saying his last name. I just can't get the dreaded M word off my lips. "And he's here to look at my computer."

"Well, take a look at mine, too, while you're at it!" my mom shoots at him, then laughs loudly. She only gets this rowdy when she's around a lot of people—and her personality becomes unleashed. I kind of like it, even though I'm miffed that she has allowed Chenille to be in her bid whist mix. She always wants me to learn how to play, but I'm more interested in tallying scores on the runway, if you catch my drift.

"I can if you want me to," offers Chris.

I squelch my automatic reflex to nudge him like I do my crew, because he's not.

"Well, how many ways I gotta say it? I do!" my mom shouts. Ramon darts his eyes in her direction. It must bother him that he can't fix everything. Lonni winks at him again.

"Well, we'll see you later," I pipe up.

"Let the man get a drink or something," bellows Mr. Chisolm. "And take your coat off, cuz Lord knows you gonna be here till the sun rises anyway. Your Pink Highness probably done jinx the thing is all!"

I hate when Mr. Chisolm embarrasses me, but he's

been doing it since I can remember. He still lives in our old neighborhood—back in the Edenwald Projects, across the street from where we used to live. We moved down here to a bigger apartment so Mom could be closer to her job, since she got a promotion. Chris takes off his jacket carefully, then folds it neatly on the black leather couch.

"Lord, hang up the child's coat!" orders Lonni. I grab Chris's jacket like it's a royal vestment and take it to the hall closet.

When we push open the door to my bedroom, Fabbie Tabby greets us. She rubs her plump body against Chris's pants leg. He just stands there. I'm impressed. At least he isn't feline phobic. He looks around my room, then rests his bespectacled gaze on the large meowverlous poster of Eartha Kitt poised in her black pleather Catwoman gear.

"Um, that's very interesting," he says, adjusting the silver-rimmed glasses on the bridge of his nose. I take another look at Chris's corny outfit and realize that fashion is not his passion. He's probably just being polite.

"She's my idol—you know, part of feline iconography," I explain, snobbily.

"Yes, I'm familiar with the concept," he shoots back.

"What do you know about walking feline?" I challenge him.

"I meant iconography—using something as a frame

of reference for what you aspire to. I'm familiar with that," he clarifies.

"Wow," I utter, involuntarily. He's *deep*. Chris stands there like he's waiting for my instruction.

"You can sit here, Mr. Chris," I say, motioning for him to sit at my desk in front of my deadbeat computer.

"Um, you don't have to call me Mr.," he says, straightforwardly.

"No, of course," I say, embarrassed. I refrain from informing him that at F.I. "Miss" and "Mr." are terms of endearment—as in "Miss Thing" or "Mr. Ninja."

Chris shifts gears quickly, as if he thinks he hurt my feelings with his polite posturing: "Actually, call me by my nickname. Everybody else does." Then he hesitates, like he has revealed too much.

"Um, what is it?" I ask, gently.

"Panda," he says, looking embarrassed.

"Oh, of course," I say, politely, then realize my response doesn't make any sense. What I want to say is *Dalmatians and pandas, oh, my! Enough with the animal kingdom already—just fix my computer, purr favor!*

I watch curiously as Chris fiddles with the switches on my computer, then checks the electrical outlets, firmly securing the wires into the outlets.

"I checked that," I say, feebly.

He nods, trying to reboot my computer. For a second a light flickers on the screen.

"Yippee!" I scream, prematurely. Okay, so I'm nervous.

"No need for yippee yet," he says, an anxious edge creeping into his voice. After hitting a few keys on the keyboard and watching various shades of blue, then black flash on my screen, he asks me a question, nervously, like my dentist did when I was five years old and had eight cavities one winter after chomping on candy compulsively.

"Um, have you downloaded any attachment files?"

My mind freezes just like my computer. Blankety blank. "Um, yeah," I blurt out like he asked me a bozo question.

"From senders you don't know?"

"Um, no," I respond, like bozo question number two just blew my way.

"Well, that doesn't matter. The real sender could have been using a Trojan anyway," he explains, taking his wire-rimmed glasses off and rubbing his eyes.

"You mean like the horse someone sent Helen of Troy as a gift but there were enemy soldiers inside ready to pop out and perpetrate an ambush?" I ask, puzzled.

"Well, yes. That reference fits exactly. Someone can send you a virus hiding behind a fake e-mail address— probably one that you recognize—but the e-mail didn't really come from that person," he further explains. He stares up at me without his glasses. I notice the dark circles around his eyes and suddenly feel guilty. He is probably kicking it 24-7 with his cyber chores.

"Oh," I respond, humbly, finally catching Chris's creepy drift. "You mean that's what froze my computer?"

"Could be. I'll do a virus scan, which will probably take a while."

"Un-freakin'-believable!" I say, revving up for a rant. "I mean, what is the point of that stupid warning that flashes when you get an attachment 'If you don't know who sent this e-mail, be cautious when opening this file'? You either download the file, or you don't, hello! It's not like you can curtsy before you hit the cursor and that's gonna prevent the stink bomb from exploding in your computer!"

"I know. And because of the tricky Trojan method, most viruses are sent hiding behind the e-mail address of someone you know, otherwise the average recipient wouldn't risk downloading the file in the first place."

While Chris runs the scan, I babble nervously about my situation. "I have to complete the hookup list for my next Catwalk meeting, then type up my assignment, which will accompany the sketches for the Design Challenge—which I have to hand in—and then the Catwalk competition itself is in June, so I can't believe this situation is happening with my computer, cuz I will be fried French toast if my circuits are burnt."

"You're funny," Chris says, nodding like he understands. "I heard about the Catwalk competition."

"Good—because there is nothing else like it," I declare. I bet all the Dalmation tekkies wish they had a front-row seat at the Catwalk competition. Keep dreaming.

After ninety minutes, Chris finally announces, "You definitely have a virus. And you're gonna lose some of your files. But don't worry, I can do a cleanup. You'll be up and running in about a year."

"One whole year?" I ask in disbelief, blinking my eyes to fight back the tears.

"Actually, a cat year, to be exact," Chris says, straight-faced.

I burst into tears, trying to cover my face with the sleeve of my pink hoodie.

Chris's tired, bloodshot eyes bulge in disbelief. "I was just joking, Pashmina," he says, apologetically.

"About the virus?"

"No, unfortunately, that's real. It's a nasty one, too—sent by an amateur," he explains, hastily. "But it won't take a year. I can clean it up in a few days—and reinstall Windows for you."

I'm so embarrassed. I wipe my eyes on my sleeve. "Who would do something like send me a nasty virus?" I wonder, twirling my hair furiously. Suddenly, I wake up and smell the catnip: since my appointment to house leader, enemy forces have been circling in cyber-space while I've been too busy tiptoeing through the tulips. "That's it—this is sabotage to ensure that I'm out of commission!"

Thanks to my excellent intel, Chris snaps out of his bleary-eyed bluster and becomes like my second-in-command: "I can look at the document history in the hard drive and see which file contained the virus, then see which files I can recover that have already been damaged," he advises.

"Execute, *pronto*," I order, getting steamed. And to think that I download files every day—from jokes to fashion forecasts and runway show photos. Who could be the culprit?

He scans through my files and e-mails carefully. "I see you get a lot of those annoying urban myth e-mails, too," he says, matter-of-factly.

"I do?" I ask, squeamishly.

"Yeah—like this one claiming that Microsoft and Bill Gates are gonna send you a refund if you forward this e-mail to twenty people within the next twenty-four hours."

"Geez—I was counting on that refund," I say, dis-appointed.

Chris cracks a smile, then reports, "This is the corrupted file—the one you downloaded with the Mercedes-Benz Fashion Week designer contact list."

"Really?" I say, trying to figure out who sent it to me, then shaking my head. "Mercedes-Benz Fashion Week contacts—is nothing sacred?"

"Not in cyberspace," Chris informs me.

"Yeah, I remember now. That was a few weeks ago. Aphro sent me that e-mail with the attachment."

Chris goes into my Internet history and retrieves the e-mail from AphroPuffs@FI-stu.edu.

I read the message in the e-mail: *Wish we were there. In the meantime, here is the designer contact list for invites for all the shows! Felinez got it from Ruff Loner and told me to forward it to you, so you can forward it to everyone in our crew "with besos."*

"Wow, I remember now. I didn't get around to forwarding the contact list to everybody yet, because I was waiting to finish the hookup list," I say, realizing that this wasn't just a sneak skirmish; it was a full-frontal attack to shut down my whole operation. Could the Dax hair grease be seeping into Aphro's brain cells from overuse? "I'm gonna kill her," I say, sweating. "That's why she kept trying to dissuade us from heading to D.T. for computer help—she wanted to shut me down!" I plop into the chair, tapping my foot. "I'd better consult with Felinez first. She's my best friend, and she's an intern at the Ruff Loner showroom," I explain to Chris. I pick up my pink Princess phone and dial her house. She answers. "Fifi, did you send Aphro the contacts for the designers showing at Bryant Park next spring?" I ask.

"What happened?" Felinez responds. That's her pat response when she doesn't know the answer to something or is nervous. I fill her in on the cyber crisis. "I never sent her an e-mail with that, *mija*," she squeaks.

"Nobody at the showroom gave you this list—and you didn't give this to Aphro to give to me?" I say, trying to jog her memory.

"Nobody gives me anything at work—except a headache. You know that!" shrieks Felinez.

Felinez is right. I *do* know that. "Do not start with the riff—Pink Head is being paranoid, okay? I think Aphro is out to get us," I confess to her.

"She has been acting weird—but I thought it was about the job," admits Felinez. "But she's our best friend. Maybe it was Liza? She is always sucking up to Willi Ninja, Jr., even though he doesn't give her the time of a twirl. But maybe that's why she's been, well, acting flaky!"

"You're right. She blew off a Catwalk meeting!" I shriek, then hesitate. "But, no, Aphro was acting weird before the job interview. When she went with me uptown, she was already chewing on gristle and wouldn't tell me what it was," I explain.

Chris waits patiently while Felinez and I continue

to hash out the horror in disbelief. "Are you gonna ask them?" squeaks Felinez.

"I'm gonna do more than that," I retort.

After I hang up the phone, Chris reiterates, "If she says she didn't send you that e-mail, she probably didn't, since she's your friend and all. Someone just used her e-mail address as a Trojan to get you to feel safe enough to download the attachment with the virus."

"I know that. But I think the other so-called friend did. Or a missing member of my house. I can feel it. What a sham-o-rama," I utter in disbelief.

Chris squints. "Sham-o-rama?" he repeats.

"Oh, it's Catwalk code," I explain absentmindedly. "It's the one place that's always open for business in the urban jungle: everywhere you turn, there is a jackal on Jump Street—ready to pull the acrylic over somebody's eyes in the name of getting ahead. What I can't believe is that that someone is supposed to be an ally in my Catwalk camp!"

"Wow. You have a very interesting take on things," Chris says, looking at me intently.

"Well, you have to—if you plan on surviving and thriving in the fashion jungle," I explain, waving off his admiration.

While Chris works on unfreezing my computer, I obsess about Aphro or Liza sending me a virus. I dial Angora. She's good at clues, but this time she offers a dim take: "Well, if either one of them did send it, they're going to deny it."

"No kidding, Inspector Chérie," I sigh, freaking out. I start sniffing my underarms while cradling the phone in my right ear. "I've got a flood again."

"What?" she asks.

I whisper about my armpits again while darting my eyes in Chris's direction. His back is turned to me as he works intently on my computer. "I'm sweating like a soccer mom!"

"Is he making you nervous?" Angora asks, amused.

"No, Inspector Chérie—someone putting a plague in my portal makes me nervous!" I say.

"I do remember something," she says, then pauses. "Liza lives by Willi Ninja, Jr., in Queens."

"Boy, that's a borough that's sure getting around these days," I hiss. "I didn't know that. Why didn't you tell me this before!"

"Because what did it matter? He is down with Dulce—and she can't stand Liza, so no way did she stand a chance of getting in his house," says Angora.

"Well, maybe she finally figured a way in—to sabotage me for him!" I shriek. "This can't be happening. Tell me it can't be happening."

"It's not happening," Angora says, obliging me. "Really, Pash, you don't know anything yet, so don't get yourself so, um, sweaty."

"Easy for you to say, cool, collected blue beret. A computer crisis plus a Catwalk competition times a date with Ice Très on Friday equals sweat squared in the armpits!" I say, driving my point home to Bunny Land.

Angora gets the message and hops off. Chris keeps staring at me between mysterious boot-ups and CD removals from the C drive.

"Sorry about that, but I'm really gagulating," I offer as an apology.

He looks at me, his eyes twinkling. "That's another very interesting word."

"Yes, it, um, means 'past freaked out,'" I explain, nervously. "Did you always like computers?"

"Did you always like modeling?" he counters.

"I'm about more than modeling, though," I say.

"I'm sure," he says, but I don't know quite what he means.

Nonetheless, I continue informing him of my vision for being a modelpreneur.

"Well, you sound like you have a clear-cut vision," he says. I can tell he's impressed.

"Yes, I do. Do you?"

"I think so. I wanna be an Internet entrepreneur. Don't think the bubble has burst on I-commerce like everybody says," he explains to me.

"Bubbles don't have to burst," I say, wistfully.

"No, they don't," Chris says, like he really agrees.

He turns and looks at me intently again. Angora is right. He does make me nervous. "I know you're busy on Friday," he says, carefully.

I look at him like he's Je'Taime's crystal ball cousin before I recall what I said. "Oh, right, you heard me on the phone?"

"I wasn't listening—just heard that part," he assures me. "But, um, you know, there is a Cyber Chic exhibit at the I-commerce trade show at Javits. I'm going on Friday and Saturday and Sunday . . . if you wanna go with me?"

"Oh, I don't know," I say, tongue-tied because I don't know what to say.

"You don't know what?" asks Chris. He runs his hand over his pants leg like he's smoothing out an imaginary crease. I can just see his room—everything labeled in neat drawers and storage options maximized to percentages, like disk-operating space on a computer drive.

I want to shriek, *I don't know anything!* Now I feel stupid. How can I squirm my way out of going out with him on Saturday when he's been so downloading with me? Just because he's too short—and his clothes are too Eddie Bow-wow—I mean, Bauer—for me.

"Um, I'm busy on Saturday, too," I say, telling a fiberoni with no finesse.

Despite Chris's almond-brown complexion, I can

tell that he's blushing because he knows that I'm lying. "Well, I'll see you tomorrow, anyway, round five," he says, wincing.

"Oh, right," I say, embarrassed.

Luckily, his cell phone rings with the old-school tune "Super Freak," by the late Rick James.

"I don't know if you should dance, or answer it," I say, guffawing too loudly. Now I sound like Aphro!

"You're funny—you know that?" Chris says, staring at me.

"Aren't you going to answer it?" I counter, embarrassed again but pleased that he has taken notice of my extensive vocabulary instead of telling me how pretty I am. Maybe he was just being nice before. I mean, why would he want to be with a girl a foot taller than him, anyway?

FASHION INTERNATIONAL 35th ANNUAL
CATWALK COMPETITION BLOG

New school rule: You don't have to be ultranice, but don't get tooooo catty, or your posting will be zapped by the Fashion Avengers!

BLACK TO THE FASHION FUTURE

Why is it that this year's annual Catwalk competition at Fashion International High School will represent black designers within the confines of its 35th annual fashion show in a more "diverse fashion" than Seventh Avenue is?

If you take an unflinching look right now at the emerging and established design houses on Seventh Avenue, you'll be pressed and pinched to find a handful of black designers with enough clout to unveil their collections in Bryant Park during Mercedes-Benz Fashion Week; or being heralded in high-fashion publications; or, last but not least, being showcased within designated selling space of our most influential retail stores, such as Neiman Marcus, Saks Fifth Avenue, Bergdorf Goodman, Barneys, Bloomingdale's, and Henri Bendel.

At the moment, plastic-covered offerings from only one such black designer can be seen being loaded into cargo trucks: Detroit native Tracy Reese. Her feminine, chic collections are sold at select retailers throughout the United States, Europe, and Asia as well as featured in magazines from *Elle* to *Lucky*. And triumphantly, Reese has finally opened her first flagship boutique, in Manhattan's Meatpacking District. The 2,200-square-foot space is a global showcase for Reese's pieces—which now include home and accessories collections to boot. But where, oh where, are the black multimillion-dollar fashion empires? The black equivalents to Calvin Klein, Ralph Lauren, Donna Karan, Gucci, Giorgio Armani, Kate Spade, or Juicy Couture? Can it be that Seventh Avenue is suffering from style amnesia? Fashion history speaks for itself: back in the seventies there was a natural alliance between the fashion industry and black designers; practically every street in the burgeoning district housed a talent who was black enough for ya. From revered designers Jon Haggins and Scott Barrie to the wonderful world of Willi Smith to Stephen Burrows, who had such colorful clout that the specialty department store Henri Bendel appointed an entire boutique to Burrows within its prestigious fashion walls. Recently there was an uprising. Seventh Avenue received flak for its lack of representation among black models during Fashion Week. That put enough of a wedge in the door for colorful maestro Stephen Burrows to stage a small collection this season. And I do mean small. Meanwhile, Italian *Vogue* proclaimed, "Black is beautiful!" Famed photographer Steven Meisel shot an entire issue of *Vogue Italia* with black models, in the hopes that other issues of *Vogue* would follow suit, or dress. But alas, what were they wearing? Well, you already know the answer: Prada and *nada* from black designers! For all practical purposes, fashion historians can claim that the black reign vanished along with the infamous nightclub Studio 54, the heyday of disco music, and the dazzling mirrored disco balls that reflected that era's hopes and dreams for multiculturalism. F.I. fashionistas are not falling for the rap tricks, either: P. Diddy's Sean John and Russell Simmons's Phat Farm and Kimora Lee's Baby Phat represent the ghetto-fabulous iconography but their collections are not so fab—from a design perspective, anyway. When the 35th annual Catwalk competition wraps in June, we hope that Seventh Avenue will follow our color cues and allow some of the emerging black talent to breathe diversity into the fashion industry. America coalesced enough to elect a black president: it's time to redefine the color of fashion—and get black to the future.

Posted by Enter the Dragon
11:23:45

7

Liza missed a week of school, but today I got wind of her return and decided to corner her after last period, since both our science classes are in the same corridor. I sneak out of chemistry class early and crouch by the door of the biology lab, waiting to see her guilty face. As soon as the house music pipes up over the loud-speaker, signaling the end of the period, I nervously pull my fuchsia felt cloche over my eyes, preparing for my attack. The door flings open and students pour out, a few giggling at my frenzied, furtive-looking state. Liza darts her eyes in my direction like I'm a test-tube baby that got away—in other words, something she shouldn't see.

"Hold up," I order as she tries to flee from me.

"Hi, Pashmina. I was going to call you," she offers weakly, surrendering like a shoplifter caught red-handed.

"Well, you could have e-mailed me from cyber-space," I blurt out against my will, "since I got your *last* e-mail, which luckily I did not circulate to any-one else."

Liza registers shock. "What?"

Ignoring her reaction, I barrel through my spiel: "I didn't know you live by Mr. Willi."

"Yeah, I do. Well, no, I don't exactly," she says, nervously.

"So you live by him, or you don't? Make up your mind." I grill her, hoping if I stay on the possible prankster, she'll fold like it's laundry day.

"We both live in Rego Park, but it's a big area. It's not like he lives near my house. That's what I meant," Liza clarifies, but she's on the verge of confessing. I can feel it.

"Are you sure?"

"Sure about what?"

"That you never see him?"

"No, Pashmina. I never see him."

"Then why didn't you come to the meeting?" I ask, bluntly.

Liza stalls for so long that I can see her formulating a fiberoni. "I couldn't make it."

"Why—too busy plotting in the palace to dethrone me?" I yelp.

Finally, Felinez arrives at the scene. She stands next to me with her arms folded defensively.

"I couldn't make it because I had to go to my job—at Vidal Sassoon!" Liza confesses.

"You didn't tell me about any job," I bluster.

"Yes, I did. I knew there was going to be a conflict

with my schedule—and there is—but I'm trying to work it out." Now Liza is close to tears. "I'm sorry. Dame already put me on blast, okay? I'm sorry. I can't do everything!"

"I'm watching you," I threaten, squinting my almond-shaped eyes into menacing slits to make my point.

Liza looks terrified and scurries away. I grab on to Felinez and we head outside. "I think she's twirling me like a sponge roller."

"She did tell us about the internship at Vidal Sassoon," recalls Felinez.

"She did?" I balk, frustrated.

"Yeah, she did," says Felinez, holding my arm to steady me.

"Now let's see what Aphro has to say," I sigh, amping myself up. We're meeting everyone outside to head on our fabric foray. "This is more exhausting than Watergate. And by the wigglies rotating in my stomach, I can tell the plot is about to thicken."

Aphro greets us with the deadpan expression she's adopted as of late. I decide to play a clueless catalyst like Helen of Troy so I can figure out if she is indeed behind the Trojan trickery. "Oh, I didn't thank you. I got the e-mail you sent me with the Fashion Week designer contacts."

Aphro looks at me blankly.

"Remember?"

"No, cuz I didn't send it," declares Aphro.

"But the e-mail said it was from you," I say, nonchalantly.

"Yeah, and the tooth fairy is real," retorts Aphro, tapping her foot impatiently. "I gotta go." Aphro decided to opt out of our Mood Fabrics rendezvous, because she wants to go to Twenty-eighth Street to buy jewelry supplies instead. Since I don't have any proof, I refrain from putting her on blast and simply hold out a twenty-dollar bill so she can snap up bangles, which will be engraved with quotes and slogans to implement our Design Challenge.

"Don't forget to bring me back all the receipts," I remind her, much to her chagrin.

"I'm not Shamu at SeaWorld, so you don't have to train me," Aphro snaps, jumping at the Jackson in my hand.

I want to snap and snatch the crispy bill right back but Felinez pokes me in the side for me to chill.

Before Aphro evaporates, Diamond manages to innocently ask her, "You're gonna embellish some of the letters with crystals, too, right?"

"You got crystal money?" retorts Aphro, letting out one of her obtrusive snorts.

Funny how I used to think Aphro's signature snort was *très* adorable, and now I just want to stick her head in a trough to relieve her sassy sinus condition. Felinez pokes me again for good measure. Chirpily, I pipe up, "With the next Catwalk installment we will be able to dig in for, um, the extras." Felinez is right: I have to squash the beef jerky with Aphro, at least publicly, or else I'll look like a hater, because everybody knows that Aphro needs a job, too—even if I suspect it's to fund her cruel campaign to outrank me.

Luckily, at least someone seems ready to stroke Aphro's ego: "Congratulations on your job—again, Miss Aphro," squeals Chintzy, rushing up to join us.

Aphro beams proudly while twirling the peacock tails on the emerald beaded lariat wrapped around her neck. "You're always so bootylicious," she coos, approving of Chintzy's tall lace-up butterscotch leather boots with clunky high heels. Chintzy always wears boots but at least these are an improvement over the white go-go ones she wore all fall.

Nole stares at her boots, too, no doubt trying to decipher the designer. "Those are Michael Kors?"

Chintzy nods, running her hand quickly over her slicked-back hair, which is perched in a thick ponytail as always. "The mane is flawless, as usual," observes Nole. "Is it yours?"

Chintzy blushes, then nods again.

Aphro looks at Chintzy's sixties-style do approvingly but is more interested in deciphering my dates.

"So, you going out with Ice Très later, I hear." I feel a tinge of paranoia coming on as I ponder her position: how is she gathering her intel? I haven't told her about the date, because it's not like she and I have been kanoodling over frothy cappuccino and convo lately.

"Yes, I am, tonight," I say, proudly. This way, I put Aphro on notice: *I may dig Dr. Zeus, but I definitely have options, okay?* For emphasis, I add, "Can you believe Chris—pardon me, I should call him by his preferred nickname—*Panda* asked me out, too? To go to some cyber shuttle in outer space, or something."

"No, you did not say *Panda?*" Nole Canoli asks in disbelief, stroking Countess Coco's wild fiery hair like a lion tamer.

"Who is he?" Diamond asks curiously.

"A lifesaver, that's who," Angora interjects, then informs everyone of our brave trip across the continental divide.

"His friends need to watch a few more episodes of *Meerkat Manor*—cuz he looks more like a raccoon than a panda if you ask me. The circles under his eyes are deep," I cut in, circling my own with a half-moon gesture. "But that's just the teaser of his circus act. His last name is Midgett and it suits him to a centimeter!"

"Miss Purr—that was shady even for you!" howls Nole.

"I'll tell you what's shady—someone sending me a

computer virus. I don't care about losing my school-work, but my Catwalk competition files?" I say, pulling the reins on my pink paranoia. "If I find out who cyber-jacked me, I'm gonna be so shady astronomers will be reporting on the eighth total eclipse this year instead of the usual seven for *eons* to come!"

"I'm out," blurts out Aphro, bidding us all good-bye.

Nole looks at me, seeming puzzled. "What's up with her, now that she has a job?"

"It's not *that* job I'm worried about," I say, suspiciously, as I watch Aphro sashay down the block, all legs and attitude. "It's her new sideline that has me worried."

"What sideline, or do you mean side dish?" giggles Nole.

"Sideline—as in *espionage*, that's what," I say, exhaling. There, I said it—out loud.

Nole purses his lips. So does Countess Coco.

"Come on, Nole. Figure it out. Why would anyone send me a virus—that I was supposed to circulate to all the members of my crew? To shut me down, okay? And who better than someone inside my house?"

"Are you suggesting one of us?" Nole asks, looking offended. He glances over at Ruthie Dragon, who is barely containing her disdain.

"No, not you!" I say, exasperated. "I'm thinking Liza or Aphro, or maybe it's Dame. That's it—he's just setting up his assistant hairstylist to take the fall—and I don't mean the synthetic ones!"

"Right," Nole replies, nodding and looking at me like the pink paranoia has finally gotten the best of me. He strokes Countess Coco's head gently, then glances at his shady assistant, Ruthie, *again*.

I glare at Ruthie Dragon, daring her to defy the chain of command. The time has come for a counterattack. "Chintzy, I want you to keep an eye out for anything suspicious. And I do mean anything. And keep an eye on Aphro *and* Liza *and* Dame for me. You got that?"

"I got it," Chintzy says, confidently, which already makes me feel at ease.

"Look, I know you have to go take care of your father," I say, realizing that I'm hogging my assistant's personal time. She already told me that she has to bail to handle her situation at home.

"Yes, I have to go now," Chintzy says, apologetically. "I can go with you, though, if you need me to."

"No, handle your business."

"I didn't know you knew your father," blurts out Nole, being insensitive, since the topic of fathers is a touchy one for me too. I may not know my father, but Nole does—and not only is he MIA; he's clearly missed.

"He left when I was little. But he just got back from

439

working for the Save the Children Federation in Malaysia and was feeling run-down, so he is staying with us, but since my mother is working all the time at the hospital, I take care of him," Chintzy says, sadly.

"Wow, there's a lot of viruses going around lately," Felinez says.

"Well, go ahead, then. We'll walk you to the subway," I offer, to counter Felinez's unnecessary sarcasm.

Chintzy hesitates, then smiles. We all walk to the Seventh Avenue subway entrance together and Chintzy heads toward the stairs for the downtown trains.

"I thought you lived by Gunhill Road," says Felinez. Both Felinez and Chintzy live uptown in the Boogie Down.

"Thank you, I wasn't thinking!" Chintzy says, but when she looks up, I see that there are tears in her eyes.

Suddenly, I realize she must be more upset about her father's situation than she's letting on. "I hope your father gets better," I say, honestly. "Don't worry—I'll show you the swatches Monday at lunchtime."

"I'm just so worried about him. I'm sorry," she reveals, then smiles sadly.

"I know, I'm sorry!" Felinez gripes, watching Chintzy cross the street.

"A computer virus is not funny. And if your father got sick, you would give birth to five purses," I scold her.

"Well, at least her father is back. Mine might as

well be in Malaysia, since he travels all the time and I never see him!" says Felinez.

She is right: her parents are on the road most weekends out of the year, performing on cruise ships and at festivals.

Angora slides her arm into mine—her way of telling me to squash it. We keep our caravan moving, and as usual, the sidewalks are Subway-sandwich thick with bustling action. Everybody is trying to get ahead in the Big Apple—in more ways than one. A group of gruff-looking shorties shoving a rack packed with plastic-covered garments almost runs us over like Mad Max. "Move it, cupcakes!" one of them bellows out.

"Awright," Angora says, blinking and swiftly moving her blue suede bootees out of the path of a wheel threatening to run over her foot, and bumping into mine.

Meanwhile, Nole Canoli spots an oncoming obvious fashion offense. "Oh, no. Herve would not approve," he mutters.

We all turn to witness a woman with wild matted hair strolling down the street wearing nothing more than a black garbage bag. It's wrapped around her body like a bandeau dress and tied with a string around her waist. She even has bags tied around her feet. No one in the fast-moving crowd even stops to look at her— but us.

"That wouldn't be part of a Design Challenge, would it?" Felinez asks feebly, reminding us that two years ago, recycling materials was the mandate for the Design Challenge in the Catwalk competition.

"I don't think so, *chérie*," comments Angora, sadly, shaking her head. "My mother would make me move back home—tomorrow—if she saw this," she confesses, clearly relieved that Ms. Ava is back home in Baton Rouge, where she belongs. "I wish we could give her some clothes."

"But we gave clothes to the Christmas drive," Nole points out. Last week, all the students at F.I. brought in clothes and stuff that will be donated to the shelters. Of course, a lot of the design majors donated stuff they'd made themselves—real works of art, if you ask me.

"I know," says Angora.

"Your mother has never been here to visit you?" blurts out Felinez.

"She would lie down in a bed of begonias naked in her backyard before she came to this 'bug-ridden manifesto in need of a makeover,' as she calls New York," offers Angora. "Just because you have a parent who is around doesn't mean they care about you."

"Well, she does care about you," I counter. "She lets you live here with your father because you want to."

"And if my father was not doing so well, she

wouldn't stand for it. I would be forced to attend Tulane 'Tulip' High School," Angora says, ungratefully.

"Is it really called Tulip High?" asks Diamond.

"No, but all the girls wear flower corsages to gym class, so it might as well be," Angora explains, sounding exasperated.

As we approach the corner of Fortieth Street to head to Mood Fabrics in the middle of the block, I can't believe we spot my snobby rival, Shalimar Jackson, standing near the curb with her outstretched arm, waving desperately for a cab.

"Don't tell me she has already stroked the bolts, or I'm gonna be in a bad 'mood,'" snarls Nole Canoli.

"Well, she's not carting any shopping bags, so I'd say she hasn't cleaned the showroom out yet!" Angora notes wisely. We all know that Shalimar has a, well, Hefty bag–sized budget to spread around for her Catwalk competition expenses, thanks to her parents.

"But that still doesn't mean she's going to win the Design Challenge, so let's keep our eyes on the prize," I warn my crew.

Since we all can't pretend that we don't see Shalimar standing there perched on her high-heeled brown suede Shimmy Choos, we keep our eyes on her—each of us unwillingly dispensing a fashionista nod, which includes a phony grimace through pursed lips. Shalimar returns a fashionista nod and, if I'm not mistaken, tries to stretch her stature by standing taller. Truth is, if Shalimar was taller, she would probably try to rip the runway. Luckily, she's *not*.

"So, where you heading—the high-heeled race?" asks Nole, snickering.

"What?" replies Shalimar, snobbily.

We come to a fashionable halt while Nole breaks down Sydney's eighty-meter race in which 260 runners sprint in hot pants and stilettos to the finish line. "First prize is five thousand," he coos. "You could buy the 3.3-pound truffle—recently discovered by an Italian truffle hunter near Pisa—with those cute coins."

Shalimar turns shady, no doubt still wincing at Anna Rex's biting blog entry about her "opulent" tastes.

"Is that in Australian dollars or American?" asks Diamond, trying to turn the situation to a Lite FM dial.

"Who cares!" counters Shalimar, waving her taxi-hailing hand more vigorously. Truth is, by four p.m. on Friday she'd have a better chance of winning today's Mega Millions lottery than hailing a cab in the Garment District. Sure enough, even a cab with its center light burning brightly (which means the taxi is available for fares) whizzes by without stopping. "I can't believe this!" shouts Shalimar. Then she stomps her foot.

"Want me to try?" asks Diamond.

"Why—do you think you'll get one instead of me?" Shalimar replies.

Diamond winces. Leave it to shady Shalimar not to realize that Diamond was just being her usual nice self. I know that Diamond wasn't insinuating that she could get a cab cuz she's white. Truth is, I'm not 100 percent sure Diamond knows she is.

"Why you tripping?" asks Nole, calling Shalimar out. "Everybody knows cabs don't stop for black people here because they think we're going to a shady neighborhood and they're gonna get robbed. How are they supposed to know you live on Park Avenue, Miss Jackson?"

Shalimar looks at Nole like she could skin him alive—the same way a fur trapper did the tiger-striped beaver whose fur collar is on her Iceberg capelet. "I'm just trying to get to Madison Avenue, then get home to change," she admits.

"We all know what's on Madison Avenue, so why don't you just say it?" teases Nole. "You're going to Jimmy Choo's for a tune-up."

"Right," Shalimar says, shaking her head and looking annoyed.

"So, you got a hot date later?" he probes.

"Yes, I do," says Shalimar. "Now, if you'll excuse me, I'd better make a call. Otherwise I might be standing here *forever*."

Diamond is still freaked out, but she waves good-bye sweetly as Shalimar whips out her cell phone to call a car service.

"Must be nice to have it like that," I utter.

"You should have told her you had a hot date later, too," Angora says, propping me up. "I bet you she'd be jealous if she knew you're going out with Ice Très."

"It's true, *mija*. She likes him—even if he did get suspended," claims Felinez.

"Honey, her family would probably have a fit. You know she'd better bring home Mr. Brooks Brothers, or bust," predicts Nole. Shalimar's family is part of New York's black bourgeois. "And he'd better come with a high-yield money market account!"

Diamond finally giggles and I'm glad.

"I'm surprised you didn't try to save her fur collar!" I tease her.

"I thought about it, but right now I'm thinking about Snickers the Sea Dog," quips Diamond.

"Is that your hot date?" chuckles Felinez.

"No. He's this cocker spaniel who got rescued by a cruise ship after being stranded on Kiribati island in the Pacific for four months! Somebody sent out an SOS, cuz they were going to kill all the orphaned animals on the island—so some workers on the Norwegian Cruise Line came and rescued him and this macaw parrot named Maxie."

"Where'd they take him?"

"To Oahu—Hawaii," explains Diamond. "Just Snickers, though, not Maxie."

"I wish someone took me to Hawaii. They could leave me stranded there, too," pines Felinez. She loves to travel. That's why the thought of winning a trip abroad means so much to us. We also plan on traveling all over the world when our business, Purr Unlimited, is a slamming success—like Betsey Johnson's fashion empire.

Diamond babbles on about Maxie's macabre experience—exacerbated by the fact that most ports don't accept exotic birds like her, so she's still stranded on the cruise till they find her a home.

When the elevator opens onto the tenth-floor entrance of Mood Fabrics, Nole drops his interest in Gulliver's travels and vies for velvets instead. He strokes a bolt of cerise pink burn-out floral velvet like he's spreading butter on a freshly baked croissant. "What do you think?" he asks, salivating.

"I can already see corsets with matching tattersall skirts sashaying down the runway. Très feline fatale," I advise.

Angora eyes the fabric like a true reporter. "Wow, how do they do this?" she utters.

"Sulfuric acid mixed right into the print paste so the chemical eats away the fiber and creates a hole in

447

the printed design. Voilà," sighs Nole. "Wish I could put some on my stomach to eat away at my pouch." He sighs again, then sucks in his gut.

"That's disgusting," snarls Felinez, who is usually fascinated by fat-burning formulas, before walking away. She starts scanning the aisles, on her mission to find materials for her totes, which will now be billed as billboard *borsas* on the House of Pashmina program. "Ay, *Dios mio!*" Felinez squeals. I rush over to her to see the source of her glee. Felinez is standing in front of a bolt of see-through pink vinyl. "I can't believe it!" she breathes to the salesclerk—a pencil-thin fashionista with crimped hair the color of Cheez Doodles.

"Wow, good work," I note. Felinez hugs me proudly. "I'm gonna make the totes really big—*muy grande*—like a L.A.M.B." Fifi isn't referring to the farm animal, but to the gargantuan L.A.M.B. tote bag big enough to hide a body. Everybody from Beyoncé to Lindsay Lohan has been seen carrying one.

"I haven't seen you this happy since you busted the piñata at your sixth birthday party," I chuckle, hugging her back.

Over her cuddly shoulder, I spot a Kasha twill in a neon pink that makes my heart stop. "Oh, me, oh, my, Miss Honey, don't you hear me calling you!" I swoon. "Strapless bustiers and matching bustle skirts!"

"It looks expensive," warns Felinez.

"Yeah, well, watch me bargain it down," I reply.

Diamond strolls over and examines the neon weave, carefully reading the label. "This one is made from vicuna?" she asks in disbelief.

Miss Cheez Doodles dashes over, putting on her red glasses attached to a silver chain around her neck. "Yes, I guess it is. This must be a leftover from the Jean Paul Gaultier collection we secured a few seasons ago."

"You know that vicuna is considered an endangered species now," Diamond informs the clerk. "PC Kasha twills should be made from cashmere blends or a fine wool."

"Nothing holds the garment better, though," the saleslady snaps.

"A few seasons ago, huh?" I say in a somber tone, setting the foundation for my price-slashing strategy. Bargaining is the one thing I learned from all those afternoons hanging out at the store where my mother worked when I was younger. She couldn't afford a babysitter, so the store manager used to let Chenille and me come there and wait till my mom finished work. The customers would inevitably comment on how adorable and well-behaved we were, so as long as we did our homework and kept quiet, everything was furbulous for my mom.

"Yes," says the saleslady.

"It's starting to pile, though," I say, pointing to some imaginary nubs on the fabric.

Flustered, the saleslady examines the bolt before she delivers her verdict: "I don't see anything."

"Oh, it must have been a shadow. Um, is it forty-five or fifty-four inches wide?" I ask, trying another tactic. Sometimes if you hesitate long enough, it wears down the salesperson's resolve to stick to the price.

"It's forty-five," she says, sensing my hesitation.

"Too bad it's not black," I say, pretending that pink isn't my first color choice. It's always easier to get a discount on colors that could be clocked as out-of-style by next season. Little does the salesperson know that pink is always in vogue in my *mundo*.

"Look, I can give it to you for ten dollars a yard—if that helps," the saleslady says, feigning ignorance of my tawdry tactics.

"Oh, that would," I say, like it was her idea.

Nole comes over and almost busts my charade with his oohs and aahs at the vixenish vicuna, but I nudge him, prompting him to stop in mid-aah. Too much enthusiasm could spoil the price reduction—and it's still a long way to the cash register.

When Nole meets my eye, I give him a wink, and he catches on quickly.

"Are you a model?" the saleslady asks me.

"I'm the leader for the House of Pashmina in the Catwalk competition, and yes, I'll be modeling in the fashion show, too," I tell her so she gets my priorities straight: leadership first, modeling second—the fabbie focus of any true modelpreneur. Just as I thought, the saleslady is hip to the Catwalk competition. Probably from dealing with F.I. fashionistas for years.

"Yes, you're the second one to come in today," she informs me.

"Someone was here before us?" shrieks Nole.

The saleslady can't seem to decide whether she should spill the refried beans, or let them simmer.

"Just tell me, was she wearing a tiger on her back?" I ask, teasing her. I'm still not convinced Shalimar hadn't already made her haul here and stashed the bags.

The saleslady just keeps smiling as she hoists the bolt to a counter to cut. "How many yards?" she asks.

"I bet you it was Anna Rex—cuz I just noticed a black hole in aisle five!" snorts Nole.

"What black hole?" asks Ruthie Dragon.

"Never mind that. Just write down that we need neon pink seam binding," instructs Nole.

"I think we should edge the bustiers in black," I say, in a nod to my favorite contrast—hot pink and black.

"Good call," says Nole.

Diamond nods enthusiastically in agreement.

Reluctantly, Ruthie also writes down *black binding* on Nole's notion list.

"How many yards?" the saleslady asks again.

"Five," I shoot, apologetically, getting back on the fabric track.

"Listen, I saw some iridescent nylon for the padded vest and tiered skirt," says Diamond, motioning across the aisle.

"What color?" I ask.

"Gunmetal gray, celadon green?" queries Diamond, hesitantly.

"No pink?" I counter.

"No pink," confesses Diamond.

"No need to point out that sore sighting," I blurt out. Diamond winces.

"Agreed," says Nole, backing me up.

"But the vest doesn't have to be in the same exact fabric as the tiered skirt. I mean, it's street gear combined with flirty, right?" I say, rethinking the contrast.

"That's true," pipes up Felinez.

"Okay, let's look," I say, giving in. I realize that Diamond doesn't have enough rough edges to take my jabs and keep moving. She's so sensitive.

I examine the smooth sheen of the nylon and decide that a gray padded down vest would set off the pink tiered skirt. "The skirt should be pink chiffon—urban meets überfabbie."

"I dig it," says Nole.

"Add heavy-duty gold zippers and down feathers to the list," I say to Ruthie.

"I already have *that*," she says, testily.

One more fire-breathing glare from Nole's assistant and I will have to refrain from using the bolt of nylon fabric I have tucked under my arm as a lethal weapon. Just one sideway swipe would topple this Dragon. For all I know, *she's* the spy in our midst. I make a note to my fashion self to share this new insight with two people who still believe in my pink paranoia: Angora and Felinez.

"We should do one vest in celadon, too," I say, deciding that Ruthie deserves one accidental sideways swipe after all. Sure enough, after I do the deed, Ruthie is knocked a few centimeters off her smug Uggs.

"Oops, my bad," I giggle. "Two vests coming up."

"Easy for you to say—me and Diamond will be sweating all weekend!" gripes Nole.

"I got it," says Diamond, cheerfully grabbing the second bolt out of the bin.

"Catsuits coming up," says Nole, smirking. He knows that this is my favorite—and not just because I'm going to be modeling one of them.

"Come on—we have to do one black one!" insists Nole.

"One black one coming up—Phallon will be relieved—but trust, I'm wearing the pink one!" I warn him.

Next up, we find stretchy knits for our hoodies and sweatpants and hot pants, which will be logo'd up with slogans to meet our Design Challenge.

"What about purple?" Diamond says, reminding me.

"The color purple," I repeat, remembering our outfit that will be tagged with the title inspired by the Alice Walker literary classic.

"I like the lilac one," I say, pointing to a cotton knit.

"You would—cuz it's purple mixed with pink," points out Felinez.

"Thank you for that color theory moment," I say, teasing her. Color theory was one of Felinez's favorite classes.

I look nervously at my Naughty Kitty Lolita watch to check the time.

"Don't worry—you're not going to miss your hot date with the Ice *Homme*," sighs Angora.

I shrug like I'm not stressing, even though I am. "I think I'm down with the Thug Nation after all," I say, getting giddy.

"Urban Thug," Angora says, correcting me on the moniker for Ice Très's clothing line.

After I pay for our fabbie fabric finds, we each grab a plastic bag, then head two blocks down to Steinlauf and Stoller for notion supplies.

Diamond grabs two bags of down feathers for the

454

zippered vests. "Whoa, we only need one," I order. "I always advise, add but don't pad!"

"No, you don't," pipes up Angora.

"Now I do," I quip back.

Nole hassles the salesclerk about the shady selection in threads. "You don't have neon pink?" he demands.

"No, we don't," says the blasé salesclerk.

"I bet if Gianni came out of his tomb and demanded it, you'd stock it like it's *haute*!" snaps Nole, referring to his design idol, the late Gianni Versace.

"I think the cerise shade would contrast cutely," I point out, hoping to squelch Nole's divo designer tantrum.

"No, it won't!" Nole says, stomping his foot. Now even Countess Coco has been shocked out of her stupor. Her ears perk up and her eyes bulge in distress. I pat Countess's head to assure her that I've got this sticky situation handled.

"It'll work—trust me," I say. Examining the cone of thread, I read the label and realize its polyester. "We need cotton," I instruct the salesclerk.

"Cotton," he mumbles.

"Yes, long-staple, mercerized, forty-weight, hundred-percent-cotton thread, please," I say.

Now Nole smiles. "That's my girl—count on her to get testier than me."

The salesclerk hops to it. "I'll bring it up."

"He'd better," huffs Nole. "He's out of stock *and* must be out of his mind if he thinks I'm working with Polly and Esther!"

"Ruthie, go get us some snaps and closures while we're waiting," I order, sending his reluctant assistant for some reinforcements for the bustier and corset panels.

"I don't trust her," I confess to Nole.

"Well, I do, Inspector Clouseau—so close the case!" he giggles.

"I can't wait till Garo Sparo sees our corsets," Diamond says, satisfied. Garo Sparo is a downtown designer who specializes in corsets. "I can't believe you turned down an internship to volunteer in the animal shelter instead," I groan.

"I felt the animals need me right now," counters Diamond, defending her decision.

"Just remember we need you more," Nole warns his second-in-command.

Then, armed with everything from interface to muslin, we decide to call it a day.

"Thank God it's Friday!" shouts Nole, strutting down Seventh Avenue.

"Not so fast," I interject, needing one more quick huddle to make sure we're on the same production page.

"I'm going over to your house on Sunday and Diamond's house next week," I explain to Nole.

"When am I going to see you?" protests Felinez.

I didn't think I had to hover over her to get the bags done; she's such a pro I know I can trust her to turn out billboard *borsas* and belts faster than a factory in China.

"Okay, well, I can after I finish at Nole's?" I ask, fondling Fifi's forearm.

"Okay, squeeze me in," she sighs.

"Fifi?" I query, like *come on, work with me*. I realize that we'd better talk. "I'll call you in the morning, okay?"

She nods like I'm kicking her to the curb.

Right now, I realize that I have to get ready if I'm going to head down to Native by seven o'clock for my date with Ice Três.

"Time to get Native," I giggle. Everybody, of course, follows my dating drift.

"Work the Ice Man for points on the Dow Jones, Miss Pashmina," advises Nole.

"Abso-freakin'," I say, nodding.

8

Standing in front of Mrs. Paul's apartment, I ponder whether I should indeed knock on her door. But then I'm swayed by the image of Eramus held hostage in a checked shirt and high-water tweed pants for two days running. This prompts my hand to move like it's being controlled by a Ouija board. I rap softly on the hollow steel door and, on the spot, conjure up my fashion game plan: I'll butter her up first, *then* ask.

Luckily, Eramus answers the door—or rather flings it open with glee.

"Hi, E.T.," I say, officially anointing him with a new nickname. He must like that, because he beams, but my heart sinks at the sight of him standing there in his overcoat with a stack of pamphlets in his hands. I know this means he's going out with Mrs. Paul to play a not-so-fun game of "knock, knock" on people's doors. In other words, his glum grandmother has already enlisted him to pound the pavement in the name of Jehovah's Witnesses, handing out *The Watchtower*.

"You want one?" Eramus asks, his doe eyes widening with fear.

"Um—" I stop myself and then say, "Sure, I'll take one."

Mrs. Paul marches down the hallway, purse and pamphlets clutched tightly in her fist. "I told you not to open the door," she scolds him, looking at me suspiciously. I want to blurt out, *Hello. I'm your neighbor*, but I know the drill. She hates us. See, one early Sunday morning she made the mistake of knocking on our door to bestow us with a pamphlet—and received a verbal thrashing from my sleepyhead mother.

"You look nice," I lie to Mrs. Paul, then blurt out my business. "Um, you know about the Catwalk competition I'm doing. I was wondering if you would consider letting Eramus audition to be one of the junior models in our fashion show."

Mrs. Paul looks at me like I'm a just-released juvvie. "Really?" squeals Eramus, excitedly, his eyes widening like pool balls.

"Come on, now," orders Mrs. Paul, walking toward the door, which is my cue to scram. Eramus looks at me, appearing frightened, like he's going out to meet the boogeyman on a Friday night and wants me to rescue him.

"Um, maybe you wanna come over tomorrow—and I'll show you some sketches for my fashion show?" I query.

"No, we're going out shopping tomorrow—over to Benny's," Mrs. Paul informs me.

Benny runs the thrift shop, Second Time Around, where Mrs. Paul does most of her shopping. Eramus looks sad that my pleas for his fashion advancement have been torpedoed.

"Okay, well, another time," I say, cheerfully, trying not to act defeated. God, that went over worse than the Maxi Coat and Hot Pants Ball at Club Vinyl. Not one ticket sold.

Inside my own apartment, I'm greeted by another tense scenario: this one between my mother and Ramon. Mom is all dressed up in a bronze scoop-neck minidress, shimmering from a bounty of iridescent paillettes. "You promised we would go dancing! And do something I wanna do for a change," my mom moans.

Ramon winces. "Who do you think I'm remodeling that bathroom for—not me, you know?" he counters, sitting slouched in a chair, wiping beads of sweat from his forehead with a cloth. My mom puts her hands on her hips, hovering over him. Little does he know that she's not going to take that dress off until she's danced thirty times to her favorite disco song, "I Will Survive," by Gloria Gaynor. Meanwhile, Chenille is hovering over her, stabbing at her frosted wig with a teasing comb, determined to get every strand in place, despite the fracas.

"Look at all this trouble Chenille went through fixing my hair!" exclaims my mom. She refers to all her

460

wigs as her hair, which I'm sure Ramon hasn't even figured out yet.

"That's right. I'm missing a client," Chenille brags. She raises a can of Aqua Net hair spray at a ninety-degree angle to Mom's head like she's coming in to the finish line.

Reluctantly, my mom puts her pounce on pause to turn and acknowledge my presence—her other, unemployed daughter. "Did you get the job?" she asks, like she's having déjà vu.

The spritz has obviously put my mom's memory on the fritz, because I already told her I didn't get the job at the Jones Uptown boutique.

"Aphro got it," I grunt.

Chenille rolls her eyes, which makes me Doublemint paranoid that she knows something she's not telling me.

"Aphro got it?" my mom repeats, looking puzzled. "I thought she was going to work for a designer. Ain't she designing something?"

"Well, she majors in jewelry design—and Laretha is gonna let her showcase her pieces at the boutique, too," I say, down for the count.

"Now I know you'd better go dancing," interrupts Chenille.

"I am," says my mom, glaring at Ramon.

"Well, I gotta go get ready," I say, quickly.

"Where you going?" my mom asks me.

"Out," I say, not wanting to also remind her that I told her I was going out with Ice Très tonight.

"With the computer guy?" she asks, teasing me.

"Abso-freakin'—*not!*" I exclaim.

"You need to be going out with somebody who can fix something around here," she declares.

"She's going out with Ice Très," interjects Chenille, matter-of-factly.

I'd like to whack Chenille with the wig brush. Instead, I just glare at her. She has the nerve to brush up against me as she saunters by me to her bedroom.

I turn quickly to follow her. "How did you know that?" I ask, demandingly.

"I know."

"Well, since you're in such a chatty-catty mood, tell me this," I badger her, "what were you trying to tell me the other day? Something's going on in the House of Pashmina? Did it have to do with Aphro?"

"Could be," Chenille says in a tone that lets me know water torture won't loosen her tart tongue.

"Could be *not*," I counter, tired of the tawdry tango.

I slam the door to my private sanctuary and commune with Fabbie Tabby for a few tranquil minutes before I decide what I'm going to wear. "Turn to the power of pink," I say out loud for Fabbie's ears only. I take out my pink pullover crewneck sweater embroidered with diagonal hot-pink hearts. As I ponder whether to pad my bra, and which pants to pair with my soon-to-be-ample hearts, my pink Princess phone starts ringing. Now my heart—the beating one in my flat chest—flutters nervously. I pick it up, half expecting to hear Ice Très's giggly voice querying me about my wardrobe choices for the evening. He's the only guy besides Zeus, Bobby Beat, and Nole who genuinely digs riffing about the fashion groove. Instead, I'm greeted by Snorty by Nature.

"Your ears must be scorching," I say hesitantly.

"On fire," Aphro says, gruffly.

There is an awkward pause, which I know means Aphro has something she wants to get off her equally flat chest. "So what do you want to tell me?" I ask, trying to get this party started.

"Hold up. Lemme finish this personality quiz in *CosmoGirl*," she says, obviously stalling.

"What for? I can tell you that without any quiz!" I snap. "You're a *bieeeotch*!"

"Oh, shut up and wait," she starts. I almost want to tell her, *Not now, please, I've had enough "reality" for one day—between Caterina and her crew, you, Benny, Diamond's designing drama, Liza Flake, Ruthie Dragonbreath, and Shalimar's shadiness*—but I hold my pink tongue and listen.

"Listen, I knew you would put me on blast about taking that job," Aphro says, defensively. Yet again, she's displaying her annoying attitude. When Aphro and I first became tight freshman year, I always allowed it, because secretly I felt bad about her situation—being in a foster home. Now I just wish I lived in a house as nice as she does with the Maydells.

"I don't care that you took the job, but you coulda given me the heads-up before I had to hear about it from my assistant—in front of everybody else in the Catwalk meeting!" I exclaim, getting my piece out before she interrupts me like she always does. And I hate that about her, too.

"Oh, hold on to your hot sauce, Miss Purr. I was gonna tell you, but you've been avoiding me like I gave you meningococcal meningitis!" protests Aphro.

"Don't be so dramatic with the teen diseases," I say, twirling my hair nervously, but what I really want to blurt out is *You gave me more than that—you sent me a computer virus!* "Well, now that you've got a job, you can kick in for supplies for the jewelry."

Although I'm half teasing, Aphro isn't. "Hello, that's what I've been trying to tell you. I went down to Chinatown today after I got a hot tip on some counterfeit Chanel ivory bangles," Aphro states emphatically. "That backroom action down there is fierce. They look like Chanel, for sure, and I did kick in so I could get two dozen of them!"

"Okay, well, whatever blows your circle skirt up," I

say, still confused. On one hand, Aphro seems down for the Catwalk twirl, but on the other, I sense she's trying to sabotage my leadership.

Right now, I'm more interested in strategizing my ensemble, so I interrupt Aphro's flow for feedback: "Should I wear the pink velvet jeans with my sweater tonight—or the leggings?"

"Wear the jeans and the pink shoes with the kitty pom-poms," she suggests.

I pull out my pink velvet jeans and search for stains. Once they pass my inspection, I plop them on top of Fabbie's head as she lies on the bed in her royal kitty pose. She loves when I do that. Why else would she just sit there on the bed and not move the cover-up till she's good and ready?

"I gotta jet," Aphro announces, abruptly.

"Hold up." Before I can press my edit button, I blurt it out: "You didn't send me that virus, did you?"

Aphro doesn't even pause. "I'ma act like I didn't hear that, cuz you're tripping. I'll see you at Nole's for the fitting."

"Right," I say, my cheeks flushed. "So are you going to tell me what is going on with you?"

"No, because there is nothing to talk about," claims Aphro.

"Okeydokey," I say, signing off. And Aphro knows what that sign-off means: I'm not buying it!

I have to get ready, so I scurry to the bathroom to start beating my face with Glam Kitty cosmetics. First I apply meowverlous cream foundation in my shade—tawny beige—then set it off with a pouf of loose powder applied with a big plump brush. After I sweep my eyelids with moody pink frosted eye shadow, I apply shy pink shimmery booty dust to the corners of my eyes and my imaginary cleavage. Bobby Beat turned me on to this feline fatale finish—and it will be de rigueur for all the models in our fashion show. *"Meowch,"* I moan to myself when I approve my handiwork.

My mom yells out from the living room, so I fling open the door to my pink palace to see what she wants. Like I thought, her plans are about to spring into action despite the original setback—Ramon's fatigue. "We're going. Don't be back later than eleven." Although Ramon has ditched the scruffy work gear and changed into a striped burgundy shirt and black pants, he still looks like he just crawled out of a bomb shelter—frightened but happy to be alive.

"I know. I'll be home," I concede, although eleven is not the bewitching hour I had in mind. I'll probably get Ice Très to walk me home, anyway. Then maybe we can make out in the stairwell—right under the goofy red graffiti: Treva 4EVER.

"Call me on my cell at ten o'clock sharp, and then

when you're back home," Mom warns me, squelching my shot at a stairwell interlude.

"Will do. You look nice," I say, smiling.

I hear my bedroom phone ringing and I run back to get it. "Hello," I answer, in a breathy voice. This time it's a distressed Angora.

"What time is he picking you up?" Angora asks, sounding concerned.

"He said seven o'clock but he hasn't gotten here yet," I say. "Should I call him?"

"Absolutely not, according to *The Rules*," advises Angora.

"Oh, right," I say, chuckling. Angora, the sound bite queen, swears by a dating manual that advises, "Never call a boy unless it's to return his call. And never e-mail him first, either. No smiley faces. No recipes. No YouTube videos! *Nada. Niente*. Nietzsche. (The last part I added for good measure.) Exasperated, I sigh to Angora, "How is he gonna call if I'm talking to you?"

"Call-waiting?" quips Angora.

"No, I mean . . . I gotta go get ready!" I blurt out before I realize that Angora probably called for reasons of her own. "Wazzup?" I ask, concerned.

"My father's freaking out," she admits. "He got his profit participation statement today from Bandito Studios and there's no money."

"What, what?" I ask, confused.

"The profit participation statement lists all the money the studio brings in from Funny Bunny everything, and how much they pay the creator—in this case, my father—after all their expenses. So the statement says they're in the *red*—they've lost money, to the tune of five million dollars!" Angora explains patiently, but she's having trouble breathing, like she does when she gets stressed.

"What a sham-o-rama. That sounds like a three-card monte," I say in disbelief. When Angora's dad first moved to New York, he went to Times Square, where these shamsters used to always be set up with cardboard boxes, ready to empty tourists' pockets with their confidence card game. In it, the mark—in this case, Mr. Le Bon—was tricked into betting his ducats that he could find the money card—for example, the queen of spades—among three facedown playing cards. Of course, the shamster had *always* perfected his sleight of hand, which guaranteed that the mark would always pick a losing card.

"Je'Taime told him that he was going to get a lot of money—and apparently, Daddy has been counting on that. So we're not going to Colombia for Christmas," laments Angora.

Now I feel bad for her, but still I can't help giving her advice: "I think maybe your father should be taking advice from a lawyer and not from his psychic. Don't you think?" I say, gently.

"I know. He's been on the phone with one all day. Now he's running around the apartment so hyper I'm worried about him," Angora confesses.

"Well, maybe I can come over on Sunday," I say, my head whirling with my weekend schedule. I have to do my homework, go over to Nole's, and see Felinez.

"I don't know what to do," Angora says, trying to catch her breath. "I don't want to call Ms. Ava. And Je' Taime spent all day making her famous gumbo, but Daddy won't eat a drop. And his eyes look crazy because they're so bloodshot."

"Well, make him some of your mint julep tea. Try to get him to calm down," I suggest.

"I know. I will. Well, have a good time tonight," Angora says, sweetly.

"Um, listen," I interject, quickly, "have you heard anything?"

"About what?"

"About anything. About Aphro. About Liza Flake. About the bubonic plague. About the computer virus. Anything," I say, exasperated.

"Settle down, *chérie*," Angora says, calmed by my cuckoo episode. "We have to be very careful how we deal with this situation."

"Now you sound like the AOL warning. 'If you don't know who sent you this e-mail, open with caution.' What a crock!" I hiss.

"I'm sorry, Pash. I'm not AOL, but I feel like saying the same thing. What else are we supposed to do except be careful?" advises Angora.

"You're right. Okay, signing off," I say, giggling. "And don't forget that I love you."

When I get off the phone, I look at my Glam Kitty clock on the wall and notice that it's seven-thirty already. I'm starving and my stomach is now fueled by jitters. And now where is Ice Très? Spacing out, I stare at the Eartha Kitt poster over my bed. I continue floating, orbiting on the image of Chris "Panda" Midgett trolling with his PC pals at the Jacob Javits Center. Well, at least he's probably having fun. I switch on my computer, which is now working, thanks to the shortie with a techno plan. I search through my files for my Catwalk competition document so I can examine the call-of-show lineup for our fashion show. Scrolling down through my files, I start to feel creepy about the corrupted file that contained the virus. When I asked at school, nobody else reported their computer going into deep freeze. Shrugging off my feelings, I numbly start reordering the lineup of my fashion show. Definitely the canvas hoodie with the graffiti cargo pants should go before the chiffon drawstring gown—and not the other way around. After fifteen more minutes, I decide to ditch Angora's advice. I pick up the phone and dial Ice Très's cell. It goes straight to voice mail. I listen carefully and leave a squeaky message. I don't want to sound like I've hit the panic button, even though I have. We were supposed to take a bus down to Lenox Avenue together so we could get to Native around eight o'clock! Obviously that's not gonna happen and he hasn't even called to cancel. Suddenly struck by lethargy, I force myself to get up and finish getting ready. There is no way Ice Très would stand me up. Nobody would primp up their plumage just to pluck out my kitty whiskers by standing me up. *Would they?*

I shake off such feline-foolish thoughts and sashay for myself in front of my full-length mirror after I'm dressed. Staring at my long reflection, I smile. There is nothing like head-to-toe pink for earning personal purr points.

"Meowch!" I squeal out loud, staring at Fabbie, who is still propped on my bed without a care in the world. I'm so glad nobody keeps her waiting. I know it would make her fluffy fur wilt.

By eight o'clock, the phone still hasn't rung, so I pick it up just to check that it's still working. Now I'm bona fried. I call Ice Très's cell phone again—and this time my message is extra-crispy. "I don't know if you've been washed up by the Pineapple Express, but if you have, I hope you've drowned!" I whisper fiercely into the phone before hanging up. Instead of feeling better, I feel guilty. Ice Très told me that the reason his family had moved from Hamilton, Washington, to the Big Apple was that their house had been flooded several times by tropical waters originating in Hawaii. Suddenly I'm flooded by horrible thoughts: What if Ice Très is trying to get back at me for getting him expelled? Maybe he sent me the virus! Nobody told him to write that corny graffiti in the school stairwell, but I bet he blames me for the Cupid misfire. Phase two of his get-even plan: he stands me up! All along I assumed it was someone in my house—but what if it's the handsome hoodwinker hovering on the horizon with twinkling eyes and dangerous dimples?

**FASHION INTERNATIONAL 35th ANNUAL
CATWALK COMPETITION BLOG**

New school rule: You don't have to
be ultranice, but don't get tooooo
catty, or your posting will be zapped
by the Fashion Avengers!

TAKE IT TO THE BRIM . . .

Some of my friends in my neighborhood out on Long Island give me static
about being in the mix at F.I. As a
matter of fact, I don't even say the
name of my school when talking to my
skateboarding brethren, because I
don't want to deal with their raised
eyebrows and silly smirks. Since the
news circulated around the bushes that
I'm competing in something called
the Catwalk competition, names like
"Sissy-rella" and "primping pimp"
have been flying around my hat, attempting to make a landing too fre-
quently for my fly tastes.

I also know that right across the
street from F.I., the dogs at D.T.
(don't see any reason to spell out
that school name, either) are barking
big-time about the male students at
F.I. Personally, I think they should
stop with the haterade conventions and
focus on student amalgamation that
would force D.T. school officials to
lighten up on their constricting dress
code. I would have a problem with attending a school that prohibits me
from wearing headgear. I know D.T.
isn't the only one with this kind of
crimp in its pimp. My cousin Demeter

goes to a school in the UK where you either lose the baseball cap or be moved out of the classroom and taught in isolation. Taking all these creative restrictions into consideration, I feel lucky to be a part of my school. I recognize that I'm a serious sneakerhead, which means I must bring the headgear—*always*. As a matter of fact, I hope that after hearing about my blog entry, the F.I. faculty will take a cue from Bell Academy in Bayside, Queens (which my younger sister, Olivia, attends—and yes, I come from a big, tight family), by instituting "Crazy Hat Fridays." At that progressive school, students are encouraged to wear their most creative headgear on a designated day. F.I. was, well, designed for that type of display in creative thinking out of the hatbox.

Wearing lids isn't about exuding attitude—it's about claiming your angle with "hattitude." These days, I've been hinged to my mink zebra-striped-brim hat, because my dad made it for me. My dad, Mr. Cronus Artemides, is an old-school tailor in every sense. The man can make a suit that would put the House of Armani out of business. I'm not bragging—this is a serious fact. My father was trained by his grandfather back in Greece. I don't think you can get that kind of training anywhere else, from what I can see. No disrespect to the fashion design situation here at F.I., either. My father could have been a world-

class designer, but he had to raise a
family and has been successfully running his own tailor shop for two
decades in Manhattan. Unfortunately,
with the escalating greed of New York
landlords, my father may be forced to
take his tailoring skills elsewhere. I
really think that's foul. Let me ask
you: how can you expect a small re-
tailer to pay $10,000—$30,000 a month
on rent for a retail operation and
still be able to pay all their other
expenses that we've learned about in
Retail 101 AND expect them to turn a
profit? You don't have to be a student
at Fashion International (okay, there,
I said it) to see that is straight-up
pimping. Now, I don't want to go off
on any retail riff here and now, but
rather get back to basics: I plan on
wearing my mink zebra-striped hat
proudly to the Catwalk competition,
where I will be taking the competition
to the brim. And hats off to the winning house, cuz there's nothing sissy-
relish, or whatever, about winning a
trip abroad and $100,000 in prize
money—which could buy some serious
Italian headgear.

Posted by Sneakerhead 14:56:45

9

Felinez freaks out when I tell her that I have to jettison the fashion pit stop to her house later because Angora requires my assisterance instead.

"I can't believe it. *Yo no lo creo!* You promised!" she hurls at me on the phone as I try to juggle my double mochaccino frappé coolatte in one hand and her vixen vibrations in the other. The heated exchange causes beads of sweat to percolate on my upper lip despite the whipping winds that are propelling me faster than my magenta suede bootees into the narrow doorway of the tenement building on East Sixty-seventh Street where Nole lives.

"Come on, Blue Boca—I'll see the bags on Monday," I plead as I take the elevator to the fourth floor to Nole's apartment.

"No, I'm on the design team, so you should have invited me, too!" announces Felinez.

"I know that, Fifi. *Duh!* I didn't think you wanted to labor through the first fittings," I protest, catching my breath when I reach the fourth-floor landing.

"Well, now I do, since you're too busy to see me! I

finished five billboard *borsas* already! What if you don't like them, huh?" she pleads in return.

"You're a genius, Fifi—you never make anything I don't like. That's why we're going to be in business together, so stop it, *purr favor?*" I moan.

"Well, I'm coming anyway. Michelette is driving me cuckoo mambo. I gotta get out of this *casa Telemundo!*" cries Fifi, sounding more like a desperate housewife than a designated designer.

"Awright then, hop on your broomstick to the East Side, cuz there is plenty of parking space over here," I sigh, eyeing the rows of fancy cars parked on the street.

"What's that supposed to mean—I'm a *bruja* now?" asks Felinez, defensively. "I only light the candles for *buena suerte*—good luck—not because I'm a witch!"

"I know that, Fifi," I say, trying to calm her down. After I snap my phone shut, I realize that I didn't even get to chew the catnip about Ice Très's espionage because I had to fluff Fifi's whiskers instead. Dragging my feet down the gray carpeted hallway, I reflect on my new reality: being in house leader mode 24-7. *"It just goes on and on till the break of dawn!"* I sing, or rather squeak, in my cackling jackal voice.

I tap rapidly on Nole's front door with my knuckles before my blurry vision rests on the tarnished brass knocker directly in front of my nose. Suddenly, I feel a stabbing pain in my chest—the familiar ache I get when my heart is hurting. I can't believe Ice Très left me in the booty dust Friday night!

My clanking the knocker full strength activates Countess Coco's shrill bark. But she's not the only one agitated: I hear someone scurrying to open the door, then yapping, "I'm so sick of all these newspapers! Why don't we just open up a newspaper stand!" The choppy tone belongs to Nole, who maneuvers the door until it is slightly ajar. Sight unseen, he orders, "Come in—and don't trip!"

I heed the command and enter. Countess Coco pops out, pawing furiously at my leggings to get my attention.

"Were you talking to me?" I ask, peering at Nole squished behind the half-opened metal door.

"Is there someone else coming in?" Nole asks.

"No," I respond, gingerly picking up the poofy, persistent Pomeranian, who weighs a fraction of Fabbie Tabby's "fluffy weight."

"Then obviously I was talking to you," he says, gently rubbing his hands together, releasing a waft of freshly applied Kiehl's hand lotion into the overheated air.

"In that case, I'm all ears to business propositions," I continue.

"Huh?" asks Nole, his big brown eyes bulging big-time, probably because he's been up all night working on the samples.

"The newspaper stand—with backdated editions? *Gen-i-us*, if you ask me," I say enthusiastically while staring at the mile-high stacks of newspapers behind him. They're lining the entire stretch of the narrow, dark hallway inside his apartment. "Who woulda thunk underneath all that Gucci garnish was all the news fit to print on the planet?"

"Don't wear out my nerves, Miss Purr. I was talking to my mother, who must think there are winning lottery numbers inside these freakin' papers—*why else wouldn't she throw them out!*" he shouts loudly, obviously unraveling.

I wince in embarrassment for his mom. I know she works in the real estate biz, so she probably has her reasons for hoarding the newspapers—despite Nole's protests.

Nonetheless, I hop on his whiny bandwagon: "I hear you. I'm definitely over my kitty litter limit today. The 'notorious tagger' stood me up Friday night. I think that's who sent me the virus. And Felinez is coming over pronto."

"What, what? Why don't we just hold the Geneva convention in my hallway? After all, who needs chairs when there are newspapers to sit on!" hisses Nole.

"What—so far all we have is Aphro coming, and now we're talking about Fifi the foodie. She doesn't sit— she noshes. Just whip out the chorizo pan," I shoot back.

"You didn't ask me if Aphro could come," Nole hisses.

"I know. I'm sorry," I say. Nole is being so hypersensitive about the designs. He doesn't want anyone to get a whiff until they pass our high standard of approval. "She insisted. I had to relent, since we're on real shaky ground, thanks to her cyber crime." So what, I'm embellishing, but it's partly true.

"I thought you said Ice Très did it," Nole says, confused.

"I know, but at this point I don't know what to think anymore—maybe they're in cahoots," I say, furrowing my brow, because I'm supa-tense. And Nole is, too.

He pats his forehead nervously. "Listen, pink panther, you're wearing me out like Inspector Clouseau. I can't think anymore."

"I know, but *you* might want to double up on the Secret today. I certainly did," I advise, then put down Countess Coco, bend my arms to flap them like a chicken, and sniff my aromatic pits for good measure.

Nole lets out one of his infectious frilly giggles— destined to land him a CFDA Fashion Award if nothing else does.

"You are sooo shady—I do *not* use Secret!" he squeals. "You know I've been working on these samples like the Red Devil hot sauce demon!"

"I know. I can *smell*—oops, I mean, I can *tell*," I giggle, hugging Nole's pudgy frame, soaking up the dampness radiating from beneath his white Gucci T-shirt.

"Speaking of secret—the only one you need to know about a busy bee is you're gonna get stung by proximity, okay?" warns Nole.

"Huh?" I ask, puzzled pink.

"Who do you think Shalimar was shimmying with in her Jimmy Choos from dusk till dawn Friday night?" asks Nole, dramatically folding his pudgy arms across his chest.

Now it's my turn to stammer: "What, what?"

"Miss Purr, I don't know how you manage to maintain your 3.5 grade point average sometimes. Hello—the Ice Man cometh—and wenteth, in this case with Shalimar. And they were cozily chomping together on conch fritters at Native Friday night!"

Now I go into deep freeze. "Native—the restaurant?" I ask, mindlessly taking one of my spiral curls hostage.

"Hello—not Native the teepee!" quips Nole, insensitive to my kaflustered state.

"He double-booked?" I say, shocked.

"Exactly. Wake up and smell the catnip—and stop yanking!" orders Nole, smacking my hand like my mom used to do when I was little to get me to stop my annoying habit. "The notorious tagger from Highway 20?"

Nole mutters, shaking his head. "Puhleez, I bet he's probably still using his first box of Crayolas!"

"How do you know about this?" I ask, standing frozen until Nole motions like a design sergeant for me to follow him into the cramped living room.

"Never mind. Just let that shady scribbler go *poof* into the night, so you can focus on the real grand prize—the Big Willie trophy—okay?"

"Awright," I say, resigned. "How could I fall for Ice Très's graffiti game—*twice?*" I'm so distracted navigating the newspaper piles and trying to avoid stepping on Countess that I stumble, falling face-first onto the bold headline 2,000-YEAR-OLD EARRING DISCOVERED!

Countess scurries away like the Road Runner while Nole kneels to my rescue, fretting. "That was not a sashay. Are you okay?"

"I'm okay," I moan, massaging my jaw. "I just hope the Jerusalem jewels will survive."

Nole quickly scans the newspaper headline in question. "Don't worry about them; they'll be on the bidding block by high noon," he declares, rearranging the toppled stack of newspapers with the story about the precious emerald and pearl antiquities on top of the heap. Wistfully, he adds, "I hope they find one of my designs buried under Egyptian ruins two thousand years from now. That would be fitting—for Chic Canoli."

"Speaking of Egyptian ruins and treasures, have you talked to Elgamela?" I ask, gingerly. I wanted her to come, too, since three fitting models are better than one, but Nole vetoed the idea. Like I said, he's supa-anxious about who sees the samples before they're feline approved—and about safeguarding against leaks in our intel.

"Stop asking me so many questions," quips Nole.

"Well, I need answers—so who told you?" I ask, knowing that Nole follows my nosy drift.

"I'm not telling you," he retorts. "Let's get back on the weave track. We need that three-hundred-dollar bonus."

"Right," I second, glancing around his living room, which looks like a cross between an old Chinatown sweatshop and a preview to a costume exhibit at El Barrio museum.

"This is nothing. Wait till we really crank it up," claims Nole, shrugging his shoulder at the cluttered chaos.

"Looks cranked up to me," I tease. For starters, the expansive faux marble table jutting out of the dining room has been turned into a cutting table, covered with patterns; then there are the numerous bolts of fabrics leaning helter-skelter against the walls, scraps littering the hardwood floor like confetti from a birthday blast. Nole's prized fashion sketches are taped everywhere on the walls and lamp shades, and one is even dangling from the corner of a framed Etta James poster.

"I dig the poster," I comment.

"My dad gave her that," shares Nole, referring to his mother. "He knew Etta back in the day," he adds, nonchalantly, but I can still tell that he's mystified by his father. Nole's dad is an old-school black jazz musician—not famous or anything, but he was definitely in the game.

"Do you ever see him?" I ask, because I can't help being nosy.

"No, but he left behind his prized collection of vinyl records," he says, pointing to the impressive rack lining the top of a console. "Got everybody from James Brown to Martha Reeves and the Vandellas."

"*Purrfecto*," I coo in approval. "I'm anxious to get my pose on to a few old-school tracks."

"He'll probably come back one day to get them. I mean, they were the only thing he ever cared about," Nole sighs, taking the two front panels of muslin off a dress form with a flourish. "If this fits you, then we're good to go on the bustier front."

"I hope my, um, dad does, too," I say, stumbling over the word uncomfortably.

"Do you know him?" asks Nole, his bleary eyes widening.

I know Nole's brains are fried by seams and dreams,

so I ignore the fact that he obviously forgot my searing saga.

"No. And it fries my frittata that Miss Viv won't tell me who he is," I admit, following Nole's and Angora's lead by calling my mother by her first name.

Nole, whose edit button is more busted than Aphro's, doesn't disappoint. "Maybe that's because she doesn't know who he is, hello?" he blurts out.

"Could be," I say, flinching. I'm not trying to hear that. "I think he's gonna just show up one day, like if I—I mean, we—win the competition and he sees me on TV and thinks, Ooooh, she's so *purrlicious*, I can't even believe she's my daughter!"

"Yeah, the losers always come running when you're too *furbulous*—and it'll be too late," predicts Nole, motioning for me to get undressed with a dramatic hand gesture.

"Why does my father have to be a loser?" I ask.

"Do you think it's gorgeous that I have to go to the store with her chasing after me in the produce aisle like the Terminator in that chair if I don't pick out the ripest tomato? Losers—that's what they all are for leaving us!" declares Nole, holding his hostile ground.

Now I feel friv for blurting out my untold tiddy like a preschooler. I haven't even told Felinez that one. Queasily, I ask, "Should I go into the bathroom to change?"

485

"No, Penelope and Napoleon are in there licking each other's paws. It's their Sunday-morning ritual," he explains. Penelope and Napoleon are Nole's prized Persian cats—so prized, in fact, that they had an official wedding ceremony that cost more than Kibbles 'n Bits.

"Even though Penelope already has experience portraying the blushing bride, I'm definitely angling for Fabbie Tabby to close our fashion show," I quip.

"Not gonna happen," snipes Nole like he's delivering a pedigree prediction. "I take verbal contracts very seriously, so don't think you can renege on our original agreement!"

To lure Nole into the divo design position in my house, I agreed that Penelope could close the show. "I guess I'm becoming a true fashionista," I coo proudly. My favorite teacher, Ms. London taught us "In fashion, everything is negotiable, then renegotiable."

But right now, Nole is not in a negotiating mood. "Today, Miss Purr!" he orders.

"Awright," I snap, to mask the fact that I feel funny peeling off layers in the middle of his living room. Leaving my pink leggings in a puddle, I stand like a dummy in my Hello Kitty bloomers and pink mesh bra. After all, this is what I'll be expected to do at designer fittings in my not-so-distant future.

"Well, hello, kitty," Nole says, leveling his stare at the iconic cutie on the front of my pink cotton briefs.

Countess Coco rests on her hind legs, cocks her fluffy head to the side, and squints, seemingly staring up at my small chest.

"Don't look, Countess—or they'll shrink!" I say sheepishly.

"Hold still," Nole orders me as he pins the seams of the muslin to fit my bodice. Muslin is a designer's best friend—and any worth their weight in Gianni Versace gunmetal rely on it to sculpt the shape of the design *before* they take a "bite" out of the actual fabric the garment will be made from. See, sketching is one thing—but putting it to the muslin test is another.

"Your mother doesn't mind you taking over the living room?" I ask. At home, I'm not allowed to work in the living room—and I have to keep my "projects," as my mom refers to my modelpreneur enterprises, confined to my bedroom.

"She minds, but the Catwalk competition is war, so I've declared a hostile takeover," snorts Nole.

Nole's mom's ears must be burning, because the whir of her Hoveround power chair signals her approach before she enters the war zone.

Although I know from reading one of Nole's Catwalk blog entries that his mom desperately needs hip surgery, I'm startled when I see her squeezed uncomfortably into the iron chair responsible for most of her mobility. She's also much bigger than I pictured her—

probably about a plus-size 24. Her piled-high frosted blond hair with wispy bangs reminds me of the retro dos favored by girl groups back in the day.

"Hi, Mrs. Canoli!" I say, my voice squeaking against my will because of my naked state.

She studies me blandly, then orders, "Don't call me Mrs., just call me Claudia. Canoli is my maiden name."

"Oh, I'm sorry," I say, even more embarrassed, because I forgot that Nole had told me his mother and father weren't married. Now I wonder what his father's last name is. I rest my weight on one bare foot instead of both, like I'm taking up too much space or something. "I'm Pashmina."

"I know," she responds, her lips finally curling into a lazy smile. "I like your boots. Magenta looks good on you."

"Wow, thank you," I say. "That's amazing you knew what color this is. Most people think it's fuchsia or pink."

"Most people are color-blind," Ms. Canoli says. Then she asks, "You want something to eat?"

"Um—no," I say, even though I'm hungry.

"I'm waiting till everybody gets here, okay?" Nole informs his mother, like he's annoyed.

"Who's everybody?" his mother asks.

"Never mind," snaps Nole.

"Felinez—she's our accessories designer," I say,

because I feel bad that Nole is being so snappy with his mom. If I talked to my mother like that, she would shorten my career's life span.

Nole shoots me a look and says, "Models should be seen and not heard!"

"Yeah, well, I don't just rip the runway, I rule it," I quip back. "I'm the house leader."

Nole's mom smiles again—but this time I can tell she's letting me know that she approves of my feline feistiness. Now I stand quietly while Nole continues to pin me in—tightly. "Does that hurt?" he asks, smirking.

"Um, no sir," I say.

"Too bad," he swipes.

"Oops, excuse me, my breasts are vibrating," shoots Nole's mom, digging for a cell phone in her blouse. "What? He wants to see it today. Tell him to be there by four," she shoots. "No. It's sixty-five hundred. Not a penny less. All right." Ms. Canoli flips the phone shut, then anchors it back under her bra strap inside her blouse.

"All right—I gotta get ready. Get those two love-birds out the bathroom—time's up. I gotta get in there!" she orders, wheezing. She commandeers her chair in the direction of the bathroom.

Suddenly, someone outside the door activates the brass clanker with more voracity than I did.

"She's early," laments Nole. "I wanted to have the skirt done, too, before anybody but you sees it."

"It's feline fabbie already," I assure Nole as he pins the puffy sleeves into the sleeve sockets. "We're lacing up the front, right?" I ask.

"Yup—and the back, too. Even Gaultier is going to gag when he sees that!" squeals Nole, running to the front door.

Aside from the late Gianni Versace, the only purrworthy designer in Nole's book is French-born Jean Paul Gaultier—especially since he designed the costumes for Nole's fave cult film, *The Fifth Element*.

"Omigod—you're early!" echoes Nole's voice from the hallway.

I suck in my stomach and scurry over to the mirror above the chartreuse velvet couch to look at how the lines of muslin are coming along. "Fabbie Tabby is going to love this," I purr. I stand on my bare tippy toes and push up my small breasts inside the bra to see if I look trussed up like a turkey.

In a few seconds, Nole's shadow makes its way down the hall. "Do you think maybe we can push up these catnip treats till they topple?" I ask him, staring at his reflection in the mirror.

That's when I notice the reflection behind him—of the only zebra-striped mink hat I've ever seen . . . on Zeus's head!

10

Zeus's mysterious cameo makes me want to zap myself into an invisible hole in the floor, but where is that escape clause when you need it, huh? Instead, I screech involuntarily, "Omigod!" Then I attempt a mad dash to the bathroom, careening around the couch, but merely manage to stub my toe *hard* on its unforgivingly obtrusive corner. "*Ouuuch!*"

"Omigod, don't try that on the runway!" squeals Nole, imitating me—and getting off on his sneaky surprise, no doubt.

"You okay?" asks Zeus, coyly. He knows exactly how to perch his brim and curl up the corners of his mouth to make me gaspitate.

"It depends," I reply, wincing.

"On what?" Zeus asks, squinting his dark magnetic eyes with curiosity.

"Are you my secret Santa?" I say, still clinging to the hope that a hole in the floor will magically appear and suck me in.

Before Zeus can answer, the whir of Ms. Canoli's

Hoveround can be heard approaching the scene of the fashion crime again.

"Oh, dear!" she says when she spots the combo of the mad hatter and me, still standing in my *bloomers*. As the convo progresses, however, I realize that her exclamatory outburst is probably more in response to Zeus's chiseled cheekbones and dark, fluttery eyelashes. "And who are you?" asks Nole's mom, blushing like a Kabuki doll, thanks to the extra helpings of rosy rouge she has poufed on her apple-sized cheeks.

Zeus humbly introduces himself—and chatters effortlessly, displaying more of his, well, digable charm. He extends his hand to Ms. Canoli and she shakes it, giggling.

"Isn't he gorgeous?" Nole says, finally warming up to his mom.

She counters with her own question: "Doesn't he look like Stavros?"

"Who?" responds Nole.

"Stavros from the support group for people who've been abducted by aliens," his mom says, nonchalantly.

"No need to spill all the refried beans!" hisses Nole.

"What? He does look like him. Stavros was a nut, but he was handsome," counters Ms. Canoli.

"You have to forgive her," Nole advises Zeus, obviously embarrassed. "She meets people in the strangest places."

"Yeah, well, that's where the best real estate leads come from these days, and I don't see you complaining when we go to the Gucci outlet," she explains, defensively.

"Um, if you'll excuse me . . . ," I interrupt, planning my escape to the bathroom to lick my wounds, but Nole isn't having it.

"Where do you think you're going? We've got work to do. Let me fit you in the tattersall skirt muslin now— or we'll be here all day!" he orders me.

"Um, where do you want me?" Zeus asks while trying not to say hello to the kitty on my bloomers.

"The sweatpants are ready—so strip down!" Nole orders. "I hope your undies are as interesting as Miss Purr's!"

"I wore my Joe Boxer smiley faces just for the occasion," he chuckles.

"Why don't I put on Aretha? I just found the early Atlantic years," Ms. Canoli interjects, then sends a swipe Nole's way: "I told you it was here. It was behind Al Green. I bet if it was *Vogue* magazine, you would have found it under the piles of Pompeii!"

"Don't be so dramatic," hisses Nole.

"You talking about the Golden Reign?" asks Zeus, his hypnotic dark eyes brightening up like the epicenter of the solar system. Suddenly, Zeus spins around and takes in Ms. Canoli's expansive record collection.

"Yes, I am," Ms. Canoli says, proudly. "I've got every album she ever made."

"Wow—this is unbelievable!" exclaims Zeus, fingering the record—*Unreleased Recordings from the Golden Reign of the Queen of Soul*—like he has discovered the Holy Grail. He scratches the faint stubble on his face in approval as he scans Ms. Canoli's expansive row of vinyl records. "This is a *serious* collection."

Nole digs through a pile of clothes and pulls out pieces of the terry cloth fabric, which he has already cut into sweatpants.

"Heh, he doesn't get the muslin treatment?" I ask.

"Not for sweatpants and a hoodie," snipes Nole, like I should know better, which I do.

What I really want to say is *Let's finish with my skirt fitting first,* but of course, that's the moment when my cell phone rings in my bag on the other side of the room. No way am I answering it. "If that's Aphro, she'd best be on her way instead of calling me to tell me about it," I gripe.

"Tell her not to be late next time," Nole orders me.

Zeus waits patiently to be fitted into the deep raspberry sweatpants. "Aren't you going to answer it?" Nole challenges me, swishing the pants in my direction.

"Nope," I say, nodding in approval at the sweatpants. "That color is so fierce."

"The pink palette will be represented in full force in the House of Pashmina," comments Nole.

"You can have this Aretha if you want," offers Ms. Canoli, her dark lashes fluttering like a, well, schoolgirl.

"Are you serious?" asks Zeus in disbelief.

"If I wasn't, I wouldn't offer it," counters Ms. Canoli. "Take it."

Zeus holds the precious album and bends down to kiss her on her full cherub cheeks.

"I got an op to spin for New Year's Eve, so I'm trying to make sure my collection is tight by then," he explains. "And this is as tight as it gets."

"I hope you enjoy it," she says, like she's satisfied that someone finds her useful; then she steers her Hoveround out of the room in a hasty exit.

"Where are you spinning?" I ask Zeus. I definitely wouldn't mind rubbing elbows—and more—with Zeus on New Year's Eve.

"Native," he says, humbly.

"You mean Native on Lenox Avenue?" I repeat in a squeaky voice. Nole shoots me a look like *This is definitely déjà vu.*

"Yeah," Zeus says. "I was there Friday night. Ice Très hooked me up with the owner for the gig. I mean, it's not a big spot—but the sound system is kicking and they get a nice crowd, apparently."

"Yeah, so I hear," I moan, then shoot Nole a look to let him know his kitty kat is definitely out of the Gucci bag. Obviously, it was Zeus who told him about the Ice Très and Shalimar sighting. Even Hello Kitty on my bloomers blushes as I ponder whether Zeus also knows that Ice Très left me in the booty dust for shady Shalimar.

Suddenly, the door clanker clanks again—and this time I simply plop onto the couch and pull a piece of the brocade bustier fabric onto my lap. "No more 'peeka-boo, guess who' surprises for *moi*," I blurt out at Zeus, then quickly divert my eyes from the bright yellow smiley faces emanating from his direction.

It takes only a *segundo* for me to realize that the loud cackling noises in the hallway belong to Felinez and El-gamela, who sail into the living room without so much as a minor mishap. "No wonder I can never find a news-paper!" squeals Elgamela, hugging Nole. Now I realize that even though she and Nole have been hanging tight, she has obviously never been to his house before. She gasps at Zeus. "I would hug you, but I can't in that disrobed condition!" exclaims Elgamela, blushing. "If my father was here, I would never hear the end of his 'chirping.' " We all laugh at Elgamela's joke: her parents are Muslim and run Chirpin' Chicken on Second Av-enue, about five blocks from Nole's house.

"Well, good thing he isn't, because I have to fit you for the bathing suit," says Nole.

I try to motion with my eyes to Fifi that I'm in distress, but she just looks puzzled, holding tightly on to the jumbo shopping bag she's lugging. I lose all sense of modesty and jump off the couch to hug her. "I'm so freaked out!" I whisper in her ear. But she pretends not to hear me.

"You've never been here before?" she asks Elgamela, who is taking in the apartment like it's a cultural exhibit.

"I know, it's weird, but Nole is quite the divo—he never has time for his friends," she says, hugging Nole again. "But I love that we get to see each other all the time now, though, thanks to the House of Pashmina!"

"Big up!" Zeus says, swooning, then ducks behind the armchair for cover as if he suddenly realizes his smiley faces are showing. That's when I'm finally sure that Elgamela and Zeus have never had any clothes encounters of any kind, or else the mad hatter wouldn't be blushing—big-time.

Nole hands me the sample for one of the evening skirts. I step into the skirt and Nole starts fitting me. "I think the waist is too high," I comment.

"No, it isn't," he snaps.

"I think it's too long," says Felinez, finally plopping down her jumbo red cotton shopping bag as if it's safe from shoplifters.

"I don't mind the length but I'd like to see a little

more sweep on the bottom—so it really shows off the ruffles," I advise.

"You're right," snaps Nole, before ordering me to step out of the skirt so he can add another panel.

"You next!" screams Nole, prompting Elgamela to stop her snake charmer act and get undressed.

"Right here?" she asks, her eyes bulging.

"Yes, your father is not here!" bellows Nole.

"Well, I'm going in the bathroom," insists Elgamela.

She waltzes off in the wrong direction—confirming that she hasn't been to Nole's humble abode before. Nole doesn't stop her but watches as she walks into an ambush. "Omigod, I'm so sorry!" we hear Elgamela yelping—obviously to Ms. Canoli, whose bedroom she walked right into. Sheepishly, Elgamela walks back into the living room with her head lowered in embarrassment. "Was she getting undressed?" Nole asks, smirking.

Elgamela nods. Nole hands her the black Lurex bathing suit and points toward the bathroom.

Felinez, who obviously can't wait any longer for my approval, pulls a flashy feline tote out of her never-ending shopping bag like she's pulling a rabbit out of a magician's hat. "What do you think?" she asks anxiously.

Nole examines the roomy tote bag like a forensic scientist. "You don't think this is too big?" he asks.

"No, I don't think so," I answer for Felinez. The whole point of winning the Design Challenge is that the audience will be able to see the handiwork."

"Stevie Wonder can see it!" counters Nole.

I grab the tote bag from him and look at both sides. "I like that it has separate billboards on each side. This is really clever!" I exclaim, gazing approvingly at the "ABSOLUTE FELINE" faux vodka ad that Felinez concocted for our purposes. On the other side is a faux ad for the Broadway play "ALLEY CATS."

"Absolute Feline—that's us," I say.

Felinez breaks into a dimpled smile, then dumps the rest of the bags and belts and hats out of the shopping bag and onto the hardwood floor. Nole snaps up one of the vinyl hats and puts it on Elgamela's head: "This looks like a dunce hat. It's so pointy!"

"No, it's not," I snap, getting, well, snappy from Nole's endless objections.

"We should do brimmed ones," he counters.

"No, we shouldn't—then you won't be able to see the advertisement as clearly," I snap again.

I stand in front of the mirror, positioning the hot-pink vinyl hat till the black cat is front and center, then decide: "I think it's *purrfect*."

I pick up the vinyl hat for the male model and stand in front of Zeus. "Oh, right," he says, smiling, then takes off his beloved zebra-striped mink hat and rests it right on top of Ms. Canoli's prized vinyl record collection.

Zeus strikes a pose and Nole quips, "Taking it to the brim."

"Brimless it is," I order.

"I still think the bag looks too beachy," claims Nole.

Felinez shows him the bucket bag and the duffel bag designed to sling over the shoulder. "Now, these work with the urban wear."

"Awright," I say, giving in. "We can use the tote bags for the swimwear segment. You happy?"

"Delirious," seconds Nole.

Elgamela comes out of the bathroom wearing the slinky black one-piece bathing suit. "Omigod, can I really walk down the runway in this?"

"I think so," Zeus says, his dark eyes beaming.

"My mother will faint—and my father will disown me," she predicts somberly.

"Do you wanna rip the runway or flip chicken wings the rest of your life?" asks Nole.

"Don't get chirpy with me," Elgamela snaps back, making me realize why I dig her so much: she is fierce, inside and out. "I'd work in a retail store if I could afford to—but my father pays me better, okay?"

"I hear you. Somebody has to bring home the bacon," I quip, because it sounds like Nole is making fun of Elgamela's family venture. "I wish I could get any job."

"Well, it's not like you've really looked," Nole says with his signature surly attitude.

Now I'm bona fried. How dare he put me on blast like that? "I have too looked, because we can't all spend our Saturdays at the Gucci outlet!"

Elgamela interrupts our claw fest with her very real concern: "I can't wear this. I can't."

"Are you serious?" I ask, also concerned.

"I can't wear a bathing suit on a runway," squeaks Elgamela.

"Yes, you can," I counter. "If your picture appeared in the dictionary, it would be in a bathing suit. 'Slinky sphinx'—those two words go together."

Elgamela covers her face with her hands, then shrieks: "You don't understand. I don't even wear a bathing suit to the beach!"

"Do you really want to be a model?" I ask her, peering into her beautiful, exotic eyes.

"More than you do," she says.

"Then you'll trust us?" I ask, earnestly.

"Okay," Elgamela says, firmly. "But I'm not wearing the bathing suit."

We stand there in awkward silence while I marinate in having a real model drama on the rotisserie.

"I can't believe you're acting so shady!" shouts Nole, stomping his foot.

"Stop stomping your foot—I'll go put it on," I blurt out, taking charge of the situation like I'm supposed to as the house leader.

"Awright," whines Nole, his chubby cheeks more flushed than prawns at a picnic. Elgamela goes into the bathroom without an ounce of remorse and hands me the bathing suit when she comes out. It's bad enough I'm having my doubts about Aphro's loyalty to our house, but now I have to deal with this, too. Slipping into the slinky number, I wonder, Where is Aphro? I realize that the vaudeville show must go on. "That is gonna look so fierce with the pink cat on the bodice."

Nole sits there, pouting, arms crossed over his shoulders, before I throw him my house leader glare, which makes him hop to it. He begins adjusting the seams at the shoulders. "You're smaller in the shoulders than she is."

"It's the black-girl syndrome," I accurately point out. Zeus snickers, then blushes. Now even Elgamela smiles. Her shoulders and hips are equally proportioned. My hips and butt are bigger than my shoulders even though I'm skinny, too.

Suddenly, I feel self-conscious that my legs aren't as long as Elgamela's. "I think the legs should be higher cut," I point out.

"Agreed," Nole says, adjusting the legs. "Always makes the legs look longer—and your legs aren't as long as hers."

"I know that," I snap, then quickly turn the dial to Lite FM. "With high heels, though, my legs will be through the roof," I predict.

"Let's keep it moving," I instruct Nole, getting tense as I start thinking about our Catwalk budget. "At the rate we're going, I'm gonna have to sell my stuff on eBay to make some money."

"I bet there would be a bidding war on those Hello Kitty, um, you know," blurts out Zeus, blushing.

"Awright, Mr. Auctioneer, let me fit you in the muslin for the vests," smirks Nole.

"Sounds like a plan," says Zeus, taking off his T-shirt.

"Whoo-hoo!" Nole swoons at the sight of Zeus's pectoral muscles, which are more chiseled than I imagined.

"Wow, your ancestors would be proud," I say. After all, Zeus is named after a Greek god.

While Nole adjusts the armholes, Felinez continues to show me the bags and belts. "Wow, this is what you call wide," I say, picking up a belt. I adjust it around my waist really tight. "I like it like this."

"I agree," seconds Elgamela.

After Nole finishes with Zeus's fittings (two more pairs of pants, one vest, and a coat), Zeus slithers back into his T-shirt and baggy pants. Not surprisingly, he also zones in on the record collection and comes across vintage James Brown. "Oh, this is a must," he declares.

Sweating profusely, Nole stops to pat his forehead with a hankie, then drops it onto the floor, which is our secret code for initiating a Pose Off. "Set it off!" shrieks Zeus as James Brown croons his old-school classic "Hot Pants." Even Felinez stops pouting long enough for us to vogue our hearts out for a few minutes. Elgamela twirls in a circle with her arms stretched above her head. I can't wait to see her do that signature move on the runway for our fashion show.

"Work it, Snake Charmer!" coaches Nole, calling the "exotic dancer" by her on-screen identity.

When the song ends, I come out of my voguing trance and realize that Ms. Canoli has been observing our relaxation ritual with a satisfied smirk. "Did you ever hear of Xenon?" she asks no one in particular, but Zeus answers the question.

"Nah, I haven't."

"That was the club I used to go to—every Thursday night. It was hopping—line around the corner, but me and my girlfriend always got in," she recalls.

"Now you know where I get my moves from," Nole informs us, proudly.

And he's not the only proud one: beaming brightly, Elgamela declares, "I *was* born to wear a bathing suit!"

"I made a pitcher of iced cappuccino," announces Ms. Canoli.

"I'd like one," I say. After drinking two full glasses, I run to the bathroom to pee, then run out of the bathroom when I hear my cell phone ring. This time I dive into my purse to answer it. "It's Angora," I say out loud after seeing the number. "I'm almost finished—and coming your way," I coo into the phone. Angora sounds even more out of breath than she did Friday night, which usually means she's seriously stressed and her asthma is kicking in. "I can't believe it," she says, barely able to contain her anxiety. "Je'Taime is taking Daddy to Magikal Mamma's to get some voodoo remedies to heal him, but I think there's something really wrong—and he's not telling me."

"What?" I ask in disbelief.

Now Felinez is hovering near the phone to hear what's jumping off.

"I don't know—Daddy seems like he's flipping out. I can feel it. Just hurry up and get here," Angora says, her voice cracking.

"Okay," I whisper. Then I ask, "Is it okay if Fifi comes, too?"

But Angora has already hung up the phone. I stand there, stunned.

"What happened?" asks Elgamela.

"More drama and kaflamma," I say, without revealing Angora's business. I scroll through the missed calls to see who called earlier. Looking at the unfamiliar number, I realize that it wasn't Angora. I read the number out loud, but no one seems to recognize it. Suddenly, I wonder if Ice Très is trying to reach out to me from a private shoe phone, or something.

"I'd better not call back or maybe he's programmed a virus into my phone, too!" I yelp.

Zeus looks puzzled but doesn't ask what I mean. Instead he announces, "I gotta jet."

"Where you going?" Nole asks, nosily. "To see your girlfriend?"

Zeus smiles, shyly, smoothing down his wavy hair, then puts on his mad hatter. "Could be."

While Nole fits Elgamela—again—in the hot black one-piece bathing suit, I stare at the unfamiliar number on my cell phone screen. Finally, curiosity gets the best of me and I dial it, hoping I don't win the booby prize in the process. Someone picks up quickly and says, "Hello, how are you?" After a few seconds I realize that the caller is Chris Midgett. Covering the phone with my hand, I mouth out loud, "It's Panda!"

"Go out with him and forget the shady scribbler," orders Nole.

I wave my hand in disgust and continue my convo with my cyberspace crony. As if he's channeling Nole's wish, Chris asks me out on a date. "You wanna go to this place uptown that I really like?" he starts.

"Don't tell me—*Native*?" I ask.

"Well, I have to be honest—I wasn't going to say Native, but we can go there if you'd like," admits Chris.

"Oh, no, let's go to the place you like!" I exclaim quickly.

"Um, it's a diner called Googies on Fifty-seventh Street," he says, sounding unsure of himself.

"Wow, *Googies*," I repeat in a goofy voice, resisting the urge to say *goo goo ga ga* instead.

Nole holds his pudgy stomach and bends over laughing. What was I thinking? Panda and his posse aren't on point with groovy spots like Native. They probably hibernate at the corny spots advertised at the Welcome to New York booth in Times Square.

"Go out with him," orders Elgamela.

I heed her advice. After all, why am I hesitating? It's not like my dates show up; they're too busy cyberjacking me.

"Awright," I hear myself saying, almost involuntarily.

When I get off the phone, Nole claps. "Bravo, Miss Purr. Now that's a fitting end to a fitting! And don't forget to bring me back the doggie bag!"

Felinez looks at me suspiciously. "Oh, come on, Fifi—I'll bring you back a doggie bag, too!"

"No, *graci-ass*," she snarls, looking at me like she's going to make me into a bulletin *borsa* with a fake milk-carton ad featuring a missing BFF.

"Well, I'm out," announces Zeus again. I love that he doesn't have to bend down much to kiss me on the cheek. Then he props the Aretha album under his arm and makes a point of giving Ms. Canoli a warm and fuzzy good-bye.

Fifi and Elgamela help clean up before we head over to Angora's. Nole pulls me aside. "Save the PR spin and just give it to me straight with no chaser—where is freakin' Aphro?" he whispers, boxing me in with his strong, chubby arms.

"I don't know," I admit.

He looks at me like my answer isn't good enough.

"What do you want me to say?" I ask, defensively.

"The truth, that's what." Nole holds my arms in place.

"These days the only messages I'm getting from her are computer viruses, okay? She doesn't even tell me she gets a job that I interviewed for. I have to find out with everybody else," I hiss, referring to Chintzy's announcement at the last Catwalk meeting.

"You'd better find out what is going on with Biggie Mouth," he warns me.

When we're leaving, Nole has shifted back to his grand self and gives me a grand good-bye and hug. "I deserve that after putting up with your divo drama for a whole day!" I quip in return.

"I know, Purrlicious One, but we did good work today."

"No doubt," I say, hugging him back like the victory belongs to both of us.

FASHION INTERNATIONAL 35th ANNUAL
CATWALK COMPETITION BLOG

New school rule: You don't have to be ultranice, but don't get tooooo catty, or your posting will be zapped by the Fashion Avengers!

SHOP IN THE NAME OF PATRIOTIC LOVE . . .

Everywhere you turn, we're bombarded with news stories about the scary state of the American economy. But nowhere is the impact of this undesirable downturn felt harder than on the retail business. This year, for example, two of Santa's ubiquitous reindeer—Dasher and Prancer—can be seen in full effect without their cheerful caribou crony Shopper in the mix. It seems this year Shopper has strayed from her usual maxing-out-the-credit-card duties and is hitting bargain outlets like Woodbury Commons and Daffy's instead. Shopper is also busy "winning" presents in eBay auctions instead of buying them at full retail price at prestigious department stores or trendy boutiques. While these guerilla tactics are helping Shopper pinch pennies, it's most unfortunate for students at Fashion International, because we rely on upscale retail operations as our main source of part-time employment. Mind you, I'm not insinuating that we're being paid fairly or anything, but those of us who don't have wealthy parents still need the measly monies

so we can at least contribute to required school supplies—though, you
try buying metallic Lycra or faux fur
pile on today's meager hourly retail
wages. Did you know that the minimum
hourly wage is a measly $6.55 per
hour? That means the budding fashionista shopgirl who helped you match the
right Gucci, Pucci, or Prada argyle
sweater to pair with your tube top and
Seven jeans isn't making enough money
to buy the same outfit as you are. To
make matters worse, the F.I. students
who really need these jobs are the
lucky ones who've been chosen as team
members in the Catwalk competition,
because we have a whole host of mone-
tary needs that some of our parents—
and the Catwalk budget—can't cover.

That's why we're constantly comb-
ing the fashion board for the coveted
jobs. And that's why, despite the dis-
graceful hourly wage for retail employees, competition for these jobs is
as wicked as ever. As a matter of
fact, good luck plucking anything off
the fashion job board, if you ask me.
Luckily for me, I have a guaranteed
part-time job working in my family
business, Chirpin' Chicken, that pays
more than the hourly wages given to
students at Fashion International for
part-time positions. And luckily for
me, my family business is booming despite the sagging economy. My proud
and hardworking family is big on gratitude. So in the name of my family, I
want to thank everyone personally for

continuing to keep the chicken economy alive, plump, and well. But please let us not forget about all the lonesome cashmere scarves and imported crocodile purses hanging desperately in department stores and boutiques everywhere—pining for a place to call home in someone's closet. This holiday season, as you celebrate Kwanzaa, Hanukkah, and Christmas, let's encourage our families and friends—and even strangers—to shop in the name of love to support our economy—and most importantly, Fashion International's fashionistas' futures!

Posted by Snake Charmer 12:34:05

Since we're so close to Chirpin' Chicken, Elgamela charms us into making a pit stop. "We can eat and ask my dad for cab fare to Angora's. It's a win-win, no?"

"It's a done-done, yes?" I second, enthusiastically.

Once inside the blazing hot and brightly lit Sphinx family–owned chicken grill, I tear past the counter toward the back in search of seating so I can unload my coat and bag; a few feet farther, I spot a small archway on the right that leads to the promised plop-down area, though it's totally dark. "Why are the lights off in here?" I ask no one in particular as I slide my hand around the wall, feeling for the light switch. I got plenty of practice using this tactile technique during the "dark" years I lived at Grandma Pritch, who habitually kept the lights off to save money on electric bills. Within seconds, I locate the switch and flip it on, only to see a man facing the wall, bent on his knees with his head bowed and hands clasped together in prayer. Mortified, I flip the light switch off and back out, walking into Elgamela, who I didn't know was right behind me. She pats my arm, assuring me, "That's just my father.

Don't worry—he's oblivious." She goes on to tell me that Mr. Sphinx prays five times a day, like most devout Muslims, regardless of his whereabouts.

Clutching my coat and bag, I run to the bathroom, then decide it's safer to sidle up to the counter next to Felinez and Elgamela, who are "oblivious" to the smoke wafting in our faces from the spit-fire grill. "I guess I can bypass my weekly Biore-strip ritual tonight," I snicker, patting my nose.

"You don't have any blackheads—except in your imagination," groans Felinez. "I get them for real— even on my *culo grande*!"

"Puhleez, don't call your butt big," I scold her.

"My butt is big—but I don't have the market cornered on blocked sebaceous glands, cuz according to Aphro, 'black girls and blackheads go together'!" Felinez giggles.

Her channeling of Aphro's angst reminds me that I have to find out why Aphro was MIA from the fitting today. It also prompts Elgamela to inquire about the whereabouts of the missing member of our "Bling Quartet," as we've been aptly named by the haterade committee at F.I. "Why didn't Aphro come to the fitting?"

Fifi rolls her eyes and snitches like a C.F.I. (confidential fashion informant). "At least she got invited. I had to invent a family tragedy to be granted VIP access!"

"Fifi, stop fibbing," I snipe back. "You don't have to invent family tragedies—in your case they *really* exist!"

Now I smile sweetly at Elgamela while I formulate my PC response to her probe, since I don't know why Aphro didn't show up—even though I suspect it's all part of her escalating espionage. "Um, it was only the first fitting. I think Aphro had to work today and I just forgot," I say, embellishing with relish.

"She did?" Felinez asks, puzzled. "I didn't know the store was open already."

I wince and don't say anything.

"Call her and tell her to meet us at Angora's, because we need her," suggests Elgamela, sounding spookily clairvoyant while sweeping her long wild hair out of her face. "I don't know why Aphrodite should join us. Let's just call it intuition from the goddess Bast."

"Oooh, citing sources for inspiration, I dig that," I say, impressed. Elgamela goes on to explicate about the famous feline goddess revered by ancient Egyptians and often depicted as a woman with the head of a domestic cat.

"She sounds like a feline fatale *maximus*," I decree.

"A lot of Egyptians name their daughters after cats," Elgamela explains, proudly. "My father wanted to name me Muit, which means 'cat' in Egyptian, but my mother's choice won out."

"They always do," I utter, involuntarily, but refrain from revealing that my name is probably my mother's choice, too, since I don't even know who my father is.

"So what does Elgamela mean?" asks Felinez.

Elgamela blushes. After hesitating, she shares: "It's Egyptian for 'the beautiful.'"

"Fitting," I decide, swayed by Elgamela's eerie energy. I dial Aphro's number, hoping she won't answer, but she does, and much to my surprise, Aphro's flipping her own switch. Not only is she all ears—instead of mouth—about my Ice Très disappointment, she is brimming with more good news for herself. "Laretha wants to hire me for the photo shoot for her Web site!"

"Are you serious?" I gasp. The Aphro I used to know would have called me on the shoe phone, *pronto*, if she had news this hot off the griddle.

"That's right—three hundred dollars for a day's shoot!" Aphro screams into the phone.

"So, is that where you were today?" I inquire, gently, trying to squelch my Gucci Envy.

"Where?" she asks, sounding puzzled.

"At Jones Uptown. Where else?" I ask, testily.

"No, why would I be there?" she asks, defensively. "The store's not open yet."

"Then why didn't you come to the fitting?"

"I had something to take care of," she says, without offering any explanation.

"You should have told me you weren't coming," I say in a crispy tone.

"I didn't know I wasn't going to be able to make it till it was too late—so it didn't matter if I called or not," Aphro sighs, unapologetically.

I can feel my throat tighten around the indisputable fact: Aphro is acting shady. "Well, can you come to Angora's?" I sputter, trying to regroup.

"I'm there," she shoots, without buttering me up on crispy toast like she prefers.

"You sure?" I counter. I don't trust her but pretend I'm catering to her incognito affairs. "I dread dragging you from the B.K.L.Y.N. into Manny Hanny for *nada*."

"Get off the phone. In another five minutes, I'll be just another black girl on the IRT—heading your way!" she claims, signing off.

I stare into the phone receiver. "I don't know what's going on with Aphro, but I think it's time to stop pretending. I'm calling a bronze alert." Felinez knows what I mean, but Elgamela doesn't, so I explain. "We need to watch each other's back from now on. I don't know what's going on—but the House of Pashmina is not falling like a deck of cards."

"We got your back—and nobody can take away our designs. We're gonna win, because we're the best," Felinez assures me.

"Yeah, but there's a force trying to sabotage our

situation," I mumble, tapping my finger nervously on the raised glass counter.

"Now you sound like Darth Vader," Elgamela says, clearly getting spooked. And I can tell that the exotic one doesn't spook easily.

"All I'm saying is, I'm sleeping with one eye open from now on," I predict, pulling my hair. "Oh—Aphro got a modeling job for the Jones Uptown Web site."

"Stop it, *mija*. We're in a restaurant," orders Felinez, rescuing my hand from my hair. "And now I get it—you're just jealous because Aphro got *two* jobs."

The portly chef offers Felinez a corn on the cob, which she accepts.

"No, I'm not." I wince. But I shut up quickly, because I am.

Felinez shakes her head at me like we're in kindergarten and I'm stealing her pink crayons out of her box again. "You gotta try this—take the cob and dip it in this mustard curry sauce."

"No. I do *not* want to get kernels stuck in my teeth. It's not a cute look, Fifi!" I exclaim, turning my head away from the incoming cob.

Mr. Sphinx, who has quietly slithered behind the counter, interrupts our cobnobbing with a polite salutation, followed by a subtle nod and a quiet smile. Elgamela introduces us, putting me on blast: "Father,

Pashmina is going to be a model, too—and she's the leader of our house."

"No, I'm the leader of the house," quips Mr. Sphinx, but I know he's not impressed. I can tell by the way he levels his dark eyes, weighed down by droopy lids, then gingerly pats his forehead with a white hankie. Elgamela and her father carry on in Egyptian. Meanwhile, Felinez has gone mum, thanks to the unwanted attention of the Haitian grill cook, who is intent on foisting another cob of corn on her, accompanied by a wink and a greasy drool.

"No, *graci-ass*," says Felinez, adamantly, letting him know she is not Poca Hot Pants who can be wooed with a few kernels and a pair of moccasins.

"Take it," I whisper.

"No way, *mija*," she says under her breath. For a few seconds, the frisky cook's hand and the cob are suspended in midair.

"Okay, so what do you want, then?" I ask, annoyed, because I want to sit down.

"Some anti-*pest*-o," snarls Felinez.

"Right." I nod, then decide to take the cob for her. "You'll thank me later."

Felinez simply pouts, following me into the seating area. "Why do all the men who like me have to be greasy and fat?"

519

"Now who's being superficial?" I hiss back.

"Look who's talking. The only reason you like Zeus is because he's a *papi chulo*, even though he doesn't like you. And the only reason you don't like Chris is because he's short, but he likes you!" she snipes.

"Ouch! Just whip out a seam ripper, why don't you?" I wince. Plopping my tray, piled high with a quarter chicken and pita bread, on the table, I counter, "It's not true!"

"Yes, it is! You don't like Chris *Midgett* because he's too short," says Felinez.

"That is not the only reason. He wears goofy glasses and tacky khakis, okay? The last time I checked my arithmetic, two fashion wrongs do not make a right!"

"We're over the Catwalk budget—so who says you can count?" hisses Fifi. Now I'm pissed. I am over budget—and she is the only one who knows it besides Angora, who secretly agreed to loan me the money until I get the next installment of the Catwalk budget. With her father's finances on the fritz, I doubt that's going to happen.

"Say it louder, so Ms. Lynx can hear you! One of these days, I really will sew your lips shut with my wicked baste stitch—but trust me, those stitches will never come out!" I warn Felinez. "Besides, now that Aphro is aggregating commerce from every corner, she can kick in for the overdraft."

Felinez stares at me.

"I'm just riffing Retail 101, okay?" I squinch.

Now Elgamela enters the fray: "My father doesn't want me in the fashion show. Period," she says, tears in her eyes, sitting down at our table.

I flop down my pita bread in protest. Elgamela bows her head, but not to pray: she's steaming—and this time the spit-fire grill is not the cause. "What happened?" I ask her, fearing that something got lost in translation with her father.

"I told him about the fitting," she says, embarrassed, "and he was furious. He's worried the clothes will be too skimpy for me to parade in front of people."

"The Catwalk competition is *not* a parade—hello! And he can't nix you from the mix just like that," I warn.

"I can help you get another model," Elgamela says, defeated.

"You can help me get disqualified as house leader, that's what you mean," I groan, swallowing hard to keep from regurgitating the dollop of dread that has been expanding in my stomach since Friday night. The Catwalk rules are Swarovski crystal clear: all deletions and additions in regards to team members must be reviewed by the Catwalk committee, which will render its decision. And that decision is final. No appeals, thank you. "It will be a wrap and a falafel."

"I can't disobey my father," Elgamela whispers, her forehead twitching. Felinez stops eating, which means she is also distraught by Mr. Sphinx's unfitting response to a Catwalk fitting.

Twenty minutes later, I still haven't managed to convince Elgamela to call off her runaway from the runway, but we have to jet, because Angora is waiting. As we exit in defeat, Mr. Sphinx nods at us politely. Felinez makes sure not to meet the gaze of the grillmeister, whose eyes are glued to her every bounce. Even after we get outside, he stares through the steamy glass front, licking his lips like a hyena waiting for a lost lamb to wander within his predatory reach.

Once we're in a taxi, I sigh deeply. "I don't think your father digs us."

"Please forgive him. He thinks modeling will lead me to the pole!" blurts out Elgamela.

"What, what?" I ask, imitating Aphro.

"A *stripper*," Elgamela says, emphatically.

"You're *joking*," I punctuate in return, because the image of Elgamela twirling around a pole in a gentlemen's strip club instead of strutting on a chic runway simply doesn't click.

"I can't even bring a Victoria's Secret catalog into the house without his throwing a fit—and falafels!" admits Elgamela, sheepishly.

I ponder Elgamela's plight, taking out my tube of

lip gloss to freshen my pout and my point of view. "So where do you get your fashion groove from? I mean, you always seem like you're flaunting the fierceness— except for the bathing suit episode today, of course," I spurt.

"I guess hanging out with you and Nole has taught me the first rule of fashion," Elgamela starts: "act like you're fierce even if you're not feeling it."

"I think you're on to something," I say. Watching her take out her tube of MAC Lipglass and press the opened applicator across her pouty bee-stung lips makes me realize that I am rubbing off on the exotic one. Brainstorming, I whip out my notebook so I can formulate another tenet for our Catwalk Credo. "The first rule of fashion: Act fierce even when you're not feeling it."

"That's a good one," Felinez says, approvingly.

"I'm beginning to realize that the second rule of being a good house leader is acting like a therapist," I think out loud. "So, Miss Feline Fatale Maximus, can I ask you to declare a moratorium on your decision for now until we can all discuss it together in a group session?"

Elgamela nods, despite the troubled glaze over the glint in her dark eyes.

"I'm not off my therapist duties just yet," I mutter, dialing my cell phone to check on Diamond Tyler. A little while ago, she left a message when her call went straight to voice mail. "I just need to make sure she's on schedule for a fitting next week."

Judging from the sound of Diamond's voice, I realize that the only thing she needs to be fitted for is a straitjacket.

"I haven't had time to work on anything!" Diamond drones on, trumped by the sound of a television.

"Oh, really?" I say, surprised. "What's that ruckus?"

Sounding flustered, Diamond hesitates, then comes clean: "I'm watching the animal news. See, Polo is the only gorilla in India who doesn't have a mate, so the zookeepers are really worried about him. They're making a global plea to help find him a mate."

"What's newsworthy about that? We're all desperately looking for love!" I blurt out, exasperated.

Felinez smacks my hand. "Speak for yourself."

"All right, Diamond—can we please put Polo's problems aside for now so I can make my own desperate plea for a fitting, tomorrow?" I say, trying to tune in to Diamond's channel.

"No, I can't, I'm sorry," Diamond says, quietly.

"Can you give me an ETA, then?"

"A what?" asks Diamond.

"An estimated time of arrival."

"Oh. Um, I don't know, Pashmina," responds Diamond, not even attempting to tempt me.

"You don't have any idea?" I ask again.

"No, but I have to get back to watching the news," Diamond says, impatiently.

"Okay, whatever. Give my regards to Polo. And maybe you should introduce him to Maxie Pad the macaw, since she's been rejected from every port. From the way things sound in India, I bet the Bay of Bombay could be an option. Problem solved, no?" I say, signing off.

Fifi gives me that look like I flubbed it. "I don't think that was a good demonstration of acting like a therapist, *esta bien?*" Fifi says, frumping her face.

"Fifi, please, she's going bananas about Polo's plight. Friday she was sending an SOS about Maxie and Snickers the sea biscuit, who are stranded on an island."

"Snickers is a spaniel," Felinez says, correcting me.

"I could kick myself. I knew I should have called her yesterday," I hiss, glomming on to one of my curls for comfort. "When the call goes straight to voice mail, your life goes straight to *hell*."

Felinez and Elgamela remain quiet for the rest of the cab ride, which makes me feel embarrassed for my outburst, so I stroke their fashion egos. "I think we did a lot of work today, no?"

Felinez and Elgamela both nod enthusiastically.

"Awright, now it's time to stroke Angora's fur," I say, snapping on a smile.

We get out in front of Angora's building on Eighty-ninth Street between Riverside Drive and West End Avenue. "Wow, it's so pretty and peaceful here, it doesn't even feel like New York," exclaims Elgamela, gazing down the quiet, tree-lined street toward the massive cluster of trees in Riverside Park.

We sail through the colorful stained-glass doors of the building lobby and smile at the doorman in the bright burgundy uniform and matching hat, both brimming with gold braided trim and tassel detail. He smiles at us, making us feel important. Then he chirpily asks, "Can I help you?"

"We're here to see Miss Angora Le Bon," I say, grandly. The doorman picks up his lobby phone to ring Angora. "There's no answer," he informs us, "but I know she's home, because I haven't seen her go out. Mr. Le Bon went out a little while ago with, um . . . ," he says, pausing like he's struggling to remember someone's name.

"Je'Taime?" I ask, guessing.

"Yes, sorry. I couldn't pronounce her name correctly," he says, looking embarrassed. "Well, anyway, they went out earlier, but I haven't seen Angora. Listen, why don't you just go up?"

"Great, thanks," I say, trying to match his cheerfulness.

Once we're in the elevator, Elgamela asks, sounding intrigued, "Who is Je'Taime?"

"She is Mr. Le Bon's psychic, visiting from Baton Rouge, but if you ask me, something is awry," I blurt out.

"Really?" Elgamela asks.

"Angora says they went out to get some shrubs—no, I think she said roots at a voodoo store," I say, scratching my head, "but if you ask me, she should pick up a few refresher pamphlets while she's there, because I don't think her psychic powers are working."

Fifi looks at me disapprovingly.

"Fifi, what's the point in doling out tiddies? Now is the time to spill the refried beans," I advise.

Elgamela looks puzzled, so I fill her in on the whole problem with Mr. Le Bon's royalties—or lack thereof—from Bandito Studios for the tons of Funny Bunny toys and merchandising and amusement park stuff that the company has made based on Mr. Le Bon's creation. "But yet they haven't broken him off a piece of the back end. In other words, he has not received any profit participation."

"You mean they don't give him any money for all the toys and merchandise and stuff they do?" Elgamela asks, rhetorically, I hope, since she's simply repeating what I just told her. "That doesn't sound fair."

"Mr. Blunt would hop on this one," I say, referring

to our fashion business teacher, who taught us that fashion designers receive royalties—an exact percentage of every single item that has their name on it. Without the royalties, F.I. graduates like Calvin Klein and Ruff Loner and Yves Saint Bernard would not have been able to build billion-dollar burgeoning empires that make budding fashionistas like us eager to hop on the fashion gravy train.

"Hollywood sounds like the Wild West," Felinez says, sounding sympathetic to artists' plight, because as a designer, she hopes to scoop up as much profit as she can with her bag designs one day.

"Yeah, it's wild, all right—and it's definitely west. Can you imagine if they tried to do that to Dolce and Gabbana or Betsey Johnson? Puhleez, they'd walk right into the department stores and lift the clothes off the mannequins!"

"Peekaboo, don't sue!" cracks Felinez.

"Guess who?" I yelp when we get to Angora's front door and see it ajar. When I don't get a response, I gently push it, but something is stopping it from opening all the way. I stick my head into the crack so I can yell through it, thinking maybe Angora is nearby and left the door ajar because she's at the trash takeaway or something. But out of the corner of my eye, I can see a paper on the floor, and when I push the door even farther, I see that Angora is lying next to it, her body flopped near the door. "Omigod!" I scream, squeezing my way through the door with more force. I bend down frantically to see what's wrong, and from her gray complexion, I gather quickly that she has probably had an asthma attack. Sure enough, Angora raises her hand and whispers faintly, "Get my inhaler."

Elgamela and Felinez have also rushed in and are hovering over her. Felinez picks up the piece of paper, which has adhered itself to her shoe.

"Is she okay?" asks Elgamela.

"Does she look okay?" I yell. "Help me look for her inhaler!"

We both scramble in search of Angora's nebulizer inhaler. I find it inside her fringe purse plopped on the kitchen counter. With her sweaty palms, Angora grabs the inhaler and places it in her mouth.

"Omigod," moans Felinez, staring at the paper in her hand. "This is an *eviction notice*."

"I'm calling 911," I say, ignoring Felinez.

"No, don't," spurts Angora, wheezing. "Just give me a few more minutes."

"Should we wait?" Elgamela asks, hesitantly, probably because she doesn't want me yelling at her again.

"If the inhaler doesn't work, then we'll call," I say, more calmly.

We wait for a few minutes, which seem like an eternity. "I'm not going to any hospital for an asthma attack unless I'm unconscious," Angora says, softly.

Now that she has seemed to regain her breath, I become interested in the probable source of her current attack. "Lemme see that," I say to Felinez, who hands me the paper. Like Felinez said, the form is indeed an official eviction notice for "failure to pay rent due and in arrears pursuant to RSA 540:2 in the County of New York."

"I can't believe this," I utter, involuntarily, reading the amount due—$11,500, or, in other words, three months' rent. Reading the notice intently, I realize that Mr. Le Bon was obviously counting on Funny Bunny money that he thought he was going to get. I shiver thinking about the stress my mother goes through with her monthly bills. Who knew that Mr. Le Bon was going through the same thing?

"I found it in his bedroom after they went out. I knew something was wrong—I've been feeling it for months," Angora says, quietly. "I was going downstairs to the building management office to see if Mr. Gahneff was there and maybe I could talk to him about the eviction notice, but then my legs got like rubber and I just couldn't breathe and I got really lethargic. I guess I freaked out." Now Angora starts sobbing. "I can't believe Daddy kept this from me."

"Don't do that. It'll aggravate your asthma," warns Felinez, trying to fight back her own tears. Angora rubs her eyes and tries to stifle her sobs.

"How am I going to keep this from my mother?" Angora asks, raising her arm for us to help her up off the floor.

"Oh, Angora. I'm so sorry," I say. Felinez and I bend down to help her sit upright against the door. I hug her gently, also near tears.

I know how much Angora dreads dealing with her mother. She moved in with her father to get away from her—and to attend F.I., of course.

"Why don't you want to tell her?" Elgamela asks, innocently.

"Because I want her to keep her hysteria on Hysteria Lane—and not here," admits Angora. "If Daddy loses this apartment, she'll make me come home and I'll have no choice, that's why."

Elgamela shoots me a guilty look, batting her long dark lashes to the beat of Morse code, like she's trying to relay a message.

My eye starts twitching involuntarily and I shriek inside. The thought of losing both of them is more than I can fathom.

The intercom buzzes and Felinez jumps to answer it. "It's Aphro," she informs us.

Sure enough, a few minutes later, Aphro enters and

she comes bearing a peace offering: she shoves a big tin into Felinez's hand. "My foster mother let me take some chicken wings and corn bread for y'all."

"Oh, we ate," Felinez says, much to my surprise.

"Thank you, *chérie*. I'm hungry," Angora says, smiling weakly.

"What happened to you?" Aphro asks, finally sensing that something is wrong. "You look pale as a ghost."

We give Aphro the broad strokes of the latest drama and kaflamma and she shakes her head in despair.

Aphro listens intently, then provides a primo example of excising payment from unwilling parties. She says that Mrs. Maydell had been plying her domestic services for the now-bankrupt rapper, Trigger Happy, who hadn't paid her in two months. "She asked him for her money while she was cutting up some apples to fry for his breakfast, and he said, 'I'll hit you up with that soon.' She kept slicing with that knife and very calmly told him, 'You'd better go cut me a check now before I cut you.' He went with a quickness to put some paper in her hand. So somebody needs to go up to the Bandito Studios and set it off, okay!"

"I heard that," I second.

"It does sound far more effective than my alternative," Angora says, wearily.

"What's that?" asks Aphro, all ears.

"Calling my mother," admits Angora, softly. "But I have to eat first."

We sit down at the table to eat—and I decide to join in so that Angora won't sit there picking, because I'm sure she hasn't eaten all day. She's been busy fretting about funds instead.

"This place is wild," Aphro says, looking around at the surroundings—Mr. Le Bon's compulsive, cluttered collection of everything from bunny bookends to velveteen rabbit coasters.

"It is," seconds Angora; then she breaks down into tears again. Probably the thought of all these floppy-eared friends hopping into storage is more than she can bear.

She reaches out for me to hug her. "Can you stay until Daddy and Je'Taime get back? I don't want to be here by myself." Then she beams at Aphro and says, softly, "I'm so glad you're here, too."

I look at Elgamela eerily. She was right.

Angora gently rubs her chin, releasing a few dainty corn bread crumbs onto her napkin. "I want to lie down now."

We go into Angora's powder blue sanctuary and she plops down on her bed, instructing us to sit nearby.

Elgamela is elated to finally meet Rouge, Angora's prized Ragdoll cat, who has been hiding behind the blue chiffon curtain panel on the windowsill like a belly dancer manipulating a veil.

"I've wanted to meet you for so long," coos El-gamela, stroking Rouge's sublimely silky white fur.

"We did good work today," I say, pulling out the copies of revised sketches from the fitting to show Angora the shapes of silhouettes to come.

"*Tres mignon, chérie*," she coos approvingly at the baby-doll dresses, which she loves the best. About thirty minutes later, the color in Angora's face returns. "Can someone sashay into my father's bedroom and make sure it's not, um, in disarray? I made a mess snooping around—and when I, um, freaked out, I didn't fix everything back."

By now, we've all grown accustomed to Angora's substituting the phrase "freaked out" for "had an asthma attack."

"Right on it," volunteers Aphro. "He won't notice an Easter egg out of place by the time we're finished." Felinez goes with her.

I pick up a delicate brush off the vanity table to fix Angora's matted hair. "I must look a mess," she says, sounding embarrassed.

"At least your locks surrender to a few strokes," I tease as her straight blond hair behaves without a fuss and lies on her shoulders.

"I'm ready for my close-up, *chérie*," she says softly. "Do you think I'm doing the right thing?"

I know exactly what Angora is asking me. "Call her. Chicken Little would agree the ceiling has definitely fallen down," I assure her.

I hand her the powder blue Princess phone, her blue emery board, and her inhaler. She rests them on the bed next to her, side by side, before she gets the courage to pick up the receiver and dial the dreaded number of Ms. Ava Le Bon.

While Angora is on the phone, Aphro rushes back into the bedroom with a stack in her hand. "You can't believe all these bills we found in his bedroom— stamped 'past due'!"

I shoot Aphro a look like *Can't you keep it Lite FM, purr favor?* Then I jump off the bed so I can go whisper to Aphro, up close and personal: "Talking to her mother is one thing, so let's not stress all of Angora's nine lives today, okay?"

"Pash, *puhleez*, the cat is already out of the bag. They about to get evicted!" hisses Aphro.

I want to hiss back, *It sure is, so don't let me drop a dime on your cyber crime!* Instead, I push her back into Mr. Le Bon's bedroom with the upsetting stack of unpaid bills. "Just put them back under whatever pillow you found them under. Let the tooth fairy handle that!"

I hop back onto the bed to hold Angora's hand while she absorbs her mother's wrath. As expected, the conversation quickly reaches a crispy crescendo. "But what about the Catwalk competition? I can't just leave school!" protests Angora, shaking uncontrollably. She moves the phone away from her ear for a second and I can hear her mother's hysterical voice, loud and clear: "I don't care about any ole competition, and after I get finished with that foolish father of yours, that will be the least of your problems!"

Angora smiles and starts filing her nails. It's a ritual she has perfected from years of fighting with her mother. After a few seconds, she puts the phone receiver back on her ear. Angora begins blinking rapidly, then curtly informs her mother, "I'm hanging up now."

Suffice it to say Angora doesn't have to fill us in on the obvious: that Ms. Ava is madder than a witch who overslept on Halloween. "And now Daddy is going to be so mad with me," she says, resigned to the ruckus coming her way.

Felinez comes back into the bedroom. She sits down in the swivel chair at Angora's desk, then fiddles with the computer. "Can I check my e-mails?" she asks.

"Go right ahead," advises Angora.

"But what about this map—do you need it?" Felinez asks, looking at the computer screen.

"No, I'm finished with that," says Angora. "Daddy

wanted me to get the directions for the law firm on Varick Street where he's going next week."

Aphro walks back in faster than Foxy Brown to add, "All those unpaid bills I saw—he's gonna need more than an attorney. He'd better hire a magician."

Yeah, to make you disappear just like you made my files, I want to shriek, but politely ask her instead, "Did you put everything back in place?"

"If that's what you call that mess in there, then yes, I did."

I glance over at Fifi for support, but she is glued to the map on the screen: "375 Varick Street—that's the same building where Grubster PR is."

"Grubby what?" asks Aphro.

"Grubster Public Relations—one of Jackson Holdings' clients—as in Shalimar Jackson's father, who has an investment banking firm on Wall Street," I say, curtly, wondering why Aphro is acting like she doesn't remember that. "Shalimar is always bragging about her father's clients."

"Not as much as that Prêt-à-Portea," Elgamela says, elegantly. "I'd like to hit her with a wet sassy-spirella tea bag—right in her eye."

"Y'all need to stop," Aphro says, glumly.

I look at Aphro like *Who are you?*

"Oh, so now you're in Shalimar's sorority?" I challenge her.

"No, but she don't be bragging about nothing to me," Aphro says, poking out her pout.

Suddenly, there is commotion at the front door. We all freeze.

"They're back!" whispers Felinez.

Angora very calmly rises from her bed like a powder blue princess, smoothing the top on her blue flannel pajamas. I help her into her blue bathrobe and we follow her out of the bedroom like she's the Pied Piper.

One by one, we sit on the ivory velvet sofa in the living room, plumping the rabbit-embroidered pillows first against our stiff backs. Mr. Le Bon and Je'Taime can be heard clattering in the kitchen. The whir of a blender becomes background noise to their high-pitched chatter.

Angora waits until Je'Taime comes out with a tray on which she has assembled various roots and a tall glass filled with a green whipped beverage.

"Is that what Daddy is going to drink?" she asks calmly.

"Yes, this will help clear his head, so we can concentrate on a remedy for this *situation*," Je'Taime says, her lyrical lilt landing on the last word. She is a tall woman who appears even more towering as a result of the colorful wrap ensconced on her big head.

"Situation?" repeats Angora.

Mr. Le Bon comes out of the kitchen, grinning

wildly. He's wearing a chartreuse rayon bowling shirt with pink flamingoes in the background. "What's going on?" he asks, looking at us, his blue, bloodshot eyes scanning us wildly like pool balls.

"I've called her," Angora says, flatly. "I saw the eviction notice."

Mr. Le Bon's grin turns grim faster than a three-reel slot machine in Las Vegas comes up with blinking lemons. "Do you realize what you've done?" utters Mr. Le Bon, without even hiding his angst from us.

"Yes, I do, Daddy," Angora says. "But do you realize what you've done? I think it's time you start taking advice from an attorney instead of Je'Taime."

"Now, there is no need for that kind of obstinacy, Angora," tsks Je'Taime, her big brown eyes bulging.

"She's going to make you go home," Mr. Le Bon warns Angora.

"Well, I guess I should be glad that at least I'll have a home to go to," Angora says, turning feistier than I've ever seen her.

Squiggles in my stomach churn at the reality of Angora leaving me behind.

"She's calling back to talk to you," announces Angora.

"Um, listen," Mr. Le Bon starts, scratching his short spiky crew cut like a rabbit with dandruff, "do you mind if we talk about this in private?"

"Um, we'll see you later," I say, jumping up, signaling the rest of my crew to rise.

After we gather our belongings, including Aphro's tin pan, we kiss and hug Angora and flee the scene of another fashion crime.

"What are we going to do?" frets Felinez once we're outside.

"I don't know, Fifi, but we have to stick together to weather the pleather," I babble.

At least Elgamela has the eerie presence of mind to lighten the blow: "Don't worry, Pash. I'm not going to leave the House of Pashmina. I don't care what my father says. Angora doesn't have a choice, but I do."

"But you said you can't disobey your father. What are you going to do?" I ask, wanting to make sure that Elgamela knows what she's in for.

"I'm not going to tell him—and when the invitation comes for him to attend our fashion show, I'll make sure my mother has enough antacid relief on hand to administer to him," she says, curling up her lips whimsically.

"I want you to know that you are now not only an officially fierce member of the House of Pashmina, but you have been granted access into our inner sanctum," I say, embracing Elgamela's shoulders in a feline fatale ritual. "Even though Angora is not here, after your support in there tonight, I know she will be in accordance, too. Are we all in agreement?" I look at both Aphro and Felinez for approval.

"Abso-freakin'-lutely," Aphro says, imitating me.

"I'm sorry we don't have any kitty litter to throw over your shoulder for this momentous occasion, but," I say as we huddle around to hug Elgamela, "we thank you. And I'm sure the goddess Bast thanks you from her kitty tomb."

12

We manage to get our Design Challenge finished before the Christmas break, despite Diamond's detour. It took a little huddling and coaxing (okay, five hours) on Tuesday to bring her to the finish line, but the furbulous results are worth it, even though I'm sooo grateful that part is over like a four-leaf clover. Now that I've just handed in the challenge to the powers that scratch 'n' sniff in the Catwalk office, we're all outside getting an update on Le Bonfire of the Insanities.

"Yesterday my father was hopping on all the counterfeit Funny Bunny merchandise being sold on eBay—and threatening the slimy sellers with lawsuits. He was sending them nasty e-mails, like 'If I'm not making funny money off my creation, then I'm certainly not going to allow you to openly commit copyright infringement!'" recounts a stoic Angora. "As for my mother, she didn't call until last night, because me being homeless is not as important to her as planting Peruvian lilies in her garden. 'Wait till you see them bloom in the spring!' she cooed, like I care!"

Angora is sprinkling on the Cajun eloquence for

Nole's benefit, since he's only now privy to the scandal. That's probably why, despite the gravity of the situation, he in turn can't resist the urge to snicker, "Break it down, Miss Blue!" which is his new nickname for Angora, despite it being confusing, since my nickname for Fifi since second grade has been Blue Boca, because of all the blue Icees she sucked down that long hot summer.

"How is he gonna pay the back rent?" Felinez asks, concerned.

"He can't," reveals Angora. "Next semester my new residence will be on Hysteria Lane."

I realize that I don't need to keep Chintzy any longer. She was helpful enough in photocopying everything so we could meet our deadline.

"Chintzy, you can go now," I inform her. "Thanks for helping me get here on time."

"No problem," she says, sweetly. "I'll see you later." With that, she bounces off, her ponytail swaying from side to side.

"But something has changed, no?" insists Elgamela, focusing back on Angora.

"*Oui*—and no. Nothing has changed but I was crying so much I couldn't come to school another day without a Too Faced Lash Injection," Angora explains, referring to her favorite brand of mascara.

"Speaking of two-faced . . . ," whispers Elgamela.

543

We all turn to observe Shalimar and her crony, cubic-sized Zirconia. They turned in their Design Challenge yesterday, but they've been lingering by the water fountain long after getting the few spurts required to quench any vampire's thirst. We didn't notice because we were so glued to Angora's five-gore story. The budding modelblogger, however, is paranoid about her father's financial follies "being leaked to the gossip gurus at Page Six," as she aptly put it. Pursing her lips, she gazes across the hallway to see if the eavesdropping duo picked up a salacious sound bite. Shalimar and CZ (her unofficial nasty nickname) start snickering up a storm, but the real reason becomes apparent when Caterina and the Teen Style Network crew surface from the stairwell.

"Don't mind us. We're just waiting for my *boyfriend*," Shalimar shouts loudly, then waves to Caterina like they have an appointed rendezvous.

"No, she didn't," gasps Felinez.

"Yes, she did," I mutter, deciding it's time to hurl the first gallstone at my Catwalk opponent: "Well, if you've managed to snare a boyfriend in your fur trap, then there's hope for us all, huh?"

"Preach, Pashmina!" snickers Nole.

Boom and the rest of the camera crew quickly proceed to aim and shoot. Caterina smiles at me slyly, like *Sorry, but it's my job to deliver the drama!*

Now Boom points his camera at Shalimar for a re-action shot. She decides to wax meekly about her Christmas plans. We decide to ignore her. Angora pulls out her nail file and we huddle back together to commence with our crisis.

"So what's gonna happen with your father?" asks Nole, impatiently.

"He'll be homeless with all his rabbit things," admits Angora.

Nole's face drops like a boom. "You've got to be joking!"

"There are no jokes here," I lament, but when I hear the sound of another opponent's voice closing in rapidly, I realize that I misspoke.

"Okay, Miss J-J-ackson, what's soooo important that I'm missing my chance to be perched early in biology class, ready and willing to dissect a cold-blooded vertebrate?" taunts Willi Ninja, Jr., sashaying around the bend with Dulce and her ubiquitous red patent Kate Spade tote in tow.

Once Willi Ninja, Jr., spots the camera crew, he bounces back and forth on his feet like a boxing kangaroo. Of course, it produces snickers all around.

"Obviously, it's time to strap ourselves in and fasten our Gucci belts for this roller-coaster ride," declares Nole, stroking Countess Coco's head. Even she snarls like she's preparing for a cat *and* dog fight.

Still feigning the fierceness, Shalimar insists, "I just wanted you to meet my new man!"

As if on cue, Ice Très emerges from the stairwell, but his eyeballs ping-pong back and forth when he sees all the parties present and realizes he has walked into a fashion ambush.

"Ice Très? Shady one, please, I already know him," protests Willi Ninja, Jr.

"Yes, but now there's *us*," coos Shalimar, gazing into Ice Très's eyes like a desperate housewife. "Who would have thought that two different fashion paths could lead to the same place?"

"Now you sound like a fortune cookie," snarls Willi Ninja, Jr., to Shalimar, keeping his eye on the prize: Ice Très's hand-painted jacket. "But I'm feeling the Ice Man's jacket. The next Graffiti Guru, huh?"

"Did you see my new Tory?" interjects Zirconia, thrusting her tote in a flagrant effort to bag five minutes of frame.

"CZ, stop swinging that pendulum of a carryall. Want my rating? I give it three and a half *oinks*," Willi snaps, disapprovingly, then ponders a poaching possibility: "But I could use it as a murse for the show if you're parting with that ole thing."

"What's a murse?" asks Caterina, angling for a dangle.

"It's a man's purse," shoots Willi, grabbing the handles on Zirconia's Tory Burch camel leather tote.

"Are we going to be seeing them in your show?" asks Caterina.

"I ain't giving you the keys to paradise, so *don't try it*," squeaks Willi Ninja, Jr., his voice rising an octave. "Let's just say I'm not trying to be too edgy, or playing it too safe. I'm just riding the line until it's time to shine—*holla!*"

Not to be upstaged, Shalimar shouts in our direction: "Speaking of graffiti—have you heard that some misguided members are scribbling on the booty for the Design Challenge?"

" '*Stink* Pink'—oops, I mean, '*Tink* Pink'!" seconds Zirconia.

" 'Kitty Trail Next Right'!" adds Shalimar. "Yeah, that will stop traffic on the runway—for real. It's bad enough they're practically running *Animal Kingdom* in their meetings, from what I hear."

I freeze, suddenly realizing that Ice Très must be the spy who came in from the cold. "I can't believe it," I say, stunned.

"But how would he know about our billboards and the sayings on the sweatpants and our display idea?" whispers Felinez.

"I don't know," I say, shuddering, "but obviously the House of Pashmina has more leaks than the *Titanic*!"

While I stand baffled, at least one person has put the pieces of the fashion puzzle into place. "Let's go.

Drama is not a major food group—and I need a real snack before I dissect of frog!" announces Willi, twisting Dulce by the arm to march on.

Felinez rests her hand on mine—her cue for me to stay chill, since Boom has the camera pointed right in our direction again.

Shalimar hits the rewind button on her Christmas plans now that she has a captive audience.

"Wait, lemme guess," chimes in Nole. "You're going to Pisa to hunt for a *five*-pound truffle!"

Caterina reveals another sly smile, like *Ding, ding, round's over.*

Now I'm ready to go another round with Aphro. "I need some answers—right now," I blurt out, getting up in her face. "Have you been talking to Ice Très behind my back?"

"Don't let me set it off up in here," says Aphro. "I can't believe how stupid I am. I was going to tell you that I talked Laretha into using both of us for the modeling shoot for her Web site, and you here still tripping when I already told you I didn't send you that e-mail!"

The hallway quiets down. Even Shalimar stops yapping as Aphro storms off.

I run after her, my cheeks burning. "You can't deny that you've been acting shady. What do you expect me to think?"

Aphro keeps marching, ignoring my glare. Leave it

to Ice Très to go for the spotlight—literally. "Hold up, Boo-Kitty, let me holla at you for a minute."

Ignoring him, I continue to sashay steadily toward Aphro, because I know that Caterina and her crew are still filming us.

Over my shoulder, I hear Shalimar whispering harshly at her thug: "What are you *doing*?"

Ice Très breaks free from her octopussy tentacles and gains on me. "Come on, Your Catness, I know you're pissed, but I can explain. Just give me five minutes," he begs me, touching my shoulder.

Instantly, my chest constricts, but the chatter in my head shouts, *I want the truth!*

"Pashmina, don't listen to him," Elgamela advises me in her eerie clairvoyant tone.

"It must be you spying on us," challenges Aphro. She points the index finger on her bangle-jangling arm in Ice Très's face and snarls, "Cuz she may be feeling you, but you don't fool me—you son of a biscuit-eating, graffiti-slinging dirty dog!"

I twirl around to face Ice Très. "Have you been spying on us?"

"Y'all are tripping," he says, smirking.

"What about that computer virus?" I say, accusingly.

"Oh, you in another galaxy now," he says, still smirking, shrugging. "I got caught up on Friday night, that's what I'm trying to tell you."

"Save it for the delovelies who read your blog!" I hiss, bringing up the radickio nickname he used for girls he likes in his blog entry. "There's no excuse for standing someone up in this age of technology—send a text message, or an SOS. Ya dig?"

Suddenly, I feel a breath of fresh air in my chest, like someone opened a window. Ice Très just stares at me, speechless, like a jackal who realizes he's arrived at the scene of the carnage too late to snag anything more than a pile of picked-over bones. As he walks away with his tail between his legs, Aphro stands there with her arms folded across her chest. "You wanna know what's going on?" she asks, defiantly.

"We sure do," smirks Nole.

"They took Lennix and put him in another foster home," she reveals, referring to her beloved little foster brother.

"Why?" Felinez asks, surprised.

"He told our caseworker he didn't want to stay with us anymore because of Mr. Maydell," she says, getting riled up. "That's why I've been acting janky lately and why I couldn't come to the fitting. He left that day."

"But why?" Felinez asks again.

"Mr. Maydell was beating him," I say, realizing that I knew all along.

Aphro doesn't deny it. "Now they won't let me see

him. They said it's better if he doesn't have any contact with us anymore."

"That's not right," Nole says, shaking his head.

Aphro's eyes water but she remains stone-faced.

"Why didn't you tell us what was going on?" I ask, hurt that my best friend couldn't even come to me and tell me the truth.

"I *hate* this drama—and nobody wants to hear about it, so I keep it to myself," Aphro spurts, seething with rage.

"That's not true. We do wanna hear about it," insists Felinez.

"What you really mean is, you don't want to talk about it with us," I correct Aphro. I know she hates being a foster child, but she never says it.

"Why would I want to talk about my business? It's not like you would understand," Aphro sputters.

Felinez wraps her arms around Aphro and I join in, because there is nothing left to say. Aphro is right. We don't understand what it's like to be a foster child.

Tears well up in Angora's eyes. "I can't imagine what you're going through, either," I whisper in her ear.

Now Nole starts tearing up, even though he still has his signature smirk on his face. "You're wrong, Miss Aphro—that's all I'm going to say. I *do* understand. Trust me. I wish I was a foster child."

"Don't say that," whispers Felinez.

Luckily, Aphro doesn't react to Nole's insensitivity. "I'm so mad with Mr. Maydell, I can't even look at him anymore," she says, fighting back her tears.

"Are you going to stay there?" squeaks Felinez.

"Yeah—where am I going? I'm not trying to be up in another foster home. And he ain't doing nothing to me, so I can deal with him," she reveals, poking out her mouth. She's starting to get defensive again. I can tell because she pulls away from us and folds her arms across her chest.

Nole senses it's time to move on. He grabs my arm and snaps, "Why you still here? Isn't Panda waiting for you outside?"

"Yup," I confess. "I'm going—thanks to all of you."

"There's a reason for everything," Elgamela reminds me, stroking my shoulder.

"You sound like a fortune cookie," I say, swiping Willi Ninja, Jr.'s riff.

"Make sure you give him my phone number and tell him to call me before my mother breaks our computer," shrieks Nole.

"I will," I tease him. I turn to Aphro. "And I'll call you later. And thank you for hooking me up with the shoot."

"Yes, that is great news," Angora says, sounding pleased.

I'm glad no one wants to escort me downstairs, because I don't want Panda meeting my friends—yet. Good thing, too, because my heart sinks the second I spot Chris outside standing by himself, his hands shoved in his pockets. He seems even shorter than I remembered, possibly because he's dressed like a Milk Dud—brown corduroy pants, bomber jacket, and rugged clodhoppers all sort of blend together on his pudgy physique into a round chocolate mass. I try to hide my disappointment, even though it's hard for me to fake the funk.

"You okay?" Chris finally asks, when we're seated in the brightly lit diner of his choice, which is packed with tourists.

"Just fashion drama," I confess. "I'm tethered to this espionage business by a reinforced nylon thread."

Chris nods but I can tell he's confused.

"The computer virus?" I remind him.

"Oh, that espionage," he says, smirking.

I wonder if he's making fun of me. "You don't think it's some unrelated incident, do you?" I grill him. "It's all connected to the Catwalk competition. If I find the weak link, the whole piece will unravel like Gianni Versace gunmetal fabric from the seventies. Sorry, you wouldn't know about that."

"I understand. There's always interface to a program," pipes up Chris, changing his tune.

I don't understand Chris's cyberspeak, so I bury my face inside Googies' gigantic laminated menu. The endless choices seem a big blur to me, but I'm gathering that the food here is probably as corny as Chris is. "What are you getting?" I ask absentmindedly.

"The hot dog," he says, sounding unsure of himself.

"Me too, with lots of raw onions," I decide, giggling at my repellant nature. Now let him try to kiss me with those crustacean lips!

"Wait till you see this hot dog," announces Chris.

"I can't wait." I grin like a five-year-old excited about a supa-dupa surprise. Then I pull out my pot of Glam Bomb and slick some more on my lips.

"So, did you finish the Design Challenge?" he asks me, curiously.

"Yup—thanks to you fixing my computer," I say, buttering him up. "I feel good about what we turned in—even though things are kinda crazy."

The ponytailed waiter brings our plates of food and plops them onto the table. "Wow—that's the biggest hot dog I've ever seen!" I exclaim. This time I'm not faking the funk. I stare at the *foot-long* hot dog topped with sauerkraut and onions and relish and wonder how I'm even going to fit it in my mouth. "It's huge!"

Chris starts cutting his with his knife and fork.

"*Duh*," I giggle, following his cue. Then I squirt lots of ketchup on my french fries, and eat one with my fingers, thank you. "Omigod, this is the best french fry I've ever eaten in my entire life."

Chris grins, looking pleased, pushing his glasses onto the bridge of his pudgy nose. "I'd like to see the stuff you did."

"You mean the designs? Oh, those are top secret—still," I quickly add so I don't hurt his feelings, "you know, just in case *you're* the spy."

"Right." Chris nods, knowingly. "I have an idea for designing something, too."

It figures. Now I realize I was delusional for thinking Panda wanted to pounce on me. He probably just wants connects. Oy. Everybody wants to be a designer—even Dalmation tekkies.

"Lemme guess—Mohawk pants with multiple utility pockets and adjustable cuff tabs to store computer-encrypted information?" I snicker.

Chris blushes, then stutters, "S-something like that. Except it was a shirt with insulated Velcro patch pockets for carrying your flash drives, and the pants have a cyber chip sewn into the back pocket. I guess everybody has ideas, huh?"

"They sure do," I say, stuffing my face. "What do you wanna call it?"

"Cyber Chic," Chris says like he's embarrassed for sharing his designing drive. "Well, I won't have time anyway."

"Why not?" I ask, unembarrassed as I lick the ketchup from my hands, one finger at a time, because now I feel like the teacher and not the student.

"I told you I have a part-time project at this PR firm. I'm helping revamp their computer programming. And it's down on Varick Street, so then by the time I get home . . . And I gotta go to school, and and then there's homework . . . ," he rattles on.

"Did you say this place is on Varick Street?" I ask, my ears perked. "What's the name of it?"

"Grubster PR—I didn't tell you I had a job?" he says, proudly. "You're the only person that I've seen from the posting, and I forgot that I even had the notice up on the school bulletin board—so when you called, I liked the way your voice sounded, and that's why I called you back," he says, blushing from his true confession.

"Oh, admit it—as soon as you heard I went to F.I., you pounced on it, *pronto*!" I squeal. Then I start thinking about the name of the firm he told me. "I've heard of that firm before." I stop to think about why Grubster PR sounds so familiar; then I remember that it's the PR firm that handles Calvin Klein and Betsey Johnson, to name a few famous fashionistas—and it's a client of Jackson Holdings, Shalimar's father's company. "Yeah, Grubster PR—that's a Big Willie firm."

"There is an intern there who goes to your school, not that she ever talks to me or anything. But you know how snobby the girls are at F.I.," Chris snickers, and now he is blushing big-time.

"So how do you know she goes to my school?" I say, becoming increasingly curious.

"Oh, um . . ." Chris stalls before he admits, "Well, I guess you never noticed, but we hang out outside your school sometimes."

"Oh, trust, I noticed *they* hang outside our school. Dalmation students are hard to miss—but I never, um, saw you in the—" I stop myself before I blurt out, "pack." Instead, I say, "crowd."

"One of my friends in school, Roger, used to drag me along. Maybe you didn't see me because I was hiding behind him," he admits sheepishly.

"You're funny," I say, returning the compliment he paid me when he fixed my computer. "So, what girl are you talking about?"

"I don't know her name, but I've seen her before—going inside the school—and I remember because she had on the same sort of tall leather lace-up boots. You know, kinda yellowy, but not really?" he says, trying to explain.

"You mean like butterscotch?" I ask in disbelief, because I think I know who he's talking about.

"Okay, butterscotch," agrees Chris. "And she's kinda short, Spanish, and her hair is really dark. She wears it slicked back into a long, thick ponytail?"

"Chintzy," I utter out loud, even though I'm still hanging on to the sliver of a shred of possibility that it could be someone else. Chintzy certainly would have told me if she'd gotten a job—at Grubster PR!

Chris picks up on what must be a blank expression on my face.

"You all right?"

"I'm sorry but I gotta go," I squeak, my hands frozen. Suddenly, I have the image of Chintzy on that Friday we went fabric shopping—when she mistakenly headed to the downtown entrance instead of the uptown one, since she was going home to take care of her sick father. It wasn't a mistake at all!

"Okay," he says, visibly saddened.

Now I feel bad, but I have to call Felinez pronto to help me with this emergency. I run outside to call, and thank gooseness she stops fighting with Michelette long enough to answer the phone. After I break it down, Felinez has an idea to set off another Operation: Kitty Litter.

"Trust me," Felinez says reassuringly. "Now go back inside and try to be nice and we'll do it tomorrow. I'm bringing that special bag—to dangle right in her face. She'll talk. You'll see."

"Oh, speaking of bag—you just reminded me—I forgot the doggie bag," I giggle.

"Like I said, go back inside!" orders Felinez.

When I walk back inside, Chris is so happy to see me that I feel like a puppy brought home as a gift on Christmas Day.

"I thought I said something to upset you," he spills.

"No, you didn't, but you did," I say, then clarify it.

Chris nods knowingly.

"I'm glad you brought me here," I say, sitting back down.

"I'm glad they didn't take your food away yet." He smiles.

"Me too." I smile back. And this time, I really mean it.

13

Right after first period, Felinez and I walk through the passageway in Building C to get to Building D, which houses the hair and makeup annex. "Yoo-hoo!" shouts Bobby Beat, who is running off in another direction.

"Holla at you soon," I assure him as we make our way to the wig arena. We look through the opened door of each of the wigs and extensions classrooms in the Hair Annex until we spot Chenille in her black overalls, propped on a stool, carefully applying rollers to a long, frosted wig perched on a Styrofoam head. She looks at me glumly, like the Grim Reaper has come earlier than she expected.

I motion for Chenille to come outside. She shakes her head, but we don't budge. At this point, a few of her fellow weavers are peering curiously at Felinez and me. A few even beam in recognition. They know that I'm the leader of the House of Pashmina—and some of them even voted for me in the Catwalk elections. A surly look of defeat washes over Chenille's face as she realizes that we're not leaving. Taking a deep breath, Chenille stands up to come outside and deal with whatever drama is coming her way via her annoying older sister.

Once she's in our faces, Chenille crosses her arms over her ample chest, hidden by her usual pair of roomy overalls. "Hi, Felinez," she says, politely, before stepping into a petulant pose to address me: "This better be important."

"It is, or I wouldn't risk bearing your wrath and grapes," I say, smiling.

Chenille blinks and looks at me like my jokes are broke.

"Okay, remember when we were fighting—as usual—and you blurted out to me that I didn't even know what was going on in my own house? You were trying to tell me something, weren't you?" I start, pleading with my eyes for her to listen.

Chenille looks at me blankly. "So?"

"Well, I'm begging you to tell me now what you were so desperately trying to tell me then," I say.

"Why should I?" shoots Chenille, like I'm truly cutting into curling minutes she can never get back.

"Cuz I'll give you the black leather fringed hobo bag that you *love*," interjects Felinez, her big brown eyes widening. She holds it up like a trophy. "This one with the luxurious white rabbit-fur lining?"

"Fifi, don't," I say, faking my protest, just like we planned. I wave my hand dramatically as if I'm shooing away her suggestion. But Felinez was right: the bribery works like Elasta QP hair glaze, smoothing even the kinkiest edges.

"Okay," Chenille says, much to my surprise.

We stand there waiting as she unfolds her arms and releases the weight of her body from the perturbed posing.

"Well, spill the refried beans already!" I advise my annoying sister. "Don't worry, nobody is going to renege."

"All right!" sasses Chenille. "Um, lemme think. Um, one day after school when nobody was in the acti-vator room, I heard somebody whispering behind the sink, so I stood by the door and listened. I mean, I was just trying to get the bottle of curl activator that I left in the supply closet in case somebody else tried to use it, you know."

"Okay, go on," Felinez says.

"So the one girl said to the other girl, 'My friend Victor knows how to send a virus—so we can send one to her.' So the other girl goes, 'Good, that'll make her flip.' Once I heard that, I moved behind the supply door so they couldn't see me. They were whispering, so I couldn't hear everything, but then I heard, 'Awright, cool. And don't worry, I got you an interview.' "

I stare at Chenille in shock. She stammers, "So th-that's it. I couldn't hear any more."

"Well, that's not worth parting with a bag you worked on for three months," I advise Felinez.

"I said I didn't hear anything else, but I saw who was talking," Chenille says, folding her arms across her chest again, triumphantly.

"Who was it? *Díganos*, tell us!" orders Felinez, impatiently.

"It was Shalimar and Chintzy."

"Are you sure?" I ask, stunned.

"She's sure!" hisses Felinez.

"Duh—I do know who they are, okay? I'm not stupid," seconds Chenille, agitated by me as usual.

"Omigod, I can't believe it. In legal terms, this is what they would call corroborating evidence to nail a suspect," I mutter, ignoring Chenille as I still try to absorb the shock. "She's a double agent? I can't believe it."

"Well, next time, you'll listen to me. I told you she was a sneaky señorita!" Felinez yells, emphatically. "They probably leaked our whole lineup to the Russians by now!"

"Can I go now?" Chenille asks, back to her petulant self.

"Yes, you can," I snarl, but then I quickly add, "Wait. Thank you. You did me a solid."

"Yeah, well, now you *really* owe me," squeals Chenille, putting me on notice that the prized hobo is only the first handout.

"I guess I do," I concede, my head whirring.

"Chintzy's in textile science class next period," Felinez informs me.

"I know," I say, trying to map out my get-even game plan. "This is very *Twilight Zone*–ish.

Snapping out of my shock, I freak out. What am I gonna do about Ms. Lynx? This could get me disqualified!" I yelp, yanking a clump of my hair and twirling it furiously. If the Catwalk Committee considers the deletion of a team member to be an infraction, it can lead to expulsion of the house leader, which means another member of the team can be voted as the new house leader. And no way can I risk this before the winner of the Design Challenge is announced.

"Phase Two of Operation: Kitty Litter should take care of that," proposes Felinez.

I pause, pondering the option. "Awright, let's get Elga, Nole, and Angora in on this and see what we can whip up like a soufflé," I say, nervously, sending an urgent text message to all three, then pat Felinez on the back. "Unlike Ice Très, thank gooseness, we haven't forgotten the value of an old-fashioned SOS—or a *tight* crew."

After school, we have to drag Angora out of Toys "R" Us before she gets arrested for battery and assault. In a fit of rage, Angora took one of the Funny Bunny rabbits and beat his head against the nearby Barbie doll rack until his motorized speech wouldn't stop yapping. We should have know when she suggested going there to wait until the coast was clear at her house that something was, well, funny. What fashionista would opt for Toys "R" Us over nearby Filene's Basement?

"I can't believe you would jeopardize our future with a juvvie charge," declares Aphro.

Angora's face remains blanched as we head to her house, which we've decided to make our central base for the second phase of Operation: Kitty Litter. Angora also wants us to spruce up the Le Bons' elaborate Christmas decorations.

"I may not be here after New Year's, but this is the least I can do for Daddy so we can have a real New York Christmas," she confesses.

When we arrive, the scents of Bayou Basil and Choctaw Cayenne Pepper greet our nostrils. Je'Taime is in the kitchen preparing dinner, which hopefully doesn't contain any of the ingredients for her infamous voodoo brew. "It's Five-Alarm Gumbo," Angora assures us.

Her father has fled to the performing arts library in

Lincoln Center to do extensive research on the spider-web of Hollywood accounting, explains Angora.

"Well, at least it sounds like he's got a plan and isn't sitting around being a basket case any longer," I assure her.

"Speaking of a plan, how was your date with Panda? You haven't told us," Elgamela says.

"Well, as you know, you were right—I was meant to be there for a reason—but I don't think for Cupid's chores," I giggle. "Every time I looked at him, I just wanted to squeeze him like he was a stuffed animal."

"Or do you mean whack him? Because that's the only thing I want to do with stuffed animals these days—especially rabbits," sighs Angora.

"Well, I don't think—"

"Just say it, *mija*—he's too short and not cute enough!" blurts out Felinez.

"Yes, Fifi—that's right—I'm superficial and thank you for pointing that out, but I had a really good time. The food at Googies is *meowverlous*. As a matter of facto, I could live in that place," I say, pining for my leftovers, which are waiting for me at home.

"Well, I wish I could, too, because we're still being evicted," Angora states, woefully.

"I know," I say, turning my attention to Angora and her plight as we pile into her bedroom to man the phone.

"We're sick about it," admits Felinez.

"So sick we can't think about it," I admit.

"I know," Angora says, sweetly.

"I think there is a solution. It will come," advises Elgamela.

"Yes, I'm sure it will—and I hope it does before the sheriff does," admits Angora.

"Okay, it's showtime," I say, jittery as I prepare to slip into the disguised voice of one of my alter egos.

"Do Mrs. Fartworthy," instructs Felinez with a giggle.

"Good choice. She's got the right professional parlance," I coo. I pull out the folder with the script in it and study it quickly. "Get me a can of ginger ale to gulp down so I can do it authentically!"

"And not the diet one, either!" orders Felinez with a giggle.

"Ah, you soothe my kitty soul," coos Elgamela to plump Rouge, whom she has coaxed to come onto the bed and cuddle with her.

When Angora returns with a tall glass of soda on a rabbit saucer, I gracefully gulp down the prescribed bubbly, then start dialing until I've connected to my appointed prank victim—the human resources department at Grubster Public Relations. "Good afternoon. This is Mrs. Fartworthy from the Centers for Disease Control and Prevention. I'm calling in reference to an employee by the name of Chintzy Colon, who reports to Adam Saunders in event marketing. Yes, she would be a part-time intern. Yes, that's correct," I say in my professional tone, then belch. "Excuse me there. Well, Miss Colon recently visited our emergency outreach center with concerns about possibly contracting chikungunya fever from her father, Eduardo Colon, who had recently returned from a visit in Malaysia."

Felinez distracts me by falling on the floor laughing, so I put my patter on pause and remove the receiver from my ear before I burst out laughing, too. In a few seconds, I resume: "Excuse me there. Sorry about that interruption—another urgent case is coming in. I wanted to let you know that Miss Colon's concern about contracting the virus has been validated, and although she has exceeded the incubation period for possible quarantine, we must insist that— Excuse me? Oh, she drank from the watercooler yesterday? Well, I don't think you should be worried— Well, the incubation period for chikungunya can be two to twelve days. Have you been experiencing any sudden fever, chills, headache—yes? Ah. Ah-ha. Well, that sounds like it could be more the end result of an annoying coworker," I chortle, then belch loudly. "Excuse me there. What about nausea, vomiting, lower-back pain? Okay, well, since there is no specific drug treatment for the *disease*, we are required by law to merely record certain incidents," I say, sighing defeatedly.

"What is your name? Yes, well, Mr. Kandor, I've completed the required outbreak notice and suggest that your, and the company's employees', contact with the contaminated individual be kept to a minimum. Yes, no contact at all would be best. Well, I don't think there is any need to be so direct. Perhaps you can merely convey to the employee in question that the company has been issued certain cutback and downsizing mandates. With this economic climate, there would be no cause for alarm if you follow. Yes, I would agree. No, no, that won't be necessary. The Centers for Disease Control and Prevention are merely here to serve the community and greater good," I say, very politely, belching again for good measure. "Excuse me there. All right, Mr. Kandor, I've completed the survey. And, sir, perhaps you may want to limit contact with that coworker in question—for your mental health, that is," I say, chuckling, belching for the last time. "Excuse me there. You're welcome, Mr. Kandor, and enjoy the rest of your day!"

I hang up the Princess phone receiver triumphantly and let out a real belch. "Ooops, excuse me."

Aphro, Elgamela, Felinez, and Angora laugh uncontrollably. Even Rouge looks like she's getting a few fur balls in her throat from my prank.

"*Mija*, what did he say?" asks Felinez, impatiently.

"It's what he didn't say. Let's just say Operation:

Kitty Litter was, um, *infectious* and Chintzy Colon can count down her glory days as a *Grubby* employee, because they have reached *extermination*," I announce, victoriously.

We cross paws all around. "Now it's time to deal with the dubious double agent herself. By the time we get finished with her, she better go get a job working for Castro, okay," Aphro says, itching for a battle. The plan I put into action: arranging for Chintzy to meet us at Angora's at four o'clock for an "emergency impromptu Catwalk meeting." Naturally, the Splenda-fied señorita agreed as usual, being the helpful assistant that she has been from day one.

"Three-forty-five. Let's untie the white frosted tree!" Angora says, gleefully.

"I'm nervous," I admit as we all pile into the living room to mount the glistening centerpiece of the Le Bons' Christmas spectacle.

"I'm not," insists Aphro. "She had y'all tripping all this time—thinking it was me. No, we are about to set it off up in here today, that's all I'm saying."

Elgamela stares up at the six-foot-tall Christmas tree. "Well, let's try not to hurt this beautiful creation."

"We won't," I assure her, observing how perfect it is. "I hate those towering infernos of terror," I explain, "not that I've ever seen one in our house. A shrub rejected by Santa himself is more like it."

We hold the tree while Aphro fastens the tree stand onto it. "You know, they have electronic stands now that can be computerized," she informs us.

"I don't think the rusty rabbit ornaments care one way or the other," states Angora, dusting off the tall stack of ornaments that have been in the Le Bon family for generations.

"I brought you a special one," Felinez says, excitedly, pulling out a package wrapped in red tissue paper. "I wanted to tell you all day."

"Oh, *chérie*, what is it?" Angora says, her blue eyes gleaming, because she loves presents, even more than we do. Oohing and aahing, Angora holds up the colorful stuffed dolls wearing salsa outfits.

"Since you're not going to be at the Cali Fair in Colombia for Christmas, I thought you'd like a salsa band hanging from your tree."

"You made these," Angora says, in awe.

"You know Fifi—if it's not handmade, she wouldn't put it in your hand," I say, proudly, eyeing the delicate little costumes the three ornament figurines are wearing.

The doorbell rings and Angora drops an ornament. "I'm sorry. I'm just nervous," Angora whispers as Je'Taime sails out of the kitchen to open the door. "I hate confrontations."

"I hate being disqualified even more!" I hiss to quiet

her down. We all line up on the couch like we're the Christmas decorating committee taking a gingerbread break.

At last, the unsuspecting spy is in our midst. Chintzy looks curiously at Je'Taime when she sails into the apartment. Fifi, who is sitting next to me, says under her breath, "I guess one *bruja* recognizes another." I elbow Fifi to put a lid on her witch hunt. We all have to maintain a certain poker-face position to get this rodeo on the road.

Smiling sweetly, Chintzy toddles on her beloved Michael Kors high-heeled lace-up butterscotch leather boots to the couch, where we're sitting. "*Hola*, Pashmina," she says, quietly.

"Hi, Chintzy," I say, warmly. "This won't take long, because I hate to cut into your nursing schedule. By the way, how is your father?"

Chintzy looks puzzled; then her eyes light up. "Oh, he's much better. I, um, he didn't come there. I mean, he's not at my house anymore."

"What a pity the two of you didn't have more bonding time, with him having been in Malaysia and all. How long was he there?" I query.

"Oh, I don't know," Chintzy says, squirming. "I didn't ask him."

"Well, I hope he has recovered fully from his *virus*. Was it a contagious one?"

"I don't know," Chintzy says, blushing big-time. As if on cue, Chintzy's eyes well up in tears, and she puts her hand to her face as if she's about to lose it.

"It must be very upsetting," suggests Elgamela, winding up Chintzy for a three-hankie crying jag.

"It is," Chintzy says, sitting down in the armchair directly across from us, her big brown Kewpie doll eyes widening on cuckoo cue. "I love him so much even though he was never there for us when I was little. It was so hard for my mother working and raising us by herself—four children with no help from him. That's why I'm always trying to help everyone."

"Yes, you're very helpful," I say, buttering up Chintzy's traitor toast. "That's why we wanted to see you—so you could help us with a mystery we can't seem to solve."

"What is it?" Chintzy asks eagerly, wiping away her crocodile tears.

Je'Taime walks into the living room with a serving tray and asks Chintzy, "Tea, mademoiselle?"

"Yes, please. If it's okay?"

"Of course," I second. "You like two packets of Splenda, right?"

"How did you know that?" Chintzy asks, looking impressed.

"Oh, I remember freshman year in the Fashion Café they didn't have it and you pulled out a packet from your purse," I recall. What I refrain from telling her is that that was when I first came up with her Splenda-fied smile moniker.

"I'm going down to the laundry room," announces Je'Taime.

Chintzy smiles at her and says thank you, then gingerly balances the teacup and places the saucer on the coffee table like she is glad we invited her.

"Um, like I was saying, we can't seem to figure out how Shalimar and Zirconia are so fully informed about our entire Design Challenge plans and even the theme for our fashion show," I start, trying Angora's sweet approach first. "Do you have any idea?"

"No, I don't," Chintzy says, sounding newly concerned. "How do you know they know?"

"We had an incident in the hallway—that was completely taped by the Teen Style Network, as a matter of fact. It was interesting how Shalimar and Zirconia knew exactly what time to tell the network to be there. She even invited Ice Très and Willi Ninja, Jr., to join in the frenzy—at three-fifteen, the exact same time you knew we would be handing in our Design Challenge to the Catwalk office. Do you think that is a coincidence?" I ask, curiously.

"It has to be, Pashmina. I don't think anyone knew I was going to meet you there at that time. Unless someone has been eavesdropping on me. Omigod, I didn't even think of that! I forget how jealous people are of us—I mean, you," she coos.

Now I can tell she's fluffing my whiskers. "But all the stuff about our ideas for the Design Challenge and our fashion show lineup—you didn't discuss that with anyone?" I ask.

"No, why would you ask me that? I would never tell anyone about our plans. I know how important it is to keep everything discussed confidential," Chintzy says, convincingly. "All I care about is that we win this competition. I didn't want to say anything before but I think someone has been leaking information—and obviously Shalimar found out!"

"Do you have any idea who that person could be?" Angora asks, sweetly.

Chintzy looks over in Aphro's direction and answers, "I wish I knew, because I would tell you. If you want, I can try to find out."

"I know you didn't just look at me like that, did you?" blurts out Aphro, challenging Chintzy.

"No!" says Chintzy, sounding frightened. "I didn't mean to look at you like that."

"So you don't talk to Shalimar at all?" I ask, trying to regain our upper hand.

"No, she never talks to me," Chintzy insists. "Why would she?"

"And you don't know anything about who sent me

that computer virus that almost destroyed my life," I say, getting edgy.

"A virus. Omigod—I'm so scared of getting one of those I never download attachments from *anybody*!" swears Chintzy, emphatically. "Listen, I don't know why you're attacking me like this, but somebody has obviously been telling you lies!"

"Lies? Chenille heard you in the activator room with Shalimar, talking about how you could get your friend Victor to send a computer virus! *Mentirosa!*" shouts Felinez like she can't wait to knock Chintzy harder than her birthday piñata.

Chintzy's lip trembles as she fights back tears. "You're the liar, not me!" she snarls at Felinez. "And I'm not going to listen to your lies anymore, Felinez!" She dramatically turns to march out. Felinez lunges at her, yanking her ponytail from behind to drag her away from the door. Chintzy screams. "Get off me, *loquita*, you're crazy!" Felinez won't budge. She yanks Chintzy's ponytail so ferociously that it comes off in her hand, causing Felinez to fall backward hard onto the carpet.

"You all right?" cries Elgamela, rushing to Felinez's side.

Aphro rushes to the site of the fakeness: "Omigod, your hair is *fake*—just like you!" she shouts, then jumps on Chintzy and pins her to the floor. "We know you're a double agent. Your cover is blown like this ponytail, so you'd better start talking!"

"You're crazy! Get off me, or I'm calling the police!" screams Chintzy.

"You may want to call Mr. Kandor in the human resources department at Grubster PR first. You do work there—and it doesn't take a genius to figure out who got you the hookup!" I shout, finally playing the trump card.

Chintzy stops writhing instantly. "What did you tell them?" she asks hysterically.

"About your father's trip to Malaysia and the mysterious virus he contracted that turns out to be highly *contagious*," I say, nastily.

"If I lose my job, I'm going to leak all your designs all over the Internet to get back at you, cuz I didn't do anything!" she screeches, turning even nastier. "And I'm going to tell them you're lying, because my father lives in Larchmont and he's a janitor and I can prove it!"

"So his trip to Malaysia for Save the Children was just a charade?" Elgamela says, satisfied that we finally caught Chintzy in a bald-faced lie.

"So what? I made it up!" shrieks Chintzy. "I just did that because my father never comes to see us and I wanted to impress everybody. That doesn't mean I had anything to do with that stupid virus, or that I'm a double agent. That's insulting. And you can't prove it!"

"So you're saying that my sister, Chenille, is a liar—and she didn't see you with Shalimar in the dark in the activator room plotting against me?" I reiterate for clarification.

"Get off me and I'll talk," Chintzy says, writhing again.

We let her get off the floor and Felinez throws her ponytail piece in her face. "I hate you!" Chintzy snarls.

"Not as much as we hate you!" shouts Aphro. "I can't believe you, sitting up there in the Catwalk meeting, dropping the dime on my job, but you neglected to tell us who *your* 'boss' really is!"

"I do know Shalimar. So what? I'm saying if you try to get me disqualified, I'll tell Ms. Lynx that you're telling lies because you're jealous of me and you stole my designs. Then you'll get disqualified as house leader!"

"Do you really think telling *more* lies is going to make this a better situation?" Elgamela asks in disbelief.

"I need the money and the job for my family. You would do the same thing. You don't live in a situation like I do," Chintzy says, starting up with the tears again.

"Hold up," says Aphro. "What money are you talking about? It's an internship."

"The money Shalimar gave me," confesses Chintzy, gritting her teeth in despair like she has finally gotten the dancing bears off her chest.

We freeze, staring at Chintzy in disbelief. "Wow, you don't *fabricate*, you give shades of *Watergate*," I exclaim, plopping back onto the couch in shock.

"If you try to get me in trouble, I will get you in trouble," declares Chintzy, finally playing her hand.

"So you actually want us to keep you in our house so you can continue to spy on us for Shalimar?" asks Angora, sitting straight up on the couch like she's finally registering the level of Chintzy's deception.

Chintzy doesn't respond; instead, she pulls her short hair out of the elastic band and smooths it back again. I watch in shock. All of a sudden, my mother's voice pops into my head. "Never trust anyone who always wears the same hairstyle," I say out loud, gaining the strength to play *my* next hand. "Look, all we want is you out of our house. We're thinking perhaps you can get a little more mileage out of your father's fabricated trip to Malaysia than you expected."

"What do you mean?" asks Chintzy, stone-faced.

"You're going to go to Ms. Lynx's office tomorrow and file a Catwalk competition release form so you can be excused from your obligations as a team member due to 'extended family problems and complications,'" I suggest. "Your poor father's condition has worsened and he requires your constant attention, because your mother is working and you have to take care of your brothers and sisters, too. You get my drift?"

"I'll think about it," Chintzy says, blandly, like she refuses to give up her elaborate espionage.

Aphro starts to say something nasty, but I cut her off. "Okay, you think about it. That's fair."

Somberly, Chintzy gets up to go.

"You'd better hope we don't lose the Design Challenge because of you," warns Aphro.

"It's not my fault. I wasn't trying to hurt you," Chintzy maintains.

"Well, tell Victor that virus of his is more powerful than a Russian missile," I retort.

Chintzy's face drops, and for the first time, I see the cuckoo bird popping out from inside the clock.

After she leaves, I sit stunned. "Now I understand what a psychopath is," I say, taking it all in. In psychology class, we studied personality disorders and I couldn't have been more bored. "I have just seen shades of straight-up shady. I could teach Mr. Treech's Psychology 101 class with enthusiasm."

"She is so sneaky she could sell blue Icees to the Eskimos," agrees Felinez.

After a little while we go back to decorating the Christmas tree with renewed appreciation.

"She turned more leaky than *sneaky* whenever her father came up, though," Elgamela observes.

"That's true. I thought she was going to fold like it's laundry day, but she was so convincing, she could have starred in a remake of *The Three Faces of Eve*. I sure misjudge people," Angora says, folding her arms across her chest. "Speaking of laundry, where is Je'Taime?"

The doorbell rings, prompting Angora to say, "Maybe she left her keys," and jump up to answer it. I hear her talking to a man in the hallway before she closes the door with an envelope in her hand. "That was Mr. Gahneff, the building manager. My mother wired him the arrears for the rent," Angora says in disbelief. "I can't believe it." Angora's hands shake and she starts wheezing.

"Come sit down!" We grab Angora to head for the couch. She sits there quietly for a second, the envelope dropping out of her hand. "Why can't you believe it? The only alternative would have been her only daughter and her ex-husband on the sidewalk, and despite what you say, I don't think your mother is that vindictive," I assure her.

"No, I can't believe that she's downstairs," Angora says, turning as pale as a Victorian poster child. "She told Mr. Gahneff to tell us to come downstairs and help her with her luggage—all ten pieces."

We gasp, but Angora starts giggling. "I got my secret wish after all."

"What wish?" I ask, holding her hand.

"I prayed last night that if I got to spend Christmas in New York with all of you, then I would never complain about anything again, so now God is holding me to it—and the proof is right downstairs!"

All of a sudden, the Christmas tree topples over.

"Omigod," says Elgamela, jumping up to stand it vertically again.

"Ay, *Dios mio!*" exclaims Felinez, helping. "We don't want Ms. Le Bon to see the tree like this!"

"Oh, why not?" chuckles Angora. "It'll give her something else to complain about."

"Don't think she came all this way without notice to complain," I exclaim, adamantly. "She came because she loves you, Angora. And so do we."

Now Je'Taime comes back from the laundry room. "Are you coming downstairs to help?"

"Not just yet," yelps Angora. "This is way more important."

The five of us kiss and hug each other tightly.

"Who knows what is going to happen with all this craziness?" I confess. "But this Christmas we were meant to be together and spend it in *meowverlous* fashion."

New school rule: You don't have to be ultranice, but don't get tooooo catty, or your posting will be zapped by the Fashion Avengers!

"V" IS FOR VICTORY!

As my mother would say, "the money was definitely funny this year," but I still had a *meowverlous* Christmas—mostly because I got to spend it with my crew. I'm proud that we made the commitment to strap ourselves in and fasten our Gucci belts so we could take the roller coaster ride of the season and ended up screaming our heads off together. It was a furbulous blast. Now it's the New Year, and until today, the letter "V" always stood for "vicuna," "Velcro," "Versace," "virus," and sometimes even "Volvo," the beat-up car that my old neighbor Mr. Chisolm drives. But thanks to the announcement that the House of Pashmina won the Design Challenge this year—pocketing the $300 bonus prize that others thought for sure had their name on it—"V" also stands for "victory"! Can I scream any louder? I don't think so, or Principal Mario Confardi will have me expelled! Naturally, I can't speak for the Catwalk Committee and tell you why we were chosen as the winners—nor can I let our fashion secrets out of the bag just yet—but I can tell you that this victory has given me the freedom to say that I don't care about those who aren't aligned with my goals anymore! I'm also not so afraid to stretch my kitty limbs and admit that I have always dreamed of being on the runways of the world on a grand scale—which is probably why I now have the resolve to stick to my New Year's resolution: live my life to my purrlicious potential! For me, personally, every day on earth is like New Year's, because I'm always amazed at all the abundance and interesting, courageous people who populate this planet. Of course, if you show me a Martian who isn't wearing an outfit the dreadful color of split pea—and who has purrlicious potential that I want to emulate—I can assure you that I'll become fascinated with them, too. Until then, I will continue to worship the earthly feline fatales, like Julie Newmar and the legendary Catwoman Eartha Kitt, with her infamous, unimitable purr.

But don't get it French twisted: I'm not from the suburbs and I know the earth is a dangerous, crazy place, and that's not only because I grew up in the Boogie Down and now live in Harlem, but because I also watch The Discovery Channel to stay in the loop with someone on my team who is more obsessed with the well-being of four-legged creatures on this earth than I am. But I'm proud to say that I'm part of a new breed of feline fatales, coming up ferocious and fearless, who are waiting in the wings for a chance to pounce on stardom and success and to be a shining, sparkly example from head to toe. As I wait for my turn to unleash my meowch power to the maximus, I'm surprised at what I'm most grateful for: the fact that I'm not alone. I think I'm luckier than most people on this planet, because I was fortunate enough to be appointed a house leader in a prestigious competition. This has given me access to a whole posse of purr-worthy kats and kitties from whom I can draw my strength and with whom I can share all the things that life in the fashion lane has to offer. I may fight with members of my Catwalk crew, and I admit that I was terrified over the holidays that I would lose one I adore, and I just found out that still another member—my former assistant—has already made the decision to depart due to family constraints, but I have been shown recently that I can't master my mighty plan without them and I don't intend to. So this shout-out is for my special purrlicious posse, because we're in this together till June. And to everyone else, happy new year!!!

Posted by Feline Groovy at 12:34:05

Glossary

24-7: Twenty-four hours a day, seven days a week. As in "I have to study 24-7 to raise my grade point average."

A hyphenate waiting to happen: Someone who is multitalented and can't be crunched into one category. Back in the day, the typical hyphenated professionals were model-actress, writer-performer, illustrator-photographer, et cetera, but new-school ones are model-blinger, modelpreneur, model-spinner, model-blogger, et cetera.

Assisterance: Sisterhood assistance, or aid from a sassy source. As in "Don't leave me dangling after the fashion show, because I'm definitely going to require some assisterance, *purr favor!*"

AWOL: When your designated fashion is missing in action—especially backstage at a fashion show. As in "Where is Elgamela's cover-up for the bathing suit segment? Omigod, it's gone AWOL!"

Big Willie: A major player in the fashion game. Someone who has earned street cred. Can also refer to the Big Willie statue—the prestigious bronze dress-form trophy bestowed upon the winner of the annual Catwalk competition at Fashion International High School. The award's name was chosen in honor of the school's founding father, William Dresser.

Blang: Bling squared.

Bona fried: Upset. Pissed off. Angry to a crisp. Legit. Authentic. As in "I can't believe Aphro told Lupo I'm gagulating over Zeus. Now I'm really bona fried."

Boogie Down: The Bronx is often referred to in hip-hop slang as the Boogie Down since rap pioneer KRS-One publicly cited the northernmost borough in New York City as the source of his inspiration.

Catwalk: A narrow, usually elevated platform used by models to "sashay, shimmy, and sell" designers' clothing and accessory collections during a fashion show. This British term was originally coined after designer Lucy Christiana, aka Lady Duff-Gordon, staged the first fashion show in London in the early 1900s.

Chevron formation: A procession of models in an inverted V-shape on the catwalk during a fashion show.

Chewing on gristle: Pondering a problem. As in "Don't act like nothing is wrong, cuz I can tell that you're chewing on gristle."

Churl: *Girl* and *child* rolled into one and used as a term of endearment or when putting someone on blast. As in "Churl, please, you're not the fifth element, so you best keep it moving!"

Ciao: Italian for "good-bye." Pronounced like dog "chow." As in "*Ciao, ciao,* Manny Hanny!"

Convo: Conversation. Chitchat. As in "What's up with all that convo with shady Shalimar?"

Crispy crescendo: Fiery finale that punctuates a heated convo or dispute. As in "My fight with Ice Très ended with a crispy crescendo. You can believe that."

Dolce: Italian for "sweet." Pronounced "dull-chay." As in "Next week is Spring Break. That's definitely *dolce*." Also used when referring to the dynamic design duo Dolce & Gabbana.

Don't come for me: A battle cry. As in "Don't come for me, Miss Purr. I know you wanted to go shopping Saturday, but some of us had to study for the trig test on Monday!"

Don't get it French twisted: Get it right. Leave the kiddie antics in the playground. Don't get the situation wrong, or sleep on it. As in "Don't get it French twisted. Willi Ninja, Jr., may be fierce, but the House of Pashmina is fiercer."

Du jour: French for "of the day." As in "Frog legs with asparagus is the soup du jour. Would you like to try it, mademoiselle?"

Fashionista: Someone who is true to the fashion game.

Fiberoni: An omission of truth. In other words, a pink, purple, or psychedelic lie. As in "Stop with the fiberonis. I know you've been slipping into the Fashion Lounge to avoid me in the hallways!"

Flaunting the fierceness: Knowing how to work the runway or having great style. As in "Did you see Mink's new Burberry raincoat? She is always flaunting the fierceness!"

Fries my frittata: To make angry, agitated, pissed off. "Did you hear that Chandelier tried to get her house leader nomination back after going MIA? That really fries my frittata that she doesn't just go back to the sandbox and build another sand castle!"

Friv: Frivolous. Silly. As in "I don't mean to sound friv, but when are we going shopping, cuz I'm tired of studying for this exam?"

Furbulous: Feline fatale code for "fabulous."

Gaspitate: Swoon. As in "Forget about Ice Très. I'm all over Zeus. He makes me gaspitate."

Haute couture: French for "high fashion," but technically refers to the creation of exclusive designer custom-fitted collections like those from the House of Yves Saint Laurent or Balenciaga. It originally referred to Englishman Charles Frederick Worth's creations, produced in Paris back in the day. Today, however, the prestigious term is used only by firms that meet certain well-defined standards. Haute couture collections are still staged for the runway in Paris and Rome, but they're also made-to-order for the elite customers—from Milan to Tokyo—who crave hand-executed techniques.

Homme: French for "man." Pronounced like *home* without the *h*.

In flagrante: Raw. Exposed. Caught in the act. As in "Thank gooseness Caterina came too late to film our Pose Off in the cafeteria. If Principal Confardi saw in flagrante footage, we'd be exiled to Style Siberia!"

Jean Paul Gaultier: Known worldwide as the *enfant terrible* (bad boy) of French fashion, the avant-garde designer's corsetry and leather work are sought after by everyone from Madonna to Kylie Minogue. He also designed the fierce, memorable costumes for the chic cult 1997 film *The Fifth Element*.

Juvvie: Juvenile delinquent. A person under eighteen who is arrested and charged as a minor. As in "I hear she's got a juvvie record. All I can say is that orange prison jumpsuit is *not* a cute look, hello!"

Kaflustered: Agitated. As in "I could not believe Nole went on and on about Ice Très and Shalimar—so insensitive to my kaflustered state!"

Keep it moving: Don't get caught up. Move on to the next taste sensation! As in "I can't believe Zeus didn't call me. Well, I guess I'd better just keep it moving."

Le podium: French for "runway" or "catwalk."

Lite FM: Opposite of heavy or stressed. As in "Why you stressing over Zeus? He's got a girlfriend. Just keep it Lite FM when you see him in the hallways."

Manny Hanny: Manhattan—the center jewel in the crown of the Big Apple. Also, the undisputed fashion capital of the world.

Meowverlous: Feline fabbie. As in "Elgamela looks meowverlous in the black catsuit."

Miss Thing: A term of endearment for a friend, frenemy, or opponent. As in "Miss Thing, I will feng shui the floor with your fierceness!"

Non-coloric: Colors without calories. In other words, drabby, dreary, nondescript, or just plain neutral like Switzerland. As in "Her outfits are always so non-coloric."

Pronto: Italian salutation used when answering the phone. Also means presto, soon, rapid, or quick. Pronounced "pron-toe." As in "I'd better get to class, *pronto*, or Mrs. London is going to read me!"

Purr favor: Catwalk code for "pretty please." As in "Can you help me with my Italian homework, *purr favor*?"

Purr-worthy: Passing the standard of feline fatale fabbie-ness.

Quibbles 'n bits: Fighting words flung in heated exchanges, also necessary ingredients for any fair "catfight."

Sashay, parlay!: Catwalk code for "Work it, super-model! Do your thing. Strut to success. Shimmy Choo suits you. Work it for purr points on the Dow Jones!"

Scandalabra: A scandal so elaborate it has more branches than a candelabra. "They found a beef tongue studded with straight pins in Central Park today. What a scandalabra!"

Shade boots: A hot mess with shadiness and attitude thrown in. As in "Did you see Shalimar gaspitating over Ice Très in the cafeteria? Shade boots, okay?"

Shimmy Choo to you: Catwalk code for "work the Jimmy Choos"—the favored footwear among fashionistas.

Shopportunity: A combination of favorable circumstances for the purpose of shopping till you drop.

S'il vous plaît: French for "please." Pronounced "see voo play." As in "Can we please talk about something else besides Dr. Zeus, aka Mr. Tasti D-Lite, *s'il vous plaît!*"

Swarovski crystal clear: In 1892, Czech gem-cutter Daniel Swarovski invented a machine that revolutionized the process of crystal-cutting. Three years later, he founded the company Swarovski. Paying homage to the first king of costume jewelry bling, SCC means displaying the highest level of clarity. Therefore, Swarovski crystal clear means "undisputable." Certainty beyond a shadow of a doubt. As in "The rules of the Catwalk competition are Swarovski crystal clear: get caught in any scandalabrious situation that compromises F.I.'s rep, and you're *out*!"

T and crumpets: Gossip. A riff off the word *tea*. AKA serving T and crumpets. As in "She told you what? Churl, you're wearing me out with the T and crumpets!"

Take it to the brim: Catwalk code for "bring it on," "give it your best shot."

Tasti D-Lite: A fashionista fave: more than one hundred yummy flavors of frozen dairy dessert that is lower in calories, fat, carbohydrates, and sugar than regular ice cream products are. In Catwalk code: a guy with all the flavor and without the extra calories or attitude. As in "Zeus is totally a Tasti D-Lite in my *libro*!"

Thank gooseness: Catwalk code for, "thank goodness."

Think outside the sandbox: To break the mold. To be creative and not always rely on the tried and true. To challenge yourself to be daring.

Tiddy: Tidbit. Tasty, juicy morsel of gossip. As in "Call me later so I can drop a real tiddy on you about Shalimar and Ice Très!"

Très tawdry: Sister to *scandalabrious*.

Tutti capito?: Italian for "Does everyone understand?"

Überfabbie: *Uber* is a German word for "extra," "ultra."

Wigglies: Nervous tension. As in "I got a bad case of the wigglies in my stomach right now, cuz I haven't started my sketches!"

Work it for points on the Dow Jones: Bring your A game. Do the best you can. Work the runway like a supermodel. Stay in the fashion game—and get *paid*.

Catwalk

rip the runway

Catwalk

rip the
runway

DEBORAH GREGORY

dedication

For my brother Edgar Torres, the real E.T.—
and to the real Alyjah Jade, a bona fide gem
destined for sparkle town

acknowledgments

I humbly acknowledge those both past and present who've labored in this "seamy" world of fashion:

The runway models back in the day who had a colorful impact on the industry: Jerry Hall, Alva Chinn, Billie Blair, Pat Cleveland—and Coco Mitchell and Lisa Garber (my two friends with whom I sashayed in Paris, Milan, Firenze, and New York!).

The designers bursting at the seams with something sashay-worthy: the late Patrick Kelly, who served it with buttons-and-bows bustiers. Stephen Burrows and his slinky Lycra numbers with lettuce-scalloped edges in bold fuchsia, mustard, emerald, and turquoise palettes. Isaiah loved black—poured his silhouettes in it. And Todd Oldham just loved the art of it all—may he find a new generation enamored with his unique design genius. And through it all, the flower-power disciple Betsey Johnson continues to thrive, while neon graffiti guru Stephen Sprouse's light burned bright for a time turned backward, then forward, until one day it will stand erect with all the style-worthy whose place can never be erased from fashion's eternal resting place—in the here and now.

Catwalk Credo

As an officially fierce team member of the House of Pashmina, I fully accept the challenge of competing in the Catwalk competition as well as granting unlimited access to photographers and television crews at any time during the yearlong process. I will also be expected to represent my crew to the max, to obey directions from my team leader, and to honor, respect and uphold the Catwalk Credo.

*Strap yourself in and fasten your Gucci seat belt. By entering this world-famous fashion competition, I acknowledge that I'm in for the roller-coaster ride of my young, style-driven life. Therefore, whenever I feel like screaming my head off or jumping out of my chic caboose, I will resist the urge; instead, I will tighten the belt a notch on my fears like a true fashionista.

*Illustrate your visions, but don't be sketchy with crew members. My commitment to my House must always come first. Nothing must stand in the way of my Catwalk obligations—*nada, nyet, niente,* Nietzsche! And when someone or something presents itself as an obstacle, I promise to call upon my crew to summon the strength necessary to cut off the interference like a loose, dangling thread.

*Rulers are for those who rule with purrcision. The true measure of my success will not be how I scale the terrain to fame, but my ability to align my tasks and tantrums with those of my crew. I must always remember that grandiosity could land me in the half-price sale bin like Goliath—who was toppled by a tiny but well-targeted rock!

*Be prepared to endure more pricks than a pin-cushion. Now that I've made the commitment to strive toward a goal shared by many other aspiring fashionistas, I must be prepared for catiac attacks. Therefore, I will honestly share my fears and concerns with my crew so that I can be pricked back to the reality that I am *not* alone in this not-so-chic and competitive world and will not achieve fabulosity solely on my own merits.

*Become a master tailor of your schedule. I must face the fact that my time has now become a more valuable commodity than Gianni Versace's gunmetal mesh fabric from the seventies. Despite the complexity of my tasks, I must always find the time to show up for my crew and attend my weekly Catwalk meetings throughout the year. Together we can make our dreams come true, one blind stitch at a time.

*Floss your teeth, not your ego. Now that I'm part of a crew, carrying on about my accomplishments like I'm the Lone Ranger of Liberty prints is not cute; neither is grungy grooming, or having food between my teeth. I will carry tools of my trade with me at all times, including a container of dental floss and hairbrush so that I can be prepared for prime-time purring and on-camera cues that may come at me off the cuff.

*Ruffles don't always have ridges. While everyone is entitled to an opinion, I will not allow myself to become hemmed in by well-meaning wannabes outside my crew. My individual style is only worthy when it becomes incorporated into the collective vision of my Catwalk crew. I will also resist the temptation to bite anyone else's flavor to the degree that it constitutes copying, or I will be asked to pack my tape measure and head back to the style sandbox on my own.

*Pay homage and nibble on *fromage*. As a true fashionista, I must study the creative contributions of those who came before me so that I can become the maker of my own mélange. I will also publicly give the fashionistas who came before me the props they're due whenever name-dropping is appropriate. Despite my quest for individual development, I must acknowledge that I will always channel influences from the past, present, and future.

*Click out your cat claws to defend your cattitudinal stance.** When others turn bitter, bring on the glitter. Competition always brings out the worst in foes—and even friends—because everyone will try to gobble the biggest slice of the fashion pie and no one readily settles for crumbs without putting up a fight.

*Always be ready to strike a pose.** Even though I may not be a model in the House of Pashmina, I cannot expect to strut the catwalk without getting a leg up on the competition first and saving my best riff for last. When it's showtime, I will be prepared to do my assigned task to help bring the House of Pashmina to the finish line.

*Act fierce even when you're not feeling it.** I will never let the competition see me sweat. While going through this creative process, I may feel doubts about my direction. Therefore, I will bounce ideas off other crew members, but never reveal sensitive information to anyone else! Not all fashion spies have been sent to Siberia—they hide among us, always ready to undo a dart or a hemline.

*Keep your eyes on the international prize.** As a fierce fashionista, I intend to get my global groove on by sampling style and culture around the world. To show my appreciation for the global access that style grants me, I pledge to practice a foreign language for five minutes a day and double up on Saturdays, because we're going to win the Catwalk competition and stage our fashion at a destination—to be determined—far, far away! *Ciao, aurevoir, sayonara!*

Tonight's the night. Fashion International High School's thirty-fifth annual Catwalk competition! Lincoln Center is buzzing like a fashion apiary—and the House of Pashmina fashion show is jumping off inside the hallowed fashion tent.

"Pinch me, purr favor!" I squeal giddily to my BFF since first grade, Felinez "Fifi" Cartera, who is Krazy-Glued to my side. I sneak a peek behind the curtain, watching my other BFFs, Angora Le Bon and Aphro Biggie Bright, rip the runway in front of a standing-room-only audience. The flashbulbs are popping—and the Teen Style Network reality-show crew throngs both sides of the catwalk. The Catwalk judges are seated front and center, including the ringleader, larger-than-life Catwalk director Ms. Fabianna Lynx, and her pudgy bichon frise, Puccini, clad in matching leopard outfits.

Like a heat-seeking missile, I scan the crowd until I set my sights on my major Catwalk rival—Shalimar Jackson. "Tonight's the night, all right. I'm going to tell her that I know she's the reason we couldn't get Tracy Reese shoes for our fashion show!"

While I'm riffing about shoes, a mysterious pair of hands sporting a giganto CZ ring on one finger slide under the curtain and grab the lone pair of pink kitten heels.

"One last beat, Miss Purr!" coos Bobby Beat, our makeup artist.

Angora and Aphro return from the runway and join the huddle while Fallon, our plus-size model, who's been waiting behind the scrim, sashays onto the runway.

"Our fashion show is the most fabuloso! Even if we don't win—we did it!" Felinez gushes, tightening the notch on my wide belt.

"I couldn't be a house leader without you, my catty crew. No matter what, we're in this together—Absolut forever!" I say, fighting back kitten tears.

The music pipes up over the PA. It's my mom's favorite disco song, "I Will Survive" by Gloria Gaynor, but with altered lyrics.

"What, what?" I stammer. "Zeus changed the song? Where is he?" Flustered, I search the wings for Zeus, our house's deejay and male model and my fantasy Tasti D-Lite, but he's nowhere to be found. Suddenly, Ice Très, the notorious tagger from Highway 20, who has been trying to "tag" me with his affections all year, floats toward me from the folds of the curtain like an apparition.

"Why you always checking for Zeus? I'm the one who's always been down for you, boo kitty."

"What are you doing here, Ice Très?" I hiss impatiently.

I can't believe the so-called graffiti guru who almost got me kicked out of school when he tagged a stairwell with his cuckoo Cupid notions has wheedled his way backstage!

"Pash, focus—your cue is in five seconds!" frets Angora.

Felinez grabs one pair of pink kitten heels and puts them on my feet "Go!"

"Hold up!" I protest, puzzled by the song switcheroo. I have to find Zeus.

Fifi pushes me onto the stage. "Go!"

I steady myself, step out from behind the scrim, and take a few steps onto the runway, but one of my heels collapses and I stumble. Humiliated, I fall—in slow motion. Out of the corner of my eye, I see Zeus standing against the back wall next to Shalimar and her underling, Zirconia, who are laughing hysterically. In horror, I realize that the judges are no longer perched in the front row; in their places are cats, holding the House of Pashmina programs in their paws—and hissing at me. As I land headfirst on the runway, one of the cats pounces on my back with a resounding thud.

↖ ↗

I wake up startled as my cat, Fabbie Tabbie, pounces on my chest—and meows louder than a truck backfiring on Broadway. "Oy, Fabbie!" I groan, pushing my beloved auburn-haired cat off me. "You almost gave me catiac arrest!" I slide my pink cat eye mask up and rub my aching noggin, or rather, my headful of pink sponge rollers, trying to decide if the ache is real or a figment of my imagination, like the dream.

"That wasn't real, was it?" I utter, confused.

The alarm on my cat clock goes berserk—eyes bugging, tail wagging—sending me springing into action against my will.

"I wish I was a cat right about now—so I could hide beneath my faux fur like you," I say, teasing Fabbie Tabbie, whom I love like a feline sister.

Fabbie Tabbie tilts her bushy auburn head and meows.

"Awright, your fur isn't faux, I'm so sari!" I mumble, sliding off the bed and slithering into my terry-cloth bathrobe—with the raggedy cat's head appliqué on the back that's about to explode into ninety nubby pieces—and matching fuzzy slippers. Shuffling out of my bedroom and down the narrow hallway plastered with vintage Josephine Baker and Billie Holiday posters, I start singing the altered lyrics of the Gloria Gaynor song from my dream.

> "First I was afraid
> I was petriFRIED
> Kept thinking I could never live
> Without Fabbie Tabbie by my side . . .

But as long as I know how to pose
I know I'll stay alive
I will survive! I will survive!"

As I enter the kitchen, screeching to the finish line of Gloria's anthem for sisterhood, Chenille stares at me, obviously spooked, but for different reasons than I am. "It's a little early in the morning to be scaring people with your singing, isn't it?" queries my sarcastic younger sister. The faux music critic is plopped at the small elmwood dining table in the adjacent kitchen alcove, shoveling in a jumbo breakfast that's fit for a construction worker—just like her drab outfit: long-sleeved beige waffle-weave cotton T-shirt under baggy denim overalls.

"Good morning, Vampira Sisterella," I mutter to my sister, who is a freshman at F.I.'s Hair Annex. While reaching for my Hello Kitty coffee cup, I gaze up at our old lunch boxes tucked in the corner of the cabinet. I pull one off the shelf and strike a pose like a model on *The Price Is Right*. "Can I pack you a fashionista lunch today for school—two carrots and a testy tea bag? Oops, sorry, I meant Tetley."

"Princess Potty Mouth? That was your lunch box," Chenille says with a smirk, shaking her head. Chenille doesn't hide the fact that she finds me mildly annoying, and truth is, I feel the same about her, doubly.

"Oh, right," I say, smiling fondly at the former carrier

613

of my PB&Js and dreams, placing it back on the top shelf where it belongs. Then I pour hot water for my apple cinammon tea.

My mother is also seated in the alcove, talking on the phone in her animated Miss Viv professional manner, which means she's probably talking to her boss, Roni Strauss. I wait patiently for Mom to get off the phone because I desperately need her intel about handling this Shalimar situation, which obviously has me so stressed I'm dreaming in Technicolor terror.

"You might as well open a catering hall and close the boutique—as many bar mitzvahs you've got lined up!" my mom cackles, kibitzing with Roni like a fashion storm trooper. My mom is dressed sharp, as she would say, in a bold emerald-green wool blazer, black turtleneck sweater, and black trousers. "I'll open. I'm on time. Go on. Just bring me back some gefilte fish. You know what I mean. The good stuff on that buffet table! Mazel tov!"

My mom hangs up the phone and I can sense she's picking up the pace as a result of the convo with her boss. She hurriedly takes a swig from her Belgian blend mocha coffee, which she usually sips with relish. "Roni's gotta go to Long Island to yet another bar mitzvah, so I gotta open today," she informs us with the slight Southern lilt that hints at her Georgia roots.

Suddenly, a loud roar emanates from within the wall.

"That sounds like Tony the Tiger. Or *me* practicing Spanish," laments Chenille.

Now I catch her sneaky drift—she's angling for sympathy from our mom about her heavy class load. For some delusional reason, Chenille thought she was going to spend her freshman year waffling hairstyles the same texture as her T-shirt instead of putting in hard time for the fashion crime—studying math, science, and other legit classes.

"That's probably the boiler in the basement. Mr. Darius has *got* to replace that relic with one from this century," my mom complains. "At least Ramon says he'll fix the bathroom ceiling later."

"Yippee!" I squeal. Ramon is Mom's "man friend," as she refers to him, and a professional handyman.

"And what's with that face?" my mom asks my sister sternly. "It's a big deal you got accepted into Fashion International. But you gotta take regular classes like everybody else, because it's still a regular high school." Now my mom looks at me to back her up.

"It's la-bor-iously regular. Felinez can help you with your Spanish homework," I suggest, offering the services of my übertalented BFF, whom Chenille has known since her kindergarten days.

"So, how are you going to handle the situation with that girl?" my mom asks me, obviously ready to help.

"Today is definitely the day," I say, imitating the

Shallow One's huffy self-important tone. "I'm going to confront Shalimar Jackson. That's all there is to it."

My mom looks at me blankly.

"See, Shalimar doesn't know that I know she bribed Chintzy Colon—my former assistant—with an intern job at Grubster PR—one of her father's clients—so that Chintzy would be her spy in the House of Pashmina. Apparently, Shalimar had every intention of leaking *our* design secrets to sabotage our fashion show. But we peeped what Chintzy was up to. Remember I told you Felinez pulled off Chintzy's fake ponytail when we confronted her at Angora's house?"

My mom winces like she fears for the synthetic strands on her own head—a streaked shag Beverly Johnson wig.

"Well, maybe that wasn't our finest moment," I admit. "Luckily it wasn't caught on tape by the Teen Style Network. But the upshot was that we talked Chintzy into going to the Catwalk office and dropping out of our house due to a 'family emergency.'"

"It sounds like it was the right thing to do for the sake of the competition," my mom interjects.

"I know, but Ruthie Dragon, who is now my assistant by default since Chintzy Colon got booted, is also an intern at Tracy Reese's showroom—you know, the black designer who makes those pretty ladies-who-lunch dresses—"

"I know who Tracy Reese is," my mother says tersely, waving a copy of *Women's Wear Daily*.

"Oh, right," I say apologetically. Sometimes I forget that just because my mother works as an assistant manager at a plus-size boutique—Forgotten Diva on Madison Avenue—doesn't mean she doesn't keep up with the "regular" fashion scene, especially black designers. "So anyway, Ruthie asked her boss at Tracy Reese if she could hook us up—you know, the House of Pashmina—with shoes from their closet for our fashion show. You following?"

"Right in your footsteps—go on. I swear, you can never tell a story before I finish my coffee!" my mom protests, placing her cup in its saucer.

"I'm sorry. I get caught up in the fashion flurry. Anyway, Ruthie's boss said that's not gonna happen—us snagging the shoes for our show. Due to, as she put it, 'a commitment to another house in the Catwalk competition'!"

"Okay, so the Dragon girl claims that her boss at Tracy Reese told her you can't have shoes for your fashion show because somebody else has dibs on them?" my mom asks.

"Exacto."

"How do you know that the Dragon girl is telling the truth?" my mom counters as she eyes Chenille's toast before snatching a bite.

"You mean, like it's a conspiracy theory?" I slough off the notion like reptile lotion. "Ruthie doesn't have that kind of fire power. I know Shalimar Jackson is behind this soleful deception—because Tracy Reese's company is owned by Intelco—one of her father's Wall Street clients."

"Okay, what if Shalimar *is* behind this—you still didn't get enough evidence to prove it," my mom says emphatically.

Obviously, all those reruns of *Law & Order: Criminal Intent* have finally seeped beneath my mother's wigs and into her brain. "Somehow, I have to end this reign of terror. Shalimar thinks her parents' money can buy her this competition! She walks around school like we're all her fashion flunkies. I can't take another day of her sham-o-rama!" I pat my rollers in protest.

"What's the matter with your head?" my mom asks.

"I don't know. I had the weirdest dream. The House of Pashmina fashion show? Turned into Cirque de Soleil. I think Tony the Tiger was there!" I moan. "And we were playing your favorite song for the finale! 'I Will Survive.' I would never play that disco tiddy in my show."

"Gee, thanks," cracks my mom. On Saturdays, not so long ago, she would put on a leotard and do her own version of aerobics in the living room, playing old-school disco songs—including Gloria Gaynor's. She could never get Chenille to exercise with her, but I loved jumping around and would always join in. Our little disco sessions are probably what gave me the confidence to sashay down a runway today. That and the fact that I'm tall and leggy.

"Don't mind me, I'm just goospitating about this stupid dream," I mumble. I'm on edge with my mom lately, and I don't mean to be. Or maybe I do. But not about her taste in tunes.

"Those dreams are telling you something," my mom advises with conviction.

"Like what? Don't sleep on rollers?" I pull a box of Ritz crackers from the pantry cabinet and force myself to eat a few before I hit the shower. I hate eating breakfast, but sometimes I feel light-headed by second period in school—and that's definitely not cool.

"Like in order to make your dreams come true, you have to *wake up*," Mom says, serving up her Southern wisdom.

"Well, my dream remains the same—to be a model-preneur," I quip. "So I can buy you a really nice house where you can perch your kitten heels." Suddenly I remember my dream—the rigged kitten heels. I get a somber look on my face. "Maybe the dream was trying to tell me that I have a lot of nerve going up against the Jackson dynasty."

My mom senses my conflict. "Whatever you decide,

just make sure I'm perched at that fashion show in June in a new dress." She glances at the eggshell-ivory face on her elegant crystal watch with the wide red faux-alligator band. "Right now, I'd better perch myself on the IRT!"

"Pashmina is right—Shalimar is probably behind it," pipes up Chenille, like she's testifying at a Senate hearing. "I'm the one who saw Shalimar conspiring with Chintzy Colon in the activator room to send Pashmina the deadly computer virus. I broke the whole story."

"Like Woodward and Bernstein," I say, giving Chenille her props like she's one of the two *Washington Post* reporters who broke the infamous Watergate scandal.

Leaving Chenille with her lumberjack breakfast, I head back to my bedroom to get pinkified for my busy day. Not only do I have to confront Shalimar, but after school I have a Catwalk meeting with my crew, which includes model–deejay–graphic designer Zeus Artemides. I can't help it—those dark, piercing eyes hooded by fluttery lashes, that perfect smile with big white teeth, and those taut muscles that I get to feel every time he gives me a hug are like a Tasti D-Lite trifecta. I'm not sure if Zeus still has a girlfriend, but I keep hoping that he doesn't and he likes me and will let me know after our Catwalk duties are over in June. You know, sorta like saving the best for last.

After I finish getting dressed in a pink corduroy jumper, pink turtleneck, and fuchsia fishnet stockings, I search for my kitten shoes. Fifi worked on them all weekend, embellishing them with furbulous jeweled cat clips. "Here, kitty kitties," I yell, tearing my room apart in a mad search for them, but *nada*. "Aargh. Chenille!" She must have hidden them. When we were little, we were always hiding each other's things to get on each other's nerves.

Defeated, I scrounge the closet for a consolation prize—my pink ankle boots. I zip them up and I'm ready to report for fashion duty. At today's Catwalk meeting, we'll be selecting the five junior models who will open the House of Pashmina fashion show. I've set my sights on a child-model muse. See, my grumpy neighbor across the hall, Mrs. Paul, has the cutest, patootiest grandson, eight-year-old Eramus Tyler, whom I've nicknamed E.T. Although it's risky fashion business, I just have to try to rescue him from his tawdry life in high-water corduroys and sad plaid shirts and put him in the Catwalk fashion show. But the likelihood of Mrs. Paul's hitting me over the head with the stack of Jehovah's Witnesses *Watchtower* pamphlets she carries in her purse is far greater than that of my getting my fashion wish granted.

Nonetheless, I stand outside my apartment door like I'm looking for something in my pink hobo purse until I hear Mrs. Paul exit her apartment. The sound of her jangling keys is music to my ears. Like I'm performing staged choreography, I drop my keys into my purse, then head toward the elevator bank, where she stands like a stone statue.

"Good morning, Mrs. Paul," I say chirpily.

She gives me a once-over through squinted eyes before delivering the results of her pink poll. "That's a crazy outfit."

"Thank you," I say, as if I didn't really hear her, then launch into my fashion plea. Before I can even finish, Mrs. Paul judges me guilty.

"The answer is no," she says firmly. "And you can tell your mother not to be knocking on my door, expecting me to buy any tickets for any such nonsense, either!"

"Oh, I'm not selling any tickets," I explain earnestly. "It's invited guests only."

Now it's Mrs. Paul's turn to act like she didn't hear me. She stares at the elevator ceiling, humming a hymn, clutching her black vintage purse with the gold kiss lock like it's filled with prayers. I stare down at my boots, wondering why she brought my mother into the fashion fray. My mother never knocked on her door. Mrs. Paul was the one who used to knock on our door at the crack of dawn to "deliver the word"—until my mother delivered her fiery wrath.

Sighing, I decide it's best to abort Mission: Impossible before my tape self-destructs. I press the second-floor button so that I can go to eight-year-old Stellina's apartment and confirm the audition time. Stellina is my junior model choice numero uno, and her mother has enthusiastically given her permission.

Not surprisingly, Stellina opens the door since her mother, Mrs. Warren, rarely moves from the couch in the daytime. She works the night shift as a nurse at Harlem Hospital nearby. "Good morning, supermodel!" Stellina says excitedly. "I can't wait to audition later and show you wannabes how to pose for purr points!"

"That's exactly why I'm here. Can I talk to your mother, *purr favor?*" I say, peering into the living room.

"Why?" Stellina asks suspiciously.

"I just wanna make sure it's still okay with her."

"It's okay if I say it's okay," Stellina says, whispering, since she hasn't lost all her fashion marbles.

"Who at the door, Stellina?" Mrs. Warren yells.

"Hi, Mrs. Warren. It's me, Pashmina." I gingerly step into the living room so she can see me.

Mrs. Warren is propped on the couch with a tumbler glass in her hand. She puts it down on the end table and scratches her exposed arm, right below her ladybug tattoo. "Stellina done wore me out about that audition—I know she's going with Tiara and her mother, so that's fine."

"Thank you, Mrs. Warren," I say cheerfully.

"You sure done grown," she says, eyeing me carefully. "How tall you now?"

"Um, five feet nine inches—but I think I'm done growing." I giggle.

"I think Stellina gonna be taller than that—her daddy was six four, you know," she says and hmmphs.

"No, I didn't know that," I say. Now I wonder where Stellina's father is—kinda like I wonder where my father is—but Mrs. Warren doesn't volunteer any more info on that tiddy, kinda like my mother.

"You think she could be a model?" Mrs. Warren asks.

Feeling like a model scout instead of a budding model myself, I make sure to deliver the hype. "Yes. She could prance to a payday, no doubt."

"Good—cuz you said the operative word—*payday*. She need to be bringing a check up in this house!" Mrs. Warren chuckles, shifting her bulk on the brown velvet couch.

Outside, Stellina follows me to the elevator. "Is Greasy coming?" she asks.

I know she's referring to Eramus Tyler, whom she teases for his Dax-slicked hairdo. "No," I say wistfully. "I couldn't get Mrs. Paul to see the fashion light, but I tried."

"That's cuz she got her head up in that Watchtower," Stellina says mischievously. "Don't worry—I'll get her to see the light for ya."

I'm amused at Stellina's tenacity, but I know it won't do any good. Still, I humor her. "Absolutely, super-model. See ya later."

As I walk out of my building, my stomach churns in anticipation of my confrontation with Shalimar. Luckily, my cool neighbor, Mrs. Watkins, gives me a shout-out from across the courtyard. "Hey, Pashmina, don't you look like the cat's meow!" she yells, beaming, toting her usual Piggly Wiggly shopping bags.

"Thank you, Mrs. Watkins." I beam back at her.

"When is that fashion show of yours?" she asks.

"In June—we're coming down to the finish line," I explain nervously.

"Well, if you need anything, you let me know. I got a few runway moves myself," she teases me.

"If I think of anything, I'll let you know!"

"Awright, I gotta get my Take Five. I have a feeling it's gonna be my lucky day!"

"Well, good luck. I hope it's *mine*, too!" I wave at Mrs. Watkins as I walk away. That's probably why I don't see Mr. Sunkist, the homeless man who hangs around our building, zooming my way with his shopping cart piled high with empty cans. He crashes into me and knocks me over and the cans tumble on top of me. Gagging, I mutter, "Maybe not?"

2

Getting my hustle on, I round the bend on Seventh Avenue, trying to shield the gaping hole in my fishnets from the prying eyes of fellow fashionistas. I send a text to my crew: "ETA in five. CODE PINK!" so they'll meet me *pronto* in the Fashion Lounge, our makeshift headquarters for power huddles and fashion emergencies. As usual, the D.T. dogs, who attend Dalmation Tech High School across the wide traverse, are parked on F.I.'s faux-marble steps to gawk at the female fashionistas who make up seventy percent of our student body. That includes Chris "Panda" Midgett, who has cured my computer from a nasty virus but has been angling for more than a tech tune-up ever since. I pretend I don't see Chris as I climb the stairs, but another admirer is hot on my kitten heels. Like déjà vu from my dream, Ice Très magically pops out from the crowd. "Hello, boo kitty," he says, shoving his hands in the front pockets of his baggy supersized jeans like he's searching for something—hopefully a clue.

"Hi, Ice Très," I reply, supa chilly. Inside, however, I'm wondering why the notorious tagger's delicious dimples and warm-milk-chocolate complexion have an effect on me. After all, he stood me up, and this is the first time we've said more than two words to each other since. See, Ice Très made a date with *moi* on a Friday night to hang out at this restaurant called Native. I was so amped about it, but he ended up leaving me in the booty dust—without so much as a call, a text, or even an SOS. That Sunday, I heard through the fashion grapevine (which consists of designer Nole Canoli and his Pomeranian, Countess Coco) that Ice Très was seen at Native chomping on conch fritters and crispy corn bread with the Shallow One! That's right, Shalimar Jackson.

Despite the fact that I'm furious at the dubious double booker, I hear myself say sweetly, "I got a Code Pink. Can I whisper at you later?" Then I point to the gaping hole in my fishnets.

"Oh, right. Got you, boo kitty." Ice Très winks, gathering the nerve he was obviously searching for in his pockets. "Me and my crew are gonna skate in Central Park by the duck pond later. I'ma tag the overpass for the first time. I'd really dig it if you came."

I resist the urge to find out if he's still in conch-fritters cohoots with Shalimar and attempt to keep it moving up the stairs, ignoring him. But Ice Très pleads his case. "I told you Shalimar orchestrated that foul-up. I'm not gonna lie—I needed the hookup she was dangling about financing my Urban Thug street wear. How many times do I have to tell you how seriously positively *sorry* I am about standing you up?"

Now I yield against my nasty will. Somehow I sense Ice Très is telling the truth. He's no match for Shalimar's masterful manipulation. From the day she purchased her first eight ounces of super-straight human hair, courtesy of Adorable Hair on West Twenty-Fourth Street, Shalimar has been "weaving" a spiderweb of deceit to trap the naïve and needy. To Shalimar, hair extensions are career extensions.

"Awright, stop quacking. I'll run through there with my crew—if the police aren't there first! *Ciao*, meow!"

"*Ciao*, meow!" the Dalmation dogs heckle in unison.

Ice Très shoots them a disapproving look. "Freeze it, fellas. I'm a PC."

Angora flings open one of the school doors and her big blue eyes pop at the sight of my bruised leg. "Oh, *chérie*, what happened? You saw Shalimar already?"

"No. Just another victim of fashion roadkill. Mr. Sunkist was trying to make a deposit," I explain, embarrassed. "But I'm ready for the Shallow One—even though I'm *sooo* dreading the Ice Age exchange."

"I know, it is a chilly prospect," Angora agrees, steering me in the direction of the Fashion Lounge.

"Hold up," I say, eager to get her feedback about the Ice Très exchange.

We make a quick pit stop behind the huge glass trophy case, which holds one of the highly coveted Big Willie bronze dress-form trophies, given to the winner of the Catwalk competition. But suddenly, Angora alerts me to an incoming missile. "Uh-oh, here she comes—Miss America."

I turn to see the Shallow One striding confidently in our direction—her Adorable Hair weave flapping coquettishly in the wind. I do a double take at the sight of J.B., her snippy mascot, proudly perched in the black Fendi Spy bag at her side. "I thought J.B. was banned to Style Siberia—forever?" I mumble under my breath. Last year, J.B. chewed on Ms. London's Fendi bag in model appreciation class. Principal Confardi showed his lack of appreciation by yanking J.B.'s Fashion International access pass.

"Hi, Pashmina. Hi, Angora," Shalimar says, descending upon us, her large brown eyes and white teeth sparkling on cue as she levels her sights squarely on Angora. "Um, Angora, could you give us a moment? This conversation is—*privé. Comprendez-vous?*"

"*Oui. Bien sûr,*" Angora says, graciously leaving.

"Hi, J.B.," I say, gingerly extending my hand to pat his prima donna head. J.B. snaps at my fingers like a hungry piranha. Luckily, I withdraw it before he gets his chomp on.

Shalimar glances at my frenzied fishnets before she

dives into her agenda. "Pashmina, I think you've been misinformed by your *assistant*—what's her name?"

"Do you mean Ruthie Dragon?" I clarify, going along with her charade. Even J.B. probably knows that Ruthie Dragon is my assistant now.

Suddenly, Caterina Tiburon, camouflaged in her usual khaki gear, appears with her ubiquitous Teen Style Network camera crew, ambushing Shalimar and me. The bright light flashes in my eye, causing me to squint. This constant intrusion of so-called reality is due to the fact that Fashion International's entire faculty and student body have signed a waiver permitting the crew unlimited access. That means no exchange (or corpse in the closet!) is safe from the crew's probing intentions! I try desperately to shield my frazzled fishnets from the cameraman's lens, but to no avail. And as I suspected, Shalimar uses the occasion to practice spin control.

"Um, whoever is your assistant. Sorry, I can't keep up with the turnover in your staff. But, I wanted to personally inform you that I'm not the culprit responsible for your inability to raid—I mean, secure Tracy Reese shoes for your fashion show. I mean, the House of Pashmina fashion show," Shalimar says, suppressing a smirk.

Out of the corner of my eye, I see the infamous zebra-striped mink hat on the head of Zeus zooming by.

I desperately want to turn and shout, *"Rescue me!"* And despite the fact that my cheeks are burning from yet another humiliation at Shalimar's hands—and Jimmy Choo–clad feet—I calmly proceed. "You're not using Tracy Reese's shoes in your fashion show? I mean, the *House of Shalimar* fashion show?" I add, mimicking Shalimar's haughty tone. Two can play that fashion game.

Shalimar responds, *très* tongue-in-chic. "Absolutely not. I'll be featuring Jimmy Choo shoes *only*. And that's not revealing any of the design secrets for the House of Shalimar fashion show. Everybody already knows my allegiance to the Malaysian cobbler—since *everything* about me has been dissected on the Catwalk blog almost daily."

Before I can dissect Shalimar's dismissal, an eager student vies for her attention. "Excuse me, Shalimar. I hear you're going to be in charge of the career mentorship program and I need after-school credit—"

"I haven't decided, but can we talk later? I'm in a meeting," Shalimar interupts the eager student.

"Oh, sorry, right!" The student giggles, managing to smile right into the camera lens. "And I'm rooting for you front row in June. I know you'll win!"

After the student leaves, Shalimar regains control of the convo. "Listen, I don't know which house has dibs on the Tracy Reese shoes, but I want to make it clear—it isn't mine. Not the House of Shalimar. Worry not."

"Thank you for letting me know," I say. Now I'm confused about my intel, and past experience has taught me to be cautious. See, when my computer froze a few months ago from a nasty virus, I was running around in circles accusing everyone of the cyber whammy—from Aphro to Liza Flake (one of the hairstylists in my house) to even Ice Très. (After all, he did stand me up.) It was only after Felinez and I bribed my sister to spill the refried beans that we figured out it was Chintzy Colon—at the behest of Shalimar. Turns out Chenille accidentally overheard them plotting the plague in the activator room.

I decide it's time to play my trump card. "Next you'll tell me that you had nothing to do with getting Chintzy Colon a job at Grubster PR and weren't behind the cyber crime committed on my computer."

"Your accusations are *exhausting*. Chintzy is delusional. And the last I heard, she withdrew from your house because of family problems. Clearly she has no shortage of those," Shalimar says, challenging my intel. "I suggest you look further into the shoe situation before—"

Now Shalimar's underling, Zirconia, sporting an

oversized CZ ring, cuts in. "Big problem. I can't get J.B.'s access pass reinstated cuz—"

"I told you to see Mr. Confardi— All right. Is there anything I don't have to do myself?" hisses Shalimar, who then whispers something to Zirconia out of camera range before she resumes speaking down to me. "Excuse me, Pashmina. I'd better go. Oh, one more thing. I don't think you see the big picture. When I was twelve, my father gave me a book—*The Seven Secrets to Success* by Dali Drammeh. My father attributes his success to those valuable principles. Maybe that's the difference between you and me—well, maybe you should just pick up a copy. Listen, I'm sorry, but I have to go take care of this. We'll discuss it another time."

Shaking my head in disbelief, I force a polite smile. "Yes, I'll go pick up a copy, *pronto*, of your father's precious manifesto—*The Seven Secrets of Swindling!*" Walking away, I smile warmly at Caterina and her crew, who are now turning their attention to the long-awaited return of Chandelier Spinelli, the former house leader who bailed out on the Catwalk competition when her father, Mr. Spinelli, a nurse at Brooklyn Hospital, was indicted last fall for his alleged participation in an illegal-body-parts operation. (I know, it's très bizarre.)

Over my shoulder, I hear the Gucci Guilty One, as

we've aptly nicknamed Chandelier Spinelli because of her designer name dropping and father's indictment, coo to the cameras: "I'm just *soo* glad to be back in school!"

Like I'm passing a train wreck, I can't help but turn to catch Caterina stick the mic in Chandelier's face and ask one of her usual annoying questions. "Are you upset about being disqualified from the Catwalk competition?"

"Ask me that next year when I launch my election campaign—again. But this year, I can assure you, I'll be there in June at the fashion shows rooting for Shalimar Jackson. Now that I'm no longer in the running *she's* the favorite to win!" Chandelier cackles back.

I fume at the Gucci Guilty One's predictable prediction as I swing open the gilded door to the Fashion Lounge. Angora, Aphro, and Felinez are hyped and ready for the Code Pink, which is my fashion emergency. There is a hot-glue gun plugged into the wall, and the sewing kit is arranged on the shelf.

"Hi, sugar plum," coos Angora, concerned.

"Hi, crème brûlée," I coo back.

Felinez queries anxiously, "Did she admit it? Did you tell Shalimar?"

"*I tried.* Smuggling Gianni Versace gunmetal mesh from the seventies over the Berlin Wall would have been easier. I couldn't get a word in edgewise," I lament, having a meltdown.

"I'm not surprised. When Shalimar's talking to herself *she* can't get a word in edgewise," bellows Angora.

"And what's J.B. doing back in the mix? Someone school me, please?" Aphro asks, agitated.

"That one's easy. The Jacksons' financial contributions to F.I. coffers minus Ms. London's chewed Fendi purse equals J.B.'s reinstated access pass. Do the math," I mumble. "And, just my luck, the Catty One filmed her denying the whole Chintzy thing on tape!"

"That takes shadiness to a new level," winces Aphro.

"To the glass ceiling." I shudder, wondering if Ms. Lynx's spies overheard the sordid exchange.

"So she denied calling dibs on Tracy Reese's shoes for her fashion show?" Aphro persists.

"She issued a nondenial denial."

"Speaking of shoes, where are the kitten heels?" Fifi asks, landing her disappointed gaze upon my ankle boots. "The ones encrusted with a kaleidoscope of crystal stones in the *exquisite* shape of twin Siamese-cat clips? The ones I slaved over all weekend?"

"Don't ask, Fifi, okay?" I lament. "I tore my bedroom apart like Chicken Little on a griddle. Chenille must have hidden them. Oy, what is it with shoes lately? Can't people go back to robbing cradles?"

"Forget your shoes," interjects Aphro. "So you're telling us that Shalimar isn't borrowing any shoes from Tracy Reese for her show?"

"Correcto. She claims the House of Shalimar will showcase its allegiance to the 'Malaysian cobbler' Jimmy Choo—and that we've been shoe-jacked by *another* house."

"By whom?" my crew asks in unison while aiming the handy repair accoutrements in my direction.

"I have no idea. My guess is we're gonna have to *sole*-search the shady situation," I expound, suddenly getting a whiff of inspiration. "Hold up—I do have a fishy idea, however." I grab the scissors from Angora and slip into the bathroom stall, taking off my fishnets.

"So what are we gonna do about shoes? We can't afford to buy any." Felinez gulps.

"I know, Fifi—and we sure can't make them, because the only thing we know about cobblers is they're peach," I lament, wrapping a piece of fishnet around my neck like a bib.

Stepping out of the stall, I continue mapping out my fishnets and our strategy. "Let's just pick the child models today, finish our fittings, okay? Which means I pray that Diamond brings the sketches—and leaves the animal alerts at home and out of the Catwalk meetings."

"I know, it is becoming troublesome," Angora agrees about Diamond Tyler, who is on my design team. "She seems more interested in the goings-on in the four-legged kingdom—that's why she inundates us with gory stories about their perils and problems."

"Speaking of animal updates, you won't believe the catmare I had last night—in high definition," I remember suddenly, getting creeped out again. "We were backstage at the House of Pashmina fashion show, but when I went out onstage for the finale—I fell on my face, and all the judges had turned into hissing cats!"

"That does sound weird. What do you think it means?" Felinez asks. She's always searching for omens, signs, burning bushes, Tweets—anything that can remotely serve as guidance through this complicated maze called life.

"Maybe you should ask Confucius?" Aphro blurts out to Felinez. "Check those slips from the Chinese fortune cookies you horde in your purse like shredded documents!"

I look in the bathroom mirror at my newly fashioned fishnet skullcap and matching bib. "I don't know—maybe that catmare was trying to tell me that I'm gonna fall flat on my face in front of everybody at our fashion show."

"Dreams are never what they seem—sometimes the message is convoluted," advises Angora, who studies my latest creations carefully and beams. "Pash, that looks *très* adorable."

Angora is our unofficial style expert when it comes to hats. Like Zeus, she's almost never without one. Unlike the Mad Hatter, however, Angora likes to mix them up—from powder-blue mohair berets to vintage felt cloches.

"My mom said the same thing about dreams in reverse," I tell her, pushing the fishnet skullcap farther down on my forehead. "So, Aphro, Fifi—approve?"

"Um, yeah, except for that pink sponge roller in the back of your head!" snaps Aphro, letting out one of her signature snorts.

"Oops!" I yelp, embarrassed.

Angora takes out the stray hair roller as house music is piped over the PA system, signaling the start of first period. Amidst our giggles, we exit and sashay our separate ways.

FASHION INTERNATIONAL 35th ANNUAL CATWALK COMPETITION BLOG

New school rule: You don't have to be ultranice, but don't get tooooo catty or your post will be zapped by the Fashion Avengers!

LIGHTS, CAMERA, JACKSON!

Can we cybertalk about the intrusive white elephant in the pantry closet? Unless your swelled head is buried in the pearly sands of Fiji, you've figured out that I speak in riddles about the Teen Style Network camera crew. For an entire school year, these alien intruders from the television planet have been granted the green, red, and blinkin' yellow light to follow Fashion International students and faculty members around anywhere we go.

Of course, this invasion of privacy is in the name of capturing the not-so-pretty process of the Catwalk competition by any means necessary—even if it means hiding in someone's pantry closet. Now, please don't pooh-pooh my PC (pantry closet) reference. There are those prancing among us who have a pantry closet—as well as a cook, a butler, and fine bone china for serving tea, which they've bragged about ad infinitum. (Stay awake in Latin class?)

This morning, however, the Teen Style Network camera crew (who hence-

forth shall be referred to as TSN,
which is not to be confused with TMJ,
although the two have a lot in common)
merely had to hide in plain sight in
the school's lobby to land a double
whammy of a jammy. First they captured
a not-so-chic catfight between an underling named after a shawl favored by
street vendors and a privileged member
of the "other" Jackson dynasty. The
clawfest would have been a trilogy of
terror if a Blue Beret with blinkin'
blue eyes (this one named after rabbit
hair) hadn't politely been asked to
hop along on a scavenger hunt. By the
way, what exactly does the word *privé*
mean when the TSN alien intruders can
descend upon us without warning?

At any rate, the frustrated underling named after a shawl's claims of
espionage against her house unraveled,
along with her ripped fishnets, under
the glare of the camera lens. Doesn't
she know that her only mistake was
getting elected in the first place?
See, there is only room for one house
leader in this year's Catwalk competition. Frankly, there should have been
a memo—just like the one announcing we
had to sign waivers for all the up-
too-close-and-personal video-stalking
tactics from TSN.

Milliseconds later, the TSN intruders also captured the long-awaited return of a former house leader who used
to be a brightly lit fixture at F.I.
before her father was indicted for his
alleged participation in an inter-

national illegal-body-parts ring. Come next June when the show airs, we'll all be privy to the close-ups of the raised eyebrows of students scurrying from the scene as the insecure fixture tries to ensconce herself back in the school and let the light shine on her once again by giving the camera crew a few sound bites. (Whatever happened to "No comment"? Surely it's a phrase she memorized after witnessing her father repeat it thousands of times to the reporters hiding in their bushes after his arrest?)

Unlike the TSN intruders, I've tried to be careful about protecting the identities of all parties involved, as you can see by my references in riddles. Thanks to TSN stalkers, however, we should all ponder the following fashion fodder: after the poses have been struck, will the winner of this year's Catwalk competition claim the Big Willie trophy through sheer talent, or simply because they delivered the best sound bites? Only the hairdressers will know for sure. The rest of us will have to watch next June to find out after the fur settles, the swag is regifted—and the Nielsen ratings are in the bin.

Posted by The Riddler at 15:04:12

3

After textile science class, I'm summoned to Ms. Lynx's lair.

"What do you think she wants?" Felinez frets naively.

"Duh? I put Shalimar on blast on camera?"

"Oh, right, the spies are everywhere," Fifi concedes, nervously plucking cat hairs off my top.

"I'm shedding!" Agitated, I shoo away her hands.

When we hit the third floor, I detect another reason to be fearful: down the hall, in plain sight, is my sister, Chenille, in her drab overalls, being filmed by Caterina!

"This really takes a bite out of fashion crime," I shriek like a Barbie banshee. "First she hides my shoes, now she's shrinking in the spotlight!"

I try to decide if I should bolt, while Fifi puts on a brave front and steers me forward. As we inch closer, my suspicions are confirmed. Caterina is grilling my unsuspecting sister about Catwalk business!

"I know that the hot water conked out in your house, but did the lights, too?" Fifi whispers to me.

"No, why?" I retort defensively.

"Look at what Chenille is wearing! Did she get dressed in the dark?"

I roll my eyes, exasperated. "I know. *Oh.* I told Chenille you'd help her with her Spanish homework, just so she could stop kvetching about her fumbling frijoles!"

Now Fifi rolls her eyes. "*Graci-ass!*"

Then we both watch, wincing, as Caterina probes my shy sister in her usual pushy manner: "Is it true that Chintzy Colon was acting as a spy for Shalimar and you're the one who brought this to your sister's attention?"

"Oh, please, don't let Chenille drop the quibbles 'n bits! How did the Catty One peep our intel?" I yelp.

Fifi frets. "I didn't say anything to nobody! *Te juro*—I swear!"

I sigh, resigned. "Truth is, the House of Pashmina has more leaks than the *Titanic.*"

Squealing, Chenille spills the refried beans one by one. "Once, I saw Chintzy talking to Shalimar—I mean, they were hiding in the activator room, so I told my sister. But that's it—it's not like I was spying or anything." Chenille sees us and raises her forehead like a furry chinchilla desperately sealed in a Kremlin vault, gasping with its last breath to be saved.

"*Hola,* Chenille," coos Felinez. "I hope you're taking care of that hobo?"

Chenille gulps at the mention of the "bribe." See, in order for us to coax Chenille into telling us what she overheard in the activator room, Felinez offered up her prized black leather fringed hobo with the white fur lining. True to her handygirl nature, Chenille never uses it, but the prize is simply about collecting a piece of fashion herstory. (Although she doesn't admit it, Chenille knows that Fifi and I are destined to be fashion trailblazers.)

"Oy, the fashion grapevine delivers drama faster than FedEx," I lament.

Apparently Chenille isn't delivering drama fast enough for Caterina, because the pint-size producer shifts her khaki camouflage gear in my direction and goes in for the fashion kill. "Pashmina, is it true that your sister told you about the exchange?" she yells.

"Yes, she did," I say, without adding relish to the hot dog. I walk away, striding confidently toward Ms. Lynx's office, before I realize that my strut is eerily imitating Shalimar's.

The pushy producer persists. She yells down the hall: "So is it true that Chintzy was a spy for Shalimar?"

"You heard Shalimar's explanation. Chintzy dropped out of my house because of family problems," I reiterate, shifting my gait and losing my balance slightly.

I quickly regain it as Fifi taps the face of her watch

with her finger. "*Mija*, you're late!" Then she nudges me into the Catwalk office. "Just go in there and act professional. See you later."

The house music sounds over the PA, and even Caterina knows that's her cue to back off from the students with their busy schedules. When I walk into the Catwalk office, Ms. Lynx's assistants, Sil Lai and Farfalla, are sitting together, peering at a magazine. "Pink hair is soo last year—even though I think T.T. looks good in it," confesses Farfalla.

"You're just saying that cuz she's Italian," counters Sil Lai. They're buzzing about my favorite jewelry designer, Tarina Tarantino, who has a penchant for Hello Kitty and neon fuchsia synthetic wigs in a blunt bob.

"*Non è vero!* That's not true!" protests Farfalla. "Betsey Johnson looks *bellissima* in it, too!"

I stand at the desk, smiling, and pipe up, "Pink is always in. I agree."

"You would," Sil Lai says, eyeing me like I'm a fashion felon requesting a change in the color of prison-provided jumpsuits. "Bordeaux is hot right now. I'm thinking about going red, like Alyjah Jade."

"Who's Alyjah Jade?" I ask curiously, wondering if it's a new designer or model rising in the ranks.

"She's a singer," Sil Lai says, like she's playing a trump card. Then she talks directly to Farfalla, ignoring me. "She's performing at the Lipstick Lounge next week. I so hope I can make it, but I'll still have classes at Barbizon."

I wonder what Sil Lai could be taking at Barbizon but I don't dare ask, given her chilly reception. She's not tall enough to be a model, so it can't be that—and I thought that's what Barbizon is known for. I glance at the closed door to Ms. Lynx's office, then around the office—looking right into the gaping jaw of the leopard statue in the corner.

"Your skullcap is so cute. Guess you're getting a jump on Fly Hat Fridays," coos Farfalla.

"Fly Hat Fridays?" I ask, puzzled.

"Haven't you heard? Ms. Lynx read that Zeus Artemides post on the Catwalk blog about hats," explains Sil Lai, trumping me twice. "There will be a memo."

Farfalla, who comes from the land of Dolce & Gabbana (that's Italy, nonfashionistas), sweetly fills me in further: "Ms. Lynx has decided to designate Fridays as Fly Hat Fridays in order to inspire students and faculty to wear their most creative headgear. Not that anybody here needs encouragement to be more creative!"

"But that's not what she wants to see you about," Sil Lai says not so sweetly.

I refrain from blurting out that I already suspected that. Or that I also know that Sil Lai is Ms. Lynx's personal spy, reporting every fashion bread crumb before it even drops on the ground in the enchanted fashion forest.

"And you can go in now," Sil Lai orders, pursing her thin red-lacquered lips.

"Oh, *grazie!* Thank you!" I squeak to Farfalla. No point in wasting my cheesiness on Sil Lai, even though I don't fully understand why she's so shady to me.

I step into Ms. Lynx's inner sanctum, but she is on the phone. "Hmm, hmm—that's right—*avec chanterelles, s'il vous plaît. Merci!*" Ms. Lynx coos into her leopard phone before placing it back in its cradle.

My ears prick up at the mention of such an exotic name as Chanterelle. Now, that has to be the name of a major new model, because Ms. Lynx keeps her ear to the street—aka Seventh Avenue. Ms. Lynx motions for me to sit down in the Queen Anne chair with the leopard cushion opposite her massively cluttered desk. I try to sit down like I'm poised for positive strokes, even though I feel like a lamb being led to slaughter. Especially when Ms. Lynx levels a blank stare at me like she can't remember something important—like my date of execution. Squirming, I blurt out, "Chanterelle—that's such a pretty name."

"Yes, it is—for a mushroom, which is exactly what I was ordering on my mesclun salad." Now Ms. Lynx snaps out of her trance.

Meanwhile, my cheeks burn with embarrassment—bright red! I sounded like such a fashion amateur.

"So, Miss Purrstein—there seem to be a lot of goings-on in the House of Pashmina that apparently I should have addressed sooner," Ms. Lynx says, putting on her leopard glasses, then opening a leopard folder and peering at a page carefully.

I shriek inside, wondering if it's a secret dossier she's been compiling—on me!

"I had no reason to suspect anything wrong when Chintzy Colon asked to be removed as a member of your house due to a family emergency. It was a legitimate claim." Ms. Lynx pauses. "But now am I to understand that you're accusing Shalimar Jackson of influencing Chintzy—and Tracy Reese—in some way? What's next—a Catwalk conspiracy in the Pentagon?"

Flustered, I stammer, "N-no, my assistant, Ruthie Dragon, told us that she'd be unable to secure shoes for our show from Tracy Reese because another house would be using them due to a prior arrangement."

"And? So you assumed it was because of Shalimar Jackson?"

Now it's my turn to stare blankly at Ms. Lynx.

"Did you?" Ms. Lynx persists.

"Yes, because Intelco is one of Mr. Jackson's—um—Jackson Holdings's clients," I blurt out.

"Pashmina, I know you don't major in fashion

journalism," she says, riffling through the papers in the dreaded folder again. "And your grade point average is excellent—very impressive—but perhaps you'll consider honing your investigative reporting skills before you accuse anyone of anything—especially on camera?"

"I didn't do it on camera. I mean, that wasn't my intention!" I protest.

Ms. Lynx ignores my defense and continues delivering her summation. "I called over to the Tracy Reese showroom and spoke to Rina in the publicity department. Apparently, the House of Ninja will be lent their collection of highly sought-after soles."

"How did that happen?" I ask, puzzled pink. Nervously, I yank one of my curls. Willi Ninja, Jr., has no connecs at Tracy Reese. And to my limited knowledge, no other student from F.I. is interning there now, except for Ruthie Dragon, who is on *my* fashion team— the House of Pashmina.

Ms. Lynx ignores me again. "It's not my job to find out how the House of Ninja managed to secure shoes that are eluding you. May I suggest focusing your energy on finding shoes instead?"

"I'm sorry," I apologize humbly, because I'm gagulating at this latest tawdry turn.

"Don't apologize to me. But may I suggest you apologize to Shalimar Jackson?" advises Ms. Lynx.

"But I do know that—" I stop midsentence to suppress my urge to drop the tiddy about Shalimar and Chintzy sending me a computer virus. What's the use? It won't earn me any brownie, or pinkie, points. Instead, I switch gears: "I will apologize to Shalimar. Thank you."

Ms. Lynx tilts her head at me, softening, before she puts her fashion armor back on: "I specifically asked all of you to please be careful about on-camera dialogue. The operative word is *discreet*. For the sake of our fine fashion institution. Have I made myself clear—again?"

"Understood. *Capito!*" I say enthusiastically.

Ms. Lynx smiles faintly at my Italian cheesing before administering another stern warning. "It shall remain on record that Chintzy Colon dropped out of your house due to a family emergency, but if any other member of your house drops out, I will be taking a closer look at the cause to consider shaving points off your Catwalk score."

I fight back the tears and smile, my back frozen to the chair like a Popsicle, before Ms. Lynx dismisses me.

I can't even look at Sil Lai when I exit; luckily she's on the phone. With her kind eyes, Farfalla delivers a message to me that I decipher to mean *Hang in there, cara!*

The hallway is no longer a war zone. Bolting to my

fashion marketing class, I feel grateful that I didn't reveal anything to Ms. Lynx about Chintzy—the spy who came in from the cold. For sure, that plan would have backfired, just like my plan to confront Shalimar. And at least now, I'm still in the fashion game.

4

Angora, Aphro, and Felinez are already in Studio C for our Catwalk meeting. So is Ruthie Dragon, sitting in a corner by her lonesome, pretending to be engrossed in the book *Fifty Shoes That Changed the World*. I wonder if Ruthie is trying to channel a subliminal message to me.

"What happened?" Felinez whispers.

"Let's just say Ms. Lynx put me on notice—any more pink slips and I may fall from grace," I whisper, sitting at the head of the conference table. It's a ritual I usually find royal, but today I feel like a leader about to be dethroned.

"Of course, the Shallow One is sipping up the drama like Earl Grey tea," Aphro blurts out.

I wink at Biggie Mouth with my left eye, which is Catwalk code for "Put a lid on it." This hushed convo is for our ears and fears only. I glance over at Ruthie and recall what my mom said. How do I know that Ruthie is telling the truth? Just in case, I'm unofficially yanking her privilege to sensitive info. It's bad enough that today's Catwalk blog entries have everyone yodeling from the fashion treetops about the Shalimar showdown in the lobby this morning. "I shouldn't have put Shalimar on blast till I had better intel," I croak, shifting into guilty gear.

"Well, I'm just glad somebody finally said it—the Shallow One does think she's the only viable candidate in this high-heel race!" snarls Aphro.

"And she's trying to win it with our shoes!" hisses Felinez.

"That's just it. Willi Ninja, Jr., shoe-jacked us, not Shalimar," I confess.

Angora is aghast at this tawdry tiddy. "Pash, are you sure?"

I nod. "That's what Ms. Lynx told me."

Felinez crinkles her brow like she's channeling *brujería*. "Don't be fooled by Shalimar's silence of the lamb chops. She's leading us to slaughter—I can feel it!"

"Please don't get mad, Fifi, but feelings are not factos," I advise.

"I'm not—but I had a feeling about Chintzy and I was right, *está bien*?" protests Fifi.

"*Está bien*, okay," I crow, deciding to test her *brujería* intuition. "So who exactly is the Riddler?"

"It could be anybody," Fifi responds, shrugging her shoulders like an unappreciated psychic.

"*Oui, c'est vrai*. It's true. It could be anybody hiding

653

behind a blog identity," seconds Angora. She gently smooths the ends of her long, straight blond hair. "Now all we need is the Joker."

"Speaking of true or false, does *chanterelle* mean 'mushroom' in French?" I query, hesitant about my pronunciation. Angora takes French for her language requirement.

"True," Angora says, nodding. "Technically, it's one type of mushroom."

"What about Alyjah Jade?"

"That's a mushroom, too?" asks Aphro, skeptical.

"No, she's a singer performing at the Lipstick Lounge next month—or so says Sil Lai."

"Then she must be stuck-up, or Sil Lai wouldn't be putting her on blast," snorts Aphro. "But I heard that spot is serving it cutely with red velvet love seats. Wish someone would take me there."

"Why don't you ask Lupo? You've been locking lips with him—might as well cozy up together at the Lipstick Lounge to test those love seats," I suggest. Lupo Saltimbocca is our resident photographer, thanks to Zeus, who brought the goofy Italian Francesco Scavullo wannabe into the House of Pashmina. Although he really digs Aphro, she is sticking to her sob story—that his nose is too big to be diggable.

Aphro doesn't respond to my snap; instead she starts belting out an impromptu riff like she's channeling an old-school blues singer: "So we ain't got no shoes/and we ain't got no man/but we got our slinky moves/and we're putting on a show so/everybody gonna have a real good time."

"What moves you got?" I ask, taking the Bessie Smith bait. I know that the late legendary blues singer is a favorite of her foster mother, Mrs. Maydell.

"Come over later so I can show you the pose formation I have in mind?" pleads Aphro in her normal voice.

"Yes, ma'am," I say obediently. Things have been tense for Aphro at home since her foster brother, Lennix, was removed. Aphro finally told us that Mr. Maydell and his strict discipline were too rough for Lennix's gentle nature.

More members of my Catwalk crew file in for our meeting. "Here are my models!" I announce, snapping into Catwalk leader mode at the sight of Mink Yong and Kissa Sami, who arrives with her velvety-blue-eyed little sister.

"Well, who is this?" asks Angora, beaming approvingly at our first child model prospect—yummified in a parfait-orange sweater over bubble-gum pink leggings and Pastry Kicks sneaks.

"Cherry," she says with a grin.

"Oh, Cherry, *chérie*, aren't you a style soufflé."

A puzzled look clouds Cherry's face, prompting Kissa to explain to her sister, "She likes your outfit."

Cherry grins shyly, reminding me of how insecure I used to be if I thought someone didn't like me. Now there's only one person who I wish liked me more: the Mad Hatter.

"Fly Hat Fridays! Work it out!" shouts Benny Madina, our dreadlocked male model, clapping at Zeus as he brightens the doorway with Lupo Saltimbocca and his Nikon lens.

Fallon also claps for Zeus's fashion activism. She is our star plus-size model. "Freaky Fridays! Now all we need is Big Girl Appreciation Day to set it off up in here!"

Lupo Saltimbocca lets out a snicker.

Zeus tips his brim before he takes off his black leather jacket, baring his muscled biceps in a black T-shirt emblazoned with the words DON'T FEED THE MODELS.

"We are not adding that slogan to the Urban Gear segment!" I blurt out, referring to the slogans we've stamped on the T-shirts and sweatpants in our show.

Zeus winks in acknowledgment of my cuteness. Staring at Zeus on the sly, I wonder if he was always so secure and confident. With those dark, dreamy eyes and chiseled cheekbones, he probably knew at the age of two that he was gonna be a Tasti D-lite. Or maybe that's what it's like when you have a big, tight family with a father at the helm; you get to feel warm, secure, and fuzzy inside.

Lupo, on the other hand, wears his insecurities like an itchy wool sweater plagued by pilling. His eyelids are so droopy he has to tilt his head sideways when he levels a gaze, like he's searching for his good angle. Like right now, as he sidles over to Aphro and plants a kiss on her satin-smooth cheek. "*Ciao, bella,*" he coos.

"Hey," she shoots back, angling her face so she doesn't butt heads with his Pinocchio-plus nose. Despite what Aphro says, I know she is feeling Lupo, and definitely vice versa. For a second, I fantasize that Zeus is feeling me, too—and that that's why he comes over and gives me a hug.

"Congrats," I coo, blushing. Suddenly, I start blathering about my creepy catmare. "So I had a dream that we were playing this funny remix of 'I Will Survive' in our fashion show—and you were nowhere to be found. And I was like, what's with the switch-up? Why did Zeus do that? And where is he?"

"Yeah, well, I'm right here. So, what you got?" he asks, interrupting my babble flow.

I shake my head like *Forget it*, but I can't get the song out of my head, so I start singing it in my cackling jackal voice. After all, Zeus is the deejay and will be putting together the tracks for our show.

"Oh, Lord, rip the runway, not my eardrum, puh-leez!" Aphro puts her hands over her ears.

"*Párate, stop!*" hisses Felinez. She slaps Aphro on

her arm. "Nobody stopped you when you were singing like an old-timey washbucket."

"*That* was the blues. Get your history straight."

"Go ahead, *mija*—it's really cute!" coaxes Felinez.

Because everyone else giggles, too, I shrug off my shame and resume singing like a cackling jackal.

> "*First I was afraid*
> *I was Petri-FRIED*
> *Kept thinking I could never live*
> *Without Fabbie Tabbie by my side . . .*
> *But as long as I know how to pose*
> *I know I'll stay alive*
> *I will survive! I will survive!*"

While I'm singing, Diamond Tyler, our second designer in command, sneaks into the meeting like a field mouse, quietly popping into an empty seat. When I squeak to the finish line, I record the reactions: Angora and Felinez clap loudly. Liza Flake snaps her gum loudly, then snickers until she's posy-pink in the cheeks. Aphro just shakes her head, embarrassed. Zeus's reaction is the most surprising. "I could make a track out of that. I'm not kidding," he reassures me.

"Really?" I respond, surprised. "My mom would dig that. Let's mix it." Trailing off into the outer limits, I resume trying to decipher my trippy dream. "In my dream,

I was wondering—why were you standing next to Shalimar in the audience instead of remaining backstage with us?"

Zeus shrugs his shoulders like he's lost me in the Twilight Zone. He meets my gaze, and his eyes twinkle until we're locked into a mutual adorationfest. That is, until the spell is broken by the noisy entrance of nosy Nole Canoli, model Elgamela Sphinx, and makeup artist Kimono "Mini Mo" Harris, who has brought her little cousin.

"Oh, look, it's Mini Mo Two!" squeals Dame Leeds, our lead hairstylist.

Nole is more interested in Zeus's brim victory. "Fly Hat Fridays! You'd better work, supermodel!" Nole Canoli squeals like he's Miss Piggy, whom he strongly resembles, only without the strands of pearls. "In honor of the first Fly Hat Friday, I'm making the Countess a red pillbox hat!" Nole plops down with his better half, Countess Coco, perched neatly at his side in a Prada carrier.

"That's it—we need some pillbox hats for the bomber jackets and ruffled chiffon skirts," I brainstorm.

Kissa strokes the Countess's fiery red mane. Unlike snippy J.B., the Countess has manners and appreciates attention and Lambo Lovers delicate liver treats.

"Well, if we don't win, we'll be remembered as the house that created Fly Hat Fridays," giggles Liza Flake.

When she's not popping her annoying gum, she's blowing off Catwalk meetings for her internship at Vidal Sassoon. Not once, but twice. Oy, our assistant hairstylist makes me scratch my head—and not to relieve dandruff, either. Of course, Dame Leeds, our lead hairstylist, always makes sure Liza is on time so he can avoid tangling with me.

"I think we should put a few pillboxes in the show—with the minidress segment?" I suggest, inspired by Zeus's accolade. "We don't have enough hats in the show—that's what we need—even though the Ferocious One hates last-minute additions."

"I second that motion," seconds Zeus. He tips his brim again and nods humbly again.

"Who's the ferocious?" Cherry asks innocently.

"The Big Bad Lynx!" blurts out Nole.

Aphro knocks him on the shoulder, her personal code for "Put a lid on it." The Chintzy Incident has taught us one thing: we don't know who is carrying secrets to our enemies at the Kremlin (aka Ms. Lynx's office), or where the Teen Style Network has planted hidden cameras!

"All right, sorry." Nole smirks, then beams at Cherry. "Are you ready to twirl? What's your name?"

While Nole continues to coo with Cherry and Kiki, Mini Mo's miniature lookalike, I can tell Felinez is fretting because Michelette, her older sister, hasn't arrived yet with their little brother, Juanito. "She probably has her head stuck in a *telenovela*!" Felinez moans. Michelette works in a video store. She's addicted to Spanish soap operas—mainly the Colombian *Betty, la Fea*—and sometimes has to be pried out of the recliner chair.

"She'll be here," I assure Felinez.

"Don't you have someone coming, too?" Nole asks me.

I nod. "But not to worry—nothing will keep this divette in training from a shot at model stardom!" I quip.

"I heard that!" screams Stellina, blazing through the doorway like a shooting star.

I jump up to hug Stellina, relieved that she came without Tiara, her timid best friend from Building C. Alas, I hoped too soon. Stellina turns around and looks behind herself like she's lost her bread basket in the forest. She bolts out the door. Seconds later, she returns—with not only Tiara in tow, but also Eramus "E.T." Tyler.

"Color me impressed," I shoot at her, pleased. "How'd ya pull this off?"

"I'm going with Mrs. Paul on Sunday to hand out *Watchtowers*," she says, rolling her eyes. *The Watchtower* is the official magazine of the Jehovah's Witnesses. "Miss Pashmina, you owe me—big-time."

"I get your drift," I respond quickly. What I want to

say is *This is a fashion show, not a magic show.* Even the Great Houdini couldn't pull a runway trick out of his hat to transform Tiara's fashion travesties!

"Wow, you're going to see a watchtower? Where?" Zeus asks, intrigued.

Aphro jabs Zeus in the side of his black leather jacket like *Chill for now and we'll hit you up later with that info.* No point in insulting E.T., who beams at me like I'm his Secret Santa.

"I am so glad to have you in the mix!" I quip.

"You think I could really be in a fashion show?"

"Why not?" interrupts Felinez, ready to reassure him. "My brother, Juanito, is going to be in our fashion show, too, so you won't be the only boy!"

"Well, he has to try out first," blurts out Dame Leeds, like he's in charge of model casting.

I refrain from telling Dame that Juanito's audition is merely a formality. Juanito's in there like swimwear.

"Don't worry—I'm really happy you're here," I assure E.T.

"He kinda looks like Lennix," Aphro says sadly.

"Who's Lennix?" E.T. asks.

"My brother," Ahpro says quietly. It's the first time I've ever heard her refer to Lennix as her brother. Usually she says foster brother.

"So why are you so late, Miss Diamond?" asks Dame Leeds, shifting the focus from family to feuds. I know he's really putting me on blast—not Diamond—because I put him on blast for Liza's two no-shows.

"I had to go see for myself—I heard that three coyotes turned up on the Columbia University campus," Diamond reports, like she's delivering a trend observation from the Fashion Week tents at Lincoln Center.

"Really?" Stellina asks, excited.

Diamond ignores my stare and continues like we're just sitting around having a howling good time and not conducting a Catwalk meeting. "The peak of coyote breeding season is right now, I think—so a lot of them are getting kicked out of their homes while their parents are preparing to—well, you know." She stops, embarrassed. "So anyway, the young ones migrate south along the train tracks, cemeteries, the park, and even college campuses like Columbia, because they're looking for food—you know, like small rabbits—"

"Um, Diamond—that's enough with the urban coyote tales," I say sharply. I've had it up to here with Diamond disrupting the meetings with her "tails" of woe.

"I was just trying to explain—" Diamond stops because her voice is getting shaky. "I mean, if you can talk about your nightmares, why can't I talk about what's important to me? This fashion stuff isn't the whole world."

"Yes, I know. But I'd appreciate it if you would keep your updates to Catwalk-related topics from now on, okay?" I plead. Diamond's face is beet red. "Don't get me wrong, we can talk about that kind of stuff after the meeting is over. Right now, I want to talk about this great idea we got to set off the the satin bomber jacket and chiffon skirts—what about pillbox hats?"

Diamond doesn't answer me. She sits down like a petulant child, fiddling with her sketchbook on the table, then gets up and walks out of the meeting!

"I knew it," I groan. "Today is *not* my lucky day."

**FASHION INTERNATIONAL 35th ANNUAL
CATWALK COMPETITION BLOG**

New school rule: You don't have to be ultranice, but don't get tooooo catty or your posting will be zapped by the Fashion Avengers!

HERE COMES THE JUDGE . . .

As of late, everyone at Fashion International is tethered to two "seamy" topics: 1) This year's Catwalk competition, for which the contestants are busy assembling their creations on cutting tables. 2) The ghoulish body-parts ring—members, which include the father of one of F.I.'s former house leaders—accused of running an international illegal chop shop. All related parties will face judgment day real soon. The five competing houses in the Catwalk competition will face the music when the esteemed judges cast their votes after the fashion shows are unveiled at Lincoln Center in June; the five members of the body-parts ring will face the music in Brooklyn Supreme Court after the jurors reach a verdict.

But how can we resist passing judgment in the meantime? Let's examine the sordid facts: one house leader went MIA after the chop shop scandal broke, leading her to withdraw from the competition; one house is claiming they were duped out of designer shoes; and apparently another will soon be facing charges concerning misappropriation of funds (that allegation is freshly plucked from the seedless grapevine).

As for the trial: we have discovered that Nurse Spinelli was part of a scheme to harvest corpses at funeral homes for bones, skin, cardiac valves, and other body parts to sell in the global transplant business! Skin, sold in sheets, went to burn victims. More than 12,000 people in the U.S., Canada, England, and other countries received the body parts!

Apparently, on the first day of the trial, juror #2 heaved up her matzoh-ball soup and root beer float during the district attorney's opening argument: "Thousands of people around the world are walking around with tissue and pieces of bone that were never tested for hepatitis and other diseases!" Yikes! Some trade secrets should never be leaked.

The identities of the trial jurors and the five judges for the Catwalk competition are being kept confidential, but we the people always count on leakage. (Those darn leaks in the Catwalk office must keep Ms. Lynx up at night—and on the prowl for intruders!) A grade-A reliable source has confirmed that one of the judges in the Catwalk competition is Hello Kitty—obsessed jewelry designer Tarina Tarantino—not Betsey Johnson, as certain people falsely reported earlier in the year! Coinky dinky: both daring designers wear a fuchsia wig, but we the people don't agree with the recent rumblings that a pink "influenza" will create a "color bias" in this year's Catwalk competition. Oh, glow up! There are five judges on the posh panel—and as in the cadaver trial, all verdicts delivered must be unanimous.

In summation, we the people think fashionistas should have more faith in the system. How much do you want to bet that one of the Catwalk judges will surely be color-blind—except for the color green, if you catch my drift—thereby ensuring the *shoe*-in of a certain house. (There, somebody finally said it!)

At any rate, the former house leader who sashayed away in disgrace has announced that she plans on running again next year for house leader in the Catwalk competition. Ahem, we the people think said candidate doesn't stand a prayer of even a hung jury. Come graduation time, she should just grab that cap and be glad it only comes with a tassel—and no strings attached. But hey—no judgment!

Posted by We the Fashion People at 13:45:34

5

I'm so frazzled that Diamond Tyler dissed me in front of my entire team that I start yanking my hair like an outpatient from the Amsterdam Gardens psych ward.

"Can we have one meeting without drama?" squeals Nole Canoli. "I'll go get her!" Nole plops the Countess on his chair in her Prada bag and waddles out of the room.

Ruthie Dragon can't help but throw a satisfied look at me before she bares her "sole": "It took a little digging—but I did find out at work about the shoes. The House of Ninja is going to be borrowing them," Ruthie states, like she's reporting from behind enemy lines in Afghanistan.

"Yes, I know," I say curtly.

Benny Madina, an avid Ninja hater, asks, "All I wanna know is how'd *he* steal our hookup?"

I refrain from commenting, but looking around at my Catwalk crew, I realize that I'm being called into action. "Look, I know that you've all turned in your hookup sheets—but if anyone has a shoe lead we can explore, exhaust, beg, borrow, or steal, please let me know?"

"Go Manolo or go solo, that's what I always say," quips Bobby Beat, our star makeup artist.

"Well, put your money where your mouth is," heckles Dame Leeds. "Enough with the false advertisement."

"At this point I'd take Kmart shoes and Prada manners, people," I warn Dame, sounding an awful lot like the Ferocious One, Ms. Lynx. "We've got eight weeks to showtime. Also, for the next Catwalk meeting, I need all of you to hand in your lists with email addresses for all the friends and family members you're inviting to our fashion show. Zeus will be designing the Hold the Date email announcement that Angora and I will be sending to all guests. For the purposes of top secrecy, the final invitations will be sent out to our guests a few days before our fashion show. Everyone clear?"

"Crystal," heaves Dame.

The door swings open and I jump, startled, but it's Michelette and Juanito instead of the usual intrusive suspects, the Teen Style Network crew.

"Hola!" Michelette coos excitedly.

Felinez doesn't hide her agitation. "You didn't keep Juanito waiting at school, I hope?"

Michelette doesn't answer her younger sister—subtly establishing who's in charge. See, their parents gig-hop around the world—mostly on cruise ships—

performing with their sixties cover band, Las Madres and Los Padres, so Michelette is in charge most of the time. There's also no question about who's blonder. Michelette has been streaking her hair platinum blond since I can remember. Felinez thinks it's tacky, but then again, she's not a fan of "shady" hair—she won't even use a red henna rinse on hers.

"You're going to work the runway for us?" asks Aphro, teasing Juanito.

Juanito shrugs his shoulders and doesn't respond. His curly hair is even wilder and darker than Fifi's.

"No?" prods Angora. "You're telling me someone as cute as you doesn't dream about becoming a super-model?"

"No," Juanito says, shaking his curly head.

"Then what do you want to do?" Angora quizzes further.

"I wanna be an artist," Juanito says confidently.

Now Lupo Saltimbocca, our star photographer, perks up. "What kind of artist?" He has been quietly snapping photos from his catty corner. Inspired by Juanito's stance, Lupo gets up and zooms in for a close-up of his face.

"A con artist," answers Juanito.

"Juanito!" shrieks Felinez, then covers her face with the palms of her hands, embarrassed.

"That's so funny!" laughs Stellina. Tiara stares at her beat-up brown loafers. I wonder if she laughs at all.

The ripple of laughter rises when Nole returns without Diamond. He thinks we're laughing about Diamond's disappearing act. "I tried to talk her off the ledge!"

I shrug my shoulders, letting Nole know *Not so funny.*

Zeus senses my agitation and slides out the door. I assume he's going after Diamond. If anyone can convince her to come back, he can.

"Let's all move to the left side," I instruct my crew, so we can make space for the child models to walk on the right side of the conference room.

I position my adorable child models in a single line while I quiz them. "Everybody knows what a fashion show is, right?"

Stellina throws me a look like *Don't try it,* then answers. "Yes, we're gonna wear fierce clothes and walk on the catwalk!"

"That's right—and the fierce clothes have been made by us—because you're going to represent the House of Pashmina by opening our fashion show!" I say, hyping my junior models' crucial position. "Okay, one by one, I want each of you to walk all the way down to Felinez, stop in the middle on the way back, twirl, then walk the rest of the way and make a left like you're going backstage. Everybody understand?"

My child models nod. One by one, they proceed to walk as instructed and we watch on the sidelines. That is, until we get to Kiki. She stops in the middle—and doesn't move.

"Come on, Kiki—go ahead and twirl!" Mini Mo coaxes her cousin. But Kiki won't budge. She stands there, twirling her foot in a circular motion.

"Come on, Kiki!" Mini Mo shouts again.

This time Kiki screws up her face and starts to cry.

"That's okay, Kiki. You don't have to."

"You can do it," coaxes model Mink Yong. She babbles in Japanese to Kiki.

"She doesn't understand!" Mini Mo snaps.

"Oh, sorry," Mink apologizes.

Mini Mo pulls Kiki aside so the rest of the child models can take their turns walking.

Secretly, I wish that Tiara would pull a divette fit, too, so she can exit door left. When it's Tiara's turn, she walks, all right—like a shivering penguin marching gingerly on thin ice at the North Pole!

"Tiara—walk like I told you," whispers Stellina, who has obviously been coaching her friend beforehand. Tiara stares down at her feet and walks back, embarrassed. Stellina's checks fill up like a balloon and she releases the air in a deep, disappointed sigh. Then, just as quickly, Stellina puts her fashion face on like a pro—and walks, twirls, and returns in a fluid motion.

"Now, there's a star in the making!" Nole applauds.

"Thank you," coos Stellina, blowing a kiss.

"Not so much smiling at everyone when you're on the runway, Ms. Stellina. Remember, you're a model while you're out there. Don't react to anybody, just look straight ahead and keep walking till you hit the turn to go backstage."

"Got it," she says, taking another turn.

E.T. goes last—and delivers a nice quiet little strut. Even I can't help clapping when he's finished. "That's *purrfecto!*"

"I knew you could work it," seconds Stellina, like she's been coaching her new crush.

Because Diamond has still not returned to the fashion fold, I decide it's best to take all the child models' measurements myself—even Kiki's.

Afterward, I announce to everyone, "We're going to have our runway training next week, then final fittings—for our child models, too—who can leave now if they'd like."

"So does that mean Tiara is in the fashion show too?" Stellina asks me point-blank.

"I'll work with her," blurts out Aphro. Aphro is our choreographer and runway trainer. She begins her assigned duties at our next Catwalk meeting.

"Yes, she's in," I relent.

Tiara breaks into a smile.

"Bye, supermodel!" coos Stellina.

"Is someone picking you up?" I ask, concerned.

"Yes, my mother. She's already downstairs," Tiara says, flashing her phone in her palm.

I kiss Tiara goodbye.

"Is it okay if I leave now?" asks Mini Mo.

"Yes, go ahead. I appreciate you bringing, um—"

"Kiki," says Mini Mo, filling in the blank.

Embarrassed by the lapse in my brain synapse, I continue, "Right, Kiki—but we won't be able to use her."

"Oh, don't worry about it," Mini Mo says, kissing me on the cheek. "She asked for weeks when the audition was, then she gets here and freezes. Go figure." Mini Mo shakes her head, causing the fine strands of her blunt, straight bob to flutter gently.

After Kiki is gone, Dame Leeds grunts, "You could have given that poor little girl a chance."

I decide not to respond to Dame. I've had my quota of catfights with him: over Liza, over the designs—which he has no talent for. He should stick to hairstyling. I make the creative decisions—period.

Speaking of creative decisions, when Zeus returns with Diamond, I realize we won't be able to go back to the way things were. Now I'm going to have to wrestle the evening gown sketches out of her and decide what to do about the outfits for the five child models.

Since Diamond is his second in command, Nole luckily takes the lead. "Are you feeling better?" he asks the petulant pet activist, who slithers into her seat without so much as an apology.

Diamond picks up her precious sketch pad and stares at it without answering.

I gain eye contact with Zeus and say thank you with my eyes. He winks in acknowledgment.

"Well, can we see the evening gown sketches, at least?" asks Nole.

Diamond hands him the pad without saying a word.

I look over Nole's shoulder and can't believe my eyes. "These are Grecian?" I ask, surprised, staring at the sketches for a draped one-shoulder gown and a strapless one.

"That's what you said you wanted," Diamond says, bursting at the seams.

"No it isn't," I say, remaining calm. "This is clearly goddess inspiration—not feline fatale."

"Okay, no worries—we'll start over," offers Nole.

"We're supposed to have ruffles and flirty cascading hemlines for the gowns—for the pink Lurex," I reiterate. Now I'm freaked out by Diamond's obvious meltdown, which has been coming for months.

"The draping works with the Lurex, too," protests Diamond.

"Yes, I know, but it's not feline fatale—that's all I'm saying," I reiterate. But I can see Swarovski crystal clear that Diamond doesn't agree.

"Okay, okay. Diamond, redo the sketches. By Friday. Now, let's talk about the kids' outfits," Nole says forcefully.

"We should open full throttle with our color theme—pink and black—the boys wearing graffiti tees with our slogans and the girls wearing tiered sundresses so they can twirl to the maximus," I say.

"Furbulous," says Nole. "Let's start on that this weekend—and we're good to go?"

"*Oh*. I got it—how about matching umbrellas edged in ruffles, with slogans on them, and the girls open them while they're twirling?" I say, excited.

"Genius!" coos Angora.

Everyone nods in agreement. Meeting over.

"I can't believe we got through a Catwalk meeting without you-know-who barging in," Nole quips, relieved. I know he's referring to the Teen Style Network crew.

"Hard to believe," I second, trying to take the rough edges off the Diamond disaster. "Ah, my masterful draper—what a ride. You know I couldn't do this without you." I smile at Nole. He waddles over to give me a hug.

676

Diamond shoots a furtive glance at our exchange. She was supposed to be my masterful illustrator—but I can clearly see I'm going to have to draw the line with this drama queen.

"Runway training begins next week, which means the time has come for the Pet *Pose Off*. Who's it gonna be, Penelope or Fabbie Tabbie? Time to put their paws to the test," I remind Nole. Penelope is Nole's prized cat.

"Now you're talking. Let's set it up so Penelope can wipe the floor with your dishrag—oops, I mean tabby cat," he snaps.

"I already signed up for a session to use the catwalk ramp tomorrow in the auditorium," I say. The catwalk ramp is put up in the Fashion Auditorium for Special Events.

"What is the Special Event?" Ruthie Dragon asks.

"Who knows. We'll find out tomorrow," I respond. "Good thing is, they're putting the ramp up." Whenever the catwalk ramp is assembled in the auditorium, students can schedule sessions for their own use before it's taken down and put in the storage area backstage.

"Sounds good," Nole says confidently. "Diamond, this is right up your alley. Why don't you come to the Tabbie-Penelope Pose Off—or I should say, *battle*—and be a judge? That way, you can bring the evening gown sketches, too." Nole isn't so much asking Diamond as ordering her.

For a *segundo*, Diamond registers approval and nods, but then she darts out the door like a mad matador. "I'll deal with her drama later," I mutter, shaking my head.

Now it's time to end the meeting, so we stand in a circle, holding hands, while I read part of the Catwalk Credo. My crew say their good-byes and start streaming out the door.

"What is up with Diamond's claws-and-paws attitude?" Aphro asks me.

"I have no idea," I sigh wearily.

Aphro deciphers my message ASAP and snarls impatiently, "Awright, you coming?"

"In a minute," I say, gathering my papers. No point in cutting off any Zeus interaction sooner than I have to. I always find myself lingering in his presence.

Nole lingers, too. "Don't worry, we're gonna fix the sketches," he assures me.

"I know," I sigh, frustrated that I can't do the sketches myself, but illustration is not one of my strengths. Neither is draping, even though I'm an expert seamstress and got my first sewing machine on my eleventh birthday. My gift is a clear vision. Felinez thinks I should improvise and major in design anyway, but I'm old-school—like the haute couture masters.

Now Dame Leeds tries to step in, but I'm definitely not in the mood for his March madness, so I inch over in Zeus's direction. Blathering, I ask, "So, you're going to start the fashion show mix?"

"I've already started it," he says. "I'll just do a Gaynor mix—and I was gonna have our first round ready for the runway training."

"Oh, yeah, right," I say, like I'm recalling music strategy discussed at our last meeting. Not.

My phone vibrates from a text message, so I pull it out to check if it's an emergency from my mom. Out of the corner of my eye, I sense that Dame Leeds is getting my message—and stepping off. Even if Chris Midgett isn't. The text is from him: "Sorry you didn't talk to me this morning. Can you call me? Don't want to bother you. Now it's your move."

"Not," I mumble, turning off my phone.

Zeus's next move, however, is the one I don't see coming. "Listen, you wanna go get something? I wanted to swing by the Barbiecue Hut before I head home."

"Really?" I ask. "I'm up for some Twizzlers."

Zeus chuckles. Aphro not so much. Once we're outside the Studio, I can tell from her face that she'd like to shove mine into a piping hot pizza pie. I know I told her I would go over to her house, but we've got plenty of time to formulate our runway moves before the next Catwalk meeting. I figure she can go hang with Lupo instead and get the attention she craves, since that's what she is really looking for right now—and Lupo lays it on thick like mozzarella made in his native Firenze.

"Come on, *cara*. I'll take you to your favorite place," Lupo coos to Aphro, sensing her distress.

She begrudgingly accepts Lupo's invitation to hang out at the Naughty Luna Café, which is near her house.

"That's so sweet, you're gonna trek all the way to Brooklyn," I encourage Lupo.

"Do or die, Bed-Stuy!" he giggles, turning on his supergoofy charm.

I'm secretly relieved that Lupo didn't ask to come with Zeus and me. Or maybe those two planned it that way from Jump Street.

"*Bonsoir, chérie,*" salutes Angora, kissing me good-night. Felinez and Angora both seem confused by the change in plans, but they're happy for me.

"Be good!" Felinez whispers as she hugs me.

"I will," I whisper back.

But what I really want to do is scream from the fashion rooftop: *Someone pinch me*, purr favor!

6

"There is only one thing that would make me miss my mother's cooking—the Barbiecue Hut's Mango Tango Ribs," says Zeus, his elbows propped on the restaurant's picnic-style wooden-plank table as he scans the huge laminated menu with the pink heads of adorable Ultra-Lashed piglets winking in each corner.

I shift my weight on the hard wooden bench, trying to decide if I want to get greasy in his presence.

Zeus senses my hesitation. "My bad. You're probably a vegetarian?"

"Are you kidding?" I reply heartily. "Aphro is always putting me on blast for sucking bone marrow out of turkey bones. Why'd ya think I was a veganista?"

Zeus hesitates before he spurts, "None of the models at school are into getting down and dirty."

I find myself blushing against my will at his immodest description of F.I.'s diet-obsessed fashionistas.

Zeus cleans up his act. "You know what I mean?"

"I do. Every day after lunch, Anna Rex rotates between the five stalls in the Fashion Lounge, coughing up carrots," I giggle. "I just—I dig that you're such a fly communicator—and not just on Fridays."

"You're messing with me," Zeus says, flashing his big, perfect teeth, his incisors resembling adorable fangs. Zeus places the palm of his hand on his massive chest like he's trying to put his laugh box on pause.

"And thank you for feeding me," I giggle.

Zeus taps his chest again over the words DON'T FEED THE MODELS before he gets my jab and chuckles. "Oh, right, the T-shirt. My mom got this for me at SeaWorld."

"Ha, ha." By the time the tall, wiry waiter with the electroshock-therapy bleached-blond hair comes over with our drinks, Zeus and I are both caught up in a gigglefest and I have to repress the urge to confess *Please forgive moi, but Zeus brings out my kooky side!* Instead, I clear my throat and dictate my order: "Mango Tango Ribs, please." No use worrying about squirting sticky sauce on my face at this late juncture. I've already embarrassed myself mucho today.

"Ma'am, you get two sides," says the waiter.

"Oh, right. Collard greens and mac and cheese, *purr*—um—I mean, please," I say, giggling.

"Two times on that," Zeus tells the waiter, like he's working on his mixes.

The waiter stares blankly at Zeus.

"I'd like the same sides as the señor—the kitten—I mean the lady—" Zeus explains, but now he can't even finish his sentence before he breaks out laughing again.

The waiter nods and scribbles on his pad before he leaves in such a hurry that he walks into the restaurant's mascot—Miss Barbiecue, the pink pig wearing a red and white gingham apron, perched prominently in the entrance to the dining room.

We snicker at his collision, checking out the ambience. "This place is cool, isn't it?" Zeus asks me.

"Yeah, downright freezing," I say, shuddering at the early onset of air-conditioning. "And it's not even spring yet—officially."

We go for another round of giggles, prompting me to needle Zeus. "If I didn't know better, I'd swear you put some sassy-fras in my pink lemonade."

"Ma'am, I could say the same thing to you. Think I didn't notice the foam in my root beer fizzling mighty quickly?" counters Zeus. "By the way, I'm emailing you the Hold the Date notice I designed for our show. I think you'll dig it."

"I'm sure I will," I say, pleased as punch that Zeus is doing triple-threat duty in my house. Not only is he the deejay and a model, he is also designing all our graphics. I decide to play a game with him. "Awright, tell me something about you that nobody knows."

Zeus ponders this tiddy before he responds: "My sister, Olivia, and I have this shark club."

"What?" I respond, balking.

"Serious. We went to the Long Island Aquarium when we were little and we got hooked," he explains. "Now she bakes cookies in the shape of a shark. Cuts out sponges. I got a rubber shark collection. I even made her a shark dress for her school play last year."

"That's a good one. I didn't take you for the shark type." I smile. "Or realize that you're a designer."

"Isn't everybody these days a wannabe something?" he comments. "Awright, what about you?"

I blink hard, deciding if I should throw him just a tiddy or some live bait. Against my better judgment, I do the latter. "Um, I don't know who my father is," I confess. There, I said it. I pat my fishnet skullcap. Twirl the curls on the end. "My mother won't tell me who he is. And sometimes I wonder what he looks like and if he knows that I exist. Or if I'm just a creature-feature from another planet." I decide not to tell him that I also think my father is white. I've embarrassed myself enough for one day.

Suddenly, Zeus reaches across the table and rubs my cheek with his knuckle. "You're so sparkly and cute, it has to come from inside—not anywhere else."

The room stands still. Gets quiet, too—despite all the chatter and clatter around us. I've waited so long for Zeus to give me a sign—a smoke signal, a communiqué with invisible ink, or a message in a bottle—that he likes me. But, maybe I'm hallucinating? Does he really like me—like that? The thump-along in my chest says he does. Or maybe that's heartburn, from chugging too fast? My mom says I imbibe my beverages like lightning is coming my way. Before I hit the panic button, I blurt out: "Okay, two questions, to go with the two sides. Um—"

"No, keep the babble flow going," Zeus says, coaxing me to continue.

I giggle again because I love how Zeus flips the switch to Catwalk code, which he's been privy to by hanging with our crew for the last six months. "What I'm suggesting is the following. Ahem, ahem," I continue, fumbling for phrasing. "How about we each get to ask one question and the other person has to answer it. No back-downs. No excuses."

"Cool. I can do that," Zeus agrees, smiling slyly, the corners of his mouth curling up like they do right before he breaks into his soon-to-be-a-supermodel smile. "Look, I'm sorry. I don't know why I can't stop smiling with you. Okay, hit me with the question. Felines first—go!"

My breathing quickens. I back down from what I really want to ask him, which is *Do you have a girlfriend?* Instead, I switch to a more neutral probe. "What kind of felines does the Mad Hatter fancy?"

"Oh, that's a good one," Zeus laughs. "I thought you

were going to ask me if I'm gay. I'm so sick of people calling me out like that at school."

I blush again. Unbeknownst to him—or maybe he does know—I was one of those people. The first time I laid eyes on Zeus last fall, he was coming out of voguing class in his signature mink zebra hat. I asked anyone who would listen if they knew if Zeus was on the loose, but nobody at school had reliable intel on the latest zebra sighting. He was freshly transferred from greener pastures in Long Island, specifically, Benjie Bratt High School.

Deflecting attention from my embarrassment, I shoot, "Well, you know what they say—straight male models in this business are as rare as Komodo dragons in Indonesia!"

"Very funny," Zeus says, shaking his head, then he rattles off all the male models who are as straight as peg-legged pants.

I concede to his impressive rundown by smiling demurely and tilting my head.

"Okay, well, to answer your question—I like ferocious felines like you," Zeus says, blushing.

I blush, too. Bingo!

"Okay, my turn to ask a question?" Zeus informs me teasingly.

"Bring it."

"Who texted you before when we were in the

Catwalk meeting—and caused you to make that killer kitty face?" Zeus asks.

"*Oh*, right," I sigh, stalling for a *segundo* to formulate my response. "When I got the computer virus—which I know Shalimar and Chintzy orchestrated—anyway, I was desperate for help, right?"

"Oh, I remember that," Zeus says, nodding.

"So, this Dalmation Tech guy, Chris 'Panda' Midgett—you may have seen him hanging outside on the steps with the D.T. dogs?" I inquire.

"I've seen the dogs, yes, can't miss 'em—but can't say I was checking for that, um, specific species you just mentioned," chuckles Zeus.

Trying not to laugh, I continue, "Well, Panda—that's his nickname—came to my cyber rescue and I was so grateful about it—I think that's why—I did go out on one date with him—to Googies Diner."

Zeus picks up his napkin again and breaks out laughing.

"You laugh—but the foot-long hot dogs there will make you wanna slap your mother!" I heckle.

"Oh, I doubt that—I love my mother," counters Zeus, "but go ahead."

The waiter interrupts, balancing piping hot plates of ribs in both hands. "Excuse me."

"Hit us with it, partner," Zeus goofs, looking directly up at the waiter's face.

Finally Zeus's charm has warmed even the waiter; he breaks out a tiny smile, setting the plates down in front of Zeus and me.

Zeus looks at the plate of ribs, then right back at me, signaling me to continue. I find it so diggable how he always looks at me when I'm talking—and when I'm not.

"So Chris wants to go out with me and keeps texting me, but I don't want to go out with him. And I feel guilty because I can't get with his program on any other format besides his cyber skills, if you follow me," I spill in candid fashion. "So, long story short—that's why I turned off my phone in the Catwalk meeting."

"Okay, I follow. So you're saying he's a little corny for your taste, like most of the D.T. dogs?" Zeus asks, like he's enjoying making me squirm.

"Yup—and a little too short," I add for good measure.

"I get it. Short like Lupo."

I almost bite my tongue from embarrassment instead of the pork rib. "I'm sorry—I really like Lupo. He's an amazing photographer, too."

"He's really flipping for Aphro."

"I know."

"Well, did you know his father runs the largest shoe factory in Italy? All the Italian shoe manufacturers subcontract his factory's services. And for every pair they sell, they give away a pair to the homeless in Third

World countries," explains Zeus proudly. "He's a seriously righteous man. I mean, a CEO who treats his employees and consumers with respect."

"Really," I say, amazed. While I'm wondering why Aphro never told me that tiddy, I'm spooked by the dream again—me falling flat on my face on the runway because my kitten heel gives out—*kaboom!*

Zeus's gaze zaps my frightmare like Kryptonite. "Come here," he whispers. He leans over to kiss me.

I obey. Mesmerized, I move in closer. I feel the watchful eyes of patrons at nearby tables, but I don't care. "Um, you're not going to bite me, are you?" I ask, smirking.

Zeus doesn't answer. He moves in like a shark on a mission. I relent like a willing victim, meeting Zeus's dreamy lips for my first real kiss. With Mango Tango sauce. We keep kissing, sliding down the rabbit hole like we're the only two people left in the restaurant, besides Miss Barbiecue herself, congealed into a lifeless ceramic statue, winking at us. I imagine Miss Barbie whisking us with a checkered napkin in her pudgy paws through a portal at the bottom of the rabbit hole that leads into a secret, silent passageway. And when Zeus's tongue touches mine, we're finally alone—the only two people left anywhere on the planet, period. Alone in paradise lost.

FASHION INTERNATIONAL 35th ANNUAL
CATWALK COMPETITION BLOG

New school rule: You don't have to be ultranice, but don't get tooooo catty or your posting will be zapped by the Fashion Avengers!

HERE, KIDDIE KITTY . . .

A certain ambitious house in the Catwalk competition seems to have more than a few tricks up its sleeve—not to mention a "cat in a zebra hat," but we won't talk about that right now—even though we're all wondering who's scratching his belly and if he's declawed. Now back to the house in question that Arm and Hammer built.

First off, what offends us most are those annoyingly adorable and endless feline references that make us want to scream *Ciao, meow!* already. Secondly, there are the ubiquitous feline symbols—everything from goo-goo grommets to appliqués applied everywhere. And we do mean everywhere. If you haven't had the pleasure of changing for gym class with members from this house, consider yourself lucky to be spared the annoyingly sappy sight of cutesy briefs with a Cheshire cat grinning on the rear view.

But today was the last straw in the fun house: there was a recent procession of miniature models scampering in the school building. Okay, letting the cat out of the bag: it's obvious we will have to endure kiddie kitties on the runway in a certain house's fashion show.

It's also obvious that some of us will stop at nothing to reinvent the fashion wheel with their kitten-size talent—which will no doubt nauseate judges and guests in the process—in order to get their grubby paws on the prizes. We can only hope this feline flops like the ill-hatched marketing idea of recycling Scoop Away.

It's bad enough that the fashion business has always taken a lot of flack for, well, overheating its formula, ever since 1980, when Brooke Shields appeared in the controversial Calvin Klein jeans print and television ads at the ripe age of fourteen, proclaiming, "You want to know what comes between me and my Calvins? Nothing."

That's right, not all of us fall asleep in fashion advertising class, but some of us really should take a catnap to conjure up some new hat tricks for recyling the same ol' ball of yarn, before the panel of judges take their front-row seats at the Cat-walk competition fashion shows come June.

Posted by Spadey Sense at 13:55:23

7

I wake up to the sound of my mother yelling in the living room. My bedroom is dark and I'm sprawled across my bed, fully dressed. I strain my eyes to see what time it is on the cat clock across the room. Ten o'clock. Rubbing the crust out of my eyes, I remember the afterglow of floating on the subway, encased in my pinkalicious bubble in Zeusland—until I came home and was hit with the sight of Chenille in drab gray. I barked at her, "Where are my shoes? I know *you* hid them!"

But now that I've been rudely awakened, in more ways than one, I try to drown out who my mother is yelling at in another room; it's obviously someone on the phone, because the heated exchange is limited to her booming voice.

I prop myself on my fifty pink velvet and paisley pillows, gazing peacefully at Fabbie Tabbie, who is perched in the chair at my desk, gazing at the computer screen, where the Catwalk blog is still up. I was reading the blog because I was paranoid that there would already be rumors about my Zeus rendezvous posted online, but I drifted over to the bed, daydreaming about said rendezvous, before I passed out. Now I realize how silly that is—not the daydreaming part, but indulging in paranoia as a pastime. Or maybe not? Good thing Fabbie Tabbie is keeping tabs for me.

"You'd better keep up, Fabbie Tabbie," I mutter in approval. "Because in fashion, one day you're in—furballin' with the Fendis—and the next day you're out with the kitty litter."

Fabbie Tabbie slowly turns her head, gazing at me with those *Avatar* smoldering eyes. I still don't move. Not yet. I'm determined to languish in my daydreams about Zeus until I'm forced to face my dreary reality, but I can't wait to give Fifi a finger-lickin' report tomorrow at school—and to see Zeus and fall down the rabbit hole all over again. I'm also bringing Fabbie Tabbie to school tommorow for the Pet Pose Off. "You have to look *purrfecto*," I coo to Fabbie Tabbie. We've been practicing prancing together for months in the courtyard. I don't understand why Nole Canoli is putting my paws to the fire on this one. He doesn't even let Countess Coco's paws touch the ground, let alone those of his two cats, Penelope and Napoleon. How does he think Penelope is going to maneuver on a runway? "*Mañana*, we're gonna knock Penelope back on her haunches."

Right now there's a soft knock on my bedroom door,

but I don't answer. I'm still not in the mood to deal with Chenille, who probably wants help with her *holas*—or maybe this time it's her English homework.

"Pashmina?" my mom calls out, entering my bedroom without waiting for a response.

I sit straight up, noticing that her eye makeup is smudged so she looks like a raccoon. Clearly my mom is rattled about something. I just hope it has nothing to do with me.

"Fabbie Tabbie—go to bed!" orders my mom. Fabbie hops off the chair and scampers to her bed. Now Mom turns her stern attention to me. "I called you earlier, but you didn't answer. Why didn't you pick up your phone?"

"Oh, I turned it off. What's wrong?"

My mom slowly sits in the chair, folding her purple satin bathrobe across her legs like a trained geisha. "Can you show me how to use that Facebook thing?" She dabs at the corner of her eyes in a feeble attempt to remove the smudges without looking in the mirror.

"I tried to show you how to do Facebook before, remember? It's really easy. Even you can learn it. Sorry, I didn't mean to say that," I apologize, rising from my bed.

"Not now," she insists.

"What's wrong, Mom?" I ask again. I plop back down against the pillows on my bed. She's got me spooked.

Slowly, my mom starts in on her tale of woe. "You

remember Aradora, who worked with me but I had to let her go because, um—" My mom stops. Obviously she's too rattled to talk. She starts massaging her forehead, like she's trying to formulate her scrambled thoughts.

I decide to help her. "You had to let her go because she was scratching herself all the time—like she was a victim of the current bedbug epidemic?"

"That's right. You remember. And I brought Lonni over to her house once to play cards with Aradora and her husband," she continues. Lonni is one of my mom's girlfriends; she runs a dance studio in Brooklyn—the Dancing Diablo. "Actually, Aradora was supposed to come over here to play cards. Remember that time we were playing cards and you came in with that guy to fix your computer?"

"Yes, Chris Midgett." I don't want to think about him now and feel guilty. I just want to think about Zeus.

"So anyway, that time I brought Lonni to Aradora's house was the only time they ever met," my mom explains carefully.

"I got you, Mom. Go ahead," I say, nodding.

"Aradora called me today and told me that Lonni contacted her on Facebook, trying to add her as a friend."

"Yeah, that's what you do—you can contact any member on Facebook and ask them to add you as a friend."

"Well, that doesn't make any sense—someone is either your friend or they're not," my mom says.

"It's just a social networking thing, Mom," I explain, wondering where the story is headed.

"All right—whatever. So Lonni is saying to Aradora on this Facebook thing, 'Let's get together for drinks, girl, and you can meet my new boyfriend.' So Aradora was like, 'I thought you were married.' Lonni responds, 'No, I'm separated and I have this new boyfriend—and I'm in love.'"

I nod for my mom to continue. *In love.* That's exactly how I feel about Zeus after tonight, but I realize that now is not the time to tell my mom that tiddy.

"So Aradora was asking Lonni about the boyfriend and Lonni said he's really handsome—Dominican and Jamaican—and a fabulous interior designer. So Aradora is thinking, That's funny, isn't Vivian's boyfriend Dominican and Jamaican? It's not like you hear that combo platter every day of the week. So anyway, she asks Lonni what is her new boyfriend's name, and where did she meet him? And Lonni was acting all cagey and cryptic with that information, so that's how Aradora knew something was 'frying in fish town.' That's what she said," my mom says, letting me know she thinks Aradora's phrasing is corny.

"Go ahead."

"So Aradora tries to milk Lonni for more information, like do you have a photo of him up on Facebook? Lonni says she did have some photos up, but she took them down because she's trying to be sensitive to other people's feelings. So Aradora thought maybe she meant the ex-husband, but something didn't feel right, so she contacted me and told me the whole story. And she asked me to go on Facebook and she would show me the stitches of what Lonni said—or something like that—which I didn't understand."

"You mean, the thread of the conversation?" I probe.

"I guess so," my mom says, crumbling. "I told her I didn't go on any Facebook thing, but I appreciated her letting me know."

"So what do you think is going on?" I ask, even though I dread the answer.

"Lonni hasn't said anything to me about having a new Dominican Jamaican boyfriend, or one from the hinterlands, for that matter."

Suddenly, I remember that time when Lonni was here playing cards, so was Ramon. There was something about the way Lonni winked at Ramon. I saw the exchange. But I thought Lonni was just being Lonni—kinda wild and in your face. After all, that's what Mom has always liked about her. Lonni used to be a customer at the Forgotten Diva before she lost fifty pounds from dance classes and then started working at the dance studio where she now teaches hip-hop.

"So you think Lonni is, um, seeing Ramon?" I ask, shocked.

"Well, I tried to reach him all day to find out. And I called her, too. She finally picked up the phone and brushed me off, denying it. Said she couldn't talk because she was busy," my mom says, choking back her tears. "That was him on the phone just now. He said you can't own people, and he is a grown man and what he does is his business."

"So in other words, he was saying he is, um, seeing Lonni?" I ask, puzzled.

"That's what it sounds like to me," my mom says, defeated. "I just can't believe it. Interior decorator? He ain't nothing but a handyman who works at a Queens hardware store. She'll get hers. Lies always catch up to you. Always."

Suddenly, I shriek. "Omigod, Ice Très! I forgot I made a date with him to watch his wheelies at the skating rink—I mean, the duck pond." I jump up and get my purse to turn my cell phone on. Sure enough, there are five text messages from Ice Très.

"Why did you forget?" my Mom asks.

"Because I ended up, um, hanging out with Zeus—the model, deejay, and graphic designer on my Catwalk team," I explain carefully. Now is not the best time to tell Mom that our relationship has progressed. Embarrassed, I pick up a pillow from my bed to cover my face. "What a sham. That's what I am! Ice Très is never going to stop quacking about this!"

Suddenly, my precious missing kitten heels fall from behind one of the pillows. "Oh," I say, surprised.

"Well, I guess the other shoe has dropped after all," my mom observes. "Go apologize to Chenille."

"Right," I say sheepishly. I completely forgot that I had hidden my heels from Chenille in the first place. Fretting, I ask my mom, "So, what should I do about Ice Très?"

"Well, whatever you do, tell him the truth. I can't take any more liars around me. Never again," my mom says, getting up from the chair. She tightens the sash on her purple robe as if she's tying up loose ends. "I'm going to bed. You'd better go ahead and call that boy back."

"No, I'll see him tomorrow at school," I say, like a coward.

My mom glares at me.

"Okay, I'll call him now."

"I think maybe you're taking on too much. You always do that," my mom warns me.

"You think that's what the dream was trying to tell me?" I shriek. "That I'm going to fall on my face?"

"So you told Shalimar, I take it?" my mom asks.

"Yes, I confronted her—or I should say, she confronted me and turned it into a showdown at the okie-dokie—right on camera!" I inform her. "Should I apologize to her?"

"That would be a good idea," my mom advises me.

"Oy, I hate groveling."

"Don't we all."

I send Shalimar a text: "Sorry about the shoe mix-up. Please accept my sincere apologies. Pashmina."

"So what are you going to do about the shoes?" my mom asks, concerned.

"Oh, I'll tell Fifi I found them. She was pissed, too."

"That's not what I meant. I meant the shoes for your fashion show."

"Oh, right." I take a deep breath. "Well, we still don't have any."

"You'll figure it out—you can do anything you put your mind to . . . ," my mom says, her voice trailing off. I can tell she just got a bolt of inspiration. "You know what? I'm calling Ramon back. You can't fault someone for telling you the truth—but enough with the lies already."

My mom closes my bedroom door. I'm haunted by what she said: "You can't fault someone for telling you the truth." It reminded me of what Ice Très said to me outside school today. He was telling me the truth about the Shalimar situation, even if he was embarrassed. "She dangled, he angled." I smile, thinking about Ice Très's goofy smile and how much I relate to him. I'm just as desperate as he is to make it—big-time. But right now, I can't think about Ice Très because it's all about Zeus. My mom is right. Enough with the lies.

I pick up the phone and dial Ice Très's number, hoping he doesn't answer. But he does.

"Where you been?" Ice Très asks, concerned.

"I got caught up in the Catwalk meeting," I quaver, losing my courage to be honest. I blather about the Diamond drama before I blurt out the truth. "Then afterward I went with Zeus to the Barbiecue Hut."

There is silence before Ice Très responds. "Oh, so you can go out with him, but you can't go out with me?"

Now I feel guilty. "Okay, I can."

"Let me take you to the Lipstick Lounge, this new—"

"I know all about it," I interrupt. "But this isn't going to be a repeat of Native, is it?"

"I knew you would say that," he moans. "No, there will be no repeat of the Native no-show. Just give me the chance for us to sit down and talk. That's all I'm asking. If after that, you don't want to have anything to do with me, I won't ask you again, not even for a soda pop in the Fashion Café, okay? Do we have a deal?"

"In principle," I say, stalling. Now I feel guilty for different reasons, like I'm doing something behind

Zeus's back. But that's ridiculous. I owe Ice Très this much for standing him up tonight.

"Okay, we have a deal. And a date. But if you stand me up this time—then we will really be even!"

"You won't regret this, boo kitty. I promise."

I hang up the phone and sigh. I hope I won't. One thing is for sure: I don't regret my date tonight and how sparkly Zeus makes me feel inside.

If I had known how quickly my sparkles were going to fade, I would have bottled the sensation. The next day, Shalimar Jackson wastes no time in flaunting my apology in my face. "Thanks for the 'heartfelt' apology. Don't you wonder—how did cowards communicate before there was texting, huh?"

My cheeks are burning, but I keep my mouth clamped shut.

Shalimar eyes Fabbie Tabbie by my side in a large mesh carrier. "Oh. Since when are cats allowed?"

I opt not to reveal sensitive creative info about the Pet Pose Off to my Catwalk rival. I can hear Angora's gentle voice ringing in my head: "*Chérie*, sometimes the truth is just plain inappropriate!" Shalimar brushes off my silence as another dis and flounces through the security checkpoint with J.B. in tow. It burns me that Flex, the security guard, doesn't even ask her for J.B.'s access pass.

But in my case—no such privileged posturing. "Access pass, please," he barks at me.

"Fabbie Tabbie's only here for one day," I protest. "And I'm checking her into the Petsey Betsey Lounge until she has her, um, business appointment after school."

"She needs an access pass," snaps Flex. The towering security guard rolls his large eyeballs like he's heard better explanations from preschoolers.

I don't want to go to Principal Confardi's office to procure the pass but I have no choice since Flex isn't flexible.

"I thought Chenille was bringing Fabbie Tabbie to school?" Fifi asks me as we inch toward Mr. Confardi's office.

"I did ask her. She curtly informed me that she is not my assistant in the House of Pashmina!" I relay.

Fifi holds the carrier while I fumble in my pink suede bag for Fabbie's health documents. "Maybe you should apologize for accusing her of hiding your shoes."

"Maybe I should apologize for being taller, too."

In the administrative office, we gingerly plop down on the bench outside of Mr. Confardi's office.

"You know, she's just jealous of you," Fifi advises.

"I know," I say, weary from the stress of sibling

rivalry. "It's not my fault Chenille didn't get into any of the houses. But what did she expect? She's a freshman with no track record except in drab attire."

"She thinks you should have let her be an assistant hairstylist in our house," Fifi points out.

"I couldn't! Dame Leeds insisted on Liza Flake—and Dame came giftwrapped with the Nole Canoli package—although I'd like to jetsam his arrogance overboard into the curdling Black Sea." I shake my head. "I'm caught between a curling iron and a crimping rod."

Felinez nods, defending my decision. A slender blond student swathed from head to toe in black walks into the office, staring straight ahead. Although I can't remember her name, I can tell she's a disciple of my Catwalk rival, Anna Rex. Ignoring us, she stops at the counter, glued to the techno gizmo in her hand.

"Can I help you?" asks an administrative assistant.

Without looking up, she mumbles: "Yes, I'm here to make an appointment with the Internet addiction counselor."

The administrative assistant places a clipboard in front of the obvious BlackBerry addict for her to sign.

Suddenly, Mr. Confardi's booming voice wafts out the open door of his office. "I did not order the zap-it ultra-bright white. I'm Italian American, honey, people pay money to get the color of my complexion. It's the wrinkles I can't stand! Never mind. I ordered the anti-aging defense serum. You sent the wrong product—so why should I pay the return postage to send it back?"

"Another case of misappropriation of funds?" I whisper to Fifi.

Hanging up the phone, Mr. Confardi lets out a bark, "Aarrgh, do your job, people!"

"Speaking of keypad strokes, you don't think they were talking about us in the blog, do you?" I drill Fifi.

"What happened?" Fifi responds.

"The suggestion that someone has sticky fingers with the Catwalk budget?" I prod.

"Oh, right. I bet you it's Moet Major," says Fifi.

"Why?" I ask. Moet Major slid into a house leader slot by default after Chandelier Spinelli disappeared from school following her father's chop-shop indictment.

"She looks like she has sticky fingers," says Fifi.

"And sticky hair products." Moet Major, my least fave Catwalk rival, is a petite tomboy with burgundy spiked hair and asymmetrical bangs glued to the sides of her pointy face. In short, she's heavy on the superhold gel and light on talent.

"So what happened?" Fifi asks.

"Awright—you asked for it." I proceed to add relish to the details of my magical evening with Zeus. "It was surreal how connected I felt to him—like this crazy energy just sucked me up and I went tumbling down a rabbit hole. The whole thing made me feel like Cinderella."

"When we were little, you said that Cinderella was stupid, because who would run off dropping a shoe, let alone a glass slipper?" Fifi reminds me.

"Fifi, we were in first grade—I didn't realize the depth of the emotional complexities," I explain, flustered. "Now I can see the big picture."

"Now you sound like Shalimar," Fifi says, scrunching her nose like she's caught a whiff of a repellent odor.

"What I'm saying is Cinderella was upset—that's why she lost her slipper, not because she was stupid, okay?"

Fifi shakes her head. Suddenly, I think about the nightmare again—falling on my face on the runway because my kitten heel gave out. "Maybe I'm a reincarnation of Cinderella?" I ponder, spooked again.

"You're cuckoo," snaps Fifi.

Our Cinderella debate is cut short by the receptionist's command. "Go in now, please."

Mr. Confardi takes one glance at the carrier in my hand and balks. "Pashmina—you know cats are *not* purse-sized pets!"

"I know, Mr. Confardi," I apologize, explaining about the Pet Pose Off, which is the reason for Fabbie

Tabbie's presence. "Until then, she'll be checked in downstairs in the Petsey Betsey Lounge."

"I see." Mr. Confardi softens, smiling slyly, like he approves of our feline finale idea for our fashion show.

"Nole Canoli will be bringing in his cat, Penelope, for the same purpose. They're dueling it out," I explain earnestly.

"Just make sure I don't see Fabbie Tabbie catting on the runway with the special guest!" he warns me.

"What?" I respond, puzzled.

"There'll be an announcement," Mr. Confardi barks, shooing me away.

As we leave the administrative office, Nole Canoli rushes in—late, as usual—with Penelope in a black carrier. "Make sure Fabbie Tabbie rests all day," he warns me. "Penelope is going to wipe the floor with her later."

"We'll see."

Nole brushes against me to crowd his way into the reception area. "Oh. I hope it's not you who's misappropriating funds for our Catwalk budget, is it?"

"Yeah—I bought myself two first-class tickets to Fiji," I snarl. "You caught me pink-handed."

8

By lunch period, we're all sitting in the Fashion Café searching for chic clues to the mysteries: 1. Which house leader is being called out in the Catwalk blog for perpetrating funny business with funds? 2. What is the Special Event in the Fashion Auditorium today?

An announcement over the PA instructs all current Catwalk competition team members to convene in the gymnasium for fifth period.

"Well, now we know the Special Event pertains to us," I observe nervously. "No biology class for *moi* today. Yippee." While I'm delirious that I won't have to go to biology, Angora is happy, too, but for the wrong reasons.

"And no voguing class for *moi*." Angora sighs delicately, ogling her dessert—a stylish houndstooth cupcake with Bavarian cream filling.

Meanwhile, Felinez has her eye on sucking up Aphro's: a green tartan plaid cupcake soaked with Madagascar vanilla. "Which one did you get?" she asks, even though she already knows the answer.

"Never mind, you ain't getting it," snaps Aphro. She never shares her food, and who can blame her: she has had to contend with the grabby hands of other foster kids since the ripe age of four.

Suddenly, I get a cupcake special delivery. Ice Très comes up behind me and hands me a striped cupcake that reminds me of Fifi's fave pj's. "No pink ones?" I tease him.

"Nah, but wait till next Friday—you're gonna love the taste of the Triple Pink Pussycat cocktail at the Lipstick Lounge," he says, kissing me on my cheek. I flinch, embarrassed. Suddenly, my cheeks seem to be in big demand.

"Later," says Ice Très. He jets, sensing that he'd better not push his luck—yet.

"Houndstooth, camouflage, and plaid cupcakes? No, *merci*." I pass my cupcake to Fifi. "All yours."

"What happened with Ice Très?" Angora asks.

"Nothing yet. I made a date to go with him to the Lipstick Lounge—it was the least I could do after standing him up last night," I confess.

"Ah, the mystery place. Wish I was going there," Angora says wistfully. "Anywhere but to my job."

"We're all working girls now," I remind her.

"You do look exhausted," Aphro says, delivering an observation as blunt as her bob.

"*Merci*." Angora says, embarrassed. Like Aphro and me, Angora was forced to get a part-time job—luckily landing one at the lovely Anthropologie boutique in

SoHo—after her father's Funny Bunny cartoon empire turned into a basket of rotten eggs. Now the Le Bon family is learning to live on a budget—with strings attached, thanks to the watchful eye of Ms. Ava Le Bon, who came up from Baton Rouge to rescue her only daughter and her "irresponsible ex-husband," as she refers to him, when the Funny Bunny finances fell apart last Christmas.

"Zeus is on the loose," signals Aphro. I turn to witness Zeus's arrival and automatically wave him down.

"No, don't. Wait until he comes over on his own," advises Angora. "Remember, you're supposed to be in demand, *chérie*—so many suitors, so little time!"

"Right." I smirk.

Angora subscribes to the dating principles from an old-school guide called *The Rules*.

"So many suitors!" Fifi giggles so hard, she chokes on her cupcake.

"And so many crumbs," adds Angora, handing Fifi a napkin. Ms. Ava Le Bon also runs a charm and etiquette school back home—and it's rubbed off on Angora, whether she likes to admit it or not.

"Actually, you do have a point. Why am I waving him down?" I ponder. Zeus smiles at me but heads over to Lupo's table instead of ours. Nole Canoli rushes right over there, too, fawning over Zeus and babbling.

I stare at him blankly, trying not to feel slighted.

"Why didn't he run over to be with your pinkness?" taunts Aphro.

"Who cares," I fib. I glance around the lunchroom, catching sight of Chintzy Colon sitting by herself—wearing a fishnet skullcap and matching bib, my Code Pink–inspired creation.

"Look who's biting your flavor," observes Aphro.

"At least she stopped wearing that annoying fake ponytail," comments Fifi.

"Ice Très would like to bite your flavor, too," chuckles Aphro.

"Maybe." I sense Ice Très's watchful eyes turning in my direction. Nonetheless, I pretend I don't notice and continue gazing at Zeus, who is locked in animated convo with annoyingly pushy Nole Canoli.

"Nole is sure acting shady today," Aphro says.

"He's not happy about the Pet Pose Off, but they don't call it a competition for nada. Why shouldn't Fabbie Tabbie be given a fair chance before I concede to Nole's nefarious nepotism?" I explain, defending my position.

"I hear that," Aphro agrees.

Much to my dislike, Zeus stays at the table with Lupo and Nole for the rest of lunch period. Meanwhile, I babble to my crew about every detail of our date together, which consisted mainly of gazing into each other's eyes.

Suddenly, Fifi cringes. "My father used to look at my mother like that." She screws up her full cheeks and bursts into tears.

"Oh, no, *chérie*," sputters Angora. She takes a napkin to wipe the cupcake cream off Fifi's upper lip.

"I worked so hard to be in this fashion show—and if they both don't come to see me, I will never forgive them. *Never*," she announces. Now Fifi covers her face.

"What are you talking about?" I ask Fifi.

"He's moving out!" Fifi blurts out.

"No way, José," I respond.

Fifi breaks down and tells us about the *telenovela* she's been keeping to herself. I was so wrapped up in my own *telenovela* that I didn't even notice something was wrong with my BFF. I had no idea the Carteras, her musician parents, were having trouble in cruise paradise.

Now everyone at the nearby table is looking at us. I hug Fifi and whisper in her ear, "I will never leave you. I promise you that. Best friends, *pura vida*. Just like we promised each other."

Fifi moans, "I'm gonna make you keep that promise."

"Good," I confirm. "I like keeping promises."

I look up and spot Diamond. She is like an animal tracker—someone who senses when the wounded are in need of help. I can tell she is dying to come over, but she keeps her distance, hovering nearby, then darts over to the table where Elgamela Sphinx is lunching with

Dame Leeds and Mini Mo Harris. "I really need to speak to Diamond about the progress of the evening sketches," I mumble.

Struck by paranoia again, I ask my trusted crew: "What do you think is going on? Does everybody think I'm the house leader misappropriating funds? Is that it?"

"So what if they do? We know the truth," Aphro assures me. "Read between the weave—it's Shalimar!"

I waive off Aphro's prediction. "Misappropriation of funds? Why would she? She has the money."

"Who else could it be? Wanna bet?" Aphro dares.

"All right, Biggie Mouth—you're on," I state. "Why you want to part with your hard-earned coins is an Agatha Christie mystery to me."

Aphro and I now both work part-time at the Jones Uptown boutique. For meager hourly wages (seven dollars an hour, to be exact). Given the sorry state of the retail industry, however, I'm grateful to Laretha Jones for finally changing her mind and giving me a job. Laretha was pleased purple (her favorite shade) with the modeling shoot Aphro and I did for her website. I got three hundred dollars for my first professional modeling job, too.

"Oh, we're not betting money," Aphro informs me. "You cover my shift on Saturday so I can go visit Lennix."

"They're letting you see Lennix?" Felinez asks, forgetting her parents' problems.

"Yeah, but it has to be on Saturday," says Aphro matter-of-factly. I can tell she's trying not to get excited, but she must be. Originally Aphro's caseworker told her she would not be allowed to visit Lennix in his new foster home.

"Wow, that's great," I second. "I'll cover your shift, no problemo. But if you lose, then you cover my shift on Sunday." Not that I have anywhere to go on Sunday besides working like a demon on the Catwalk collection. As a matter of facto, I'd work at the boutique 24/7 if I could—because I need all the ducats I can get.

"Oh, you just want to see if Zeus is gonna ask you out on Sunday," Aphro teases me.

I blush, shaking my head in the negative.

But Aphro isn't buying it. "So what was it like kissing him?"

"How did you know I kissed him?" I respond, feeling icky. "Houndstooth and plaid cupcakes, putting my smooches on blast—is nothing sacred?"

"You should have known Zeus would tell Lupo," Aphro says. By the smirk on her face, I can tell my bossy BFF is pleased with herself for landing such a zesty zinger.

"Who knew he was the kiss-and-tell type?" I utter. I stare over at Zeus for life support, but he's still deep in convo.

When lunch period is over, I want to go running after Zeus—and Diamond, for that matter—but my kitten heels turn to Silly Putty. Against my will I find myself waiting to make eye contact with Zeus as we pour out of the Fashion Café. I figure I can glom onto that fast-moving cluster of Catwalk contestants who are migrating to the Auditorium for the Special Event.

At the doorway, Nole breezes by, banging into me—on purpose. "Oops, sorry. Miss Purr, you must be gaining weight. Not so smart before the fashion show, no?"

"Today, Mr. Nole, you are working all of my real hair follicles." I shake my head of kinky curls. Then I snap back into leadership mode. "We're working on the children's outfits tomorrow, right?"

"Yes, Miss Purr," he says, sighing. "So many orders and so little time."

I suck up to his charade. "Can you please tell Diamond that I expect her to be at the Pet Pose Off with the sketches in hand for our evening segment?"

"It's already done, Miss Purr," Nole says. "Stop trying to ruffle her feathers. She wouldn't miss seeing Penelope win our Pet Pose Off for all the urban coyote tales in North America."

"Right," I mumble, tight-lipped. My lips loosen, however, at the sight of Zeus heading in my direction, finally. I gaze at him steadfastedly, blotting out Nole's prickly patter.

Zeus's piercing dark eyes twinkle like black diamonds. Inches away, he says, proudly, "I've got something for you." I'm hoping it's a kiss, but instead Zeus reaches into his messenger bag and pulls out a CD in a clear plastic sleeve. "Now, if you don't like this, tell me the truth and I'll run it through another remix."

I stand there speechless. Zeus waits for a response.

"Oh, right—yeah," I stammer, sidetracked by my latest bout of insecurity. Arrgh.

Now Zeus is distracted by Dame Leeds, who is bending his ear. After Dame jets ahead to catch up with Liza Flake, I can't resist asking. "What was Dame serving?"

"He thinks something is about to go down. Never mind. We'll see," Zeus relays, shrugging off my concern.

So I move on to another concern. "You're coming to the Pet Pose Off?" I ask, biting my lip.

"No doubt," Zeus assures me. "But go ahead to the auditorium. I gotta take care of something first."

I nod, then catch up with my crew. Lupo sidles up to Aphro and puts his arm around her waist.

I need Angora. "Zeus is acting weird," I whisper to her.

"That's how guys are. Maybe he's thinking about buying a new pair of sneakers and doesn't have the money. Maybe it has nothing to do with you."

"That's radickio," I respond.

"That's why you have to really get to know a guy

before you decide if he's right for you," Angora adds sweetly. "In *The Rules*, it says girls always close off our dating options too soon. We meet a guy we like and bam, closed for business! But you can't."

"Wow, that's deep," I say, shaking my head at Angora's dating wisdom.

"She's right, *mija*. All of a sudden he likes you? So what—you don't have to fall all over him," Fifi warns me. "You didn't fall all over Ice Très, and now he's chasing after you, right?"

I think about what my crew is trying to tell me, but I'm just puzzled pink. "You're both right, you know. I guess I don't trust Ice Très—but I just really trust Zeus, that's all," I confess.

"Why? Because he's a Tasti D-Lite? He has to earn your trust—that's what it says in *The Rules*," adds Angora, capping her argument. Little does she know, in many ways, she is just like her mother—always dispensing advice.

FASHION INTERNATIONAL 35th ANNUAL
CATWALK COMPETITION BLOG

New school rule: You don't have to be ultranice, but don't get tooooo catty or your posting will be zapped by the Fashion Avengers!

WHO YOU CALLING A WEB-A-HOLIC?

No self-respecting fashionista could care one glass tiger eye about the goings-on directly across the street from us at that grungy hole in the universe known as Dalmation Tech High School. (As a matter of fact, could someone please do us the community service of submitting that gray mass of a mess to the television show *Extreme Makeover: Home Edition*?) But with the recent news that one of the D.T. students hanged himself after being constantly cyberbullied, you've now got our attention because you've stepped smack into the middle of our fashionable Twitter-jitter blog-obssessed terrain.

At F.I. the hallways may be our runways, but the Internet is where we take the gloves off, ripping apart character seams and cutting close to the hemline. Read the entries on the Catwalk blog on any given day to witness the malicious and therefore delicious rants and raves we direct toward each other. Any way you slice the grosgrain ribbon, our endless Tweeting, gossiping, and name-calling should be called exactly what it is: cyberbullying.

In memoriam of the now deceased D.T. student, who we've learned was named Bernie Rifkind, let's call a moratorium on using technology as terrorism. If you have a conflict, corned beef, or another type of angst with a fellow fashionista, may we suggest that you put the keypad down and confront the situation face to face, or mano a mano. And to all you two-fisted gizmo users whose hands are too full with your electronics, do us all a favor and head to the administration office to sign up for a session with our newly appointed Internet addiction counselor. There, I said it—right to your screen.

Posted by Twitter Teen at 05:21:16

9

We pour into the Fashion Auditorium under the watchful lens of Caterina Tiburon and the Teen Style Network crew.

"Hi, Teen Stylers!" I wave at the camera crew.

My gleeful shout-out pales next to Willi Ninja, Jr.'s: upon sight of the ubiquitous lens, Willi vogues to his seat with a dramatic flourish. "Follow the winners, churl!"

"Follow the show-offs," Aphro chortles in response.

"Aphro, wait till they see your moves on the runway," Angora offers in support. Truth is, Angora needs as much of Aphro's support she can get—and luckily, Aphro can give her just that in our runway training sessions.

"Trust I will bring it," Aphro says confidently.

But not as confidently as Shalimar Jackson strides into the style snake pit: she releases a sparkling smile, waving like a First Lady at a political fund-raiser.

As usual, Shalimar's PR antics (as in public relations, not Puerto Rican) make me shudder. "I want no more leaks," I whisper to Angora.

"No more leaks. Got it!" she responds, like she's my spin-control aide taking notes.

Ms. Lynx takes center stage with her pudgy bichon frise, Puccini, clad in his matching leopard outfit. He plops down right by her side, panting heavily, like he's getting too old for this horse-and-furry show. "Could everyone please sit in the front rows," orders Ms. Lynx. "Only contestants in the Catwalk competition should be present. If you aren't currently a member in one of the five Catwalk houses, please sashay to your regularly scheduled class." Ms. Lynx motions to her assistants, Sil Lai and Farfalla. They immediately scan the aisles and carefully eyeball every seat to weed out strays—aka Catwalk wannabes or has-beens.

After a few more moments, Ms. Lynx reveals what we're all anxious to find out. Or not.

"I know you're all wondering why you've been selected to participate in this Special Event, but first let me dispense the instructions for your next challenge."

We the unwitting unleash a collective groan that rises to the rafters of the cavernous Fashion Auditorium.

"The blind side. I didn't see that one coming," I gripe to Angora, who is seated on my right.

By the satisfied smirk on Ms. Lynx's MAC-attacked face, we can tell she relishes our response. "Yes, that's right, another challenge. That's why it's called the Catwalk *competition*, fashionistas!" she chuckles, then drops the other shoe. "This will be your last challenge, and it should be incorporated into your fashion show at Lincoln Center," Ms. Lynx says proudly. "This is called the Wild Card Challenge, because we want you to surprise us by introducing an unpredictable element into your fashion show—something we don't expect, but that correlates with your theme. Naturally, it can be interactive or not, *but*—and here is the big but—"

A few well-deserved snickers emanate from Benny Madina. Bet Ms. Lynx didn't see that one coming. Touché.

"*But* you must have fun with it!" Ms. Lynx adds. "I know. You probably are looking for more guidance in executing this random request—but that's why it's called the Wild Card Challenge."

A few of us shoot our hands straight up in the air. Ms. Lynx shoos away our concerns with her dramatic hand gestures. "Each house leader must submit a brief outline of your Wild Card Challenge to the Catwalk office a few days before the fashion show so that the judges will know what they're looking at."

Moet Major raises her hand fervently.

"Yes, Moet," Ms. Lynx says, calling on my petite Catwalk rival.

"How do we know if we do the Wild Card Challenge right?" asks Moet.

"If you don't go over budget, then you've succeeded,"

Ms. Lynx says, content with her brevity. Another collective groan rises to the rafters, but this time it's followed by a few good snickers.

"That's the spirit," chuckles Ms. Lynx. "And please remember, each house leader must permit the Teen Style Network crew to capture an aspect of the execution of your Wild Card Challenge on camera, when you will discuss your choice and the reasoning behind it."

Now Ms. Lynx calls on another student, who is in Willi Ninja's house. "So the winner of the Wild Card Challenge will be chosen after the Catwalk competition is over? Will there be a prize?"

"That's the best question so far!" quips Ms. Lynx. "Yes, of course. The winning house of the Wild Card Challenge will be given a Buy-a-Book-a-Week Go Wild gift card from Barnes and Noble Booksellers, with a maximum annual value of one thousand dollars. Consider that: all those books on the houses of Gucci and Versace you always wanted to buy but couldn't afford!"

We clap wildly. Angora's pupils widen with delight. She could sit in a bookstore for hours massaging pages.

"Please keep in mind, like the winner of the Design Challenge—which was the House of Pashmina—the winner of the Wild Card Challenge may not necessarily be the winner of the Catwalk competition. The winner of the Catwalk competition will receive an all-expenses-paid two-week trip to Firenze, where they will open the

Pitti Bimbo collections by staging their fashion show again. They'll also receive a five-piece luggage set by Louis Vuitton to transport their Catwalk collection abroad in grand style!" Ms. Lynx suppresses a squeal herself. "Okay. That's enough incentive for now. Without further ado, let's get on with our Special Event."

We clap wildly. Now I'm supernervous. "I don't know if I have another challenge in me—wild or otherwise," I utter. Peering down the row, I catch Zeus's eyes. He is sitting next to Lupo. I smile at him coolly. Angora is right. I should dangle the carrot in the rabbit's face instead of forcing it down the rabbit's throat. At least, I think that's what my BFF was trying to tell me: play it cool.

Just like Ms. Lynx is doing right now as she delves into the rest of the afternoon's agenda. "I know there has been lots of speculation about the judges for this year's Catwalk competition—yes, I read the Catwalk blog with gusto," Ms. Lynx informs us. She is now talking into the microphone, which has been positioned to accommodate her six-foot stature. "Well, I'm very excited that one of this year's confirmed Catwalk competition judges is also the guest of our Special Event."

Willi Ninja, Jr., claps and shouts. "Bring it!"

Ms. Lynx does just that. "I'm pleased to have with us today posing instructor Benny Ninja! After being selected as one of this year's Catwalk judges, Benny asked if he could visit the school to see the contestants before the fashion shows. That's what I call a win-win. Please, let's give a warm fashionista welcome to Mr. Benny Ninja!"

Everyone in the audience claps with gusto. Suddenly, I wonder if Willi Ninja, Jr., already knew who today's special guest was. "First the shoes, now this. How is it he always seems to be one step ahead of us?" I fret to Angora.

She shrugs while I turn to look at the object of my current Gucci Envy. I can't help but notice a strange expression on Willi's face, one that I can't quite decipher. Puzzled pink, I turn back quickly so I don't miss Benny Ninja as he prances onto the stage. Posing grandly, Benny, who is tall, slender, light-skinned, and bald, is wearing a gray iridescent jumpsuit with aviator glasses.

"That's the same fabric as our vests!" exclaims Fifi.

For our Urban Gear grouping, we designed iridescent nylon padded vests in celadon green and gunmetal gray to pair with pink chiffon tiered skirts.

"Maybe we should have made jumpsuits!" I whisper back to Fifi before Benny interrupts with his rah-rah rant.

"Hello, fashionistas!" Benny Ninja squeals, waving to the audience. "I know you're ultra excited, because it's about to be on. The only thing I love more than a fashion show is one that comes with prizes—and a trip, okay! And I'm honored to be a judge in this year's Cat-walk competition!"

We clap again.

Turning to Ms. Lynx, Benny Ninja coos, "I *love* the introduction of the Wild Card Challenge into the competition, too! Bring it!"

Ms. Lynx nods with a satisfied smile.

"And I know you fierce fashionistas are not going to let us down, okay!" Benny says, hyping our ambition. "But today you're not here to be judged. I'm here as your personal pose coach because I want each of you to bring it in June. I've been to many fashion shows during fashion week at Lincoln Center, and it is truly an experience—and an honor." Benny Ninja strikes a few poses emphatically. We clap in approval.

"If nothing else, I want to emphasize how important the element of posing combined with runway skills will be to your fashion show—as it is to all fashion shows from here to Paris to Milan to Taiwan," instructs Benny Ninja. "Awright, now I want each of you to show me today what you plan to offer the audience while your models are on the ramp. Therefore, some of you are going to battle each other in poses. I need two volunteers to come up here on the ramp with me now, please."

I look down at Zeus, but he isn't budging. Without thinking, I raise my hand. Benny Ninja motions to me.

"Okay, fierceness, come up here with Miss Naomi next to you." Aphro realizes he's talking about her and jumps up, too. We walk onto the stage.

"*Me-ouch!*" someone in the audience snarls.

I want to sit back down, but it's too late—I stepped up to the challenge. Sweating, I smile nervously at Benny. He turns to the audience and says, "What's important to remember when you're staging a fashion show is that every model on that runway should have a moment where they exaggerate their pose—strike it for maximum effect, okay? This is a business—and in a fashion show, you're selling fashion."

Benny walks down the ramp as if he's in a show and demonstrates various poses. When he's finished, everyone claps. "The poses that you choose to exaggerate are dictated by the segment or groupings of outfits in the fashion show. Like makeup and hair, your poses are tools to represent the mood and purpose of the collection.

"Okay, so you two will battle doing *face* poses," he instructs Aphro and me. "The primary purpose of face poses is serving beauty, which is an important element of every designer's presentation. Okay, go!"

Aphro and I walk down the runway and strike poses that emphasize our faces, then we walk back down the runway, stop in the center and pose.

Benny claps. Pointing to Aphro, he says: "You're a

natural at posing—serving the lips and eyes. Did everyone see that?"

A few students shout out. "Yes!"

"Okay, Miss Naomi in a few years . . . thank you! And you, too, are serving the cuteness." Benny beams at me, and Aphro and I both leave the stage and go back to our seats.

Benny Ninja calls up two new models for each of the four additional battles: shoe poses, handbag poses, on-the-floor poses, and evening wear poses. "So while all of you are working on your runway training and choreography for the show, keep in mind, what else are you going to be working on? Anybody?" he asks.

I raise my hand. "Exaggerating our poses in each segment?"

"That's right, cuteness," Benny Ninja shouts. He waves at all of us wildly again. "I'll see all of you in June! And may the best house *win*!"

Suddenly, I wonder why Benny didn't call on Willi Ninja, Jr., for anything. After all, since day one Willi has pranced around the school bragging about his voguing pedigree—that he is the adopted godson of the late voguing legend Willi Ninja. (May he R.I.P. and posthumously accept my heartfelt gratitude for incorporating voguing classes into F.I.'s physical education curriculum.)

That mysterious question is answered pronto. When the clapping dies down again, Benny Ninja asks: "Is there someone here who calls himself Willi Ninja, Junior?"

A silence drops over the auditorium. "What happened?" whispers Felinez, as confused as everyone else is by Benny's strange question.

Willi Ninja, Jr., lets out a deep sigh and raises his hand.

"Could you stand up, please?" Benny instructs him. "What is your name?"

Willi Ninja, Jr., pauses before he hesitantly spits out an unexpected reply: "Curtis Clyde."

"Good—let's let Willi rest in peace," suggests Benny Ninja, like he's delivering a sermon. "There is only one House of Ninja—and now I'm the father. I'd like to talk to you for a minute—school you about a few things—if that's okay?"

Willi Ninja, Jr., stands by his chair like a deer caught in a borrowed Balenciaga ball gown. Benny Ninja dramatically gets down from the stage to walk toward him. A flustered Ms. Lynx rushes back onstage with Puccini waddling right behind her. "Okay, everyone, I'd like to thank you for coming," she says, heaving like she's trying to catch her breath. "And will the five house leaders please make sure to come to the Catwalk office by Friday to pick up your next installments of the Catwalk budget."

Caterina heads right over to the left aisle with her

mic and her crew following like mice to capture the exchange between Benny Ninja and Willi Ninja, Jr. While I can't hear them, I can tell by their stances that each is deadlocked into his own position. With a dramatic gesture, Willi sweeps his hand by his cheek, wiping away—crocodile tears? Aphro and Angora stand frozen, trying to comprehend what is going down before our very batty lashes. Fifi and I inch our way out of the rows of seats, closer to the aisle, so we can hear Benny and Willi, but Ms. Lynx beats us to it.

She rushes over to the ensuing disaster, wedging her large stature between the two like a referee. Ms. Lynx orders, "The two of you come to my office—*now*."

"What is going on?" Aphro blurts out.

"Watergate? Willigate? I'm not sure," I whisper.

Meanwhile, Zeus and Lupo are a few feet away from "Willigate." Lupo is busy snapping photos with his Nikon.

Fifi slips her arm through mine as if for security when Ms. Lynx escorts Willi Ninja, Jr., and Benny Ninja out of the Fashion Auditorium. The lithe voguer doesn't get too far, though, before a swarm of students descend upon him like locusts on corn stalks, thrusting notebooks and pens at him for autographs.

"Not now," Ms. Lynx warns the needy throng.

Leaving the rest of us in the booty dust, Caterina and her crew focus their cameras on Shalimar and her sidekick, Zirconia. Shalimar beams at Caterina, ready for her close-up, but what she gets is a comeuppance instead.

"Shalimar, is it true that you're being investigated by the Catwalk Committee for misappropriation of funds?" probes Caterina in her shrilly voice.

"Misappropriation? That is utterly ridiculous," Shalimar responds, flustered.

"Ding, ding. Caterina scores once again with a catty sound bite," I report, glued to the breaking scandal.

Patting the strand of white pearls around her neck, Shalimar regains her cool composure for round two. "Tell me one thing. If I used my own personal funds—and I'm not saying that I did—how can that be defined as misappropriation of funds?"

"Then tell us exactly what did happen?" Caterina asks, probing further. "My understanding is that each house is given a Catwalk budget and is required to provide receipts for all expenses—"

"We're given a Catwalk budget, and if I choose to spend my own funds, that should not be considered misappropriation," Shalimar says sharply, leveling one of her sophisticated stares at Caterina—the one in her repertoire that conveys I'm Shalimar Jackson. Need I say more?

"Okay, but if you didn't provide the receipts for the items purchased—which far exceeded the amount of your allotted Catwalk budget—that is against the Catwalk rules and regulations, isn't it?" Caterina insists.

"It shouldn't be. If I choose to allocate my own funds for something that I feel will best represent the vision I have for the House of Shalimar, why should I be penalized?" Shalimar challenges.

"So you're not denying that you spent more than is allotted for your show?" Caterina says, hemming her in.

"I didn't say that. I simply said what if?" Shalimar states coldly.

Now it's Angora's turn to report: "Oh, she's pulling her classic—issuing a nondenial denial."

"Can I say something?" Zirconia interjects, flashing the annoyingly large fake diamond ring on her middle finger as she moves closer to the microphone.

"No, I've got this," orders Shalimar, dissuading her underling from following in her Shimmy Choo steps. "Right after we leave here, I need for you to go to Showroom Eight and pick up the hosiery they're lending us. Like I asked you."

Zirconia nods obediently. "Okay."

Issuing a direct order puts Shalimar back in her poised position. She takes Caterina on. "I'm abiding by all the rules of the Catwalk competition, and no one can prove otherwise." As she and Zirconia march off to the beat of their budget, she glances in my direction, hurling a shallow snippet: "Some of us are getting by with the budget of a stick of Wrigley's. Now, that's what should be frowned upon!"

I stand glued to my spot. Frozen. Zeus inches closer, his warm body radiating heat. And so does Aphro's big mouth. "Nice sound bites—but you still got caught!"

Turning to me, Aphro demands: "As for you, pay up." Of course, Aphro is referring to the wager we made in the Fashion Café. "You should have known she was the source of the misappropriation scandal. The Shallow One never disappoints."

"You won by a mere technicality—the blog wasn't one hundred percent accurate," I blather.

Aphro cuts me off. "Yeah, and where's the news flash in that—hello?"

"She didn't misappropriate funds—which technically alludes to embezzlement, theft, or using appropriated funds for personal use," I go on, ignoring Aphro's bluster. "Actually, what she did is the reverse—she used her own money for the purpose of the House of Shalimar's fashion show."

"Yeah, whatever—the offense in question was still attributed to the Shallow One, so it's the same thing. Honor the bet."

"Awright, basta with the pasta—I'll work your shift on Saturday!" I cave. "We've got way bigger fish to fry. As a matter of fact, we'd better be bringing up some sharks, okay?" I turn to gaze at Zeus. "No offense."

"None taken," he returns, basking in our secret.

"Oh, what are you hyping now?" demands Aphro.

"The Wild Card Challenge—*hello*?" I remind her.

"That's true, *chérie*. We'd better brainstorm," Angora says, supporting me.

"Forget about a brainstorm—we're going to need a mighty hurricane to pull this one off!" I state. "I need all of you at the Pet Pose Off later so we can sharpen our claws for a game plan."

"I hear you," agrees Aphro.

Fifi looks like she's going to cry. "I can't come. Mami wants me to be at home. Papi's supposed to come move his stuff out later!" She starts bawling right in front of Zeus and Lupo. I feel obligated to finally let everyone in on the Cartera crisis.

"Her parents are splitting up," I whisper.

Zeus flinches, then nods. He hugs Fifi and she surrenders in his arms, releasing buckets of tears on his leather jacket.

"Fifi, you don't have to come. We'll handle this," I assure her.

"I want to help," Fifi croaks between sobs.

"Are you kidding—you're the Elmer's to my glue," I shoot back. Fifi has been working herself to the bone with her parents' costumes and our accessories for the fashion show.

"*Está bien*. I'll see you later," she moans, wiping away her tears.

"Good thing you never wear makeup," I blurt out, realizing that it sounds insensitive.

Zeus lingers behind. "You'll help us with this one—I'll see you at the Pet Pose Off later?" I beg him.

"Yeah, I'm there, but you've got this. A Wild Card Challenge? You were born for this," he assures me.

I try to suppress my smile, but a wink gets away anyway. "I hope you're right." I smile nervously.

Zeus doesn't blink. "I am."

10

I arrive at the Fashion Auditorium at three-fifteen on the polka dot with Fabbie Tabbie in tow, only to be upstaged by a Catwalk contender who has already snagged enough face time for one day. I'm puzzled pink why Willi Ninja, Jr., is running the ramp with the ten models in his fashion show during my time slot. The superlimber models are practicing poses incorporating Ninja moves and star-shaped origami shurikens instead of the lethal metal ones used by ancient ninja warriors. Lupo and Zeus are standing in the back row watching the choreography intently. Annoyed, I try to get Willi's attention so he can take his rodeo on the road.

Zeus breaks away for a second to give me props about my ninja moves at the Special Event. "Your face poses were on point."

"Thank you. I got nervous at the prospect of posing for *the* Benny Ninja—but I tried to work it," I admit.

"Well, you did. And say what? Benny's posing is like poetry in motion," observes Zeus, impressed.

Now it's my turn to provide Zeus some strokes. "Thanks for supporting Fifi. She's in freak city about her parents splitting up—and the sudden death of their cover band, Las Madres and Los Padres."

"I can't imagine." Zeus shrugs his shoulders, like he's shaking off the possibility of such a scenario going down between his parents.

What I'm trying to shake off are the repercussions for the House of Pashmina. "If her father doesn't come to the fashion show, I don't know what's going to happen."

"Are you serious?" Zeus asks in disbelief.

"*Molto* serious. Fifi will unravel, along with our fashion show!" I say emphatically.

"No, I mean are you serious her father is really not coming to the fashion show?"

"Fifi's mother told him he can't come unless he moves back into the house—Los Padres costumes and all," I confirm. "I can't believe I'm saying this, but Mrs. Cartera is using our fashion show as leverage. Like dangling a carrot." I wince, recalling where I got that metaphor from: Angora's dating advice with regard to Zeus.

Now Lupo listens in, acting concerned, but I can tell he's more interested in stroking his crush. "Aphro was *fantastico* at the Special Event, no?"

"That's why she's in charge of runway training."

Lupo returns to the action on the catwalk, perplexed by Willie's lineup. "Why does he have so many male models in his show? *Non capito*. I don't understand."

"You wouldn't," Zeus says, teasing his BFF, who prefers to aim his Nikon lens at girls. "He's making his ninja-style statement, and I kinda dig the deployment angle. If you ask me, this could be a tiebreaker come June." Zeus strikes a ninja pose and pretends to throw a well-targeted shuriken at me. "Inside secret? For the Design Challenge, Willi put notes inside the shurikens."

"Now I know why the House of Ninja lost," I shoot, referring to the Design Challenge, in which each house had to incorporate things we see every day into our collection. "The only people sending notes in shurikens these days are Hattori Hanzo wannabes!"

Zeus raises his left eyebrow.

"Fifi's brother, Juanito, schooled me—he's thumbsup with the ninja video games on his PlayStation," I admit, divulging the source of my ancient ninja warrior shout-out.

Finally, Willi Ninja, Jr., acknowledges my presence. "You booked the ramp?" he shouts from the catwalk.

"Obviously," I respond politely. "One look in the Catwalk appointment calendar would have told you that."

"I did look, Miss Purr. Please forgive me? I figured we'd get a little runway rehearsal in before anybody—I mean you—got here," Willi explains apologetically. He puts his hands on his hips. "Can you give us one minute? Then we'll wrap this up like a sushi platter to go."

"Without the wasabi, I hope?" I tartly reply, referring to the greenish root of the Asian herb of the mustard family, possessing a bite as pungent as Willi's.

"You're so raw." Willi sashays back into action.

I'm puzzled pink by Willi's flip from ferocious to feeble. The Willi Ninja, Jr., we know prances around school like he's the prince of the voguing ball and we're just shabby extras.

The handler of my four-legged competition arives: Nole Canoli. Sweating profusely, he releases a loud fart as he plops into one of the joined padded seats. "Excuse me," he mumbles, placing his precious cargo—Penelope, in a padded carrier—by his feet.

"*Excusez-moi* is right," says an embarrassed Angora, scrunching her sensitive nose. Once Diamond Tyler and Aphro arrive, the three are all over the furry felines.

"I love Persian cats," Diamond says, fawning over Penelope's round face and shortened muzzle—which I'm convinced is the result of a botched nose job. Stroking with satisfaction, Diamond coos, "They both have such beautiful toffee-red fur. I love it."

"Toffee-red—next fall's scorching shade," I predict. "She's a typical tabby in her own special way."

Now Dame Leeds waltzes in with attitude to spare. The only reason I've invited him is because I'm desperate for input for the Wild Card Challenge.

Dame, however, thinks his presence is required on

all matters. "The finale of the show? Oh, no, Miss Purr—I get to vote on these scragglers, too," he snipes at me. He eyes Penelope and Fabbie Tabbie with disapproval. "Although I'm not so sure about this idea of yours. I don't see a standing ovation between the furry likes of these two."

"Got any ideas for our Wild Card Challenge?"

Dame doesn't bother to answer, but Diamond has plenty to say about his outburst.

"You shouldn't say nasty things about Penelope and Fabbie Tabbie. They can hear you, even if you think they don't understand. And they are precious."

"Honey, I saw *Precious*, the movie, okay? There is another word you should use when referring to these two." He rolls his eyes, unconvinced about my finale idea.

"Well, precious Penelope did not approve of the Betsey Petsey Lounge." Nole pats his forehead with a monogrammed hankie. "Too many strays for her tastes."

"Have a good run-through," yells Willi, waving as he sails up the aisle with his mostly male model caravan. Surprisingly, Willi also says goodbye to Nole, whom he despises more than Mardi Gras beads made in China.

"Yeah, right. Bye, Mr. Willi Ninja, Junior," Nole says.

"Oh, about *that*. You can call me C. C. Samurai from now on," Willi informs Nole humbly.

Nole stops fluffing Penelope's hair. "What, what?"

he asks, imitating Aphro, his full cheeks ballooning from this hefty incoming tiddy. "Excuse me, but who changed the channel to *Invasion of the Body Snatchers*? I thought we were watching *Strike a Pose*?"

As Willi disappears through the swinging doors, Zeus and Lupo step up with intel about the Ninja sneak attack that occurred earlier. "We first peeped the situation in photography class. Like a minute ago."

"Like when?" Nole asks for clarification.

Zeus turns to Lupo and asks, "What day did we go to the Francesco Scavullo retrospective?"

"Two weeks ago. *Lunedi*—Monday," Lupo confirms.

"Right. So anyway, Toro and his crew—they're all Photography majors—" Zeus explains.

"Like me," interjects Lupo.

"Right. So Toro and his crew were photographing the voguing balls—that's for their final project," Zeus continues. "Anyway, they got to photograph Benny Ninja and his house—the real House of Ninja—at the Body and Soul vogue ball. So Toro came back to school and was telling us in class how he met Benny Ninja. Toro bragged to Benny that he went to Fashion International with Willi Ninja, Junior. But Benny's response was like, Willi Ninja, Junior, who?"

"So Toro knew something was *pazzo*—crazy—*capisce*? You understand?" Lupo says, with his dramatic hand gestures.

741

"*Wow*. So Willi Ninja, Junior, isn't really the adopted godson of the late Willi Ninja?" I ask in disbelief.

Zeus nods. "*Exacto*, as you would say. His name is Curtis Clyde, but he changed his name to Willi Ninja, Junior—and nobody was hip to this because the late Willi Ninja is, well, you know—deceased."

"I wish I was a fly on Willi's jumpsuit so I could hear what Benny Ninja said to Willi when he cracked his face."

"I heard Willi—I mean C. C.—tell Benny that Willi wouldn't mind because he was only paying *fromage*. How do you say that French word?" Lupo turns and asks Zeus.

"He said he was only paying *homage* because he wanted to be Willi Ninja's adopted godson," Zeus clarifies.

"No, Lupo was right. The correct word is *fromage*—because the whole thing sounds cheesy," Angora quips.

"Maybe if he had asked Benny if he could join the house? I mean, since he's the father," Zeus notes. "But now Benny is like, 'You and the house of Ninja—*not*.'"

"This is thicker than *Six Degrees of Separation*."

"*Che cosa?* What do you mean?" Lupo asks innocently.

"It was a movie about this guy who was posing as Sidney Poitier's son—which gave him entrée into elite circles to scam the rich and famous," I explain.

"Oh, yeah, I remember. Will Smith played the guy in the movie," Zeus adds.

"So what's Willi going to call his house now? The House of Willi Wannabe?"

"Maybe he just should just call it Willigate—I mean, he's got nothing on Nixon," Aphro says, aghast.

"Did you see Ms. Lynx freak out when Benny put that wannabe on blast? I thought she was going to keel over—timber!" squeals Nole.

Anxious to deflate Nole's hubris, I snap back into leadership mode. "Okay, let's set it off with the Pet Pose Off now. And right after, we need to brainstorm about the Wild Card Challenge. I hope everybody is okay with this, because we may have to pull an all-nighter."

Diamond shrugs her shoulders like she's gonna have to flee for an animal emergency, which prompts me to prod her for the evening wear sketches. "Diamond, do you have anything to show us?"

"Um, can we talk about that after?" squeaks Diamond.

Biting the inside of my lower lip, I realize I'm going to have to deal with Diamond's "sketchy" behavior. For now, we have to finish the Pet Pose Off before the ramp is disassembled and stored backstage.

Nole Canoli, however, still wants to chew on the gristle from the Special Event. "That drama with C. C. Karaoke was just the appetizer," he chortles, inhaling.

"Now I'm ready for the main course—what happened with Shalimar? Somebody better serve the T and crumpets.'"

I bite the inside of my lower lip again, trying to be patient as helpful Angora plays hostess with the mostest. "Jimmy Choo is only lending Shalimar ten pairs of shoes for her fashion show, but she wanted twenty. So somebody leaked to the Catwalk office that Shalimar was spending her own money to get the extra ten—which is against the Catwalk competition rules and regulations."

"So what's going to happen to the Shady One?" Aphro asks abruptly.

"I overheard Shalimar in the Catwalk office last period. She was trying to squeak by on a technicality: she claims that after the show, the extra ten pairs of shoes are going into her personal collection, so why should it matter?" reports Angora.

"Oh, puhleez, Rapunzel could have spun a better weave than that one. Miss Adorable Hair bought shoes in different sizes, okay, so how could they *all* be for her?" Aphro blurts out. "For starters, Zirconia wears a size eight. The other model, Pretensia, wears a size nine—I know cuz I tried on a pair of her shoes one day—and Shalimar wears a size ten—hello, Bigfoot?"

"She should have said she was going to donate the shoes to charity—like my father does at his factory for every pair of shoes they sell to a store," Lupo points out proudly.

"Puhleez. Like father, like daughter—the only charity angle her family comes up with is if they are getting something in return, like running this school!" Aphro claims adamantly.

"You know, that wouldn't be a bad idea—us hyping some charity angle at our fashion show," chuckles Zeus.

"Hyping what, shoes? We still don't have any!" points out Dame, striking the panic button.

Luckily for me, another chord is struck: "A charity angle—wait a second. I dig that—that could be the answer to the Wild Card Challenge!" I exclaim, excited.

"Charity? We're the ones who need shoes—how's that charity?" Dame Leeds asks with annoying bluster.

"Because when we send out our brilliant invites to the House of Pashmina fashion show, we will ask guests to bring a pair of shoes to donate to the homeless—you know, like St. Martin's Homeless Shelter on Ninth Avenue?"

"Wow, I dig that," says Zeus, rubbing his chin.

Everyone stares at me, ingesting the idea. "By adding a charity angle to our fashion show, we can incorporate that into our theme—Feline Fatales Empower Themselves and Others," I state, bringing my concept to the finish line.

"That's good, Pash. *J'adore*. And we can put our

charity program on the back cover of the House of Pashmina program, too—on every seat!" adds Angora, getting excited.

"Wow, that's true. Everybody has a pair of shoes they don't want but someone else can use—someone who needs them," Zeus says, rubbing his chin some more.

"Now check this. What if we have a fierce cart in the lobby of the fashion show, manned by two members of our crew—we'll decide later who will be the designated shoekeepers—who collect the shoes? That way when guests enter, they'll see this furbulous cart and deposit the shoes. We could hype that."

"Wow, Pash, I really adore this idea. This could make a community impact, too," mulls Angora.

"Heels on Wheels! That's it—that's the name of our charity incentive!" I say solefully, looking at my crew for a reaction.

"That's perfect! Heels on Wheels. We'll stencil that on the front of the cart with some fly shoe graphics. *Boom!*" exclaims Zeus.

"Okay, Mr. Deejay, now you're cranking," I squeal.

"Oh, about *that*," Zeus squirts, imitating C. C. Samurai. "You can now call me a mixologist."

"Duly noted. You'll be credited as such in the Catwalk program," I utter.

Lupo slaps his hand to his forehead. "Oh. *Mamma mia!* I love this idea—my father would love it!"

I turn to gauge Aphro's reaction. "It's on," she says. "And Shalimar can't top that for the Wild Card Challenge. Hmmph, what's she gonna do—throw shoes at guests in the audience from the runway? That would be her idea of wild. Wildly extravagant. You know what I'd really like to do after we graduate? Rip those orange extensions right out of her head and donate *them* to charity!"

"Right," I second. Suddenly, I conjure up the frightmare at my fashion show—hair extensions flying and me falling on the runway from rigged heels. "Please, everybody make sure to check my kitten heels three times before I hit that runway?"

"You're *not* going to trip," Angora states, knowing exactly what runaway train I was on in my brain.

"I don't mean to be a thrill killer whale—but isn't a cart expensive?" Nole asks, bringing us back to the basics: Catwalk budgetary constraints.

"No. See that's the thing—it's not going to cost us one sordid *dinero!*" I say, screwing up Spanish currency. "My neighbor, Mrs. Watkins, works at the Piggly Wiggly supermarket near my house, and she already told me she can help—just ask."

"That's right! Mr. Sunkist is always stealing the carts from the Piggly Wiggly, right?" Angora asks, remembering my run-in with the homeless cart crasher.

"Well, yeah—he 'borrows' the metal shopping carts

from Piggly Wiggly, then comes back with empty soda cans to get the deposit money. I mean hundreds of cans. But I'm not talking about those shopping carts. I'm talking about the wooden-lidded carts the delivery guys use when they are bringing the groceries to the customers' homes," I explain. "Maybe I can get Mrs. Watkins to give us one of those and we can paint it *screaming hot pink*!"

"Whoa, that is not a brainstorm, that is a hurricane." Zeus beams at me with bravo. "I can go with you to pick up the cart and help you paint it."

"Okay," I say, delighted that Zeus has volunteered. Now a pang of guilt settles into my midriff. "Maybe Fifi will be finished and she can come help, too?"

Zeus nods like that's cool. Now I excuse myself to make a call to Mrs. Watkins at the supermarket to execute our get-ahead game plan.

Just as I had hoped, Mrs. Watkins is true to her word. "Anything for you, Pashmina!" she whispers into the phone.

I click off my phone, deliriously hyped. "*Yes*, it's on!" I scream to my crew, just as the Teen Style Network barges into the conference room. But this time my nerves aren't even jangled. I greet Caterina and crew with gusto: "Hello, Teen Stylers, you're just in time for some real furry footage."

Of course, Caterina's idea of footage is always a lot

more hairy. "So, what did you think of Benny Ninja confronting the Ninja imposter in front of all the Catwalk members?" Ms. Caterina asks bluntly.

"It was really wild," I say carefully, "and speaking of wild—we just hatched our idea for the Wild Card Challenge, which you can be privvy to later!"

Caterina's eyes glaze over, but she lets me explain the concept for our Wild Card Challenge before she takes a fork on the thorny road. "So, have you come up with any ideas for securing shoes for your show—since Curtis Clyde snagged your source?"

"That's yet to be determined," I say coyly. Diverting from that drama, I make an appointment with Caterina to come to my house tomorrow night so she can see us paint our *Heels on Wheels* cart. Caterina barges over to Nole to get a sound bite on the Ninja drama, instinctively sensing the discord between the two rival designers.

"Benny was looking out for his own agenda. Being a judge in the Catwalk competition is major props for him—so he had to out the shadiness!" After delivering his sound bite, Nole lets Caterina know that he is anxious to get his game plan in action: pushing Penelope for the finale. "Come on, Miss Penelope, let's get those pretty, tiny little feet ready for the runway. We both know you should be pattering to a pose instead of that fat heffa with big paws!" he gripes. Nole combs

Penelope's hair for the tenth time, cooing, "And you don't need some silly stage name like she has, either."

Now I render my own imitation of C. C. Samurai. "Oh, about *that*," I inform Nole. "You can now call Fabbie 'Fabbie Tabbie,' which is spelled *T-a-b-b-i-e*. Think how chic that will look on the House of Pashmina program."

"Yes, so chic I'm going to throw up from my beak! But first Fabbie Crabby has to win!" Nole marches onto the stage with Penelope. He fluffs Penelope's feet and dresses her in a black coat dotted with dangling, shimmering crystals.

"Um, I pray that's not what you think she's wearing—if she wins?" I ask.

Nole ignores me.

"Um, I'm serious. That contraption makes her look like a traveling jewelry salesman," I badger.

"She'll wear a wedding gown, just like we discussed—before you reneged!" snaps Nole.

"I did not renege!" I shout back.

"Yes, you did, but I'm a team player, which is why I'm going along with your charade," he says, offended. "Penelope only walks like a star when she's dripping in jewels! So if you don't like it, get pink earplugs!"

"Whatever makes you clever," I shoot back, puzzled by his dis. Nole agreed to do this Pose Off. It was only fair. Suddenly, I realize it would also be fair to get feedback on Zeus's remix. "Oh, wait!" I yell, putting a halt to the Pose Off. "I want everyone to hear the remix Zeus did of Gloria Gaynor's 'I Will Survive.' Let's play it so that we can decide if we should use it for the finale."

"Excellent choice." Zeus beams, accommodating my request. He heads over to the tech booth and puts in the CD. We all wait until the bass kicks in—and the singer belts out the lyrics. "Ooh, I like the singer's voice. Who is that?" I ask Zeus.

Zeus hesitates before he answers: "Oh, she does vocals on a lot of my tracks. So you like it?"

I nod approvingly. "I really dig that singer's voice—she adds this haunting quality to the house-music vibe."

"Yeah, she's an amazing vocalist," agrees Zeus. I can tell he's reluctant to tell me more, so I let it go like disco. Maybe it's an industry thing—not revealing your resources. I can understand that.

Aphro starts to shake a tail feather, singing over the track: "At first I was afraid, I was petrified!"

Lupo's eyes widen like pool balls. He starts snapping away with his Nikon, mesmerized by Aphro's tantalizing moves. Now Elgamela joins the fray, gyrating her hips like a belly dancer. Nole shakes his head. He puts the jeweled collar around Penelope's neck with the matching leash. "Penelope dances better than that," he snipes. Nole positions Penelope to get ready to rip the runway.

"Okay, on the count of three," I instruct him. "One,

two, three." Nole proceeds to walk down the runway, but Penelope doesn't take the nibble. His pampered Persian won't budge a single long hair on her plump body.

"Come on!" Nole whispers.

Forcefully, Nole tries to drag Penelope, but she lashes out with a paw and hisses.

"Don't do that!" shouts Diamond. Agitated, our resident animal activist jumps out of her seat, insisting, "Nole, let me try. You can't treat an animal like that!"

"No, I don't want your help. I can do this myself!"

Diamond ignores Nole and climbs onto the stage, displaying more enthusiasm than I've seen her muster in months. She takes the leash from Nole and tries to walk the runway with Penelope. Penelope latches onto Diamond's leg, clawing her ferociously!

"I knew this was a bad idea!" screams Dame Leeds.

Zeus cuts off the music as Nole grabs Penelope and pulls her off Diamond's leg. He screams at Diamond: "She hates you! I told you to let me do it!"

A tearful Diamond protests, "I was trying to help!"

"Well, you didn't!" Noel continues, screeching. He holds Penelope, trying to quiet her trembling furry body.

"Diamond, it's not your fault," I say, trying to reassure my hysterical second designer in command.

Now Angora and Aphro are examining Diamond's wounded left calf, which is scattered with faint red welts and scratches. "I think she should go to the infirmary," advises Angora.

I feel like an eel in a pair of kitten heels, but I have to ask: "Diamond, can you wait till we finish?"

"No, my leg really hurts. I wanna go now!" she cries. "This is cruelty to animals, putting them in a fashion show. I should never have agreed to this!"

"But we're just closing the fashion show with a cat—it's our personal statement for the House of Pashmina," I balk. "And it wasn't your decision!"

"Nothing is ever my decision!" whines Diamond. "I can't take it anymore—all you people care about is winning a stupid competition and becoming famous. Fashion isn't everything, you know?"

"Really—then what is?" Nole challenges.

Diamond's eyes widen in horror. "Listen, this is really too much for me. I feel guilty working so hard on a fashion show when all anyone cares about is winning prizes and money and a trip. There are animals that are sick and dying all over the world—they don't have enough food to eat. I mean, they need our help, but nobody even cared when I mentioned the coyotes wandering in Central Park scavenging for food."

"I feed my cats fresh liver—what are you talking about?" Nole protests.

"I don't think this fashion business is really for me. I mean, I don't care about this stuff," Diamond confesses.

Now we all realize what has been bothering Diamond and why she's been acting so weird. I also realize in horror that the watchful eyes of the Teen Style Network camera crew are upon us. Before Diamond does any more damage, I pull her to the side so that we can finish our convo without their probing lens.

"Look, Diamond, we understand," I console her. "This is a lot of pressure. But this means a lot to us. Ever since I can remember, I've dreamed of being a model. For me, this is about helping my family. I'm in this with my crew, and I need for you to stay until the competition is over."

I look at Angora, Aphro, Felinez, Elgamela, and Zeus. They beam at me approvingly, so I continue. Caterina is entertaining herself by getting more sound bites from them. I turn my attention back to the ego of my wounded designer. "And I do care about animals just as much as you do. I love Fabbie Tabbie more than life itself."

"That's what I want to do. I've decided," Diamond says. "I want to devote my life to helping animals. I mean, that's all I really care about."

"Okay, but can you just hang in there until the competition is over so we don't get penalized?" I whisper.

Diamond nods. Dame Leeds nudges into our conversation, but for once, he does a reverse. "I'll take Diamond to the infirmary."

"Thank you, Dame," I say gratefully.

Diamond limps out of the auditorium with Dame.

I motion for my Catwalk crew to huddle together. "Listen up. We got lucky that this incident happened behind closed doors—meaning there's no one in here but us—and them," I explain, rolling my eyes toward the Teen Style Network crew. "So let's make sure this *stays* between us, since that footage isn't airing until after the competition is over!"

"Absolut. Another one bites the dust," Nole says, exhaling deeply, his hefty midsection rising to the occasion.

"We can't afford to have another house member leave—next time I will get penalized!" I snap.

"I don't mean Diamond," Nole snaps back. "I mean Penelope!"

"Are you conceding defeat?" I ask in disbelief. "I mean, it's only fair that Fabbie Tabbie continue the Pose Off."

"That's true. You're right—we probably have two furry failures on our hands, not one," he says defiantly. "And we should rethink the finale. Maybe get a goat, like Mexicans do for their weddings?"

"Oh, now it's on," I hiss. I motion to Zeus. "Hit it!"

Zeus puts on the remixed house-music track again. Confidently poised, I stand with Fabbie Tabbie's leash in my hand. As soon as the lyrics kick in, so do I: I gently pull Fabbie Tabbie forward and we sashay down the runway together. Fabbie Tabbie takes each step like a true star, just like we practiced all summer in the courtyard! When we reach the end of the platform, she rests on her haunches, posing prettily. I smile and bow like we really are at the fashion show and I'm being showered with affection from the audience. Lupo clicks away furiously. Everyone claps. "Bravo, Pashmina! Work it, Fabbie Tabbie!"

For good measure, I stare right into the lens of the Teen Style Network and strike a final pose; then I walk back, beaming, and Fabbie Tabbie doesn't miss a furry step. Now Nole's face is cracked. I almost feel bad for the helium-inflated Canoli. Nole simply hates being defeated. In more ways than one.

Caterina rushes right over to get a sound bite from Nole with regard to his four-legged failure. "Let Penelope have her private moment, okay?" he orders.

Folding, Caterina and her crew wrap it up and exit.

Afterward, I take the time to console Nole and take responsibility for the Diamond disaster. "Look, Diamond is cracking under the pressure," I whisper to him.

"Who are you telling?" Nole whispers back, patting himself with his monogrammed hankie. "I'll deal with her—I know exactly how to smooth those ruffled feathers."

"How?" I wince, trying to get the image of Diamond's weltered leg out of my mind.

"We're going to give her design credit—even though she's a disaster. That's how. In return, she has to stay—and she can be one of the dressers backstage. No one will be the wiser if she just seals her penguin lips," Nole orders.

It's a solid plan, and at this point we have nothing to lose but the Catwalk competition. "Let's try it," I agree, then throw him some well-deserved kibbles 'n bits. "Fifi and I will make the evening wear without the sketches."

Nole nods his head, pleased. "Good, because my plate is full. You do the evening wear. I'll finish the pillboxes, which are killing me! Of course, Fifi can finish those, too."

"Fifi is overworked!" I balk.

"Well, then I guess you'd better free up your schedule from smooching sessions with Zeus and put the pedal to the metal!" orders Nole.

I pause, like a good negotiator, then agree. "Done and done."

FASHION INTERNATIONAL 35th ANNUAL
CATWALK COMPETITION BLOG

New school rule: You don't have to be ultranice, but don't get tooooo catty or your posting will be zapped by the Fashion Avengers!

MOVING ON UP?

Like Mercedes-Benz Fashion Week, not everyone is deliriously delighted that Fashion International's annual Catwalk competition has moved from Bryant Park to Lincoln Center. But after a long and contentious battle between the designers and park management, Seventh Avenue has taken their show on the road. To the critics and snobs who pooh-poohed the fervor, flash, and gridlock, claiming that Mercedes-Benz and other big-time corporate sponsors turned the business of fashion shows into nothing more than a commercial for a car dealership, I have one thing to say: it's the naïve who don't realize that larger budgets and marketing power are what make the dream of becoming a designer possible. And that sometimes it's just time for an upgrade—especially if you can afford it.

Which brings me to another source of not-so-chic contention: the budgetary constraints forced upon Catwalk competition contestants with regard to their expenditures for their respective fashion shows. Is it really necessary to penalize a Catwalk house for not adhering to overly strict budget constraints? Or to require house leaders to provide expense reports and receipts for every cent spent down to a stick of gum? Why shouldn't a specific house leader be allowed to contribute funds directly to their fashion campaign if they so desire? If you ask me, it's time for an accounting upgrade so we can put on a real fashion show worthy of the status that comes with the new location: Lincoln Center, home of the American Ballet Theatre and the Metropolitan Opera. Oh, and the Big Apple Circus.

Posted by Shimmy Choo to YOU at 14:15:43

11

Nole is furious that Fabbie Tabbie won the Pose Off, but I can't deal with his ego right now, because I'm desperate for an update from Fifi. Zeus and I wave good-bye to Nole and the rest of my crew as they toddle down the yellow-brick road away from school.

"I feel guilty about dragging Fifi to my house, but that's the problem with brainstorms—and hurricanes: they always come at inconvenient times," I confess to Zeus.

"That's the problem with breakups, too," Zeus offers about the Cartera family crisis.

"This is doubly true, but Fifi's gotta help us with decorating the Heels on Wheels cart—especially since the Teen Style Network is visiting my dank basement," I fret. "We always do everything together."

"You're lucky, you know. Fifi's been there for you since first grade, when you were swiping the pink crayons out of the box," Zeus chuckles.

I land a well-deserved jab on Zeus's sturdy chest, but I'm impressed by all the little details about *moi* he seems to remember. "I know, I'm lucky. But that's because I plied her with delicioso Coco Helado ices for five years to assuage my guilt about sucking on her talent." I marinate on Fifi's father being kicked out of the hornet's nest. "In a million years, Fifi never imagined her parents breaking up. She wasn't happy about them being on the road all the time with their band, because that put her older sister Michelette up in her hair—literally—but she really cares about her family."

"That's probably why the two of you are so connected," Zeus philosophizes. "You're more like sisters to each other than your own sisters are to you."

I ponder his astute observation while twirling my curls; I use my other hand to call Fifi on the celly. For five minutes I listen to Fifi drop a hyperfrenzied earful.

"As soon as Papi got here, Mami threw his clothes out the window! The police had to come!" she yelps on the other end between bouts of tears about the horror-frying experience. Apparently, Mrs. Cartera suspected that a scantily fringed dancer on the Princess cruise ship was the root of Mr. Cartera's last tango in Tahiti. "Mami saw the text messages he sent her," moans Fifi.

"Oy, technology seems to be at the core of every tawdry takedown these days," I lament. "I showed my mom how to use Facebook this morning. She's determined to catch Ramon in his cyberacts of finagling with her friends."

Fifi blathers on. "I can't believe Mami flipped like this. She threw him out!"

"I know, boo kitty," I say, consoling her.

Fifi laughs. "Now you sound like Ice Très."

"I know, boo kitty," I repeat, giggling.

"So what happened at the Pose Off?" Fifi says, switching gears for a fashion FX.

After I fill her in on Fabbie's paws-down victory, I map out our game plan for the Wild Card Challenge.

"Wow, *mija*! How did you come up with that?" she says, regaining her artistic edge.

"With some assisterance from Lupo and Zeus, actually," I say proudly, filling her in on Lupo's father's shoe factory.

"Wow, I didn't know that. Do you think Mr. Saltimbocca could lend us some shoes?" she jokes.

"The customs charge on that would be a fortune," I explain to her. In fashion merchandising class, we learned that imported products are hit with a hefty forty percent surcharge. "We're in desperate need of a domestic loan."

I can tell Fifi is depleted, but she puts my guilt pangs at ease. "I'll leave now so I can be at your apartment after you get the cart from the Piggly Wiggly—so Mami doesn't start throwing *my* stuff out the window!"

"You sure?"

"She would. *Te juro*. I swear."

"No, I mean you sure you want to be just another girl on the IRT right now?" I ask.

"*Mija,* I said I'm sure!"

"You are the best BFF. I love you so much, I could whack you like a piñata," I coo. "Oh, don't forget to bring your paintbrushes."

After I hang up, Zeus is smiling, waiting for an update. "All the ducks are lining up."

"A few got thrown out the window with the bathwater," I sigh, recounting the flying clothes story.

"Ouch," winces Zeus. He puts his arm around my shoulder and I find myself in a trance, following my personal Pied Piper to the pungent aromas of the Fashion Hot Dog Cart on the corner of Seventh Avenue. "Excellent idea—hitting the hot dog cart before we head uptown to snag a cart!"

Pedro Posse smiles at us even though he doesn't get my inside joke. I smile back. I've got nothing but respect for the bespectacled hot dog connoisseur, who stands in the same spot five days a week, rain or shine, manning his Fashion Hot Dog Cart. Thanks to Pedro Posse's strong work ethic, designer hot dogs are the backbone of every aspiring fashionista's diet.

"I'll take one Donna Karan Diggity Dog," Zeus tells Pedro. Turning to me, he asks, "What do you want?"

"A Roberto Cavalli Cherry Dog," I decide. I always opt for the dog with the sliced red peppers. "I'm a one-dog phony—oops, I mean pony!" I reach into my bag to pay and notice I have a text message.

Zeus shakes his head. "I got this."

I take out my phone to look at the text, in case it's from my beleaguered mom, but it's not. It's a text from Ice Très: "We're on for Friday. How did it go today?"

Zeus sees the expression on my face. "What's up?"

"*Nada* to the *niente*." Feeling guilty—this time for telling a fiberoni, I peer down at Fabbie Tabbie's carrier.

"Nothing for the cat?" Pedro asks, grinning, as he hands Zeus his change.

"A Juicy Couture Chili Dog for Fabbie, maybe?" Zeus asks, humoring me.

"Abso-freakin' no," I assure him.

"Take a bite," coaxes Zeus, moving his dog in my direction.

I shake my head. "Last night the deejay saved my life. Don't want to push my luck. Oh, sorry, I meant the mixologist," I chuckle, envisioning the embarrassing barbecue sauce stains on my fishnet bib at the Barbiecue Hut, which may be apropos, given the joint's drippy name.

Zeus is digging the drippy quotient once again, diving into his Donna dog, which runneth over with melted cheese.

"Speaking of meltdowns, do you think Diamond is okay?" I ask, trying to assuage my Twitter jitters about another online posting putting our house on blast.

"From the scratches? Oh, yeah. They weren't *that* bad," Zeus assures me. "From the other thing? I think she had a moment of truth about the direction she's heading in."

I pause, amazed at Zeus's depth.

As a matter of fact, I'm standing still for so long outside the Piggly Wiggly that Zeus recommends, "We'd better go in before Mr. Sunkist steals our cart."

My eyes twinkle at the fact that Zeus remembers the name of the homeless man in my hood.

"I remember the hole in your fishnets, too," Zeus reveals, winking. "*Both* are unforgettable."

I take a swipe at Zeus's leather jacket, my hand landing on his unyielding bicep. "Ouch," I joke.

Mrs. Watkins is behind the register in the 10 Items or Less aisle, furiously attacking the foil on a Take 5 scratch-off ticket.

"Darn!" she exclaims, disappointed at the reveal of the losing numbers. Mrs. Watkins looks up and instantly the mischievous light in her bulging brown eyes is ignited at the sight of Zeus, like she's just received the consolation prize for lotto losers.

"You haven't met Zeus before?" I ask her tentatively. In the fall, Zeus came to my apartment for our first unofficial Catwalk meeting, which was taped by the Teen Style Network crew to capture each house leader in their "natural habitat."

"No, I sure haven't had the pleasure," she says, grinning wildly at his zebra hat. "Is that real?"

Zeus nods. "I know some may think it's unethical, but my father made it. Otherwise, I don't believe in killing animals for their fur."

I wince, conjuring up Fifi's fondness for fur, like the prized fur-lined hobo she made and doled out to Chenille for the infamous bribe. "Yeah, but we're fashionistas—and the fur business makes up seven billion dollars of retail sales," I blather defensively. "Every business has its shadows. Right, Mrs. Watkins?"

Mrs. Watkins shakes her head sharply and purses her lips. "The lottery is as crooked as a Chinatown hem, because I know for a fact I sure should have won by now, as many tickets as I've bought!"

Mrs. Watkins fixes her gaze on Zeus's hat. "I sure would love to have one of those. You must be used to all the attention."

"Yeah, I am. I've had it for a year," Zeus says warmly, fluttering his eyelashes like an obedient geisha girl.

"No, I meant about being so handsome," quips Mrs. Watkins.

"Oh, thank you."

"Don't thank me. Thank your mother," cajoles Mrs. Watkins. "I bet you and Pashmina are both gonna be famous models one day. I know it as sure as I know I'm going to win the Take Five—one of these days!"

Zeus chuckles. Mrs. Watkins motions with her eyes toward the Plexiglas-encased booth. "Mr. Beach is going on break in five. So y'all go meet me by the back exit."

"Okay. Thank you, Mrs. Watkins," I say gratefully, picking up Fabbie Tabbie's carrier.

"Don't thank me yet. Better see if any of them carts got wheels left, the way those delivery boys be riding like it's the Wild West!" she warns us.

My heart sinks at the thought of another busted scenario like the Tracy Reese shoes getting absconded right under our kitty noses. Zeus, on the hand, beams with hope. Like he always does.

When we see the beat-up delivery carts, Zeus smirks. "She sure wasn't lying. These carts look like they're used to deliver tiger milk to residents in a Bangkok prison camp!"

We giggle, checking out the carts carefully until Mrs. Watkins sneaks to the back, opening the padlocks to release them.

"You decide," I instruct Zeus. "They all look the same to me."

"Nah, some are in worse shape than others. The hinges are rusty on this one. I'm not gonna open it in case bats fly out."

"Oh, Lord," says Mrs. Watkins.

Zeus opens the lid on another cart, closes it, and

points to a cart on our left. "Let's take this baby—she'll be a real fixer-upper."

"We're going to paint it pink," I inform Mrs. Watkins excitedly.

"Ask me why I'm not surprised," she chuckles. Mrs. Watkins relocks the rest of the carts. "Now y'all get out of here before I get fired!"

"Thank you!" I coo gratefully. "You'll be sitting front row at our fashion show. I promise. Two tickets on the house!"

"I can't wait. I've never been to a fashion show before," Mrs. Watkins announces.

Zeus wheels the delivery cart across the street to my building. "The coast is clear," I say, relieved. "I don't want to tangle with Mr. Sunkist tonight. He'd probably think we stole this cart from him."

Out of habit, I gaze toward the second floor of my building. Sure enough, Stellina is in position. "Hey, the other supermodel!" Stellina says, waving at us. "Fifi's in the lobby! What you doing with that delivery cart?"

"You'll see—it's a surprise for our fashion show!" I tell her excitedly.

"I can't wait!" she screams.

"Don't forget—your fitting is on Saturday," I yell to Stellina.

"Forget? I'm not sleeping till then!" Stellina swears.

"Chenille did my mother's hair today. She got ten dollars!"

"Your mother paid too much," I mumble under my breath, waving good-bye to Stellina.

Zeus chuckles. "You don't like your sister much, huh?" he asks.

"She treats me like I'm some pretentious model in the making," I balk. "And she doesn't like the things I like because she has the attention span of a poodle."

"But she digs doing hair," Zeus offers, locking in her hairy position.

"Well, it doesn't dig her—I'd never let her touch mine," I start in before realizing I'm sounding like a poodle myself, a snooty one.

Zeus rolls the cart into the lobby and greets Fifi like she's his long-lost sister. I hug her tightly. "It's gonna be all right."

"No, it isn't—Papi isn't coming to my fashion show! And I think he's moving in with the flamenco dancer!" she cries, getting upset. Fifi's eyes are bloodshot, and her normally unruly hair is hopelessly flat, like it's been depleted of all its moisture.

"I thought you said she was a tango dancer?" I ask, confused.

"Whatever—she's making moves on Papi!"

Zeus seems uncomfortable and doesn't say anything.

He pushes the cart into the elevator so we can descend to the dark, dank, nefarious basement to paint it.

I chatter nervously. "Luckily, there's enough space down here to store the cart until the night of the fashion show. Mr. Darius always lets us store stuff down here."

"You sure it's going to be safe?" Zeus asks, hesitant about my idea. He looks around like he's been here before—in his frightmares.

I point to the caged area that Mr. Darius keeps locked. "I'll come down in the morning so Mr. Darius can lock it in the cage. Nobody has a key but Mr. Darius and his assistant."

Zeus nods, still intent on eyeballing the dankness. "This place is creepy. I bet you there are a few bodies buried down here somewhere."

"Yeah, and I bet Mr. Darius put them there," I say, spooked.

"Stop trying to scare me!" frets Fifi.

I swat Zeus on his arm again, but this time I'm prepared for his taut muscles. Or so I think. "Ouch. You're like a man of steel," I chuckle. "Okay, you stay here. I don't want to leave the cart for a second. We're going up to my apartment to drop off Fabbie and get the supplies."

"You sure you don't need help?" he asks.

"With a can of paint, some brushes, and a drop-cloth?" I retort. "Fifi and I can manage."

Once we're inside my apartment, I realize that my mom is still not home from work, but Chenille is there.

"Hi, Chenille!" says Fifi, back to her bubbly self. Chenille is sitting at the kitchen table, struggling with her homework. I quickly point out: "Wish I could help, but I'm on Catwalk duty. We got this great idea for the Wild Card Challenge—but I can't tell ya, cuz then I'll have to silence ya."

"Ha, ha," snarls Chenille. She taps her pencil on the table impatiently.

"Have you heard from Mom?" I know she must have called home at least once and Chenille would have picked up the phone. I take the quart of pink lemonade out of the refrigerator and some paper cups from the pantry to bring downstairs. Chenille watches me curiously. I don't tell her that Zeus is in the basement—she'd probably think his hat belongs to Tony the Tiger.

"Where are you going?" she asks nosily.

"I told you it's top-secret. So did she call?"

"Yes. And she's depressed," Chenille shoots back, tapping her pencil on the table more rapidly. Craftily, she blurts out: "God, I can't believe how much homework I have."

"Let me see the Spanish homework," volunteers Fifi.

While Fifi is helping my conniving sister, I pick up the phone to call the Forgotten Diva Boutique. This whole Ramon situation is bananas. Why can't my mom meet someone diggable like I have? My mom answers, and she sounds oddly enough like a deep-sea fisherman struggling to talk from fifty leagues below the sea.

"Are you okay?" I ask her, concerned.

"I guess so. Thank you for showing me how to do that Facebook thing," she says, sighing deeply. "I caught them in the act. Lonni had the nerve to put up photos on her Facebook page: 'Our Memories at Brighton Beach.' I guess I should be glad Ramon found somebody who would go to the beach with him—in Brooklyn."

My mom's idea of going to a beach is vacationing in the Carribean.

"Well, you're right," I assure her, "there is nothing worse than a liar."

"Or than being alone. I'm so tired," she reveals. "If I didn't have you and Chenille, I would just call it a day, I swear."

"Don't say that!" I'm horrified. All my mom wanted was for Ramon to take her to the Copacabana on Thursdays for Eighties Boogie Night. And now he's watching the rise and fall of the waves with loony Lonni. I hope he gets bitten in the crotch by a Brooklyn crab. "You'll meet someone else. You'll see." I repress the urge to tell her that I have. Now is not the time.

"You know what my horoscope said today?" my mom asks, and continues without waiting for a response. "A single black woman over forty has a better chance of getting struck by an airplane than meeting a man."

"No, it didn't. You're just spouting statistics," I gripe, keenly aware of my mother's fondness for finding frightening stats. One of her faves: tracking the number of sexual predators on the loose in New York City.

"It is true," my mom insists.

"No, it isn't—there are lots of available men on the prowl in New York, just licking their chops like hyenas on the horizon," I say teasingly.

"Yes, you're right. There are," she relents. "Today a man with his belly popping out of his paisley shirt came into the store after staring at me through the window all morning. Mr. Popover gave me his business card, winking as he told me 'I love big women.' I bet you he wouldn't like it if I told him what kind of men I like."

"What kind?" I ask, taking the bait.

"Men who take me shopping on the first date!" Now my mom releases a laugh, which reminds me of her old self. She has the craziest laugh I've ever heard besides Aphro's. Like a pink flamingo in a fun house.

"Zeus, Fifi, and I are painting the cart now," I tell her, after filling her in on our Wild Card Challenge.

"That does sound like a great idea. It's amazing how you just come up with this stuff," she says, impressed.

"Well, my crew helps—especially Fifi," I assure her.

"How is she doing? Her mom throw her dad out yet?"

"Um, we'll talk about that later," I say, not wanting to talk about it with nosy Chenille within earshot. "We have to get our project in gear, because the Teen Style Network is coming over to watch us preparing for the Wild Card Challenge."

"They're not coming in that apartment!" she freaks.

"No, no—the basement. That should put the fear of Halloween in them," I chuckle. "But I'll make sure to pull down the cobwebs before they get here!"

"Awright then, I'll be home in a little while," she says, before rushing off because a customer needs her assistance.

After I hang up the phone, Chenille badgers me. "What'd she say?"

"That you must be exhausted from all that whining about your homework," I quip.

"Whatever," snaps Chenille.

"I'm sorry about the shoes. I know you didn't hide them," I say, breaking down. I do owe Chenille an apology.

"Whatever," Chenille repeats.

Feeling absolved, I motion for Fifi to wrap it up like a falafel to go. My sister doesn't even thank Fifi for her efforts and doesn't look up from her homework so I can glare at her disapprovingly. Fifi and I head to the hallway closet to retrieve the paint supplies. "Bingo." I'm eyeing two full gallons of Passion Pink paint left over from painting the dresser in my room last summer. We found the discarded dresser on a sidewalk on the Upper East Side and turned it into the pink anchor of my bedroom. "Another fixer-upper, presto pronto." I take the dropcloth, two paintbrushes, paint thinner, a scraper, coarse sandpaper, and an empty pail I fill with water.

As we head into the elevator, Fifi says softly, "You shouldn't be so mean to Chenille."

"Why not? She loves it," I reply unapologetically.

Zeus is pacing the basement when we return. "I thought you two ran off to Petticoat Junction with the Beverly Hillbillies," he riffs.

"What's the matter, pussycat, were you scared?" I tease him. "My mom is freaked out about Ramon, so I called her to offer some assisterance."

"Assisterance, huh? What's the matter?" he asks, concerned.

"Ramon took her best friend, Lonni, to Brighton Beach in Brooklyn. She's freaked out."

Zeus clams up. That's the second time. I guess guys don't like to hear stuff about other men two-timing. It's bad for their image. Now I feel embarrassed for breaking out my family drama. Fifi, on the other hand, uses the blank space to bend his ear with hers. She vents big-time while the three of us carefully spread the plastic dropcloth on the dirty cement floor. Zeus rolls the delivery cart on top. I open the can of paint and stir it. "Nice color," he comments. "The darker, the better. We should still do two coats, though," he advises.

"I know the drill," I inform him. "We painted the dresser in my room this same color. It came out de-lovely." Suddenly, I think of Ice Très—*de-lovely* is a word he uses—in referring to me.

Zeus nods, his eyes twinkling. Turning to Fifi, he beams. "I can't wait till we put on the graphics and your hand-painted illustrations. You're such an artist."

"*Graci-ass,*" Fifi says humbly.

"How come you don't do sketches?" Zeus asks.

"I'm not into sketching designs," Fifi admits. "I don't know why, but I'm not."

"Well, let's get this rodeo on the road before the Teen Style Network crew comes. They'll be here pronto soon."

"Are you stressed about the designs now that Diamond dropped the ball?" Zeus asks candidly.

"Yes. Mostly about those darn shutter-pleated dresses and the pillbox hats, I guess. Fifi, we're going to make them without sketches, okay?"

Fifi nods like Superwoman and we start sanding down the cart to smooth out the rough edges and remove the splinters. Now it's my turn to vent: I fill in Fifi about the Diamond drama. "We can't afford for Diamond to drop out. Ms. Lynx already warned me—any more shenanigans and I can take our fashion show on the road."

"You caught Chintzy with her hand in the cookie jar—that's one thing. What was she gonna do—go running to Ms. Lynx's office to get you disqualified?" explains Zeus. "But Diamond? She starts in with that doe-eyed earnestness about animal rights and even I start questioning what we're doing this for."

"Gee, thanks for that vote of confidence," I balk.

"Hey, come here," says Zeus. I lean in and Zeus kisses me on the cheek. "You're doing an amazing job."

"But we're still shoeless," I say, kissing him back. "And there's no tip-toeing around that."

"But we're not without a house," Zeus chuckles.

I think about Mr. Sunkist and shudder. "Being homeless. That's my mom's biggest fear," I reveal. "She left me and Chenille at Grandma Pritch's house when we were little. I thought my mom was never going to come back. And when she did come back, two years later, she never told us what happened. Where she was. Not to this day. But I see her worrying all the time about paying the bills. She's so stressed, I can feel it."

After I finish my babble, I sigh deeply, relieved that I told Zeus. Fifi already knows this sordid story.

"Now what's going to happen with Mami if she's not in the band anymore with Papi?" Fifi asks, fretting.

"Your mom is talented—and in full bloom. With all her flower power, she could get a job singing to tulips," I say confidently. "People would pay just to see her outfits!"

We continue sanding the wooden cart, smoothing the splintered surface—and my fears of being homeless.

"Now, that's a nice job," I say proudly.

We each take a brush and apply a coat of Passion Pink paint to the cart. "Heels on Wheels forever," I giggle. "I wish I could paint everything pink."

Zeus is more interested in washing his hands, and goes to the sink. "Well, we can start in on the basement tomorrow if you want," he challenges me.

I wrap my paint-smeared hands right around his neck. "Oops," I tease, pulling away.

He taps my nose with his index finger. "Got you back, Pinky."

"What time is it?" I ask, checking my cell. As if they're reading my mind, my phone rings and I answer. It's Boom from the Teen Style Network crew, making sure they're supposed to descend in the elevator.

"Yup, that's right—just take it to the tomb level!"

Boom laughs, but once the crew arrives, I can tell Caterina is creeped out by the basement, as if the

Candy Man is going to make a cameo with his hooked hand.

"So," says the pint-sized producer, "what are you doing for your Wild Card Challenge?"

"Well, first I thought you might tell us what the other fabbie four have got up their sleeves?" I heckle.

Caterina smirks. "You're the first one we're filming."

"Yippee!" I say, psyched. "So much for saving the best for last!" And this time I mean it.

New school rule: You don't have to be ultranice, but don't get tooooo catty or your posting will be zapped by the Fashion Avengers!

WE ALL PLAY THE NAME GAME

At Fashion International, we're encouraged to adopt monikers for our fashion identities that reflect our respective vision. (Gucci and Pucci and Prada, oh my!) Some of us, however, have taken that mission so far down the yellow-brick road we must have passed out in the poppy fields along the way! What else could explain the soaring rise in identity theft? Today's Special Event in the Fashion Auditorium bore witness to an extreme example of this name-snatching syndrome, which has become as tacky a trend as two-fisted gizmo users flexing their technology (hence the reason there's such a long waiting list for Internet addiction counseling!).

Those among us who weren't summoned to the Fashion Auditorium at high noon today shall remain nameless, but you shouldn't remain clueless—so allow me to break down exactly what transpired. The special guest was Benny Ninja, aka Benjamin Thomas, the appointed father of the House of Ninja and a fierce posing instructor who has appeared on major television shows such as *Keep It Fierce* and *Rip the Runway*. Catwalk director Ms. Fabianna Lynx (aka the Ferocious One) thought it would be a special treat to give this year's Catwalk contestants the chance to meet one of this year's judges. And who better to show these competitive contestants how to strike a pose categorically—face poses, hand poses, purse poses, on-the-floor poses, and finale poses—than the revered Benny Ninja?

Little did anyone know that Benjamin Thomas had another agenda: to expose an imposter at our school. It was more PRICELESS than a MasterCard commercial witnessing wannabe Willi Ninja, Jr.'s face—SNAP, CRACKLE, POP, POP, POP!—when he was called out by a real Ninja!! That's right, Willi Ninja, Jr., is NOT the adopted godson of the late voguing legend Willi Ninja! While dozing off in the poppy fields, the imposter Curtis Clyde must have gotten the confused idea that wanting something desperately enough is the same thing as being entitled to it. (With a clunker of a name like Curtis Clyde, however, can you blame him for perpetrating identity theft? Have some sympathy, fashionistas.)

When Benny Ninja popped Curtis Clyde over his head with a purse pose ("BOP, wake up!"), he snapped out of his trance and got a crash course in street marketing. Take a peek at C. C.'s crib sheets.

LESSON NUMBER ONE: Don't be bogus and hide behind someone's brand identity. Just because you're a fan (or a copycat) doesn't mean you can legally co-opt yourself into an entity that has already been created, manufactured, and marketed. (You'd think someone majoring in fashion marketing, like C. C. Wannabe, might have gotten a whiff of that during the first semester of his freshman year.)

LESSON NUMBER TWO: Do your homework before you adopt a moniker for your fashion identity. Every rapper knows, if you want to be a part of the Wu-Tang Clan, you have to give them a call first and ask! Or if you've come up with your own TAG, then do your legal research and make sure no one else has already claimed that name. Therefore, Curtis Clyde (aka Twirl Happy 1992 on-screen) should twirl—RIGHT NOW—to the copyright office and see if anyone has already trademarked his new moniker—C. C. Samurai—before he finds himself engaged in another stealthy sword fight.

LESSON NUMBER THREE: Build your own brand identity. Contrary to popular belief, the fashion game is NOT all about the faux. Yes, there is plenty of flavor biting going on, and counterfeiting is on the global rise to the tune of six billion dollars annually, but these tawdry tactics give

all of us a bad name. Add this rule to
your repertorie—and it's guaranteed to
open the doors to the Magic Kingdom:
set your sights on becoming an original before you get crushed as a carbon
copy.

Posted by Squash the Squabble at
14:66:19

12

A week later at our runway training session, Aphro finally spills the refried beans about locking lips with Lupo. "Okay, so we kissed once," Aphro confesses.

"I knew you were feeling the Firenze flavor!" I squeal. "How was it, bella bronzina?"

"His nose kept getting in the way."

"Ooh, you're bad. *Très mal*," Angora protests.

"I said I like him, but I can't be seen in public with him. Okay?" balks Aphro.

I look at her, surprised. "Lupo is goospitating over you. And what are you giving in return?"

"The truth, that's what. Oh, I'm supposed to pretend I don't notice Lupo's shorter than me?" Aphro challenges, leveling her Bed-Stuy stare at *moi*. "You wouldn't be fawning over Zeus if he wasn't 'a tall Tasti D-Lite.'" Aphro renders her best kitten imitation of *moi*.

I throw my Catwalk notebook down on the chair next to me. "You're the one who told me to 'stop acting like the Princess of Pink in my Chicken Little Castle and get with Zeus already.' And that's a direct quote!" I retort, twirling my finger Aphro style. "Now you're insinuating that I'm sticking to him like a pesty puffer?"

"You're always on the dribble-drabble about your agenda. After the competition is over, you should get a talk show on the Teen Style Network and tell the world!"

"The world is not enough," I giggle.

Angora scavenges for her own reality scraps. "Fifi says you kissed him in the basement when the three of you were decorating the Heels on Wheels cart."

"That was *before* the Teen Stylers got there!" I admit, blushing. "I relish—um—the hot dogs we ate. Awright, I could kiss him till the break of dawn."

"You might get to do that, Sleeping Beauty, if we don't find some shoes for our fashion show!" warns Aphro.

"*Oh*. It's not enough that I brainstormed a Wild Card Challenge guaranteed to earn us purr points? *And* have been working around the clock on its feline fatale execution?"

"Don't take all the credit. Zeus and Fifi helped hook it up. *And* Lupo is the real inspiration behind it!" counters Aphro. Now she stands up for her *huomo*.

"If I hadn't gone out with Zeus to the pig trough, I wouldn't known Mr. Saltimbocca had a shoe factory that donated shoes for every pair they sell! You never told me!" I balk.

Aphro levies a lame retort. "You never asked."

"Look, you don't have to huff and puff like the magic dragon," I insist.

Ruthie Dragon, my fire-breathing assistant, throws me a look like *Hold on to your hot sauce there*.

"Sorry, Ruthie," I apologize politely, then turn my attention back to my blustery BFF. "I handed in the one-pager for our Wild Card Challenge to the Catwalk office today."

"What'd Ms. Lynx say?" Aphro asks, wide-eyed.

"Well, she was standing by Sil Lai's desk, so I put it in the in-box—I mean, she didn't say anything, but I saw her glance at it and she looked pleased."

"Oh," says Aphro, disappointed.

"Look, I'm on kitten-heel patrol twenty-four seven searching for signs of available soles. Okay? Fifi is even asking the publicity director at Ruff Loner."

Aphro sucks her teeth. "Ruff Loner wouldn't loan out a bedtime story to a foster child. Felinez couldn't get a day off during spring break!"

This is true. Fifi snagged an intern gig at the Ruff Loner showroom, and her boss is *ruff* around the edges.

"We're also sending out letters this week to all the showrooms," I add authoratatively.

"You might as well send out good vibrations to the Travelocity roaming gnome!" Aphro snarls at our efforts.

Fifi flinches at Aphro's sole attack.

"Awright, I'm gonna shut up." Aphro backs off in fear of Fifi's fragile state over her parents' separation. At least for a *segundo*. "But that does not mean I'm gonna stop worrying until I see some lizard slingback sandals to go with the chiffon multi-tiered ruffled skirt and bomber jacket, for starters."

"Lizard. Really?" I glaze blankly at Aphro like *Keep hope alive!* That is, until I'm hit by good vibrations of the design nature. "OMG—I just got a fashion zap. Fifi, the faux leather we got for the tote bags? We can use it to make a tiered ruffled miniskirt to set off Aphro's bomber jacket!"

"No way, José!" Fifi says, stomping her foot. "We're behind in our production schedule already!"

"I know, Fifi—I'm sorry," I spurt. Now I back off. What was I thinking? But I can't help it when it comes to my fashion zap attacks.

Neither can Fifi. Her bushy eyebrows rise to high noon. I know what that look means: Fifi loves a texture tease. "I really like that combination," she admits.

Even Angora goes into fashion reportage mode: "I can see the two different textures glistening under the bright lights. And the colors—yum, yum—black faux leather in contrast with the gunmetal gray satin, sublimely set off by the hot pink tank underneath."

"Yes, yes, can't you just taste it—I mean, see it?" I goof, trying to whet my crew's appetite.

Aphro digs it, too. Even though she acts nonchalant. "Chiffon. Or faux leather. They'll both set off the lariats wrapped three times around the neck." Aphro primps like a peacock because she has already finished her allotted task: making the jewelry for our show.

Fifi senses it, too. "You should stop showing off like a factory worker who finished first on the assembly line!"

"Well, I did finish," Aphro boasts, twirling the purple lariat wrapped around her neck.

Now my stickler assistant wants a bauble breakdown. "So what do we have?" Ruthie Dragon asks. Officiously, she takes out her notebook to record the jewelry sequences even though we're filling out the "run of show" sheets next week.

"Well, we've got the long multicolored seed-bead lariats for the Chic Meets Street segment, dangling crystals for the Belle of the Fur Ball evening wear segment, and the inscribed bangles for the graffiti Urban Gear segment, which opens the show after the junior guest models take their twirl on the runway," Aphro reports.

"That's all? *Está todo?*" attacks Fifi.

At that moment, Zeus and Lupo enter the fashion fray. Lupo's camera is already hanging around his neck as if he's ready for action. I wink my left eye twice at Aphro and Fifi—our Catwalk code to zip it. Lupo smiles wildly, like he's glad to be in the mix so he can click away *pronto*—and squeeze in a cuddle or two from his *bella bronzina*, his unofficial nickname for Aphro.

"Hi, Dr. Zeus," Angora says warmly. "We were just talking about your hatness. When are we going to see our Heels on Wheels charity creation? I can't wait!"

I refrain from reminding Angora that the mold and other mildew mayhem in the dank dungeon could aggravate her asthma.

Oblivious to Angora's sensitive nose, Zeus answers, "Come over anytime. Wait till you see the graphics and Felinez's illustrations. I mean, we hooked it up. Seriously."

"Oh, good. I was beginning to wonder if that spooky basement was reserved for smooching?" quips Aphro.

I jab Aphro in the ribs, but I should have saved it for Nole Canoli. He saunters in out of breath and chirps like a parrot. "When am I gonna see this Heels on Wheels cart? I have to approve it, too!"

Following Zeus's lead, I crack: "You can come over anytime to my Tomb Raider basement. We're open twenty-four seven, like any respectable sweatshop."

Zeus beams at me, curling up the corners of his lips like a court jester.

"Awright, let's get down to business." I whip out my *Teen Elle* magazine so I can babble about Babette Epaulette, a designer on Long Island making audacious shoulder ornaments.

Aphro gazes curiously at the fringes, chains, and feathers that can be harnessed onto the shoulders of jackets. "Now, that's what I'm squawking about," she says approvingly.

"Good—because I'm putting them on the bomber jackets! Chic Meets Street. Seriously."

My trio of BFFs gaze curiously in my direction like they're watching a drunk sailor about to flotsam and jetsam a ship's entire cargo overboard by accident.

Nole decides to haze instead of gaze. "Whoa, Miss Purr—enough with the last-minute design choices. I need a minute to digest this—cat appliqués on the back of the jackets, fringes on the shoulders? The only thing you'll need is two canaries perched on the front pockets!"

I can't resist returning an uppercut. "Look who's still sore about his perils with Penelope."

"I don't know, I kinda like it. I don't think it's too *mucho*," Fifi interrupts, raising her eyebrows again in approval.

While I smile victoriously, the seven remaining models and five kiddie guest models pile into the expansive conference room for our first runway training session. Stellina is bouncing off the walls. "I don't know why you want me to come. I am *trained*!" Tiara doesn't even smile. I fret, doubting my decision. Can Aphro really turn Tiara into sashay material?

"I like your outfit," E.T. says appreciatively.

"Thank you," I say. "Wait till you see your outfit at the fitting next week. You're gonna love it."

E.T. grins like he is genuinely grateful for another golden opportunity to get away from his grandmother Mrs. Paul's clutches.

I clear my throat to deliver my motivational model mantra. "Awright, everyone, it's back to the business of the show," I order. "The time is almost near—for our highly anticipated function at Petticoat Junction."

"Well, I'm not wearing any petticoats. Let's clear up that confusion right now!" Fallon mouths off. Lupo lets out a nervous round of laughter. He points his camera and clicks photos of Fallon in her sassy posturing mode. She's wearing a red leather jacket and leopard leggings covered by a short black Lycra skirt. At a size eighteen, Fallon is representing the higher end of my every-size philosophy, which is essential to my fashion vision. That's why I ignore the fact that Fallon gives us grief at fittings.

As usual, Angora is the first to reassure. She gently caresses Fallon's plump arm. "No petticoats *pour vous*."

I continue to sashay through my speech. "I know all of you—except for our junior models, of course—are quite familiar with walking the runway. And if you're like *moi*, you've probably dreamed about it since you were in designer diapers."

"*Mija*, what are you talking about—we were six!" Fifi blurts out, giggling.

"Oh, right," I say, shaking my head. "Um, like I said, during the sandbox reign. Anyway, we've called this session today to show all of you how to represent on the runway for the House of Pashmina."

Everyone claps. "Yeah!" squeals Stellina, flapping her arms like a chicken. Actually, she looks like a buttercup about to be plucked in her yellow cotton turtleneck and olive-green leggings.

"The feline fatale concept behind the House of Pashmina collection must be conveyed every time you step out on that runway. The junior models will open the show, and the rest of the models each have three assigned outfit changes," I explain carefully. "Aphro, as you know, is one of the models, but she's also our runway choreographer, so today she will show us how to work the runway to represent our theme."

Aphro comes up and stands next to me to walk the run of the room. We pushed aside the conference table so that we have plenty of room to conduct our runway training.

"I want everyone to memorize the tenets of our feline fatale concept: fun, flirty, fierce—the latter is imposed to convey our catlike prowess. What this means in terms of practical application is—there will be no trotting like horses on the runway!" I emphasize.

I do a quick exaggerated demonstration of the gait that I despise, up and down the length of the conference room. "I don't care how hot this style of walking is on the runways in Paris right now. You can save that galloping gait for Gaultier, okay? That is, if you're lucky enough to get booked in his show—and from what I can see, every male and female model I've handpicked in this room would be Gaultier-approved."

"What's Gaultier?" asks Juanito, confused.

"He's a con artist!" shouts Stellina.

"Okay, Miss Buttercup?" I scold Stellina. "Jean Paul Gaultier is a revered French designer. He even designed costumes for Madonna's worldwide tours and Britney Spears—and he designed the costumes for the movie *The Fifth Element*."

"Fierce cult classic," Nole shouts out. "If you've never seen the movie, rent it!"

"Anyway, he's not the only one. A lot of designers have their models working this equestrian style of walking in their shows," I explain. "All you need to know now is, it's the exact opposite of feline fatale."

"So we're supposed to be slinking down the runway, too?" asks Benny Madina, a hot chocolate model with shoulder-length dreadlocks and brilliant white teeth. (He was Aphro's pick.)

"Look—I know we have a lot of haters," I admit, sensing the uneasiness among my models. "They think our whole feline fatale concept is too frilly. Let our haters be our motivators. We are participating in this competition for our shot at fashion stardom. And don't think for a second we're going to misfire because of cyberbullying."

Everyone claps. "That's right, bring it," Benny says, regaining his confidence.

"So back to serving what *we* do. I want all my male models to think of yourself as male cats. So, Benny— you're a black male cat. Can you envision how he walks? Slow, graceful, with purpose—and the exact opposite of a ninja warrior, okay? We'll leave those moves to C. C. Samurai's models!" I explain, in an effort to motivate my Catwalk models to think outside of the litter box.

I look at Benny's and Zeus's faces and can tell that my motivational speech is sinking in. "Now Aphro is going to guide each of you through the training."

Aphro walks up and down the run of the room, demonstrating the feline fatale style of runway model- ing we approve of. She loves walking the runway, so she can't resist unleashing a tiny smile.

"Work it, *bella bronzina*!" coaxes Lupo.

Stellina is mesmerized by Aphro's style. Even at her tender age, she can spot what any trained fashionista can see: Aphro works it for purr points on the Dow Jones—and her long, muscled legs and arms give her a panther's edge.

"Notice that Aphro never puts her hands on her hips—which you see a lot in fashion shows," I point out. "The House of Pashmina does not throw shade—or attitude!"

"Not on the runway, anyway," interjects Nole.

"Right. Think playful, flirty, and accessible. Oh, but that does not mean girly. And our male models can convey this playful attitude, too.

"So rule number one—never put your hands on your hips when you're on the runway," I announce.

"Okay!" shouts Stellina.

We line up the child models first. Aphro begins by providing Tiara with the extra instruction she needs. She gently tells her to stand straight with her shoulders back, walk slowly, and smile.

E.T. is up next. He fidgets while standing at the makeshift stage. "When you first come out on the runway, stand completely still," Aphro tells him. E.T. listens and follows Aphro's instruction to the letter.

My cell phone vibrates in my sweater pocket, so I take it out to glance at it. Another text from Ice Très: "Counting down the days. You and Me. Sipping Pinktinis at the Lipstick Lounge." I put the phone back in my pocket and continue to watch Aphro training E.T. He walks up and down very smoothly.

"Smile a little more—okay?" Aphro coaxes him. "And take slower steps. Remember, just envision how a cat walks. Keep that image in your mind while you're walking on the runway. Nice and easy. That's what fe-line fatale is all about."

"Meowch!" hisses Benny Madina.

Training Tiara, of course, is not as easy. She has to walk the runway five times before Aphro finally gets her to smile softly. It's obvious she is going to need another session. But for today, she has made some serious strides.

After she's finished, Angora coos at Tiara. "Bravo, you were really good. Did you like it?"

Tiara nods. Stellina is waiting for some strokes, too. "And you were good, too. *Très bien.*"

I hand Tiara a cup of pink lemonade, which she guzzles faster than a paratrooper falls out of a plane without a parachute.

Now Aphro is ready for the bigger fashionistas. She turns her attention to Benny Madina and breaking him out of his butch stance. He's a little stiffer than he was at the model tryout sessions. "Doesn't he seem bigger?" I whisper quietly to Angora. She nods. I wonder if he's been bulking up from weight training or something but decide it's better not to ask him. Male models get even testier than female ones about their measurements. Finally, Aphro gets Benny to relax enough to create a runway presence that aligns itself with our fe-line fatale concept. After a few rounds, Benny lets go and stands at the end of his walk with a natural grace.

"Benny, that was on point," I say, encouraging him. "Can I make one petite suggestion? We need for everyone to be aware and smile a little more—like you know a secret nobody else knows and you're dying to share it with the audience—but you can't."

Our exotic model Elgamela Sphinx, known online as Snake Charmer, is up next, and slinks down the runway, serving it sublimely. I love her mysterious image. Elgamela is Egyptian American with dark curly hair, superthick eyebrows, and dark doll eyes.

At first, I was sure that Zeus was feeling Elgamela, but now I know he isn't—at least not like that.

Aphro places her hands on Elgamela's slender hips to adjust them forward slightly. "Lean back when you're walking just a little more," she advises.

"For your first outfit, you can walk even slower than that, because you're going to be wearing a bathing suit—and flat sandals," I add. Suddenly, I cringe at the mention of footwear again. I should have known that Aphro would not miss another op to hop on the blame train.

"That's if we ever get them," Aphro blurts out.

Everyone else zips their lips. Elgamela smiles at me like she knows, we're all supa-tense. She concentrates on her walk carefully. After she finishes, she exclaims, "The slower I walk, the better, so I don't jiggle—and make my mother faint!"

We all laugh uneasily at the mention of her strict

parents. Unlike Fifi, Elgamela is happy that her father won't be at the fashion show. See, Mr. Sphinx is a strict Muslim, and he has forbidden his slinky daughter to model in the Catwalk competition. At first, Elgamela was going to comply, but last Christmas after Angora and her father almost got evicted because of funny money business with his Funny Bunny cartoon franchise, Elgamela made a New Year's resolution: to sashay toward her dreams. With the covert help of her mother, Mr. Sphinx will be serving grilled chicken at their family-operated eatery, Chirping Chicken, on the Upper East Side, while Elgamela is serving style on the runway with us in the fashion tents in Lincoln Center.

After Elgamela finishes her sultry sashay, Nole claps. "Bravo! Work it, Snake Charmer!"

Secretly, we've all got our fingers crossed that the devout Mrs. Sphinx doesn't confess to Mr. Sphinx at the last minute. Gingerly, I query: "Isn't your father happy there is the first Muslim Miss U.S.A.?" (Last year, Rima Fakih, a Queens-raised daughter of Lebanese immigrants, became the first Arab American to win the sparkly crown.)

"Are you kidding? He keeled over when he saw the photo of her in the newspaper, wearing that bikini under the Miss U.S.A. sash!" shrieks Elgamela. "He was so upset, he prayed that she doesn't win the Miss Universe pageant so she doesn't disgrace herself any further by letting the whole world see her parading onstage in a bathing suit!"

"Okay," I say, disappointed. "But you're sure he's not coming to our fashion show?"

"Oh, I'm sure, because my mother has agreed to not say she's going until the day before—that way he can't get anyone to cover for him at the restaurant!" Elgamela confesses.

"Sounds like a Code Pink plan," I say, still unsure.

Zeus is next up for petite tutelage from Aphro. I watch, mesmerized by his every move. Kissa, the Finnish model, blushes while watching. I can tell she digs Zeus, but for once I feel sure about one thing: Zeus likes *moi*.

After all the models have finished, Angora plays hostess and pours pink lemonade for everyone.

"Congrats! Catwalk cocktails all around," Aphro squeals, psyched by the runway training session. She always seems happier when she's doing what she loves: working the ramp. Relieved that the session went well, I begin to chill—and think about Ice Très's text. I wonder what Pinktini cocktails are?

I haven't told Zeus that I'm going out with Ice Très. I smile at Zeus, who is talking with Kissa. Fifi tries to smile, but she's frazzled, too. I feel so helpless seeing the wounded-fawn look on her face.

At last, Aphro finally reveals what's been making

her act so shady. Collapsing into the chair next to mine, she lets the information simmer slowly. "It didn't go so well on Saturday." Aphro sighs like she's been waiting to exhale all day, then takes a gulp from her drink before she continues. "Lennix's new foster mother is a trip. She was grilling me about what happened. But I was like, why should I tell her about that? What happened at the Maydells' has nothing to do with her, you know? That's our business."

"I agree. Why should you tell her?" I second.

"Well, she was all about playing Detective Do-Right. After she couldn't get anything out of me about the Maydells, she starts grilling me about my background. I was like, *Hello—you're not taking me in as a foster child.*"

"What did she ask you?"

"Where was my mother and did I have a father? Frankly, I was like, *Not only do I not know you, but why would I tell you if I did? Hello?*" Aphro swings her left leg like her reflexes are being tested in the doctor's office.

Now Angora sits down, sensing that something is wrong. Aphro clams up for a second, but Angora rubs Aphro's arm like *Be for real, it's me,* chérie. The three of us were there when Angora needed us.

"Then finally she was asking me questions about

what I plan on doing when I grow up. So I told her, I'm going to be a model and travel. Then I told her about the Catwalk competition and asked if Lennix could come." Aphro pauses, and I wonder why until she starts sniffling.

"Oh, *chérie*," coos Angora.

We wait quietly for Aphro to regain her feisty flame, which she does in a few seconds. "So, she was like, 'Modeling? Well, you should think about getting an education. And you shouldn't be allowed to walk around in that outfit, because your skirt is too short. And I don't know what kind of foster parents you have—well, obviously I do know, because that's why Lennix was removed—but he certainly is not going to any fashion show.'"

"She sounds mean," I say, squirming.

Fifi squirms in her chair, too. Although Mrs. Cartera is far from mean, she sure threw Mr. Catera's shoes out the window with enough brute force to hit an innocent bystander on the head.

"Oh, trust, I wasn't scared of her. Then she looks me straight in the face and says, 'Lennix is going to college. I'm going to make sure of that. And if your foster parents cared about you at all, they wouldn't allow you to indulge in this nonsense, and they'd make sure that you go to college, too—and make something of your life.'"

"She said that?" Angora asks in disbelief.

Aphro snaps. "Why would I say she did if she didn't?"

I come to Angora's defense. "She didn't mean that—"

"I know. I'm just tripping," admits Aphro, covering her face with her hand and swinging her leg more forcefully.

I glance over at Kissa and Zeus, who are still at the other end of the conference room, flirting, from what I can see. I realize I'd better wrap up our runway training session so everyone can spread to the four winds of NYC. I get up to address my models. "Um, everybody— that was great. So next Thursday will be our fitting for the evening wear segment. *And* Fabbie Tabbie's wedding gown," I squeal. "Okay, *finito*. That's it—you did great."

"Can I come?" begs Stellina.

"No, it's just for the regular models," I tell her.

"So Fabbie Tabbie is a regular model and I'm not?" she challenges me.

"Oh, let her come," Aphro insists. "We can do the kids' fittings and the evening gown segment at the same time. Why not?"

"Oh, I do not want to be doing a fitting around any kids," blurts out Fallon. "No disrespect."

"We'll do the junior model fitting and Fabbie

Tabbie's evening gown together. How's that?" I suggest. Compromising, as usual. But that's my job as house leader: greasing the fashion wheels—and everybody's ego.

"That's okay with me," offers Felinez.

"Okay. Kissa, you'll have to bring Cherry an hour earlier. That's okay?" I ask.

Kissa nods yes. Her sister, Cherry, smiles. She doesn't talk much, which I guess most designers would approve of. According to Nole, models are meant to be seen, not heard!

Zeus, on the other hand, has gotten an earful, and I can tell he seems a little jittery. I try to sense what's going on. "Um, I have to take care of something," he says.

I feel my heart sinking but concede. I know that Aphro wants me to come over. I can tell even though she doesn't say it that she really needs my assisterance right about now.

"All right, we'll resume tomorrow," I say, trying to keep the situation Lite FM.

But when Zeus pecks me on the cheek, I sense something is off. After he leaves, I sit back down with Angora, Fifi, and Aphro. "Did you notice anything strange about Zeus?"

"Ray Charles could see that," states Aphro.

"I don't know. Sometimes he's all over me, then other times, he seems so distant. I feel confused."

"*Chérie*, that's just guys. I told you. Read *The Rules*," preaches Angora.

"No, Pash is right. There is something weird going on with Zeus," says Fifi.

"Angora is right. Ice Très is beating down my phone—probably because I ignore him, I swear," I reveal. "And he is so looking forward to our date."

"You should be, too. Give yourself a chance to see if you like Ice Très now that Shalimar doesn't have her hooks in him anymore," advises Angora.

"Puhleez, everyone is on the shady Jackson payroll," Aphro says with a snarl.

"So, what was the upshot with Lennix?"

"She said Lennix can't come to any fashion show—and I got the impression I wouldn't be allowed to visit him again," Aphro says, poking out her pouty mouth.

"I wish Lennix's new foster mother could see you in action. How amazing you are with kids. You worked Tiara like a lion tamer. Amazing," I profess, giving props.

"Thank gooseness, or we would have to rename our show the March of the Penguins!" barks Nole.

Suddenly there is a knock on the door. "Oh, Lord, look who is tardy to the party," cracks Aphro.

"Caterina?" I mumble. But when I open the door, C. C. Samurai is standing there without a shuriken—his weapon of choice. "Oh, ye cometh unarmed?"

"Can I come in for a second?" he asks.

I look over to Angora. "Oh, sure," she says, quickly shifting into her hostess mode.

C. C. Samurai takes a deep breath, like he's anchoring himself. Ruthie Dragon sits straight up in her chair. Even I'm waiting for the other shoe to drop. And does he ever drop it.

"In light of the recent incident with Benny Ninja, I've had to rethink my strategy. I don't want the Tracy Reese shoes. They're yours—you borrow them."

"Why would you do that?" I ask suspiciously.

"After what happened, nothing matters more to me than regaining my credibility," confesses C. C. Samurai.

"So what are you saying?" I ask, stunned.

"The name of my house has changed, but the theme remains the same—urban warrior fashion. But my models won't be wearing shoes, because style warriors go barefoot in the urban jungle," C. C. Samurai spins.

"It's your Wild Card Challenge!" blurts out Nole, pleased as a piglet with a snout stuffed with truffles.

C. C. Samurai is startled, like he swallowed an overweight canary. Carefully, he constructs his thoughts. "Look, I'm willing to let you have the shoes—as long as you don't go blasting my show secrets on the blog. I only agreed to borrow the shoes because she wanted to make sure you didn't."

"You're talking about Shalimar, aren't you?" says Aphro, demanding a response. "Aren't you?"

Now C. C. looks like a canary with heartburn.

"See, I told you not to be fooled by Shalimar's silence of the lamb chops. She is trying to steer us to slaughterhouse five!" Fifi says righteously.

Like Fifi, Aphro is running helter-skelter with accusations of espionage. She tries to force C. C. to confess: "Come on, tell us. It was Shalimar. It makes perfect sense. How else could you have gotten access to Tracy Reese shoes if Shalimar wasn't behind it?"

"I will not get in the middle of any catfight. My lips are sealed." C. C. Samurai strikes his usual pose. "Don't shoot the messenger, just sign for the delivery, okay?"

I decide I'd better dive into this drama before the gift of the shoes—which are made for walking—struts out of our reach. "You're right," I say cordially, comprehending his metaphor. "We want the shoes, and in exchange, your Wild Card theme will not be leaving this room. You have our word." I gaze at everyone in the room to make sure we're on the same page.

"I'm counting on that. I'm just grateful that this crisis gave me such a fabulous idea for my Wild Card Challenge." C. C. Samurai flexes, like he's superior because of his decision but still anxious to mark this particular amends off his to-do list.

Now Aphro sits straight up in her chair, like she's saying *Don't do it!*

But I'm in charge, and my job as house leader is to put my pride in check for the collective good of my team. "So you'll make sure that the publicist at Tracy Reese is aware that we'll be borrowing the shoes instead of you?"

"Will do," C. C. Samurai assures me.

"Thank you," I say gratefully.

"You're welcome. I feel if I'm going to win this competition, then I want to win it in my own right."

I can tell by the glint in Nole's eyes that he admires C. C. Samurai's new attitude. I do, too. Apparently, the Benny Ninja beatdown has been a catalyst for this unexpected episode of C. C. "sole" searching. And C. C. is right about one thing, which I utter out loud: "You're right. May the best house win."

13

What I love most about the Carteras' cramped digs on the Grand Concourse in the South Bronx: the spicy, aromatic smells of Latin food wafting through every room and the dizzying whir of electronics, phonics, and gadgets in concert. Fifi, of course, is always putting the pedal to the metal on her sewing machine. Her younger brother, Juanito, plays his keyboard or video games, and practices his ninja antics. As for Michelette, she keeps the apartment amplified with the simultaneous blare of Latin music and Spanish *telenovelas*.

Today, however, the Mardi Gras mood, along with Mr. Cartera, is absent from 5555 Grand Concourse. In its place, a tension you can cut with a chorizo knife. Determined to make our final fittings fun, however, Mrs. Cartera has been cooking up a carnival in the kitchen, even though right now she's taking a break and hovering over Fifi in her bedroom with a purple paisley blouse in her hand.

Seated in front of her sewing machine, Fifi screams: "Mami, stop bothering me. *No me jodas mas!* I told you I have to get the stuff ready for our fashion show! Why don't you wear the yellow jumpsuit and fly away like Big Bird!"

Fifi's reference to the costume she constructed for her mother's Las Madres persona doesn't go unnoticed. Mrs. Cartera flinches, becoming embarrassed that her paisley request is for our eyes only. Nonetheless, she continues to grovel: "I know, *la mia preciosa*— just two little darts? I look like a sack of *papas fritas* in this. I'll love you forever."

"I know. That's what worries me," moans Fifi, blowing stray strands away from her face.

Mrs. Cartera waves off Fifi's faux foreboding with a flick of her tiny wrist, which is weighed down by wide wooden bangles hand-painted with delicate flowers. I've witnessed this tango between the two *mucho* times before. Fifi caves and her mother hands over the blouse. Humming softly, Mrs. Cartera waits patiently, shifting the weight on her fuchsia stiletto slides with tinted hydrangea flowers on the toes. When it comes to her accessories, Mrs. Cartera is always in full bloom.

"I have such a headache," says Fifi, rubbing her forehead. Fifi won't admit it, but she's so stressed about her parents' separation and our fashion show, she has nothing but headaches and stomachaches most of the time.

"I'll get you some vinegar," her mom suggests.

"Vinegar?" I ask curiously.

"It's an Andean remedy—lowers your blood pressure,

gets rid of the headache *subito*," she explains, snapping her fingers. I watch as Mrs. Cartera sashays out of the room, her heels clicking on the hardwood floor.

Fifi relents to the pounding pain, cradling her head in her hands until her Mom returns with a bottle of white vinegar and a tablespoon. "I hope you don't mind. I took the scale out of the oven so I can cook, *está bien?*"

"Just put it back after you finish—without any grease stains, *por favor!*" orders Fifi. She keeps the scale hidden in the oven, but takes it out every morning, moving the scale around on the linoleum like a Ouija board, searching for the spot where the indicator is tricked into showing she weighs less than 150 pounds.

"You're coming to our show?" I ask Mrs. Cartera rhetorically. Why'd I do that?

Mrs. Cartera puts her hands on her hips defiantly. "Oh, I will be there, but *he* won't."

Fifi snaps again. "Mami, *párate!* Just stop."

"Why don't you tell him that? I wasn't the one in the Coco Loco Lounge in Santo Domingo in front of everyone taking pictures with *her!*" Mrs. Cartera shoves a spoonful of vinegar into Fifi's reluctant mouth. Fifi swallows, squinting disapprovingly.

Now it's Mrs. Cartera's turn to cave on cue. "Okay, *mija*—I will stop."

Fifi shoves the blouse back at Mrs. Cartera, who

walks over to the full-length mirror on the door and holds the blouse to her chest, pleased. Humming a little louder, Mrs. Cartera gets starry-eyed, like she's fantasizing about serenading guests on a cruise ship, but at least this afternoon she will have a captive audience with us.

Involuntarily, I blurt out a compliment. "Purple makes your complexion snap, crackle, pop!"

Mrs. Cartera nods knowingly, then plants a kiss on Fifi's throbbing forehead: "I thank you, my daughter, in the name of the rumba, the mambo, and the cha-cha-cha!"

With that, Mrs. Cartera cha-chas out of the bedroom, happy for a fleeting moment.

"She's addicted to alterations," swears Fifi.

"And we're addicted to purrfection," I utter. "Everybody needs something to get them through the day—that's what Miss Viv always says."

Fifi gives me a knowing nod that secretly communicates *Thank gooseness we have each other.* Then she resumes sewing the cotton drawstring pants to be worn by our two boy junior models. While my hands are busy cutting the strips of fabrics for the ruffles on the girl junior model's tiered sundresses, my nose is being treated to the intoxicating aromas of fresh *fritangas* sizzling in cauldrons of oil—grilled beef and chicken, pigs feet, leg of lamb, ribs, and different types of chorizo sausages, longaniza, murcillo blood sausages, and *chunchullo*—fried cow intestines—with mini potatoes and *arepas*.

"She is making enough *comida* for the Spanish Inquisition," moans Fifi, licking her lamb-chop lips.

"We'll go down in Catwalk history as the one house that always fed our models," I snicker, reflecting on Zeus's DON'T FEED THE MODELS T-shirt. "Oy. I wish the Mad Hatter was coming over today."

"You're going tomorrow night to the Lipstick Lounge. I wish I could go there," confesses Fifi.

"I wish you were going, too," I admit. "I'm psyched about seeing this singer, Alyjah Jade."

"That's nice Ice Très is taking you. I like Ice Très more than Zeus. He's better for you."

I know better than to argue with Fifi's Santeria sense. "Awright," I concede. I glance quickly at all the candles Fifi has perched around her bedroom. Lately, she's been burning them at night, searching for guidance. "I don't know. Ice Très is so goofy. He kinda reminds me of my bathrobe with the cat's head falling off the back—I know I should sew it back on, but I don't want to mess with its tattered charm."

"All you have to do is put him back together like Humpty Dumpty!" prompts Fifi.

"Yeah, right. Where's the faux faux?" I ask, referring to the last precious piece of faux leather.

Fifi points to the battered rustic wooden crates branded with the words *Arancias de Colombia* that are stacked in the corner. I remove the top crate and spot the huge pile of postcards in the crate beneath. These were sent by Mrs. Cartera from all over the world. I glance quickly at some of the postmarks—Guadeloupe; Nassau, Bahamas; Lima, Peru. I put the postcard-filled crate on the floor and dig through the third crate until I find the supple black faux leather, which I need to make the tiered ruffles for my furbulous new creation.

Cutting the strips perfectly straight, I get jagged feelings about Ice Très. "Ice Très makes me feel comfortable. When he isn't lying."

"He told you the truth—Shalimar was using him. Did you tell Zeus you're going to the Lipstick Lounge?"

I shake my head. "No way, José."

Suddenly, Fifi bursts into tears. "I wonder if Mami will ever be happy again like she was when she and Papi were performing together around the world."

"I wonder if my mom will ever be happy again, too. Why didn't Ramon just pick a mermaid in Coney Island instead of flapping his fins in Brighton Beach with Lonni, her best friend?"

Fifi giggles. I giggle, too. I didn't even realize I was so upset with Ramon until now. "*And* he didn't even fix the bathroom ceiling. Now all I hear is drip, drip, drip!"

We giggle again, sitting at the sewing machine to

stitch the strips of ruffles, which will be adhered to the sundresses after the fitting. Fabbie Tabbie meows like she's grateful we're making progress. She is plopped in the center of Fifi's bed, while Fifi's prized Bengal cat, Señorita, is crouched on the floor below. "Fabbie Tabbie! Get off the bed!"

I pick up Fabbie Tabbie's white chiffon wedding dress for the finale and put it on her. Fabbie paws at me in protest, but I tap her head to stop it and slip the dress over her wide girth. "Oy, Fabbie. You should concentrate more on the bits and less on the kibble." I pat her pudgy stomach. "Maybe I should put her on a diet like a model right before Fashion Week?"

Fifi doesn't respond. She is basting the gathers on the chiffon ball skirts. I tighten the elastic in the middle of the wedding gown and contemplate whether the train could use more ruffles. "Do you think the train is long enough?"

Fifi glances over and nods.

"You sure? I want that train to screech to the finish line. You only get to be a bride once," I coo.

"That's not true," Fifi winces. "Daddy is going to marry that tango tramp and she's already been married three times. I heard Mami talking about her on the phone to Nona!" Nona is Fifi's grandmother in Colombia, who takes out her false teeth at night but keeps her common sense close to her heart.

"Fifi! You don't know that," I chide her.

Fifi puts down the skirts and parks herself in front of a candle, lighting it, then closing her eyes. I don't say a word until she finishes and resumes sewing. Two hours later, we're finally ready for the model fittings—and ready to chow down. While we wait for the models to arrive, I carefully press the shutter pleats on Mink's and Yong's fuchsia evening dresses.

My cell phone rings. "Aarrgh, it's Panda," I moan, staring at the screen. "Why can't he just send a text like a normal person?"

"You should talk to him," advises Fifi.

"Fifi, come on. I can't talk to him now," I protest.

I put the phone down on Fifi's dresser.

"Have you called Diamond?" Fifi asks.

"I will," I say, sighing.

"She's probably trolling the slaughterhouses looking for sheep to rescue," snipes Fifi, shaking her head. Once Diamond Tyler came to a Catwalk meeting upset because a sheep with a USDA clip hanging off its ear escaped from a slaughterhouse on Tremont Avenue. The sheep was running on the Grand Concourse, causing a traffic jam.

"Wait till Diamond hears about Señorita's pedigreed Bengal lineage—then she'll get her rough hide over here," I decide. Never mind that Fifi secured Señorita from the ASPCA. I dial Diamond's number, but she doesn't answer, so I leave a message, dangling the Bengal pedigree like bait.

"Knock, knock," yells Juanito from the bedroom door. He has pried himself away from his ninja games so he can be fitted for his Catwalk outfit.

"You're going to dig your outfit," I tell him.

We cart all the junior models' outfits to the living room to prepare for the model stampede. Juanito can't wait to try on his graffiti T-shirt with DON'T MAKE ME PURR printed on the back and the matching cotton pants. "This is cool," he says, letting loose with a disciplined kick. "They look like karate pants."

"They're not!" cautions Fifi.

"Okay, help me put the food out," shouts Mrs. Cartera from the kitchen.

"Tell Michi—I'm busy!" snarls Fifi, exasperated. Michelette senses the incoming disturbance and rises from the couch and saunters into the kitchen. Turning to Juanito, Fifi snaps, "And you can't wear these before the fashion show, so don't ask! *Entiendes?*"

Juanito doesn't answer his sister. Instead he keeps practicing his ninja poses.

"Don't worry," I soothe Fifi.

We're keeping all the clothes for the fashion show at my house in plastic garment bags to protect them. I motion for Juanito to cut it out so I can pin the bottom of his pants to make them shorter. Juanito is tame compared to Stellina. She's so excited when she sees the sundress, she jumps up and down like she's on a trampoline.

I show the girl junior models the matching umbrellas they'll be carrying. "And when you get to the end of the runway, each of you will open your umbrella and twirl it so everybody can see the slogan stamped on it."

"Oh, that's fierce!" exclaims Stellina, gazing at hers, which says I'M FELINE GROOVY.

I'm struck by another idea. "As you pass each other on the runway, you cross paws, okay?" I show them the Catwalk handshake. Even Tiara giggles.

"Do we have to do that?" groans Juanito, obviously disappointed he won't be doing any ninja poses.

"Yes, you have to do it, Juanito!" exclaims Fifi.

"Awright. I'll do your stupid boring handshake."

"Juanito, we worked really hard on your outfits. The least you can do is appreciate it!" screams Fifi.

Like a mother hen, Mrs. Cartera zooms from the kitchen with a spatula in hand. "*Que paso?*" she asks, her heels clacking on the wooden floor.

"*Nada.* Nothing," I pipe up. "It's time to eat!"

Fifi cracks a smile. I hug her and we all sit down at the big dining room table. The doorbell rings and I jump up to get it. The rest of the troops have arrived. I glare at Aphro like *Where were you when we needed you?*

"What's up with you?" she snarls.

"Fifi is having a cheddar cheese meltdown—so please, be nice to her," I warn Aphro.

"I'm always nice to her," she responds bluntly.

"Oooh, good, I'm hungry," says Fallon, following her nose to the dining room table. She sits down and dives in.

Elgamela is equally happy with the feast. "Oh, Mrs. Cartera," she coos. "The food is so good. I've never eaten anything so delicious!"

Mrs. Cartera beams with pride and explains in detail how she prepares the *fritanga*. If there is anything she loves more than dressing up, it's cooking and eating. Like mother, like daughter, because after Fifi polishes off the *platanos*, she regains her sweet nature. That is, until Juanito asks the wrong question.

"Is Papi coming to the fashion show?"

"No, he is not," barks Mrs. Cartera.

"But I want him to see me on the runway!" Juanito says in protest.

Fifi starts bawling again and jumps up from the table. Now Aphro's eyes soften, like she finally gets why I was fretting. She jumps up and follows Fifi. The rest of us eat our lunch in silence.

After we finish, Fifi and Aphro come back out so we can finish our agenda: the fittings. I figure it's best to get Fallon's fitting out of the way first. I hand her the pink bustier to put on, and just like we imagined, she has a hissy fit at the sight of her abundant cleavage, which isn't even spilling over. "I told you I do not want to leave my tatas on the runway!" she exclaims.

"Fallon, I'm adding a ruffle at the *top* of the bustier—you're not going to see anything," I assure her. "This is just a fitting—the bustier is *not* finished!"

"It better not be—or you can let Fabbie Tabbie shake her tail feather in this one, okay?" she hmmphs.

I smile sweetly and keep pinning Fallon, because I've learned my biggest lesson as a house leader: when others fret, keep your lips sealed. Fallon loves getting the last word in edgewise and otherwise.

Alas, it's a lesson that Aphro hasn't caught on to yet. "Miss Fallon, no one is interested in ruffling your feathers," she adds.

"Oh, so now I have feathers like *Big Bird?*" she asks defensively. "You don't know what it's like to wear a size 40D bra and have guys staring at your tatas."

"I know what it's like," counters Fifi. "I hate it!"

"Oh, awright," Fallon says, giving in. "Just don't start crying again, please."

Fifi giggles. "I won't if you're happy with your outfit."

"Delirious," snaps Fallon.

"Awright, you're up, supermodel," I coo to Aphro. "I have to fit you for the faux-leather skirt. I'm so excited. When others said I would fail, I went faux and pulled it off!"

Fifi shoots me a look.

"I didn't mean you, Fifi—I meant Nole!"

"Ooooh, don't y'all get me caught up in any catfight," warns Aphro as she slips into the skirt.

"We won't, trust," I assure her, ogling my handi-work. The skirt fits Aphro like a glove. "I admit the brainstorm was a late entry—but the faux-leather miniskirts instead of chiffon ones was a good call, no?"

"But I love the chiffon," says Angora, the Southern belle.

"Yes, for the evening skirts—but we don't have to OD on the flimsy, do we?" I ask.

"Nor the flimflam," points out Aphro.

Fifi darts her eyes over at us—again. Every sound bite spreads suspicion about her parents' separation. I feel for her. Everyone in her five-story building is buzzing about it—thanks to the clothes flying out the window.

Left to Fallon, the chiffon ball skirts could fall by the wayside, too. "This doesn't make my hips holla?"

Now Fifi frets. She examines the waist like a foren-sic scientist. "We could take out some of the gathering."

"No, I like it—it's very Marie Antoinette," I say with conviction.

"Who is that?" asks Fallon bluntly. "And why don't you let her wear it?"

I refrain from filling Fallon in about the former

queen of France and focus on the ball skirt. "Fallon, can you trust me—the poufiness is really flattering."

Flustered, Fallon rolls her eyes. Now Mink and Angora step into their chiffon ball skirts. Fallon eyes her slimmer counterparts slipping into the same silhouette. Surprisingly, she likes what she sees. "Oh, it is cute, kinda princessy," she relents.

"And wait till people see the three of you swooshing down the runway in a princess procession," I add quickly.

"We love princesses!" giggles Mink.

"Now it's your turn," Angora says, excited. She's referring to the feline fatale ensemble I'm wearing for my one memorable turn on the runway with Fabbie Tabbie—the furbulous finale. I'm determined to cast aspersions on Dame Leeds's doubts. "This has to be the ultimate sendoff."

Aphro agrees with me. "Trust—you are saving the best for last."

"You're not jealous, I hope," I query seriously.

"Get over yourself. Just because you're going to the Lipstick Lounge . . . ," swipes Aphro.

"You are?" Elgamela asks, excited.

"Thanks for letting the cat out of the bag."

"Spill the refried beans, already!" coaxes Elgamela.

"Ice Très invited me to the Lipstick Lounge to hear this singer, Alyjah Jade, perform," I say, smiling.

"Wow, I so want to go to that place!" coos Mink Yong. "Sil Lai told me all about it! She's going!"

"Oh, right," I say, like I didn't remember that Sil Lai and Mink Yong are friendly—and part of the Asian clique at our school. "Um, I thought Sil Lai said she still had classes left at Barbizon and can't go?"

"Oh, right," Mink Yong says, like she forgot that tiddy. "She's not sure yet."

"What does Sil Lai go to Barbizon for?"

"She's training to become a Barbizon model instructor. She wanted to be a model really badly, but she's too short. So if you can't be one, you can teach them," Mink explains matter-of-factly.

"Oh, right," I say, finally grasping the reason why Sil Lai shows me shades of Gucci Envy.

Bluntly, Aphro voices what I'm thinking. "So she's just another shortie in the model haterade convention?"

My cell phone rings. I pull it out of my purse to answer it. "It's Diamond Tyler," I mouth to Aphro and Angora. The rest of the models remain quiet while I speak to the touchy animal activist. I tell her about our evening-gown fitting and she calmly replies: "See, I knew you could pull this off without me."

"I need a favor from you, Diamond," I admit, desperate to contain this situation. "I need for you to keep this drama between us—can you do that and not let on to the Catwalk office?"

"Yes," says Diamond. "I'll be at the fashion show—I'll help as a dresser."

"Well, I was thinking—I have a far more important task for you and your design talents."

"I told you, I can't handle the designing stuff," she balks.

"I know, I know. That's not it. Would you mind attending the other fashion shows and reporting back to us at the run-through what you saw? We're not going to get to attend the other four fashion shows, but we at least want to know what they're doing," I stress, appealing to Diamond's SOS sensibility. "Please, come to our rescue?"

"Oh, I would love to do that," Diamond says humbly. "But I thought Ruthie Dragon wanted to?"

"She does, but I want you to be my eyes and ears at the other fashion shows because you're a designer at heart," I say, selling it hard. "Ruthie is better suited for manning the Heels on Wheels cart in the lobby instead." Of course, what I haven't told Diamond is that my fiery assistant doesn't know about her Wild Card assignment.

"Oh, okay, I'll do it," Diamond says, like she's trying her best to be agreeable since she has us caught in her crosshairs.

"Purrfecto," I sigh, super relieved. "I knew we could find a mutually agreeable task. We're a team. And I want it to stay that way. If word of another defection got out, the House of Pashmina would be fried, finished, and flotsamed!"

I hold my breath for a second, secretly hoping Diamond will just jump back into the fashion fray, but after a few more seconds of steely silence I realize we've passed that stop at Petticoat Junction.

"You're so funny, Pashmina. I'll be at the fashion shows, then come to the run-through. I promise," she says, referring to the term used for those precious few and highly frenetic hours in which we rehearse before the actual show.

"I thank you in the name of the rumba, the mambo, and the cha-cha-cha," I say, relieved.

Diamond chuckles. "What is that supposed to mean?"

"It's the highest order of thank-you from the Fritanga dynasty," I jest.

"What do you think Ruthie Dragon is gonna say when she finds out you dumped her for Diamond?" Aphro asks.

I balk. "Do you know what an honor it is to man the Heels on Wheels cart?"

Leave it to Aphro to squash my schemes and dreams. "Well, I sure hope she thinks so."

"Never mind," says Fifi, who is anxious for me to try on my purrlicious pink creation for my fitting. After washing her hands, she pins me into the fuchsia tatter-sall skirt with matching bustier.

Stellina's eyes pop. "I wish I could wear *that*."

"You are definitely the Princess of Pink now," confesses Aphro.

Everyone beams at me while Fifi pins me in all the right places into my pinkness. I stare back at my reflection in Fifi's living room mirror. "The Princess of Pink. I could get used to that title!"

FASHION INTERNATIONAL 35th ANNUAL
CATWALK COMPETITION BLOG

New school rule: You don't have to be ultranice, but don't get tooooo catty or your posting will be zapped by the Fashion Avengers!

DON'T CALL IT A COMEBACK

The invited few didn't know why they were being beckoned to the Fashion Auditorium for a Special Event. Like an ermine caught in a mink trap, I got caught up in the unscripted turn of dramatic events. Of course, the Teen Style Network thought they were living in a field of ratings dreams when the Benny Ninja vs. pseudo Willi Ninja, Jr., battle was staged right before their nosy lens. Frankly, all the catty students at Fashion International should send me thank-you notes in origami shurikens for providing an extra helping of drama to their boring lives—and giving them something JUICY to run home and tell their friends and families about besides the Spinelli chop-shop trial.

But it's time to set the record straight. I may have changed my moniker to C. C. Samurai, but my agenda is still the same: to win the Catwalk Competition. Only difference is, I won't be attempting to accomplish this task by any means necessary—unlike

certain tawdry, ambitchous others who
shall remain nameless. See, due to my
recent drama I learned a valuable lesson: I don't have to play dirty to get
what I want—and rightly deserve. I can
stay on my game AND be true to my
vision—and mine always was, and always
will be, to be serving men's style
without traditional boundaries. My vision was not a lie. I know I adopted a
false moniker out of deep admiration
for what Willi Ninja stood for—so keep
basking in that admission of guilt until you get caught in one of your own.
But don't call it a comeback, okay,
because I never left the game. And
please don't believe your own hype:
everybody has their own shades of
truth, so keep coloring with Crayolas.
I'm just here to publicly tell you
that I've put my Crayola box of ficti-
tious crayons away and don't need to
draw with them anymore to get what I
want. I'm not saying I don't love the
drama—if I didn't, I wouldn't be attending a school that could rightly be
named Drama Central—but I've discovered that I like winning better. And I
have what it takes to be a real contender in this game of fashion,
whether the haters like it or not. So
I want to publicly thank the revered
Benny Ninja, father of the House of
Ninja, formed by the fierce late Willi
Ninja, for pulling the sleeve on my
warrior outfit. And like a certain

Catwalk contender told me the other day: may the best house win!

Posted by Twirl Happy1992 at 21:43:17

14

I definitely dig SoHo, the artistic downtown section south of Houston Street in New York City, where the most feline fatale designers in the galaxy, like Anna Sui, Tarina Tarantino, and Betsey Johnson, have their flagship boutiques. Within these five square blocks of prime Manny Hanny real estate lies a veritable design mecca where I hope the flagship boutique for my dream retail chain, PURR UNLIMITED, will also be in the mix one day. I can dream, can't I?

The grooviest restaurants and clubs are also in SoHo, and right now I'm headed to the tartiest new addition: The Lipstick Lounge on Broome Street. Even though it's coming down to the wire for my Catwalk team and our fashion show, I had to put this on my checklist so I can make things right with Ice Très. At least, that's what I've been telling myself. But with Diamond Tyler acting skittish, like a sheep with a USDA clip hanging on her ear; shady Shalimar setting her sights on a serious sabotage mission; and cuckoo Chintzy Colon on the loose like a rogue CIA agent, I can't risk any more negative energy ricocheting around the House of Pashmina until the winner of the Catwalk competition is chosen and goes home with a Big Willie trophy.

Speaking of negative energy, the Shrek-sized bouncer manning the door of the Lipstick Lounge has it in Kate Spades. "Are you on the guest list?" he asks like a professional bully.

Ice Très didn't mention anything about a guest list. I hide my flustered reaction and smear on the charm like moisturizing lipstick in the shade Please Let Me In. "Um, I'm a friend of Abraham's?" I pull a five-dollar bill from my pink leopard-print denim shoulder bag and wave it like a white flag, the internationally recognized truce symbol.

With a military poker face, the seven-foot-tall giant looks at me like I'm a freshly minted cuckoo and orders: "He's definitely not on the list. Step aside, please."

Switching gears pronto, I stutter: "I'm sorry—um— I'm supposed to be meeting a friend here—Ice Très Walker?"

The bouncer doesn't say a word or crack a smile, but I've obviously said the magic password, because he parts the Red Sea—aka the velvet rope—and nods for me to enter paradise.

"Thank you!" I say, relieved.

Once inside, I scan the hypervamped room with its decor straight out of a Lady Gaga video: feathered red lampshades plopped on end tables with carved legs and glistening disco balls hanging from the ceiling. Searching for signs of Ice Très and coming up empty, I plop down in the nearest vacant red velvet love seat, which is as enticing as a lush poppy field. Nervously, I pull out my cell phone to see if Ice Très has sent another text, but he hasn't. Still unsettled, I reread the last text he sent me to make sure I didn't miss an important message in the bottle: "Boo kitty. On my way. Can't wait to see you!" Ressured that I'm on the right kitty trail, I decide to sit tight, taking a deep breath and sinking into the plush velvet cushions. Adjusting my eyes to the dim, moody atmosphere, I turn and gaze at the empty stage, slowly focusing on the shadowy figure of a girl with long, sparkling ruby locks peeking from behind the folds of opulent red velvet drapes in the left corner. Now the girl with the ruby locks emerges a few more inches from behind the fold in the drapes and the profile of her haughty aquiline nose emerges. I watch her, fascinated, wondering if it's Alyjah Jade, the singer who's performing tonight. Tall and slender, she's dressed in a tight black minidress with over-the-knee black boots, and is having an animated conversation with someone who still remains behind the drapes. She tilts back her head, laughing—all pale ivory skin, ruby red lips, and blazing bordeaux hair with iridescent glints galore. As I ponder whether the singer's waist-length hair is courtesy of Mother Nature or Adorable Hair extensions, the person with whom she is kanoodling also emerges from behind the curtains and embraces her in a tight hug. My mouth drops at the zebra sighting—the mink hat that belongs to none other than Zeus Artemides! I freeze inside, wondering why Zeus didn't tell me he was migrating to the Lipstick Lounge tonight. Then I remember that I never mentioned to him that I was coming, either, or even more salacious—that I have a date with Ice Très! Furiously, I calibrate the plausibility of my explanation: *It was a last-minute thing. I didn't even know I was going before six o'clock.*

Seeing them locked in their embrace, I wonder if Alyjah Jade is one of Zeus's childhood friends, or a friend from his old high school, Benjie Bratt. Zeus is superaffectionate, so I try not to trip about how up-close and personal he is with the redheaded Goldilocks. He gets touchy-feely with Elgamela Sphinx, too, which used to make me think they were dating until I found out for sure that they aren't. I sit frozen like a pink statue, wondering if there's an escape clause or a secret trapdoor into which I can vanish. As I contemplate how to handle the situation, I'm distracted by a familiar voice streaming from my left.

"Hey, boo kitty, sorry I'm late!" says Ice Très, bending over to kiss me on the cheek before he slithers next to me on the sofa.

I don't know how Ice Très always manages to sneak up on me, and this time I blurt out this observation.

"That's because no one ever pays attention to graffiti messengers—we just sort of blend into the background, along with the plight of urban decay," he says, like the last street poet.

"I see," I respond, slowly digesting Ice Très's gift for dropping knowledge.

Prattling on, Ice Très reveals the holdup. "My uncle Ray-Ray gave me a ride, but somebody ran over a skunk on the FDR and things definitely got a little hairy."

"And here I thought you were skateboarding to SoHo," I respond nervously, trying not to look in Zeus's direction.

Ice Très grins, setting off his goofy smile with dimples to match—positively infectious.

"How do you know it was a skunk that got run over? You saw it?" I ask, trying to distract myself from the Zeus sighting.

"Nah, but I smelled it—and so did half of Manhattan," Ice Très says, scrunching his nose in disgust.

"I don't know—this gory story sounds like a Diamond Tyler tale," I tease, while watching Zeus and the girl with the ruby hair out of the corner of my eye on the sly.

"Come on now, you think Diamond's the only one with close encounters of the animal kind? It's a jungle out there, boo kitty. You know that," jokes Ice Très.

"Actually, I do," I concede. "Speaking of, how did you get a hookup on the guest list here?"

"Oh D-Man at the door lives in my building," Ice Très says proudly, focusing on the unique design of my pants. "Wow, I dig those pants—did you make them?"

"Yeah, I did—I'm really into unconstructed edges and puzzle-piece design these days. You know how it is as an artist, you're always on to the next new thing," I say, riffing.

Zeus suddenly spots us in our cozy corner like *he's* looking for the next new thing. Now I'm try to decipher the pieces of the puzzled expression on his face as he walks toward us.

"Hey, what are you two doing here?" asks Zeus, his eyes darting from Ice Très to guilty *moi*.

"Same thing you are, I guess," quips Ice Très. "Checking out the new establishment."

I wait for Zeus to offer his explanation, but he doesn't. He stands there, looking slightly distressed. I squirm on the velvet love seat, wracking my brain trying to think of something to smooth things over like Velveeta cheese. "Um, I heard about this singer from Sil Lai," I pipe up feebly. "Do you know her?"

"Um, yeah, I do," says Zeus.

"Oh, is that her? The girl with the ruby locks?" I muse, just checking to make sure she is Alyjah Jade, although the possibility of two girls in the same room with long sparkling ruby—not red, mind you—hair is about as low as two wearing my unique puzzle-piece hot-pink pants.

"Um, yeah, that's her," Zeus confirms. But he still doesn't elaborate.

I'm dying to ask Zeus how he knows Alyjah Jade, but I'm too busy wondering if he's upset with me because I'm here with Ice Très. Zeus fidgets with his brim, confirming my suspicions. Obviously he is thrown off his Mad Hatter axis by this unexpected scenario.

Unaware that he has been dropped into the Bermuda Triangle, Ice Très keeps the frothy flow going. "I hear she's an amazing songwriter, too," he offers. "My cousin goes to the same high school she does—Ocean County Vocational Tech."

"Oh, really?" Zeus asks, surprised.

"Yeah, Kite Walker—he's a senior there. She's a sophomore now, right?"

"Um, yeah," Zeus responds, still fidgeting.

"Wow—look who else is here," Ice Très announces, motioning across the room. "It's an F.I. reunion."

We all turn around to witness Sil Lai and Farfalla being seated in the cushy love seat directly across from us.

"The spies have arrived," jokes Ice Très.

"What do you mean?" I ask, paranoid.

"You know, they work for Ms. Lynx, boo kitty—but it's a joke," Ice Très clarifies upon noticing the freaked-out expression on my face.

Zeus seems freaked out, too. "Listen, I have to take care of something, but I'll see you two in a few."

Zeus smiles as he exits but refrains from winking at me like he usually does. I feel crushed. No way José did I have any intention of hurting him. Now I'm sure. I like Zeus *mucho*.

After Zeus bounces, Ice Très exhales, like he's relieved. "He was acting a little weird, wasn't he?"

"Um, yeah," I reply guiltily.

Upon dispensing his observation, he wastes no time getting back to his own agenda: impressing me. "I'm glad you came," he says sweetly. "It means a lot to me."

"Um, yeah," I repeat, still perplexed. "But what were the odds of running into Zeus? They had to be one out of two hundred sixty-nine million—just like the chance of winning the New York Lottery Mega Millions jackpot." (My mom isn't the only one who can ply innocent bystanders with statistics, okay?)

"I want you to check this out," Ice Très says, like a man on a mission. He pulls out a rumpled sketch pad to show me his latest graffiti art—charcoal abstracts with shadowy words in the background: *Black. Born. Bred.*

I examine Ice Très's art, and for the first time, I really look at his interpretations and the complexity of the designs, the moody subtext. "Wow, these snap, crackle, *pop*," I critique honestly.

"This is part of my new series called 'Black and White.' I'm gonna put them on canvas, and on the back of white denim jackets," he explains proudly.

"Wow—Urban Thug. I can see your whole concept now," I observe, examining the graffiti-inspired art. "I see the whole collection: wearable art from the street. I dig it."

Ice Très peers at me as if he's trying to figure out if I really like his work, so I reassure him.

"This is really amazing. You have such a gift for tactile realness," I offer, trying to run it through my mental art catalog. "It reminds me of something."

"Basquiat?" asks Ice Très.

"What?" I respond.

"Jean-Michel Basquiat," he repeats.

I conjure up an image of Jean Paul Gaultier and respond, "Is he a designer, too?"

Ice Très looks alarmed. "You're sleeping on the greatest graffiti artist of the twenty-first century. Jean-Michel Basquiat."

"Oh, right," I say, suddenly remembering snippets about the late legendary artist from Brooklyn who ran with the Andy Warhol crowd. He was the darling of the eighties art scene. "Please forgive me. I got confused."

"Forgiven," he says. "Basquiat is my idol.

Brooklyn-born—and an integral part of the New York art scene. He ran with Julian Schnabel, too."

"Brooklyn-born. You dig that," I tease him.

"Well, artists born anywhere in New York, actually—like you. You take it for granted, being raised here. As for me, I'm soaking it up." Ice Très beams at me intensely. "Washington State? Nothing like this. Only thing I miss is that overpass on Highway Twenty, where I drew my first tag. That'll always be my touchstone."

"Yeah, I know. Now tell me something about you that nobody knows," I say, squelching the déjà vu feeling from my date with Zeus. And the guilt.

"Oooh, boo kitty, that's a good one. Awright. I was going to enroll in Dalmation Tech High, which is how I came across Fashion International on the other side of the street. My father wanted me to be an electrical engineer, just like him."

"Wow," I say.

"Yes, I'm most gifted in the electrical arena, just like my dad—but I have the soul of an artist," he humbly explains. "I still always have my tools with me, though, just in case." Ice Très opens his messenger bag to show me a melton cloth holding some tools. "Always be prepared for life's emergencies. That's what my Dad *drilled* into me."

I chuckle at his pun. "Wow, you're amazing. And it's so amazing how you draw. It really is."

"You're amazing, too," Ice Très adds.

"Not being able to draw well is the reason why I could never call myself a legit fashion designer. Call me old-school, but sewing or draping is one thing. Capturing the architecture of a garment in an illustrative blueprint—now, that's paramount," I explain humbly. "I see myself more as a modelpreneur, because I can bring all the elements together."

"Wow. You broke that down—just like an artist," Ice Très assures me.

"Really?" I ask, gazing into his eyes for approval while still trying to hide my guilt.

Ice Très senses my discomfort. "What's on your mind?"

Suddenly, the lights dim. "I was thinking that either I'm going blind, or the lights are getting dimmer in this joint," I joke, deflecting from my internal drama.

A waitress in a slinky red Lycra minidress comes over and smiles. "*Bonsoir.* Can I get you anything?" she asks.

"Two Pinktinis," orders Ice Très.

"*Merci,*" she says as she smiles and walks away.

"You're going to have one?" I ask, grinning.

"Why not? When with Pink Head, I should drink pink," he quips.

"How did you know my nickname is Pink Head?" I ask, surprised.

"I know a lot of things about you," Ice Très informs me, pleased.

"Like what?"

"That you don't trust me because you think I was playing you—but I wasn't. I liked you from the very beginning, but Shalimar was gassing me up and telling me that she was going to help me with my Urban Thug line as long as I didn't have any contact with you," explains Ice Très candidly. "But I was stupid, so I listened to her. I figured that way I wouldn't get the two of you caught up in a catfight. I thought I could keep the two things separate—business and realness."

"Too late about the catfight," I say, miffed, because now I have another piece of corroborating evidence about Shalimar's espionage intentions.

Ice Très comprehends the catty situation. "Shalimar is jealous of you. Maybe it's that hair," Ice Très says with a smirk, stroking my curls.

"Yeah, real hair—and a real mess," I giggle uncomfortably.

"And a realness, period. She was constantly talking about you," he reveals.

I suppress the urge to ask what Shalimar said about me while Ice Très continues breaking it down.

"She's got the big-time backing, no doubt, because of her father, but you're a lot more honest—and adorable. And trust, she knows that."

I smile, basking in Ice Très's compliment. Nervously, I can't help glancing around the room, secretly wondering whether Zeus has returned, but I don't see him. "I wonder where Zeus had to dash to that was so important," I say nonchalantly, trying to keep my concern Lite FM.

The music pipes up over the loudspeaker—a song by the artist Pink. I smile at Ice Très and he smiles right back.

Now our red waitress returns. "*Pour vous*," she says chirpily, placing two menus in front of us.

"Do you speak French?" I ask her, impressed.

She keeps smiling. "A little. *Un peu.*"

While scanning his menu, Ice Très asks me, "Do you really like my work? Your opinion is important to me."

"Yes, I do," I say, nodding.

Ice Très grins, sliding his precious notebook into his sleek black carrying case.

"I really do," I repeat. "You're really talented."

"So are you."

The room is completely full now, and Alyjah Jade appears center stage in front of the microphone with a guitar in her hand. A band joins her, assembling in the background.

"Awright now," says Ice Très. "Nothing I dig more than real instruments."

Alyjah Jade starts strumming the guitar and singing

a beautiful song. Her voice is pure, sparkling clear, like Swarovski crystals line her throat. Suddenly, I realize that I know that voice. "That's the girl singing the remix of 'I Will Survive' that Zeus produced for our fashion show!" I whisper to Ice Três.

He nods approvingly while I get a creepy feeling inside that I can't shake. *Why didn't Zeus tell me that the singer on the track was Alyjah Jade? I would have been so impressed.*

Ice Três smiles at me, quieting the chatter of so many questions in my head. I'm hypnotized, listening to Alyjah Jade singing and basking in the presence of true artists—both her and Ice Três. After she quietly finishes the song "One Bright Penny," she talks to the audience, letting us know that she writes all her songs. She also points out her father—one of the musicians accompanying her in the background. I feel a twinge of sadness in my chest for my unknown father. Ice Três looks at me seriously, as if he knows what I'm thinking.

Now Alyjah Jade coos into the microphone, "This next song, 'He's Mine,' which I wrote last fall when I began my freshman year, is dedicated to my one true love—my boyfriend, Zeus."

Ice Três smiles, nodding his head in a eureka moment, as if he finally grasps what brought Zeus to the Lipstick Lounge tonight. "Oh, I got you."

Meanwhile, I freeze inside like a Dominican

Popsicle, wondering if maybe I heard Alyjah Jade wrong. No way she said what I think she said. I'm so stunned that I can't even speak without my voice cracking to ask Ice Très if Alyjah Jade just said "my boyfriend, Zeus."

I look around furtively in the dark, desperately trying to spot the mink zebra hat that I've come to know stripe by stripe. Ice Très looks around, too, like he wants to give the Mad Hatter a shout-out.

"Where'd he go?" Ice Très asks.

I sit frozen, my mind floating above me; then I stare down at my puzzle-piece pants, trying to piece together the puzzle of Zeus. I rack my brains, trying to remember whether I ever asked Zeus if he had a girlfriend. Meanwhile, Alyjah Jade has just finished the song she dedicated to her one and only, and she proceeds to melt into another one of her original songs. "Now, this song, 'These Lies,' I wrote for my old boyfriend," she chuckles, then strums the guitar slowly, introducing a haunting melody. And as she sings, her voice is filled with layers of disturbed emotion.

> "Pinocchio, it's time to shrink your nose—
> It's stretching across the universe.
> And don't, don't you know if you don't let go
> These lies will break the curse?
> These lies. These lies. These lies. These lies."

Against my will, I become unfrozen, the torrent of warm tears streaming down my face melting away the icicles of shock. *How could Zeus hurt me like this?* I try to remember every conversation we ever had. Suddenly, I remember his shark collection. Now I know why he likes sharks—because he himself is a girl-eating, flesh-tearing, predatory shark. Suddenly, it doesn't matter whether I asked him if he had a girlfriend. He should have told me all about his girlfriend with the ruby locks and the achingly beautiful voice. He should have told me! As Alyjah's singing strikes more chords of dissent within me, I recall my fashion frightmare. Zeus left me backstage—he wasn't there for me when I needed him. I shriek now, thinking about the Catwalk competition. What am I going to do?

Alyjah Jade continues singing, strumming my pain with her verses:

> *"You can only keep a perfect straight face on*
> *for so long.*
> *You're about to lose it. Is this all a joke,*
> *Just a hoax? I don't know, but the pieces fit.*
> *And you don't see that it's so obvious, and*
> *I know, I know."*

Tears continue to pour down my face like a never-ending faucet. Not a dribbly faucet like the one in my house, but one with full hydraulic force. Out of my Niagara Falls stream, I can see Sil Lai and Farfalla looking over at me curiously, but I don't care. Ice Très reaches over and touches my hand, squeezes it hard. He probably thinks I'm deeply moved by the song, which I am, but not for the reasons that he assumes. After Alyjah Jade finishes, everyone claps in appreciation. Everyone except us, because Ice Très won't move his hand from on top of mine. I don't move his hand away, either. I turn and look at him, my eyes wet with tears. He smiles at me. I smile back at him.

"Please don't lie to me anymore. I can't take anyone else lying to me," I say, breaking down into another round of fresh sobs.

"I promise. I won't lie to you ever again. You mean a lot to me," whispers Ice Très.

I can't stop sobbing, and Ice Très doesn't try to stop me or flip out about my freak-out. He just sits there, steady as a rock with his hand on mine, until the show is over, and so are my tears.

15

The fashion grapevine at Fashion International has more thorns than a vampire's rose garden, so I wasn't surprised that my Catwalk rivals—and everyone else at school except my immediate crew—had a field day with my embarrassing episode at the Lipstick Lounge. As for me, I've refused to clog or blog the Catwalk channels with tart grapes of wrath. For the next few weeks, I keep my exchanges with Zeus to Catwalk business.

"Honey, you should have known, Zeus is on the endangered species list: a shark in a zebra-striped mink hat," warns Nole, flicking the salt from his fingers each time he dips them into the bag of potato chips with vinegar. "Feline fashionistas, beware!"

"Why don't you say it a little louder so he can hear you," I hiss at Nole, who is sitting near me in Studio C.

Right now, Zeus is staring at me from across the room. He can't stand that I've put him on deep freeze.

"If it wasn't for Zeus, we wouldn't have trumped the Wild Card Challenge. Otherwise, I would have burned him like a frittata," I whisper to Fifi.

"I know, the Heels on Wheels cart turned out amazing," she responds.

"He should still apologize," insists Nole. Aphro can't resist—she reaches over to take a few chips out of Nole's bag.

"Yeah, like right about now," I decide. We've just finished our last runway training session before the fashion show, and enough time has passed since I got *smeared* at the Lipstick Lounge by the shocking discovery that Zeus has an übertalented girlfriend, Alyjah Jade, who has been strumming his übersized ego since seventh grade.

Of course, Angora tries to talk me out of confronting the Mad Hatter. According to her *Rules*, you're never supposed to let a guy see you perspire. "Pash, you've been ignoring him for weeks—and see how obsessed he's become with you? Guys love being ignored," claims Angora.

"Who cares?" warns Fifi. "Don't say anything to him about it, because he's going to squeeze the life out of you like an octopus!"

"No, he won't, because he's already given me a shark bite," I profess calmly. "He does owe me an apology, and now I'm ready to listen."

Meanwhile, Ruthie Dragon is vying for more attention, too. I told her I have something to discuss with her, and the truth is I can't put it off any longer, but I know she's not going to be a happy kitty after our convo. "Gimme a sec," I tell her.

I edge my way over to Zeus just in time to catch that familiar glint in his dark dreamy eyes.

Ignoring the sparks, I announce my agenda. "Listen, I just want to clear the air so we're on point next Friday at the fashion show."

"Awright," Zeus agrees, grinning slyly.

"Why didn't you tell me that you have a girlfriend?" I ask bluntly.

"You never asked me if I have a girlfriend," he insists, upon being catty-cornered.

"You never asked me if I wanted you to kiss me, but that didn't stop you from doing it!" I retort, grinding my teeth. "I just wish you had told me you've had a girlfriend since your sandbox days, okay? Can you dig that?"

"You know how much I dig you," Zeus coos, his eyes twinkling, trying to soften my serious stance.

But I'm not budging. "I dig you—not so much that way, okay? Soooo, just be on the premises three hours before the show and that will be the end of our gory story."

Zeus nods, smiling like he's impressed. It's obvious he still appreciates my diggable digs, if you catch my swift drift.

"So you'll report for triple duty for the run-through three hours in advance?" I confirm again.

Miffed, Zeus nods. He's so used to getting his charming way he can't understand why I won't let him butter me up. "Yes, I'll be there. And I still care about you. Deeply."

To keep my emotional distance, I purse my lips instead of puckering them. Amazingly, this self-help trick works better than a cold shower. "I should really thank you, because if it wasn't for you betraying my trust, I would have never allowed Ice Très to show me his true colors. And that would have been *my* loss."

Zeus flinches against his will. Now I realize he didn't know that inside tiddy about my Ice Très hook-up. Too bad.

"Oh. And you know what I dig about Ice Très—deeply? He doesn't divide his 'deep feelings' in half so he can share them with *two* girls!" I add for good measure.

Zeus starts to say something but backs off, leaving me to fumble with my Catwalk folders so I can wrap up this horse-and-phony show like a Venus flytrap.

Fifi, who has been hovering, helps with my paper trail. "At least you found out sooner rather than later," she offers as a booby prize, carefully placing the glossy magazine pages of selected hairstyles into the appropriate folders.

"*C'est vrai.* That's true," seconds Angora.

"Is it true you like these hairstyles?" I ask, changing the subject back to the fashion track.

Angora gazes at the chignon tear sheets I've collected. "Pash, bravo on the hairstyles. Only you would have thought of putting pink extensions in the ponytails and chignons," commends Angora.

"Thank you," I say, pleased, remembering the source of my inspiration—Alyjah Jade. Her burgundy locks sparked my own color cues. "What can I say? Inspiration really does come from everywhere—even during our darkest hour."

"You're so dramatic," snorts Aphro. "But I love the *I Dream of Jeannie* braid."

"Yes, I know—purrfect look for you, Miss Chiseled Cheekbones," I sigh.

"I'm just happy the pillbox hats came out. Making a pyramid would have been easier," Nole says, sweating. He takes out his monogrammed hankie to wipe his forehead. By instinct, Dame Leeds comes over, peeved, his spadey sense working overtime.

"I'll give you that—the pillbox hats are cute. But we still could have gone with the bob for the Chic Meets Street segment," he says belligerently.

"That's too much work—putting the hair up in braids, then removing the braids for a bob," I counter. Truth is, I vetoed most of Dame's butch-looking hairstyles because I didn't dig them.

Now Dame's second hairstylist in command, Liza

Flake, comes over to put in the same three cents. "Bobs would have looked cute."

"Ponytails are cuter," I insist.

The two breathe venom in my direction, which I ignore. "I'll see you two next Friday?"

"I guess so, even though I don't know why you don't just do the hair yourself since you don't listen to our opinions!" mumbles Dame.

"I absolutely need the two of you next Friday—will you be there?" I reiterate.

"Wouldn't miss it for the world," Dame says, relenting.

"We can't wait till next Friday," seconds model Mink Yong, tossing her bangs out of her eyes. She picks up her ever-present green Juicy drawstring tote and slings it over her shoulders like a sack of potatoes.

"Everybody ready?" I squeal. Now that all the models are ready to leave, I realize that it's time for my final pep talk. "This is our last meeting before our run-through on the day of the fashion show," I announce, hyping my models. "And we're ready as we're ever gonna be. Aren't we?"

"Yeah!" scream Kissa, Elgamela Sphinx, and Mink Yonk.

"So. Come next Friday, everyone must be at our designated tent in Lincoln Center three hours before showtime. Okay? *Tutti capito?*"

All my models nod. "You heard that—three hours before?" Nole says, nudging Zeus.

I smile tersely at the Mad Hatter, who stands in place—obviously he won't leave without an acknowledgment from me. Thankfully, my house leadership skills automatically kick in despite myself. "I'll see you next Friday—and thank you for everything. Without my models and my crew, I've got nothing but clothes on hangers."

Zeus nods in approval. "No, thank *you*," he says humbly.

I smile at Zeus and bite my tongue. I need him for next Friday night. And luckily, not before, thanks to Ice Très.

As if reading my mind in reverse, Zeus offers, "You sure you don't need me to come over and move the Heels on Wheels cart with you?"

"Nope. We got it under control—and thanks to you again, it's gonna be the Wild Card surprise of the evening," I spin confidently. "Ice Très's uncle Ray-Ray is coming by with his van to help us load." I neglect to mention to Zeus that this particular set of wheels also comes with the faint smell of skunk juice. Nonetheless, I love the sound of having my own personal transport. Zeus not so much, because he twitches nervously. Kinda the way I did right after I found out about Alyjah Jade.

"Oh, right," he says. "The Ice Très factor."

Frankly, I couldn't have gotten through the Zeus ruse without Ice Très stroking my fur and wounded ego every step of the way, every day. See, I finally broke down and told Ice Très what had happened. Ice Très was so upset, one day during lunch period in the Fashion Café he had to refrain from zapping Zeus with a chilled glass bottle of Nestea. But after having gotten suspended once for tagging the stairwell with that stupid cupid professing his love for me, Ice Très learned one thing: how to keep his cool in school.

"Awright, I gotta wrap this up like a falafel," I sign off. I motion around the room to all the paper cups and disarranged chairs.

Finally!" shouts Nole. For once, I don't mind his boisterous attitude. I'm just glad he has recovered from the shock of not dominating the fashion: Penelope is out; Fabbie Tabbie is in. But the truth is, now that I've slayed one dragon, it's time to deal with another. Ruthie Dragon sidles over, bright-eyed and bushy-tailed. Angora senses that fire-breathing tactics may ensue, so she motions for Aphro and Fifi to come to my defense.

"This is so exciting," coos Angora, smiling warmly at Ruthie. I love Angora for always knowing how to prime the fashion pump.

"I was thinking maybe we should have regular

Coca-Cola backstage, too, in case anyone wants it?" queries Ruthie Dragon, pen in hand, notebook poised.

"No way, José!" vetoes Fifi. "I'll drink it by the gallon—and I'm already going to be nervous enough!"

"Um, Ruthie, we're going to stick with water and Diet Pepsi for now. And I've got that all covered. It's at my house," I inform her, stalling.

"Oh?" she says, making a checkmark on a list in her notebook.

"Um, but I was thinking—you know, we've got enough dressers backstage, and Fifi is going to take over assisting me for the run of the show. So you know what would be the most awesome responsibility I can give you?"

The blood drains out of Ruthie's face like she's recovering from a slap. A hard one. "You're *not* telling me that I'm *not* going to be backstage to help with the fashion show?"

"I want you to have the honor of manning the Heels on Wheels cart in the lobby," I announce.

"Why would I want to be in the lobby instead of backstage!" she yelps.

"Are you serious? It would be an honor. You would be representing the House of Pashmina—meeting all the important guests and judges up close and personal, while we'll be in the back slaving away," I spout, trying to sell my position.

"And our charity angle for Heels on Wheels is so important," seconds Nole. "You'll be collecting all the footwear for the homeless shelter—that's such an important cause. I'd want to be hobnobbing with the guests if I could!"

Ruthie Dragon interrupts our sales spiel. "If it's so important, then why can't Felinez be out there in the lobby?"

"I need Fifi," I blurt out, before realizing how unimportant that makes Ruthie sound. "Fifi is a designer—if something goes wrong, we need her backstage to help!"

"Well, if you don't want me backstage, then you obviously don't need me," Ruthie fires off.

"Hold up—I thought the whole point of being on a team is to be a team player," Aphro interjects.

"The only thing the so-called team is doing is ganging up on me!" shouts Ruthie Dragon. "You can do that to Chintzy Colon, but you ain't doing that to me, okay?"

"Oh, Ruthie, that's not fair. Chintzy was a spy—we had no choice," balks Angora.

"Well, I've been treated like one," Ruthie Dragon confesses, finally revealing the root of the tension between us. "If Nole Canoli didn't want me here, you wouldn't even have put me on the team."

"And you were hired as an assistant, so why aren't you assisting?" needles Nole. "You saw *The Devil Wears*

Prada—you're lucky none of us asked you to fetch us ice cream cones from the North Pole!"

"Well, I'm not a dog, so I'm not about to roll over," hmmphs Ruthie Dragon. "If I can't be backstage, then I'm not doing anything."

"S-so you're not coming to the fashion show," I stutter, my cheeks burning from her fiery attack.

"I didn't say that. Do I have to repeat myself?"

"No, you don't," I relent.

Ruthie leaves us singed.

"What are we going to do?" Fifi frets.

"Light one of your candles," I sigh, defeated. "Then pray for a miracle."

"Meanwhile, can we please just go to Staples and pick up the Xeroxes of the program?" offers Angora.

"Oh, right," I say, flustered. That's what I love about Angora—she always knows how to press the Easy Button.

⌃⌐

On Wednesday, Angora comes over my house so we can email the House of Pashmina fashion show invitations to the guests from our combined crew lists. Then we fold the three hundred House of Pashmina programs in half. They'll be placed on the seats for the guests at our fashion show. "Oy, what a bummer we can't have goodie bags like Betsey Johnson has at her fashion shows," I gripe.

"Well, when you have Betsey Johnson money, you'll do just that," my mother yells from the kitchen. "And aren't you two going to eat with us?"

Chenille is already seated at the table. "Oy, she could have helped us fold the programs," I whisper to Angora, but motion with my eyeballs to tense Chenille, who has her arms crossed on her chest like she's guarding against any incoming requests.

"We're almost finished, and it was fun," Angora whispers back. "This neon pink really makes a statement."

"I know," I say gleefully, reading one of the programs for the millionth time. "The Heels on Wheels charity statement on the bottom makes the program look so much more, well, important."

"*C'est vrai*. It's true. *Très* important." Angora says sweetly.

The phone rings and my mother picks up the extension in the nook to answer it.

"Pashmina, it's for you," she yells.

"Oh, maybe it's Ice Très," I say, smiling. "Now, there is someone who wants to help every step of the way."

After a few moments on the phone with Dame, I realize that's exactly what I'm gonna need—*help!*

"This can't be happening!" I scream into the receiver. "It's *not* happening!" My knees buckle, so I plop down in a chair at the dinner table with my mom and Chenille, who suspends her forkful of green peas in midair, looking at me like I'm the cuckoo she always suspected.

"What's wrong?" my mom asks.

Ignoring her, I press my forehead with an open palm like I'm trying to rearrange my brains. "So what does this mean?" I ask sharply, demanding that Dame provide further clarification on this unexpected, unanticipated, unwanted Code Pink call.

"What part of 'Liza Flake fell down a flight of subway stairs' don't you understand?" Dame Leeds snarls back.

"So you're telling me she can't come to the fashion show—not even on crutches?" I shriek in disbelief. I feel my face flush with rage, and my left eye instantly starts twitching.

"Houdini couldn't come to the fashion show with a broken leg—hello!" snaps Dame Leeds.

At last, the levee has broken and the dam of tension that has been building up between Dame and me since day one is flooding the phone wires. "We have a fashion show to put on and no assistant hairstylist. Get a replacement!" I scream hysterically.

"Pashmina, you don't have to shoot the messenger!" snaps Dame Leeds.

"If I had a BB gun I would!" I snap back, twirling my hair uncontrollably.

"I'm going to ignore your unprofessional behavior like I always do," snarls Dame Leeds, "and I'll try to find a replacement. But it's not going to be easy. I don't like amateurs."

"Who does!" I snap.

When I release the phone back to its cradle, I try to explain to my mother what just happened, but as soon as I open my mouth, I burst into tears.

Angora rushes over. "What happened?"

Chenille resumes shoveling forkfuls of peas, releasing a sly smile. My mom waits patiently for me to regain my composure so I can tell her. "That was Dame Leeds, my lead hairstylist. He claims that Liza Flake, his second in command, has fallen and she can't get up," I say, releasing another round of sobs.

"What?" my mom asks, still not clear.

"She took a tumble on the IRT and missed her stop—at fashion stardom!" I start in. "I knew she was going to be a problem—I just knew it! But I had to hire her because Dame insisted. He also claimed she is the snap-in extensions queen, but the only thing I ever saw her snap was her Wrigley's gum, which annoyed me to no end!"

"So what are you going to do?" asks my mom. I should be used to her pat response after I whine about a problem, but it still jars me. In my mother's world, when there is a problem, all she wants to know is: what's the solution?

"I told him to find a replacement!" I blurt out defensively. "Oh, I knew that Liza Flake was going to be a problem. Maybe I'm psychic, too, like Fifi, because I swear I knew it!"

My mother brings me back to more practical matters. "You sure you want to leave something so important for him to do? I know when one of the salespeople flakes out—oh, sorry, I didn't mean to use that word."

"Oh, please, any word at this point is helpful," I say tearfully.

"Well, when one of the employees at the boutique doesn't show up for work, I don't wait for Roni to tell me what I know has to be done. I handle the replacements myself if I can," my mom explains.

The room gets quiet. I sit pondering my mother's advice. Racking my brains, I try to think of a qualified hairstylist who isn't already in another house, but I can't.

Angora has other ideas. "Why don't we let Chenille do it?"

I dart my eyes at Angora like *Why don't you stick to the dating advice, please!*

"I'll do it," pipes up Chenille. "Show me the hairstyles."

My mom looks at me like *Don't even think about saying anything stupid.*

"Okay," I agree. I go get the sketches for the

hairstyles. "We're slicking back the hair, then mixing the ponytails with pink hair extensions," I explain carefully.

"I can do that," Chenille says confidently.

"For the Chic Meets Street segment, the models are wearing pillbox hats," I add. "Then for the evening segment, we're leaving in the pink extensions but turning the ponytails into chic chignons pinned under."

"I can do that, too," Chenille says in the same deadpan tone.

"You sure?" I squeak.

My mom looks at me sternly.

"I'm sure," says Chenille.

I pick up the phone and dial Dame back to let him know the Code Pink has been handled.

"Now tomorrow I have to file a member replacement form with the Catwalk office," I say to him, still in shock. "Wish me luck."

"You'll need more than that," admits Dame Leeds.

This time I don't snap at him, because he's right.

⌐ ⌐

The next day when I go to the Catwalk office to file a replacement form to officially record Chenille as Liza Flake's replacement, I can't help but notice the smirk on Sil Lai's face, even though she is trying to suppress it.

I get paranoid, wondering if she knows about the Diamond drama or the run-in with Ruthie Dragon.

Luckily, Sil Lai tips her hand like a bad poker player. "Did you have fun at the Lipstick Lounge?"

Leave it to slippery Sil Lai to dredge up month-old drama. "Yes, I thought Alyjah Jade was amazing," I report, taking the high fashion road instead of resorting to refried gossip, which Sil Lai craves like leftovers. "But not as amazing as the House of Pashmina fashion show is going to be."

As I race out, Farfalla coos behind me. "Good luck. *Buona fortuna!*"

"Thank you!" I shout back, because luck is exactly what I need.

New school rule: You don't have to
be ultranice, but don't get tooooo
catty or your posting will be zapped
by the Fashion Avengers!

WILD THINGS

Next Friday, the place to be will
be watching the five fashion shows in
the Catwalk competition. Yes, all bets
are on: in the biggest pot so far, the
winner snags a BlackBerry Torch. Luckily, not everyone in New York City
knows about this hot ticket happening,
otherwise F.I. fashionistas would not
be able to vie for front-row seats
(all right, second-row) in the fashion
tents at Lincoln Center.

As in all coveted contests, however, you can always count on a few
leaks. We thrive on leaks. So here's
the leak of the week: everybody is
trying to figure out what each house
is doing for the Wild Card Challenge.
Each house was told to incorporate an
element of surprise into their fashion
show that reflects their theme. Huh?
Ms. Lynx was working those spots overtime to come up with that one. Anyway,
we hear one house is gonna pop the
fake fizzy for guests to sip while the
models serve fashion on the runway.
(Serving bubbly style, get it?) Another house has lost their shoes (or
their mind), because their models are

going to be barefoot. Now, this one we don't get—and maybe it would be a good idea if the fashion shows were still held at Bryant Park instead of Lincoln Center. (Barefoot in the park, get it?) Frankly, it sounds too *Into the Wild* for our stylish tastes.

Of course, everyone wants to know what that certain overfunded house is going to incorporate into their show, because frankly, they're a "shoe-in," but so far the intel has been shaky. We do hear it has something to do with ambition, possibly to go with their theme. (Step on Everyone to Get Ahead?)

That brings us to an update, since one contestant is out of commission and won't be fulfilling her duties in the Catwalk competition. Apparently, Liza Flake is in traction, holed up at her house in Never Again Land. The question is, how did Liza Flake break her leg? We hope the rumors are not true—that someone sent Liza flying down a flight of subway stairs. (So much has been going on in that catty house, we don't know what to believe!)

That's it for now—except you know that expression break a leg? Let's not jinx anyone else by using that expression at the Catwalk competition, okay? So, to all the contestants, we'll see you on Friday, and please, don't break a leg!

Posted by Givers and Takers at 05:07:10

16

When we park the Heels on Wheels cart in the lobby of the fashion tent on the appointed Friday afternoon, four hours before SHOWTIME in capital letters, we're still not sure who is going to helm it.

"I've left Ruthie *mucho* messages. What else can I do?" I complain about my assistant, who is MIA.

"You should have told her sooner she was exiled to Siberia," hisses Nole, panting as he pushes one end of the cart.

"I was still singed from her last fire-breathing blast, so forgive *moi* for waiting," I retort. "Besides, I don't need her backstage—I need her in the Wild, and that's what being a team player is all about, okay?"

"You know I'd do it, but then you'd get disqualified," offers Ice Très.

"Aw, how sweet—sickeningly sweet. Now I'm going to be ill," grunts Nole, letting go of the cart handle and panting.

Ice Très stares at our groovy charity creation with his artist's eye, then maneuvers it perpendicular to the entrance for maximum exposure to incoming traffic.

"Wow, this really is a kickin' cart," he says, satisfied, examining Fifi's hand-painted shoe illustrations. "She's got serious skills."

"I know. Fifi really put her foot in it!" I boast. Out of the corner of my eye, I see a team of security guards and Farfalla milling around the entrance for the other fashion shows; Farfalla is talking into her headset and holding a clipboard. Eyeing the cart, I order: "Cover it up!"

Ice Très drapes the dropcloth over the cart pronto. "And you gotta go. *Now.* Stop quacking." Only the members of my team are allowed backstage, and I don't want Ms. Lynx, or the beady eyes of her spies, spotting any irregularities on my already blemished—okay, bruised and battered—Catwalk scorecard.

"I'm gone—like graffiti. But I'll resurface right when you need me. You'll see," Ice Très says, planting a kiss on my forehead.

"Right, Houdini. In my dream? You appear backstage floating out of the curtain folds like that psycho in the movie *When a Stranger Calls Back.*" I giggle.

Ice Très's dimples deepen. "You just gave me an idea."

As he darts off, I squinch my nose, puzzled. "Okay, but I hate that movie."

Sally G., one of our designated dressers, also has an idea. "You guys head backstage for the run-through, and I'll wait here till you need me for the rehearsal."

"Yeah, that'll work," I say, snapping into leadership mode.

Zeus zooms into the lobby with Lupo, both with their respective equipment. I hand them the package of House of Pashmina programs to place on the guests' chairs. "Make yourselves useful—and don't miss a chair!" I coo.

"Will do. See you in a few," Zeus says, winking. Some habits die hard.

"See, the pep talk worked," adds Angora with a wink, imitating Zeus.

"Thank gooseness something is working!" I fret. "Do you think Diamond is really gonna go to the other fashion shows and spy for us? I hope she doesn't blow us off to attend a rhino rally."

"Stop it, Miss Purr. I spoke to D.T.—she's already 'in play,' as the operatives say in the CIA," barks Nole. Giggling, Felinez, Nole, Angora, and I head backstage with our precious cargo—the clothes and accessories, which have been kept under tighter wraps than the ancient Egyptian artifacts at the Metropolitan Museum.

Once backstage, Nole and I place the clothes on the two long racks in the order they'll appear in the show. Meanwhile, Felinez and Angora clip the Xeroxes of the line-up sheets above the garments in each segment. Each outfit has been given a number, and next to each number is the model who will be wearing that outfit.

"Okay, our first segment," I say, pointing to the kiddie-wear clothes. "We line up the graffiti T-shirts and pants for the boys and the ruffled sundresses and ruffled pants and tops for the girls."

"Where are the umbrellas?" Fifi panics.

"I thought you had them!" I shriek.

Fifi looks tearful. "No, I don't!"

"I have them, remember me?" shouts Aphro, barreling backstage with a huge plaid Chinatown shopping bag.

"Oh, right," I say. "We put them with the jewelry."

Aphro takes out the umbrellas and hands them to me, then plops down the cellophane bags holding the jewelry for each designated outfit. For the girls, pink ribbon bow necklaces with cat pendants get placed in bags and hooked on the back of the three junior girl models' hangers. Meanwhile, Fifi places the girls' neon pink sneakers and the boys' black sneakers at the base of the rack. Because Tracy Reese didn't have any children's footwear, we sprang for the sneakers at Daffy's. "I'm pleased as punch that we've still come in under our eighteen-hundred-dollar budget and three-hundred-dollar Design Challenge bonus."

"I don't believe that Shalimar has. Her reports are rigged," professes Aphro.

Zeus pops in. "My deck is set up. Need anything before we begin rehearsal?"

"Look who's so helpful now," I tease him.

"Not now, Miss Purr!" snaps Nole. Nole takes the two down vests—one pink and one green—for the Urban Gear segment from a garment bag and fluffs them out. They get paired with the graffiti-stenciled pink leggings and T-shirts. I hold up a long stenciled tank top, which gets paired with the pink velour capris stenciled up the side with our slogans.

"Billboard *borsas* and knapsacks, please!" I shout at Fifi. For the Urban Gear segment, the female models carry totes with our faux ads inside them—my favorite is the fake movie poster for *Run, Pussycat, Run!* The male models have billboard bowling bags. For jewelry, Aphro inscribed bangles with our slogans—to be worn by the armful with each outfit in the Urban Gear segment.

"Next segment—Cinch and Sparkle!" I shout. Nole hands me the skinny mini-T-shirt dresses with our slogans printed on them—STYLE SHOULD MAKE YOU PURR and MEOWCH FOREVER!—to be worn cinched at the waist with superwide vinyl billboard belts.

"Why are there four billboard belts?" Nole asks.

"We decided the black and pink catsuits will be worn with the wide belts, too, and long over-the-knee boots."

"When did we change that?" balks Nole.

"Not now, Mr. Canoli," I bark at him. "It's been

done. Elgamela is up with Fallon in the bathing suit segment after that—it's easier for her to slip out of the T-shirt dress and sandals than the catsuit and thigh-high boots!"

"Oh, right," he says, imitating me.

"God, I love those boots. Can we keep them?" Angora jests.

"Let's just say we owe Tracy Reese our first-born fashions from Purr Unlimited," I predict, taking the two inscribed cuff bracelets for the bathing suit segment and bagging them. Next, I place Elgamela's black maillot with high-cut thighs and cat-appliquéd booty on a hanger. Fallon will be wearing a tankini beneath a hot-pink and black flowing cover-up with a cat appliqué on its sheer nylon back.

My phone rings. "Omigod, it's Diamond!" I yelp, answering.

"Um, I know I maybe shouldn't tell you this, but I saw Willi Ninja—sorry, I mean, C. C. Samurai—unloading. He said to tell you he doesn't appreciate that you broke your promise," Diamond says, squeaking.

"What?" I respond, the blood draining from my face. Then it hits me like two tons of flubs! C. C. must think someone from my crew leaked that Wild Card barefoot tiddy posted on the blog.

"You tell him I didn't. We didn't!" I blubber. "A deal's a deal. I would never renege!" After an awkward silence, I realize that Diamond gets the drift. "Awright—hit me with a report."

"Okay. It's true—the House of Moet served fake bubbly in plastic flutes to the attendees," she reports. "Four attendants walked around—two guys, two girls— wearing black satin jackets with *House of Moet* in mustard yellow letters embroidered on the back. The guests were each given napkins—white ones—that had the image of a champagne flute on it and *Celebrate!* in black letters. Oh, and the napkins were paper."

I tap my foot impatiently, waiting for the good part, and notice the two floppy straw hats in the corner getting buried. Flailing my arm at Felinez, I point and mouth, *Hats for the swimwear—clip to the hangers!*

"Are you there?" asks Diamond.

"Yes, with bated breath!" I respond.

"The predominant colors were yellow and black— actually, there was too much black in the show," Diamond says, digressing. "But I really liked the eye shadow the models were wearing—navy blue shaded to the lid and below. Sorta eighties-looking."

"Wait—the judges—who are they?" I interrupt.

"Vanna Snoot from Snooty Models."

"Right, I knew that."

"Tarina Tarantino—she looked bored sometimes, but she'd catch herself. I swear I saw her checking her pink iPhone in her lap. And um, Benny Ninja—which you know—and Ms. Lynx—and um, sorry I forgot his name, but he's vice president at Macy's, or maybe president?" Diamond says apologetically.

"What? That's not fair! Macy's is owned by Federated Stores, and Anna Rex's father is an executive there!" I yelp. "So, no Betsey Johnson?"

"Nope, no Betsey Johnson."

"Oh, we are deep-fried," I predict, my armpits suddenly sautéing in perspiration.

"Do you want to hear about the clothes?" Diamond asks, hesitating.

"Yes—that's the main course!"

"Two short-short overall jumpsuits—no, three, one each in white, black and yellow, with polka-dot hankies tied around the neck, or hanging out the back pocket. Cotton hankies tied around the head went with jean leggings—lots of studs and grommets in the whole collection. Up the sides of the denim skirts and leggings. Baseball jackets that said *Majorette* on the back. The collection was very sporty—even the evening outfits, long denim strapless dresses with grommets. And a denim wedding gown with a veil. No pets."

"So, did you like it—not the part about no pets, obviously," I joke nervously.

"Yeah—I thought it was kind of one-note—very strong, um, sporty element. But I think it was supposed to be a statement about hip-hop—because—*Oh*, she played hip-hop songs through the whole show. But they closed with the song 'Celebration' by Kool and the Gang—you know, the white denim strapless bridal gown with calf-high white patent-leather boots."

Farfalla steps into the backstage area. I hurriedly get off the phone, whispering to Diamond, "Okay, call me back!"

Farfalla scans the area and I wonder what she's looking for. She glances down at the clipboard clutched in her hands and smiles officiously. "Everything okay?"

"*Yes!*" I squeal.

"Good. The Teen Style Network is coming your way to tape some footage of your rehearsal," she reports. "Just want to make sure everyone will be decent?"

"In every way!" I assure her. "We begin our run-through in one hour. Maybe they want to come then?" I ask, sweating profusely.

"I'll tell them," says Farfalla. "If you need anything, just have one of the security guards come look for me or Sil Lai."

"Yes, thank you, Farfalla," I coo. After she exits, I mutter under my breath. "Sil Lai? No thank you!"

While we finish lining up the looks, I'm dying to know what has been unveiled at the other fashion shows, but Nole wants an update now about Moet's. I fill him in while we finish lining the garments up in order. "Anna Rex's show finished now?"

Nole looks at his watch. "Almost." He rubs his weary, bulging eyes before he gazes steadily at the faux-leather miniskirt with tiered ruffles that I'm so proud of.

"Green with Gucci Envy?" I ask.

"Can't wait to see that one on," he admits. "You did good. My mother will be proud of us."

"My father won't," barks Fifi.

Fearful of another Fifi fretfest, I quickly shoot, "None of this could have been done without you."

"She's a genius," seconds Nole.

"Okay, Chic Meets Street segment—satin bomber jackets with chiffon miniskirts and one faux-leather skirt for Aphro," I read off the run-through sheet. Then I put the ruffled purple tank top with Aphro's skirt. One orange and one neon pink bandeau top for each of the jackets.

Nervously, I look at my watch. Where is Diamond's next call? "Where is she? Anna Rex's fashion show is over, isn't it?" I fret to Fifi.

"No, it isn't, Pash," reports Angora.

"Yes, it is. Just ended," claims Ruthie Dragon, entering backstage and the fray.

I glance at my AWOL assistant, trying to read her like the *New York Times*. Is she open or closed? The answer comes like lightning. "I went to Anna Rex's show—boring!" she reports, not showing an ounce of remorse for disobeying a direct order from a superior style officer.

Clenching my teeth, I force myself to acquiesce: "Tell me, Ruthie, we're dying to know."

Ruthie pulls out her notebook like a buyer or fashion reporter with oodles of notes taken for professional purposes. "You are not going to believe what Anna Rex did for the Wild Card Challenge. Well, I think it was for the Wild Card Challenge—or maybe that was her Design Challenge concept?"

While Ruthie ponders a point she didn't consider during her unassigned spying spree, I repeat myself. "Tell us what you saw."

"Well, here is the House of Rex program," Ruthie says, shoving the pale gray program into the palm of my hand like it's the Holy Grail.

Angora rushes to my side to peruse the program with me: "The Double Duty Roster of Rex: Every woman wants to own fashion that works as hard as she does. The shirt that doubles as a tote. The jacket that can be transformed into an evening skirt. Each of our models is wearing one item that can be transformed before your eyes. Your guess is as good as ours. To prove it, the guest who picks the ten items out of ten will win an item from Rex's Double Duty Roster collection, to be claimed after the show."

"Wow, that's quite a gimmick—more contrived than the Easter egg hunt at the White House," Angora says, pursing her lip.

"So what did Rex turn into—a rooster purse?" I ask impatiently.

"She didn't model in the show at all. Just came out at the end and bowed. Oh, someone from the audience gave her a bouquet of white roses. She waved like a vampire Miss America."

"I'm sort of surprised," I reveal. "I was sure she was going to close the finale like I am."

"Okay—I think the Rex Roster—the winner, anyway—is the long black mesh skirt that could proba-bly be made into three different items. It looked like it could become a head wrap or hat, a tube top, and a shoulder bag," rambles Ruthie. "Oh, everything was black and white, of course. No color at all, except for gray and a little beige—no, it was more like khaki—the skirts with the adjustable strings up the side. Oh, that was one, too—like a parachute or laundry bag."

"She should have had more color, I think," offers Angora. "Color always saves the day." Angora gets a text and looks at it. "My parents are on their way. 'You can never be too early!' says Ms. Ava. But not to worry, she knows she cannot come backstage before the show."

"Oh, we're not worried about that," I sigh. "Just about everything else."

"Well, she can sit next to my mother and Michi— maybe teach her how to talk to people without a TV re- mote control in her hand!" sputters Fifi.

"Do you want me to text Ms. Ava back and tell her to look for your mom and Michelette so she can sit next to them?" Angora asks, taking Fifi seriously.

Fifi doesn't answer. Now I'm more interested in an- swers from Ruthie Dragon. "So, are you just passing through?"

"I guess so, because I'll head out now to stand at the Heels on Wheels cart," she informs me. "Now that I've seen Rex's Wild Card Challenge, I understand how it could factor into winning the fashion show!"

"See," Nole says, pursing his lips in satisfaction. "Now you know why I had to have her. She thinks five steps outside the kitty-litter box!"

Ruthie smirks with satisfaction. "So don't worry, every guest walking into the door tonight is going to know about our Heels on Wheels cart."

"Good job!" I spout, imitating Nole. I hug Ruthie Dragon. "Thank you."

"Don't thank me yet. When that cart is full and

Lupo has snapped the photos proving it, then you can thank me!" Ruthie Dragon says, sailing out.

"The shirt, Pash, isn't she gonna wear a shirt?" Fifi hisses.

"Oh, right!" I mutter. "Ruthie—you have to put on one of our Catwalk T-shirts, STYLE SHOULD MAKE YOU PURR. Remember?"

Ruthie takes the shirt, staring at Nole like *Please turn around*.

Nole walks over to the garment bags to take out the evening wear outfits.

"Please tell Sally G. to come on back," I instruct.

"Hello, everyone," says Dame Leeds when he arrives. He doesn't make eye contact with me, just starts taking stuff out of his leather cases and pretending he's caught up in the fashion flurry.

I decide to cut through that ex-tension cord with my freshly sharpened scissors: "Dame, Chenille is on her way with the hairpieces and our finale model, Fabbie Tabbie."

Sure enough, the announcement of my feline royalty gets a rise out of him. He winces, then sighs, so I decide to pile on an extra helping of humble pie.

"Wait till you see what Chenille did with the braids—she got this great idea to intertwine pieces of pink chiffon into them."

Dame Leeds looks down and nods like *Whatever*

878

makes you clever. Luckily, when our makeup artists, Bobby Beat and Kimono Mini Mo, arrive, they raise the quotient of air-kissing to the ceiling. Then the dynamic duo lay out their assortment of selected makeup for the House of Pashmina models like they're Renaissance artists preparing to attack a blank canvas. "Think Pink. I've been saying that to myself all morning!" coos Bobby Beat.

I can't resist ogling the extensive pink palettes— cream and powder eye shadows, loose glitter, lipsticks, glosses, powder blushes—all arranged with choreographed care. "I can't wait for my first Bobby Beat beat," I squeal.

"We are saving the best for last, Miss Purr," Bobby Beat jokes, arranging his brushes.

"No way, you've got pink brushes, too!" Fifi squeals.

"Girls, where have you been? Obviously not at the Sephora counters lately—exclusive home of the Tarina Tarantino collection and the one and only purveyor of pink makeup brushes!"

Before I can even open my mouth to ask, Bobby Beat retorts, "Fifty-nine dollars for a five-brush set. Now, if we win this lunch money today, children, I can purchase sets for everyone."

"We're going to hold you to that," swears Fallon, arriving with the rest of the models, right on time for rehearsal and to indulge in the pure pandemonium of preshow jitters. "Ooh, I was so nervous getting here. I was going down the subway stairs and this group of rowdy sailors running up the stairs almost knocked me over. I held on to that banister real tight going down, praying, 'Please, God, don't let me fall. Don't let lightning strike twice on the IRT'!"

Of course, we all know Fallon is referring to the subway line taken by Liza Flake—but we're all too superstitious to comment, except Aphro, who blurts out, "It *is* Freaky Friday."

17

Chenille arrives backstage with a duffel bag slung over her left shoulder and Fabbie Tabbie in a carrier. If I didn't know better, I'd assume she was an army recruit reporting for duty, by the looks of her attire: drab green khaki pants to match the duffel bag and a dark green cotton hoodie over a tank. The only thing missing: dog tags dangling on a chain around her neck.

"Aww, the star has arrived," coos Angora.

"Yes, she has," I reply, beaming at Chenille. Then I motion to Fifi to harness the junior models—and watch them like a hawk, as it's time to address my troops. "We're doing *two* run-throughs. Also, junior models, you're only appearing on the runway once; then you will walk out at the end in a procession with all the models."

The junior models nod. Stellina grins wildly. "We know that!"

"For the rest of my models—each time you come back from the runway, stand backstage with your dresser, who will tell you when it's your turn to go out," I explain. "And after you have walked on the runway in your third outfit, keep it on. Remember, the Teen Style Network is out there—so give it all you've got! See you on the runway!"

"See ya, supermodel!" shouts Stellina.

Sure enough, Caterina and the rest of the Teen Style Network are already stationed by the ramp, ready to shoot. I stand by the ramp with Nole and Fifi. Lupo is in position, too, snapping away with his trusty Nikon camera.

We wait for Zeus to turn up the lights to begin the run-through. First up, two of my junior models—E.T. and Stellina. They sashay to the end of the runway, then veer off, one to the left side and the other to the right. Stellina stands for her single pose, then turns.

I motion to her, making the gesture for the umbrella. "You open the umbrella, twirl!"

"Oh, sorry!" she shouts.

"Don't worry—we're doing two run-throughs."

Caterina motions to me. I tell Nole and Fifi to take over while I go chat with her.

"The Heels on Wheels cart looks amazing," Caterina congratulates me. "I think I was your first donation. I donated a pair of Vivienne Westwoods with platform heels." She chuckles like a disco queen. "Do you really think guests will bring shoes to donate?"

"Well, we sent out five hundred invites to our friends and families—hopefully they plan on helping."

"You think you'll win the Wild Card Challenge?"

"Excuse me," I say, distracted. I want to give further instruction to my crew. "Benny's supposed to drop his barrel tote when he gets to the end of the runway," I shout.

"He knows—mind your business!" Nole shouts back.

I dart my eyes back to Caterina. "Yes, the House of Pashmina will win the Wild Card Challenge. I think so."

"What makes you so sure?" Caterina probes.

I resist the temptation to reveal my intel, or my source, who is stationed on the fashion front.

"Have you already gotten reports from Diamond Tyler? She ran from me after the Moet Major fashion show," Caterina informs me. "Isn't it against regulations for team members to stray from their designated area?"

Buckling, I don't attempt to brave a fib-eroni. Instead, I blast through my sound bite. "I'm going to win the Wild Card Challenge because everybody likes the givers and not the takers."

"Pashmina!" yells Sally G. I look back and she's holding my cell phone.

"Are we done?" I ask Caterina, desperate to escape.

"For now," she replies. "Can you tell Dame Leeds I'll need five minutes?"

"Oh, okay," I shriek, then toddle away.

When Sally G. hands me the phone, I bark at her.

"You can't leave your station now—you've got to make sure your models come out in order!"

"I know, Pash, but it's Diamond. She says she's gotta speak to you," Sally G. says, miffed.

"Awright, I got it," I say apologetically. "Yes, Diamond?" I answer, anxious.

"Shalimar's show was amazing," she reports.

"Oh, really?"

"Yeah, the Wild Card Challenge was executed very well. She divided the show into the Seven Principles of Style Success. And on each guest's chair was the faux book."

"What book? Wait, hang on." I motion to Dame Leeds. "Caterina needs five with you."

Dame doesn't jump to my command, so I glare at his back until he does. He saunters out of the dressing room.

I put my ear back to the phone and Diamond breaks it down. "Well, it was a booklet called *The Seven Principles of Style Success*. I couldn't get my hands on one since they were on the guests' chairs and I was hiding in the back, but it was really the show's program."

Suddenly, I remember Shalimar telling me the reason I wasn't on the fast track was because I hadn't read *The Seven Secrets to Success*. "Bingo, I know where she got that from—from the book her father read," I recall.

Diamond continues, "The first model in each segment came out and held up a sign with an element from Shalimar's must-have list, like 'Military Enlistment. Dress with disciplined purpose.' That segment had a red wool three-quarter-sleeve peacoat with eco-friendly wool faux-fur lining. Another model had on an anorak and slouch pants. And the models marched, by the way."

"Did Shalimar model in the show?"

"Yes, she came out in the Eco-Friendly segment. 'The hunt is over for the hue of choice. Go hunter green.'"

"So was her show packed?" I ask, succumbing to my own shade of green—envy.

"Yes, to the rafters," Diamond rattles on, but I'm distracted by the commotion at the hair and makeup station. Bobby Beat is under the counter, fooling around with outlets.

"*Oh.* Did you see C. C. to tell him I'm not the one who leaked his Wild Card Challenge?" I ask, fretting.

"Pashmina, I've already had a close call with Caterina—she almost caught me on camera!" objects Diamond.

"I know, stay below the radar—we're almost in the homestretch. Call me back," I plead with her. I'm so distracted I can't even listen to any more of Diamond's report from the fashion front.

"*Ciao*, meow," Diamond signs off.

"Wow, she really does have a sense of humor underneath all that faux fur," I mumble to Bobby and Mini Mo, then recount the blow-by-blow from the House of Shalimar show.

"Why is it so dark in here?" I ask, noticing that the makeup and hair station is dark.

"We've been trying to turn on the makeup lights at the counter to prepare for the stampede of models coming our way!" Bobby Beat explains, exasperated.

"The switches aren't working," seconds Mini Mo.

"And someone needs to get that taken care of before I plug in the hot comb to no avail," Chenille chimes in.

The run-through is finished and I fret to Fifi and Angora, who return backstage. "What's wrong with the outlets? Please, somebody help me!"

Now even Zeus, who has also returned backstage, tries to get into the outlet action, but he comes up short. "The lights went out on the runway, too. I don't know—all the lights seem to be out."

I get down on my knees and plug the hot combs into different sockets, but *nada*, nothing happens. No lights, no camera, no action. "Oh, come on, don't get shady with me now!"

"Omigod, *mija*, what are we going to do?" Fifi screams, hysterical.

"We should get Farfalla," orders Aphro.

"No way. I need Ice Très," I snap.

"But he can't come back here," frets Angora.

"Where's Diamond? She can find Farfalla," suggests Aphro.

"*No.* You don't move. We can't afford to have any more members MIA!" I shout. I pull out my phone and send Ice Très a Code Pink text: "I need you NOW."

"Do you think he'll come?" asks Dame, who has returned to the fashion fray. "Or maybe we should just send an SOS and pray to be rescued from Gilligan's Island."

"Not to worry. Ice Très always manages to find a way to get to me," I say, my heart pounding.

"I'm gonna call my dad," frets Angora. Her father is an animation whiz, but mostly when it comes to Funny Bunny rabbits. "Maybe he can talk us through it."

"Well, the clock is ticking and tocking—Angora, let me start with you," frets Bobby Beat. He pats the back of his makeup chair like a mad scientist.

"Not now, *s'il vous plaît,*" she says anxiously.

"Just as well—I can't see what I'm doing, so unless we're going for the Big Apple Circus look, I might as well surrender my brushes," Bobby Beat says, frustrated.

"That was not necessary," I snap.

"Well, we are under the same tent—I thought it was fitting," he says, flicking his hair out of his face.

Suddenly, Ice Très appears backstage just like in my dream. "How did you get past the security guards?"

"I told you I'd be here for you. So, what's the Code Blue?" he says, customizing the Catwalk emergency code to a shade he prefers.

"Help me, please," I say, breathing heavily. "We can't figure out what's wrong with the outlets!"

"I got it," Ice Très says confidently.

He takes the melton cloth holding his tools from his messenger bag and opens up the circuit board.

"Wow—forget the fashion emergency kit. We gotta start rolling like that?" Aphro blurts out, amazed.

"Get dressed!" I command her.

"What? In the dark?" she counters.

"All right—I got this situation under control," Ice Très shouts from behind the panel.

Suddenly, the lights on the makeup bureau pop on.

"Oh, thank gooseness!" I squeal.

Ice Très checks the lights behind the runway scrim. A few minutes later, he comes backstage and gives me a hug. "Look, I'm not Con Edison, but I'll tell you this— that short-circuit situation didn't happen by itself. Somebody intentionally rerouted those wires."

I fall backward. Angora tries to catch me. "Omigod, the dream—I think I know what it was trying to tell me," I realize, like I'm having a vision. "It's not that

I'm going to fall on my face. My shoes were rigged in the dream."

Angora, Aphro, and Fifi stare at me, and just like a crew who are as tight as we are, we utter the dreaded word in unison: "SHALIMAR!"

"That's what the dream was trying to tell me—not to fall for any of her tricks!" I say triumphantly. "She's been out to get us from day one!"

"I've been trying to tell you that," blurts out Fifi. "I was right! She found another way to sabotage us—and it almost worked!"

"Yeah, it almost did," I realize, calmed by the revelation in the eye of the fashion storm. Now I turn and squarely face Zeus as another revelation sinks in. "And I'm not going to fall for your tricks, either. That's why you weren't backstage in my dream. You changed the tune—and deserted me because you can't be trusted!"

Zeus gives me the evil eyeball. "Yeah, well, I can leave now if that's how you feel."

"Hold up," Ice Très says, calming us all down. "We—I mean, you guys have a fashion show to put on. You've worked all year for this. Keep your eye on the prize. You're a team. Don't fall apart now—then Shalimar will have won."

We stand around silently, soaking in the objective

advice. Even Dame suspends his hairbrush in midair. "He's right—let's get to work! We got a show to put on."

Ice Très hugs me tight. "You're going to win this," he whispers in my ear.

"I've already won—because I've got you," I whisper back, tears in my eyes.

Ice Très gives me a long kiss until Bobby Beat insists that I succumb to his powder brush.

"Good luck, boo kitties!" Ice Très shouts as he sneaks back out.

After another hour of preparation, the five child models and ten adult models line up to get ready for the first procession.

Stellina is bouncing off the walls. "Pinch me, Miss Purr, please. Pinch me."

I almost oblige to keep her still, but Dame is yanking my hair. "Your sister is good, I must say," he confesses.

"I know," I admit, beaming at Chenille proudly, but she is still no-nonsense, as usual. She's sitting in her hairdresser slot waiting for the second procession, when we will put up the ponytails into chignons.

"Not too much pink!" I squeal. "I'm watching you, too."

"Yeah, well, our eyes are watching God," Dame says, motioning upward.

"Good idea," says Fifi. "I would have brought my

Love candle to burn back here, but it's missing from my room."

"Really?" I ask. I'm sure I saw a whole roomful of candles at Fifi's house two weeks ago.

"I think Papi took it since he can't be with me," Fifi says, holding back her tears.

Diamond enters the backstage area.

"I knew you'd be back," shouts Nole. His pudgy cheeks fill out with pride.

"Yes, I wanted to tell you that Ruthie Dragon is not happy about manning the Heels on Wheels cart, but it looks like it's filling up!" Diamond reports, her eyes beaming, full of charity.

"You mean there are people out there already?" shrieks Angora.

"Yeah. Just waiting in the lobby! *Oh.* I saw this guy bringing like two shopping bags—no, I mean they were *Hefty* bags—filled with shoes," adds Diamond.

"Wow—we need a few more guests like him, huh?" I say, getting unbelievably hyped.

"Anyway, he gave me a card to give to Felinez," Diamond continues.

Felinez grabs the envelope and opens it. She reads the card, and tears stream down her cheeks. "Papi is here!"

"Really?" I shriek, my eyes tearing up, too. "Read it so we can hear!"

"It's in Spanish, but I'll translate," Fifi says, choking back the tears. "'My precious daughter, I would not miss this day for anything in the world. I will be coming back home because I cannot live without you and my family. When you were born I prayed that you would have all your fingers and toes, but God gave me so much more in you. You are so talented in so many ways, and the best daughter I could have wished for. Love, Papi.'"

I look around at all my crew—even the models are trying not to cry. "You two—stop crying!" I shout at Angora and Aphro, who are on the verge of ruining their makeup. Even Bobby Beat has gotten teary-eyed.

"Who could live without you? I can't." I kiss my BFF on both cheeks; then we hug.

Diamond is moved, too. "I didn't know that was your father," she says, touched that she was the messenger. "He just asked Ruthie if he could give her the card to give to you, and Ruthie said no, she couldn't leave the cart. He looked so helpless. I told him I would do it."

"Did he look okay?" Fifi asks, concerned.

"Oh, he looks really nice—he's wearing a black suit and tie," Diamond reports.

"No, I mean does he look okay?"

"Oh, yes, he looks happy. And he shaved," adds Diamond, wondering if she's said the desired words yet.

Obviously she has, because Fifi snaps out of her

Kodak moment, reignited with a passionate purpose, and squeaks: "Okay, we gotta get ready!"

"Yes, let's get in position, fashionistas. It's almost showtime!" I shout for good measure.

"Yeah, well, you—in position in my chair!" Bobby Beat orders me. "It's time."

"Oh, you look so beautiful," I coo at my junior models, who are all dressed and ready to rip the runway. They are standing in order. Waiting.

After fifteen minutes, my makeup is done and it's time for my hair. Nole has steamed my pink satin bustier and skirt. "This is a showstopper." He gets Fabbie Tabbie's wedding gown ready. "Should I dress her now?"

"Yup, let's all get into play."

As I'm getting trussed up in my bustier, the models for the Urban Gear sequence are ready and waiting. Elgamela and Fallon are also ready for their bathing suit sequence. Fallon even looks happy to be wearing her bathing suit. "You know, I could wear this to the beach. I would even take off the cover-up," she whoo-hoos.

Now we can hear the crowd swelling outside the runway scrim. "Is it crowded?" I ask, hyperventilating.

"We can't look, how do we know?" barks Nole. He is fretting with Fabbie Tabbie, making sure she looks perfect. "Omigod, I feel like she's my own," he says nervously.

Farfalla comes backstage. "Everybody ready?"

"Yes, we're ready!" I shout.

"You start in *five. Buona fortuna!*" she says with glee.

"*Buona, buona!*" Bobby Beat shouts back.

Zeus activates the music tracks, then takes his place in line.

"You look hot," Nole says, eyeing the Mad Hatter.

I want to kick him, but I'm afraid to lift up my evening skirt or move too suddenly. Fifi brings over my kitten heels. "You're sure they're not rigged?" I ask her.

"No, Cinderella, they're not!" she quips, carefully slipping my feet into the pink mules with crystal flowers. Fabbie Tabbie is perched on a high chair so she can stay out of the way until the finale.

"Showtime!" I squeal as the music comes on.

The junior models are released toward the bright lights, and immediately we hear a roar of clapping.

"Yes!" I cheer, flooded suddenly by the welling of tears. Bobby Beat is looking right in my direction and points his big pink powder brush. "Don't you dare, Miss Purr!" he threatens me.

I break out smiling and fan my eyes with my hands. Bobby Beat quickly comes over and fans me, too.

The junior models have finished and they come back sweating. "I'm going to be a model!" announces Stellina, like she has figured out her destiny.

"You already are!" I coo at her.

The models for the Urban Gear segment are working

the runway. Benny Madina and Mink Yong are the last two to return. "It's a full house, honey!" shouts Benny.

Now Elgamela and Fallon go out for the bathing suit segment, and this one gets the most applause so far. But Elgamela comes back in tears. "My mother fainted right in her chair!" she screams. "I can't go back out there!"

"No, no, come on, put on the dress!" hisses her dresser, Fabunique.

We realize that Elgamela is not joking, but the show must go on. "Are you sure your mother fainted?" I ask in disbelief. The lights are so bright on the runway, how could she possibly see anybody in the audience?

"Stop that train at Petticoat Junction immediately!" barks Bobby Beat. He runs over with Mini Mo to mend the ruined eye makeup. "Pull it together, Elgamela. Your mother will survive, like Gloria Gaynor!"

I'm so nervous that I burst out laughing. So does Zeus. "At least my mother is gonna be happy," I giggle. "I picked her favorite disco song to close our show."

Now Elgamela laughs. "You're right—that's probably not my mother, but someone else wearing traditional Muslim headwear!"

The absurdity is not lost on us. Elgamela is turning pro. The models for the Chic Meets Street segment are on the runway. Elgamela gets ready for her evening outfit—the tattersall skirt and bustier. Relieved that another crisis has been averted, I can't help but ask, "Has anyone laid eyes on Shalimar out there?"

"Oh, yes, she's standing in the back with Zirconia, green with envy!" reports Aphro. "I glared right at her, but don't worry, I didn't miss one turn, pivot, or sashay."

"Trust—I'm not worried," I say, fretting inside.

The evening wear models head out onto the runway. "You look great!" I coo to Fallon, who was so worried about spilling out of her bustier.

"Ruffles really do have ridges!" jokes Nole, patting Fallon on her chest.

I breathe deeply, getting ready for my finale.

Fifi and the other dresser, Dominique, truss me up in my finale dress even tighter. "Oh, you look like a fairy godmother!" Fifi says, her eyes watering.

"So does Fabbie Tabbie," coos Angora.

I stand behind the curtain waiting for the music cue, holding Fabbie Tabbie's leash tightly. "Fabbie Tabbie—it's showtime."

Fabbie Tabbie scratches at her ear like the veil is bothering her.

"Oh, *purr favor*—not now. We're almost there!"

Fifi bends down and adjusts the veil, patting Fabbie Tabbie on her head to calm her down.

Right on cue, the remixed version of "I Will Survive," sung by the übertalented Alyjah Jade, cranks up, signaling my grand finale with Fabbie Tabbie. Suddenly,

I wonder if Alyjah Jade is in the audience. Smiling inside, I hope she is.

Fallon is back from the runway. "We have survived!" she squeals. I beam at her, pleased that my plus-size model ripped the runway without a wardrobe malfunction. "See, I told you you could do it!" I whisper to her.

"I know!" she whispers back, excited. "Wilhelmina Plus-Size Division—here I come!"

My heart pounds in my chest as the last model returns and I stand ready to rip the runway.

When I walk out, the paparazzi are flashing their cameras like crazy and the crowd is a blur. I try not to look at the judges sitting in the front row, but I can't help noticing Tarina Tarantino's shocking-pink wig, which is even brighter than I imagined it. She is seated with Ms. Lynx and the other judges, and I sense that she is beaming at me brightly. The audience claps loudly with each step Fabbie Tabbie and I take. When we get to the end of the runway, Fabbie Tabbie sits on her haunches like a true supermodel. I feel tears in my eyes again, but I will them not to fall—not now. I firmly stand on my kitten heels, knowing they will hold up. Just like Fifi, Angora, Aphro, Nole, and even Diamond have, I have survived through all this. I return backstage breathless. "OH, MY GOD!!!!" I shout. "We did it!!!!"

After I recover, my models and the rest of my crew march out on the runway in a long procession. The audience goes wild. They give us a standing ovation. I walk out holding Fabbie Tabbie in my arms. I search the audience, looking for my mother. She is sitting in the second row next to a handsome older man in a gray pin-stripe suit. "Bravo!" she yells. "Bravo!"

I pose for the cameras as flashbulbs pop wildly, and wave to Caterina. Now my crew turns toward me and claps. "Bravo!" they scream. I am so overwhelmed, my lower lip trembles. Fifi's father hurries to the end of the runway and shoves a big bouquet of pink roses into her arms. "*Te amo.* I love you," she says to her father. Then she turns to me and we hug each other so tightly, she crushes her beautiful rose bouquet into my bustier. "I love you."

18

Standing still. That's what I'm having the most trouble doing right now. Against my focused will, I shift my weight on my pink kitten heels, staring down at the jewel-encrusted cat clips slaved over by my bestest Fifi for my tootsies only. It's Monday evening, exactly seventy-two hours after our triumphant fashion shows in Lincoln Center, and I'm on the cavernous stage in the Fashion Auditorium with the four other rival house leaders in this year's Catwalk competition: Shalimar Jackson, C. C. Samurai, Anna Rex, and Moet Major.

The five of us are lined up in a row like soldiers of style while the Teen Style Network crew pans our every twitchy expression with their handheld cameras. Gazing up at us from their cushy position in the front-row seats are the five prestigious judges of this year's Catwalk competition, including Ms. Fabianna Lynx, the director of the Catwalk competition and Fashion International High School's assistant vice principal.

Also permitted on the premises for this very special judgment day: the remaining members of the five Catwalk houses, quarantined to the back rows and given a gag order by Ms. Lynx's trusted assistants, Farfalla and Sil Lai, and two hefty security guards. Although quiet as church mice, everyone in my crew is present and purring, including my younger sister, Chenille, who didn't join the fashion fray until the not-so-chic Liza crisis but delivered like an *unbeweavable* pro and will be treated as such from now on.

Forcing myself to focus, I stare straight ahead beyond the glare of the bright klieg lights onstage, but I'm distracted by Aphro, who is waving her arms wildly, trying to get my attention, forcing me to supress a tiny smile.

"Good afternoon, fashionistas. Thank you for joining us," Ms. Lynx finally addresses us.

"Good afternoon!" we the fabbie five shout back in unison.

"I'm Fabianna Lynx, the Catwalk competition director. Joining us today is our panel of prestigious judges—jewelry designer Tarina Tarantino; posing instructor Benny Ninja; Vanna Snoot, president of Snooty Models Inc.; and Fred Sitomer, senior vice president of marketing for Federated Stores."

The judges nod at us, and we beam back with sparkly smiles. Luckily, Shalimar Jackson, who is channeling a passenger-from-the-doomed-*Titanic* look— because what else could explain her wearing a slinky bronze metallic gown and long strands of pretentious but real Mikimoto pearls—doesn't embarrass us by also releasing one of her signature First Lady waves.

"Today we're here to announce the winner of the Wild Card Challenge—as well as the winner of Fashion International High School's thirty-fifth annual Catwalk competition," Ms. Lynx says proudly, her strong vibrato generating fever-pitch excitement. "What's at stake? The winning team for the Wild Card Challenge will receive a Go Wild gift card from Barnes and Noble with a buy-a-book-a-week value for up to one thousand dollars. This year's winning house will receive an all-expenses-paid two-week fashion trip to Firenze—Florence, Italy—where they will open the spring Pitti Bimbo collections by staging their fashion show. The members of the winning house will also divide the one-hundred-thousand-dollar cash prize, three one-year twenty-five-thousand-dollar modeling contracts with Snooty Models, Inc., and three full scholarships to the Fashion Institute of Technology, and last but not least, a five-piece luggage set by Louis Vuitton to carry the winning collection overseas in luxurious style."

The five judges clap, so we join in and the Teen Style Network cameras zoom in for close-ups.

"House leaders—for the Wild Card Challenge, you were asked to introduce an element of surprise into your fashion show that correlated with your show's overall theme. I'm delighted to report that the judges were incredibly impressed with the choices made by each of you. C. C. Samurai—the absence of footwear to underlie the warrior spirit of urban wear was a brave choice. We've never witnessed that before in any collection. However, we felt that message was too subtle—and was therefore lost on your audience," Ms. Lynx explains gingerly.

"You didn't mention this at all in your fashion show program—which means that in essence, you left your buyers barefoot and without direction," adds Fred Sitomer.

"Moet Major, the introduction of bubbly beverages to accent your theme of Celebration was appreciated, but where was the celebration in the collection, whose overall focus was urban wear?" asks Ms. Lynx.

"Can I explain?" balks Moet Major without waiting for a response. "Urban wear, street gear, is what my generation wears to celebrate. We don't have to dress up anymore if we don't want to." Moet Major shifts in her burgundy Adidas sneakers from her left to right foot, then folds her arms defensively across her chest.

Ms. Lynx nods in disagreement and keeps it moving. "Anna Rex—recyling fashion is an excellent platform, and you somehow found a way to interpret that in your Wild Card Challenge, but what you were really offering was a collection with pieces that served more than one purpose. A skirt that could be turned into a head wrap: excellent idea. The top that doubles as a shoulder bag: I loved it, but it really did not reflect recycling even in the choice of fabrics, which were not recyclable."

"I liked the offering of a prize to customers—that's always a great merchandising strategy in retail," adds Fred Sitomer. "But I agree with Fabianna—what you were really offering were double-duty pieces, not fashion that's recycled."

A flustered Anna Rex tries to explain, "That is the point—my idea of recycling is assigning more than one duty to an item in your wardrobe."

The judges ponder Anna Rex's response as if they're weighing it into their decision. Meanwhile, I can feel the perspiration beads cluster in my armpits. I press my arms closer to my torso in protest.

"Shalimar Jackson—your execution of the Wild Card Challenge was closely correlated to the theme of your collection. Bravo. Very well done. And it was an unexpected surprise. Having a style guide—*The Seven Secrets of Style Success*—for a customer to follow, telling her exactly the trends she should incorporate into her wardrobe this season? I loved it." Ms. Lynx beams.

"I loved the sixth secret—'The Structured Handbag: Lock down your look with a style guarantee.' That's clear advice for any customer, telling her exactly what to buy—a polished handbag. And that not only will this addition to her wardrobe complete her outfit, but it will benefit her career as well. Fabulous direction," seconds Vanna Snoot.

Mr. Sitomer seems the most amped about Shalimar's style mandates. "What is really genius about this concept is you could give buyers at your show a clear guideline every year—a mandate about their buying options for the season. Now, that's a well-merchandised collection."

"Like I said, choosing the winner for the Wild Card Challenge is very difficult," Ms. Lynx quickly adds before turning her attention to me.

Taking a deep breath, she gazes at the index cards in her hand, then looks up at me. "Pashmina Purrstein, you took the element of surprise and gave us exactly that—a truly surprising element."

"I've never been to a fashion show that had a display specifically designed for charity purposes—in this case, the Heels on Wheels cart. It was adorable," coos Vanna Snooot.

"And it was successful—I couldn't believe how many people actually donated shoes!" belts out Benny Ninja.

"Bravo—the color was awesome!" Tarina Tarantino says, clapping softly with a fuschia feather plume pen gripped in her left hand.

"While we adored the surprise, we weren't completely convinced that it correlated directly with the theme of your collection."

My face flushed with hot coals, I try to explain: "Our feline fatale theme is empowering ourselves and empowering others. The feline fatale customer is fun, flirty, and fashion-conscious, but he or she is also community-conscious."

"Yes, we get that—it was fun, I liked it," Benny Ninja says definitively.

"Thank you, house leaders. Please give us five minutes before we make a decision," Ms. Lynx informs us.

While the judges whisper among themselves, Boom the cameraman breaks away from the Teen Style Network pack and steps up onto the stage, zooming in for close-ups of the five house leaders that are too close for Southern comfort, if you ask me. Alas, no one was asking. Suddenly, I feel the nerves in my jaw tensing up like I've eaten an overly tangy tart.

"Okay, we're ready. We've made our decision," announces Ms. Lynx.

We the fabbie five stand silent as church mice. Even our crew members in the back are collectively holding their breath.

"The winner of the Wild Card Challenge is . . . the House of Shalimar. Congratulations," announces Ms. Lynx.

Shalimar shrieks, clutching her pearls like a beauty-pageant winner. "Thank you!" she gushes.

Like déjà vu, I feel my knees buckle like I'm about

to go under because I am a passenger on the ill-fated *Titanic*. I cringe inside. *I should never have made that snide comment to myself about Shalimar. I jinxed myself!*

Fighting back the tears, I wait for Ms. Lynx to continue.

"Now, one of you will be the leader of the winning house in Fashion International High School's thirty-fifth annual Catwalk competition. But please remember you are all winners—the fashion shows this year were exceptional in execution, design, and overall theme. Anna Rex—your silhouettes were classic and stream-lined, and incorporating double-duty designs into your collection made it extremely utilitarian."

"I could honestly see myself wearing the black mesh duster—throwing it over everything for work, and going out afterward," adds Vanna Snoot.

"I thought the only element missing was the element of surprise in design," says Tarina Tarantino.

"And color—even for the New York customer there was too much black, gray, and ivory—it made the collection too heavy," claims Benny Ninja.

"Yes, color was definitely needed—the tube knit dress, for example, could have easily been offered in a teal or burgundy option," suggests Mr. Sitomer. "Customers don't crave that level of simplicity. Every silhouette was so simple it could easily be used as something else. While that type of utilitarian element is commendable, it doesn't appeal to the customer's desire to own it—or to buy it right now."

"And the average consumer already has a black dress, skirt, top, and leggings in her closet," adds Vanna Snoot.

"Okay. Moet Major. Your theme was Celebration—the celebration of hip-hop style," Ms. Lynx clarifies. "But it was obvious to us the only things you were celebrating were slouchy, unflattering silhouettes for a lazy customer."

Benny Ninja interrupts, "Even the urban customer, the street kid, wants an option for that one night they're gonna break out to the prom or a birthday party. It's ridiculous to think they would actually show up to a special event dressed in a hoodie and baggy pants."

"I found the overall collection to be a celebration of one look—and you didn't bring any design elements to that look, either. Even urban gear has bouncy style elements—where were they?" says Mr. Sitomer.

Moet Major shifts back and forth on her Adidas again, holding her arms captive across her tiny chest.

"Pashmina Purrstein—you exhibited a lot of fun in your collection, and lots of color," commends Ms. Lynx.

"I loved the color—I could have drunk the neon pink catsuit with a straw!" squeals Tarina Tarantino.

"Oh, we know you loved it," jokes Benny Ninja. "What I loved were the design surprises—the faux-leather skirt with the tiered ruffles paired with a satin bomber jacket. It was as cute as anything I've seen on the runway in Paris."

"The flutter-pleated evening dresses nailed it—any woman, young or older, could wear that dress to a special occasion and feel, well, feminine—which is in keeping with your theme of feline fatale," Vanna Snoot says with a nod.

"Shalimar Jackson—the collection, as we mentioned, was highly conceptualized with its themes—the military influences, chic outerwear to wrap up your career choices, capes, ponchos. Luxurious choices. A real career woman's wardrobe. What we didn't see was that surprise design element," claims Ms. Lynx.

"It was all predictable—but very pretty," agrees Tarina Tarantino. "I loved the elegant appeal, even though I wasn't sure the clothes would be flattering on the average woman—only a specific body type, extremely slender. Same with Anna Rex's collection."

"C. C. Samurai, your collection was innovative. Kimono wraps over trousers is a fresh sporty option that I've never seen. But again, like Anna Rex, you shied away from color, providing customers with safe options," explains Ms. Lynx.

"The dashiki tops were cute—I would wear one of those even for performing," claims Benny Ninja, observing the house leader with fresh eyes.

"I loved the jumpsuit, but it needed more structuring—it was too baggy and unflattering for the average man," observes Mr. Sitomer.

"I did not design that for the average man," bellows C. C. Samurai.

"Contrary to popular belief, the average customer is extremely size-conscious—always looking for pieces that will flatter their fit," reports Vanna Snoot, crossing her legs.

"Actually, only one house designed a collection that could be flattering to women of all sizes. Pashmina, the addition of a plus-size model who actually wore clothes that fit sublimely—the pink satin bustier and skirt that draped to a flattering length—was innovative. I could carry the collection with confidence that it would sell," Mr. Sitomer weighs in.

"Contestants, give us a moment to confer," announces Ms. Lynx. We nod like helpless lambs. I glance at Shalimar to convey my congrats. She smiles weakly.

A few minutes later, the judges gaze at us. "Okay, judges, have we made a decision?" Ms. Lynx queries, looking at each of her professional judges.

"Yes," says Tarina Tarantino, smoothing the edges of her fuchsia wig with her long acrylic-tipped fuchsia nails accented by diamond-shaped rhinestones.

"The winner of Fashion International's thirty-fifth

annual Catwalk competition is . . . the House of Pashmina," announces Ms. Lynx.

"Omigod!" I shriek involuntarily. Much to my chagrin, I also grab my cheeks with my palms, resembling a preschooler trying on her first pair of ruby slippers.

Aphro lets out a banshee shriek in the background, despite the warning to be seen and not heard.

"Congratulations. Your collection was packed with personality—I loved it," says Mr. Sitomer, beaming at me.

Standing up, Ms. Lynx instructs: "House leaders, I'm going to ask if you would please leave the stage now—except Pashmina."

C. C. Samurai winks at me as he leaves. Shalimar Jackson looks like she'll be spending the evening shooting off letters to everyone from her attorney to the style Supreme Court in a vigilant effort to get this decision overturned. After the four house leaders head to seats in the audience, Farfalla comes up the side steps to the stage with a bronze Big Willie trophy, artfully crafted like a dress form, in her hand. She hands me the trophy and hugs me.

I'm so tearful, I can't hide it.

"Will the rest of the members of the House of Pashmina please come to the stage," Ms. Lynx orders.

My crew heads down the side aisle and makes their way to the stage to stand with me. Farfalla is holding Lupo's camera and shooting the photos for our Catwalk competition scrapbook. The Teen Style Network continues rolling until we are all in place on the stage.

"Despite the turns and twists that were experienced this year, you really came through. Pashmina, Nole, Felinez, Diamond—the vision was exceptional in every way. And I want to commend the entire team for doing an exemplary job. You represent the essence of what William Dresser, our founding father, had in mind—continuing the outstanding legacy of the fashion industry."

The judges clap loudly.

"And I want you to remember this: the experience you have shared together as a team over the course of this school year is essential to your success in the fashion industry. There is no question you all have bright futures. And they were made even brighter by the invaluable insider peek you were given preparing for your fashion show. You cannot be a member of the fashion industry—a fashion, jewelry, or accessory designer, a model, photographer, or buyer—if you do not believe in working together as a team. Fashion is a collaborative effort, and no one person creates the vision that ultimately drives the commerce of the six-hundred-billion-dollar fashion industry. Remember that—and thanks to your experience in the Catwalk competition, you probably always will. Congratulations. This was the chance of a lifetime, and you won. Enjoy it. And we're going to have the experience of a lifetime in Firenze, Italy—I guarantee you!"

We clap loudly. Nole, who is standing closest to me, whispers, "The first round of gelato is on you, Miss Purr. I won the bet."

"What bet?" I ask, confused.

"You're always reneging, Miss Purr," Nole says, shaking his head. "Always reneging."

"I beg to differ," I retort.

"Oh, really?" Nole says, waiting to hear.

"Really. I told you we would win the Catwalk competition if you stuck with me!" I squeal proudly.

"Yeah, you sure did. But I told you if I guessed the color of your bloomers, you'd have to buy the first round of gelato! Now, if you don't mind getting unstuck, I'd appreciate it," says Nole, sweating and pulling away.

"Yeah, but you didn't have to guess—you saw them at the first fitting!" I protest.

"Whatever!" squeals Nole.

Fifi moves in closer and so does Angora. "The competition may be over, but we're going to be a team forever. Promise?"

I kiss Angora and Fifi, my best friend since kindergarten, even though she swears it's the first grade, and I make a promise I plan on keeping: "*You* two are stuck with me for life, like it or not."

FASHION INTERNATIONAL 35th ANNUAL
CATWALK COMPETITION BLOG

New school rule: You don't have to be ultranice, but don't get tooooo catty or your posting will be zapped by the Fashion Avengers!

CIAO, MANNY HANNY!!!

Talk about the wildest ride in the history of the style amusement park. According to the press coverage, this year's Catwalk competition was the closest in the competition's history. Okay, believe that. OH. Sorry. In case you haven't heard, the winning team for this year's Catwalk competition is the HOUSE OF PASHMINA! That's right, right now we're busy packing for our trip to Firenze, Italy, where we will stage our fashion show for the second time as the opening for the Pitti Bimbo collection.

But hang on, I know it's the tradition for the house leader of the winning team to offer some words of wisdom for next year's candidates, so I will fulfill that duty without any grudges. Here's some battle-plan advice: Make sure to pick your team members carefully, because you will be stuck with each other for a whole year—and things will get *unbeweavably* hairy. To that end, no question to potential applicants is off-limits. Try these questions on for size: Do you have a portfolio? Do you have a girlfriend? That's right—ask that latter question in braille, Swahili, and sign language just to be on the safe side. My sordid experiences have taught me that some fashionistas get a thrill out of withholding valuable information on their applications—dating and otherwise! Secondly, pick people who are good at what they do—not at what they *want* to do. Then let your team members do their assigned tasks so that you don't get overburdened with the little stuff.

For the rest of my advice, see my next blog entry, which I'll be posting when I arrive in Italy. (I'm going to share with you the Catwalk Credo my house created. You should create your own credo to distribute to your team members, but hey, feel free to bite my flavor, too.) Last but not least, remember, every generation of fashionistas has been inspired by those who came before them. So I guess you're it!

Okay, forgive me for being Hello Kitty, good-bye, but I've got five pieces of Louis Vuitton luggage to fill with our Catwalk collection before the team members of the House of Pashmina hop on a plane. I guess I only really have one thing left to say: *Ciao,* Manny Hanny. For two long, memorable weeks, I'm going to miss you and all your inhabitants!

Posted by Feline Groovy at 06:30:10

Glossary

Adorable Hair: New York's premier locale for purchasing human hair sold by the ounce, used for weaves and extensions. Everyone from Naomi Campbell's hairstylist to Jessica Simpson's has been spotted at Adorable's.

Aka: Also known as. As in "Did you see Shalimar Jackson, aka the Shallow One, posing on the school steps this morning like she was Michelle Obama at a press conference?"

Awky gawkster: A boy who is awkward and prone to gawking. As in "Why would I go out with Panda and his crew? They're just a bunch of awky gawksters."

Babble flow: Talking in a stream-of-consciousness style that doesn't quite connect all the dots. As in "I don't mean to interrupt your babble flow, but I gotta catch the train to get home and clean my room before my mother has a meltdown."

Basta with the pasta: Enough already. As in "*Basta* with the pasta. You have to help us come up with a Wild Card Challenge that will knock Shalimar out of the running!"

Brujería: Spanish for "witchcraft, sorcery." As in "Come on, Fifi—isn't there a *brujería* spell you can place on the judges so we can win the Catwalk competition?"

Cara: Italian for "sweetheart, dear." As in "Hang in there, *cara*! You're *furbulous*!"

Catmare: A vividly horror-frying dream in Technicolor, involving scary creatures.

Chérie (or chéri for a boy): French for "sweetie, dear, precious, darling." Pronounced "sher*ee*." As in "Oh, *chérie*, I wish I was tall like you so I could be a model, but I hear the circus is always hiring—so don't worry about me!"

Chill to the maximus: Relax; act like a veggie. As in "Win or lose, after the Catwalk competition is over, I intend to chill to the maximus."

Code Pink: To call an urgent meeting with your crew in order to remedy a time-sensitive problem or strategize a future course of action. Aka Code Blue, for crews who prefer a less girly hue.

Coinky dinky: A coincidence of the highest order. As in "How is it possible that Shalimar happens to be at the same club where I was meeting Zeus? That's quite a coinky dinky, don't ya think?"

Connecs: Connections; hookups. As in "Do you have any connecs for woven metallic leather? All I need is a yard—and I'd appreciate your assisterance, *mucho!*"

Dribble-drabble: Blather; babble. As in "Stop with the dribble-drabble about Zeus. We know you're hooked, lined, and *sinking!*"

In flagrante: Latin phrase meaning "caught red-handed." As in "Yesterday, my nose was twitching, so I picked it and Caterina and her crew caught me *in flagrante!* Nowhere is safe in this shantytown—not even the school stairwell!"

Faux pas: From French for "false step." A social boo-boo. Pronounced "foe pah." As in "You were supposed to meet me at Dingoes Diner at eight. I can't believe you left me standing there with the hoodrats. That was a major faux pas!"

Ferocious feline: A fierce female. A ferocious feline is a force of nature to be reckoned with.

Gagulating: To be super upset. As in "Did you see Zeus canoodling with Alyjah Jade in the corner booth at the Lipstick Lounge after she performed? I was gagulating!"

Goospitate: To break out in goose bumps; to swoon over someone; to become breathless or hypnotized by someone. As in "Benny Madina is cute—but Zeus is the one who makes me goospitate. Too bad he has a girlfriend already!"

Kaflammatory: Inflammatory squared; inciting drama. As in "It's not a good idea to yell 'Fat girls need love too!' outside a Jenny Craig center. That's *très* kaflammatory, don't ya think?"

Keep it moving: To avoid getting caught up in drama and kaflamma. As in "Someone just told me they saw Ice Très with Shalimar at Googies Diner. I don't know why he stood me up, but I'm gonna keep it moving."

Kibitzing: An affectionate Yiddish term for "yakking, schmoozing, joking, shooting the breeze." As in "Would you stop kibitzing already with Ms. Lynx? She's not gonna let you slide on the Design Challenge—and we gotta get to Mood Fabrics before they close!"

Kvetching: A yiddish term for complaining or whining. As in "Stop kvetching about how hard your day was in school. My feet are killing me from waiting on customers all day so I can pay the bills around here!"

LV: Louis Vuitton—considered pretentious by some, prestigious by others, but the most knocked-off design house around the globe. As in "When your own initials are not enough, strive for status strokes by toting real instead of Chinatown fake LV."

Modelpreneur: An enterprising model like Heidi Klum or Kimora Lee Simmons who builds a fashion empire.

Moi: French for "me." Pronounced "mwah." As in "Are you going to Bloomingdale's *sans moi*? How could you?"

Not cute: Catwalk code for appearing out of place; being caught in an embarrassing, uncomfortable, awkward situation. As in "Did you see Shalimar trying to get in the mix with Ice Très at the Lipstick Lounge? Not cute!"

Peep: To uncover intel or clues. Also *Bo Peep:* to uncover clues or intel—big-time. As in "Did you Bo Peep that situation with, ahem, Curtis Clyde and Benny Ninja in the auditorium? I couldn't believe it!"

Pinkizzily: Catwalk code used to express the power and influence of the shade of pink. As in "I've got a date with Ice Très—time to get pinkizzily!"

Schmooze: A Yiddish word for sucking up, cheesing. As in "Shalimar is always schmoozing with Mr. Confardi, just to keep the extra Kibbles 'n Bits coming her way!"

Serving it cutely: To wear something furbulously; to be decorated beautifully. As in "I just saw the new Betsey Johnson pink floppy sun hat. I could serve that cutely!"

Sham-o-rama: The one place that's always open for "bizness" in the urban jungle; everywhere you turn, someone is trying to pull the acrylic over someone else's eyes in the name of getting ahead. Don't fall for it!

Spill the refried beans: To kiss and tell; to gossip. As in "I saw you hanging out with Zeus. Were you getting smoochy? Come on—spill the refried beans, already!"

Très: French for "very." Pronounced "tray." As in "You look *très* tasty today in the go-go boots!"

Vampira Sisterella: A perpetual early riser who awakens at the crack of dawn to shower—sucking up all the hot water—scarf down the leftover lemon meringue pie, and snag the choicest items at designer sample sales.